1001 Dark Nights
Bundle Seven

1001 Dark Nights Bundle 7
ISBN: 978-1-682305-69-0

Published by Evil Eye Concepts, Incorporated

1001 Dark Nights Bundle Seven

Six Novellas
By

Shayla Black
Laura Kaye
Lara Adrian
Heather Graham
and introducing
Skye Jordan
and CD Reiss

1001 Dark Nights

EVIL EYE
CONCEPTS

Sign up for the 1001 Dark Nights Newsletter
and be entered to win a Tiffany Key necklace.

There's a contest every month!

Go to www.1001DarkNights.com to subscribe.

As a bonus, all subscribers will receive a free
1001 Dark Nights story
The First Night
by Lexi Blake & M.J. Rose

Table of Contents

One Thousand and One Dark Nights

Once upon a time, in the future…

*I was a student fascinated with stories and learning.
I studied philosophy, poetry, history, the occult, and
the art and science of love and magic. I had a vast
library at my father's home and collected thousands
of volumes of fantastic tales.*

*I learned all about ancient races and bygone
times. About myths and legends and dreams of all
people through the millennium. And the more I read
the stronger my imagination grew until I discovered
that I was able to travel into the stories... to actually
become part of them.*

*I wish I could say that I listened to my teacher
and respected my gift, as I ought to have. If I had, I
would not be telling you this tale now.
But I was foolhardy and confused, showing off
with bravery.*

*One afternoon, curious about the myth of the
Arabian Nights, I traveled back to ancient Persia to
see for myself if it was true that every day Shahryar
(Persian: راير*هش*, "king") married a new virgin, and then
sent yesterday's wife to be beheaded. It was written
and I had read, that by the time he met Scheherazade,
the vizier's daughter, he'd killed one thousand
women.*

*Something went wrong with my efforts. I arrived
in the midst of the story and somehow exchanged
places with Scheherazade – a phenomena that had
never occurred before and that still to this day, I
cannot explain.*

*Now I am trapped in that ancient past. I have
taken on Scheherazade's life and the only way I can
protect myself and stay alive is to do what she did to
protect herself and stay alive.*

*Every night the King calls for me and listens as I spin tales.
And when the evening ends and dawn breaks, I stop at a
point that leaves him breathless and yearning for more.
And so the King spares my life for one more day, so that
he might hear the rest of my dark tale.*

*As soon as I finish a story... I begin a new
one... like the one that you, dear reader, have before
you now.*

Pure Wicked
A Wicked Lovers Novella
By Shayla Black

1001
DARK
NIGHTS

PURE WICKED
A Wicked Lovers Novella

NEW YORK TIMES BESTSELLING AUTHOR
SHAYLA BLACK

Chapter One

Wasn't regret a bitch? In fact, Jesse McCall couldn't remember another time in his life when it had come off its leash and humped his leg so thoroughly.

As he emerged from the modern, mostly glass hotel, flashbulbs burst in his face, blinding him. He paused as reporters shouted questions his way. Beside him, his shark of a publicist, Candia, barked "no comment" in a nonstop loop as she led him to the waiting limo at the end of the crowded walk.

Jesse glanced at the big blue sky. Late afternoon blistered. Had it already been more than twelve hours since everything had gone so wrong? Why hadn't he asked more questions or hung around longer? Something that might have prevented this fucking tragedy...

Raking a hand through his hair, he squinted as he dragged his gaze over the surrounding skyscrapers. He was in some downtown area. Austin. Yeah. Half the time he woke up and didn't know what day it was, what city he'd preformed in, or who the hell he was lying next to. The life of a musician was frenetic and nomadic. Jesse had sold out one stadium tour after another since age sixteen. Twelve years later, he didn't know any other way to live.

He reached into his pocket and tossed on a pair of Armani shades, thanking god he wasn't hung over. A year of sobriety had ensured that, but still Candia strode beside him on her usual platforms, tense and waiting to flay him alive with her tongue the second they were alone.

When the limo driver opened the door of the sleek black stretch, Jesse climbed in behind his publicist as she settled into the leather seat and smoothed back the professional twist of her dark hair. Their chauffeur enclosed them together in the back of the car, and Jesse counted down to Candia's imminent explosion.

"Damn it, we're still on tour. The album just dropped last week." She tossed her gray Prada briefcase onto the floorboard and shot him a frustrated stare. "The bad-boy image has always worked for you because you're young and hot. But the public will view this as over the line. You want to give me the whole story now?"

As if she hadn't heard every word he'd told the pair of detectives over the last three hours. Did she honestly think he'd held back? The interview had finally ended when they'd realized he knew nothing and hadn't been in any way involved. Then the paunch-bellied one with the scowl had asked him to sign an autograph for his teenage daughter. With a few strokes of his pen, Jesse had been out the door.

"It's already public knowledge?" He'd hoped she could keep a lid on this until he could figure out what to do, how to process, what to say.

"TMZ and Perez Hilton are all over this shit. You even made CNN."

So that was a yes. He sighed. "I swear, I don't know anything else. After the show last night, Ryan caught me as I was leaving my suite. He said he'd met a girl and asked to borrow my room since he couldn't find the key to his own. He was in too much of a hurry to get under her miniskirt to fetch another one from the front desk."

Of course Ryan had invited him to join in, too. Girls and drugs, just like the good ol' days. Jesse had declined and begged Ryan to come with him. No dice.

"Then you went out for a ride?" Candia asked.

He nodded. "Cruising around on my motorcycle helps clear my head after a show."

And kept him away from the partying that had nearly ruined him over ten years of his career.

"Did you get a good look at her before you left?"

"You mean, did I know she was only sixteen? No. I barely glanced at her but I would have pegged her at well over twenty-one." Definitely not a sophomore in high school.

"If you'd made him go to the lobby, maybe someone would have stopped him... Maybe he would have used the head up north." She pressed her thumb between her eyebrows, obviously fighting off a headache. "Maybe... But it's done."

He wanted to be pissed that Candia had put this off on him, but she hadn't voiced anything he hadn't already thought. "At the time, I figured if Ryan was screwing some cute blonde, maybe he wasn't getting high."

Jesse scoffed at the terrible irony of that.

"Oh, he absolutely was. And he got her high, too."

Yes, his bandmate and old buddy had overdosed the girl—in Jesse's room. So naturally, everyone assumed he'd been involved.

"The press is having a field day." At barely four thirty in the afternoon, Candia already sounded damn tired.

Jesse could guess who they'd cast in the role of scapegoat, even though he hadn't been in the building when Ryan had pumped his jailbait hookup full of heroin and taken her to bed. Then, once his backup vocalist had realized the girl was unresponsive, he hadn't called 911 for medical help so she might have lived. No. He'd apparently panicked and shot himself in the head, doubling the tragedy.

Besides being a PR nightmare, Jesse had lost a friend he'd been trying to save. And the staggered, grief-stricken looks on the faces of that girl's parents when they realized their daughter was gone would haunt him forever.

"So, I guess social media is firing up with condemnation and hate." He stared out the window at the thick traffic.

"Enough to make me nervous. You've got sympathy from the hard-core fans but... We have to cancel the rest of the tour," she murmured. "The noise is too negative. You look like an insensitive asshat if you continue on as if nothing terrible has happened."

"We had six shows left." It could have been more, but he wished it had been fewer.

"Yep. That's well over a hundred thousand disappointed fans. And those are merely the ones who held tickets. It sucks." She hesitated. "You'll be thirty in less than eighteen months. I'm starting to think the time has come to tone down your bad-boy-gone-wild image."

She was right. Jesse didn't bother asking if his parents would be proud. They'd cashed out on his fame years ago. His dad now played golf with celebrities. His mom trained other stage parents and gave interviews about where they'd gone wrong with their only son. He hadn't talked to them in forever. But none of that mattered at the moment. Bottom line, Jesse wasn't proud of himself.

He hadn't been in a long time.

"We need a distraction," she told him. "You should start an anti-gun crusade."

Jesse shook his head. "Too political."

"What about a series of PSAs about suicide prevention?"

"Ryan didn't want to take his own life. He was simply too high to realize he shouldn't. Besides, doing either of those things will look like I know I should have done more."

Candia gave him a deflated sigh, then began chewing on her bottom lip as if sorting through the problem. "I'll keep working on solutions."

"While you think about my public image, find out how we can help the Harris girl's family, like providing funeral expenses or whatever else they need." He paused. "Have my lawyers work up a confidential settlement and set these folks up for life."

"But you had nothing to do with her death."

"All those parents know is that the last time their daughter walked out the door, she was coming to my concert. She'll never be home again because of the choices my bandmate made. They will never recover from that loss."

Candia got quiet. "I'll take care of it."

"Great. I appreciate you coming with me to talk to the rest

of the band." They'd all been devastated but not stunned when he'd broken the news. "And when the police contact Ryan's parents and you get the details of his funeral, let me know."

She nodded. "Absolutely."

"Thanks. So…I guess you're canceling my appearances for a while?" When she nodded, the career-driven part of him grimaced. The rest of him exhaled in guilty relief. He hadn't had a day off in years.

"I'm afraid you won't be visiting Jimmy Fallon with this album," she quipped. "I think it's better if we proactively back out on these appearances for now, citing grief over the loss of your friend. We'll have an easier time rebooking in a couple of weeks, once this crap has died down."

"Wait. Maybe I should use those appearances to tell everyone that I had nothing to do with it." But he couldn't deny that on plenty of nights in the past, it could have been him—and everyone knew it. The fact that Maddy Harris had died in his hotel room simply splashed another stain on his already bad reputation. And it sure as hell made him feel shitty, too. What a waste of life…

"That's not what they want to hear. *'Rock Star Overdoses Underage Fan on Sex and Heroin'* makes for a juicier headline. Until the police finish their investigation and release the details, people will assume you had a hand in the incident."

He sighed. "So what do you want me to do?"

"I'm going to issue a statement expressing your grief and deepest apologies to the Harris family. You're going to disappear—way off the radar—until I say otherwise. No swanky resorts. No high-profile outings with Taylor Swift. And absolutely no intoxication. Think sober monk."

No one would ever believe that.

"I've got it." She snapped her fingers and excitement lit her eyes. "You can go to rehab."

Jesse scowled. "I'm not an addict."

"But it would look good. Repentant."

"It would also be pointless. Everyone goes to rehab and no one cares. No." He glared her way. "If I hole up, this dies down."

"All right," she said grudgingly as the limo stopped in front of the executive airport outside the city. "But I don't want to see a Twitter or Instagram pic of you for at least the next two weeks. Once we're back in L.A., hide out in your house. That should work. I'll tell you when it's safe to come out."

His ultra-contemporary house was decorated with every luxury and technological delight known to man, not to mention blessed with sick city and ocean views. But it had never felt like home. Despite the place being eight thousand square feet, Jesse couldn't imagine being cooped up there for the next fourteen days. It would only remind him of everything wrong with his life.

"Paparazzi know where I live. If I get on that plane with you and go to L.A., they'll figure it out. So will fans." Even now, he imagined that if he looked at his phone he'd find a full voicemail box and hundreds of text messages. He couldn't deal with anyone else's expectations right now when he'd done so poorly at meeting his own. "If you really want me to disappear, we'll have to come up with another plan."

"You're well known on every continent but Antarctica. The press would spot you almost anywhere you travel, especially if you take a security detail. They seem to have eyes and ears at every airport. I…" Candia huffed. "I need to think about this."

"I'll give it some brain power too, come up with a few ideas." Though he had no idea what to suggest, Jesse did know that what he'd done in the past—disappearing into the bottom of a bottle with some recreational blow and a woman under each arm—wasn't going to do a damn thing to clean up his image.

"Ideas?" She sounded as if that horrified her. "You? No."

"I'm a grown-ass man. And I've learned a few things over the years." He lowered his sunglasses and stared at her over the rims. "Go. You handle the press. I think I might know how to disappear."

When the driver opened the limo door, Candia grabbed her bag and turned to him. "You sure? Can I really trust you not to fuck this up?"

"Yeah. I know how much is on the line. Call me when the coast is clear."

* * * *

Jesse wiped his palms down the front of his jeans, then rang the doorbell. Hell, he didn't even know if Kimber was home. And that scary bastard she'd married—had it really been almost five years ago?—wouldn't be thrilled to see his wife's ex-fiancé, especially this late at night. If he was lucky, Deke Trenton would slam the door in his face. More likely, the big operative would try to beat the shit out of him.

After a gut-tightening moment, the porch light flipped on and the door swept open.

Deke towered in the doorway, a beefy forearm braced against the jamb, blue eyes raking him with a scathing glare. Then Kimber's husband sighed and looked over his shoulder, back into the living room. "Kitten, your personal Bieber has decided to drop in."

"Jesse?" He heard her familiar voice.

Deke stepped back, and she appeared in the doorway a moment later. Well, her pregnant belly edged into view. The rest of her followed an instant later. He hadn't talked to her in so long, he hadn't even known she was pregnant again. Didn't that make him feel even more like a shit?

Deke wrapped an arm around her—both a reminder and a warning. Jesse was relieved that seeing the man's hands on her no longer made him twenty kinds of jealous.

"Oh my gosh!" Kimber's hazel eyes widened as she pulled him into a quick hug. "You really are here."

Jesse held her in return for something slightly longer than a moment.

"Yeah. Sorry to drop by without calling." Clearly, he was intruding on their happy domestic scene.

"Not at all. Come in." She opened the door wider and stepped back.

He could have sworn he heard Deke growl. But the guy let Jesse enter. Now that he'd interrupted their evening, he'd talk fast, thank them, and be gone.

As he cleared the foyer, flashes of light told him the TV was on, but he suspected it had been muted because he didn't hear a sound coming from the box. Children's toys filled baskets and shelves around the room—balls, books, trucks, stuffed animals. Kimber had given birth to a son almost four years ago and was obviously about to be a mother again.

"Sit." She waved him over to the couch. "Can I get you something? Water? Coffee?"

Reluctantly, he sank into a chair, leaving the couch for the two of them. "No thanks. How are you?"

"Pregnant. It's a girl this time." She smoothed her hand over her distended belly with a serene smile. "I'm due at the end of next month. Otherwise, I'm fine."

"And you're on bed rest until then so you don't go into premature labor again. Feet up." Deke hustled her back to the sofa and lifted her lower legs and placed her heels on a pillow strategically positioned on top of the coffee table. Then the man pinned Jesse with a stare, shaking his head. "So I'm guessing this isn't a social call. Your buddy Ryan fucked up and bit it last night."

Kimber gasped, then elbowed her husband. "Deke!"

"Am I wrong?" Deke looked his way.

Jesse raked at his hair. He hated wearing it to his shoulders and filled with "product." The stylist he paid a small fortune for insisted it looked both cool and hot. Same with the scruff on his face. Sometimes he just wanted it all gone. "Nope. I wasn't there."

"*Access Hollywood* suggested something similar about an hour ago," she said.

"Which I don't watch," Deke cut in. "You came here for a reason. What do you need?"

Tugging at his ear, Jesse grimaced. These damn earrings weren't him, either. Crap, he shouldn't have come here. He didn't want to risk bringing the press down on them, especially if Kimber was having a difficult pregnancy. She didn't need the stress.

"Nothing." He stood. "You've got your hands full. I assume your son is in bed. And I... I'll figure it out."

"You need a place to go?" Deke barked.

Jesse opened his mouth to admit that's why he'd come, then he snapped it shut again. Deke's buddy Jack had some isolated cabin deep in a swamp, and it sure would come in handy about now. But Jesse hadn't done anything for himself since fame had hit—not kept his schedule, answered his calls, or styled his hair.

Hell, he'd barely wiped his own ass. Simply rehabbing his image wouldn't cut it. As Candia had suggested, the time had come for him to change everything.

He was too damn unhappy to spend the rest of his life this way.

"No. I've got a place in mind," he lied. "Before I headed that way, I wanted to spend time with someone who…" *Knows I'm not the sort of man to corrupt and overdose a teenager.* But one of the last times he'd seen Kimber, she'd walked in to find him balls deep in an intoxicated, barely legal girl while chugging a fifth of bourbon. Deke must know that. "Someone who wouldn't bullshit me. Someone with a solid word of advice."

"Well…" Kimber wrinkled her brow in thought. "I've always told you that you have to decide what you want your life to be and make it happen."

Deke shook his head. "Kitten, I think he meant me."

When she glanced at him for confirmation, Jesse sent her a half grin. "Yeah, man to man. Or something like that."

His answer clearly surprised her. "Oh. Sure."

While it was no secret that Deke had never been a fan of his, and Jesse really had no right to ask for even a word from the man, he was thankful Kimber's hulk of a husband seemed willing to give it.

"Sit." He waited until Jesse complied. "I get it. Good times and fast women are easy to come by and hard to turn down." Deke sat back and took Kimber's hand. Though the overhead lights cast a glow on his golden hair, no one would ever mistake him for an angel. "But you've got to stop acting your age in rock star years."

"Rock star years?" Jesse frowned. What the hell was he talking about?

"Cut your age in half and add one." Deke cracked a smile.

Jesse shook his head. "I'm not fifteen."

"Then don't act like it. Life isn't about getting high or laid. Obviously, you've got an incredible career. It's your character everyone is questioning. Stop behaving like a douche. Start being a man. It's not complicated."

Well, he'd asked for it, and Deke had never been one to

candy coat.

"I've been sober for a year. Actually, almost thirteen months."

"That's great!" Kimber praised.

The other man simply cocked his head and leveled him with a hard glance. "Women?"

Jesse didn't want to answer with Kimber in the room. His wandering penis had only been one of the reasons she'd left him. He hated to admit how little he'd changed since their breakup. "I'm no saint."

"Hmm," Deke mused. "Last bed partner?"

He hesitated. "A couple of cities ago."

"You remember her name?"

"No." Jesse grimaced.

"So she didn't mean anything to you?" Deke quizzed.

"Nothing."

"Then why did you do her?"

She'd been eager and pretty and willing and… "I don't know. I didn't have a reason not to."

"If you want your life to have meaning, you have to treat all the parts of your life as if they're meaning*ful*."

Deke's advice surprised Jesse. His words had almost sounded philosophical. Kimber's husband had always struck him as being long on intimidation and short on principles. Clearly, Jesse hadn't looked past the brawn.

His former fiancée wore a scowl. "Deke's right. When was the last time you wrote music? And recorded it? That used to mean everything to you."

He sucked in a breath and winced. "Longer than I'd like to admit."

"Your new album doesn't sound like you. It's great. Catchy and fun. Edgy. Clever." Kimber flushed. "That came out wrong. I know you can be fun and clever and all that. It's just…some of your best hits were soulful ballads about finding yourself and following your heart. You wrote those before you hit it big, and I haven't heard a song like that from you in forever."

She was right. Between the two of them, Jesse heard the message loud and clear that he'd lost his way, personally and professionally. This sabbatical away from the limelight had to be about becoming a whole new him. He couldn't wait. Getting the opportunity to change his partying, sex-god image—and himself—couldn't come soon enough.

"You're right. And I needed the honesty." Jesse stood. "Let me know when you have that baby. Thanks."

Chapter Two

Texarkana, Texas

"How have you not committed double murder?"

Bristol Reese stared into her beer, then glanced at her best friend. "They're not worth twenty-five to life. But don't think it hasn't crossed my mind."

Jayla scowled, her dark, expressive eyes both disapproving and dismissive. "Girl, that's restraint. He's a player and she's batty as hell."

"Which is why they deserve one another. I'm sure they'll have a short, miserable life together," she shot back, then chugged some of her brew, ignoring the clapping and laughter from the group gathered at the large table in the center of the restaurant.

Her friend's expression softened, her mocha skin glowing under the muted amber lights above the bar. "What about you? You gave that man sixteen months of your life. I really thought he intended to propose to you."

"I did, too. But I guess Hayden decided that Presleigh is better wife material."

Jayla snorted. "No, he thought having Miss Lafayette County on his arm would make him look like the shit with his buddies. That beauty pageant skank might look good in Victoria's Secret, but she's not you."

Bristol nodded. "Actually, I think that's something Hayden appreciates about her. And she's not a skank. It pains me to admit it, but she's sometimes sweet."

"She stole your man!"

"I don't think she had to try very hard," Bristol pointed out. "Hayden was dazzled by her short skirts and her adoration…and that was that."

Jayla pulled what she would have called her stank face. "His bitch ass needs to be taught a lesson."

Her friend was probably right, but Bristol had to take part of the blame. Her pride stung when she realized she'd buried her head in the sand and ignored her instincts about Hayden because she'd wanted him to be everything he wasn't—sweet, helpful, caring, capable of compromise. God, why was she so idealistic? A sweeping, romantic gesture bowled her heart over every time. She wanted Mr. Darcy to move heaven and earth to marry her, sought an Edward Lewis who was willing to conquer his fear of heights to rescue her so she could rescue him right back, hoped for her own Johnny Castle to tell her parents that nobody puts Bristol in a corner, ached for an Edward Cullen who knew his soul well enough to take one look at her and realize she was "The One."

She was a hopeless romantic, and it hadn't brought her a damn thing but misery.

"I'm not sure he's worth the effort." Bristol sighed.

"And Presleigh has no spine." Jayla was getting indignant on her behalf, slamming a fist on the bar.

"Another fact Hayden appreciates, I'm sure. I wouldn't conform enough for him. He always tried to change the way I dress, and all but bullied me to shut down my 'silly' business. He would have much preferred that I teach Sunday school at the church, maybe sell some Mary Kay on the side, and be blissfully happy to be Mrs. Hayden Vincent the third."

Jayla looked disgusted. "That's not you. You're too passionate about life to do nothing but keep a clean house, spit-polish up the kids for Christmas photos, and scrapbook your life away."

"Agreed." She drank more of her beer, then lowered the mug to the nearly empty bar with a sigh. "But you basically described Presleigh. Hell, maybe they are a perfect match."

"Ugh. He's falling for an empty package."

Bristol shrugged. "But he doesn't have much depth, either. I let myself be dazzled by a few roses and charming words from the most eligible guy in town. I mean, he's Lewisville, Arkansas's version of a Kennedy. I had a crush on him in high school something fierce. And he looked good in his football pants."

Jayla tilted her head. "I'll give you that."

"I appreciate you being mad on my behalf, but honestly...I'm more humiliated than heartbroken. I'm over him."

For the foreseeable future, no more entanglements of the heart. Flings only. If she kept the length of her relationships to a night—a weekend, tops—she couldn't make the same mistake again.

Bristol simply wished she didn't have to see Hayden and Presleigh together all the damn time. But in a town of twelve hundred people, avoiding them wouldn't be easy. Even if she moved away, she'd come home to visit and run into them eventually.

"A toast," Corey, one of Hayden's football friends from high school said, standing in front of the rest of the gathering. "Raise your glasses, everyone. To Presleigh, the most beautiful girl in Lafayette County. May you always follow your heart and be happy. To Hayden... Cheers, man. You're one lucky bastard."

As the crowd laughed, Bristol looked on with a sigh...then spotted her mother bustling over, her Pepto-Bismol pink suit looking more suited to Easter Sunday services than an engagement party.

"You're being rude," her mother chastised. "This is Presleigh's event, and you're sitting at the bar, sulking. Come give her your love and support. After all, she is your sister."

Bristol tightened her grip on her mug. "I closed my restaurant early and drove forty-five minutes down the road to celebrate her upcoming nuptials to the man who dumped me for her. I think the fact that I'm here at all is enough."

"You sound bitter," her mother tsked, her hair not blowing at all as the air conditioner kicked on.

She wasn't. She and Hayden hadn't been a good match, and she hadn't wanted to admit it. In truth, he'd done her a favor by falling for someone else. Bristol just wished that someone hadn't been her younger sister. At nineteen, Presleigh was too young to get married and too pampered to know what the word compromise meant.

"Mama, leave it. Please. I'm not making waves. I'm still speaking to her. And to him. Anything more will take time."

Her mother frowned. "At least come sit with the group. Food will be served soon, and the rest of the family is asking questions."

Because keeping up appearances with her Aunt Jean, a distant cousin, and the rest of the townsfolk was far more important than any potential heartbreak or misery her own daughter may have suffered.

Beside her, Jayla rolled her eyes. She and Linda Mae Reese had never gotten along. Her best friend had always sworn that her mother favored Presleigh. Bristol had never experienced that as vividly as she was right now.

"We'll be there in a few minutes, Mama. I'm just waiting for a friend." Maybe the others would be done eating before she had to admit that her "friend" hadn't shown up—what a shame—and she joined the party as it wound down for the evening.

"Who?" Her mother frowned. "We didn't invite anyone else, Bristol."

In her mom's vernacular, that meant that Bristol asking someone new to join the party without her knowledge bordered on unacceptable.

Jayla gave Linda Mae a sweet-as-pie smile. "Her new boyfriend."

Bristol whirled on her barstool. "Are you crazy?"

What the hell was she going to do when no new man showed up except look more pathetic?

Her pal gave her an apologetic grimace. "It slipped out."

Quickly, Bristol scanned the few men nearby to see if any might be suitable fake boyfriend material. Maybe she could bribe him with a few drinks to play nice for an hour. But no guy fit the bill. Predictably, most folks in a restaurant near the five p.m. mark were at least old enough to be social security eligible or were married with children.

"Oh." Her mother reared back, obviously surprised. "I

didn't know you were seeing someone. Who is he? Where did you meet? What does he do? Where does he live?"

The more her mother asked questions, the more suspicious she sounded—with good reason. It wasn't as if Lewisville had a huge pool of eligible bachelors, and Bristol didn't make the trip west to Texarkana often.

She shot Jayla a glare. Her friend shrugged in silent apology. She appreciated Jayla wanting to prevent her mother from continuing the bitter-hag routine, but this lie simply didn't help.

"Mama…" Bristol sighed, knowing she needed to swallow a choking bite of humble pie and admit that she was totally single. But damn, she wished she didn't have to.

Behind her, she heard a shuffle and turned to see an absolutely gorgeous guy emerge from the shadows. His tight black tank framed an amazing set of muscled shoulders, one of which was covered by a tribal tattoo. He had a strong jaw, wore a black skullcap and a pair of expensive-looking sunglasses, along with a smile that made her breath catch.

When he removed the shades to stare at her, his dark eyes danced with amusement. "Hi, honey. Sorry I'm late."

* * * *

Jesse knew he should have resisted butting in, but the cute little brunette had clearly been through hell with her sister and the ex-asshat. Her mother's haranguing only seemed to make her sink down on her barstool more, as if she wanted to escape. He knew what it was like to have shit coming at him from all directions. That lesson felt particularly fresh now.

He had sneaked a peek at the entertainment news on his smart phone when he'd wandered into town a few hours ago…and wished he hadn't. If he could go back in time and stop Ryan from tragically ending two lives, he'd be eternally grateful. Sadly, a miracle wasn't in the cards for him, but he kind of hoped the girl at the bar saw him as one. She wasn't crying in her beer yet, but if he couldn't give her some breathing room soon, she absolutely might.

When he spoke, her green eyes, tucked under the sun-kissed fringe of her bangs, bounced from the bar, up to his face. She blinked, stared. Jesse worried that covering his shorn hair, shaving the scruff, removing his earrings, and not wearing leather wouldn't be enough to disguise him. He knew damn well he'd taken a big, impulsive risk by showing himself in public— but who could resist a dive called Bubba Oink's Bone Yard?— and jumping in to Bristol's situation. Thankfully, he didn't see recognition on her face, merely confusion.

"I'm not too late, am I?" he prompted.

She swallowed, and her pretty African-American friend discreetly nudged her ribs with an elbow. The brunette slid off the stool. "Ah…no. We haven't eaten yet."

"What's your name, young man? My daughter hasn't mentioned you." Her mother, who had a serious case of helmet hair, sent him a frown somewhere between puzzled and disapproving.

He stuck out a hand and improvised. "My name is James, ma'am. Most of my friends call me Jamie. Nice to meet you."

Her mother took his hand. Her soft skin felt cold. "James. I'm Linda Mae."

"I'm Jayla," Bristol's friend added with a friendly handshake. "So glad I finally get to meet you."

"Pleasure." He nodded at the women, then took the pretty brunette's hand in his. "It's good to see you, Bristol."

Surprise widened her eyes even more. He liked the way she wore her emotions on her face, the way freckles dusted her nose, the way her pouty lower lip shimmered under the lights.

"Um…you, too, Jamie." She sent him a stilted smile.

Linda Mae shook her head suspiciously, then huffed back to the others.

"We should join the party," her friend suggested and grabbed her by the elbow, hauling her toward the gathering. She gazed past Bristol to him with a wink. "Thanks for joining us."

He grinned back and followed. "You're welcome."

The long table around which everyone else sat looked fairly cramped, and Jesse didn't think Bristol wanted to get cozy with these folks anyway. So he pulled up seats at the empty table directly behind it. He placed Bristol between him and her friend, then looped a casual arm around the back of her chair, brushing her long ponytail as he did. He'd enjoy his knight-in-shining-armor routine for an evening, then he and Bristol could have an amicable "breakup" before he continued down the road in search of somewhere to spend the next couple of weeks. But for tonight, she'd have a reason to thumb her nose at her mother and sister.

On the far side of the party's table, a blonde wearing too much makeup and a gaudy engagement ring made googly eyes at a twerp with light brown hair and a condescending expression. Bristol had dated *him*?

The rest of the party sent him glances ranging from curious to suspicious. He waved. "Hi, everyone. I'm Jamie, Bristol's new boyfriend."

After a brief round of introductions, he settled back into his chair and watched his supposed new squeeze. She was built on the petite side, but he'd already noticed when she rose from her barstool that her jeans hugged the curves of her really pert ass. The pretty little thing also had a noteworthy rack.

She glanced his way, then leaned in to Jayla, speaking softly. "Did you set this up? Hire him or something?"

The other woman shook her head. "No. He just appeared. Like a fairy godfather."

"Without the glitter and wings," Jesse quipped in low tones.

"Seriously?" She swiveled her gaze in his direction. "Why would you help me?"

"Because you needed it, and I can't resist a damsel in distress." He flashed her a smile filled with the dimples that had been getting him laid since he turned fifteen. He probably shouldn't but he hoped they were working now.

Bristol frowned, looking uncertain. Did she wish he hadn't butted in?

He leaned back to give her space. "Do you want me to go?"

She chewed on her bottom lip and stared as if trying to figure him out. "Who are you?"

A splash of adrenaline spiked his bloodstream. Had she recognized him after all?

"I'm Jamie." Well, that was his cousin's name, but he'd at least turn around if someone shouted it. Hopefully. He leaned closer and whispered in her ear. "I'm not a crazed rapist or ax murderer, if that's what you're worried about. I overheard your dilemma and decided to help. I just want to see you smile, okay?"

"Everything all right?" a male voice called from the next table.

The groom-to-be tried to stare him down, narrowing his eyes to something he probably thought resembled a Hollywood action hero's most intimidating glare. Jesse tried not to laugh.

"Great," he assured the dickwad.

Bristol's sister latched onto her fiancé's arm and looked up at him as if she sought all the answers of the universe in his eyes. Jesse didn't have anything against love or adoration. He didn't know much about them, but he didn't think her insipid expression was a good representation of either.

"Is that guy bothering you?" Bristol's ex asked her, nodding his way.

Jesse tensed, waiting to see what she'd say. She glanced away from the fidiot and over to him again. She tucked her hand in his and squeezed. "Why would you think that? I'm great, Hayden."

"She's just put out that I'm late," Jesse lied smoothly. "Carry on."

Hayden did so reluctantly, telling everyone at the gathering about the moment he'd realized he was in love with her sister over punch and cake, right after Presleigh risked herself to rescue the neighbor's kid from an angry hive of bees.

"Is he talking about Ben Bob?" When Bristol nodded, Jayla rolled her eyes. "C'mon now. That kid threw rocks at the hive because he wanted to see what the bees would do."

"Yep. He even admitted that."

Jayla frowned, as if remembering an annoying but key fact. "Didn't that happen at *your* birthday party?"

"It did." Bristol nodded with an acid smile.

So Hayden had thrown her over for her vapid sister when he'd come to celebrate her big day? "What a raving douche."

"You got that right," Jayla put in.

While Jesse couldn't deny that he'd pulled some dick moves when he had been briefly engaged to Kimber, that had been years ago, when he had been young, intoxicated, and stupid. Back then, he'd believed the world owed him a good time.

How had anybody tolerated him?

"Thanks for that assessment, babe," Bristol tossed back at him, wearing an intriguing hint of a grin.

"If hearing me diss your ex makes you happy, I'll be glad to do it more."

Her grin widened, almost becoming a full-blown smile.

Before Jesse could coax one out of her, the waitstaff began bringing everyone glasses of sweet tea and trays full of beef brisket sandwiches, coleslaw, baked beans, and bread. Bottles of wine followed. Hayden called for a bucket of beer. People dug in, conversation ensued, and the bride and groom looked at each other as if they couldn't wait to be alone. Jesse wondered if they realized how incredibly insensitive they were being. Probably not. Even if they did, Jesse suspected they wouldn't care if they hurt Bristol. Obviously, they'd disregarded her feelings some time ago.

Thankfully, the restaurant began piping in music, a kind of modern country tune that Jesse didn't hear often but liked. He eyed Bristol as she bounced in her chair to the beat. Her gesture looked completely unconscious, as if she didn't expect anyone would be watching her. He kind of found it adorable.

When the waiter began taking the food away, she'd barely touched hers. Instead, she peered at him as if he was a riddle she needed to solve. The intelligence on her face, coupled with an unconsciously sultry thing she had going on, piqued his interest. Blood rushed south. Against his better judgment, his cock stood up and saluted her.

Shit, he'd jumped into this situation to help—nothing more. He'd just rolled into town and wasn't sure what to do with himself. He hadn't cast himself in the role of her boyfriend in the hopes that she'd let him fuck her.

Everyone around them was laughing and imbibing. The engaged couple kissed again. Bristol tried not to look at them. Jesse wanted to wring their necks.

"Walk with me?" he leaned closer and asked in her ear.

She turned his way, her big green eyes snaring his gaze. "Where?"

"I don't know. I've never been to this place. Where can we talk without technically leaving the party?"

She paused, then turned to Jayla. "Will you distract my mother for a few minutes, pretty please?"

"You did *not* just ask me to do that." Her bestie crossed her arms over her chest and gave her a glare full of attitude.

"I'll make you a whole batch of peanut butter blossom cookies," she wheedled.

Suddenly, Jayla gave her a dazzling smile. "Deal."

"I think I got played," Bristol told him with a fond shake of her head.

"I'd say so." He held out his hand.

She tucked her cell phone in her pocket, leaving her purse with her friend, then she placed her hand in his outstretched palm as they strolled the perimeter of the restaurant/bar. "So…what made you jump in? Did I look like a sad spinster, so you decided to end my singledom for a night?"

"No. I'm a sucker for engagement parties. Can't you tell? I saw all the white balloons with the cute pictures of the bride and groom attached and I couldn't resist. If I'm lucky, maybe we can catch another sappy speech and drink some terrible champagne."

She sent him a skeptical glare. "Have you ever been to an engagement party?"

"Not since my neighbor's daughter married an alpaca farmer. I was twelve," he admitted.

Bristol laughed, and Jesse loved hearing the light, lyrical sound. That giggle was a music all its own. "Made a big impact on you, huh?"

"The cake did. But the marriage lasted about as long as I think your sister's will."

"It took me longer to decorate the 'save the date' cookies she asked me for tonight than the whole marriage will, I suspect. The wedding is next month. Mama wanted her to be a June bride. Presleigh isn't ready to be anyone's wife."

"And he's no Prince Charming."

She nodded. "There is that."

"Why did you date him?"

"That's a good question." Bristol hesitated. "He found me after I broke my ankle and took me to the doctor."

"You felt as if you owed him?" Jesse asked.

"No. I liked him—or I thought I did. But that was before I actually knew him."

"How did you get hurt?" Even in the dimming light, he saw the flush in her cheeks, and Jesse sensed a story. "Okay, 'fess up."

"Well, I bought this aerobics video and I was trying it out but…"

"Your ankle snapped, did it? Were you doing some crazy *Insanity* shit?"

She twirled a section of her hair around one finger and looked anywhere but at him. "Um, no."

"So…what were you up to?"

Biting back a smile, she sent him a coy glance. "It was supposed to be pole dancing but I didn't have a pole, so I used a column in my apartment. I didn't know it was hollow and wouldn't hold me. I landed wrong and…it was embarrassing."

He gave a hearty laugh. "I don't mean to make light of your pain, but you have to admit that—"

"No, it totally sounds funny. And if anyone could have seen it, I'll bet it would have been hysterical."

Maybe, but he'd bet that before her fall, he'd have found her sexy as hell. "So he took you to the hospital?"

She nodded. "Yep. He also brought me roses while they set the cast. Then he filled my prescriptions and took me home. He even tried to pet my cat, Shakespurr."

"That's what you named your cat?"

"Yeah, he's a feline so he's clever and creative. And just like the Bard himself, before I had Shakespurr fixed he liked older women."

"Right." Jesse enjoyed her sense of humor and quick wit. He wondered how many of the women he'd taken to bed over the years he might have liked if he'd bothered to get to know them. Probably none. This one seemed really different. "So you decided you liked him because he tried to pet your pussy?"

She tsked at him and sent him an annoyed glare, hands on her hips. But the fact that she was about a foot shorter, coupled with the smile she couldn't repress, took all the starch out of her censure.

"That's not all. Hayden also told me that he had a crush on

me in high school."

"And you fell for him?"

Bristol heaved a long sigh. "Totally. I sound like an idiot."

Jesse didn't like hearing her put herself down when she'd done nothing wrong. "No. You sound like a woman who trusted the wrong guy because you wanted to believe the best about him."

"I really did."

Now she sounded sad, and he wanted to turn her frown into another smile. "Since you've been so honest, I guess I'll tell you something true." He squeezed her hand. "I saw you sitting on the barstool talking to Jayla and thought you were beautiful. If you've once thought you're not simply because the ex-jackass tossed you over for your younger sister, trust me. It's not you; it's him. I can already tell you're way smarter. I also suspect you're a better human being. So if he made you feel lousy, forget it. I've traveled all over the world and met a lot of women. You seem pretty awesome to me."

She blushed again. "Thanks."

"Like I said, just being honest."

A comfortable lull fell between them, and Jesse finally scanned his surroundings. He'd played a number of places with this vibe when he'd first started singing. It hadn't taken long before a random YouTube video had brought him to the attention of record producers. He'd been too nervous to appreciate the valuable learning experience and too young to join the revelry that would inevitably happen here later. Right now, a band dragged in their instruments and readied themselves for their Saturday night set.

Besides maturity and experience, the other thing that made his trip to this joint different was the fact that he held Bristol's hand in his. He liked the simple touch, liked knowing she was there with him step by step. She didn't have any expectations that he'd find the nearest room away from his screaming public to get in her panties. Bristol seemed perfectly content to simply be with him.

Conversely, the fact that she wasn't squealing to sleep with *the* Jesse McCall really made him want her. Or was there just something about her that did it for him?

"So…since you saved me from social hell tonight, are you expecting money?"

If she only knew how much he didn't need it. "Nope."

"Sex?" She quirked a brow at him.

Jesse couldn't help but smile. "I wouldn't turn it down…"

"Oh, yeah?" Her smile dipped. "And you're not interested in Presleigh?"

"God, no. She's pretty in that plastic way, like a Barbie doll. Sure, she's cute and has a nice bod. But I've met a million girls like her. She's not interesting."

"And I am?" Bristol quizzed, looking a bit skeptical.

"So far, yeah."

"You don't really know me," she pointed out.

"Fair enough. But you seem real. Unlike your sister, it's pretty clear you didn't spend all afternoon preening in front of the mirror and dressing for attention."

"What does that mean? Maybe I did."

"I guess that messy ponytail with the chunk that didn't make it up—nice scrunchie, by the way—was on purpose. And who wants to wear a skirt so short that a stiff breeze could reveal your underwear when you could go the rumpled jeans route? Much sexier. And that patch of flour on your neck here." He swept his fingers over the spot and felt her pulse jump. "Hmm, honey. It's a turn-on."

She gave a tsk of self-disgust and swiped at the flour, then dragged the elastic band covered in pink polka-dotted fabric from her hair. The multi-hued brown strands bounced past her shoulders and brushed her arms, the ends a shade much closer to blond. It wasn't any sort of ombre dye job, simply a natural byproduct of the sun. Her tresses framed her delicate face.

"Okay, so I'm not *Vogue* ready."

"But like I said, you are pretty, no matter what you're wearing," he told her. "You know, since I'm your boyfriend for the evening, I should know more about you. I mean, in case people ask? At least the vitals."

"That's a point. My mother may have paused her interrogation, but she'll be back." She seemed to gather her thoughts. "I'm twenty-four, my middle name is Alexa. My dad died when I was ten. We used to bake together when I was a kid.

I dropped out of college in my sophomore year to start a little coffeehouse in my hometown called *Sweet Cinns*. Making ends meet each month is touch and go, but I love what I do and wouldn't change a thing. What about you?"

"I'm still trying to find myself. I got a GED at sixteen. I had this crazy idea, but it didn't work out the way I thought. So...right now, I'm seeing the country and trying to figure out where to go next. Where's your hometown?" He changed the subject before she could ask him for details.

"Lewisville. That's in Arkansas, about thirty miles east. You've never heard of it."

"I haven't," he admitted.

"It's a tiny town, so small that we had to come here to find a restaurant big enough for the party."

"Do you have a lot of competition in the restaurant biz there?"

"Well, it's not like Starbucks has come to town, so that helps. But we also don't have a morning rush hour. I'd love to have cars wrapped around the building, but it isn't equipped with a drive-thru. No other place in town is open for breakfast or makes everything from scratch. I don't stay open for dinner because I can't compete with Burge's Pit Bar-B-Q or Scooter's Pizza Shack."

He nodded as they meandered closer to the band. "Wise business decision. I'll bet your goodies are delicious. I'd love a taste."

His voice had gone low and husky, and Jesse wondered if she'd heard it.

She raised her gaze to him, lashes fluttering flirtatiously. "Is that right? Well, my hot buns are fabulous."

"I have no doubt they are." He winked. When she giggled, he wished he could stay around long enough to take a bite of whatever she offered.

A few moments later, the collection of musicians grabbed their instruments and started playing a lively contemporary country love song with a three-four meter. It wasn't like anything he played in his vault of songs.

"Dance with me?" he asked, stopping at the edge of the floor and drawing her closer.

"You waltz?"

Not really. "Sure."

Mostly, he just wanted to hold her close.

She bit her lip. "I'm not much of a dancer."

"I'm pretty decent. I'll go easy on you. Say yes." He skimmed a palm down her back.

She exhaled, her breath shaky. Her stare never left his face. "Okay. They're your toes."

"You'll do great."

Jesse took her hand in his and brought her closer. Every one of her curves seemed to align perfectly with him, each contour fitting to his like pieces of a puzzle. That sounded cheesy, even in his own head, but he'd never been more aware of a woman's every dip and swell, of his heart racing simply because she stood near and their palms touched. He wasn't at the eighth grade formal, slow-dancing with a girl for the very first time. He'd long ago lost track of how many women he'd slept with. But she made everything seem new again.

Were his palms actually sweating?

They fell in time to the music together, Jesse mimicking the sort of waltz his grandparents used to dance. Bristol seemed a bit stiff at first, but with every step she relaxed more into his arms.

"Where did you learn to dance?" she asked.

He couldn't say that his very first manager had hired dance instructors to work with him to perfect his on-stage moves and that, more recently, he'd hired a "male entertainer" to show him how to make his moves sexier. Instead, he opted for something he could tell her.

"My grandparents owned an Arthur Murray dance studio. I spent my summers there. When I was thirteen, I thought it would be the happening place to pick up girls, so I paid attention. I learned a lot."

"I'll bet you were smooth even back then."

"I thought I was." He smiled at her. "I see the pictures now and think 'dork in braces.'"

She laughed. "I can't imagine it."

"True story."

Because he wasn't digging even the small bit of distance between them, Jesse flattened his palm to her back, sliding down to the sway in her spine, bringing her petite frame and sweet curves even closer. He didn't usually have any trouble controlling his cock. Now it had a mind of its own, and he ached to slide all of her against every inch of him too badly to care if she felt that.

When he arched into her, she gasped, then flattened herself against him. The friction as they swayed together blew his mind. She glanced up at him, and he curled a finger under her chin to bring her face beneath his. He really had to restrain himself from grabbing her ass. Public displays didn't bother him but that sort of thing might bug her. And he wasn't supposed to be drawing attention to himself.

"If you don't want me to kiss you, say something now."

"I…I can't."

Jesse eased back, trying not to let the surprisingly visceral disappointment consume him. "You can't let me kiss you?"

"No, I can't say anything."

His entire body tensed. He wanted to throw her to the ground and get inside her in the next thirty seconds. Sure he liked sex. Loved it. But this compulsion to take off Bristol's clothes and make her scream out his name seemed way beyond any normal urge.

He took her face in his hands. God, she was so small in his grip. Delicate. Lovely. Her stare clung to him, her green eyes so open and earnest. She wasn't playing a game, wasn't merely interested in him because of who he was. She seemed to like *him*.

Now was a really crappy time to decide that he seriously liked a girl. Jesse knew he should walk away. But Deke had advised him to make all the parts of his life meaningful. Bristol Reese might be the most meaningful thing he'd felt in years.

Chapter Three

Bristol fought to catch her breath. When Jamie cradled her face and looked into her eyes as if nothing in his life meant more than this kiss, an electric spark had sizzled down her spine. The answering jolt darkened his hungry stare.

She hadn't felt important to anyone since her father. She wasn't unhappy being alone, but her ill-fated relationship with Hayden had taught her that she couldn't play second best anymore. Looking back, she saw that he'd always gravitated to Presleigh. Too often, he'd been happy to forego an evening with her to have dinner with her mother and sister. Jamie could care less that her beauty queen sibling was anywhere in the building.

"Good. I'm going to kiss you." His voice sounded husky, rough. His grip on her tightened as if he didn't want to let her go. "I'm going to make you open to me so I can taste every corner of your mouth. I want to know what it feels like when you melt against me and moan in surrender."

Her heart picked up speed until she could hear its beating in her ears. "Sure of yourself, aren't you?"

He shook his head. "I'm banking on the hope that this pull I'm feeling toward you isn't one-sided. The way you're looking at me says it's not. If I'm wrong, tell me."

"You're not," she breathed. "This is crazy. We met an hour ago." But she still felt as if she knew him in some weird way on a soul-deep level. Jamie made her hormones swirl and did something she couldn't quite classify to her heart. Walking away from him now simply because they hadn't had a requisite date at Chili's before sharing a movie didn't make sense. It didn't have any bearing on whether they slipped into bed.

Hadn't she vowed earlier to have flings? Jamie seemed as if he'd qualify as the perfect one.

He leaned closer, his gaze focused on hers as his lids shut. Her breathing stopped. Her heartbeat stuttered, then lurched. Bristol wanted to know how being close to him would feel. He wasn't her "type" and that didn't seem to matter at all.

"Bristol?" She'd know that sharp voice anywhere.

"Yes, Mama?"

"Hayden and Presleigh have a few words to say to everyone. And she'd like you to pass out the cookies."

"Damn it," she muttered under her breath. When Jamie smiled down at her, his hands still cupping her face, his warmth went a long way to squelching her disappointment. He wasn't letting her mother ruin their first kiss. She wouldn't either. "I'll be right there."

"And Aunt Jean wants to know what she's doing wrong with her chocolate sheet cake."

"I'll bet she tried to use two-percent instead of buttermilk again," she murmured to Jamie. "Sure thing. I'll be right there."

The sound of her mother's heels clicking away was a relief.

"Does she do that a lot?" he asked.

"Interrupt my love life. No. I don't have much of one."

"Excuse me while I have a Neanderthal moment and tell you I'm glad to hear that." He chuckled. "I meant does she try to direct you."

Bristol rolled her eyes. "All the time. She's from a really old-fashioned family. If you're not a wife and mother, you're not really an adult. There's no such thing as being a single woman who can look after herself in this neck of the woods."

"I'll bet you have an independent streak."

"Always have," she said wryly. "But I need to get back or she'll badger me."

"Then let's go." He took her hand and led her toward the others.

"Thanks for not bailing."

He scoffed comically. "I'm your boyfriend for the night. What kind of asshole would that make me to dump you in the middle of a party?"

"Someone more similar to Hayden than I'd like."

He laughed. "Not the image I'm going for."

As they reached the gathering, Presleigh was still clinging to Hayden as if he was her sun and moon. He flashed a smile down at her, as if he wanted everyone to know that he was enamored with his bride-to-be. Bristol had once seen that expression directed at her, and she wondered what her younger sister would do if someone new caught his eye.

Presleigh spotted her and smiled. "Thank you, everyone, for coming. Invitations are in the mail, but Bristol also made delicious cookies and frosted them with our wedding date. She's so clever." Her sister sent her an earnest expression. "In fact, she's one of the most important people in my life. Bris, I'm hoping you'll be my maid of honor."

Bristol felt her eyes widen and tried to keep the horror off her face. Wasn't it enough that she'd given Presleigh her man and baked her engagement cookies? Now she had to stand next to her sister as she married the man who had once been hers?

"Are you fucking kidding me?" Jamie muttered under his breath.

"I thought you wanted me to bake your cake." Bristol didn't know what else to say.

"I do," Presleigh assured with an excited shake of her head. "But you've always stood next to me in childhood. I want you to stand beside me as I become a wife."

"It would mean a lot to both of us," Hayden added.

Was this really happening? "Didn't you already ask your friend Shea?"

"Yeah, but she and Corey"—she pointed at Hayden's friend—"had that ugly breakup. Now they won't even speak two words to each other. I finally decided that it was fate telling me that you should be the one to stand beside me. Mama is going to walk me down the aisle since Daddy isn't here. Please... It will be perfect."

What a lovely piece of emotional blackmail, wheedling in front of almost everyone she knew so that she'd look like a bitch if she refused. Never mind that she was apparently second choice. "Um…"

"I've already picked out a dress and ordered it. It will fit perfectly and look fantastic. Please…"

It would probably look awful since she and Presleigh had polar opposite tastes. Bristol took a deep breath. It didn't matter. As Daddy had always said, family was family—and they came first. As much as she didn't want to do this, Bristol also didn't want to start a family feud over her pride.

"All right. I'll do it."

Jamie scoffed beside her. Yeah, she would have liked a graceful way out of this mess, too. But this commitment would last one day, over and done. Then she would step back and let Hayden and her sister live their lives.

"Thanks, Bris." Presleigh looked as if she was going to tear up. "It means so much to me."

Bristol smiled and tried to make it look genuine. "You're welcome. On that note, the cookies are in the storage container in front of you if you'd like to pass them out."

"They're your cookies. Don't you want to?" Her sister looked confused.

Her ego could pass up the stroke of hearing the cookies were pretty. A sugary shortbread topped with white icing and black piping to draw the June calendar, the treats had come out well.

"I'm good." Bristol shook her head. "Jamie and I are going now."

If he seemed surprised by her proclamation, he didn't show it.

When her mother scowled in disapproval, Jamie acted as if her sour expression didn't exist. "She promised to spend some time with me since we're still getting to know one another." He reached across the table and snagged a cookie out of the red plastic container. "Nice to meet you all."

With that, he grabbed her purse from the table and led her out of the restaurant, taking a big bite of the pastry as they hit the door. Just outside, he stopped completely and moaned. "Oh, my god. Are you kidding me? This is a foodgasm. Amazing."

She grinned up at him. "Did you doubt me?"

"If I ever did, I won't do it again." He moaned once more. "I understand why Jayla manipulated you for cookies. I may have to learn strategy from her."

He wouldn't be around that long since she only did temporary relationships now, but that was all right. He could flirt all he wanted. "How about an ooey-gooey cinnamon roll? They're what I'm known for. I'll make you a pan…" She took a deep breath. "If you're still with me come morning."

He froze altogether again—everything except his eyes. They came absolutely alive. Dark, focused, demanding as he scanned her face to see if she was serious. God, he really was hot. She couldn't wait to see him without the black skullcap, without the clothes that hid what she felt sure would be a breath-stealingly hard body. Not to mention that he was funny and nice and…seemingly on the same wavelength as her.

"Your place?" he asked.

"Is that a yes?"

He grabbed her shoulders, pressing their foreheads together. "That's a hell yes. Lead the way. I'll follow you on my bike."

Bristol didn't wait for Jamie to change his mind. She dug her keys from her purse and leveled him with a sexy stare full of come-hither. "Keep up."

"I will," he vowed. "Then once I have you naked and under me, I'll get deep inside and fill you up. You won't have a single regret."

Bristol refused to regret anything. She was determined they would make this a night to remember.

She hopped in her car, and he followed her on some sleek black-and-chrome motorcycle. Watching him lean over the machine, his thighs hugging the bike as it roared and purred, seeing him handle it with an enticing male grace and agility, totally revved her desire. She'd always dated seemingly good guys…who never turned out to be quite as good as she'd believed. Jamie was all bad boy.

Bristol couldn't wait.

A few miles shy of Lewisville, her phone rang. Jayla's contact appeared, and she answered the call right away. "Hey!"

"I tried to save you, but your mama wouldn't listen."

"Save me?" Her stomach tightened with worry. "Uh oh. What does that mean?"

"She wants you to come to dinner on Tuesday night—and to bring Jamie."

"No. Absolutely not. He's my Saturday night fling."

"Well, your mama thinks he's your new man."

"And whose fault is that?" Bristol groused. "So he and I will have to break up before then."

Jayla got quiet. That was never a good sign.

"Spit it out. What's the issue?"

"Your mama invited half of Lewisville, and the townsfolk are starting to think that you're not interested in hanging onto a man."

Bristol gripped the steering wheel. "I'm not—not anymore."

"But you know how they think. You're either a good girl looking to get married or a ho-bag who doesn't deserve their business."

Shock pinged through Bristol. "Seriously?" Then she thought it through and cursed. "Never mind. I know it's true. So basically, I have to look ready to pair up with Jamie until death do us part before he dumps me horribly—much later—so I can win their sympathy or else no one will buy another mushroom omelet or peach cobbler from me, right?"

"That's pretty much how it is."

This debacle would probably be crazy to anyone who didn't live in a tiny town. But here, where everyone knew everybody and their business, Jayla's reminder was irrefutable.

"Damn it." Bristol shook her head. "I'll deal with it. Thanks for the warning."

"Thanks for not shooting the messenger."

Jayla rang off, and Bristol tried to decide exactly how to plead or bribe Jamie into coming to dinner on Tuesday night. Since it sounded as if he was between jobs, hopefully it wouldn't be a problem. Normally, that would bother her since she preferred to date guys who were gainfully employed. But she wasn't planning a long-term relationship with Jamie, just sex.

She glanced in the rearview mirror. He still sat about twenty feet off her back bumper as they headed east on Highway 82.

Maybe she could sweet talk the man or feed him incredible desserts to make him stay through Tuesday. Or tie him to her bed. That had appeal. Though she'd like it better if he tied her down.

And if the townsfolk found out she fantasized about that, they'd absolutely die.

Still, she imagined what she and Jamie might do together, her autopilot keeping her compact on the highway. When she looked up again, they were cruising into Lewisville. Along the town's main drag, on the corner, she saw her shop and pulled into the parking lot behind the building as the sun dipped toward the horizon. Lewisville looked its best this time of day. Even then, it still appeared older, sometimes a bit neglected. Most children raised here left the moment they could. Bristol wondered why she'd stayed. Concern for her mother and sister? Memories of Daddy? Or being too afraid to leave everything she'd ever known?

Shaking off the thought, she stepped out of her car, purse on her shoulder, as Jamie climbed off his bike.

"Cute little town," he said.

"Small."

"Quaint," he corrected.

"That's a nice way of putting it." She gestured to her place. "Want the tour?"

"Sure."

She let them both in the back door. She mostly kept supplies here, along with a small office in the corner. Flipping on lights, she led him into her kitchen, which sparkled—just as it did every day after the close of business. Her industrial oven and mixer gleamed. Pristine stainless countertops covered the length of two walls, waiting for her to create the next yummy treat. She'd had to get a loan from a bank in Texarkana since the town's one financial institution had refused to loan funds to a "kid," but she'd done it on her own. And she was proud.

"So this is where the dough happens?" He winked.

"Yeah. And up front here…" Bristol directed him through the next door and into the front of the shop with its display cases and bistro tables. "This is the customer area. I can only seat twenty since the building is a converted brownstone and this room is the former parlor. But I'm proud of it."

Jamie looked around, seeming to take in every nuance. His eyes gleamed with appreciation. "It's got a lot of charm. Most places I go have none."

She frowned. "What has you traveling so much?"

"Gotta make a buck." He shrugged. "So do you live somewhere near your shop?"

She wondered what he did for a living but got the feeling he didn't want to talk about it. And did she really need to know if they were simply going to have a fling? "Upstairs."

Maybe it didn't seem smart to take a stranger home, but instinct told her Jamie wasn't dangerous. Besides, her family and friends knew who she'd gone home with. Jayla would no doubt check on her.

Bristol took Jamie's hand and guided him back to her stock room and to the staircase along one wall she and Jayla had restored to its original gleaming wood, just like the floors.

Together, she and Jamie charged up to her apartment, and she unlocked the door. As it creaked open, the last golden rays of the day illuminated her rustic chic space—the cozy white sofa, the glass table built on whiskey barrels, the braided rug under her grandmother's dining room table.

He glanced around, then cocked his head in thought. "It's you."

She smiled and shut the door behind them, flipping on the overhead lights. "Yeah?"

"Comfortable, happy, unvarnished. I like it."

"Thanks." He seemed to get her, and that did Bristol's heart a world of good. Hayden had hated this place. He liked things grander and more formal, not an eclectic grouping of her favorite things. He called antiques "recycled junk." "But you didn't come all the way to Lewisville to comment on my decor, right?"

"No." He turned to her, his hands suddenly engulfing her hips, his stare drilling down into her eyes. "I did not."

"So what did you come to do?" she challenged.

He gave her a panty-melting grin as he pulled her closer, fitting her flush against his body where she could feel every inch of him. "Make you glad you let me follow you home."

Bristol swallowed and lifted her face to him. "Are you finally going to kiss me?"

"Eager?"

She gave him a coy shrug. "A little."

"Let's see if we can make that a lot." He took her face in his hands.

She flashed back to the bar, in the instant before their lips had nearly met. Heart pounding, blood racing, need reeling... Yeah, she'd cursed her mother's interruption. But since then, her anticipation had grown. She wanted him more now. Maybe Mama had done her a favor in the long run. They wouldn't be interrupted here.

"You're welcome to try." She gave him a wicked grin.

He didn't say a word, just dipped his head toward her. Bristol held her breath. Her heart felt suspended in the moment and too filled with anticipation to beat. No man had ever excited her so much with a mere word or smile. She wondered how she'd handle his kiss.

"Look at me," he insisted, his voice gruff and low.

Her lashes fluttered open, and she peered up at the deepest, darkest eyes she'd ever lost herself in.

"That's it," he encouraged. "I wanted to see you, get closer to you. This may be temporary but it isn't impersonal."

"It's not," she whispered.

He caressed her face, shifted a hand behind her neck, fingers sifting through her hair. Bristol hadn't thought it possible, but he looked even more serious. "Good."

Finally, he brushed his lips over hers, the touch full of gentle command and electric thrill. A sizzle flashed over her skin. Her heart started thumping again, now beating a rapid tattoo against her chest.

Jamie pulled back enough to stare down at her again, searching her face for something. He caressed her other cheek with his warm palm. "God, I've got to taste your mouth, your skin. All of you."

Before she could say a word, he captured her lips once more, this time crashing into her, hungry, demanding, as if he couldn't get to her fast enough. He took her mouth as if he owned her, and Bristol wasn't prepared for his onslaught. His touch made her dizzy. No, *he* did. His musky scent surrounded her, dangerous, sexy, as he pressed his chest to her beating heart and consumed her.

He was above her, around her, all over her. Reaching up on her tiptoes, she threw her arms around his neck, every bit as desperate to get to him, and gasped into his kiss.

Bristol wrapped the hem of his tank in her fists and tugged up. He grabbed her wrists and swept them over her head, forcing them against the wall as he stared at her, panting, searching, naked hunger tightening his face. "Bedroom?"

The dark snap of his voice made her tremble. "End of the hall."

"Let's go." He bent and lifted her, wrapping her legs around his hips and covering her mouth with his again.

But instead of heading in that direction, Jamie shoved her to the wall and pressed himself against her. She swore she could feel his heart beating wildly. Then she forgot everything when he tightened his grip on her thighs and fitted his hips between them, rocking against her sex, right where he'd made her ache for him most.

Bristol gave a soft moan and writhed against him. It had been a while since she'd had a lover, but she had never felt anything so explosive, so connected. So right.

She pulled at his shirt again, perfectly happy with the idea that they might not make it to the bedroom. Here against this wall would be every bit as amazing, she'd bet.

He tore his mouth from hers. "How the fuck are you undoing me so fast?"

"It's…" *Chemistry.* "Something's happening between us. I…" *Need you.*

"Yeah. Me, too." He plowed her mouth again, his tongue surging deep, his kiss thorough, as if he meant to stake his claim. "I'm glad we're alone. I want to please every part of you. I want your body to know who owns it tonight. I want you to equate me with pleasure until all you have to do is hear my voice to get wet. I don't want you to have the slightest urge to ever say no."

"I can't imagine ever refusing you anything, Jamie…" She couldn't catch her breath, and it didn't matter now. Not as long as he was touching her.

He mumbled a curse before smoothing out his expression. Then he started down the hall finally, every step providing friction between them in the most delicious places. Fresh tingles erupted. Desire settled between her legs—an ache so sharp it stunned. They were still fully dressed. He hadn't done anything more than kiss her. But Bristol already suspected he would be the man by which she measured all others.

Jamie kicked the slightly ajar bedroom door open wide. Shakespurr scrambled off his perch on the windowsill with a startled meow, then scampered out of the room. Bristol barely noticed because Jamie carried her to the bed and tossed her to the mattress, following her down and covering her body with his own. He broke their kiss only long enough to tear her lacy shell from her torso and toss it across the room. Then he took her mouth again, nipping at her bottom lip and stealing inside, shredding her sanity.

Bristol tugged at his tank, frantically sliding her hands under the cotton to reach the supple skin over hard muscle. She longed to feel him, drink him in, make him a part of her for however long she could.

Finally, he tore his shirt off, sitting up enough so she could get a good look at him. Bristol nearly swallowed her tongue. Oh. Dear. God. The longer she looked at him, the more the dizzying fever of desire spun inside her. She raked her palms up the ridges of his abdomen, over the bronzed bulges of his torso. She traced the tribal tattoo on his shoulder, sucking in a breath at his iron flesh beneath her touch. Unable to resist, she skated her fingertips down his chest again, taking the time to circle one of his nipples. She delighted in watching them both go hard. Goosebumps broke out all over his body.

"Don't push me too hard, Bristol. I want to do this right." He panted, his breath coming fast as he gripped the button of his fly and tore it open. "Let me give us both a good time."

He didn't wear anything beneath his jeans. Bristol saw a shadowy hint of hair-dusted male flesh and shivered. Pressed against her earlier, he'd felt big.

"Hurry." She reached for the snap on her own jeans and tore it open, then tugged the zipper down and shoved the pants over her hips, at least until his body impeded her striptease.

Quickly, he stood, shucking his own denim.

Bristol got instant confirmation about his size. Well-endowed was putting it mildly. Or maybe she'd been handling nothing but small pricks like Hayden. Literally.

"That's it, honey. Take it all off so I can get to you. I want to see that pretty skin and silky pussy before I devour them both."

No man had ever talked to her that way. His words were gritty and raw, but there was nothing dirty about them. He made her feel sexy, like a woman should.

For the first time in her life, she wanted to give a man every part of her.

She doffed her pants. Her panties followed before she reached for her bra and unhooked it. When Jamie began prowling toward her like he meant to take her in every way that would give her pleasure, her nipples peaked tight. Her sex clenched.

Heart pumping, feeling eager, she spread her legs for him, planting her heels wide on the bed. "You're too slow. Come here so I can touch you."

A hint of a smile lurked at the corners of his lips. "You're awfully bossy. Or is that impatience?"

"Would you rather debate what I'm feeling or…" She ran her fingers up the insides of her thighs, nearly brushing her own wet flesh. "Get to the good stuff?"

Jamie paused, as if debating for a moment. Then he dropped all pretense and focused his potent gaze on her. "Good stuff. In fact, let's see how good we can make it."

Before she could say a word, he covered her body, flattening her against the mattress again. Their naked chests pressed together as his face hovered over hers. The heat of his body enveloped her, warming her seemingly from the inside out. He thrust his fingers into her hair as he stared into her eyes. This might be a temporary fling—the first of her life—but somehow he managed to make her feel special with a single, searing glance.

"Kiss me," she whispered, unable to look at him without wanting more.

He dipped his head and seized her lips with his own. When he closed his eyes, he might have broken their visual connection, but his kiss gripped her heart and squeezed. He came at her as if desperate to possess her. The intensity jarred Bristol. She'd never felt like the focus of any man's desire—until now.

Then she stopped thinking altogether because he urged her lips apart with his own and plowed inside, his tongue curling against hers. Their lips mingled. Their breaths entwined. Bristol arched against him. Jamie wrapped his arms around her more tightly.

"You're so fucking sweet. And small. I don't want to break you."

She lifted her hips, rubbing against his unflagging erection. "You're big." When he laughed, she had to join him. "I meant that you're tall and all buff. It's just...when you're near I can't—"

"Not touch you?"

"Yeah," she breathed against his lips.

"I know exactly what you mean."

"This is intense."

He paused. "Very."

Relief slid through her. So he felt it, too. "I've never experienced anything like this."

Was that too honest?

Jamie glided a palm down her side, thumbing the edge of her breast, hugging the curve of her waist, before taking her hip in hand. "Truthfully, neither have I."

And he looked as if that puzzled him. Warmth oozed through her bloodstream, tugged at her heart. Shouldn't she have felt this and more with the guy she'd once hoped to marry before he'd chosen her sister? Probably, but if she wanted to keep this connection to Jamie fleeting, then she needed to stop dwelling on her feelings and start focusing on the pleasure.

She closed her eyes and kissed her way up the strong column of his neck. When he groaned, she nipped at his ear and traced her fingertips down his spine. He braced both hands on her hips and started moving, rocking his erection against her.

"Yes." She urged him on, digging her fingers into his steely shoulders.

He captured her lips again, focused and intent, as if nothing was more important than lavishing attention on her mouth with one frenzied kiss after another. Bristol drowned in his taste, let her head get dizzy with his scent. The ache between her thighs turned sharp and sweet. She had no doubt that only he could sate it.

Then he worked his way down her body, leading with his mouth, worshipping her skin as he kissed a path down her throat and over her collarbones before he zeroed in on her breasts. He paused, his hot breath exhaling over her nipples. They tightened even more. Desperation crept through her. Her ache turned urgent.

"Touch me," Bristol pleaded.

He skimmed his knuckles across one turgid peak. Sensation pinged through her body, reverberating down to her toes. She gasped.

"So perfect. So beautiful," he murmured.

Then Jamie took one hard bead in his mouth, sucking her deep. She hissed at the pull of sensation and tore off his skullcap. She'd hoped to sink her fingers into his hair and bring him closer. Instead, the dark buzz hugged his scalp and made the angular hollows of his face even more pronounced. He was all male. Another shiver of anticipation rolled through her.

He stared down at her as if he waited for something. A reaction maybe? When the moment passed in silence, he bent his head and took her other nipple in his mouth, giving this one a sweet tug, too. Then he shifted his weight onto the bed, angling himself against the side of her body so he could smooth a palm down her stomach. Bristol held her breath, her heart tripping in the seconds before he cupped her mound in his hand. He slid his fingers over her slick skin, teased at nerve endings already screaming for more. Jamie could have no doubt that she wanted him bad.

"You're wet." His voice had gone deeper, huskier.

"I'm ready," she choked out, spreading her legs for him.

Maybe she should be more modest or wait for him to make the next move, but that was the old her. The her who let herself be misled and jilted. The woman who'd emerged from those ashes demanded what she wanted without apology.

He thumbed her clit a few times, then dragged the digit through her moisture. She moaned, her mouth gaping open at the need that one mere touch sent through her body. Another few seconds and she'd probably go over the edge. *Please, yes...*

"Next time, I'm going to take you slowly and savor every bit of you. Right now, you feel so damn good. I can't wait." He bounced off the bed, then prowled to his jeans, pulling a condom free. He rolled it on virtually one-handed and frighteningly fast.

Clearly, he'd done this a lot.

Bristol felt a moment's trepidation, then stopped herself. They weren't having a relationship, merely a hookup. It didn't matter if he was a well-practiced manwhore. The only thing she should care about was pleasure.

She smiled at him. "I can't, either."

Jamie climbed back on the bed, settling his knee between her legs as he pushed her flat again. "Can you take it hard? Fast? I'm not going to be happy until you're screaming for me."

"Stop talking and start living up to your promise."

His cock jerked. Then he settled his body between her legs and gripped her hips, thrusting the head of his erection against her aching sex in one swift move. When he'd settled unerringly against her opening, he shoved forward. Hard.

His first few inches stretched her, and a sweet sting flooded her veins with drugging need. She surged up to him, her head arching back on a moan. He gripped her tighter as he eased back, then pushed deeper.

"Oh...fuck." His voice dropped lower, his raspy tone making her feel as if he was coming apart, just like her.

"More," she barely managed to squeak out.

"Yes," he growled. "Now."

Jamie delivered, withdrawing before he plunged in once more, shoving his way deeper inside her, inciting a riot of tingles. The head of his cock rubbed against her most sensitive spots. She grabbed at his shoulders, frantic to hang on as he took her close to the edge, amazed at how completely he filled her.

When he pulled back, he dragged his hard flesh over those same screaming nerves. Her heartbeat resounded in her ears. Bristol didn't care if she ever took a deep breath again. The feel of his hands on her body, of his cock working back into her would keep her more than happy.

"You're so tight. So…made for me right now. Take more." His voice deepened with dark command.

No way she could have refused him. Instead, she lifted her legs around his hips and arched closer. "Yes."

He wrapped his fingers even tighter around her hips and plunged forward again. He filled her once more, seeming to take up all the empty space inside her while relieving none of the ache. In fact, it only grew until her head swam with dizzying desire.

But he paid no heed, merely kept pressing in, squeezing another inch of his erection into her clenching flesh. He gritted his teeth, totally focused on her. Sweat dotted his temples as he shoved in yet another inch. Then a bit more.

Bristol gasped at the foreign sensation, as if he not only opened her body completely for the first time but owned it.

Finally, he tilted his hips down, fitting himself utterly against her, inside her. She writhed under him, at once frantic to end the maddening ache…yet make it last forever.

Jamie sucked in a couple of heaving breaths before he swooped down and stole into her mouth. He attacked her lips, claiming them as he withdrew his cock. She cried out in protest at his loss, but he swallowed the sound with his kiss. Then he stroked deep inside her again, stretching her to accommodate every bit of him, drowning her objection with more desire. He took down all her defenses.

He made her forget that Jamie Last-name-lacking was nothing but a fling who would be gone in a handful of days.

She didn't know how to hold anything back when he thrust into her, falling into a deep, fast rhythm that made her ancient bedframe squeak, her old floors creak, her heart thunder, and her pleasure receptors overload. Everything about him called to her, from the slightly tangy flavor of his kiss, to his scorching palms roaming her overheated skin. With every stroke, he seemed to anchor himself deeper until she would have sworn that with the feverish rise of her orgasm, he was also unzipping her skin and turning her inside out, forcing her to show every bit of the vulnerability and need she'd rather hide.

Her headboard hit the wall. Thrill zipped through her as he filled her again.

He positioned her legs up and against her body, spreading her wider, allowing him deeper. "Wrap your hands around the headboard. Don't let go."

Her heart fluttered, skipped a beat, as she complied. His triumphant smile made the ache in her sex tighten. She clamped down on him. "I'm close."

"Oh, honey. You have no idea how seriously I'm riding the edge."

Bristol didn't have a chance to say anything before he came at her again, his rhythm harder, faster, as if he'd allowed his need off a seriously tight leash. Every thrust told her that he didn't have any intention of holding back anymore.

Frantically, she grabbed at the spindles of her old brass headboard, giving Jamie what he demanded. It felt good to give in, to surrender. He rewarded her with more pleasure. Sex with him felt like embracing a thunderstorm, riding a wild bronc. She absorbed him, savoring the rising crescendo of desire as every muscle in her body tightened for the imminent explosion.

"There you are. That's it. Yeah." He gritted his teeth, staring down into her eyes, the storm there stealing her breath. "Everything about you fucking turns me on. Come for me."

She couldn't have held back for anything. Blood rushed, tingles converged, the universe parted. Angels freaking wept.

As he tensed and slammed into her again, Bristol's world crashed open, blotting out all but him. The pleasure that twisted her body wiped away everything in her head. The orgasm was too big to hold inside. She opened her mouth to beg Jamie for some way to handle the battering ram of ecstasy. The only sound that came out of her mouth was a low-pitched, animal wail.

He followed her with hammering strokes and a long, raspy growl that sounded an awful lot like her name as he shuddered.

Then he stopped, all but collapsing on his elbows above her. He planted his face in her neck, his panting breaths rolling over her skin.

He'd stolen everything from her and made her feel as if she'd been run over by a train. She didn't have the energy to even open her eyes, but she did let go of the headboard and wrap her arms around him.

"What the fuck was that?" he muttered.

"No idea." And somehow she wondered if her world would ever be the same.

Jamie lifted his head, his dark eyes shining with mischief. "Whatever it was, we definitely have to do it again."

Chapter Four

Bristol bent to bag a few cookies from the display case for Mrs. Barton's three kids and swallowed back a moan of discomfort. But putting up with the occasional twinge was a small price to pay for the enormous pleasure Jamie had given her last night.

True to his word, after that first gotta-have-it rush, he'd slowed the pace down and loved her with finessed, insatiable perfection. As their damp bodies glided together in a furious passion, he'd taken her over and over, leaving her breathless and stunned...yet still aching for him.

Clearly, he knew his way around a woman's body.

As she secured the cookies in the little white bag, Bristol sighed.

The Barton kids whooped and cheered as she handed the confections to their mom. "Thanks. Enjoy!"

After a cheerful wave, the family tumbled out into the sunshine. Once they were gone, Bristol's thoughts drifted back to the previous night. She should wipe what was probably a stupid, sappy grin from her face. But her body still hummed with a well-loved satisfaction she'd never imagined.

And when Jamie hadn't been touching her last night—which seemed constantly—he'd talked to her. About her family, her coffeehouse, her favorite movies, fondest memories...everything. He didn't talk much about himself. In fact, he'd artfully dodged most of her attempts to learn more about him. She knew some about his childhood and that, as an adult, he was a wanderer. She knew he considered his number of true friends very small. The man obviously preferred privacy. And Bristol didn't pry. As much as she enjoyed being with him, as much as he intrigued her, Jamie wouldn't be in her life past Tuesday night, provided she could even get him to stay long enough for her mother's dinner. She didn't want to find out everything about him and like him even more. She had to think fling. Temporary. Not getting attached. Romance really was nothing more than a fairy tale. Hayden and every guy she'd dated before him had proven that.

The door chime resounded overhead. And speak of the devil…

Hayden entered her shop, looking flushed. From the heat? She glanced at the clock over his head. Twenty minutes until she closed, and he knew it. When they'd been dating, he'd come by about this time when he had something on his mind. He knew it was her slowest time of day and that she couldn't end the confrontation by walking away until she locked her doors at quitting time.

Bristol tensed. "What's up?"

Hayden didn't pretend this was a friendly chat. "Is he still here?"

"Jamie?" she asked as if she had more than one man in her life. No way did she want Hayden to think she sat around pining for him. Nothing could be further from the truth.

"Yeah. I didn't appreciate you bringing him to our engagement party."

"He was my 'plus one,'" she fibbed. "I RSVPd."

"No, Jayla was your plus one," he reminded her, holding up a stern finger.

Okay, that was true but… "Why does it matter? It's not as if you ran out of food or chairs. The party wasn't negatively impacted because Jamie came."

"I didn't like it. I don't like him for you." Hayden crossed his arms over his chest.

Now that Bristol had seen Jamie do nearly the same thing—while naked—her ex seemed on the scrawny side, not deeply masculine or shiver-worthy. Seeing Hayden in the buff had never incited her to tear off her clothes and plead for his touch. But Jamie...

As she crossed the room with careful steps to straighten the bistro tables and chairs—mostly to avoid looking at Hayden—she felt that sappy smile creep across her face again. "Too bad. I do."

"That expression is making me sick. He's obviously a player. And why are you walking so funny?" He scowled, then he gaped. "Are you sore because he—"

"I won't discuss my relationship with Jamie, especially not with you, Hayden. You're engaged to my sister now, so what I do is absolutely none of your business. Did you have a reason to come here, other than to harass me?"

He pulled down on his Sunday-best navy sport coat. "To check on you."

"I'm fine. Don't you have someplace else to be? Isn't there a church potluck this afternoon?"

"I skipped it."

Hayden never missed an opportunity to play the role of "big man in town." Bristol stared at him suspiciously. Why was he sweating? "So you could come here and bug me?"

"No." He sent her an annoyed scowl. "I stopped by Corey's house and... That doesn't matter. Watching you leave with that guy last night worried me. He won't stay, you know."

Bristol shrugged as if it didn't matter. Jamie wouldn't stay, and she was okay with that...mostly. Not seeing him after Tuesday night's dinner at her mother's house sounded horrible right now, but she was in a sex-induced infatuation bubble, right? By the time she was done with him, it was possible they both would have found a hundred ways to crawl on one another's nerves. By then, they'd realize how wrong they were together. Then she'd be ready for her next fling. No muss, no fuss. No problem.

It just didn't feel that way now.

Get it together, girl. You are not getting your heart involved again.

"You didn't stay either, and I survived," she pointed out.

"He's only using you for sex," Hayden added.

"I'm okay with that. At least he's putting a smile on my face.

I finally understand what the big deal about sex is." She gave him a tight smile. "Shouldn't you be focusing on your sex life? After all, you and Presleigh are getting married next month."

"You know she's a virgin. We're waiting for our wedding night."

Seriously? Hayden hadn't wanted to wait ten minutes with her, and he was willing to wait over a year for her sister? *Wow.* That still didn't explain why he'd come—and why he sounded more than slightly jealous, unless…

She shoved her hands on her hips and faced him. "So you don't like Jamie here because—"

"I'm in the bed he wants to occupy until he marries his sweet little bride," Jamie called from behind her, standing in the doorway of the kitchen.

When he stepped into her restaurant, Bristol breathed a sigh of relief. She knew he couldn't leave the building without first passing through her kitchen, and she figured he'd been sleeping after their vigorous night. But seeing him now, clearly intending to get Hayden off her back, thrilled her all over again.

Jamie skirted the display cases and headed toward her. "He's got a case of blue balls and hoped that you were pining for him enough to help him cheat on your sister so that he could dump you again when they got married. Or did you plan to just continue the bump and grind behind Presleigh's back after the wedding?"

"That is not true!" Hayden insisted. "I still care for Bristol deeply. And I'm going to make sure you don't use her and break her heart."

"You mean like you did?" Jamie prompted.

Hayden gaped like a fish out of water, the shock on his face overdone and ridiculous. "I did not. We were simply not suited—"

"We weren't, but I think you felt that way long before you bothered to share that fact with me," Bristol pointed out. "You blindsided me by telling me that you were in love with my sister. Two days later, you were dating her. Until then, you made me believe that you cared and"—she held up her hands—"You know what? It doesn't matter. I don't care if you don't like Jamie for me because *I* like him for me right now. Tomorrow may be another story, but I'm an adult. It's my life and my business. But don't for one second think you're going to waltz in here and whisper a few pickup lines, seduce me out of my clothes, and use me to pass the time until your wedding. In fact, I'd better not see or hear from you again until you say 'I do' or I'll be having a long talk with Presleigh about the likelihood of you not staying faithful."

Hayden lunged at her, his hand balled in a fist. "I wasn't hitting on you."

"Bullshit." Bristol tensed, ready to fend him off if necessary.

"And technically, I never cheated," he insisted, edging closer.

Jamie put himself squarely between them, towering over Hayden, his shoulders a formidable barrier. "I'll bet that's bullshit, too. And she *will* talk to Presleigh if you don't get the fuck out. I'll back her up."

Hayden leaned around Jamie and scowled, his expression asking her to be reasonable. She didn't see why she had to defend her decision, especially since he was acting like a jealous bully. He was the one who'd betrayed her trust. No, she couldn't prove that he'd come here today to crawl between her sheets again. But his reason certainly didn't have anything to do with concern. Was he bored? Did he need to feed his ego by wooing her into bed again? Whatever. It wasn't happening.

"Bris…" He huffed at her. "You two have known one another for…what? Ten minutes? We've known each other most of our lives. Of course I'm worried about you."

She scoffed. "I know you too well to believe that. Now go away. You know I take goodies up to the kids at the county hospital on Sundays. You're in my way."

He refused to budge.

Jamie grabbed Hayden by the shirt. "She told you how she feels. You need to respect that. Turn your ass around and leave."

"You're really going to let your boy toy talk to me that way?" Hayden demanded, shoving Jamie away. "We're practically family."

Yeah, thirty days from becoming his sister-in-law, and he wanted to nail her. No thanks. "Just go."

"I'm not leaving you here with this thug." Hayden shoved

his fists on his hips and stood his ground, despite the fact that Jamie stood a good six inches above him and outweighed him by fifty pounds of muscle.

"You know, you sound tired, honey." Jamie glanced at her over his shoulder, his concern evident.

He totally ignored Hayden to check on her. Bristol tried not to let that make her a little giddy. He was merely a decent guy doing the right thing. It wasn't a romantic gesture. He might have done the same for any woman with her ex breathing down her neck.

"Three thirty this morning came early." Especially after last night. Even the thought of it made her face flush hot.

"Why don't you go upstairs and rest?" Jamie suggested.

She shook her head. "I need to lock up."

"Is it more complicated than turning the latch on the door over there." Jamie thumbed in the direction of the glass entrance.

"No. It's just…"

"Something you always do. I'll turn off the lights, too. I can handle it. Honestly."

"I have to clean up the kitchen." She glanced back at the messy space. Usually she cleaned up after herself as she cooked. This morning, she'd been too flipping tired. A night with Jamie was enough to wear out any girl, but especially one who rose at the ass crack of dawn for work.

"Go shower and eat something. It'll sit until you've rested." Jamie assured, then turned his attention back to Hayden.

Suddenly, she got it. He wanted to put her ex in his place, man to man. Bristol bit at her lip. She should tell Jamie that she could fight her own battles because she could. But the idea of a shower, a meal, and a way to avoid her ex were too much to pass up. Besides, she had the feeling he would only keep insisting.

"Sure." She smiled. "Thanks."

"Don't do this," Hayden protested. " You're making a big mistake. Talk to me."

"You let me go, so it's my mistake to make. Bye."

After a sarcastic smile and a wave, Bristol turned toward the back of the shop and headed for the stairs, feeling as if Jamie had lifted an enormous weight from her shoulders—at least for now. Come Wednesday, she'd be alone again, and Jamie would have moved on. But today, he could chase Hayden off, lock her door against the little insect, and hold her tight.

It wasn't romance, she assured herself. But it felt pretty damn good.

* * * *

Jesse heard Bristol's footfalls fade as she headed upstairs. When the door closed, he turned to Hayden with a blistering glare. "Leave her the fuck alone."

"Or what? You're not going to stay. And I'll still be around."

Hayden had him there. Jesse knew he couldn't remain indefinitely, even if sharing a bed—hell, a kiss—with Bristol was one of the most singular pleasures he'd ever experienced. For a well-seasoned hedonist, that was saying something. Still, her ex was trouble, and Jesse was determined to make sure that the asshole gave Bristol a wide berth even after he was gone.

"Are you nothing but an entitled tool who thinks you should have everything you want, and fuck everyone else?"

The scrawny guy reared back as if the question shocked him—or slapped him across the face. "What does that mean?"

"I used to be one, so I know all the earmarks," Jesse assured. "Why else would you pursue Bristol if it's only going to hurt her? You *left* her. Now she doesn't want you anymore. Obviously, that makes you feel lousy, but no one gives a shit about your pride. And young, naive Presleigh would be crushed if she had any idea you were here, sniffing around her older sister. You either care about your fiancée enough to be faithful or you're not ready for marriage."

Listen to me being all wise and shit…

"It's none of your business," Hayden shot back. "You might have spent last night with Bristol, but you don't care about her."

"And you do?" he challenged. "If you could dump her for her sister, then come back looking to get laid, I don't think you care at all."

Hayden managed to look indignant. "I came to check on

her, not for sex."

"But you wouldn't turn it down, would you?"

"I I wasn't thinking that. I…"

Hayden's seemingly perplexed expression was bullshit and told Jesse that sex with Bristol might not have been bobbing on the top of her ex's frontal lobe, but it had been swimming somewhere in his brainpan.

"The hell you weren't."

"You don't know me," Hayden finally snarled. "Fuck you."

With that, he turned and pushed out the door. The bell rang with shrill violence. The heavy glass slammed behind him.

"Good riddance," Jesse murmured, locking up and killing the lights before flipping the sign on the door to read CLOSED.

But the asshole brought up some really good points, namely that in a few days, Jesse would be gone. Right now, he didn't dig the thought of leaving Bristol behind. Kimber was the only woman he'd felt any actual emotion for in the past, and at the time he hadn't cared enough about her—or himself—to fly right. The punk he'd been years ago would probably have related to Hayden's dilemma, still being hot for one girl while engaged to another. In fact, Jesse vividly remembered the night he'd been in that position. He'd chosen wrong, siding with booze and easy ass, rather than love or respect. The decision had haunted him ever since because he knew he'd fucked up and hurt someone special. He refused to let Hayden do the same to Bristol.

While pondering ways to make the prick keep his distance, Jesse's phone buzzed in his pocket. He pulled it free and saw Candia's contact pop up on the display. A quick glance told him he was still alone in the little bakery.

He pulled up a bistro chair and answered. "Hey."

"Where are you?" She sounded frazzled.

"Did you already figure it out?" Had someone at the restaurant last night recognized him after all?

"No. You're so quiet it's eerie."

With a grin, Jesse leaned back. "Told you I wouldn't fuck it up."

"I'm actually impressed. It's a good thing you disappeared for a while."

"So things are still ugly? Why aren't the police releasing

details?"

She sighed, and he heard her exhaustion. "The investigation is still ongoing. The fact that Maddy Harris died in your hotel room was bad enough. Now I've learned that she'd helped herself to the T-shirt you wore at that night's concert. She was wearing it when she died."

"Oh, shit." He could only imagine what the press were saying about that.

"Exactly. An anonymous source leaked pictures of her body at the scene. I'm betting on a cop looking to make a quick buck. Then some Photoshopping genius positioned an image of you singing that night and her lying dead in the same fucking shirt side by side. It's circulating all over social media. *ET* and *Huff Post* aren't exactly being kind in their speculation, either. But I have no doubt it's helping their numbers." She paused. "Ryan's funeral is scheduled for Tuesday morning in Shreveport. His next of kin was his great aunt. She lives there."

"I'll be there."

"Until the police conclude this investigation and some time goes by, I'm not sure you should do anything but lay low."

"I won't miss his services, Candia. If I did, I'd look like an unfeeling prick. And I need to say good-bye. He might have had his flaws, but he was my friend." He shook his head and struggled against tears. "I wish to fuck I'd been able to save him."

The rock star life looked like good-time glitz to outsiders. Living it was something else completely. Different countries, different hotel rooms, transient "friends." Jesse's schedule was never his. Indulging in his goofy side wasn't good for the badass sex-god image he'd cultivated over the years. Yeah, it sold albums, but he never quite relaxed. Music critics and a changing industry complicated everything. And the really suck-ass part was the paparazzi hovering, just waiting to snap pictures if the temptation to dive into the ever-present girls, booze, and drugs ever became too much to resist. Not for one minute did he forget that virtually everyone around him was making a buck off his vocal cords. If he lost his voice or died tomorrow, his fans would care. But would any of the people he saw day in and day out give two shits?

Not so much. Candia was the closest thing he had to a friend now, and she was a career woman first and always. If she didn't have him, she'd mourn for thirty seconds, then pick up the phone and schmooze multiple job offers before choosing one and moving on.

No wonder he'd really enjoyed his time with Bristol. She didn't expect him to be sexy or perfect or charming or anything except nice. And while he suspected she was a tad gun-shy after Hayden, she had opened up to him and shared parts of herself, like the fact that she was named after her dad's Connecticut hometown and that she watched *Buffy the Vampire Slayer* reruns whenever she caught one on TV.

"Ryan made his choices," she murmured, her voice heavy.

Jesse gritted his teeth. "When he was so high, he barely knew his own damn name."

"Sorry. I know he'd been a part of your band for years and you used to be tight." She hesitated.

Tight? They'd shared both women and parties for years. Nothing more intimate than drinking out of the same bottle while both balls deep in the same chick. He and Ryan had grown apart after Jesse had stuck with his decision to stay sober, but that didn't mean he'd cared about the guy less.

"Thanks," he muttered.

"Maddy's funeral is that afternoon in Round Rock."

He winced. What a tragic waste. Sixteen was way too young to die.

"Did you get a hold of her parents?"

"I did. They don't want anything to do with you, your apologies, or your money. And they definitely don't want you showing up to their daughter's funeral and turning it into a media circus. They want to grieve in peace. They don't blame you for what happened. Apparently, Maddy had been through some trouble with drugs in the past. But they don't want you or any token of yours around as a reminder of all they've lost. If you really want to make a gesture of some sort, I think your best option is to start a scholarship fund in her name or shoot an anti-drug PSA."

That would cost him almost nothing. Jesse wished the girl's parents had been more demanding…but forcing them to take from him would only serve to make himself feel better. "Done. Set it all up."

"Will do. Beyond that, I'm still thinking about your image and how to rehab it. Give me time." She sighed. "So where did you go after you dropped me off at the airport?"

Jesse described his road trip to see Kimber. "But I couldn't intrude on their domestic scene any longer, so I split. They won't tell anyone. Kimber understands the pressure, and Deke just wants me gone." He shifted in his seat. "After that, I went back to the hotel and grabbed my bike off the equipment truck, then took off. I pulled over to sleep at a park off the road. Then I rolled into Texarkana and found an old-school barbershop. No one in there was under seventy, so I doubt they had any idea who I am. I'd already rented a craptastic motel room and shaved. I'd taken out my earrings and slid into the jeans and a comfortable tank I keep in the saddlebag. They cut my hair without blinking. Now I'm a new man."

"So you're in Texarkana?" Candia didn't sound thrilled, and he heard her tapping on her keyboard. "Because someone there will recognize you. According to the most recent census, the city has a population of over thirty-six thousand people. Even if you've changed your appearance—"

"I was only there a few hours. I went to a nearby barbeque restaurant the barbers raved about to grab some dinner and..." Saying he'd met someone was going to launch Candia into a righteous fit. On the other hand, she seemed to have spidey senses. His publicist would figure it out, and when she realized that he hadn't clued her in, he'd have hell to pay. Besides, she couldn't help him improve his image if she didn't know how he might be impacting it. "I sort of...met a woman."

"Oh my—" she huffed. "Seriously? You think now is the time to get laid? How long before she sells you out to the tabloids? I can see the headlines now. *McCall 'grieves' with skanky one-night stand.*"

"First of all, she's not skanky and she's not a simple lay. Her name is Bristol Reese. She bakes for a living. And she's really damn sweet. Second, she has no idea who I am."

"Get real." Candia was jaded on a good day, and this wasn't a good one at all.

"I'm totally serious. She was in the middle of a weird family situation and I helped her out. She didn't recognize me. No one did. Look." He took a quick selfie of his shorn hair and clean face, bare of all leather and jewelry. Then he sent it her way. Jesse studied the image. He looked like a normal Joe.

A few moments later, he heard a ding. "Wow, that's you? Holy shit, you clean up nice. Okay, I have to admit, I barely recognize you. Your face looks leaner, more chiseled with your hair buzzed. We should talk to Jackie about making this look permanent. It's a surprisingly cool change."

Jesse didn't want to talk about his stylist now. "It's sure a shitload easier. So anyway, I'm in this small town in Arkansas. Lewisville. Barely a thousand people live here. I'm more likely to be given a sideways glance for being a newcomer than for being an international star. Relax."

She paused. "You know, maybe it's not a terrible idea for you to hang low there for a few days. I mean, if this girl has no idea who you are and you really won't see other people, that little pissant town may be the perfect place to hide."

Candia's proclamation made Jesse smile. He didn't have to give up Bristol yet. Reality would intrude soon enough, but he could enjoy her company a bit longer. He wished he could confide in her, tell her about his problems and his grief. She would listen well and give good advice, he'd bet.

"Admit it. I did the right thing," he ribbed Candia.

"In theory. It's early days. Just keep your new bug all snug in your love nest so she can't squeal. We'll talk soon."

Before he could even say good-bye, she hung up. With a shrug, Jesse pocketed his phone. In their world, time was money, and he didn't pay her to shoot the shit. He'd rather have her figuring out how to assure the public that he hadn't played any part in the girl's death and that he was sorry as hell that she was gone.

Jesse made his way back to the upstairs apartment. Not a noise disturbed the space. Shakespurr prowled closer, staring him down before he gave a disdainful meow and trotted off. But he didn't hear a sound out of Bristol.

When he crept down the hall, he found the bathroom door open, steam still clouding the mirror over the basin. A few steps more, and he stood in the door to her bedroom. She lay across the bed, dressed in a faded gray T-shirt about five sizes too big with some terrycloth turban thing wrapped around her hair. And she was fast asleep.

A fond smile crawled across his face. After her shitty evening with her family, he'd kept her awake more often than not before she'd had to slip out to work. She'd still put in almost a twelve-hour day and confronted her ex head on. His girl had smarts, stamina, and spine.

Well, she wasn't his, like, forever. But his for another day.

He'd love to wake Bristol and prove exactly how much he appreciated her, in every way he could show her. But right now, she needed sleep. If he intended to spend half the night inside her again—and he did—she'd need it. Along with some food. Then he'd have to figure out how to persuade her to let him stay for a while. He'd slip away for Ryan's service and try to avoid the press. The rest of the time, he'd spend with Bristol. That made him smile. And bonus, he would be around to fend off Hayden the half-wit. Win-win.

After pressing a light kiss to her forehead, Jesse headed downstairs again to the restaurant's kitchen. Hands on hips, he surveyed the room. It looked as if a bomb had gone off. He sighed. He was no expert with this stuff, but it couldn't be impossible to clean. It would also save poor exhausted Bristol a whole lot of effort and allow her to spend the rest of the evening with him.

As he filled the sink with soapy water and dumped all the dirty utensils inside, the events of the past few days rolled through his head. Oddly, despite the fact that his career was in turmoil, his life upside down, and his surroundings unfamiliar, he felt completely centered. Thoughts of Bristol circled, dive-bombed. She was the reason for his Zen attitude. She amazed him. She inspired him.

A melody shot across his brain. It kind of reminded him of her—pretty, haunting, somewhat unexpected. He hummed it as he cleaned a few attachments from the standing mixer and set them out to dry. He moved onto spoons and baking pans, scouring them clean. As he wiped down the counters and display cases, Jesse realized that, despite all the crap in his life, he was smiling. Bristol did that for him. The song rolling around in his head made him kind of happy, too.

With his grin widening, he plucked his phone from his pocket and started recording the music in his head. For the first time in weeks, maybe years, he felt almost happy.

Chapter Five

Bristol awoke well after dark. She sat up with a start and found herself alone in the rumpled queen-size bed. A glance at the clock confirmed it was nearly two a.m. She'd slept ten hours. Holy cow, she never did that. Jamie had worn her out the night before, and she'd fallen into an exhausted slumber. But at least she was up early for work.

OMG, work! She'd neglected to make sure he'd locked the front door. In fact, she didn't hear any signs of him prowling around her apartment. Was he even still here?

The thought that he might have left without saying good-bye upset her way more than it should.

Scrambling out of bed, Bristol pulled on a pair of shorts and righted the towel turban on her head, vaguely wondering how bad her hair would look once she removed it. She shoved the thought aside and stumbled down the hall.

In the living room, she found Jamie. She breathed a little sigh of relief when she spotted him on her sofa with a pair of buds shoved into his ears, his phone in hand, and a notepad and pen perched on his thigh. He looked deep in thought, and she wondered what had him concentrating so intently.

When he caught sight of her, he clicked off the phone, closed the cover of the notepad, and shoved everything onto the table in a heap. "Hey, how are you feeling?"

"Kind of groggy, but otherwise all right. You hanging out? Everything okay?"

"Yeah. It's cool."

She didn't quite believe that since he gave off the vibe that she'd interrupted something. But he didn't look guilty, more like distracted. "Did Hayden give you a hard time yesterday?"

"What makes you think I'd let him?" He scoffed. "I told the little asswipe to back down. He suggested that I fuck off but I declined. It took restraint to let him walk out the door undamaged, but I let him because I didn't think mopping the floor with his face would help your situation."

Bristol didn't have much doubt that Jamie could have. "Nonviolence was probably the better choice. Sorry I crashed on you. I was beat."

He shrugged as if it was no big deal. "It's fine. You needed sleep."

Yeah, but the fact that he'd hung around waiting for her to wake up both embarrassed and excited her. Since he didn't have a job right now, it was possible he had no place else to go. Or maybe he just liked her and wanted to spend more time together. That wasn't good for her fling thing, but she'd end it soon. Any minute now… "Sorry."

"Hey, it's not a big deal. Really."

Bristol smiled when she realized he meant it. "Thanks."

"Hungry? I tossed together some stuff for sandwiches and salads last night, using your leftovers. Hope that was all right."

"Sure." She normally didn't neglect to feed her guest for over twenty-four hours. Geez, she really had been tired.

"I'll make you a plate."

She cocked her head at him. Hayden had never been half so helpful. Or caring. As soon as they'd begun dating, he'd expected her to feed him more often than not after cooking all day. He'd claimed that all his pencil pushing behind a desk exhausted him, so more often than not he'd preferred to end the day with a blow job. Less effort on his part than actual sex.

She and Jamie hadn't done more than share a bed and some skin for a few hours but already he was far more considerate. Giddy little butterflies began dancing in her belly, and Bristol had to remind herself that being a nice human being didn't mean he intended to be romantic. And they were *not* having a relationship.

"That would be great." She smiled his way.

"Give me a minute and I'll get you fed."

"Thanks. I'm going to dry my hair now and hope that I don't look like Medusa when I'm done."

"I'm pretty sure that's impossible since you're gorgeous, but go for it."

Bristol rolled her eyes at the compliment. "I look terrible. You don't have to butter me up, but I appreciate it."

As she turned for the bathroom, Jamie grabbed her wrist and snapped her around, flush against his chest. "I'm serious. I think you're beautiful. You're not calling me a liar, are you?"

His silky tone warned her that would be a bad idea. Bristol swallowed against the sudden tension in the air. "No. I just…"

"Don't take compliments well?" He raised a brow at her as if he already knew the answer. "As long as I'm around, you need to start accepting them. And believing them."

She stared up into his dark eyes in breathless disbelief. He may not be trying to romance her…but he was certainly making her heart flap and quiver. Which made her feel like a twit. She had to stop reading happily-ever-after into his nice gestures.

"Sure. Okay. Thanks." She pulled gently at her wrist, eager to leave the room before she made an idiot out of herself.

Jamie was slow to release her. "I'll have your food ready in ten. Then we can talk."

What did he want to say? She'd rather they simply had sex. She didn't find tangling between the sheets with him nearly as confusing as watching him defend her against Hayden or staring back into his eyes as he complimented her. But she had a few things to say if she was going to persuade him to go with her to dinner on Tuesday night at her mom's house, then move on afterward.

"Sounds good." She nodded his way vaguely.

After managing to brush her hair and somewhat tame the strands with a blow dryer, she tossed on her work clothes and spruced up with a dose of mascara and lip-gloss. When she tiptoed into the kitchen, she found Jamie setting a plate of what looked like a ham sandwich on thick sourdough and a mixed greens salad with some mandarin oranges and feta crumbles.

She sat and blinked down at her plate. "You did this?"

"Yeah." He shrugged. "My parents worked a lot when I was

a kid. I learned how to fend for myself by foraging from the fridge. This is easy. It's not as difficult as making turducken. Or your fabulous cookies."

But she really couldn't think of the last time anyone had cooked for her. It was a small gesture. Maybe this was his way of thanking her for letting him crash here. But that intent gleam from his dark eyes sparkled with something far more personal than gratitude.

Her breath caught. Her heart loped into a gallop. "I'm sure it's great. I really appreciate it. And I'm, um…glad you didn't bail while I slept."

"About that…" For the first time since she'd met him, Jamie looked uncomfortable. "Look, if you don't need me to go, I'd love to stay a few days."

Did he need money? Was he between jobs or houses? Did it really matter since he only wanted a few days and she needed him to stick around that long? No, but everything felt more complicated because some silly part of her didn't want to let him go.

Bristol studied him. "You okay?"

He pulled at the back of his neck. "Yeah. I'd like to spend some time with you before I go back to work."

"So you do have a job?"

Jamie laughed. "Yeah. I'm…taking a vacation right now. I haven't had one in years."

"And you travel a lot. What do you do?"

"No offense, but one reason I'm taking this vacation is so that I don't have to talk or even think about work for a while. You understand, right?"

As someone self-employed, she understood the constant pressure, the stress of being unable to simply have a few days off. If someone had given her that golden opportunity, she probably wouldn't want to talk about her job, either. Besides, unless she was going to move him into the "relationship" category, she didn't need to know everything about him. "Sure. Totally understand."

"Thanks. I want to use this time to be with you because I…like you. A lot. That probably sounds corny. It's been rough lately but being with you is peaceful. Nice." He shook his head.

"I'm saying it wrong. I feel good when I'm with you."

That insidious butterfly took up residence in her tummy again, but Bristol couldn't seem to squash him. She felt a bit like the cute guy in school had told her that he wanted to "go" with her.

Wiping the smile off her face proved impossible. "You made me feel pretty good last night, too."

He grinned. "We were damn hot together. But even hanging with you is great. We...click."

"I should disagree. After all, we're just hooking up." But she felt a school-girly grin cross her face again. "But we do click. So if you're going to stay, would you come with me to my mom's house for dinner on Tuesday night?" She winced. "She told everyone you would be there."

"And you don't want to brave it alone?"

"Not really. Please..." She sounded as if she was wheedling because she was.

"Well, I don't want to leave you alone with the wolves. Will Presleigh and Hayden be there?"

"Yep, along with half the town. I'd really appreciate it. As Jayla put it, if I come alone I'll look like a ho-bag who's not interested in keeping a man." Bristol realized that made her sound as if she might be looking for some commitment. "And I'm not interested in hanging onto anyone after my shit with Hayden, but I'm really not eager to be the center of town gossip, either."

A frown wrinkled Jamie's brow before he bent and pressed a lingering kiss on her lips. Affection with a teasing hint of passion. One touch, and Jamie made her ache for more.

He eased back, staring down into her face. "I'll go with you. Now eat. I'm going to grab a shower, if that's cool."

Bristol let out a sigh of relief. "Yeah, help yourself. And if you want to wash some clothes, I've got stackable units in the closet in the hallway."

"I appreciate it." Jamie nodded, heading for the bathroom.

She grabbed a coffee, devoured her meal, then found her shoes shoved half under the bed. Downstairs, she began flipping on lights, grabbing ingredients as she made her way from the stockroom toward the kitchen, not looking forward to the cleanup she'd neglected yesterday. It would tack on an extra hour to her day, but she'd obviously needed the sleep last night. Now it was time to pay for the indulgence.

But when she entered the kitchen, nothing but clean dishes and sparkling surfaces awaited her. Her jaw dropped. Someone had cleaned everything, set up her mixer again, put away her utensils, even mopped the usually sticky floor.

Someone? The only person who could have done that was Jamie.

Her heart stuttered then skipped. Bristol might wish she could find a way to not care about Jamie…but that wasn't happening now. Why fight what was so damn obvious? She was falling for him.

Jamie looked after her and helped her out. She enjoyed his banter. The sex was so far beyond mere pleasure that she didn't have the words to describe it. Their "click" was undeniable. She'd shared much less with Hayden and considered the idea that maybe he was "the one," at least until he'd dumped her for her sister. But Jamie was so much…more.

Was it even possible for her to stop her feelings for him from growing?

Bristol pushed the question aside, at least for now. She glanced at her phone. She still had about forty-five minutes before she had to be back in the kitchen to ensure the dough for her cinnamon rolls rose properly before baking them for opening.

Shoving the phone back in her pocket, she charged up the stairs again and found Jamie coming out of the bathroom with a towel wrapped around his lean waist. Water droplets dotted his hard flesh, rolled in the ridges between his chest, and down his abdomen. A sting of need flared between her legs. She swallowed hard, then ran at him.

Jamie caught her as she wrapped her arms and legs around his waist and covered his lips with her own. He didn't hesitate, simply plunged into her mouth with a moan and cupped her ass in his hands, as he eased them back toward her bedroom. Suddenly, she felt the mattress at her back and his body covering hers.

He lifted his head, searching her face. "To what do I owe

this pleasure?"

"Thank you. Thank you. Thank you."

"You're welcome. What did I do?" He grinned. "Because if you're going to thank me this way for a sandwich and a salad, I'll feed you all day long."

She found herself honest-to-goodness giggling. "I appreciate that, too. I meant cleaning my kitchen downstairs."

Jamie brushed her hair back from her face. "So the fact that I cleaned your utensils all spick-and-span makes your ovaries flutter?"

"That makes me sound easy." She grimaced.

He shook his head. "That makes you sound adorable. You're not like other women."

"We covered this once. I know, I don't get all gussied up and pray properly to the Revlon gods."

"Screw that. I mean, you don't try to be anyone except yourself. You don't act differently to please your mother. You didn't put on a face to impress me. And you certainly had no problem telling Hayden how you feel."

Bristol cocked her head. "I guess some people don't act like themselves when others are watching. That baffles me. Seems like a lot of effort merely to be miserable."

He nodded slowly. "Let's just say I've met a lot of unhappy people over the years. Neurotic, insecure, self-absorbed. Hell, I was one for a long time. I didn't really feel like myself for a decade."

"I can't picture that." He seemed so natural, so normal. "And where are you meeting these awful people?"

"They're everywhere. I can't tell you how thrilled I am to be with someone so real."

He cut off the conversation by kissing her again, devouring her as if he was hungry, as if they hadn't touched in a decade.

Then she stopped thinking entirely when he peeled off her clothes and lost his towel. He tossed everything to the floor and grabbed a condom from his nearby jeans.

After making her scream a couple of times so loudly she wondered if everyone on her block could hear, Bristol draped herself over his steely chest, still damp from exertion, and pressed a kiss between his pectorals. At the moment, she felt too sated to do anything else.

"I'm happy, too. You're a really decent guy," she murmured, looking up his hard torso, into those dark eyes that had the power to make her shiver. "You're considerate and helpful, not the sort of douche who would deceive me, like Hayden."

He smoothed his big hand over her crown and smiled. "Are you saying you like me, too?"

"Yeah," she admitted. *Way more than I should.* That realization made her a little uncomfortable because she worried it would end up one-sided, so she slid out of bed and grabbed for her clothes. "Um…I should get to work. I'm running late."

With a promise to drop in downstairs once he woke, Jamie gave her a lingering kiss good-bye. Bristol tried not to feel that jittery, excited, falling-in-love thing. But she failed miserably because it coursed through her veins and squeezed her heart as she tiptoed down the stairs. She was so deliciously sated that she didn't care she was twenty minutes late getting back to her kitchen. Nope. She simply headed for her dough, pushing thoughts of tomorrow aside and wearing a big ol' smile on her face.

* * * *

In a ridiculously good mood, Bristol turned on the radio and swayed to the music while she made goodies for her patrons that day. The bounce in her step was probably leftover pleasure hormones drifting through her body and the happiness of knowing that she'd get to be with Jamie for another few days.

After a few crying-in-her-beer songs, Bristol changed the station from her usual contemporary country music to the happier Top-40 station out of Texarkana. She didn't recognize many of the songs and artists since this wasn't her usual thing, but this music matched her mood.

The hours slid by, and she figured Jamie would be sleeping. When she baked her first pan of cinnamon rolls, she took two upstairs and left them on the counter for him with a note. As she turned, she skirted the coffee table, heading for the door. One glance at the glass slab topping the pair of whiskey barrels proved that the notebook in which Jamie had been writing earlier was gone, but he'd left his phone behind. Bristol hesitated.

She couldn't deny a gnawing curiosity to know more about him. But peeking at his phone would be prying. Even if she blew past her principles, she would either be wildly disappointed or even more intrigued, depending on what she found. Nope. So they'd crossed into temporary friends-with-benefits territory. Maybe even a bit more. Still, that didn't mean she needed to know his deepest thoughts. Because no matter how she defined their relationship, that didn't entitle her to invade Jamie's privacy.

With a sharp nod, she left the phone untouched and made her way down the hall to find him sprawled out in her bed, one bulging arm thrown over his head, the bronzed ridges of his chest and abs bare. She cursed the sheet riding low on his hips, covering everything else.

At a glance, he looked like the dangerous sort of man, built of brawn and brute strength. If he'd lived in another time, Jamie could have slayed his enemies with a quick slice of his sword before he claimed his woman with a ferocious kiss. God, she really had to stop the over romanticizing, even if she did have an amazing man in her bed.

When he sighed in his sleep, Bristol couldn't help the fond smile that crept over her face. He was more than gorgeous. He had a kind side. And he liked her. Having him here felt comfortable. Right. And it wasn't simply because she didn't want to be alone and he would do. Hayden had been here many times, and she'd always been a bit relieved when he'd left. No, around Jamie she simply felt grounded, like life was as it should be.

Dangerous thoughts.

Shaking her head, she headed back downstairs. The buzzing alarm on her phone reminded her when it was time to open the shop, so she started her first pot of coffee and waited for old Mr. Jones, who was eighty if he was a day. But he came every morning like clockwork at six thirty.

Sure enough, as soon as she unlocked the door, he ambled in. Sun began streaming through her windows. He took a seat and she set a mug of coffee in front of him, along with a bowl of sugar and a cinnamon roll, as always. She watched him doctor his coffee with somewhere north of a half dozen teaspoons of sugar.

"You know too much sugar is bad for you." She grinned Every day, they gave one another a hard time about something. She usually let him win.

He waved her away, his old black hand gnarled with arthritis now. "When you're my age, you feel like you've defied death for years. Bring it on, I say."

Bristol laughed. "Well, if I had your metabolism and didn't have to worry about the size of my hips, I'd probably say the same thing."

"You're a pretty thing. When is some smart man going to scoop you up?"

"Maybe marriage isn't for me." She shrugged. "I mean, I already struggle to do my own laundry. The thought of doing someone else's is awful."

"I married Mildred because my mama told me it was time to look after myself and I didn't know the first thing about cooking."

That wasn't entirely true, but Bristol let him talk. "Well, I know she fed you since you made it all these years."

"Yeah, but not a day has gone by since I lost my wife that I haven't wished I'd married her sooner so I could have spent more time with her. God rest her soul."

Bristol's heart fluttered. Mr. Jones's longing made her wistful for something more. Her time with Jamie had probably contributed to that, too. She really had to stop romanticizing the man. One more nice gesture on his part and she'd probably fall head over heels. Once he figured it out, he'd likely wonder what the hell was wrong with her.

"I know she would say the same if she could be with us," Bristol said softly and took his hand.

The old man closed his eyes and gave her a squeeze. "Find your someone while you're young enough to build a whole lot of years together and share the love. Houses and jobs come and go. But there's nothing better than having someone who's your home."

She gave him a smile, trying not to tear up and show him her sadness. But every word he'd said called to her heart's deepest desire. Her grandmother had once told her that she was meant to be married. But instead of baking for her husband and kids, she did so for the townsfolk. She mothered a cat. More often than not, she spent her intimate time with a vibrator.

Bristol wanted more. The insidious thought crept in that she wanted Jamie.

Nodding at the old man, she gave his hand one last squeeze before she turned away, taking an unnecessary trek to wipe off the counter next to the display case. It gave her a good reason to bow her head and collect herself.

"I would, but none of the guys of my generation are as handsome or as fabulous as you."

"You'll find someone. You're too sweet to be alone." He grinned. "And some smart fella who can't cook for himself is going to treasure you."

"From your lips to God's ears." She winked as he rose slowly from his chair, left some money on the table, grabbed his cane, and made his way out the door.

Mr. Jones had given her food for thought. She wasn't that woman who couldn't be complete without a man. She didn't hate the life she'd built for herself. She wasn't old-fashioned, and she certainly had aspirations of her own. But Bristol couldn't deny she'd like to be a wife and mother.

Someday.

With a sigh, she headed back into the kitchen and worked her way through the majority of the morning customers. One of the new schoolteachers came in for a dozen cookies for her hardworking students as the end of the school year approached. A few stay-at-home moms popped in for coffee and veggie omelets on their way to yoga. The guys from the drugstore down the street came to snag an assortment of goodies for their post-lunch treat. When she looked up again, it was nearly eleven a.m. She'd have another lull before her few lunch customers came in, so she hustled to toss together a few salads and sandwiches for the display case.

The radio still hummed in the background, now playing a new song of Jesse McCall's. She grinned when she remembered the crush she'd had on him in high school. The new song was infectious and a little biting, with a hint of sexy, but she liked it.

When it ended, the deejay took over the airwaves.

"Scandal has been good for McCall's new album. It's number one in its second week. An official statement says he deeply regrets the overdose of a fan and the suicide of his bandmate. His publicist says he's taking some time off to grieve, but a source close to the singer says no one has seen or heard from him in days. One of our listeners e-mailed this morning to say they think they saw him recently at Bubba Oink's Bone Yard, cozying up to a brunette. Anyone else spot him?" The deejay laughed. "While y'all speculate on that, I've got another tune coming your way from Bruno Mars."

Presleigh and Hayden's engagement party had been at Bubba Oink's. Bristol would have liked to spot Jesse McCall there, to see if he was as hot in person as he was in pictures. During high school, she'd had a notebook with him on the front, and she'd loved staring into his dark eyes during geometry and fantasizing...

She put the brakes on that thought. Dark eyes. Bubba Oink's. A man without a last name who was taking a little time off from work and didn't want to talk about his past...

No, that man in her bed could not be Jesse McCall. They didn't look that much alike, did they? That thought must be her overactive imagination stretching. Still, she withdrew her phone and launched her browser, bringing up images of the singer. None of them showed him with short hair or a skullcap or a clean-shaven face. But now that she looked closely, the shape of the face seemed similar. In most images he wore earrings, sometimes more than one. Jamie didn't sport any, but she'd noticed three empty holes in each ear. His eyes looked like a dead ringer for the rock star's.

Bristol scrolled a bit more, then came to an image that made her blood freeze in shock. Jesse McCall shirtless, with the same tribal tattoo on the same shoulder that she'd traced with her fingers, her tongue.

It was possible Jamie had gotten the ink to look like Jesse.

Or maybe Jesse McCall was hiding out in her apartment from the rest of the world and whiling away his time by having sex with her until his most recent media storm died down.

It seemed crazy, almost impossible. Almost...but not quite.

Either way, she needed the truth.

Trying not to shake, she brought up Jayla's contact on her phone and called.

"Hey, girl!" her friend answered.

"Can you come over here and mind the restaurant for a bit? Everything is made. All you have to do is work a cash register." Bristol's voice shook with anger. If what she suspected was true, then he'd deceived her. He'd preyed on a woman who'd recently recovered from another asshole, using her without a care for how she'd feel.

"Is something wrong?"

"Maybe. I need…" Bristol didn't want to explain now. She didn't want to do anything but get to the truth. "Can you?"

"Sure thing. I'll be there in fifteen. What are you going to do?"

"I might be giving our friend Jamie a huge piece of my mind."

Chapter Six

The sound of a slamming door woke Jesse. He sat up in bed, disoriented. Immediately, he knew he wasn't in a hotel room—thank god—but in Bristol's bedroom. The whole place smelled like her, something that teased his senses with cinnamon and woman. He glanced at the clock and frowned. Had she come back for lunch?

He heard footsteps marching down the hall, coming at him rapidly. That didn't sound like the gait of a happy woman.

Jesse swung his feet over the side of the bed and shoved on his pants. He was buttoning them when he caught sight of Bristol as she reached the doorway, looking tense and barely shy of furious.

"What's wrong, honey?" A nasty suspicion took root in his head. "Did Hayden come back? Because if he did, I'll—"

"What's your last name?"

The out-of-nowhere question made Jesse freeze. Was she onto him? "Does it matter?"

"You know it does."

So she'd figured him out. And she was pissed. Most of the women he'd known in his adult life would be thrilled to learn his identity. They'd be ecstatic to realize they'd been screwing a star. Not Bristol.

On soft footfalls, he headed in her direction. "Let's sit down and talk about this."

"I don't want to sit down." She gritted her teeth. "I want an answer. Did you or did you not lie to me about who you are?"

He rubbed at his forehead. He would have liked to brush his teeth and have some coffee before this confrontation. That would buy him some time so he could figure out what to say. The usual charm with his rock star smile and a flash of dimples wasn't going to cut it. He wanted her to understand that he'd never meant to hurt her. He couldn't let her think for an instant that he'd used her or didn't give a shit.

Because as far as he could tell, Bristol was the first woman he'd cared about in a long fucking time.

He took her shoulders in a light grip, his head racing. "I'm sorry."

She shook him off. "Maybe after we'd shared the sheets a time or two, you might have bothered to mention that I'm not sleeping with Jamie No-last-name, but Jesse freaking McCall. Were you ever going to tell me?"

Her eyes filled with tears, and the guilt gouged his heart.

"You kept hinting that we were merely hooking up." He shrugged. "At first, that was fine. I thought you were interesting and I needed a place to lay low. You've heard about my bandmate and the awful tragedy last week?" When she nodded, he reached for her again. "I wasn't there. I had nothing to do with it. My publicist told me to go underground while she worked on communicating that to the public. It made sense." He tried to smile. "Besides, she's scary. I tend to do what she says."

The quip fell flat. Hurt crossed her face. "So I was a way to pass the time while you hid from everyone? Great."

"No." He got serious again. "It would have been better for me if I didn't care about you so damn much, but from the beginning something about you grabbed onto me and wouldn't let go. It's why I jumped in to help you back at that barbeque dive. I couldn't look at your sad eyes and not want to make you happy. I still can't."

"So you feel sorry for me? Gave me a few pity fucks?"

"God, no! I like you. Remember?" Jesse more than suspected his feelings for Bristol went deeper, but he wasn't sure she would hear him now—or believe him. "But being famous, I have to be careful. People have sold me out before. Folks I've hired or I thought were my friends have taken pictures of me or prowled through my personal information and sold it. You've seen the pictures of me in the shower?"

She nodded sheepishly. "Everyone has. Didn't some girlfriend of yours take them?"

"Supposedly. Five weeks into the relationship, she chose half a million dollars over me. So you're not the only one who's felt used."

"That's terrible. I would never..." She shook her head.

No, she wouldn't violate his privacy like that. He might not have known her as long as he had Sierra before she'd betrayed him. Bristol wasn't a fame monger. She knew what being used felt like.

"I get that now," he assured. "At first, I wasn't sure, and what I did know of you... I really wasn't sure whether you wanted revenge sex so you'd have something to shove in Hayden's face or if you actually liked me."

Her expression softened for a moment, and Jesse hoped that meant he was reaching her. "I do like you." Then she toughened up again. " Or I did. If you thought I was only using you, why did you come home with me?"

"Honestly? I wanted you too much to pass you up. I meet a lot of women..."

That full mouth of hers pinched and she crossed her arms over her chest. "Of course you do. You'd said that. Now I understand."

And Bristol's expression said that she felt stupid. When she closed her eyes as if castigating herself, Jesse couldn't stand there and not touch her.

He closed the distance between them and crushed her against his body. When she struggled to break free, he held her tighter and set his lips against her ear. "Please let me hold you. What I'm trying to say is that I knew you were different immediately, and I liked you so much that I couldn't walk way. I've spent a decade with people who didn't mean anything to me. You're different. But I had to know you before I could risk telling you who I am."

She didn't say a word for the longest time, merely crossed her arms over her chest as if protecting herself. But he could see the wheels turning in her head, examining the situation. He thanked god she was too polite not to listen and too logical for his rationale to escape her.

"I hear what you're saying," she said finally. "In your shoes, I probably wouldn't have told me, either. I shouldn't be upset that you had to protect yourself from a near stranger because you didn't know if I would sell you out. But that doesn't make being lied to hurt less."

Jesse felt guilty for not believing in her sooner and coming clean, but grateful she understood, at least on some level. "Hurting you was never my intention, so I really am sorry for that. But I think you also never expected to care about me." He curled a finger under her chin but she resisted meeting his gaze. "Are you this upset because you do?"

Her eyes widened to big green pools of confusion and contrition. More tears shimmered, threatening to spill. "I swore off relationships. I'm bad with romance."

"*You're* bad...or you've tried it with the wrong people? I've made the same mistake." He took a deep breath, diving head first into the already deep conversation. "I'm going to put the truth out there. I've never felt this way with any other woman."

Instantly, she shot him a scathing, skeptical stare. "You don't have to let me down easy with a lie."

"I wouldn't bother." He anchored his hands in her hair and clenched his fists. "If you were anyone else, after the sex I would have already shrugged and walked away."

"So you're saying all those celebrities and groupies you've screwed don't hold a candle to me? Right..."

Her sarcasm bit, and he tugged on her hair. "They didn't. Everything about you makes sense to me. And let me tell you, nothing in my life has made sense in a long time—especially not relationships. You're pretty without artifice, kind even to the people who have wronged you, smart, ambitious. And you're refreshingly not narcissistic or mercenary. You admitted that we click."

Agreement crossed Bristol's face, though she didn't say it aloud. "So?"

"I'm going to ask again, are you this upset because you didn't want to care about me? Or because it shocks you that you do?"

She pulled away from him with a huff, her little fists

clenching. "Why can't I be normal? The rest of the free world can find someone and hook up for a day or two without getting involved emotionally. The first time I try, what happens? Yeah, I wind up being all giddy and excited. You walk in the room and I feel something in my stomach flutter. I can barely wait to touch you. Or even talk to you. I have to remind myself not to fall in love. And now I'm making an idiot out of myself with one of the most famous people on the planet." She shook her head. "I was already aiming high with the prince of Lafayette County because he was nice to me once upon a time and—"

"Don't beat yourself up about Hayden. He's the deficient one. He broke apart from you to be with your sister because he can't equal you in intellect, ambition, or character. He found someone more his speed. If he'd stayed much longer, you would have realized he wasn't for you."

She shrugged. "Maybe."

"He left you before you could beat him to it. He probably felt outdone by you. But don't for one second think that small-town prick split because you weren't good enough for him, so therefore you're nowhere near enough for me. It's bullshit, and I'll argue with you all day long."

"Hayden doesn't matter anymore."

"He doesn't, but we do. And I'm sorry I wasn't on the up-and-up, but you know why. I'm not letting you go over this crap." He shrugged as if his mind were made up. "I'm seriously not."

She took a shuddering breath, tears still threatening to spill. "How did I come in to confront you about lying to me and wind up feeling like the dysfunctional head case?"

He laughed. If Bristol could tell even a sideswiping sort of joke, then he must have said something that reached her. "Well, I usually feel like a dysfunctional head case and I didn't want to be alone."

She gave him a watery grin. "You suck."

"Not yet, but if you lose the clothes, I'll be happy to find some part of you I can get my mouth on."

With a playful swat on the shoulder, she sniffled. "I'm sorry."

"Don't be. I know exactly why you were upset. No one likes

to be lied to. Honestly, it's a relief to me that you know the truth. And now you can stop calling me Jamie. Every time you cry out that name during sex, I want to punch my cousin."

"Is that his name?" When he nodded, she giggled. "No wonder you grimaced a lot."

"Next time, I want to hear *my* name on your lips. And don't say there won't be one."

"I want there to be one, too." She took a deep breath. "But you've got a lot on your plate and a career to go back to. My life is here. And really, where could we take this?"

Damn, she was fighting the relationship thing hard. She had no idea how willing he was to fight back. "I don't know but I'm not giving up merely because it doesn't look obvious or it won't be easy. We're going to take it one day at a time, okay?" At her uncertain stare, he tried to bite back his frustration. "What's making you hesitate most. The fame? My crazy past? The newness of our relationship?"

She shook her head. "All of it."

Her hesitation was understandable. That didn't make him less impatient to be done with it. "First, you may not think you know me well, but I will never fuck you over like Hayden. I already know you're not the kind of girl to sleep with a celebrity simply because you can or want to get pregnant for a payday. The getting-to-know-you thing will take time. So will total trust. But I'm willing to be all in if you are."

"Just like that?"

"Yeah. Because I've tried everything else, so I know something good when I find it. The fame is fleeting and not real. I mean, yes, I have paparazzi chasing me and a monster social media presence. I've got screaming fans who don't always know how to observe proper boundaries. But this also allows me to make a hell of a nice living and to do some good in the world through various charities. I try not to take it too seriously, especially since it could all be gone tomorrow."

She gave him a shaky nod. "And the rest?"

"I can't undo my past. There was a lot of booze and drugs. I did a bunch of crazy, off-the-chain shit. Because at seventeen, nothing sounds more awesome than living the ultimate rock star fantasy." He shook his head at the waste of it all. "It took me a decade but I finally started questioning whether I *should* do any of that wild crap. So I sobered up, and that part of my life is done. Sobriety has given me a clarity about life I've never had. Losing Ryan has made me realize that life can be even more fleeting than I thought."

"I'm sorry for your loss," she murmured, reaching for his hands and giving them a squeeze.

Jesse clutched at her. "He was a friend. When I changed my ways, it pissed him off. We used to get wasted and tag team women together. I won't lie; we did it a lot. Once I decided to change, he had no one to party with. He started using more, fucking random girls more. I couldn't reach him. I couldn't stop him."

When he choked back his guilt, Bristol slid closer to him. "It's not your fault."

"No, he made his choices. Just like I made mine. But I'll always wonder if I could have said or done something different to help him. If I could have saved him."

"Don't feel guilty for surviving. You did what you had to do for you."

He nodded. "I knew if I didn't, I was going to die. The morning I woke up on a hotel balcony puking next to Ryan, five naked girls passed out around us, hung over like a bitch with no idea what continent I was even on, I knew something had to change."

Bristol withdrew her hands. "That's a lot of women."

"Yep. More than I even remember." He shrugged. "But I can honestly tell you that I've never stood in front of any of them and truly tried to work out our relationship. I was engaged once to a friend years ago. She ended up marrying another guy and they're expecting baby number two. That's the most serious relationship I've had. Until you."

"I've slept with three men in my life, including you. And obviously you've been with hundreds of girls."

Probably more. "The number doesn't matter. None of this is about genitals. It's about feelings. I have them for you. I think you have them for me."

For a long moment, Bristol looked afraid to be honest. Finally, she nodded. "Yeah."

"So we're beyond a hookup. It's up to us to figure out where to go from here. Who's watching the restaurant?"

"Jayla."

"So…you don't have to be downstairs again right away?" He sent her a smile rife with seduction.

Bristol hesitated, then pulled her phone from her pocket and dashed off a text. A ding came moments later. Then she met his stare with a challenge of her own. "Jayla says all is quiet for now, so I could probably stay another minute or two."

He prowled closer, unbuttoning his pants and lowering his zipper. "How about an hour or two?"

She stood her ground, her gaze dipping down to where he peeled away his jeans. "I don't know if I've forgiven you yet."

"I'm willing to do whatever it takes to make sure you do," Jesse murmured across her cheek as he grabbed the hem of her T-shirt and shoved it up. Before he'd whisked it over her head, he'd worked the clasp of her bra open, then peeled them both off at once. The second the garments cleared her body, he covered her lips with his own and sank inside her velvety mouth, stealing inside to claim her.

They'd spoken a lot of words to one another. She'd heard him…for the most part. But now he wanted them to communicate in a way he felt certain she'd understand completely.

"Shoes off," he insisted.

Then he set to work at the fastenings of her pants while drowning in the taste of her kiss. As he slid them down her hips, she kicked her tennis shoes aside and wriggled her hips until the denim fell to her ankles and she stood before him in nothing but a tiny pair of white lace panties.

Jesse smiled as he released the messy pile of her brown hair shimmering atop her head. As the waves cascaded around her shoulders, heat settled in his belly. Blood rushed to his cock. Yeah, this woman did it for him, excited him in ways he hadn't known a woman could. For the first time in his life, he wanted to be a better person—enough to do the hard work to improve himself, not use her for some quick fix to normalcy and improved self-esteem, the way he'd tried with Kimber years ago. He intended to be a better man for Bristol. He intended to keep her beside him, wake up every morning to her smile.

Heavy realizations. But Jesse couldn't remember a time he'd felt clearer or more certain.

"Now lose the underwear," he demanded. "Slide them down your hips slowly and let me see what I'm craving."

She cocked her head. "What if I don't take orders from you?"

Oh, now she was challenging him. He just smiled. "I can take what I want."

"I dare you," she breathed.

He understood what she was playing at. If she gave in too easily now, it would bend her pride. Instead, she challenged him to take her body and push the issue of her surrender.

Game on.

Jesse anchored his hands around the fragile undergarment at her hip and pulled. The seam unraveled for him—precisely like he intended she would under his touch.

When she stood naked before him, she shivered. He watched the shallow rise and fall of her breast, the movement of her hard nipples as the midday sun slanted through her window. Her fair skin looked luminous and golden. No spray tan for her. No chemicals that made her reek or look like an Oompa Loompa. Bristol was classic and alabaster, appearing untouchable.

But he definitely intended to touch her—and more. She wasn't leaving this bed until she knew she belonged with him.

Jesse bent and lifted her against his body, following her down to the mattress. He didn't give her an opportunity to wriggle away, simply anchored his hips between her thighs and pinned her down. She felt so small beneath him, and he braced an elbow near her head to take some of his weight off her.

She met his stare. Those leafy green eyes of hers were a sight he'd never get tired of.

"Jesse," she whispered.

The uncertainty on her face broke his heart. "Close your eyes. Yeah," he commended as she did. "Take a deep breath. That's it." He bent to whisper in her ear. "Any doubts you have we'll talk out later. Right now, I want to worship you."

Bristol gave a low moan. Against him, she trembled. Then

so slowly it made him sweat, she opened her eyes, her arms, and finally her heart to him. Given his past, he probably didn't deserve her, but he intended to do everything possible to make her glad she'd chosen him.

She clung to his shoulders, and Jesse brushed the hair from her face and worked his lips up her neck. "Feel how good we are together."

With a little shiver, she nodded. He fanned a hand over her breast, his thumb brushing her taut nipple. She arched into his touch and thrashed under him. He swallowed the sound with his kiss, aligning their bodies until he was flush against her, not merely covering but enveloping her. Jesse wanted to take all of her, make sure she knew that she was his. A sizzle shot up his spine when he thought about the pleasure of making love to her. But more than anything, he simply ached to feel her close.

Yeah, he had it bad. Never in a million years had he thought he would fall hard and fast for a down-to-earth baker. On paper, she wasn't his usual—not loud or flashy or sexually aggressive. Yet everything about her shy sparkplug of a personality fascinated him. Almost from the first, he'd felt as if some invisible wire attached them, tugging him closer and closer to Bristol. Until her, he hadn't really known that sort of pull was possible.

Jesse positioned her arms above her head, splayed on the mattress, then eased his hands up her silky flesh from elbows to palms, finally curling his fingers around her wrists. He anchored her to the bed and buried his nose in the cinnamon musk of her neck, closing his eyes as the light brown silk of her hair caressed his shoulder and teased his senses.

Beneath him, she softened, a gasp escaping her throat as she tossed her head back, as if the pleasure somehow surprised her. Jesse took the opportunity to drag his lips up her oh-so-soft skin before working his way to her mouth and dominating the sweet bow with a slanting, possessive kiss.

Endless. Timeless. The joining of their mouths went on. All the things that made Bristol unique piled on top of his senses.

She responded without artifice, exactly as she had the first time he'd taken her to bed. Her glimmering green eyes stared up at him, soft with raw emotion, as he skated one palm down the lush under curve of her pert breasts, her small waist, the feminine flare of her hips. True, she had the same basic parts and curves as every other woman he'd fucked, but she alone made him feel this electric gravity when they touched. When he was near her, his head buzzed, his dick engorged, and his heart chugged.

Jesse didn't see how he could possibly give her up.

Needing to inhale more of her, he made his way down her body, claiming the sweet expanse of her skin as he descended past her delicate collarbones, the swells of her breasts, her tight nipples begging for his tongue. He took them all, gliding his lips over the sensitive flesh before teasing with his tongue, nipping with his teeth.

Beneath him, she wriggled and moaned in arousal. The sweet music filled his ears. The melody he'd been writing for her played in his head, and the bridge that had stumped him last night suddenly rolled across his imagination. It sounded like a more sensual rhythm than he'd been chasing yet so perfect. So her.

The notes played a soundtrack in his head as he dipped down again to nibble at her hipbones and drag his lips over the slight curve of her belly. Jesse even liked that she wasn't perfect and didn't have the sort of personal training regime that made him feel as if he was cozying up to a bodybuilder rather than a woman.

"Spread your legs," he murmured as he caressed her mound, using his thumbs to open her folds for him.

Bristol's breath hitched. She hesitated before slowly revealing everything he desired to his ravenous stare.

Jesse hissed. She was already wet and swollen. He glanced up her body, into her eyes. They were glassy and unfocused. Her cheeks looked flushed. The sight of her arousal slammed him in the chest. He'd fucked politician's daughters and porn stars. But he'd never been with a woman he wanted to please this badly.

He dragged his fingers through her wet flesh, focusing on the little bud hardening more with every circle of his practiced fingers. "You're pretty."

After breathing in her velvet scent, he dragged his tongue through the wet groove of her sex, lingering exactly where she would be sensitive, igniting nerve endings he knew would drive her wild.

Beneath him, she thrashed, swinging her head from side to side. He knew she wasn't negating the pleasure as much as she was trying to assimilate it. He often felt the same way as soon as she put her hands on him.

"You're sweet," he muttered in between strokes of his reverent tongue.

Bristol murmured an incoherent sound and dug her heels into the mattress. Her hips lifted restlessly. Her body writhed. Jesse didn't stop, didn't let up. When she began panting, he slid his palms up her body and rubbed the turgid points of her nipples between his thumb and forefingers.

When her body tightened and her skin flushed, he knew she rushed toward climax. Her heavy breathing turned to keening wails.

"And you're mine." He slid up her body, his thumb still working her clit as it hardened to stone. "Aren't you?"

"Yes."

"Say my name," he demanded. "I want to hear you scream it as you come."

"Jesse." Her voice broke as she strained toward the pleasure.

It was one of the most beautiful sights he'd ever seen.

But he wanted to be with Bristol, inside her and a part of her, share ecstasy with her. The two of them together. Now. Always.

The melody he'd been writing for her turned louder in his head. As he reached for a condom and rolled it on, lyrics began pelting his brain. Words they'd spoken to one another. Words they hadn't yet exchanged but he hoped like hell they would. Words of reverence. Promises. Vows.

She cried out in protest because he'd lifted his hand from her moments before bliss crashed over her, but he had something better. Thank goodness she was close because seeing her unabashed, honest pleasure was undoing him fast as fuck.

"Take me," he growled, sliding between her taut thighs.

Bristol eased them open as he shoved them wide. In seconds, he'd aligned his cock with her slick channel and tunneled in.

Sensation rained down on him. Bristol felt hot and tight, yeah. But so much more. Receptive and giving. Alive. Perfect. She was everything to Jesse, and he couldn't believe that he'd found her mere days ago. In the first hour, he'd known that she was different. By the end of the first night, he'd suspected she was truly special. Now he felt an urge all the way to his soul to make her his.

Gripping her thighs, he plunged in to the hilt. A sizzle shuddered down her spine. He plastered his hands flat on the bed and tried to make his way deeper, crawl all the way inside her. He rocked against Bristol as she whimpered in his ear.

"Jesse…" Her high-pitched voice sounded desperate, and that did all kinds of things to him.

He lowered himself to his elbows and slanted his lips over hers, slipping inside her mouth as he thrust deeper. He synched up both motions, making love to her mouth as he did her body. And god, she made love back to him, clutching at his shoulders, her thighs clinging to his hips, her female flesh gripping him so tightly that every move he made incited friction that ignited pleasure.

The music spun in his head, their rapid breaths and hearts mingling in a thumping backbeat that drove him up higher. The taste of her sweetness spilled onto his tongue. The rest of her body fit against him as if she'd been molded to be his. Somewhere in the back of his head, Jesse realized he was being more fucking poetic about a female than he ever been in his life.

But he finally understood why people had been writing songs about love for millennia. It wasn't just a jolt that rattled him. It was a mammoth force tearing through his every preconceived notion about the meaning of life, about devotion. The feeling was dense and enormous. It sat on his chest like a weight. Yet the thought of sharing his tomorrows with her freed him. He could breathe when he was lost inside her. In fact, Jesse began to wonder if he could ever really breathe again without her.

Her nails dug into his back now. She broke their kiss and looked up at him with worry and wonder and tears as he sank into her again and again. Damn if he didn't feel answering tears in his eyes. Damn if this didn't feel like forever.

Bliss overtook her face as her mouth gaped open. She clenched around his shuttling cock. Her body tensed. Her lids fluttered shut and she raced toward the pinnacle.

Jesse wanted to fall over the edge with her.

He ramped up his pace. "Say my name."

"Yes. Yes! *Jesse!*" she cried to the rafters.

Bristol bucked underneath him, her sex pulsing and clutching, clinging as he rode her through the mewling orgasm. But his own desire roared to the fore, smashing his defenses like a freight train. As the climax hit, it shocked then flattened him. He felt crushed. Yet he soared. And he clutched her as if he'd never let go again. With the sound of her cry ringing in his ears and the music he'd been crafting for her lilting in his head, he groaned long and low as he released, relinquishing way more than his desire.

He gave her his heart.

As the last wave of pleasure settled, Jesse caught his breath and looked into her eyes. He had no doubt that she was the thing that had been missing from his life. She was the one who would hold his hands for the rest of their days.

He dragged in a ragged breath. "Bristol Alexa Reece, I love you."

"Really?" She bit her lip, her lashes fluttering against her rosy cheeks.

"Yeah. This isn't merely some post-orgasm glow. I know the difference. I enjoy being with you. I'd rather be with you than everyone else." He shook his head. "Hell, I'm writing a song for you, about you. I haven't done that in years. You amaze me. You inspire me."

Bristol's face tightened. Her mouth turned down. Tears flowed. "I love you, too." Then she laughed. "God, we sound crazy."

"I'm about to sound crazier." He swallowed. "Marry me."

Chapter Seven

"He proposed!" Bristol squealed as she rushed downstairs to relieve Jayla of her temporary duty, anxious to bend her bestie's ear.

"Hayden? Because if he did, I'm gonna kill that jerk." Jayla finished putting some cash in the register, then turned to look at her. "Never mind. Hayden didn't do that to you." She grinned. "He couldn't do that. Jamie did, I'll bet. Girl, you look more like he propositioned you. And you accepted—thoroughly."

Bristol flushed. "That's not important."

"Orgasms are always important."

She looked around the restaurant to make sure no one else was nearby. "Jamie isn't Jamie. He's… You should sit down." She dragged a gaping Jayla to the nearest table and all but shoved her in a chair.

"What the hell? Who is he?"

"Jesse McCall."

Jayla looked blank for a second, then she scowled as if Bristol had lost her mind. "You're sure."

"Completely. When I figured it out, he fessed up."

"You're saying the world-famous singer bailed you out at Bubba Oink's Bone Yard and pretended to be your boyfriend, then went home with you and rocked your world before he proposed?"

When Jayla said it like that, the notion sounded absolutely crazy. Some of Bristol's excitement deflated.

"Yes."

"After knowing you for only a few days? And you mean he proposed marriage, right? Not some crazy three-way like he used to have."

"Marriage." She winced. "Yes."

"And what did you say?" Jayla leveled her with an insistent stare.

"I haven't answered him yet." She bit her lip. "It sounds ridiculous. Romantic, even. But I want to say yes."

"But you didn't. Something stopped you. There's a reason."

"I don't know. On the one hand, it feels sudden. But...when I'm with Jesse, I'm so happy. He's not the guy we see in the press. He's changed."

Jayla shot her a skeptical scowl. "They all say that. Why does he want to marry you?"

"He says he loves me. I-I think I love him, too. I realize we haven't known one another long and I still need to learn tons about him but...he's a better man than Hayden. In some ways, he even reminds me of Daddy."

Her best friend took her hand. "What would you do about this place?"

That had been one of her hesitations. "I don't know."

"Would you go on the road with him, like another one of his groupies?"

Now Jayla's voice sounded soft. It held notes of pity that made Bristol cringe. "I don't know. I guess we could figure it out. He says he's sober and wants to change his life—and he wants me at the center."

"Or more likely he wants to change his image. Girl..." Jayla squeezed her fingers. "An international star says he loves you and wants to marry you after a few days and you're not suspicious? C'mon, now... He's in a tough spot. His album is doing well but he's getting skewered in the press. The late-night hosts have made him into a punch line. What better way to convince people that he's changed than to tie the knot with a pretty little country girl who bakes sweets for a living? If he did, the whole narration about his character would change overnight. Right now, the story is party monger and manwhore sinks to a new low. But if he married you, suddenly they'd talk about how, after learning some hard lessons, he'd discovered an uplifting love in the face of tragedy. He'd be a role model." She snorted. "A freaking hero."

Everything Jayla said was true—and Bristol didn't want to hear it. "He wouldn't do that."

But did she know him well enough to say that for sure? How far would a man with a career as big as his go to save it?

"I'm not pointing this out to hurt you. I'm only saying it because I love you. Hayden mostly hurt your pride, but I think you've really fallen for Jesse. He could tear out your heart. Be really careful."

The message Bristol heard was that she couldn't possibly be interesting enough to keep a man like McCall, who jet-setted around the world and slept with beautiful people. She bit her lip, fearing Jayla was right. Everything had seemed so clear and real and natural when she'd been with Jesse, discussing their future. He adored her lack of worldly ways.

But was that true for his heart or merely his image?

"I don't know what to do," she murmured. "He wants to get married right away."

"Did he mention a prenuptial agreement?"

She frowned. "Actually, I'm the one who brought it up. People like him don't get married without one. And I just thought..."

"People like him? If he's going to be your husband, he's supposed to be your equal." Jayla's expression softened as she shook her head. "Think about this. Rushing you to the altar only benefits him. But you're putting yourself in an awkward position if you marry him without thinking this through. If he's not one hundred percent serious about being in love with you and he can't follow through as a real husband, you'll get dragged through the press. There are only two ways that goes: Either you're the naive little girl he grew bored with and everyone will pity you. Or you're the whore who broke his heart because you didn't stay by his side when your hoo-ha could have healed his emotional boo-boos. Either way, your life will never be the same."

Bristol sighed, her shoulders slumping. "Why are you always right? You were right about Hayden, too."

Jayla shrugged, her hair in black waves that dipped behind

her shoulders. "Because I'm not in the middle of your situation, I can be more detached. Don't forget how much of an ass I made out of myself about D'Shaun last year."

Despite the concern swimming in her head, Bristol gave her friend a wry smile. "That was epic."

"So unless you're trying to one-up me, I think you should proceed with a whole lot of caution."

Suddenly, every muscle in Bristol's body ached as she stood. "Do you mind closing up for me?"

"What are friends for?" Jayla hugged her. "Think carefully. Do what's right for you."

Yeah. Now Bristol had to figure out what that was.

* * * *

Jesse emerged from the bedroom and donned his pants, searching the cozy apartment for his phone. He had to record all the new stuff about the song that had rushed through his head while he'd been making love to Bristol. And he supposed he should tell Candia that he might be getting married. Maybe.

Hell, he wished he knew how to convince Bristol that the amount of time they'd known one another didn't matter and that all the details would work themselves out. He'd help her find a way to either keep her bakery open here or open another elsewhere—or do whatever she wanted. All he cared about was making sure she was happy...by his side, as his wife.

But he understood her hesitation, her need to think things through. He just didn't like it.

During his search, he spotted the cinnamon rolls she'd left him earlier wrapped in foil. They were still a bit warm, and the icing dripping off them had his mouth watering. If he didn't love this woman for what was in her heart, he'd probably love her for her baking talent alone.

The first bite made him moan, and he leaned against the counter, head back, eyes closed. All this goodness from Bristol, both her words and her pastries, was good for his soul.

When he opened them again, he spotted his phone across the room on the coffee table. Dashing over to the device, he punched in the security code. His texts popped up. Candia had left him a message about two hours ago.

Morning! I've been researching your new girlfriend. Cute. Clean. The press will like her. I had a powwow with some of my peers. We all think she's good for your image. Announce that she's your new girlfriend. Or better yet, your fiancée. That will go miles to taking the attention off the crap about Ryan and the Harris girl. If you're up for it, a real wedding would totally improve the public's perception of you. I know it's quick but think about it...

Jesse sucked in a breath. Was she kidding? Ask someone to marry him for show?

Hell no! He wanted Bristol to marry him because he loved her and they would be good together. She would fill his heart, and he would fill her life.

With an impatient growl, he punched up Candia's contact and hit the call button. After three rings, the call went to voicemail. "Are you crazy, woman? I'm not going to pretend to marry Bristol for my image. I know your job is to worry what people think of me, but that's fucking out of the question. And over the line. I'm finally in love and I'm grabbing her with both hands. You can either be happy for me and get on board or hop the fuck off the train."

Jesse hung up and realized that Candia probably thought he'd gone crazy or been whipped by some magical unicorn pussy. But when she met Bristol, his publicist would love her, too. Yes, Candia knew exactly how to spin this to his advantage. She was like a killer shark scenting chum sometimes, and he didn't expect to curb her instinct, but he wasn't going to deceive Bristol to make his life easier.

Shoving the thought aside, he dashed to the sofa and quickly recorded the song that had been dancing in his head since making love to Bristol. He could hear the soft build of a steel guitar, something he never used. But it lent the song a heartfelt, somewhat country feel that reminded him of Bristol. The romantic strains of a piano accompanied as the bridge built to the chorus. He hummed where he didn't yet have lyrics, but the whole melody flowed naturally. It was beautiful and perfect for him.

Just like Bristol.

Yeah, he definitely sounded like he'd been whipped by some magical unicorn pussy. But he'd finally felt a real connection to a woman that didn't begin and end with his penis. Seeing her smile made him feel warm inside. Hearing her laugh thrilled him. So fucking sue him if he was feeling all Hallmark. He was happy. After over a decade of misery, he couldn't wait for the next ten years.

When he closed the app, he glanced at the clock. Shit, Bristol would be closing her bistro and coming upstairs soon. Since she'd never gotten to the hospital with those goodies yesterday, he thought they could run them up today—and start planning a wedding. She hadn't said yes yet, but he'd do or say whatever until she did.

Shakespurr chose that moment to jump on him and dig his dainty paws onto Jesse's lap, as if looking for a comfortable place to nap. He set the phone aside and picked up the feline. He'd never been much of a cat person, but Shakespurr met his gaze with an inquisitive stare before his lids turned heavy. Jesse stroked the cat, who immediately lived up to his name by letting loose a loud, dramatic purr.

With a laugh, he carried the cat into the bathroom, then eased him onto a rug and started the shower. The feline darted off at the sudden gush of the running water.

"Not a fan of baths, huh?" He chuckled and doffed his jeans, diving under the warm spray.

As he washed up, he hummed a few bars of Bristol's song, wondering if he could hire someone like David Tutera to pull off a huge wedding by the fall. Then again, that may not be what Bristol wanted. And the thought of speaking vows over helicopters hovering to get a shot of the ceremony wasn't his idea of romantic. Maybe a destination wedding in the Caribbean or Europe. No, she'd want her family near her. As crappy as they could be, Bristol was a girl who valued family, and she wouldn't get married without them. He made a mental note to ask Jayla about a pretty barn or church nearby and see if Bristol wanted to pledge her life to his there.

As he rinsed the last of his shampoo, he heard what sounded like his phone ringing. Candia most likely. Besides being dripping wet, Jesse didn't want to tangle with a Latina woman who had a temper to match after he'd left her that scathing message. He'd call back when she calmed down. But on the third ring, it stopped. With a shrug, he soaped up and rinsed off, then stepped out of the shower and wrapped a towel around his waist.

When he peeked out the bathroom door, he saw Bristol sitting on the sofa, holding Shakespurr to her chest and crooning to him.

"Hey, honey. Jayla closing up for you?"

She paused. Froze, really. He frowned, watching as she petted the cat one more time and set him on the cushion beside her. She didn't meet his gaze. "Yeah. But she had some questions for me. They're valid, and I think we should talk about them."

Jesse didn't like the sound of that but he'd do whatever it took to ease her fears. "Sure. What do you want to ask?"

"This marriage is really sudden. Why me?"

"Because I love you." Jesse crossed the room and picked up the feline, setting him on the back of the plushy couch so he could sit beside her.

"After only a few days?" She sounded skeptical.

He wanted to give Jayla a piece of his mind for planting doubt in Bristol's head, but if any of his friends had ever said they wanted to get married after a few days of "dating," he would have thought they were insane, too. "It may not sound logical, but it's love. It's not predictable. Sometimes when you know, you just know. I've spent way too many years being cynical. It's great to finally listen to my heart."

"What's the hurry to get married?"

Her guarded expression whacked him like a pain in the chest. "What's the point of waiting? I love you. You love me. If you want to plan a big event, we can. Or hell, let's elope. I don't care if we say our vows bungee jumping. But when you've lived with the superficial as long as I have and something real comes along, it smacks you in the face. I don't want to wait any longer to spend our lives together."

"And you're not asking me to marry you for a simple fix to your image?"

Dread detonated in the bottom of his stomach and spread

outward. How was he supposed to erase this doubt when marriage would so obviously help him? "What did Candia say to you?"

"What does that mean?"

Her face had no expression, as if she was determined to keep it unreadable. There was definitely something going on in her head.

Jesse scowled. "Somehow, she's made you think that you're nothing to me but a quick fix for my PR problem. And it's total, utter bullshit."

"I don't think so." Tears trembled in her eyes as she held up his phone. "I read the text she sent you."

Oh, shit. "Bristol—"

"Not a word, you snake. You can't deny this." She sniffled. "When I came in to talk, your phone was ringing. I didn't think and I grabbed it to answer, but I was too late. Before I put it down, her text appeared. She told you to propose because I would be perfect for your image rehab."

"You've got this wrong."

"I don't think so." She stood, fists balls, face flushing with anger. "You lied to me. You used me. All your pretty words…"

"That's not how it happened. I'd already proposed when she sent that message."

"No. She sent it hours before your little impassioned speech."

"I was asleep when she sent that message," he pointed out.

She scoffed. "Or you pretended to be."

"Seriously?" He stood and stared down at her, water dripping from his hair. He swiped it away with an impatient hand. "You think I would flat-out lie to you after I know what you've been through? After I've poured out my heart to you?"

"I think you have a career to preserve and millions of fans to make happy. Who cares about my feelings when all that is at stake?"

"I do. If I didn't, why would I have jumped in to help you save face in front of your family the night we met? Why would I have chased Hayden off? Why would I do my best to tell you how special you are? Why would I have bothered to get to know you or tell you I love you? If all I wanted was to improve my fucking image, I could have paid someone a hundred times over to pretend to be my fiancée."

She had to see that logic. He'd been in far worse PR scrapes—the time with the three hookers in Rio came to mind—and hadn't resorted to a fake wedding. Didn't Bristol get that if he wanted a facade, he could find one anywhere?

"I don't know." She jumped up and paced. "I don't understand anything. It's all happening too fast and the timing is a bit too coincidental. I can't..." Bristol shook her head, plopping his phone onto the glass table. It pinged and rattled as she headed for the door. "I need to think."

"Where are you going?" he demanded.

"Away." She sobbed and sniffled.

"You're leaving?" he marched after her. "Don't do this. Honey, I meant every word I said. I really do love you."

She wrenched the door open and paused outside the threshold, then turned back to him with tears in her eyes. "I love you, too. And that's what hurts the most. I don't know if you're the love of my life...or my biggest mistake."

Before he could say a word, she slammed the door behind her. He would have given chase, but he wore only a towel. By the time he dressed, she'd be long gone. Already, he heard her footsteps pounding down the stairs, then across the wooden subfloor of the stock room. A door slammed. He looked out the window, watching her flee to her car and drive away.

"Well, fuck." He pounded a fist into the door, then grabbed his phone and reread Candia's text. Yeah, that would look bad out of context. Damn it.

Jesse sighed. He wanted to be pissed but he understood her reservations. Trust was hard for her after Hayden had screwed her over so thoroughly. Jesse knew she had no way of knowing the man he'd been without her, and he wasn't sure how to prove that he couldn't be more serious about their marriage. But he had to start thinking fast because he didn't intend to lose her.

Chapter Eight

With a sinking dread, Bristol parked down the street from her mother's yellow Victorian and crawled out of her crappy compact. Tuesday evening dinner, and clearly she was one of the last to arrive since everyone else's cars lined the crumbling tar road on both sides.

She closed the door and leaned against the vehicle, head bowed, and let out a rough breath. Might as well end this circus. The sooner she told everyone that "Jamie" had ditched her, the sooner she could start living with the label of Lewisville's sad sack ho-bag/spinster and get back to her small apartment where she'd see Jesse everywhere and wonder again if she'd been stupid to run him off.

From the direction of her mother's house, Jayla came sprinting across the wide, open yard. "Have you heard from him?"

Bristol had no doubt which "him" her bestie was referring to. "No. Nothing."

After their argument, she'd left, taking a ride over to the Sonic Drive-In east of Lewisville, in the town of Stamps. A milkshake and a good cry later, she'd headed back to her apartment, ready to work things through. Jesse—and every trace of him—had been gone.

Only then did she realize that she didn't have his number. And it wasn't as if she could simply hit up his website or Facebook page and leave a comment that read, *Hey, Jesse proposed to me. Could you tell him I want to talk so he should call me?*

Jayla curled an arm around her. "I know you thought you loved him but…maybe him leaving so abruptly was his way of admitting that the jig is up."

"Yeah." Admitting that possibility seemed to take all of her breath. After that, she didn't have any air for the rest of her body. Her shoulders slumped. She felt half dead inside. Last night, she'd had to change the sheets before she could sleep because they smelled like him.

And his absence had torn her in two.

"It'll get better," her friend promised.

"It's just…he defended himself so vehemently. He swore that he loved me and wanted to get married. He said I was trying to make matters of the heart logical, and when I was drowning in my banana cream pie milkshake, I kind of wondered if he was right. I still do."

"Hang in there." Jayla hugged her, and Bristol reveled in her friend's embrace for a silent moment. The woman might not be her biological sibling, but she was the sister of her heart. Bristol felt blessed every day to have her.

"I'll try. Thanks."

"I'm glad you're here. I might have mentioned to Presleigh that Hayden came to see you after church on Sunday. Apparently, he told her he was going home to take a 'nap.'" Jayla held up air quotes.

"He only stayed a few minutes, and nothing happened, except that he behaved like an ass."

"That's nothing new," Jayla drawled.

"Nope. Besides, he'd been to see Corey before me." Or that's what he'd said. "He probably spent most of his time there."

"What?" Jayla pulled a disapproving face. "Corey left on Sunday morning to go meet that girl he met on the Internet, the one who lives in Arkadelphia."

"Oh, that's right. I forgot. Maybe Hayden did, too." She shrugged.

"Or he remembered that Corey's lonely little sister quit University of Arkansas and moved back home."

Bristol wanted to say that Hayden wouldn't cheat on

Presleigh…but she knew firsthand that he totally would.

"Whatever happened on Sunday, Presleigh is having one hell of a righteous snit right now. Hayden is trying to suck up but…"

"He's terrible at it."

"You know that's right." Jayla shook her head.

Bristol had to grin. She could just picture five-foot-two, eyes-of-blue Presleigh's tizzy. Then she tried to imagine self-absorbed Hayden struggling to grasp why his fiancée might be upset. She rolled her eyes.

"Well, that's something to look forward to." Because Bristol certainly wasn't eager for the rest of dinner and having to explain to everyone that her "boyfriend" had left. "Let's get this over with."

Jayla turned and started leading her toward the party. "I saw on one of the entertainment websites today that Jesse attended his bandmate's funeral this morning. He spoke. It was really touching."

Yeah, she'd look that right up on YouTube. Not. Well, all right…she probably would. "I'm glad he went. I think he needed that closure."

And maybe that would enable him to start the rest of his life with a clean slate so he could find a way to be happy. Bristol wanted that for him more than anything.

As she and Jayla crossed the yard together and opened her mother's bright-white front door, the wreath of silk daisies nearly bapped her in the face and stirred up a little cloud of dust. But as soon as she heard the shouting from inside, the sneeze burning in her nose dissipated.

"I'm going to kill you," a man growled on the far side of the foyer wall, seemingly from inside the kitchen.

Bristol didn't recognize that voice. She whirled on Jayla, her gaze asking if she knew who was making the threat.

Her friend shrugged.

"Wait a minute." She recognized that insistent voice. Hayden's pal, Corey.

Jayla absently smacked the front door shut, then grabbed her arm to haul her toward the action so they didn't miss anything.

"Was this going on when you came out to get me?" Bristol whispered.

"No, girl. If it had been, you would have been on your own. You know how to find the door." Jayla grinned.

Together, they rounded the corner to find a crowd gathered and Hayden up in Corey's face, his shirt in her ex-boyfriend's fists. "How the hell could you do this to me?"

Do what? Bristol couldn't tell by looking at the two of them.

Then Presleigh ran across the room, tear-splattered mascara running down her face. "Bris... Help me."

Automatically, she opened her arms to her younger sister, who crashed into her and began sobbing anew. Presleigh held her tightly, all but cutting off Bristol's breath. Absently, she stroked her sibling's blonde curls and slanted Jayla a confused glance.

"Now, boys..." Her mother tried to step in. "Let's talk this out."

Hayden snarled at Linda Mae. "Butt out."

Her mother jumped back with a startled gasp and a hand over her mouth.

Corey looked around the crowded kitchen as if frantic for a lifeline. No one came to his rescue.

"What's the matter?" Bristol murmured to her sister.

Presleigh stared up at her with big blue eyes, swimming in angst. "I'm pregnant."

Hadn't Hayden said two days ago that she was a virgin waiting for her wedding night? Bristol frowned.

"Why is Hayden mad at Corey? Did he tell everyone about the baby before you were ready?"

"No." She gulped then hiccupped. "Corey is the father."

When Presleigh dropped her gaze in shame, shock slid through Bristol. She snapped her stare around to Jayla, who looked equally stunned.

"When did you find out?" she murmured to her sister.

"This morning. Hayden came over to talk to me. I..." She shook her head. "I wasn't thinking. I left the home pregnancy test in the trash can. And he saw it."

Holy cow! Talk about the unexpected... Bristol's head

reeled.

"When did this thing with Corey start?"

"When Hayden started screwing my sister about three months ago," Corey cut in, jerking away from Hayden's raised fist with a glower of his own. "Sarah came crying to me one night that Hayden wouldn't break it off with Presleigh even though he hooked up with her almost every day. I knew talking to Hayden wouldn't do me any good, so I called Presleigh."

"I didn't believe it at first, but when he started going over to Corey's house a lot when Corey wasn't there, I knew. Besides, Sarah always shot me mean glances and had hickies on her neck."

Bristol grabbed her sister by the shoulders and held her at arm's length. "Why didn't you call off the wedding?"

"At first, I hoped I could turn it around. Then...I kind of fell for Corey. But the invitations were already out and the dress was ordered...and I was confused."

"All this time you kept telling me that you were waiting so your first time could be on our wedding night, you were sneaking around behind my back and giving it up to my best friend."

"Don't go there, asshole!" Presleigh charged toward him.

Bristol held her sister back. She'd rarely seen the girl raise her voice and never heard her swear, much less see her with a violent tendency.

Jayla reared back and did a double take, too.

"You started kissing on me while you were still dating my sister," Presleigh accused. "Everyone tried to tell me you're a manwhore, but I didn't want to listen. When I found out you were sleeping with Sarah, I got mad. Then I got drunk."

"And Corey helped you out by taking your virginity?" he asked snidely.

Her sister tore off her engagement ring and threw it at him. It bounced off his chest and pinged to the floor. "To hell with you! He's twice the man you'll ever be."

"How do you know? You never tried me." Hayden gave her a cocky smirk.

"Shut your mouth," Corey insisted, curling his hand into a beefy fist and punching Hayden in the nose. "You'll never deserve her."

Bristol resisted the urge to clap. Instead, she watched Hayden stumble back against the refrigerator door. Corey ran toward Presleigh, arms outstretched. He kissed her, grabbing onto her as if she was the most precious thing in the world to him. She melted against him as if he was her knight in shining armor.

What the hell?

With a sharp elbow, Jayla jabbed Bristol in the ribs. "You had no idea?"

"None." She'd kind of been avoiding them both after their betrayal. She'd have to learn to forgive her sister someday. Hayden... She smiled. Looked like he was history.

Linda Mae stepped forward again and picked up Presleigh's engagement ring from the floor. "I think you should be going."

He took one look at Presleigh and Corey, still sucking face in the middle of the commotion, then gritted his teeth. "Gladly."

On his way out, he bumped Bristol's shoulder as if he wanted to punish her, too. She'd had more than enough of him and grabbed the annoying jerk by the collar. "I'm sorry. You were going to say that, right? I know an apology must have been on the tip of your tongue. Because you certainly couldn't be so rude as to bump me on purpose when you're the cheating bastard who left me for my own sister, then ditched her for an easy lay. Tell me you aren't that big of a rat bastard."

Hayden stared as if poised to say something but then reconsidered. "Bristol, what's gotten into you?"

"A whole lot of anger. Thanks to you, I was stupid enough to let myself lose—"

The doorbell cut her off, and Bristol fumed that she didn't get a chance to lay into Hayden about how he'd done a number on her ability to trust and most likely contributed to the reason she no longer had Jesse beside her.

But Hayden decided he'd been saved by the bell and darted away when she loosened her grip to peer around the kitchen wall, back into the foyer. He sprinted out as if someone had set his ass on fire.

Standing next to her, Jayla laughed. Corey and Presleigh came up for air.

Linda Mae looked on. "It's not too late for that June wedding. We'll simply have another groom."

Bristol tried not to roll her eyes. Since it seemed as if no one else was interested in answering the door, she used it to make her escape, striding around the corner to find Hayden hustling down the walk and a very polished brunette in a gray business suit standing at the portal.

Her heart stuttered. Bristol hesitated, staring at the stranger. "Can I help you?"

Please let her have some connection to Jesse.

"Hi." She stuck out her hand. "I'm Candia."

Bristol blew out a jagged breath. She wasn't shocked…but she wasn't thrilled, either. "Don't tell me you're here to plead his case about any sort of fake marriage. The answer is no."

"I'm here to apologize," she clarified, hands clasped, face contrite. "May I come in so I can explain?"

What the hell? The night had already turned into a freaking sideshow. "Sure."

Candia stepped in, and Bristol shut the door behind her, looking around for some privacy. Obviously, they couldn't talk in the kitchen with everyone listening in. So she guided the woman into the empty parlor off the foyer to the right and shut the door. Instantly, the noise level dropped.

"Why are you here?" The more Bristol thought about it, the more she wished she'd shut the door in the woman's face. "You know, I'm a real person with feelings who doesn't appreciate you trying to manipulate me in order to make your client's life a little cushier. He can go to—"

"Before you finish that sentence, you should know that marrying you was his idea first."

Knowing that Jesse McCall thought it was no big deal to twist her heart around and pretend to be enough in love with her to share a lifelong bond pissed her off. "Great. Thanks for the FYI. You're both horrible human beings. Will you get out of my house, please?"

Well, her mother's house, but she was splitting hairs. The worst part was, even as Candia was throwing Jesse under the bus and all but admitted they'd conspired to use her to improve his image, Bristol still wanted him, missed him. Kind of even loved him.

Exactly why she hated romance. She did it so spectacularly bad and always wound up hurt. From now on, she was banning both romance *and* flings. Instead, she'd become the crazy cat spinster who baked cookies for the whole damn town. Maybe it wouldn't bother her in a few years.

Yeah, when you're sixty.

As she reached around Candia to open the door and show the woman out, Jesse's publicist shook her head. "That's not what I meant. The idea to marry you because he loves you was his. I had the same idea, though for the more obvious reason I stated in my message. I texted him…which I hear you read. When he read it first, this is what he had to say." She held up her phone to reveal the screen that listed her voicemails. One from Jesse appeared three messages down, the date and time stamp shortly after he had made love to her and proposed.

"Are you crazy, woman?" Jesse sounded really agitated. No, super pissed off. "I'm not going to pretend to marry Bristol for my image. I know your job is to worry what people think of me, but that's fucking out of the question. And over the line. I'm finally in love and I'm grabbing her with both hands. You can either be happy for me and get on board or hop the fuck off the train."

Candia stopped the voicemail, then flipped to her texts. "You can see clearly here what time he read my message." She shoved the screen in Bristol's face. Based on what she remembered, Jesse hadn't read Candia's text until after he'd asked Bristol to marry him.

Her heart seized up. Regret poured through her. Had Jesse actually meant everything he said?

Had she completely screwed up?

She jerked her stare up to Candia's face, her heart racing. The sort of cold sweat that came with a terrible realization hit her. "You're not here to try and convince me to marry him for his image?"

She shook her head, looking contrite. Given Candia's polished-within-an-inch-of-her-life appearance, Bristol was pretty sure she didn't show anyone her vulnerable underbelly very often.

"I'm here because Jesse is not merely a client; he's a friend. He was also right. What I suggested was over the line. I didn't understand how you could have possibly made such an impact on him in such a short period of time, but since he circled back with me last night, he's set up a scholarship for recovering addicts in Maddy Harris's name. At about one this morning, he filmed a PSA about the dangers of recreational drug use and experimenting. I can't tell you how many favors he called in for that. Then he sat me down and told me everything wonderful about you. In the four years I've known him, he's never connected with any woman on anything beyond the physical level. But you, he can't stop talking about. To hear him, you're practically a saint. Since you agreed to be your sister's maid of honor after she stole your ex, I'd say that qualifies." The woman sent her a wry grin.

"They just broke up. I'm off the hook." Bristol blinked at the other woman, confused. "I'm sorry. So...you came here to tell me what a great guy he is and how much I screwed up?"

"No. He wanted me to be sure you understood that what I said in that text wasn't his idea, but mine. All mine. And he wants to talk to you."

Bristol bit her lip as her heart skidded to a stop. Jesse didn't hate her for lacking trust and assuming he was screwing her over? For once, she didn't hesitate. She knew exactly what she wanted. "Yes. I want to talk to him, too. I wanted to talk to him after inhaling my milkshake."

When Candia looked at her blankly, Bristol tried not to curse at herself. The conversation had rattled her. She needed to be clear before the woman decided she was crazy and tried to change Jesse's mind for good.

"Sorry." She grimaced. "That didn't make sense."

Candia suddenly grinned. "No, I get it now. After a breakup, men cry in their beers. Women consume empty calories and have a good cry."

The woman's words gave Bristol pause. "He didn't break his sobriety, did he?"

"No. In the past, I think an emotional loss like that would have sent him to a bottle and some blow with a couple of bimbos. Last night, he was completely determined to get you back."

Her words made Bristol's heart swell and beat faster. The misery that had dragged her down since she'd returned from Sonic to find him gone had magically disappeared. In its place? Hope.

"So will he call me or something?"

"Something," she replied vaguely, then held out her hand. "It was really nice to meet you."

Bristol shook it, then Jesse's publicist exited the parlor and whisked her way out the front door. She stood, gaping after the woman. That was it?

Suddenly, Jayla appeared at her side. "Who was that?"

With a frown, Bristol started to explain. Granted, in slow, halting sentences because she was still trying to grasp it all herself. But the hope was shimmering brighter, like a shiny bangle dancing a jig in her brain.

Then the doorbell rang again, and she let out a sigh of relief. Maybe Candia had returned.

But when she wrenched the door open, Bristol found Jesse McCall standing there, looking far more like his rock star self than he had during his days with her. He wore combat boots and black leather pants—and he wore them well. A tight charcoal tee stretched across his muscled chest and hugged his bulging biceps. A fresh scruff now darkened his jawline, lending him a gorgeously disreputable look. A guitar strap crossed his torso diagonally, and the instrument rested on his back. The neck stood out, angled above one shoulder. He didn't look merely gorgeous, but as if the professional and personal side were finally happy together in his skin.

Bristol swallowed her tongue.

"Hi, honey. Sorry I'm late." He echoed the words he'd first spoken to her and sent her a searching smile, complete with those dimples that made her heart melt.

A thousand things she could say to him crossed her brain at once. A simple "hi" didn't begin to convey everything in her heart. But she didn't want to get into all the gory details of their relationship in the foyer of her mother's house while anyone could simply walk in. As it was, Bristol figured that only a miracle—or a major ongoing drama in the kitchen—was keeping everyone from running to the front door to see who'd arrived.

Jayla elbowed her, reminding Bristol that she hadn't said anything at all.

But her mouth didn't seem to be working. Instead, she launched herself at him, linking her hands behind his neck and plastering her body against his. "I'm sorry."

He banded a beefy hand around her waist and bowed his head until their foreheads touched. He stroked her crown with a soft palm. "It's all right. I understand. Hayden's crap, Jayla's questions, Candia's text…"

"They messed with my head," she agreed breathlessly.

"I sent Candia to explain since she had all the evidence on her phone. You better now?"

She nodded, then looked around to see that her best friend had melted into the background, probably in the kitchen doing crowd control. Bless her.

"Much." Bristol smiled brightly. "You're here."

"You ready to talk?"

"Yeah." But she wanted to make one thing clear first. "I love you."

"I love you, too. That song I was writing for you at your place? I finished it this morning. Can I play it for you? You'll be the very first person to hear it."

Her heart flipped and fluttered. "Please."

With the warmest smile she'd ever seen him give, he twisted the guitar strap around his body and anchored the instrument against his chest. He strummed and looked at her. He was all man, but she saw the uncertain boy under that who hoped she'd like his gift.

After he cleared his throat, he began singing in the beautiful tenor that had made him millions.

"You turned me on
Like a light bulb
With just a smile
And all your charm

You made me hot
My heart was frozen

All but closed down
Then you sparked me with a touch

And now you're gone
I'm so lost
Looking for a way to carry on

I can't go back
To who I was
To who I'd been
Don't want to hear 'God, remember him when…'

Before you
I didn't know what I wanted
Or know about love
I didn't understand
You're all I've dreamed of
But now you're gone
And I live with regret
I'm just not ready to handle it yet.

Before you
I didn't know you would change me
Or show me the way
I didn't understand
Why my pride wouldn't wait
But now I see
I understand
You've made me into a better man."

As he repeated the chorus, Bristol teared up. The drops rolled down her cheeks. He'd written those words about her? "It's beautiful. Oh, my gosh… I'm so honored. Touched." She choked. "In love with you. I wish I had something to give you in return."

"Right now, I only want one thing." He got down on one knee and drew out a pretty blue box from his pants.

She gasped. When she untied the white bow and pulled off the lid, a sleek black velvet box lay inside.

"Open it," he insisted softly.

She did so—and absolutely lost her breath. Inside was an exquisite Tiffany engagement ring. It wasn't beautiful because of its size or overwhelming dazzle, but because of its sparkling simplicity. It looked like something she would have picked out for herself.

She looked at him, fresh tears sparkling. "I love it."

"Marry me, Bristol Alexa Reese. We'll wait as long as you want to announce our engagement and tie the knot. We'll get married however you want and live wherever you want. I'm dissolving the band to go behind the scenes and focus on my songwriting. I swear no getting wasted or getting laid. I just want everything to be you and me and our lives forever."

Tears ran down her face quickly now. She sobbed at the feeling swelling in her chest, but she managed to choke out one word to him. "Yes."

A grin broke out across his handsome face. "No doubts?"

"None."

"What are you going to tell your family about me? About us."

"That I'm in love." She gave him a watery smile. "And to butt out."

He took the box from her shaking hands and settled the ring on her finger. "It's a perfect fit."

She raised up on her tiptoes and pressed a tender kiss to his lips, melting into him now and always. "Just like you are for me."

* * * *

Also from 1001 Dark Nights and Shayla Black, discover Forever Wicked and Dirty Wicked.

About Shayla Black

Shayla Black is the New York Times and USA Today bestselling author of more than forty novels. For over fifteen years, she's written contemporary, erotic, paranormal, and historical romances via traditional, independent, foreign, and audio publishers. Her books have sold well over a million copies and been published in a dozen languages.

Raised an only child, Shayla occupied herself with lots of daydreaming, much to the chagrin of her teachers. In college, she found her love for reading and realized that she could have a career publishing the stories spinning in her imagination. Though she graduated with a degree in Marketing/Advertising and embarked on a stint in corporate America to pay the bills, her heart has always been with her characters. She's thrilled that she's been living her dream as a full-time author for the past seven years.

Shayla currently lives in North Texas with her wonderfully supportive husband, her teenage daughter, and a very spoiled cat. In her "free" time, she enjoys reality TV, reading, and listening to an eclectic blend of music.

Connect with me online:
Facebook: https://www.facebook.com/ShaylaBlackAuthor
Twitter: https://twitter.com/Shayla_Black
Website: www.ShaylaBlack.com
Instagram: https://instagram.com/ShaylaBlack/
YouTube: https://www.youtube.com/channel/UCFM7RZF38CqBlr6YG3a4mRQ

If you enjoyed this book, I would appreciate your help so others can enjoy it, too.

Recommend it. Please help other readers find this book by recommending it to friends, readers' groups and discussion boards.

Review it. Please tell other readers why you liked this book by reviewing it at Amazon or Goodreads. If you do write a review, please send me an e-mail at interact @ shaylablack.com so I can thank you with a personal e-mail.

Also from Shayla Black/Shelley Bradley

EROTIC ROMANCE

The Wicked Lovers
Wicked Ties
Decadent
Delicious
Surrender To Me
Belong To Me
"Wicked to Love" (novella)
Mine To Hold
"Wicked All The Way" (novella)
Ours To Love
Wicked and Dangerous
"Forever Wicked" (novella)
Theirs To Cherish
Wicked All Night
His to Take
Coming Soon:
Pure Wicked (e-novella)
Wicked for You (October 6, 2015)

Sexy Capers
Bound And Determined
Strip Search
"Arresting Desire" – Hot In Handcuffs Anthology

The Perfect Gentlemen (by Shayla Black and Lexi Blake)
Scandal Never Sleeps
Seduction in Session (January 5, 2106)
Big Easy Temptation (May 3, 2016)

Masters Of Ménage (by Shayla Black and Lexi Blake)
Their Virgin Captive
Their Virgin's Secret
Their Virgin Concubine
Their Virgin Princess
Their Virgin Hostage
Their Virgin Secretary

Their Virgin Mistress
Their Virgin Bride (spring/summer 2016)

Doms Of Her Life (by Shayla Black, Jenna Jacob, and Isabella LaPearl)
One Dom To Love
The Young And The Submissive
The Bold and The Dominant
The Edge of Dominance (winter/spring 2016)

Stand Alone Titles
Naughty Little Secret (as Shelley Bradley)
Watch Me (as Shelley Bradley)
Dangerous Boys And Their Toy
"Her Fantasy Men" – Four Play Anthology

PARANORMAL ROMANCE

The Doomsday Brethren
Tempt Me With Darkness
"Fated" (e-novella)
Seduce Me In Shadow
Possess Me At Midnight
"Mated" – Haunted By Your Touch Anthology
Entice Me At Twilight
Embrace Me At Dawn

HISTORICAL ROMANCE (as Shelley Bradley)

The Lady And The Dragon
One Wicked Night
Strictly Seduction
Strictly Forbidden

Brothers in Arms
His Lady Bride, Brothers in Arms (Book 1)
His Stolen Bride, Brothers in Arms (Book 2)
His Rebel Bride, Brothers in Arms (Book 3)

CONTEMPORARY ROMANCE (as Shelley Bradley)
A Perfect Match

Wicked for You

Wicked Lovers Book 10
By Shayla Black
Now Available!

Ever since he rescued her from a dangerous kidnapper, Mystery Mullins has wanted Axel Dillon. When he returned her to her Hollywood father and tabloid life, she was grateful...and a little in love. Mystery wasn't ready to let Axel go, even after the soldier gently turned her away because, at nineteen, she was too young.

Now, six years later, Mystery is grown, with a flourishing career and a full life—but she's still stuck on Axel. Disguised, she propositions him in a bar, and the night they spend together is beyond her wildest dreams. Mystery steels herself to walk away—except the sheets are barely cold when her past comes back to haunt her.

Once he realizes Mystery isn't the stranger he thought, Axel is incensed and intrigued. But when it's clear she's in danger, he doesn't hesitate to become her protector—and her lover—again. And as the two uncover a secret someone is willing to kill for, Axel is determined to claim Mystery's heart before a murderer silences her for good.

* * * *

Axel Dillon . . . Even the thought of him turned her inside out.

Mystery glanced around the bar again, easing farther inside. Some biker types in the far corner playing pool eyed her. The bartender still stared down his pierced nose at her. Three cops huddled together all focused on her. Did they think she was casing the place for a robbery? She had to stop standing in the middle of the room like an idiot. Take a seat and order a drink.

Finally, her head forced her body to obey, and she eased into a little booth near the back. Once she'd seated herself, everyone around her started talking again. And from her new vantage point, she could see the back half of the bar, previously obscured by the wall of televisions.

There he sat, absently staring at ESPN and sipping a beer,

his profile strong. As usual, his rugged face was unreadable. He still kept his dark-blond hair military short. And he still looked like the side of a mountain. Somewhere around six foot five, he'd always been built big, but in the last few years, she'd swear he'd put on another slab of muscle. His tight black T-shirt hugged every hard swell and lean dip, tapering past a flat belly to narrow hips. She had to hold in a sigh. Even a single glance of him made her heart knock against her ribs and everything below her waist tingle. Mystery swallowed.

He didn't once look her way. Somehow, she'd hoped their stares would lock. He would approach her, want her, and whisk her away for a spectacular night of unbridled sex that would blow away both her panties and her mind. That had been another one of her fantasies. Right now, he clearly had no idea she existed.

On shaky knees, she stood again and headed in his direction. She tried not to stare. A glance up at the television proved he watched a recap of a pro basketball game. With a grunt, he glanced down into the neck of his beer bottle as she slid onto the empty stool beside him.

Now that he was so near, Mystery could feel his body heat, smell him—rugged earth, cut wood, musk. Damn, being this close made her feel both safe and weak.

"Something on your mind?" He turned to her, his stare expectant.

She searched his expression and didn't see a hint of recognition on his large, blunt face. What a relief. But the cleft in his chin and his bright blue eyes still made her feel weak and wanting. That instant chemical attraction she'd felt years ago hadn't waned in the least.

"There is." She mimicked the British accents she'd been surrounded with since she'd fled the U.S.—and him—over six years ago.

Her assertion obviously surprised him. Though he narrowed his eyes, they pierced her.

"I'll bite. Lay it on me."

The bartender chose that moment to come around and plunk a napkin in front of her. "Now that you found a seat, you want a drink?"

A glass of vino sounded heavenly. "Do you have a wine list, please?"

He snorted. "No. I got three types. red, white, and pink."

Mystery paused. She hadn't expected anything private label, but surely more of a selection than that.

"Is the white a pinot grigio?"

The bartender looked as if he was losing patience. "I don't know what kind that is, but the jug of white I have is as close as I've got. You want some or not?"

That could be seriously terrible booze. She'd been willing to give up designer for the night and leave her Tiffany baubles at her hotel, but she'd spew if she drank the equivalent of Boone's Farm.

"Then I'll have a glass of water, please." Better to keep a clear head, anyway. "Thank you."

As he turned and grabbed a glass, the bartender shook his head and muttered something to himself. Mystery really didn't want to know what.

"I'm not sure what threw him off more, your accent or your request." The corner of Axel's mouth lifted in amusement, giving her a flash of dimples.

She'd forgotten the way his smile could soften his harsh face. She grinned back. "He seemed quite ruffled."

A moment later, the young, pierced guy set a glass in front of her with lots of ice and a bit of water, sans lemon. She blinked, and her colored contacts jabbed her eyes with a reminder of their existence. Or maybe it was a warning that her plan would likely fail spectacularly.

"So do you," Axel said. "I won't point out that I've never seen you here, but I'll guess you've never been to a place like this."

"Never," she admitted. "What gave me away?"

He chuffed. "Leaving the door open so you could gape with barely disguised horror was a start. I particularly liked the way you turned slightly green when you stared at the guys about to do to body shots with Trina." He nodded to the corner where the bearded men and the woman in the halter top all laughed. "So why are you here?"

She'd forgotten how observant he could be and how

accurately he could draw conclusions. He did it in an instant, as if nothing in the world shocked him anymore. The world still shocked her all the time.

She hadn't, however, forgotten how direct he was.

"Curious," she lied and held in a wince at her lame answer.

He shrugged. "Let me try another way: The place is more than half empty, so why did you sit next to me?"

Brutally direct, she mentally corrected.

Mystery gaped for an answer. "Why not?"

In retrospect, she could have been a little less obvious and a little more coy in choosing a seat. Maybe she should have sat a few stools away, ordered some terrible wine, and seen if he'd struck up a conversation. But she'd taken one look at him, and any thought of careful or logical had flown out the window.

He leveled her with a disbelieving stare. "That's all you've got? You couldn't even have come up with a good lie?"

Not really. She could have gone the "You look familiar" route, but that would have been too close to the truth. As far as she could see, that only left her one tactic.

"You're very attractive. Pardon me for being interested."

A little smile lit up his eyes before he took another swig of beer. "I didn't say you being close upset me. You're attractive yourself." He stared a moment longer, then glanced down at his empty beer before he shifted his attention to her untouched glass. "You sure I can't get you something stronger to drink? I can't believe a girl like you would risk life and limb to come to this dive for a swig of water."

Truth was, drinking didn't hold a lot of appeal for her. In the past, she pretended otherwise, but . . . "While I appreciate the offer, I'm actually not interested in alcohol." She forced herself to meet his inquisitive stare. "Would you like to find somewhere more private to . . ."

"Talk?" He gave her an ironic curl of his lips.

"No." She sucked in a shaking breath. "To fuck. Would you be interested?"

Hard As Steel
A Hard Ink/Raven Riders Crossover
By Laura Kaye

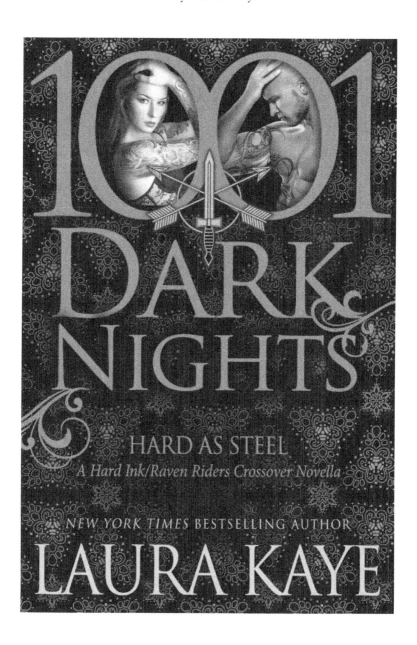

1001 DARK NIGHTS

HARD AS STEEL
A Hard Ink/Raven Riders Crossover Novella

NEW YORK TIMES BESTSELLING AUTHOR

LAURA KAYE

Author Acknowledgments

When Liz Berry called and invited me to participate in the 1001 Dark Nights project, I couldn't have been more thrilled. Getting to work with passionate, creative, amazing people has been one of my favorite things about being a writer, and everything about 1001 Dark Nights delivers that and more. So my first thanks must go to Liz Berry, M.J. Rose, and the other fantastic Dark Nights authors. I'm so glad to get to be a part of this with you and to bring my readers more stories from the Hard Ink—and new Raven Riders—worlds.

Next, I must thank my Avon editor Amanda Bergeron for helping me make Hard Ink the amazing experience it's been and for allowing me to contribute a Hard Ink story to 1001 Dark Nights. Everything about working with Amanda has been this author's dream come true. Thanks, Amanda!

My next shoutout goes to the awesome Jillian Stein, an amazing friend, blogger, and social media manager for 1001 Dark Nights. You bring such fun and grace to everything you do for me and so many others, and I really appreciate it.

As always, I'd never finish a book without the encouragement and support of writer friends Lea Nolan, Stephanie Dray, Christi Barth, and Jennifer L. Armentrout. My publicist KP Simmon and agent Kevan Lyon are amazing and indispensable parts of my team, and so often help me make what I do go as smoothly as it can. Thanks, too, to my husband and daughters for always pitching in to help when deadlines loom—you guys are the most supportive family ever and I thank you for that from the bottom of my heart. I appreciate all of you so much!

Finally, I must thank my Heroes for being so awesomely generous with their time and friendship. And, last but not least, I thank the readers for taking my characters into their hearts and allowing them to tell their stories again and again. ~LK

Dedication

To the readers, for wanting more Hard Ink! You guys rock hard. So hard.

Chapter 1

Jessica Jakes had been lusting after Ike Young from almost the day she met him, back when she was a newbie piercer at Hard Ink Tattoo and Ike first came looking for a job as an artist. Which meant she should've been thrilled that her thighs had been wrapped around his hips for nearly an hour. Except she wasn't in his bed. She was on the back of his bike. And she was running for her life.

The Harley's roar ripped through the warm May afternoon as they drove country roads, piercing through farmlands and forests. But Jess couldn't begin to appreciate the scenery. Not when her whole world was falling apart. She hugged her arms tighter around Ike's broad chest, and he gave her hand a squeeze like he knew she needed it.

She did.

Ike banked the motorcycle to the right, pulling into a narrow gravel drive sheltered by trees. Jess wasn't entirely sure what to expect. All she knew was that they'd ridden about forty-five minutes west of Baltimore into the rural rolling mountains near where Ike's motorcycle club, the Raven Riders, had their compound. Around a sharp bend, the sparkling green-blue water of a lake further down the mountain came into view. The water quickly disappeared behind another copse of trees before they reached their destination, a tiny white house with a detached garage behind it.

With a columned front porch, dark-red front door, and brown stone chimney and walkway, the place sat sheltered in the shade of several tall, old trees, and had a quaint charm about it. For the first time since she'd learned that she was in danger, Jess smiled. Because hard-ass, no-nonsense biker man Ike Young had a cute little cottage. Who would've thought?

Ike parked, killed the engine, and gave Jess a hand off the bike. She was still wearing a grin when she lifted the helmet from her head and shook out her black hair.

"What's funny?" Ike asked, eyeballing her as he scrubbed his hand over his bald head.

Jess gave Ike a long, appreciative glance—and there was so damn much to see. Besides being *way* over six-feet tall, Ike had a black abstract tribal inked onto the left side of his head, the sharp blades of another abstract tribal reaching out of the collar of his black T-shirt, and tattooed sleeves running down both muscled arms. He was a feast for her eyes. One that her hands and mouth had always longed to join.

"Nothing's funny. Your house is just so…cute." She released her helmet into Ike's big hand.

He frowned as he looked at the house, like he was trying to see it through her eyes. "It's not cute. It's a damn cabin."

Jess smirked. "Okay, well, it's a cute cabin then. Do you even fit inside this place? Because standing next to it, you look even freakishly bigger than usual."

Of course, most everyone looked big compared to Jess. At five foot one inch tall, she made up for in snark what she lacked in height. But that was okay, because she *liked* big. Ike's kinda big.

Ike shook his head and gave her a droll stare, then turned to pull her duffle from a leather saddlebag on the back of the bike. He hiked her bag over his shoulder. "House rules for as long as we're here," he said, staring down at her with those piercing, dark eyes. "One. No leaving without my permission—"

"Where would I even—"

"Two." His eyebrow arched, and he nodded toward the porch, beckoning her to follow. "If anyone comes to the house, stay out of sight."

Jess climbed the two steps and waited while Ike unlocked the door—at three different places. Under any other circumstances, she'd have teased him about being overly cautious, but given her current situation, those locks seemed more reassuring than funny. "Anything else, boss man?" she asked with more bravado than she felt.

"Yeah." He pushed open the door, then stood aside and gestured for her to go first.

She stepped inside, her eyes struggling to adjust to the dimness. The house was warm from being closed up, the air still.

Ike turned on a lamp, casting golden light over the small first floor. The living room consisted of an overstuffed brown couch facing a rustic stone fireplace. A flat-screen television hung over the mantle. A console table sat behind the couch, and not too far from that a two-seater wooden table made up the entirety of the dining room. With its white appliances, cabinets, and Formica countertop, the galley-style kitchen was old school all the way, but clean and neat. Brown paneled walls, wide plank floors, and exposed wooden beams made the house feel like the cabin Ike said it was.

Still cute, though.

A series of clicks brought Jess's gaze to the locks on the door.

You're safe, Jess. You're with Ike, out of the city, away from…whoever the hell broke into your house and tried to grab you. Just breathe.

Right. Breathing. Check.

Except, she couldn't help but feel that she'd brought this whole damn situation on herself. Still, how the hell was she supposed to know that the man she'd picked up at a bar last Friday night had been a bad guy intent on using her to get to her friends? Just thinking of it made her skin crawl and her stomach toss.

"Three," Ike said, apparently not realizing she was having a mini-meltdown in the middle of his living room.

"Three? I might need to write these down," she quipped, hoping her voice sounded lighter than her chest felt. Because

Jess *hated* to be scared. She despised feeling helpless and cornered and trapped. Once, she'd fallen apart and let fear get the best of her.

Never again.

Ike was in front of her in an instant, a scowling, unamused wall of muscle and ink. "I'm not fucking around here, Jessica. Take something seriously. For once."

Sweat dampened her neck under her long hair, and anger lanced through Jess's chest until her bones nearly vibrated with it. Anger about the danger Jeremy and Nick Rixey—her employers and friends for the past four years—were in. Anger about the fact that their tattoo shop had been bombed and closed…until God only knew when. Anger that her own house was a shambles, too, after a middle-of-the-night invasion that sent her scurrying like an animal into the crawl space at the back of her bedroom closet.

Anger about being targeted and used and hunted by the very animals that had attempted to hurt her friends.

It was all too damn much.

"Wow, Ike. Thanks for clarifying how serious this situation is. Because I was really confused about what the guys with the guns ransacking my apartment last night meant. So much clearer now." She crossed her tattooed arms over her chest and nailed Ike with a glare. Anger felt *so* much better than fear.

Ike's gaze narrowed, but then his face relaxed and his shoulders dropped. "Fuck. Didn't mean to—"

"Yeah, yeah. Whatever," she said, blinking the sting out of her eyes. No way was she crying in front of Ike. He already treated her like an overprotective big brother as it was. And that was really freaking annoying because it meant her fantasies of climbing him like a tree and having her wily way with him weren't ever coming true. Unrequited lust sucked big hairy donkey balls. "So, what's three?"

"No cell phone, no e-mail, no using credit cards," he said in a gentler tone. "In fact, give me your cell. Just to be sure."

The only reason Jess didn't gripe was because she knew enough about Nick and Jeremy's über-scary mercenary enemies to know they could probably find her easier than she wanted to think about if she didn't stay off the grid. She fished the smartphone from her bra and smacked it into Ike's palm.

His eyebrow arched as his gaze moved from the phone to her breasts and back again.

"What?" she asked, more comfortable with him ogling her boobs than giving her that serious, concerned look he wore a moment ago. "I was afraid it would fall out of my back pocket on the bike."

Ike shook his head and slipped the cell into the pocket of his jeans. Which immediately made Jess jealous of her phone because her hands would burrow the fuck into those jeans if he gave her half a chance.

But alas...

"Anything else, warden?" she asked.

"You're not funny," he said.

"I'm a little funny," she said.

"You're a little pain in my ass," he said.

Jess schooled her expression. Because she wouldn't be surprised if there was more than a little truth behind his words. She and Ike had worked together for years and become friends, but all this was way, *way* above and beyond. When the scumbags who'd broken into her home finally left last night, she'd been too scared to come out of the crawl space behind her closet and hadn't been sure who she should trust. The police were out because Jeremy and Nick had learned that the authorities were in bed with at least some of the bad guys who'd attacked Hard Ink. It was mindboggling to believe that an international drug ring that had injured Nick and killed six of his Special Forces teammates in Afghanistan over a year ago had spilled over into Baltimore. And that Nick's investigation with his surviving SF teammates that had been operating out of the Hard Ink tattoo shop had exploded all over Jess's life. But that's exactly what was happening.

Crouched in the dusty darkness of the crawl space, she'd finally settled on calling Ike. Given his protectiveness of her, his all-around bad-assness, and that he already knew all about the Rixeys' troubles, he'd seemed like the natural choice. But when she'd called, she'd never expected the barely restrained rage that vibrated off Ike as he gently coaxed her from her hiding place, nor the way he tugged her into his arms and just held her once she was out. And she'd certainly never expected him to put his whole life on hold like this. For her. "Yeah, well," she said, forcing the thoughts away. "I'll try harder next time."

Ike's smirk held a hint of amusement for the first time since they'd arrived. "No doubt. So, last rule. No busting my balls."

"I wholly object to that one. I'm already going to die of boredom out here. You have to let me have *some* fun."

Ike got right up in her space, so close that she had to tilt her head way back to look him in the eye. "You think I don't see how you use humor to deflect when you're scared? But I see it, Jess. I see you. So let me be clear. You are *not* gonna die. Not on my watch."

A riot of reaction erupted inside Jess's head. The uncertainty of being laid so bare. The scary satisfaction of being seen when Jess always worked so hard to only reveal what she wanted of herself. The red-hot lust caused by Ike's hard body being pressed so close to hers.

Despite the heat inside the house, Jess nearly shivered at the intensity Ike was throwing off. She became aware of him the way you become aware of the electricity in the air before a summer storm—slowly, insistently, magnetically. Her lips parted as she scrambled for a response, but her nipples were pebbling against his chest, which made her wonder if he'd be able to feel her piercings there.

Ike took a small step backward, but it was enough to break the crazy physical connection pinging between them. Had he felt it too?

"Okay, so, no dying," she said. To her own ears, her voice sounded like a throaty purr. "And, um—" She swallowed hard, trying to gather her wits about her. "—the boredom part?" She peered up at him, hoping against hope that she wasn't the only one as affected by whatever had just passed between them.

Ike's eyes narrowed as if he was on to her game. "Nick and his team know what they're doing. Hopefully this situation will get resolved fast and you won't have to be here that long."

"Right," she said. Jess hoped that, too. She wanted her

friends safe and their enemies to be gone. For good. Still, she couldn't help but wonder if Ike was eager for her to be out of here. In all the years she'd known him, she'd never been to his apartment in the city, nor had he ever invited her out to the Ravens' compound for any of their parties or the races they ran at their dirt racetrack. It had always felt like, on some level, Ike held her at a distance. No doubt a guy as hot as Ike had plenty of offers, but Jess didn't think his reserve with her was because he had a girlfriend tucked away somewhere. In all the years she'd known him, she'd never once heard him mention a relationship, nor had he ever brought anyone around. Still, she couldn't help but feel that there was a part of his world he didn't want to share—with her, at least.

And now, here they were for the first time ever, hidden away from the world in a tiny cabin. All alone.

Get a grip, Jess. This isn't some romantic cabin getaway.

Right. Ike wasn't here with her because he wanted to spend time with her, he was here because she'd asked for his help, because he was a good guy, and because he knew she needed protection.

When Nick's team finished its investigation and nailed their enemies, she'd go back to her regular life, and she and Ike would go back to being friendly colleagues with tons of sexual tension and flirty innuendo buzzing between them. It was already embarrassing enough that everyone knew she'd unknowingly slept with one of the bad guys. The last thing she needed while they were stuck together here was to make it clear just how much she wanted and cared about Ike—not just as a friend, or even a friend with benefits—which she'd half-jokingly suggested once in a moment of tipsy weakness. No, she wanted Ike much more than any of that. Despite the fact that she had no chance with him whatsoever.

Which meant Jess needed to put her fantasies about Ike Young aside. Once and for all.

Chapter 2

Ike needed to get the hell out of there before he ended up giving Jess a hands-on demonstration of all the ways he could distract her from the shit storm that had become their lives. Because a distraction of the his-skin-on-her-skin variety was the last thing either of them needed.

No matter how hot Jessica Jakes was—and she was like goddamn molten lava with her tight little body, inked porcelain skin, and smart mouth—she was precisely the kind of woman Ike had vowed never to get twisted up with again. A woman in trouble.

Been there, done that, still had the shrapnel lodged in his heart. Fuck you very much.

Even if Jess did have piercings in places Ike would've given his left ball to see and tongue and suck. Just once. And even if she looked at him with all kinds of invitation in her eyes. Which she was doing. Right now.

But he couldn't just drop her there and run without at least showing her around the place. He wanted her to feel comfortable for however long they had to be there.

"So, here's the dime tour," Ike said. "TV has cable." He pointed to the flat-screen that hung over the fireplace, then crossed the room toward the kitchen. He pointed to cabinets and drawers as he spoke. "Cups. Plates and bowls. Silverware.

Basically, just feel free to poke around for whatever you need." One by one, Ike unlocked and lifted the sashes to two windows in the kitchen. "There's no air conditioning here, but the breeze off the mountain usually keeps it comfortable."

"No worries," Jess said, her eyes following him as he moved around the open space of the main floor. "I don't mind the heat. We didn't have air conditioning when I was growing up, so I'm kinda used to it."

Ike nodded. "It'll be nice in here at night, though." Next, he opened the window to the left of the fireplace, and the cross-breeze immediately swept through the cabin. Work as the club's betting officer—the man who took off-site bets on the Ravens' racing events, and collected debts when owed—originally sent him to Baltimore six years ago, and then his job at Hard Ink made it a permanent move. Right from the start, Ike had been into Jess, but he figured the daughter of a cop, even recently deceased as he'd been then, was the last person he wanted to bring into the Ravens' fold. They weren't outlaws, but they weren't angels, either.

He breathed in the clean air coming through the window. Four years later, the city had become home, but Ike always appreciated any chance to get away from the grind and return to the peace and quiet of the mountains, and to his brothers in the club.

He just wished he was there under better circumstances.

Shoving the thought away, he reached into the small room beside the stairs and flicked on the light switch. "Bathroom. There are some towels under the sink."

"And the bedrooms are upstairs?" she asked.

"It's a loft," Ike said, nodding her toward the steps. The second floor had a pitched ceiling that followed the slope of the roof, and one wall that stood only waist-high, making it so that you could look down onto the living room and kitchen table. A queen-sized bed filled most of the brown-paneled space. A small nightstand and a stuffed brown armchair made up the only other furniture in the room.

Jess's gaze took in the small room, and Ike could see the question on her face before she gave voice to it.

"This will be yours," he said. "I'll sleep on the couch. My

clothes are in the closet there, but I'll pull some things out so you can have privacy."

Jess's eyes cut from the bed to him. "I'll sleep on the couch."

"Jess—"

"You're way bigger than me. I'll be more comfortable there than you will."

Ike shook his head. The last thing he needed was to be able to see her as she slept. "This is yours for as long as you're here."

"Ike, you're already doing enough for me."

"If I was doing enough, you wouldn't be in trouble in the first place." Ike wanted to bite back the words the second they escaped his mouth. Jess didn't need to know how protective he was of her and how much he really cared. Just the memory of the fear in her voice when she'd called last night and how badly she was shaking when he'd pulled her out of her closet made his blood boil.

Her brow furrowed and she stepped closer. "How were you supposed to know this would happen?"

"Given the situation, I should've planned for the worst-case scenario and had you stay at Hard Ink with everyone else. Jeremy's employees being targeted for information wasn't that big of a leap."

"Ike," Jess said, compassion and affection plain in her voice. She closed the gap between them and rested her hand against his chest. The soft touch shot through him, setting his body on edge and making him want so much more. "None of this was your fault. You can't think that it was."

He wasn't going to debate it with her. Ike wasn't a boy looking to duck his responsibilities, he was a thirty-five-year-old man who fully owned it when he'd fucked up. Because, Jesus Christ, when he fucked up, he did it spectacularly. What happened to Lana proved that. And the same thing had almost happened to Jess. What would Jess think if she ever learned Lana had died on his watch? How safe would she feel right now if she knew how badly he'd let another woman down?

Sonofabitch.

Jessica's hand gripped his shirt, and she softly beat her fist against his chest. "Ike, tell me you know I'm right."

Ike cupped her fist in his big hand and pressed her fingers against his chest. For just a moment. Problem was, he liked her touch. He wanted more of it. And restraint had never been his strong suit.

He looked over her shoulder to the bed. In his mind's eye, he walked her backward toward it, his hands in her hair and his mouth claiming hers. Desire roared through him.

Shit. Time to fly.

"Listen, I haven't been up here for a while," Ike said, giving her hand a squeeze and then stepping away, breaking the contact. "I need to pick up some food for us. Any special requests?"

"Aw, look at you being all domestic," Jess said, a playful, ball-busting grin on her full red lips. "I'm seeing a whole other side of you."

Ike rolled his eyes, pretending like he didn't enjoy her taunting even though he did. Jess was fun and adventurous and the kind of woman who grabbed life with both hands and didn't let go. She played hard and loved freely, and he admired her for both. She didn't let other people's expectations run her life or set her agenda. She wore her heart on her face and in her eyes and on her skin. And she was brave and loyal, too—things that meant everything in his world. Those were core tenets of the code by which the Ravens lived and died.

"What-the-fuck-ever," Ike said, starting down the steps. He needed some distance from her. And he sure as hell needed to get his head on straight and his body under control. "Just some damn groceries. You have special requests or not?"

Her footsteps followed behind him. "I'll just go with you—"

"No," he said, his tone harsher than he'd intended. He turned to watch her make her way down.

Standing on the next-to-last step, Jess planted her hands on her curvy hips. Hips that would feel so damn good in *his* hands, provided he ever let himself off the leash where she was concerned. Which he hadn't. And wouldn't. "Why the hell not?" she asked, brown eyes flashing.

Shaking his head, Ike gave Jess's body a long, slow once-over, from her wavy red-streaked black hair, to the fucking luscious cleavage created by the red lace push-up bra she wore under the form-fitting black V-neck shirt, to the knee-high Goth boots she wore over a pair of torn-up black jeans that wrapped around her thighs like a second skin. Against all the black, the color of the tattoos on her arms and chest stood out like sun breaking through the clouds.

That *his hands* had put a lot of that ink on her skin? Made him more possessive of her than he had any right to be.

"Can't chance having the wrong person notice and identify you. You don't exactly blend in to the crowd." Understatement of the year, right there.

She smirked. "I can tone it down when the situation calls for it."

Ike immediately hated the thought. Jess was loud, vivid Technicolor in an in-your-face kinda way. Exactly the way it should be. "Not a chance. You could shave your head and wear a paper bag and I'd still know exactly who you were from a football field away."

"Ooh, kinky." Her smirk slid into a sexy grin.

Her word choice sent Ike's brain to all kinds of places it didn't need to be. Like envisioning Jess ass-up over his bike wearing only her ink and a pair of heels while he buried himself deep from behind, or imagining Jess with a ball gag taming that smart-ass mouth of hers while he made her come with his mouth and cock until she was boneless and more satisfied than she'd even been in her life. With black fastening straps and a red ball, the gag would match her hair. Something about that image pleased him greatly. And proved he'd fantasized about it a few times before today. Okay, a few thousand times. Whatever.

Did he always have to be so fucking attracted to women in trouble? Because he wasn't any fucking white knight, that was for damn sure. Cop father and friends, drug-addict-cop-killing friends, stalkerish ex-lovers who wanted more—Jess had been in one form of trouble or another for as long as Ike had known her. "Special requests or not, Jakes? Jesus Christmas."

She laughed, and Ike tried to ignore the way it lit him up inside. Despite her size, Jess had a big belly laugh so infectious it could make you chuckle even if you weren't in on the joke. Sometimes it even included snorts that would set her off laughing even harder. "You're too easy to rile up," she said through her laughter. Finally, she calmed enough to add, "Okay, okay. I'll be serious. Let's see…I'd love it if you could get iced blueberry Pop-Tarts or Lucky Charms for breakfast, and, like, pepperoni pizza Hot Pockets for lunch and dinner. Oh, and diet Coke. That would be awesome."

Ike frowned. "Anything else?"

Her eyes went distant for a second and then wide with excitement. "Oh, Doritos, too, please. Might need a couple of bags."

"Why do I feel like I'm talking to a nineteen-year-old frat boy right now?" he asked.

"Dude, you asked what I wanted. I can't help my junk food proclivities. I'm a terrible cook and Hot Pockets are freaking good. But wait. How are you going to get all that on the bike?"

Ike shook his head and pulled a key ring from his pocket. "I'm not. I've got a truck in the garage."

"Oh, okay. Well, I really would come help."

"I know you would. Just stay put. I won't be gone long. Use the house phone if you need me." He pointed toward the end of the kitchen counter, where the handset for the landline sat.

"I will," she said quietly, looking over her shoulder toward the phone.

Something about her tone made Ike pause, despite the fact that he could really use a breather from the sexual tension that always seemed to crackle between them no matter how unaffected he tried to act. "You okay being alone?"

Jess made a face. "Of course. You don't have to worry about me."

If only it was that easy. Especially when he could've lost her not twenty-four hours before. He might not want her for himself—no, that wasn't quite true, was it? He wanted her. He'd *always* wanted her. But he couldn't let himself have her because he'd never be able to give her all of him. Jess deserved a whole man. And Ike hadn't been whole for almost eighteen years, when a part of him had died along with the first woman he'd ever loved.

And that wanting? That's why he needed to get the hell out of this house for a while. He turned on his heel. "Remember the rules," he said over his shoulder. "And lock the door behind me."

"Aye, aye, captain," Jess said, the snark back in full force. Then Ike was out the door. "Don't forget the Doritos. Lots and lots of Doritos," he heard as he closed it behind him. Fucking Doritos.

Ike walked his bike back toward the garage—no need to advertise his presence here. Except for the Hard Ink team and the Ravens' club president, Dare Kenyon, no one else knew where Ike and Jess had gone. And Ike was happy keeping it that way for now. He even planned to go to a store on the edge of Frederick instead of the more convenient one that was only a few miles from the club's compound.

He parked the Harley on the side of the garage and then unlocked the side door to the small one-car-wide building. The black and silver 1975 Ford F-250 gleamed where the sunlight streaked through the door and onto the steel and chrome. Ike had restored it a decade before and it was in pristine condition.

He was for shit at taking care of people, but he could take care of machines on wheels like nobody's business.

Enough, he thought, slamming the truck's door harder than necessary.

Enough thinking about the past. About how he couldn't save Lana. About wanting Jess and not being able to have her.

He had a job to do and that was all that mattered. *Jess* was all that mattered. Keeping her alive until the clusterfuck with Nick's Special Forces team was resolved once and for all. Until Nick's enemies no longer posed Jess any threat for being able to identify who at least one of them was. That was what Ike's brain needed to be focused on. And nothing else.

For fuck's sake.

The moment he turned out of his driveway and onto the road, an unwelcome anxiety settled into his gut. He didn't like leaving Jess alone. But he'd only be gone for an hour. Even Jess could keep herself out of trouble for that long.

Chapter 3

Jess watched Ike walk out the door, all the while keeping her *Fine, fine, I'm totally fine* expression plastered on her face. The moment he was gone, her shoulders sagged under the weight of being alone in a strange place not that many hours after strange men had proven that not even familiar places were safe.

Stop it, Jess. You are *fine. Or, at least, you can fake it until you make it.*

She nodded to herself. Had plenty of experience doing that, didn't she?

Step one was locking herself in nice and tight, so Jess crossed the room and threw all three locks.

Standing with her back to the door, she surveyed the cabin, wondering what to do with herself next. She sank into the couch and turned on the TV. Daytime television pretty much sucked ass, though, and it was amazing that so many channels existed and yet almost all of them were filled with crap. She paused on a house hunting show she liked but the husband wanted absolutely ridiculous things including a skateboarding park in the backyard. Like, an actual skateboarding park. So she turned the idiot box off and dropped the remote onto the cushion next to her.

At a loss for what to do, she wandered into the kitchen and got a glass of water. The breeze coming through the windows was fresh and fragrant, like flowers and pine needles. Clearly, she wasn't in downtown Baltimore anymore.

Turning, her gaze fell on the duffle she'd quickly packed in the middle of the night. She'd been so shaken and anxious to hurry, she wasn't even sure what the hell she'd thrown in the bag. For all she knew she had twenty panties and no pants. Which would make things really interesting around here if it were true...

Jess smirked and put her glass in the sink.

She carried the duffle to the bathroom and unpacked her toiletries and makeup, and then she went up to the loft to put away her clothes. Ah, damn, she had in fact brought pants. And shirts, too. No parading around naked to drive Ike crazy, after all.

Warm air hung in the loft like a wool blanket, so Jess turned on the ceiling fan and opened the room's only window, which overlooked a small backyard that sloped downward toward the woods. Not too far off, she could see the lake she'd noticed when they'd first turned on to Ike's property. It was weird to think of Ike in a place like this when almost all of Jess's associations of him were at Hard Ink, a tattoo parlor in a gritty and largely abandoned industrial area in Baltimore.

Turning away from the window, she couldn't help but focus on the bed—the most prominent piece in the room. A hunter-green comforter covered it, and four pillows with green-and-blue-striped cases sat piled at the top of the bed. The idea of Ike sacking out on the couch still didn't sit right with Jess, who wasn't sure how much more sacrifice on her behalf she could take from the guy. But the feeling of being a burden was a dear old frenemy she didn't have a prayer of shaking any time soon.

Sighing, she emptied her bag onto the bed. Among the pants, shirts, sleep shorts, tank tops, and underthings, she found a strappy little red dress. *Why* she'd brought a dress, she had no idea. In her haste to grab and go, she'd mostly pulled things out of a basket of folded laundry sitting on her bedroom floor, not realizing it was among them. The closet was pretty full of Ike's clothing, but Jess managed to find a free hanger for the dress. She stared at it sandwiched between a steel gray button-down and an old, frayed sweatshirt. It was stupid, but she liked seeing her clothes comingled with Ike's...

Ugh, Jess. Now you're *the one being ridiculous.* Only, unlike the TV, she couldn't simply press a button to get away from all the crap in her own head.

The sound of kids screaming and laughing echoed up from the lake and pulled her out of the inane thoughts. It was a sound of such pure innocence that it simultaneously made Jess smile and tear up. Despite the fact that her mother had run off when she was eight, Jess's dad had been *awesome.* He'd been busy as hell as a Baltimore police detective, but he was always attentive and funny and loving. He'd bought her first hair dye kit and gotten his fingers all stained purple helping her do it. He'd taken her dress shopping for proms and homecomings, and never said a word that her fashion choices trended toward combat boots and skulls. He'd given her an amazing childhood, and the laughter made her think of him. And miss him. And feel guilty all over again. Because he'd been killed four years ago. Protecting her.

Just like Ike was doing now. And the situation was equally—if not more—dangerous. Jess shivered.

More screams from the lake. Except...

Awareness shot through Jess and chased away the haze of memories and the tangle of troubled thoughts. Someone was screaming...and it sounded different now. Not playful, but panicked. She ducked her head into the opening in the window...and heard a faint but very clear shout for help.

Jess's scalp prickled and a chill ran down her back.

One moment, she stood paralyzed, and the next she was barreling down the steps, through the kitchen, and out the back door. She paused in the backyard long enough to hear more desperate cries and spotted a trail that cut into the woods from behind Ike's garage. Jess made a beeline for it, stopping every so often to make sure she was still headed in the direction of whoever was in trouble.

It seemed like she was running down a hallway that just keep getting longer and longer, but eventually the trail turned and opened up, providing a straight-on view of the water. Sweating and breathing hard, Jess broke through the edge of the trees and skidded to a halt. Scanning the lake, she saw someone splashing and trying to hold onto what appeared to be a small, overturned boat. Cries also came from a dock a little ways around the lake, where a lady was calling out to the person in the water. Jess took off toward her.

The woman noticed Jess first and flung an arm over her head. As Jess got closer, she noticed that the woman was older, her braided, pale-blonde hair all shot through with gray. In jeans and a white blouse, she was also pretty, and she reminded Jess of an old-time country-western star. A lawn chair sat behind where she stood on the dock.

"Can you swim?" the woman called, her voice strained with fear. "I can't and my little guy can't either, and I'm afraid Ben's gonna pull Sam under trying to keep himself above water. I've called my husband but I don't know how long it'll take him to get here. Oh, God." The words spilled out in a jumbled rush.

Jess's boots pounded on the wooden planks as she closed the distance between her and the lady. "I can swim," Jess said. "How deep is it?" She bent to unzip her tall boots and inhaled deeply, trying to get her breathing under control.

"Oh, I'm not sure. Not too deep here, but deep enough out there that they won't have a chance of touching." The woman paced, her hand against her forehead to shield her eyes from the sun. "Hang on, Sam!"

The minute both boots were off, Jess climbed down the metal ladder at the end of the dock. The dark-green water immediately soaked through her jeans, much colder than she expected given the warm day. Fuck, she should've taken the denim off, too, but it was too late to worry about that now.

"Oh, hurry!" the lady cried.

Jess pushed off with her feet against one of the slimy wooden pylons and swam as fast as she could. That it had been a *long* time since the last time she'd gone swimming was immediately clear, but she couldn't worry about that right now. She couldn't worry about the bite of the cold water or the drag of the heavy denim or that she was already tired from the uncharacteristic run from Ike's house—not to mention the fact that she'd only gotten about two hours sleep before the noise of someone breaking into her house had sent her scurrying for a hiding place.

Legs kicking, arms plowing into the water, Jess pushed herself for long minutes until finally, *finally* she was close enough to talk to the boys.

"Hey guys," she said in a breathy voice. "I'm Jess."

"I'm Sam," the bigger boy said, fingers gripped around a handle on the edge of the boat. "This is Ben," Sam said. Crying, the little boy stared at her with wide, terrified eyes, his arms wrapped tightly around the other boy's neck.

"Hi, Sam." She swam closer, close enough that her hand grasped at the boat's aluminum bottom. "Ben. Do you think you can—"

The little boy dove at her and clutched her around the neck. His legs wrapped around her belly like a vise.

Unprepared for the extra weight, she nearly went under. Jess grasped the same handle onto which Sam hung, pulled herself up, and shook the water off her face. Ben wailed into her ear. She had to get him calmed if she had any chance of getting him back to shore. She rubbed small circles against his back. "It's okay, Ben. I've got you. I'm gonna give you a tow back to the dock, okay? But I need you to calm down first."

"I caaaan't," the boy cried.

"He thinks he saw a snake after we flipped the boat," Sam said.

Oh, fuck. Snakes were great as tattoos and jewelry. In real life, not so much. Jess schooled her expression and forced a smile. "Even if you did, he's long gone by now. All the noise we're making would totally scare him away." Hopefully. Please, God.

Ben's crying turned into a breathy whimper. "Weally?"

"Really," Jess said. "And if you could stop crying, I bet it would make the lady on the dock feel a lot better. She's really worried, and now that I'm here, there's nothing to worry about. Right?"

"G'amma's worried?" Ben asked, his breath hitching as he looked over her shoulder.

"She is, but it's all okay now. Right?" Jess continued to rub circles against the boy's back and, slowly but surely, his breathing evened out and slowed down. Finally, he heaved a big, tired-sounding sigh. "You ready?"

"I dunno," he said, fear plain in his voice.

"I'm gonna do all the work. All you have to do is hold on to my arm," she said. "Can I show you how we'll do it?" Just when she was sure Ben was going to refuse, he nodded. "Okay, great. You're being really brave, Ben. I'm gonna turn you around and hold your back to my front. But I promise I'm not gonna let go."

"Promise?" he said, the strain of tears returning to his voice.

"I totally promise." Jess hooked her arm around his neck and across his chest, her hand finding a hold under his arm. She hadn't used her teenage lifeguard training in years, but when she was younger, she used to love to swim. Of course, after her dad died, she no longer had access to his gym, and Jess had sorta let the swimming go…along with so much else. When Ben finally relaxed against her again, she shook away the thoughts and looked at Sam. "Will you be okay while I take him back?"

"I can swim back myself," Sam said.

"Are you sure?"

He looked toward the shore, the doubt clear in his eyes.

"I'll come right back for you, Sam. You were holding Ben up all this time, so you've got to be tired." Jess ignored her own growing exhaustion. *Suck it up, buttercup.*

"O-okay," Sam finally said. "I'll wait."

"Good man. All right, Ben. Here we go, nice and easy, okay?" She lay back in the water, using her free arm and her legs to propel them shoreward. It was slow going, to be sure. Jess's lungs burned and her shoulder muscles felt like Jell-O. Ben whimpered and sniffled and occasionally lifted his head to see how far they'd gone, but Jess was impressed by how he'd managed to calm himself down. He really was a brave kid. They both were.

When Jess had nearly reached the dock, the low *whirr* of an engine reached her through the sounds of her own splashing and heavy breathing, but she couldn't divert even a moment's worth of energy away from getting Ben to safety. As it was, she was already starting to worry about how she'd get Sam in, too. But one thing at a time.

The aluminum of the ladder against her palm felt like the biggest victory ever. "Here we go, Ben," she said.

"Oh, thank goodness." Ben's grandmother extended a hand down to the little boy.

"Don't worry, G'amma," he said, clutching the metal and hauling himself up.

The woman laughed and hugged the boy into her arms, getting herself soaked in the process. It didn't look like she minded one bit.

"Okay," Jess said, clutching the ladder with cold fingers. "I'll go get Sam now." Heaving a deep breath, she pushed off the dock.

"Wait," the grandmother said. "That's my husband and Doc coming."

A few feet out, Jess treaded water, her gaze scanning for the incoming boat. Sure enough, a small motorboat was making its way toward the overturned rowboat. The older woman yelled and gestured, and Sam swam around the end and waved until one of the men waved back.

Jess looked up at the other woman. "I'll still go out if you think I should."

"No, hon. You've done enough. Come on out of there now."

With a glance back at Sam, Jess returned to the dock. Climbing the ladder took way more effort than it probably should've, but she forced herself up and out of the water until she was finally standing. A puddle of water formed all around her bare, ice-cold feet.

As they stood watching, the motorboat pulled up along Sam. One of the men hauled him out of the water and wrapped him in a towel, and then it took both of the men to right the rowboat. They slid it alongside them and slowly towed it back to shore.

The older woman put her arm around Jess's shoulders and hugged her in. "I can't thank you enough. I'm Bernie, by the way, but everyone calls me Bunny."

"You're welcome, Bunny. I'm Jess," she answered, and

then she mentally kicked herself for revealing her real name. Maybe it didn't matter, or maybe it did. Either way, *that* was the exact moment it occurred to Jess that she'd pretty much broken every one of Ike's rules in about a fifteen-minute time span.

Oh, shit.

Chapter 4

Ike unlocked the front door then scooped up the bags of groceries he'd dropped at his feet. Hands full, he made his way inside and headed straight for the kitchen.

"Yo, Jess. I'm back," he called, settling the bags on the counter. He inhaled to call her name again when he noticed something that shot ice through his veins—the back door stood open. "Fuck!" He darted out the door and onto the small back porch, but the yard was empty. "Jess!" he shouted. "Jessica!"

Sonofafuck.

Ike didn't know whether to be terrified that something had happened to her or angry that she'd left the house, and the combination of both emotions flowing through him was like a noxious, dangerous cocktail that had taken him from sober to fucked up in two point five seconds.

He tore back into the house and hauled ass up the loft stairs—just to be sure. Empty. As was the rest of the house. On the back porch again, his brain raced as his eyes scanned. The only thing back there was the trail to the lake.

The low growl of a motorboat's engine sounded in the distance. And though it was probably a ridiculous reaction, dread settled over Ike like a second skin, but he was too used to worst-case scenarios actually coming true.

His feet were in motion before he'd made the conscious decision to move. Partway down the trail, the surface smoothed out to mostly dirt, and that was when Ike noticed the shoe prints. He slowed to a walk. Just one set. Small foot size. Which meant... He was gonna kill her. He really fucking was. Right after he pulled her into his arms and made sure she was okay.

Ike ran the rest of the way into the clearing, his gaze quickly settling on a grouping of people down at the Aldersons' old dock. And there, in the middle of the group, was a very petite woman with black hair wearing all black.

That was his girl.

Well, not his.

Whatthefuckever.

He took off in the direction of the dock. Before he even got there, he made out the identity of the others—Doc, Rodeo, Bunny, Sam, and Ben—all members of the Ravens' family in one way or another. Ike's brain scrambled for a rational explanation for the scene in front of him, but he was too fucking angry and worried and worked the hell up. Rational might as well have been a foreign country.

"Hey, Ike," Doc called, giving a wave from where he stood at the end of the pier. Tall and wiry, Frank "Doc" Kenyon had shoulder-length white-gray hair on his head and his face. He was the club president's grandfather and half-owner of the compound that included the Ravens' clubhouse and the racetrack. Dare Kenyon, the club prez and Ike's good friend, owned the other half and would inherit everything when Doc decided he was done with this world and everyone in it. Some days, that seemed like it might happen sooner rather than later because the old man's hip and knee replacement a few years back gave him all kinds of difficulties and—worst of all—kept him from riding much anymore. Ike was pretty sure he'd want to go before reaching that day, so he couldn't really blame the guy.

Ike slowed to a walk as his boots hit the wooden planks. He held his hand toward Doc's but his eyes were all for Jess...who was soaking wet. What in the ever-living hell? "Doc," he said, giving the older man a quick handshake. He moved past Doc just as quick. "Hey, Ike, wait..."

But the roar between Ike's ears was too loud for listening. He marched right into the group of people crowded around the end of the dock and bore down on Jess. Clipped, angry words spilled out of him. "You want to tell me why you're down here? You know, given the motherfu—" He swallowed the curse word when he noticed Ben's wide eyes staring up at him. "Given the situation and our conversation earlier?"

The sum total of Jess's initial reaction was a single eyebrow lifting into an arch. Just the left one. The movement made him take in the droplets of water trailing down her face from her wavy, wet hair, the smudges of mascara below her lashes, and the shiver of her lower lip. Finally, she said, "I had a good reason."

"*Jessica*—"

"Ike, honey," Bunny said, smiling. Despite being in her sixties, Doc's sister still had her looks—and plenty of sass. "Your Jessica was a total heroine just now. So slow your roll before you say something you regret. Besides, Dare called earlier to let us know you were bringing someone up here for protection. So don't worry. Jess didn't spill any beans."

Amusement spilled into Jess's brown eyes, and then she chuckled. "Bunny, I think you might be one of my favorite people, like, ever."

Bunny put her arm around Jess's shoulder and hugged her in. "Us old ladies got to stick together."

Old ladies? Oh, for fuck sake. Ike wasn't sure he could ever see himself making that leap, and certainly not with Jessica "I can indeed find trouble in less than an hour" Jakes.

A headache bloomed behind Ike's eyes as he looked between the two women, and then to Doc and Rodeo, Bunny's second husband whose son Slider was Ben and Sam's dad. The two other men stared back at him with a mixture of amusement and sympathy.

Ike threw out his hands. "Could someone please explain what the hel—heck happened here?"

"Miss Jess rescued Ben and me after we flipped the rowboat," Sam said, his shaggy dark-brown hair and green eyes so much like his father's. "Or, at least, she would've rescued me, too, if Doc and Pop hadn't shown up first. But she got Ben back before he completely freaked out and drowned me while he was at it."

"Did not freak out," Ben said.

"Did, too," Sam said.

Ike ground the heel of his hand into his eye, a vain attempt to relieve the throbbing there. The story still didn't make much sense to him, but if what Slider's boy said was true, what Jess had done was big. The only thing the club valued as much as taking care of its own was taking care of those who couldn't take care of themselves.

"I heard them screaming for help from the house," Jess said. "I should've thought twice about running down here, but I…" She shrugged, then shivered. "I just acted."

Ike gave a tight nod. Her words took the edge off of his anger, although his insides were still keyed up from the fear-based adrenaline flooding through him. Not to mention, the more people who knew Jess was here, the more Ike worried that a single unintentional slip could put her in danger. Again. Of course, everyone here knew that the club had allied itself with Nick and his friends—an alliance that Ike had helped broker given his close relationship with both. And certainly everyone understood what was at stake, especially after an enemy attack on the Hard Ink building had collapsed part of the roof on the large L-shaped building and killed Harvey and Creed, two of their members, two of their brothers. So it wasn't a question of any of these people putting Jess in danger knowingly. But Ike couldn't be too careful, not where Jess was concerned. Not given how lethal the mercenaries were that the Ravens and Hard Ink team had been fighting.

Ike heaved a deep breath. "You boys okay now?" he asked, looking between Sam and Ben. They both nodded, and then turned to thank and hug Jess. Ike watched as she interacted with the kids, her behavior so natural and comfortable with them. And it did something…funny to him. Made him think. Made him wonder. Made him want.

And it certainly made him look at Jess in a whole new way—and not just because his mind was playing with the image of her belly rounding with a child. Okay, *his* child. But because she'd risked herself for someone else's kids. Given everything Slider had already lost, Ike knew how much those boys meant to the guy, which meant what Jess had done was going to mean a lot to him, too.

Bunny was right. Jess was a hero.

"Well, we'll get 'em back home now," Rodeo said, waving the boys into the motorboat.

Ike nodded. "Roger that."

Bunny stepped in front of Jess and wrapped the younger woman up in a big hug. "You ever need a *thing*, don't hesitate to ask. I owe you, Jess."

"It was nothing. Really. I'm glad I could help," Jess said, her voice subdued, not to mention a little shaky.

Bunny shook her head. "It wasn't nothing to me." As Jess nodded, the older woman gave her husband a kiss. "My car is up at the Alderson's old place. I'll meet you back at home."

With longish gray hair and a beard, Rodeo always half looked like he was smiling, but never more than when he was with Bunny. "All right, darlin'." She reached for a lawn chair sitting on the dock and he put his hand on it. "I got this." Bunny gave him another kiss and took off.

Doc limped toward Ike and clapped him on the shoulder. "Good to have you back in our neck of the woods, Ike. Can't wait 'til everyone's back."

"Me, too," Ike said. Because it would mean that the war someone was waging against his friends—and now his club—would be over. Once and for all. "Thanks, Doc."

"Don't thank me. Thank your little lady." Doc winked at Jess, earning him a smile from her.

And then they were all in the boat and easing away from the dock, the boys' rowboat tied behind them. Ike returned a few waves and then turned to Jess.

"You're pissed," she said. "Ike, I'm—"

Without a word and without warning, Ike grabbed Jess around the thighs and heaved her body over his shoulder, lifting her into a fireman's carry. He retreated down the dock, scooping up her boots as he went, and ignoring the fuck out of the hooting and hollering he was pretty sure he heard from his friends in the boat.

"Oh, my God, you cretin! Put me down!" She beat her fists against his back and kicked her feet.

Ike used his other arm to still her legs. "No."

"Ike, what the fuck? I don't freaking need you to carry me," Jess yelled, using her arms to try to push her body up.

"Too bad. I need to carry you," he said. He regretted the admission but couldn't deny the truth of the words. He *needed* her in his arms. He needed the proof of life.

"But your big-ass shoulder is in my gut and I'm probably going to puke all over you," she said, apparently not impressed by his words.

"No you won't."

"Oh. Well, if you say so. For fuck's sake." She kept up a steady stream of grumbling the whole way home, but it didn't bother Ike one bit. Because she was warm and whole and safe in his arms.

Finally, he climbed the steps to the back porch and carried Jess into the kitchen. He secured the door, then slowly lowered her to her feet to stand against the wall behind the door. He braced his hands on either side of her, boxing her in, forcing them close, making her see him, *hear* him. He ought to walk away, clear his head, get himself under control. But he couldn't force the distance between them, no matter how much he should.

He bent down, way down, so that his eyes were aligned with hers. "That's the second time in twenty-four hours that you've scared the fuck out of me," he said, nailing her with a stare.

For a long moment, her expression was filled with uncertainty and confusion, and then her gaze dragged down his face and settled on his lips. She licked her own, and Ike couldn't help but track the movement and want to warm her body up with his—starting with that sweet, smart little mouth. "I didn't mean to. Either time," she said.

He just stared at her, his head too tangled up to articulate all the things he wanted to say—and to figure out which of those he absolutely shouldn't say. Ever. Because he understood enough about himself to realize that he was this wound up for a reason. He cared about Jess. A lot. And if things were different... *But they're fucking not.*

Right.

Suddenly, Jess's cold hands were on his cheeks. Where her touch was tentative, her eyes were filled with heat...and challenge. "Kiss me," she whispered as she slowly leaned in.

"Don't," he said.

"Why not?" she asked, so close now that her breath caressed his skin.

Yeah, why not? Traitorous brain.

She ghosted her lips over his, mimicking the act of kissing while purposely keeping a hair's breadth between them. Ike's blood flashed hot and his cock was instantly rigid in his jeans. "Taste me," she whispered.

Fuck, he wanted to. He wanted to kiss her and penetrate her and claim her. In any and every way.

Ike forced himself back. The space unleashed an ache inside his chest—but better a little pain now than a lot later. That was a lesson he'd learned over and over. "I need to keep my eyes on the prize, Jessica. And that's you, safe." He scrubbed his hands over his face. "I'll, uh, I'll get you a towel."

Chapter 5

What the hell just happened?

Still pinned to the kitchen wall, Jess watched Ike walk away. Twin reactions roared through her—hurt at his rejection, and appreciation for the fact that he wanted to take care of her. At least he hadn't been as mad at her as she thought he'd be— well, once he understood why she'd left, that was. She probably should've thought about what she was doing when she went flying out of the house—not to mention what Ike would think about it. But, damnit, she was her father's daughter, and there was absolutely no way she could hear someone in need and stand by without helping.

Ike, of all people, had to understand that.

"Here," he said, returning with a big beige towel.

"Thanks." She grasped the terry cloth. He didn't let go of it right away, and it made her look up to his face—where she found his dark eyes absolutely blazing down at her. Jess didn't think she was imagining the raw need she saw there, especially when she finally dropped her gaze only to find herself staring at a prominent bulge in the front of his jeans.

Holy shit!

Abruptly, Ike turned away and busied himself at the counter.

Dazed with lust and confusion, Jess scrubbed the towel

over her face and hair and then wrapped it around her shoulders. The dry warmth of the cloth made her realize how chilly she was in the wet clothes. "I think I'll take a shower," she said. "Warm up."

Ike nodded. "Good. I've gotta get the rest of the groceries from the truck."

As he made for the front door, Jess retreated into the bathroom and quietly closed herself in. For a long moment, she just stood there, back to the cool wood. And then something occurred to her. Ike hadn't said he didn't want to kiss her, or even that they shouldn't. He hadn't really rejected her, had he?

Or maybe she was reading into her memory of the moment what she wanted to see.

Probably.

Then again, he'd been hard. And he'd looked at her like he wanted to eat her. And she was totally game to be his buffet.

She knocked her head against the door. Twice, for good measure. Because it didn't matter how much his body reacted if his brain was telling him to stay away.

Crap. How long were they going to be trapped here together? Because being so close to what she wanted twenty-four/seven but not being allowed to have it was going to suck ass. Big time.

Jess lingered in the shower longer than strictly necessary, but the warm water felt so good on her sore, tired muscles that she couldn't force herself out. By the time she toweled off, she was yawning and her limbs felt like they'd gained twenty pounds each. She hung her wet clothes over the shower curtain bar and secured the towel around her torso. Being upright was nearly painful after so many hours awake, so Jess could do little more than stumble out of the bathroom.

She walked right into a wall of strong, hard muscle that woke her right up.

"Oh. Ike. Sorry. What are you doing?" she asked, stepping back. Arms crossed in a way that highlighted the thick mounds of his biceps, Ike was leaning against the jamb, his broad shoulders covering most of the doorway. Like he'd been waiting for her to come out.

"I handled that all wrong," he said.

Jess blinked, her brain scrambling to figure out which "that" he was talking about. The scent of him, all masculine spice and summer air, didn't help, either. God, she wanted him. "Uh, handled what all wrong?" she managed.

"What you did...Doc was right. I should've thanked you, not yelled at you. Fuck, Jess." He nailed her with a stare nearly as intense as the one he'd given her in the kitchen. Though, where that one had been full of heat, this one seemed softer...affectionate? Or was that more projecting? "Those boys mean the world to Slider. I owe you."

She sighed. "Ike, you're putting your whole life on hold for me. You totally do not owe me anything. And I understand why you were worried. I should've let you know where I'd gone. Oh, well, I guess I don't know how I would've done that without my cell, but, anyway, I get it."

He pulled something from his pocket. Her phone. "That's why I'm giving you this back. I should've trusted you to not use it unless it's an emergency. And that way, I can reach you, too."

Jess accepted the phone into her hand and nodded. "Thanks."

And then they just stared at each for a long moment. Jess went from feeling amused to awkward to observed...and that made her hot. Especially as she was standing there in nothing but a towel.

As if he could hear her thoughts, Ike's gaze slowly ran down her neck to her chest. She wiped at something there and the wetness on the fingers told her it had been a droplet of water from her hair. Ike watched the movement of her hand openly, hungrily, and his desire made her bold, daring, hungry in return.

Without giving herself time to second-guess the idea, she reached out and lightly dragged her wet fingers against his bottom lip.

And it was like she'd unleashed a beast.

Ike grabbed her wrist and hauled her to him. He was on her everywhere. His hands in her hair, on her back, grabbing her ass and lifting her up so that her legs circled his hips. His tongue licked the exact route that water droplet had taken, from chest to neck to ear. And then he was kissing her, fucking her mouth with his tongue, absolutely devouring her.

Jess held on like her life depended on it, and at some point she became aware of the breeze on her bare skin. She'd dropped the towel, which meant she was totally buck-ass naked in Ike's big arms, and she couldn't have cared less.

Ike licked her mouth, sucked her tongue, nipped at her lips. He turned with her still in his arms and made for the stairs, and Jess thought she might die from sheer joy and anticipation. He tasted like strength and sin and sex, and she tightened her legs around his hips as he carried her to the loft, eager to see if all of him tasted so good—or even better.

When they reached the second floor, Ike growled low in his throat and his grip tightened on her ass, his fingers digging in. She moaned and—

Cool air from the ceiling fan washed over Jess as Ike dropped her onto the bed—and promptly turned around to leave. Jess was so stunned she couldn't speak. Just as he hit the top of the steps, he said, "Don't fucking tease me, Jessica. I'm trying to do right by you, but I'm still just a goddamned man."

* * * *

Ike felt like a bomb waiting to go off.

For one goddamned second, he'd let himself off the leash, and he'd been all over Jess.

For two glorious minutes, he'd held her and tasted her and had his hands and mouth all over her.

For the past three hours, he'd worn a path in the wooden floor of his cabin, wanting more but holding himself back from taking it. And feeling hungry and empty and desperate, like a man who'd just had his last meal and would now be forced to go without for the rest of his life.

After the stunt he'd pulled, he was also worried about Jess. Because after he'd dropped her curvy little ass on the bed— trying like hell not to put a visual to the fucking incredible physical sensations he had from carrying her naked body up the stairs, she'd never come back down.

She hadn't said a word or made a sound, either. And combined with the chaos roaring through Ike's body, her silence was driving him stark-raving mad.

Man-up, Ike. You created this problem. Fucking fix it.

He walked to the bottom of the steps. "Jess?" No answer. "Jess, I'm coming up." Nothing. He frowned, but then he was in motion, his boots thudding against the treads as he made his way to the loft.

The sight that greeted him sucker-punched him right in the heart.

Jess was curled into a little ball on her side, her hands tucked under her face. She'd folded the blanket over her, but it had slid down, leaving her shoulder and breasts exposed.

God, she was fucking beautiful.

Maybe it made him a pervert, but Ike was drawn to the bed. He crouched down beside it, his gaze drinking Jess in. Her skin was a work of art. Her right arm had a swirling watercolor rainbow and waterfall running the whole length of it, flowers and fish woven in. Her shoulder and biceps had an ornate Mexican *calavera* skull, the detail done in reds and golds and dark blues. Ike remembered every one of the after-hours sessions they'd spent together doing these pieces, Jess telling him one colorful story after another. The time with her had made it simultaneously easier and harder to go home to his empty apartment—easier because her liveliness and passion filled up some of the dark, lonely places inside him; harder because he never felt more empty and alone in his apartment than after spending a night with Jess talking his ear off. Smiling at him. Teasing him. Making him want.

On her other arm, Ike could just make out the black and dark-green leaves surrounding the wide-open faces of a half-dozen bright-pink roses. She'd already had part of that sleeve done when Ike first met her, but he'd expanded it for her over the years.

His gaze skimmed over her chest, where a constellation of different sized dark-blue and black nautical stars spilled over her right collarbone, down her chest, between the curves of her breasts, to finally end in a sweeping flourish on the right side of her ribs. She was fascinating and alluring to look at, and that was saying absolutely nothing about the little silver hoops piercing through her nipples. Jesus.

Ike reached across Jess and pulled up the blanket, covering her.

What was even more fascinating, though, was her face. Usually so animated, colorful, and just fucking *alive* with emotion, she looked peaceful and oddly young sleeping, her face bare of makeup. And it made him feel even more protective of her.

With gentle fingers, he pushed a wave of black and red hair off her face—and was surprised to feel how warm her cheek felt. He pressed his fingers to her forehead and found her warm there, too. Someday he'd get around to installing air conditioning in this old place, but he spent so much more of his time in Baltimore that he hadn't made it a priority.

Sighing, Ike made his way back downstairs. At least she hadn't come back down because she was avoiding him. And now that he thought about it, he was fucking tired, too. Jess had called him around four in the morning and he'd made it to her apartment on the second floor of an old row house within twenty minutes. After he'd gotten her out of that little shit hole of a crawl space and held her in his arms to prove to himself he hadn't lost her, they'd packed a bag, gone back to his apartment so he could pack and grab some extra firepower, and made their way to the remaining part of the Hard Ink building in time for the team's morning brief about their investigation.

He kicked off his boots and stretched out on the couch, intent on catching a little shut-eye himself. Except the minute his eyes closed, a movie started playing on the back of his lids. The terrified and embarrassed look on Jess's face during that morning brief when she saw the projected image of a tattoo worn by one of their enemies—and she realized she'd slept with someone wearing a tat just like that a few days before.

His eyes blinked open again and his gaze settled on the ceiling's exposed wooden beams.

Given the way Ike had always felt about Jess, he didn't love hearing about her sexual exploits—which were many and often colorful. Not because he disapproved, but because he wished he could be the one making her come, making her shake, making her scream his name. Otherwise, he didn't get a fucking say in who Jess gave her love or her body to, and he knew it.

But Ike did get to be pissed that someone had apparently picked her up for the express purpose of using her for information about Nick and Jeremy, and then came back days later, after attacking and destroying part of Hard Ink, to tie up loose ends. As if Jess was just so much disposable trash.

Ike's hands fisted.

The only thing he hated about protecting Jess right now was that it kept him from being a part of the fight back in Baltimore...where Ike might get the hands-on opportunity to find the man who had done these things to Jess and teach him some manners—or put him in the grave. Ike didn't really care which.

Ike wasn't aware of finally drifting off to sleep. All he knew was that he opened his eyes to total darkness. He flew into a sitting position. Momentarily forgetting where he was, he reached for the lamp on the nightstand that wasn't there. Because he wasn' t in his apartment back home, he was at the cabin. With Jess.

How the hell long had he been asleep?

He reached for the lamp on the console table behind him and flicked it on.

Across the room, the kitchen clock hanging on the wall said it was almost nine thirty. Jesus, he'd slept all day.

On a big yawn, Ike rubbed the heels of his hands against his eyes, and then he heaved himself off the couch. His eyes went immediately to the loft, which was as quiet and still as it'd been earlier in the day.

"Jess?" he called. Nothing. And then...was that a small moan? He crossed to the steps. "Jessica, you up?"

"Ike," she said in a croaking voice.

Ike took the steps two at a time and found Jess lying on her back. In the dim light cast by the lamp downstairs, he could see that she'd pushed the covers down below her belly button. As he closed the distance between them, she pulled a pillow over her breasts, and the movement looked like it took an inordinate amount of effort.

Ike frowned and sat on the edge of the bed. Before he even touched her, he could feel the heat radiating off of her. And it had nothing to do with the lack of air conditioning in the cabin because the night air had cooled the place down by a lot. "Hey. You okay?"

She shook her head. "Feel bad."

He put his hand on her forehead. Her skin was on fire. "Jesus, you're burning up."

Jess grasped his hand in both of hers and pressed it more firmly to her forehead, then her cheek, then her neck. "Hand is cold. Feels so good."

"Besides the fever, what else feels bad?" he asked.

"Just hurt everywhere," she said, looking up at him. The pain on her face and in her eyes slayed him.

"We need to break this fever. I'll be back."

She clung harder to his hand. "Don't leave."

He kissed her forehead. "I'm not. Just getting something to make you feel better."

"'kay," she whispered. As he rose, she turned onto her side, balling herself around the pillow. Drawing her knees up pulled them out from under the covers, exposing the big, intricate dream catcher that started on her hip and ran beaded feathers down the outside of her thigh.

Ike had done that piece, too.

God, it was like he could measure his life these past few years in the moments he spent putting ink on her body.

Downstairs, Ike made quick work of gathering some Ibuprofen, a glass of water, and a wet washcloth. When he returned, Jess was in the same position as when he'd left, her heavy eyelids making it clear she'd nearly fallen back to sleep.

He needed to get drugs in her first. "Hey, Jess. Can you wake up? I have some medicine for you."

She pushed herself onto an elbow and downed the pills and some water. "Thanks." When she settled down again, he placed the cold washcloth against her forehead. She moaned and covered it with her hand. "That feels good."

Ike nodded and cleared his throat. "You know, uh, you never got dressed before you fell asleep earlier. Want me to grab you a T-shirt? Or something?"

"Too hot," she whispered. "Is it bothering you?"

Given the amount of ink he'd put on her body, he'd seen *a lot* of her up close and personal—he'd done the stars running around her right breast, after all. And he knew how much it pleased her that he appreciated what he saw, too. So, under other circumstances, he might've suspected her of being coy, but there wasn't an ounce of mischief in her right now. "No. Just don't want to make you uncomfortable."

"Never could," she said, eyes drifting shut. "You're a good man, Ike Young. The best."

As much as he couldn't agree with the sentiment, he also couldn't deny liking hearing it. From her.

He grasped the washcloth to turn it over, only to feel it soaked through with the heat of her fever. This time when he left, she didn't notice. He cooled it down in the bathroom sink, then returned to her bedside and laid it against her forehead and the side of her face.

In her sleep, the corner of her mouth curved up.

Ike sat on the edge of the bed for a long while, and then he moved to the old brown armchair that sat in the corner by the window and pulled out his phone.

What's the word there? He shot off the text to Dare.

Dare's response popped up a minute later. *We set up some snipers' roosts to get better eyes on the area. Holed up in one for the night. Got the guys organized into watch units. Otherwise things are quiet.* Dare was a good choice for lookout—he was one of the best shots Ike knew.

Sorry I'm not there, Ike replied.

Do the job you need to do, Dare said. Of all people, Ike knew Dare wouldn't question his need to protect Jess. No one knew the full extent of the shit that had rained down on Dare as a kid, but the man seemed to have devoted his life to making up for it by taking care of as many people as he could. Hell, Dare had put it right there in the Ravens' motto: "Ride. Fight. Defend."

Another message from Dare: *Jeremy accepted responsibility for Harvey and Creed's deaths today.*

What the fuck? Why would Jeremy think he was

responsible for the Ravens' deaths? He wasn't the one who'd shot a missile at the Hard Ink building in a predawn attack— that was all on the mercenaries masquerading as legitimate defense contractors that the team had identified at the morning's brief. Former military guys who worked for Seneka Worldwide Security, Nick's teammate had said when he'd showed the image of the tattoo that had set Jess and him off on their flight out of the city.

And on top of it all, Jeremy had nearly been killed when part of the warehouse's roof collapsed. Responsible for Harvey and Creed dying? Hardly.

OK, I'll take care of it, Ike responded. He knew the hell that guilt for someone else's death caused. He'd dealt with it for years. Only, for Ike, it was deserved. No way was he letting Jeremy, his best friend outside the Ravens, think any of that burden lay at his feet.

On a sigh, Ike dropped his head against the back of the chair. Fuck, he was tired. And not just because of the disrupted sleep and the crisis he'd helped manage back at Hard Ink the past few weeks. Ike was tired of the weight of the guilt he bore. He was tired of living half a life. He was tired of being alone— and knowing he didn't deserve more.

His gaze drifted over to Jessica, still balled in the center of the bed.

She definitely deserved more than he was or he could give. Which, in a twisted way, probably meant it was a good thing she'd gotten sick. Ike wouldn't be tempted to jump her the way he had this afternoon when she'd come out of the bathroom, skin still warm and damp and pink from the shower. And if he kept his hands off, he wouldn't give her the mistaken impression that they could be anything more than they were.

Just friends.

Chapter 6

A long, low moan had Ike's eyes snapping open. He wasn't the slightest bit disoriented this time. Instead, his gaze cut immediately to Jess, who was moving restlessly on the bed, though she still seemed to be asleep.

Ike woke up his phone to see that it was nearly three in the morning.

Another moan, so high-pitched and needful it was almost a whimper.

He crossed to the bed and pressed his hand to Jess's forehead. If he'd thought she felt hot earlier, it was nothing compared to now. Jesus, she was uncomfortable to touch.

"Jess, wake up. Time for more medicine," he said.

Bleary, unfocused eyes struggled to look up at him, and then fell closed again.

"Jess." He shook her gently by the shoulders, but all that got him was another agonized groan. "Fuck," he bit out. He had to get this fever down. He rarely got sick, so he didn't have a thermometer there to see just how high her temperature was. And, damn it all to hell, the situation they were in would make taking her to a clinic or emergency room risky anyway. A few weeks before, someone had nearly abducted Nick's girlfriend from an ER in Baltimore, and the Hard Ink team had been avoiding them ever since. Granted, he and Jess were outside the city now, but hospital admissions created digital records and paper trails that those with the right capabilities—and questionable ethics—could follow if they were motivated enough. And these mercenary sonsabitches clearly were just that.

Which meant Ike needed another plan.

In a flash, he ran downstairs to the bathroom. He ripped the shower curtain open and knocked Jess's clothes out of the way, and then he turned on the cold water. Christ, given how hot her skin had felt, he worried the water might be *too* cold, so he made it just shy of lukewarm and hoped that would do the job.

Back upstairs, he pulled back the covers and scooped Jess off the bed. She moaned and turned into him, her face burrowing against his chest. "I'm gonna take care of you," he said. Though the sheer heat soaking into him everywhere they touched was picking at those never-healed places inside him from the last time he'd made a similar promise to a woman he cared about—and failed.

The tub was about halfway filled when he got back downstairs. Gently, he lowered Jess into the water.

Her whole body seized on contact. Groggy eyes flew open and her hands flailed and splashed water over both of them. Formless words spilled out of her.

"Hey, it's okay. We gotta get this fever down. I know it's cold but it won't be long," he said, his hand stroking cool water over her forehead.

"Ike," she whimpered, a tear spilling from the corner of her eye. "Wha's hap'ning?"

"Sshh, don't you worry. We're gonna get you feeling better. Okay?" God, he hoped this worked.

"So cold," she said, her teeth chattering. Goosebumps broke out across her flushed skin.

"I know," he said, reaching behind him for the towel she'd used earlier. He submerged it into the water and then covered her with it, both to bring the coolness up onto the parts of her skin not yet under water and to give her a little privacy. He scooped handfuls of water onto her shoulders, her throat, her face. He wet her hair. He rubbed her arms when she shuddered so hard he worried she'd hurt herself.

Shit. If this didn't work, he wasn't going to have a choice about getting help. But he couldn't let himself go there yet. He'd cross that bridge if and when he had to.

After about fifteen minutes, Jess was shivering nonstop, but her eyes looked at him with more clarity and awareness. "I'm really cold, Ike," she said. "I think it worked."

He pressed his hand to her forehead. Better, but still warmer than normal. "Can you stand it a few more minutes?"

Her shoulders sagged. "Okay."

"That's my girl," he said, his brain not well filtering the words coming out of his mouth. Obviously.

But then Jess smiled at him. Just a little bit. And the fact that he could do something to make her feel even the smallest amount of happiness or pleasure in the midst of her illness chased away whatever regret he might've felt.

Jesus, he could be a sap. He gave her shoulder a squeeze. "Let's get some more Ibuprofen in you and then I'll get you back to bed."

She nodded.

"Don't go anywhere," he said with a wink.

She smirked and rolled her eyes.

There was his girl, sass still alive and well. Thank God.

He returned quickly with the meds and she downed them with a whole lot of water. He let her nurse as much of it as she wanted. Last thing she needed was to get dehydrated on top of the fever, which seemed like a real possibility given how bad it was.

"Ready?" Ike asked, hitting the lever to drain the tub.

"Yes, please," she said, her voice weak.

Ike tossed his damp T-shirt onto the bathroom counter and pulled a few towels from the cabinet under the sink.

When he turned back around, Jess blatantly stared at his chest and waggled her eyebrows. It made him chuckle. Even sick, she was still flirting and busting his balls.

He held up a dry towel longways, blocking his view of her. "All right. Kick off the wet towel and I'll cover you with the dry one."

Jess chuffed out a small laugh. "You carried me down

here, right?"

"Uh huh," he said, already knowing where she was going with the question.

"So, you've already ogled all the goods."

He'd tried not to, he really had. Besides, for once, sex had been the last thing on his mind when he'd felt how much her fever had spiked. "I kept the ogling to a bare minimum. I promise. Now would you let me switch out the damn towels already?"

She pulled the cloth out of his hands and covered herself, the wet towel balled between her feet in the now-empty tub. "All the naughty bits are covered. Better?"

Ike gave her a droll stare, but he couldn't deny feeling some major relief that the cool soak had brought back the old Jess. He handed her another towel. "For your hair."

She squeezed it out as best she could. "I'm so tired," she said.

"That's good. Sleep is probably the best thing for you. Ready?" He threw another towel over his shoulder. When she nodded, he gently slipped his arms beneath her knees and around her back and lifted her from the tub. God, she was a little slip of a thing in his arms, even with all her curves, and he fucking loved the feel of the bare skin of her side against his abs.

Even awake and aware, she curled her face against his chest. She pressed a kiss above his heart. "Thanks, Ike. Sorry I'm always such a pain in the ass."

"Don't say that," he said, carrying her back up the stairs. "You're not a pain in the ass."

An expression flitted over her face, one that said she didn't believe him.

He hated that she thought for even a second that he minded taking care of her. "I mean it, Jess. I wouldn't want to be anywhere else than where I am. Right here, with you."

* * * *

The good news was that her fever seemed to have broken, but now Jess was absolutely freezing and, no matter how many covers Ike added to the bed, she couldn't get warm.

"Any better?" Ike asked, sitting on the edge of the bed.

Jess peered up at him. "A little."

His eyes narrowed. "You're still cold, aren't you?"

She shivered and pulled the cover tighter around her shoulder. "Yeah."

"Fuck." Ike scrubbed a hand over his bald head and mumbled something she couldn't quite make out. "Maybe I shouldn't have put you in the tub after all."

"I think it was the right thing, Ike. I was so out of it. It is better than it was before." She worked at a small smile. No matter how bad she felt, the last thing she wanted was to make him feel bad given everything he was doing for her. As if he hadn't already gone out of his way in giving her a place of refuge and his personal protection for as long as she needed it, now he had to play freaking nursemaid to a sicky. Which, on top of everything, was super attractive.

The only upside to that ice-cold bath was that Ike had gotten wet and tossed his shirt, and Jess thought she might be willing to be sick more often if it meant getting to see him shirtless. Because, holy bad-ass tattooed biker on a stick, he was so freaking hot. Cut muscles, ink everywhere, two insanely delicious indents low on his waist. And scars Jess had no idea how Ike had gotten.

All that goodness and Jess couldn't even see the big Ravens tat that she knew covered Ike's broad back. But she'd seen it before, back at Hard Ink when Jeremy occasionally did a new piece for Ike. She'd seen it enough to know that she'd love to have a good reason to dig her fingers into that tat…

Oh, for fuck's sake, even sick she couldn't stop fantasizing about what it would be like to be with Ike. Just once.

"Jess?"

Her gaze snapped to his eyes. "Huh?" Hopefully the warmth crawling up her cheeks would pass for a fevered flush. Because she was so busted.

"I, uh, asked if you thought it would help if I got in with you." The expression he wore said he was dubious about the idea.

And as much as Jess loved the idea, she didn't want him

doing anything with her that he didn't really want to do. "That's okay. Why don't you go get some sleep now? It's gotta be almost morning."

He looked at her for a long moment, and then he tapped his hand against her arm. "Scoot over."

"Ike—"

"Damnit, scoot your scrawny ass over already." He cocked an eyebrow, humor sliding into his eyes.

"Well, I'll scoot over," she said as she made herself move. "But you and I both know there ain't anything scrawny about my ass."

"Jessica?" Ike said as he got in next to her wearing only his jeans.

"Yeah?" The minute he was down, she nearly dove into the crook of his body, her forehead against his neck, her breasts against his ribs, her bare legs intertwined with his denim-clad ones. She wasn't sure where to put her hand, because the not-sick part of her brain wanted to touch him everywhere right now. Oh my God, I'm in bed with Ike! But she settled for resting it on his chest, the hair on his pecs ticklish against her fingers.

"Shut up and go to sleep." He took the edge off the words by clasping her hand in his and pressing it more firmly to his skin.

"Be nice to me. I'm sick," she said, burrowing in further.

Ike wrapped his arm around her shoulders and pulled her tighter against him. God, he felt good, warm and hard and strong. "Woman," he said, his voice full of gravel. "This is me being nice."

* * * *

Most of the next two days were a blur to Jess. The fever had come back, so she'd alternated between long sleeps and short periods of wakefulness where she choked down enough medicine and water to let her sink into unconsciousness again. Ike was still beside her every time she opened her eyes, taking care of her in every way she needed.

Ike's attentiveness did funny things to her insides—it

wasn't something she was used to. Her dad had been great, but he'd never been overtly affectionate and certainly never fussed over her when she'd gotten sick. Hell, he went to work with fevers, migraines, and bullet wounds, and was pretty much of the mindset that if you weren't bleeding out, you were good to go.

After her dad died, Jeremy had played a big role in helping Jess pull herself together. Luckily, she'd inherited enough money to take care of herself, but it was really the job at Hard Ink that finally forced her to start getting dressed again and face the world. Day by day, with Jeremy's constant friendship and encouragement, things had gotten easier, life had gotten better, and the hole inside her shrank—at least a little. Getting back on her feet had given her the strength to start to forgive herself for falling in with a crowd of friends who'd been into way more trouble that she'd known—trouble that had gotten her father killed in the first place. She wished like hell he was still around to say "I told you so," because he'd been a hundred percent right.

In her whole life, besides her father, no one had been there for her more than Jeremy and Ike. And that made them the two most important people in her world.

Stretching her aching limbs, Jess blinked open her eyes. Ike was sitting on the edge of the bed, shoulders hunched. "Hey," she said.

He looked over his shoulder and gave her a smile. "There you are. How ya feeling?"

"Sore. And tired. And really freaking disgusting." She adjusted Ike's big T-shirt on her shoulders as she turned over onto her stomach—during one of the periods where the broken fever left her shivering, Ike had dressed her. "And I hope you bought a couple bags of Doritos because I swear to God I could eat every single one."

"Maybe you ought to start with some toast," he said, eyebrow arched.

Fair point, given that she'd only had the broth and a few noodles from chicken noodle soup the day before and part of a banana that morning. She asked Ike to get Pop-Tarts and Hot Pockets at the store, and he came home with fruit. Go figure.

"Toast is boring. Doritos are life."

Ike shifted toward her on the bed. "Yeah, but Doritos will be way worse coming back up." He pressed his hand to her forehead. "Feels like the fever's gone."

"I think so," she said, rubbing her eyes. "Which is good because that really sucked."

"Apparently, you got taken out by a six-year-old. I talked to Bunny earlier and Ben's been sick, too."

"Aw, hope he's okay," she said. It had to be terrible watching a little kid be so sick.

Emotions Jess couldn't read moved across Ike's rugged face. "If you want to grab a shower, I'll throw some dinner together for us."

"Sounds like a plan," she said. "I need to get out of this bed anyway. I'm not even sure what freaking day it is at this point."

Ike rose and offered her a hand. "Tuesday."

"Wow," she said, allowing him to help steady her as she got out of bed. Ike's shirt was so big on her it nearly hit her knees, and part of her was sad to change out of it. But, honestly, it should've probably been burned at this point.

"You okay to go it on your own?" he asked, half looking like he expected her to fall on her ass.

Jess grabbed a few things from her bag and made for the steps. "I'm good," she said. "Though if you still feel inclined to carry me around everywhere, I won't complain. A girl could get used to that, you know."

She threw a smirk over her shoulder and he shook his head.

When she was clean and dressed in actual clothes for what felt like the first time in forever, she met Ike in the kitchen where she found two plates on the counter. One with very lightly buttered toast and a banana, the other with a big-ass ham and cheese sandwich and a mound of Doritos. Her Doritos.

She planted her hands on the counter. "That is so not fair, Ike Young."

He scooped the plates up and transferred them to the table. "Better?" he asked, throwing a single chip onto her plate.

"You are not funny," she said, glaring at him as she sank into the seat.

He held his hand up, thumb and forefinger a centimeter apart. "I'm a little funny," he said, stealing her words from the day they'd arrived.

"Have you heard from anyone at Hard Ink?" she asked as she took a bite of her toast. Amazing how something so simple could taste like heaven after days of not eating much.

"I've talked to Dare a few times. Seems like things are in a holding pattern right now as they track down some leads. Guys are getting antsy." Ike tossed a chip in his mouth and made a big show of enjoying it.

"You suck," Jess said. "Better save me some, too."

Ike chuckled and gave her a wink. "I bought three bags."

"Good." They ate in silence for a few minutes as Jess wolfed down her food. When she was done, she brushed off her fingers over the plate. "I'm worried about everyone."

"Nick and his team know what they're doing, and the Ravens can handle themselves. Don't worry." Ike gave her a look full of confidence.

It helped. Jess nodded. "I know. But these aren't any run-of-the-mill criminals they're up against."

"True enough," he said. "But the neighborhood around Hard Ink has been cordoned off and no one is getting in or out without our guys knowing it."

"Well, that's good," she said. "It's just…" Jess hesitated to finish the thought, but given the danger they were all in, it felt like it should be said. "You and Jeremy, and even Nick…you guys have become my family the past few years. And I couldn't take it if anything happened to any of you."

Chapter 7

The only thing Ike didn't like about Jess feeling better was that he no longer had an excuse to sleep with her. Selfish bastard.

They'd been sitting on the couch for a few hours trying to find something to watch. Cop and military type shows were out—too much like real life. The Walking Dead marathon was out, because people you liked always died on that show—too much like what they feared life might become. Ike had suggested the World Series of Poker, but Jess thought watching people play cards was boring. She'd suggested a dancing reality show, but Ike put the kibosh on that idea with a single look. Ike's desire to put off sleeping alone again had him finally agreeing to a house hunting show Jess liked where the couple saw three houses and had to decide which to buy.

Ike's conclusion: people were idiots sometimes.

"Should've picked the older house. More character," he said.

"Right?" Jess said, smiling. "You can fix up an older house, but it's harder to give a newer house that kind of character."

"I knew I liked you for a reason," he said, giving her a wink.

"Because I'm awesome." She turned toward him on the couch and propped her elbow on the back of the couch.

Well, Ike couldn't disagree with that, but he probably shouldn't agree with it either. Lest it lead them into saying—or doing—things they probably shouldn't. Now that Jess was feeling better, Ike's brain kept resurrecting the memory of their fucking amazing kiss as Ike had carried her to the loft. And his body was completely on board with the idea of picking up where they'd left off.

Ike stretched his arms over his head and yawned so big his jaw cracked. "Man, I'm dragging."

Jess peered up at him. "Can't imagine why. It's not like you've lost any sleep the past couple days while taking care of anyone."

He shrugged. "I don't know if you remember me telling you this the other night, but I really didn't mind, Jess. Still don't."

She nodded, her gaze assessing, maybe even hopeful. "You know, you could still sleep in the bed if you want."

Oh, he wanted, all right. "Nah. Be fine here."

Hell, if the disappointment that flickered across her face wasn't a kick in the gut. But he was doing the right thing for both of them. Besides, he'd rather have Jess in his life as a friend—even if he wanted more—than fuck things up with her one way or another and lose her altogether.

Her words from before still echoed in his head. You guys have become my family the past few years. And I couldn't take it if anything happened to any of you.

Ike felt the same way about her and Jeremy. Since he saw and worked with them every day at Hard Ink, he'd come to be as close to them as he was with the Ravens, who he'd known for over a decade.

And Ike knew for goddamned sure that he wouldn't be able to take it if anything happened to Jeremy or Jess, but especially Jess—whose safety and protection rested squarely on his shoulders.

Thus why he would not be sleeping in the bed again.

"Okay, then," she said, rising. "I'll go up so you can get some rest. Besides, I want lots of sleep tonight so I have enough energy to sit on the couch all day tomorrow eating Doritos and watching trash TV."

"It's important to have goals," Ike said, shaking his head.

Jess chuckled. "My thoughts exactly."

When she disappeared into the bathroom, Ike took the opportunity to grab a pillow and blanket from the closet in the loft as well as something to sleep in and clothes for the morning. By the time she came out, her wavy red and black hair pulled into two low pigtails that sent Ike's thoughts right into the gutter, he'd made up a bed on the couch.

"Night," she said, heading up the steps.

"Night," he replied, watching her hips sway in a pair of silky black shorts. Combined with the form-fitting black tank top and those perfect-for-grabbing pigtails, she was going to make it damn hard for him to fall asleep tonight.

Damn hard, indeed.

He turned out the light and went horizontal, the soft couch so comfortable against his sore back even though it was a little too short to fit his whole body. He adjusted his erection, willing it to get with the no-sex-with-Jess program. Problem was, in the quiet darkness, Ike could hear her moving around in the loft. Soft footsteps on the wood floor. The shifting of covers. The squeaking of the box spring. And all that did was invite his imagination out to play. Easy, since he had so much material to work with after sleeping with Jess wrapped around him the past two nights.

His shoulders and chest knew what the silk of her hair felt like when it skimmed over his skin. His hip knew the heat of her core when she slept with her knee across his thighs. His hands had memorized the curve of her lower back and the shape of her biceps and just how much of her luscious ass he could fit in his palms.

Ike knew what her mouth tasted like, how tight her legs could wrap around his waist, and how fucking beautiful the combination of ink and steel was on her skin.

Jesus, his cock was never going to let him go to sleep at this rate.

And was it fucking hot in here or what? He tossed the cover off, wishing he had a ceiling fan downstairs, too. Something for the to-do list around this place.

Ike sighed and flung his hand over his head. And

wondered why the hell he was torturing himself this way.

He could just go up there and get in the bed—and take what he wanted, and what he knew Jess would be only too happy to give. Neither of them was immune to the mutual attraction that had always been there between them. And her reaction to his kiss the other day made it crystal fucking clear that she was waiting for him to make his move.

Jess had plenty of one-night stands and casual hook-ups. Ike knew she was perfectly capable of handling that kind of relationship.

Except.

Except Ike wasn't a clueless idiot, and he wasn't in the habit of doing things he knew damn right well would hurt someone he cared about. Jess wore her emotions like she wore her ink—out loud and unapologetically. He had a pretty good idea that she was rocking some more-than-friendly and more-than-physical feelings for him. Right now, she thought them unrequited, and that kept a kind of sexually tense equilibrium between them. But if he let himself off the leash more than he already had—even just once—he'd very likely raise and dash her hopes, give her all kinds of mixed signals, and screw things up royally between them.

He shook his head and heaved a deep breath. If he wasn't going to go the distance with her, he had no business taking the first step.

End of.

* * * *

Oh, fuck. He was dying.

Pain throbbed in every joint and the bass beat of his pulse pounded against the inside of his skull. Dizzy and disoriented, he reached for the lamp—

Thud. The floor body-slammed an agonized groan out of him. What the fuck just happened? Where was he? Why was it so goddamned hot? His face, his neck, his chest were all damp with sweat.

"Ike, is that you?" came a soft voice. Somewhere above him, soft golden light glowed.

"Jess," he rasped, his throat feeling like sandpaper.

"Oh, my God. Are you all right?" Footsteps raced down the stairs, and then Jess was kneeling on the floor beside where he still lay. Her hand fell on his shoulder, so cool against his skin. "Oh, no. I made you sick."

"I don't get sick," he said, and then he realized how ridiculous the proclamation was given that he was currently laid flat-out on the floor. "Not usually."

"Let me help you up," she said, barely budging him.

He shook her off. "S'okay. Get me drugs?"

"Of course." While she rushed toward the bathroom, Ike heaved himself back onto the sofa, the effort it took to move his ass like he'd just done an extreme weight-lifting workout. "Here you go," Jess said as she settled next to him on the couch.

He accepted four little red pills and a glass of water into his hands and choked them down. The water was both a blessing and a curse—the cold brought relief, but even just water against the back of his throat was torture.

"Lay your head back," Jess said.

When he did, she draped a cold, wet washcloth over his head from eyebrows to bald crown. "Fuck," he said.

"I'm so sorry," she said. She pressed a second cold cloth against the side of his neck.

Ike groaned. "Don't be. That helps."

"Good." For a few minutes they sat in silence, Jess moving the rag over his neck, his face, his chest. Touching the one lying on his head, she said, "These are warm already. Let me wet them again."

He tried to nod, but the movement sent the room on a Tilt-A-Whirl. Ike wasn't sure how long it took before the combination of the cold compresses and the Ibuprofen made him feel good enough to stretch out and doze off. What he did know was that every time he woke up, Jess was right there, sitting on the floor beside the couch, ready with more drugs or a soft, soothing touch.

As the gray light of early morning streamed through the windows, Ike found her asleep with her head resting on her arms by his hip. Shit, she'd sat on the floor all night. For him.

He pushed himself up onto an elbow. The walls stayed in place, which Ike took as a good sign. As he stood, Jess didn't react to his movement at all. No doubt she was exhausted after mostly pulling an all-nighter right after being so sick herself. He had to get her off the floor.

Curling his arms around her back and legs, he lifted. Annnnd the walls started spinning as the floor went wavy beneath his feet.

"Ike?" Jess grabbed onto his arms, steadying him. How fucking pathetic was he? "Did you fall off the couch again?"

"Was trying to put you back to bed," he said, shifting to sit his weak ass down.

Jess pushed herself up to sit next to him. "In case you didn't get the memo, it's my turn to take care of you right now." Ike dropped his face into his hands on a groan, and Jess's cool hand massaged his neck. "Oh, my God. You're so hot."

He chuffed out a small laugh. "Why, thank you."

Jess chuckled. "You realize you don't have to fish for compliments, right? Not from me. Because I will straight-up tell you that the sight of your Ravens tat stretched over all these muscles gives me a lady boner." Her fingers traced the design across his shoulder blades—a spread-winged raven perched on the hilt of a dagger sunk into the eye socket of a skull. The block letters of the club's name arched over the menacing black bird.

He threw her some major side-eye. "I know I'm sick because the perverted part of my brain just heard you say my ink gives you a lady boner."

She waggled her eyebrows and laughed. The sound was so free and playful, he almost eked out a smile in return. Right before he thanked God that he was too sick to react to her saying something so ridiculously hot. Under any other circumstances, he had no doubt he'd be popping a boner of his own after hearing that spill from her lips.

"I didn't know your brain had any other parts," she said, grinning.

Fuck, smiling hurt. "Stop making me laugh."

"But I like to make you laugh."

Ike groaned. "I'm dying."

Jess's expression was full of sympathy. "I know. Think you could stand a cold shower? Might help."

He barked out a laugh that turned into a scratchy cough. If she knew the shit that had been going through his head, she'd realize how ironically appropriate her question was. "Yeah, I'll try that."

Ike stood under the cool shower for a long time, his hands braced against the white tile, his head hanging on his shoulders so that the water rained down on his neck. By the time he was done, he was freezing, which he took as a good sign. The fever must've broken. At least for now.

Having just witnessed Jess go through this, he knew it wasn't likely gone for good. Dried off and wearing a pair of dark-gray boxers, he found her leaning over the kitchen counter eating a blueberry Pop-Tart. "Breakfast of champions," he said.

"Pop-Tarts make me happy," she said around a bite. "Want some?"

He looked her over from pigtails to short-shorts. He wanted a bite, all right. "Ugh, no. Thanks, though. Happiness is all yours."

She chuckled. "Go upstairs and take the bed for the day. The more you sleep, the less aware you'll be of how shitty you feel."

He frowned. "Don't wanna leave you alone."

Jess rolled her eyes. "You'll be right upstairs."

"Fucking hate this," he said. She nodded, no doubt thinking he meant being sick when what he really meant was not being able to do the job he was here to do—watching over her. Goddamn, he hated giving in to weakness, but the sooner he got better, the sooner he'd have his head back in the game. Finally, he nodded. "All right. Call me if you need me."

Chapter 8

Jess reached her hand into the Doritos bag only to come up empty. She looked inside the foil. Annnd, yup, she'd polished off the whole thing over the course of the day. Oops.

She was going straight to caloric hell for that.

So worth it.

Besides, she hadn't eaten for the better part of three days, so noshing on the crispy nacho cheese goodness of Doritos was her way of celebrating not dying of the fever from hell.

Speaking of which…

Her gaze drifted to the loft. She hadn't heard from Ike since he'd called down for more medicine around four. It was now pushing ten thirty.

Jess turned off the TV and cleaned up her mess. In the bathroom, she washed the neon orange off her fingers and brushed her teeth for good measure. And then she went up to check on Ike, meds, water, a wet cloth, and his cell phone in hand—it had buzzed incoming messages all evening.

When she settled on the bed's edge, his eyes popped open, bleary and unfocused. "Hey," she said. "How are you feeling?"

"Like I've just gone ass over handlebars and eaten some major asphalt," he rasped, rubbing his hands over his head. "Think it's getting worse again."

"Drugs," she said, handing over the pill bottle. He

swallowed them down.

"What time is it?" he asked.

"Going on eleven. Thought you might want to check your messages," she said. "Phone went off a few times."

On a groan, Ike pushed himself up and worked his fingers over the screen. "Shit," he bit out.

Dread curled into Jess's belly. "What happened?"

"Nothing yet. For some reason the commanding officer from the team's base in Afghanistan—the one who oversaw their trumped-up discharge from the Army—is in town. And because he was friends with her father, he called Becca and asked to get together. She's gonna do the meet tomorrow morning. They're sending her in wired, just in case." Becca Merritt was Nick's girlfriend, the daughter of his Special Forces A-Team commander who'd died last year.

Worry curled into Jess's belly. She'd gotten to know Becca over the past few weeks. She was nice and sweet and she smoothed Nick's sometimes too-hard edges. And the woman had been through a fuck-ton already—way more than Jess, that much was for sure. "Man, Nick must be flipping out."

"No doubt." Ike tossed his phone to the mattress beside him. "I'm useless like this. I gotta get out of this bed." He shifted like he meant to get up.

Jess planted a hand in the center of his red-hot chest. And not the good kinda hot, either. "Not 'til you're better." The fact that she was able to so easily push him back down proved he still needed to be in this bed.

He sagged back into the mattress and his eyelids fell closed. "Don't like being apart from you."

Even though she knew he meant that in the protective sense, warmth still bloomed inside her chest. "Want me to stay?" she asked.

His lids flipped up and those dark-brown eyes peered up at her. "Yes."

He was sick and flat on his back, but something about the quickness of his answer and the intensity of his gaze sent a ripple of awareness through her body. "Well, then scooch over, ya big lug."

"You say the sweetest things," he said, voice like gravel.

"I know, right? I'm such a peach." Jess stretched out beside him, just barely resisting the urge to curl into all that hard muscle and inked skin. But it wasn't like she could still use the excuse that she needed to steal his body heat.

He stretched out an arm toward her and patted his chest. "C'mere."

"I don't want to make you too hot." She said the words even though she really didn't want him to change his mind.

"You make me feel good," he murmured.

Jess settled right into the side of his body, not minding the heat radiating off of him one bit. She tried not to feel so pleased by what he'd said. She really did. But she was pretty much giddy inside.

The sigh he released was full of comfort and satisfaction. Because of her.

Gah!

Okay, Jess. Don't be ridiculous.

She'd still been talking herself down from reading into his words and actions when she'd apparently drifted off to sleep...

Voices woke her. No, one voice.

Ike. Talking and restless in his sleep. She couldn't understand the slurred words, so she turned onto her back and closed her eyes. Ike's body followed hers. He turned on his side and curled himself around her—close enough to feel that his cock was totally hard against her thigh.

The heat that shot over her body had nothing to do with Ike's fever.

God, he felt big and thick against her. Her hands itched to stroke him. She licked her lips, her mouth hungry to feel his heaviness on her tongue, against the back of her throat. She shifted her hips, her core clenching at the thought of feeling him penetrate her, open her, ride her. Hard.

Nearly holding her breath, Jess stayed still. His erection would go away and her heart would stop racing, and then she'd fall back to sleep and forget this ever happened.

As if. In the dark, she rolled her eyes at herself.

There were cocks and then there were cocks. This one did not feel forgettable, thank you very much.

"Jess," Ike whispered.

"Uh, hey." Because it wasn't weird at all for them to talk while his hard-on was touching her.

No answer. And then: "Fuck, Jess." His hips rocked, grinding his erection against her thigh. He released a rough breath and nuzzled his face against hers. His lips dragged across her cheek until he was pressing his lips against her ear.

Holy fucking shit.

"Uh, Ike?" she said. Was he awake? If not, did she want him to be?

A hand dragged up her stomach, pulling her tank top with it. He squeezed her breast, hips grinding, harsh breaths in her ear.

My God, she was gonna die from how fucking hot this was.

He mumbled something that sounded a helluva lot like "need you," and Jess was pretty damn sure if he kept this up, she was going to come without him getting anywhere near her clit.

Not to mention, if he was dreaming about being with her and needing her, what did that even mean? Something? Nothing? Everything?

He didn't give her time to debate it. Ike shifted, his body rolling partially on top of her. It was too much weight on her thigh and knee, which she forced up and out from under him—unintentionally putting her thigh under his waist and his big body between her legs.

He rocked against her, but this time his cock ground against the very top of her thigh. Fuck, so close to where she was absolutely throbbing for him.

She didn't want this to stop, but she couldn't let it go on, either. Could she?

The blunt head of his cock pushed closer to home, and the only thing separating them was the cotton of his boxers and the silk of her sleep shorts. On the next thrust, his length ghosted over her clit. But it was enough to make her moan out loud and clutch at his shoulder.

"Aw, yeah. S'good," he whispered, his hot, sweaty cheek pressed against hers. God, he was on fire. What if he realized this happened and regretted it?

What if you *regret it?* No, she wouldn't. If this was all she would ever get of him, she'd tuck the memory away somewhere deep inside her and hold on to it tight.

Ike's hips moved a little faster, shifted closer, ground harder, until his cock stroked her pussy on every single thrust.

Fuck it.

Jess dug her nails into his shoulders and met his hips thrust for thrust. "Yes, Ike," she cried.

His movements slowed. Stopped. And then every single part of his body went rigid.

"Don't you fucking stop," she said, breathing hard. "I'm so close to coming I might die."

"Jess—"

"Ike, you want me. I want you. So have me. It doesn't have to be more than what it is," she said, an uncomfortable twinge going off in her chest. But Jess didn't care. The pleasure would be worth whatever pain she'd carry from knowing how good they were together while being denied anything more.

"I didn't mean to…" His words drifted off and he trembled above her, as if holding still took great effort.

But Jess was done with Ike holding himself back. "I know. I don't care. I need to come." She kissed his forehead, his cheek, his ear. "Please make me come."

* * * *

The room spun. His brain was dazed. His feverish body was strung tight.

And Jess was begging him for something he'd yearned to give for so fucking long.

Ike hadn't meant to start this, but now that he had, he couldn't seem to make himself do the right thing. More than that, he could no longer figure out what the right thing was in the first place.

His head hurt, making it so hard to think.

So he followed his gut and went with *feeling* instead.

"Not like this," he said, pushing himself down the bed. If he was going there, he was going all the way. His movements were jerky and imprecise, but his hands fumbled their way to stripping her bare. He wished the light was on so he could see her, but maybe the darkness was better. It made it feel more like the dream he'd thought it was.

Goddamned coward.

He shoved the thoughts away as he pushed Jess's thighs wide. "Thought of this so many fucking times," he said. And then he was done with talking. He absolutely feasted on her. Licking her cunt, plunging his tongue deep, sucking her clit— her goddamned pierced clit. Over and over.

"Ike," she screamed, his name turning into a low moan as her thighs tried to close around his head.

Her muscles pulsed and she came on his tongue. He sucked down every delicious drop.

It was like he'd been starving and now that he'd had a bite of food, he needed to gorge himself in case he never had more. The minute her body stilled, he dove right back in, his lips sucking her clit while his tongue strummed it, toying with the little hoop piercing there. She was so wet he could easily sink two fingers inside her, then three. Jess whimpered and moaned, clutched and pressed at his head, rocked her hips and rode his fingers. Fuck. He knew she'd be like this—passionate and fierce and unapologetic in her pleasure. It was goddamned fantastic.

His cock was hard as a rock and his balls ached with need, but he'd be content giving her as many orgasms as she could stand having. Her juices ran down onto his hand and he slipped in a fourth finger, nearly fisting her.

"Fuck, yes," she cried. "*Damn* that's good, Ike."

He couldn't agree more. He lost count of how many times she came on his mouth and fingers, but at some point he became aware that she was whimpering and almost chanting something under her breath.

"Fuck me. Fuck me. Please fuck me. Oh, God, I want you to fuck me."

"Jess?"

"Jesus, Ike, get in me. Please."

The plea hit him in the gut, making him want nothing more than to satisfy her. But hadn't he already taken more than he should?

Chapter 9

Jess was too needy to worry about pride, and they'd gone too far to avoid things getting awkward between them if that was going to happen. She needed him inside her, just this once.

"I want to fuck you, trust me," Ike said, voice gritty. "But I'm...that's what it would be for me. So I get it if—"

"That's what it would be for me, too," she lied. "Just for tonight. As often and in any way that you want. In the morning, it'll all have been a fevered dream," she rushed out, her mind racing. "And we'll be the same friends we were yesterday." She nearly held her breath waiting for him to make up his mind.

And then he was pushing off his boxers, climbing up her body, mounting her. There was no pretense about it. His cock found her opening and sank deep. Jess's head snapped back into the pillow on a long moan because, *omigod*, him being inside her was a total freaking rush—one Jess had never thought would happen. And, God, he was big. It was so damn good, so much better than she'd dreamed.

"Fuck, that's a tight little pussy," Ike ground out—and then he froze. "Shit, protection."

"On birth control," she said, wrapping her legs around his hips. Now that she had him, she wasn't letting go. "Take me, Ike. Don't hold back." Just this once.

He didn't. He plowed into her like there was a place inside her he needed to get to but couldn't quite reach. His pubic bone pounded into her clit, her piercing making her so freaking sensitive. His balls smacked against her ass. His hands groped and squeezed and gripped her body—her breasts, her shoulders, her hair.

"Just tonight," he rasped.

She ignored the pang around her heart. Normally, Jess was a sex-with-the-lights-on kinda girl, but tonight she was glad for the darkness. It would be her ally in masking her true feelings for him. "Just tonight," she agreed.

Ike groaned in her ear, and then his hips absolutely hammered into her, the sweaty smack of their skin loud in the otherwise quiet room. He was almost frenzied in his movements, and he shoved her hard toward another orgasm.

"Gonna fucking come in you, Jessica," he said, voice strained with need.

Those words pushed her the rest of the way there. "Fuuck, yes, Ike," she moaned, and then the orgasm stole her breath and she held on as her body thrashed and convulsed beneath him.

The shout of his orgasm was one of the most erotic sounds Jess had ever heard. His cock kicked inside her, and she could feel the jets of his come again and again. He shook and cursed and jerked as his body moved through his release.

Breathing hard, he held himself above her, cock still buried deep. They were a sweaty, hot mess, and Jess loved every moment of it.

"Turn the fuck over," he growled, pulling out. "I'm not done with you yet. Not by a long shot."

She reached out in the darkness…to find him still hard. "Oh, God," she said, her heart beating in her throat. She might not survive this night, but what a way to go.

"I've got four years of pent-up fantasies about you," he said, flipping her over. "I'm gonna make them all come true tonight or pass out trying." He was so much stronger than her that he could pretty much move her however he wanted. He lifted her hips until she was on her knees, and then he pressed her upper body down with a big hand in the center of her back.

"I'm all yours," she whispered, not sure if he heard her or if he'd even understand just how true the words were if he did. Just then, he penetrated her pussy to the hilt. She felt so much fuller this way and it was mind-numbingly good.

He gripped her hips—hard—and started to move in a series of rough, punctuated thrusts. Jess had never been one for soft caresses or gentle fucking. She liked it rough, dirty, messy, raw. Ike gave her that in spades.

And she knew he would, she knew he'd be everything she needed in bed—just like he was in every other part of their lives. Shit.

Hands on her pigtails forced her onto her hands and pulled her out of her thoughts. Ike transferred both strands of hair into one hand, and the burn on her scalp was so freaking delicious. His other hand gripped her shoulder, giving him leverage to fuck her hard and shifting their position so that he drilled into her G-spot on every stroke.

It didn't take long until Jess was moaning, concentrating, coming and shaking and grinding back against him, wanting him to fall apart just like she had.

Ike pushed her flat beneath him and followed her down to the mattress, his cock pistoning deep inside her. He clutched her shoulder in one hand and her hair in the other, and then his mouth latched onto the side of her neck and sucked. Hard.

The thought that he might mark her had her trembling again. "Fuck, do it harder," she said.

His grip tightened, his mouth sucked more intensely, his hips slammed into her ass.

Jess came until she saw starbursts in her vision, until she barely knew her own name.

Ike shouted out his release. "Shit…take…all of me."

God, she so would. For as long as he'd give himself to her. Because…because she loved him.

Aw, fuck, Jess.

But was this *really* news? No. No, it wasn't. Not if she was honest with herself.

When their bodies stilled, Ike collapsed behind her, but he didn't let her go. Arm around her waist, he pulled her back tight against his front. "Gotta sleep," he said, sounding like he was already halfway there.

And that was okay, because Jess was right there with him.

* * * *

Eyes still closed, body still trying to hang on to sleep, Ike reveled in having had the best dream of his whole damn life— fucking Jessica to the point that they both passed out.

Except…slowly but surely, his body came back on line and he became aware of warm, fragrant skin. Soft, silky hair. His hard cock nuzzled between two sweet ass cheeks.

Ike opened his eyes to find Jess pressed up against him, just as they'd fallen asleep. It was just shy of dawn, which meant there was enough light to make out the curves and shadows of her, but not much more.

Jessica. It hadn't been a dream.

The whole night rushed back to him—him making out with her in his sleep, her begging him for more and saying words that made it all okay, the best sex he'd ever had.

The heat of his skin and the ache in his head told him he still wasn't well, but that didn't keep his hips from moving and pushing his cock into the cleft of her ass.

He wanted more. No, he needed more. More of her.

Taking his cock in hand, Ike found her pussy and rocked into her until her wetness coated him and she moaned her awareness. He grasped and lifted her thigh, opening her to his invasion.

"Make yourself come," he whispered against her ear. "I wanna watch."

"Jesus, Ike," she said as her hand traveled down the front of her body. She squeezed a breast, tugged at a pierced nipple, and stroked teasing fingers over her soft stomach until her fingers toyed with the silver hoop pierced through her clit.

"Such a pretty fucking pussy," he said in her ear. "So wet for me."

"Yes," she said, her face pressing back into his. "For you."

The words unleashed a deep male satisfaction Ike probably had no business feeling, but that didn't keep it from being there. He wanted all her pleasure to be for him, because of him, with him. Why did she have to be so fucking perfect and so goddamned wrong at the same time?

Knock it off, Ike.

Forcing himself out of his head, he watched her find a circling rhythm over her clit. The sight had him fucking her faster, deeper, harder, loving the sounds spilling from her mouth, sounds that told him she loved it every bit as raw as he did.

And then she blew his mind. Slowly, she worked two fingers into her cunt with his cock. It made her tighter and added a whole new sensation to being inside her, and it stimulated the dirtiest, raunchiest part of his mind.

"That pussy is so damn hungry for me, isn't it?" he said.

"God, yes," she moaned.

"Tell me how much you want me, how much you need me," he said. He wanted to know despite the fact that knowing would make resisting his desire for her so much harder.

Her other hand slid down to rub her clit. "Oh, I do. I want you, Ike. I need you," she said, her voice breathy and deep. "Want your cock everywhere."

The words drove him harder. "In your mouth?"

"Yes." Her fingers moved faster.

"In your cunt?" he gritted out, eyes on her hands.

"God, yes," she moaned.

"In your ass?"

"Fuuuck," she said as her pussy contracted and her orgasm detonated. Her body shook and for a moment she didn't speak, didn't breathe. And then she moaned out, "Yes, yes, in my ass."

Ike almost came right there. He pulled out and banded his fingers around the base of his cock—hard.

Jess pushed off the bed, and Ike frowned—until she started searching her small purse and came up with a packet of something. She tossed it to him—Aquaphor, one of the small sample packs they gave out for new tattoo after-care at Hard Ink.

Basically petroleum jelly. Goddamned perfect.

"You sure?" he asked, cock still steel in his hand.

Without a word she bent over the edge of the bed, and

then she stared, eyebrows raised, dark eyes full of invitation, the sexiest fucking expression on her face. "I said you could have me any way you wanted, and I meant it."

Ike shoved away the dizziness that threatened when he went vertical, but he held on to her until the unsteadiness passed. He tore open the packet and coated two of his fingers with the ointment, and then he rubbed circles against the rosebud of her asshole. Having her here would make the claiming total, and that roared a deep and dangerous satisfaction through him down to his very soul. Because it was an illusion if he kept his heart out of it, wasn't it? But that was more thinking than his fever and his cock would allow him to do.

When her hips started to move, Ike sank a finger deep, then two. He finger fucked her until she was moaning and shaking her hips and reaching between her thighs to rub her clit.

"I'm ready, Ike," she said.

He moved behind her and stroked lube all over his length. God, she was small. He didn't want to fucking hurt her, which meant he really needed to know. "Have you done this before?" Part of him didn't want to learn the answer, didn't want to think of her being with anyone else before him.

Or, worse, ever again.

Fuck.

"Yes," she said. "I can handle you. Promise."

He lined the head of his cock up with her rear opening, and damn if it wasn't erotic as hell to watch himself push into her, sink deeper, disappear inch by fucking mind-blowing inch into her luscious ass.

"Shit, shit, shit," she said, her back arching, her thighs shaking.

"Too much?" he rasped, trying to hold himself back, to restrain himself from just taking every piece of her.

"Yes," she moaned. "But it's so good, too."

"Your ass is so tight," he said, watching himself withdraw and then sink back in even deeper.

A stream of sexy, desperate babble spilled out of Jess's mouth, some of it muffled against the covers as she lowered her upper body to the bed and reached back both hands to grab her ass cheeks.

This girl was going to be the death of him. She really was. "Jesus, that looks good," he said.

When she started pushing back onto him, Ike moved faster, harder, until he was hunched over her on the edge of the bed and digging in deep. They grunted in unison, the sex raw, animalistic, the best of his entire fucking life.

Without warning, he pulled out, pushed her body further onto the bed, and then was right back on her again. "Hold your ass open," he said, tone harsh, urgent.

Crouched above her, he plumbed her ass, holding his cock downward so he could sink deep, then pulling all the way out so he could enjoy the wide gap of her hole. So goddamned hot.

In, out, gape. In, out, gape. Until they were both sweating and cursing and Jess was thrashing beneath him.

On a groan, she pulled one hand away and shoved it beneath her, and the very idea of her masturbating while he fucked her ass had his balls boiling.

Her body bore down on his and she screamed into the mattress, her back going rigid as she came and came. Ike couldn't hold back another second. He sank onto his knees and hammered his cock into her ass until he was shooting in her, filling her, making a mess of her inside and out.

Jesus, she stripped him bare and turned him on his head and absolutely rocked his world.

His Jessica.

His smart-ass, flirtatious, fun-loving, brave, sometimes maddening, always loyal Jess.

One of his very best friends. Who was in trouble...which was his fucking Achilles's heel. *So check yourself, Ike. Right fucking now.*

Right.

He was in check, or at least he would be when he had to be. But the sun wasn't all the way up yet, which meant technically it was still the night.

On a shudder, he eased out of her. Despite his aches and fever and shakiness, he carefully cradled her into his arms and carried her down to the bathroom. An arm still around her shoulders, he turned on the shower water nice and warm. He might not be able to keep her, but that didn't mean he wasn't going to take care of her every way he could—for however much longer he had.

Just tonight.

He ignored the fuck out of the ache in the center of his chest. *So much for claiming her, huh, asshole?*

As they stepped into the shower, neither of them said a word. Ike positioned her so the water would mostly stream over her and threaded his fingers through her hair until it was wet. He washed her hair and her body, working to keep his thoughts a nice steady blank.

"How do you feel?" she finally asked.

"Exhausted. Not complaining, though."

Her pleased smile was full of mischief and satisfaction. She wore both really fucking well. She grabbed the soap and worked her lathered hands over his skin. "You still have a fever," she said.

He nodded.

She peered up at him with such softness. "You need the sleep you didn't get last night."

"Yeah." Not that he could bring himself to regret not getting it.

When they were done, Ike wrapped her in a towel and dried himself off while she did the same. As she brushed her damp hair at the sink, Ike came up behind her.

Damn, he'd given her a hickey on the side of her neck. He traced his fingers over it, then met her watchful gaze in the mirror. For just a second, her eyes were completely open books. And revealed a boatload of emotion he didn't want to see, *wasn't strong enough* to see, if you wanted to call a spade a spade.

It made him an asshole. He knew it did.

But then she gave him a flirty, playful smile, and the shutters dropped back over her expression. Letting him off the hook, allowing him an out.

And because he was a coward and a bastard, he took it.

Chapter 10

Jess was really glad Ike had slept all day. It gave her plenty of time to perfect her air of nonchalance about what had happened the night before. Namely, the best sex of her entire life. Not the best because Ike's cock was a thing of wicked beauty. And not just because Ike was skilled at the same kind of rough sex she craved.

It had been the best sex of her life because she found all that with the man she loved.

Oh, Jesus. I'm in love with Ike Young.

Sitting in a ball on the corner of the couch, Jess dropped her forehead into her hands, the revelation sucker punching her anew.

"You are so screwed," she whispered.

She'd known she had feelings for him, but somehow she'd chalked them up to things like being close friends, and being like family, and being in lust.

And all those things were true. But it was so much more than that. At least for her.

Jess *loved* the stubborn, overprotective, bald motherfucker. And she'd willingly made an agreement that they'd pretend that nothing had happened—and that it wouldn't change a thing between them.

In the morning, it'll all have been a fevered dream. And we'll be the same friends we were yesterday.

She was such an idiot.

A screwed, screwed idiot.

Upstairs, a cell phone buzzed a few times. "Yeah?" Ike answered, his voice rough.

Oh, shit. He's awake. Butterflies whipped through her belly.

Because it was show time. She had to make good on what she'd told him because there was no freaking way she was letting last night harm their friendship, no matter how difficult it was to bury her more-than-friendly feelings.

While Ike was still on the call, Jess hopped off the couch and checked on the frozen lasagna she'd put in the oven over an hour before. She wasn't sure if Ike would be up for real food yet, but she'd made it just in case, and she could always reheat it for him later.

Plus, after a *whole night* of incredible sex, Jess had been ravenous all damn day.

Her ears listening for the sounds that revealed Ike was making his way downstairs, Jess set the table and sliced up part of a loaf of Italian bread he'd bought. She needed to be ready to act normal. Annnd even thinking that almost guaranteed that she would fail, didn't it?

She sighed.

Footsteps on the stairs.

Jess turned to find Ike stepping down into the living room wearing jeans and a ratty gray Van Halen T-shirt. At least most of that delicious inked skin and hard muscle was covered. That helped.

"Hey," she said. "How ya feeling?"

For a split second, she felt him analyzing her, like he was wondering if things were truly going to be normal between them. It made her think of that look he'd given her in the bathroom mirror this morning—after he'd carried her downstairs and washed her freaking hair. How she was supposed to keep her stupid heart out of things when a guy did that for her *after* giving her a crazy number of mind-blowing orgasms, she didn't know.

"Better, actually." His gaze slid from her to the oven to the table. "Smells good."

"Think you can eat? I made the lasagna."

He nodded. "I'm actually kinda starving."

"That's how I was, too." She waved him closer. "Let's feel that forehead."

He eyeballed her like he was suspicious of her intentions. *Soooo* glad things were totally normal. Jess just barely refrained from rolling her eyes. Finally, he closed the distance between them.

She pressed her hand to his face. Much cooler than it had been. Relief flooded through her, easing some of the tension in her shoulders. "I think it's gone. At least for now."

"Yeah," he said, taking a step back. Away—from her. "Good news, huh?"

"Yup." She turned and peeked in the oven. The cheese was bubbling and brown. Perfect. Look at her being all domestic. She lowered the door and grabbed two hand towels, and then she lifted the pan with the lasagna out of the oven and rested it on top the stove's burners. "Aw, look at that."

He came up next to her, but not so close that they were touching. "I'm going to demolish that."

Jess chuckled. "Good."

"Lemme go get cleaned up while it cools," he said, already heading to the bathroom.

"Okay," she said, grabbing a diet Coke from the fridge.

The minute he closed himself in the bathroom, Jess sagged against the kitchen counter. Was that awkward or was that awkward? Or did it just feel awkward to her because she felt all different around him now?

Jess wanted to bang her head against a wall.

Instead, she finished taking everything to the table, grabbed a drink for Ike, and then sat her butt down to try to chill the fuck out.

He came out seconds later and joined her at the table. "Thanks for doing all this."

"No worries. Neither of us have eaten much this week so I thought we could use a real meal."

Nodding, he scooped her a big portion, then gave himself an even bigger one.

"I don't mean to be nosy, but was your call news from

back home?" she asked.

He cut a piece of lasagna with his fork. "Yeah. The team confirmed that their former base commanding officer lied about why he was in Baltimore, and a tracking device they put on his car showed that he went to a location known to be part of their enemy's business. They also found a tracking device in Becca's purse after she met with the guy, and the Ravens had to provide a diversion to keep her from being followed."

"Oh, my God," Jess said. "Is everyone okay?"

He nodded. "The team also got their hands on some new incriminating documents, so things are coming to a head."

"Well, I guess that's good news." She took a bite of food that she barely tasted.

"It is. But this Army officer is a highly decorated general with all kinds of political connections. Who the hell knows what kind of resources someone like that might have. Shit's about to get real."

God, if it wasn't real already, Jess didn't want to know what real looked like. After all, two Ravens died when the roof at Hard Ink collapsed last weekend. And it didn't get any more real than that.

"You know," she said, the words getting all tangled in her mouth. She rarely talked about her dad to anyone because his memory was all caught up in the worst mistake of her life. But this whole crisis had her thinking about him more and more recently.

"What?" Ike said, studying her.

She shrugged. "Was just thinking that I wish my dad was still around. He would've been able to help Jeremy and Nick. I know he would. And then they would've had someone in the police department they could trust for sure." Early in the team's investigation, they'd found solid evidence that the people they were fighting had at least some BPD in their pockets. "Dad is probably rolling in his grave knowing there are dirty cops working in the department he loved."

"I don't think I've ever heard you talk about your father before," Ike said as he took a bite of bread. "Were you close?"

Jess smiled. "We were. My mom split when I was eight, so it was just the two of us."

"Probably explains why you eat like a guy."

She laughed. "Probably. He wasn't much of a cook either." She pushed a piece of noodle around on her plate, then she took a deep breath and let the words fly. "I don't talk about him that much because…it's my fault he's dead."

Ike froze with his fork halfway to his mouth. His gaze narrowed. "I don't believe that."

She dropped her fork and sagged against the back of her chair. "It's true," she said, twisting her paper napkin in her fingers. In her mind's eye, scenes from that night took form like some macabre silent-era movie. "I'd fallen in with a bad crowd. I didn't realize how bad at the time. I just thought they liked to party. They seemed cool, fun, like they didn't have a care in the world. After living at home with my super serious, everything-by-the-book dad—even while I went to college part time, I was itching to be more independent. I made every wrong choice you could—loser guys, getting drunk, trying drugs. I was working all day at the tattoo parlor where I first met Jeremy and partying all night. My dad and I fought all the time. I was actually planning to move out of the house." Jess shook her head.

"What happened?" Ike asked in a quiet voice.

"I came home one night after work and walked in on two of my so-called friends robbing my house. They'd broken into my dad's gun closet. They had my mother's jewelry and her rare coin collection, and a bunch of rare comic books I'd picked up over the years."

Jess rubbed her hand over her left forearm, where her rose-and-vine tattoo surrounded a tattoo of Harley Quinn, a comic book villainess with red and black hair who wore a red and black costume. She'd been driven mad by the Joker and fallen in love with him, and then devoted her life to making him happy. It was one of Jess's earliest tattoos, one inspired by her love of comics and this dark character in particular.

"I was arguing with them and threatening them. I felt so betrayed because I'd told them about these things in casual conversation, never thinking twice about it or that they'd violate my trust like that. Hell, if I hadn't come home then, I never would've known it was them who'd done it. This guy named Marx pulled one of Dad's guns on me and threatened to shoot me. He said they needed the money or someone would hurt them. I learned later that they'd been dealing drugs and someone had double-crossed them and stolen some, which put them in debt to the dealer above them. I had no idea they were dealing." She looked at Ike. "I mean, I get it, using is bad enough. But I didn't know that."

Ike nodded. "And…your dad walked into the middle of this fight." He didn't phrase it as a question.

"Yeah," she said, her gut clenching. "I didn't even hear him come home over all the commotion. Marx shot first, and Dad dove in front of me, taking the bullet. He knocked me down in the process and managed to get off a shot and hit Burton. When Marx raised the gun to shoot again, my dad threw himself on top of me."

The memory sucked her back into the past, right back into that horrible moment. Jess smelled the hot scent of the gunfire, tasted the tang of iron in her mouth from where she'd bit down on her tongue when she fell, and heard its deafening thunder and the screams and shouts.

"Two shots went off at the same time, but my dad was on top of me and I couldn't see what was going on. And then it got very quiet." Jess met Ike's solemn gaze, a knot lodged in her throat, tears burning the backs of her eyes. She blinked again and again to keep them from falling. "My dad was dead before the ambulance arrived."

"Aw, hell, Jess. I'm so fucking sorry." He reached out and grabbed one of her hands. "Yeah, you made some mistakes, but it's not your fault he died."

Jess shook her head. She'd heard it all before, and the repetition didn't make it any more true than the first time someone had tried to convince her. "He told me my friends were trouble. If I'd listened, he'd still be alive."

"Every parent in history has probably said that about their kid's friends at some point or another. Trust me when I say I know what it is to be responsible for someone else's death. And you absofuckinglutely were not."

* * * *

Aw, fuck. What the hell was Ike doing? Besides Dare and Doc, no one else in his life now knew about how he'd failed to protect Lana. Which meant, honestly, no one else really knew him.

"What do you mean?" Jess asked in a quiet, surprised voice.

Ike debated for a long moment, and then he decided that if she could lay her greatest failure out on the table, so could he. And doing so had some extra benefits. First, it might alleviate some of the guilt she carried for her father. Second, it might make her look at him in a way that wasn't so damn affectionate—because if she thought she'd been hiding her emotions from him since he'd come downstairs, she was all kinds of wrong. And, third, it would make her see that Ike wasn't a good person—that he was just like the people her father had warned her away from. The first one was all for her, but the latter two were things he really needed to have a chance to put the colossal misstep of last night behind him, to get them back on the track they should've stayed on.

Sonofabitch.

As if Ike could have that taste of her and not want more. As if he could make it just about the fucking and keep his emotions separate—problem was, the whole time he'd been operating on feelings, not thoughts, and it was his goddamned feelings that had led him to give in to his body's demands in the first place.

As if he'd be able to stand any other man looking at her, let alone having her.

Jessica Jakes was his. Only she wasn't. And that mindfuck had no cure.

He pushed his plate away and folded his arms across his chest. "My father was trash. Working with Mexican cartels, he made his money as a coyote smuggling Mexican migrants into the country across the Arizona border. That was his business. And the expectation was that it was the family business. Me and my two older brothers were all to work for him. I hated it. I hated the intimidation, the exploitation, the separation of kids and parents. I wanted no part of it. One time, I got up the courage to tell my father I wanted to leave after I graduated high school. He beat me so bad I couldn't see for three days because of the swelling."

"Oh, Ike," Jess said, her expression so full of sympathy.

"Senior year, a girl came through on one of our transports. She stayed with some cousins in Tucson, one of whom was my girlfriend, Lana Molinas. Lana and I had been together since freshman year. I loved her," Ike said, nailing Jess with a stare.

Jess didn't flinch at that information. She just nodded.

"Lana's cousin started talking all over town about having been raped and purposely separated from her parents and little brothers. Lana supported her and went to the authorities, which was the right thing to do, of course. But it put her on my father's radar. On the cartel's radar. Bad shit started to go down. My father told me to break it off with Lana or he would. If I'd listened, Lana would still be alive. But I loved her, and I didn't want that life anyway. So we planned to run away."

"Jesus, Ike. I had no idea," Jess said. "What a horrible position to be in."

He frowned. She still wasn't getting it, but she would. "I promised her I'd keep her safe until we got out of town. She trusted me." Ike hated the sympathy he saw on Jess's face. That wasn't the reaction he was going for. He didn't want her to feel bad for him—he wanted her to be pissed at him, disappointed in him, repulsed by him. All the things he felt about himself. His words came out clipped and angry. "My oldest brother, Aaron, called Lana and told her I wanted her to meet him. She probably thought he was helping us escape. But my father sent Aaron to rough Lana up, scare her away, intimidate her into doing what he wanted and shutting her cousin up while she was at it. I found out about the meeting from my middle brother, David, but I got to her after it'd started."

Ike shook his head as the images of Lana's bleeding lip rushed to the fore. She'd been sprawled in the middle of an abandoned barn about a mile from their school, crying and clutching at her stomach. God, the sight had felt like a jagged blade to the gut.

"Aaron and I got into a knock-down, drag-out fight, and

he pulled a gun. I hit his arm as he pulled the trigger and the bullet went wide."

Fists and jaw clenched, Ike could still see the slug tearing into Lana's throat, the blood pouring from the wound.

"Lana took the bullet meant for me and bled out in my arms. Last thing she said to me…" Ike shook his head as pain bloomed in his jaw from how tight he clenched it. "…was that she was pregnant with our baby. I killed two people that day, two people I was supposed to protect," he rushed out. So he'd failed as a man and a father, as a lover and a protector. And it had cost the only person he'd ever loved everything.

"Ike," Jess whispered, pulling her chair closer to him.

He held up a hand, stopping her. He didn't want compassion from her. Or from anyone. He hadn't deserved it then and sure as fuck didn't now.

But there was more Jess needed to know. "I wanted to kill Aaron with my bare hands. But I was too fucking scared. Coward that I was, I ran instead. Eventually, I met up with the Ravens, and Dare took me in. Ike Young's not even my real goddamned name."

Jess went to her knees in front of him and pushed her body between his thighs. It was too close, too intimate, too damn much for Ike to handle. She grasped his face in her hands. "You were a kid and your father and brother were criminals. If I didn't cause my father's death, you didn't cause Lana's." Her thumbs stroked his cheeks. "Ike, I'm so sorry."

"You're not hearing what I'm saying," he said, knocking away her hands, anger boiling up inside him. Jesus, the pain of Lana's death and his failure was still so fucking sharp.

But Jess didn't back off. Instead, she pushed herself closer. "I hear you loud and clear. You and Lana were both victims of a horrible situation."

"I wasn't any goddamned victim," he bit out, shoving his chair back and springing to his feet.

Slowly, Jess stood.

"I was weak and stupid and a fucking coward. And Lana paid for it with her life. I didn't even get her vengeance," he yelled, pacing between the dining area and living room. Fucking hell, there wasn't enough air in here. Not with his words echoing around the cabin. Not with Jess staring at him.

"Yes, you did," Jess said, her voice rising. "You survived. You didn't give in to what your father wanted. You got free," she said, walking closer, and a little closer still. "Living life on your terms is the sweetest vengeance of all, and you did it without making a seventeen-year-old kid bear the awful weight of murder."

Ike glared. He was going to lose his freaking mind. He really was. "Aaron fucking deserved to die."

"Of course he did," Jess said, her expression fierce. "But you deserved to live without the guilt of killing someone more."

"I did fucking kill someone!" he roared.

She shook her head. "No, you didn't."

Jess's words, her defense of him, her compassion—Jesus, they hurt. They picked at messy scars and painful scabs inside him. He couldn't breathe. He couldn't stand still. He couldn't bear the weight of the vulnerability. And he didn't want to examine the why of it too closely—because while it'd been hard to tell this story to Dare and Doc, Ike hadn't felt this damn exposed with them. "You're wrong."

"Ike—"

"Just stop," he said, his chest so tight he had to gasp for air. "You're not listening to me. You're not hearing me." And not just about Lana, either. Jess was looking at him with so much damn emotion in her eyes that he could barely meet them. He had to make her hear him. He had to make her understand. Telling her the greatest shame of his life wasn't doing the job on Jess he needed it to do, so he was going to have to be more blunt. He gestured with his hand between them. "You and I?" Ike shook his head and ignored the burning pain in his chest. "We'll never be anything more than this. Relationships aren't my thing anyway, and definitely not with a woman always in so much damn trouble." He was the world's biggest asshole, he knew he was, especially as hurt flashed across her face. "And last night? That was just fucking, just scratching an itch. So whatever you think it meant, Jessica? It didn't. Not even a little. Not to me."

Chapter 11

With a raw, jagged hole in her chest where her heart used to be, Jess watched Ike storm out the front door.

How the hell had that conversation gone so badly so fast? Why had he lashed out at her like that? What did she say that was so wrong?

His words echoed in her brain, doing more and more damage as they sank in. She'd been nothing more to him than scratching an itch? As if she'd just been a series of holes to get him off and nothing more.

Fuck. Him.

Jess fisted her hands as anger crashed over her head like a violent wave. You know what? Let him go. She wasn't chasing after his ass, not when he was being such a gigantic freaking douchebag. He didn't want a relationship with her? Fine. It wasn't like she'd pressured him for one. And it wasn't like she'd started shit between them last night anyway. That had been all him.

But to say being with her had meant absolutely nothing? That didn't just negate what they'd shared, it negated their friendship, too. No friend talked to or looked at you that way. With friends like that... She chuffed out a humorous laugh. Exactly.

Except, fuck, his words were absolutely slicing up her

insides. That he could say shit like that after she'd opened up with him hurt. Jeremy was the only other person in her life now who knew what had happened. And now Ike. And it felt like he'd thrown all of it right back in her face.

Not that she planned on letting him see even a single drop of blood.

A half hour later, Jess had cleaned up dinner all without smashing anything, which seemed like some kind of a victory.

Ike still hadn't returned.

Through the open window over the sink, she heard loud, angry heavy metal music coming from the garage, along with an alarming number of crashes and bangs. Jess had no idea what the hell Ike was doing out there, but if he needed a time-out in the corner for a while, she wasn't going to talk him out of it.

Three hours later, she was sitting in the dark on the couch staring at the front door. Knees pulled up to her chest and chin resting on folded arms, Jess's head was a hot mess of sadness and anger and memories. And she got angrier with every hour that Ike stayed outside.

By the time she nuked a Hot Pocket for dinner the next evening, Jess was exhausted and strung-out and downright livid.

If anyone was responsible for changing their relationship, it wasn't her. She'd handled her shit. He was the one giving her the silent treatment after tearing her head off—and her heart out.

Standing at the kitchen counter, she'd just pulled a pepperoni out of her sandwich when the front door flew open. She didn't look up as she popped the saucy morsel into her mouth.

"Get your things together. We've leaving," Ike said as he clomped toward the bathroom.

Jess took another bite. Chewed. Savored. Swallowed.

Ike stopped outside the bathroom door. "Did you hear me?"

"I'm eating," Jess said. Okay, it was childish, but she had to admit she took pleasure from defying him. There was no way he wouldn't know she'd be ten kinds of curious about why they were leaving, so if he couldn't talk to her like a normal person, she wasn't going to listen.

He marched up to the kitchen counter, and she felt his gaze on her face almost as if it were a physical caress.

She took his challenge and looked him right in the eyes, working hard to make sure her face showed nothing but a careful, carefree blasé. "I'll be done in a few."

He looked at her for a long moment, long enough for her to see he was doing the careful blasé thing, too. "I want us out of here as soon as possible. The team has set up a meeting tomorrow with the assholes who ruined their military careers and attacked Hard Ink, and I want the extra protection the Ravens' compound will afford while all that's going down. Just in case."

Jess's insides went on an uncomfortable loop-the-loop at hearing what was about to happen and knowing what kind of danger that likely posed for Nick and his team. But all she said was, "Okay. I'll be ready in ten." After all, it wasn't like she had much to pack.

He gave her a single tight nod, and then turned on his heel and disappeared into the bathroom.

Ridiculously, tears chose that moment to threaten. All night and all day, she'd sat dry-eyed, too mad to let herself cry. She stared up at the ceiling and blinked the urge away—no way was she giving in to the urge in front of him. Frankly, she didn't want to give into it at all.

Before Ike emerged from the bathroom, Jess rushed to the loft to stuff all her clothes in her duffel. Downstairs again, she waited until he came out and gathered her toiletries in the bathroom. And then she was ready.

"Got everything?" he asked, a bag of his own hanging from his shoulder.

"Yup." She followed him out the front door. His bike sat in the sun by the front porch, and she had the weirdest moment of déjà vu. In so many ways, the scene was the mirror image of when they'd arrived almost a week before. In reality, so much had changed.

Ike handed her a helmet, stowed their bags, and mounted the bike. The engine growled to life, the sound cutting through the springtime air. Jess got on behind him, and then they were off. Heading out of the long driveway, turning onto the curving mountain road, and riding to another place she'd never before been—the home of the Raven Riders Motorcycle Club.

* * * *

Normally, being in the saddle of his bike cleared Ike's head and fed his soul. Not today. Not when he'd purposely hurt the person he cared about most in this world, and the only woman he'd developed any feelings for since Lana.

Because he was a fucking coward.

Ike leaned into the turns and sped up on the straightaways as they made their way over the mountain, the bike cutting through the warm evening air. Jess's hands grasped lightly at Ike's waist, though she didn't wrap herself around him the way she had on the way out of Baltimore last week. The distance between them felt like a steel bar sitting on his shoulders, making it hard to breathe, hard to even sit upright.

But he couldn't blame her for erecting a wall between them. After all, he'd handed her the bricks and taught her how to build the goddamned thing—right after he'd thrown so much hurtful bullshit right in her face.

Around a bend in the road, the Ravens' compound came into view. It was a huge piece of property—pushing 300 acres if Ike recalled correctly, and it could be accessed from two directions—the front, public entrance that led to the Green Valley Speedway, and the rear, private entrance that led more directly to the large clubhouse building, the chop shop, and the cottages. The latter was the heart of the Ravens' MC.

Ike took them around to the private entrance since they were meeting Bunny, Doc, and Rodeo at the clubhouse for dinner and staying there for the night. Most of the Ravens were in Baltimore helping Nick's team, but some of the Old Timers from Doc's generation who couldn't much ride anymore and some of the newer and prospective members had stayed behind. In case the shit hit the fan, those extra hands were better than nothing. Ike felt more secure having Jess behind the Ravens' guarded walls until the fight in Baltimore played out.

And, frankly, it was probably better for both him and Jess to be surrounded by other people given how badly Ike had fucked things up—and to keep him from fucking them up even more.

He'd hated staying out of the house the previous night, but he'd been too raw, too angry, too torn apart—about so many things. And he didn't know how to make any of it right. Jess's easy acceptance, forgiveness, and understanding of what he'd done to Lana had been so fucking hard to take. Because Ike had none of those things for himself, and that made him want Jess—and want everything she had to give—even more than he already did.

And, Jesus, he did. He wanted Jess. Not just in his bed, although that had been fucking fantastic. He wanted her in his arms. By his side.

But Ike...Ike was fucking terrified that he'd let himself fall...only to have it all ripped away again.

It made him realize that he'd been living half a life since the day Lana died—closed off, not taking chances, not feeling half of what he should. Which meant he'd wasted so much time. But he didn't know how to change, how to put the past behind him, how to fucking man-up.

And now he'd screwed things up with Jess royally. But, what did he know? Maybe it was better that way. For her.

Ike banked the bike onto the mountain road that led to the private entrance. You could tell when you hit Ravens' property, because the road narrowed and signs told you to turn the fuck around. Ike rolled up to a card reader with a mounted camera. They might be bikers, but they had some tech where it counted—and security was definitely one of those areas. He slipped his card into the slot and waited while the gate slid open.

When he had enough room, Ike shot through the breach and followed the road a short distance to where it opened up into a large parking lot. It was weird seeing it so empty of bikes and cars when it was usually hopping. The chop shop across the lot appeared quiet, too. Ike parked in one of the spaces right in front of the clubhouse, a long two-story, brown brick building with a front porch that ran the length of it. Back in the day it had apparently been some kind of mountain inn, and now it housed the club's main social spaces, a kitchen and mess, their meeting room, a workout room, and some rooms upstairs where people could crash or fuck or otherwise find some privacy.

"This is it," Ike said over his shoulder.

"Okay," Jess said, dismounting the bike. Without looking at him, she handed him her helmet. As she took in their surroundings, Ike couldn't help but run his gaze over her. Tall black boots. Tight black jeans. A slinky, see-through red shirt that had a wide neck prone to sliding off one shoulder or the other, and a tight black tank revealing a lot of cleavage underneath.

The dark purple and red of the hickey was visible depending on how she moved her hair.

God, he felt like such a shit.

Clearly, he wasn't any damn hero. That much was for sure. Not like her father. Ike's jaw was clenched as he unloaded their bags. If her old man had thought some partying, low-level drug dealers were the wrong kind of people for Jess to run with—and they were, no doubt—Detective Jakes would've hated Ike on sight. Ike Young—who came into this world as Isaac Yeager, the son of a violent criminal who had no problem being in bed with the worst of the Mexican cartels. Ike's actions—and his inaction—had caused the death of his girlfriend and unborn child. After that, grief and fear had turned Ike into a drifter until he met Dare Kenyon, who fed him and took him in and gave him a whole new family—and the papers for a new identity, too. And now Ike handled bets, debts, and enforcement of collection when necessary.

Ike chuffed out a humorless laugh. What a fucking prize.

Jess eyeballed him for a long moment. "What's funny?"

"Not a damn thing," he said, lifting their bags to his shoulder. "Look, Jess. I wanted to say—"

"Jess! Ike!" Bunny chose that moment to rush out the door and down the steps. She drew Jess into her arms. "Come in, come in. I hope you're hungry. Ike told me he was bringing you up here tonight, and I love any excuse to cook a big meal."

"I appreciate that," Jess said, humor in her voice.

"Bunny, you know you have volunteers to eat your cooking pretty much any time you're in the mood to do it," Ike said. Looked like he'd have to find another time for that apology.

The older lady laughed. "I know it. Y'all are like wolves."

Ike and Jess followed Bunny through the front entrance hall that was now a lounge to the mess hall off the right side. The décor throughout was mountain kitsch meets biker memorabilia, which pretty much meant mounted deer heads hung next to vintage metal road signs and neon beer lights. American and POW/MIA flags fluttered from the thick, exposed wooden beams overhead. Above the tall, stacked-stone fireplace—one of many that existed throughout the joint—hung a big carved wooden plaque of the Ravens' logo inked on Ike's back.

"Everybody," Bunny said to the group of people already seated around the big table, "this is Ike's friend Jessica." Then Bunny went around the table. "Jess, you remember Doc and Rodeo." Jess waved hello to the men she'd met at the lake. "And then there's Scooter, Blake, Jeb, and Bear," Bunny said, pointing to each of the men in turn. Blake and Jeb were probies, prospective members still proving their chops, commitment, and loyalty to the club. Scooter was the Ravens' newest member, his unfortunate nickname coming from the fact that he actually owned a fucking scooter. Bear was another Old Timer, though he could still ride.

"Nice to meet you all," Jess said.

"And these two ladies are Haven and Cora. They're visiting for a while," Bunny said, pointing to two pretty blonde-haired women sitting together at the near end of the long table. Ike gave them a nod as Jess said hello. He'd met the two cousins a little over a week ago when Nick and his SF teammates had rescued them from a Baltimore street gang with a side business in human trafficking.

The Ravens had invited the women to hang there where it was safe while they figured out what they wanted to do or where they wanted to go. It was one of the things the club did, part of its mission. All thanks to Dare.

"Well, all right, then," Doc said, looking down the table from his seat at the head. "Can we eat now or are we gonna torture Jess by seeing if she remembers everyone's names?"

Chuckles filled the room.

"No torture," Bunny said. "Just lots and lots of food."

Words of approval were quickly followed by praise for the feast of pork barbecue, mashed potatoes, corn on the cob, coleslaw, and cornbread that got passed around. Normally, Ike would've been thrilled to sit among his brothers and dig in to an excellent meal, but when Jess chose the seat between Bunny and Cora, that steel bar of guilt he'd been carrying hit him upside the head all over again.

But what could he do? He'd made his cold and empty bed, and now he had to fucking lie in it.

* * * *

Jess enjoyed the dinner with Bunny and the Ravens a lot, in part because she could keep her distance from Ike and try to forget about their fight—at least for a while. When it was over, though, she was worried that she and Ike were going to be stuck together again—and didn't that say a helluva lot about where they were? Bunny and Rodeo went home, and Doc and Bear—who apparently lived somewhere on the compound—left for their places. Cora and Haven seemed super nice but on the shy side, and they pretty quickly retreated to their rooms upstairs.

Thankfully, though, the younger Ravens saved Jess from the possibility of more fighting, awkwardness, or one-on-one drama with Ike when they invited them to play pool in one of the other rooms. Jess was only too happy to accept. Drinks, music, and pool sounded like the perfect distraction—not just from Ike, but from worrying about whatever fight was looming tomorrow for her friends back home.

Blake fired up the coinless jukebox while Jeb racked the balls on the felt. A hot, driving beat spilled into the room.

Away from the dinner table, Jess could better study the denim cuts they wore with black leather patches and badges. "How come your cuts only have the club's name on the back but not the logo?" she asked.

From where Ike sat on a stool at the bar behind her, he said, "Because they're prospects. They don't get patched until they've been voted in and earned it."

"Is that when you get the back tat?" Jess asked, directing the question to Blake and Jeb.

Jeb looked across the room to Ike, clearly prepared to defer to him to answer. When Ike didn't, Jeb nodded. With shoulder-length brown hair and a lanky body, he was a cute guy even though he had a total baby face. "That's right. Same time."

"Who does your ink?" Jess accepted a cold bottle of beer from Blake and took a long sip.

"I do," Ike said, nailing her with a stare when she turned to meet his gaze.

Heat ran over Jess's skin, and she hated the way her body reacted to him even when he was being an ass. And she really hated how hot she found it that the younger guys here so clearly respected Ike *and* that Ike was responsible for their ink. It was like seeing a whole new side of him, this man she'd known for the last four years.

Blake swept his dark-blond hair out of his eyes and held out a cue to her. He had a whole surfer vibe that she found appealing, though his eyes were harder and more serious than she'd noticed at first glance.

"All you," she said, waving off the cue. She wanted to assess the competition first. "I'll play winner."

It didn't take her long to determine that Blake was the better shot. He ran the table pretty handily against Jeb, which meant Jess might actually have some decent competition tonight. Her dad had made sure Jess could hold her own at pool, foosball, air hockey, and pinball machines—all his favorites. No one ever expected her to be any good, though. Back in college she had a lot of fun with the misperceptions.

"All right, Jess. You're up," Jeb said, coming to stand beside her. His elbow gave her arm a little tap. "He's brutal though, I'm warning you."

Jess smiled. "I'll see what I can do."

Blake racked and broke the balls, sinking a solid on his

first shot. He sank two more in quick succession before missing a bank shot that set Jess up very well.

"What should we bet to make this more interesting?" she asked, bending over the table and eyeballing her options.

Blake joined Jeb at the side, which she knew put both of them right behind her and probably staring at her ass. All part of her evil plan. "How 'bout five dollars," Blake said, slapping a fiver on the edge of the table.

Jess shrugged. "Sure, why not. I'm good for it," she said, winking.

"I bet you are," Blake said.

One, two, three, four balls down in quick succession.

"Damn," Jeb said. "She's gonna smoke your ass."

Blake's gaze narrowed, and it made Jess laugh. "Thirteen in the corner," she said. She lined up and took her shot, but the orange-striped ball caught the bumper right next to the pocket.

Back up again, Blake sank two more before not giving himself much of a shot on his next turn, so he used it on a Hail Mary of a bank shot that screwed up her balls.

"Gee, thanks," she said.

The look he gave her communicated more than some friendly ribbing. He was interested. "Any time, Jess. Any time."

Part of her wanted to be interested in return. Objectively, she could look at him and think, *That's a hot guy. I'd totally do him.* But her body wouldn't get on board with anything more than visual appreciation, not with Ike in the room. Not with Ike owning her heart.

Love fucking sucked.

But at least she handily won the game, running the rest of the balls straight through. "Thank you," she said, swiping the five off the table and making a little show of tucking it into her bra.

"I think we need a round of shots," Jeb said. "Make this more interesting."

"Bring it on," Jess said. "If you think it'll help."

From behind the bar, Jeb grabbed a bottle of tequila, a container of salt, and a baggy of lemon wedges, then lined up three shot glasses. "Ike?" he asked, holding up a fourth glass. Ike just shook his head.

What the hell was wrong with him anyway? "Come on," Jess said. "Have some fun."

"I'm good," he said, gaze narrowed at her.

Jess turned back to the guys as they each licked and salted the side of their hand and lifted their shot. "Lick, sip, suck," she said. And then she was licking the salt, swallowing down the golden liquor, and sucking hard on the lemon. A shudder rocked through her.

"One more for good measure," Jeb said, pouring and passing the salt again.

They did the second shot, and Jess could already tell it was a good thing she'd eaten a big dinner. Warmth bloomed outward from her stomach, and her head got just a little bit light. It felt damn good after the stress of the past week.

Jess won the second game of pool, too, and that one earned her a twenty. Blake insisted on two more tequila shots to even his odds, and Jess laughed as she teased and taunted him. Her muscles loosened and her body felt flushed. The guys were funny and flirty and the tequila made them even funnier.

Best of all, her troubles floated away and Jess could just *be* and let all the crap go. At least for a few hours.

* * * *

Ike watched Jess play pool with the prospects for over an hour. She was damn good at the game and sexy as fuck bending over the table in those tight jeans and flashing cleavage down the front of her loose shirt—where she kept stuffing her winnings. In typical Jess fashion, she was sarcastic and full of trash talk and flirting nonstop. Ike had been sporting a semi for a long time now, and he was starting to go a little out of his mind.

And he wasn't the only one getting turned on. Blake and Jeb were eating Jess's antics up, not to mention looking at her like they wanted to spread her out on the table between them and make a meal of her. They made no effort to hide their appreciation of her assets when she took her shots, and if Blake adjusted his junk while watching her one more time, Ike was going to punch him in the fucking throat.

"Bunny said you might be staying here for a few nights,"

Jeb said, sitting on the side.

"I don't know how long," she said, studying Blake as he tried to make a hard shot. "But definitely tonight."

"Nice," Jeb said. "Where are you staying?"

"Oh, uh, here?" She looked to Ike, her gaze shuttered, her expression that careful neutral she'd been wearing around him all day. It was making him insane and causing a feeling in his chest like someone had punched him there and yanked out some important stuff. "I've never been here before, so…"

Ike studied her eyes, but he couldn't get a read on her. He couldn't tell what the look meant. Was her question purely informational? Was she wondering if she and Ike would sleep together? Was she looking for his permission to sleep wherever she—or her and the prospects—might want?

Fuck if that last possibility didn't make the blood go from a simmer to a low boil in Ike's veins. He almost felt like the fever was back, though he knew it wasn't. This heat was coming from the possessive, territorial part of him. The part that said, *She. Is. Mine.*

He squeezed the neck of the beer bottle hard enough that he feared it could break in his hand. "We're upstairs," he bit out, not including the detail that Bunny had given them separate rooms. Or that Ike had requested it be that way.

"While most of the club's away," Blake said, "we're upstairs, too." He gave her a look that made Ike want to break things. "Your turn." The guy winked at her.

Jess grinned as she lined up what should've been an easy shot—and missed. She was a little thing and had now thrown back part of a beer and four tequila shots. Ike had only seen Jess drunk a handful of times, not enough to remember how fucking fluid and sensual her body got under the influence. She had him gritting his teeth and aching in his jeans.

"Aw, shit," she said at her miss, making the guys laugh.

"'Bout time I give you a spankin'," Blake said, his gaze very obviously skating down to her ass.

Jess raised her eyebrows in challenge. "Think so, huh? Do it if you're man enough." She used the pool cue to hold herself steady.

"Better get that ass ready for me," Blake said.

Annnd that's when something snapped inside Ike's brain. "Game's over," he said, shoving off his stool. "You two, clean up and get the fuck out."

The fact that the prospects hesitated before following his order ratcheted up his pissed-off factor by about ten. The fact that Jess was glaring at him like he'd ruined her fun—and her chance to get laid—had him wanting to destroy things with his bare hands. The fact that Blake paused in the doorway like maybe he was thinking of asking Jess to come with him pushed Ike all the way to homicidal.

"What part of get the fuck out don't you understand?" Ike said, glaring at the prospect. The kid disappeared into the hallway, the door swinging shut behind him.

"What's your problem?" Jess said, hands planted on her hips.

A few pages past rational, Ike got right up in her face. "What's *my* problem? Really?"

"Yeah. Really," she said, tossing her cue on the felt.

Ike backed her up against the pool table. "You wanna fuck that guy?" he bit out, knowing he was being an asshole but unable to keep all the noise inside him buttoned up tight.

"Are you shitting me right now?" she said, eyes narrowed, cheeks flushed.

"No, I'm fucking serious. You've been flirting with the pair of them all night. Shaking your ass in their face, hanging on them, getting fucking drunk."

Fury blazed from Jess's eyes. "First of all, I haven't done a damn thing wrong. Second of all, I'm an adult and you don't get a fucking say in who I do *anything* with. And third of all," she said, planting her hands against his chest and shoving him, her volume escalating. "You made it crystal freaking clear we're not together and never will be, so why does it matter to you who I wanna fuck anyway?"

Everything she said was true, but the shit storm in his head wouldn't relent. He got right back up in her face. "Because...I..." He shook his head.

"What?" she shouted.

"I... *Fuck.*" He dove at her. Clasped her face in his hands and devoured her mouth with every bit of denied desire he had inside him. He was rock hard and aching and out of his mind.

Together, they were an angry, roiling flash fire. Jess clawed his neck, bit his lip, and sucked on his tongue until he saw stars. Ike gripped her hard—squeezing her breasts, clutching her ass, pulling her hair.

He tore her jeans open and forced them down around her thighs, and then he kicked her feet apart and sank a finger deep into her pussy. "Tell me you're so wet for me," he growled, finger fucking her fast.

"You're an asshole," she rasped, her hips moving with his hand.

"Yeah," he said, claiming her mouth again. Jesus, he had to get in her. It was the only place he felt like he wasn't starved of air and solace and life.

Ike spun her around, bent her over the pool table, and freed his cock from his jeans. A twinge of something shot through him—guilt? Uncertainty? Concern, for her?

"Jesus, Ike, are you going to fuck me or not?" she asked, anger clear in her voice.

He pushed his cock into her until he was balls deep.

On a groan, he fucked her hard, fingers digging into her hips. Jess was screaming and cursing and moaning loudly—and Ike hoped Blake heard every fucking sound.

She. Is. Mine.

The thought had his hips snapping faster as his cock worked that pussy so damn good. Planting a hand on the felt, he hunched himself around her, bearing down on her, going deeper. The tenor of Jess's moans became more desperate, more urgent.

"Come all over my cock, Jessica. Fucking come for me."

Her orgasm was goddamned glorious. Her pussy fisted him again and again and again and her come coated his cock and ran down his balls. And then he was right there with her, shoving into her deep, but not deep enough. Never deep enough. He came so long and so hard that he got light-headed.

For a long moment, their harsh breathing was the only sound in the room.

Jess pushed herself into a standing position and pulled free of him. Without looking at him, she drew up and fastened her jeans.

Eyes glued to her, Ike did the same. Dread snaked into his gut.

"Can you show me where I'm sleeping?" she asked, that careful neutral back on her now-flushed face.

Ike fucking hated it, but he nodded. He grabbed their bags from where he'd dropped them in the front lounge and guided her upstairs. Theirs were the first two rooms on the second floor. "You're here," he said, pointing at the first door. "And I'm there." He indicated the next room over.

"Okay." She reached for her bag, and Ike handed it to her.

"Jess—"

"What happened tonight," she said, turning the knob and cracking the door open a little. "You should know, it didn't mean anything to me. And it won't be happening again. But thanks for scratching *my* itch."

With that, she disappeared inside the room and closed the door in his face. A click told him she'd engaged the lock.

Ike was so fucking hosed.

Chapter 12

Ike had been lying in bed for hours and hadn't once drifted off to sleep. His brain was so full of churn and burn that it wouldn't shut the fuck off and give him even a minute of reprieve—from the guilt, from the grief, from the soul-deep knowledge that he'd been kidding himself where Jessica Jakes was concerned.

Not just since he'd slept with her. And not just this week that he'd been alone with her. But pretty much for as long as he'd known her.

He'd been a hundred and fifty percent sure he'd been doing the right thing when he'd made it clear that they'd never be more than friends. But now that *she* was the one pulling the full stop...

Funny thing about having choices taken away from you—it tended to make things all kinds of crystal clear. You either felt relief all the way into your bones because it was the right decision even if you hadn't made it, or every cell inside you cried out in rebellion and loss and regret because you learned—too late—what it was you really wanted.

Ike shifted in the bed, kicked off the covers, and stared unseeingly up at the dark ceiling. On a sigh, he threw an arm over his head.

He wanted Jess. But he'd fucked things up with her more than once, and now she was done with him.

And though he still had all kinds of bullshit about his past and his failures and his shame whirling around in his brain, knowing she wasn't even a possibility now cut right through it all—and made it clear that a lot of the rationale he'd been clinging to all this time was nothing more than fear-turned-convenient-justification. Which it turned out Ike was really fucking good at since he'd been working at it for the last eighteen years.

Sonofabitch.

One of the things in particular that Jess said yesterday had really been shaking things loose in his head.

You survived. You didn't give in to what your father wanted. You got free. Living life on your terms is the sweetest vengeance of all...

Prickles ran over every inch of Ike's body.

He'd gotten free of his father physically, but not mentally, not emotionally.

Jesus. He hadn't been living life on his own terms, had he? Not really. Because he was still running from his father. Still internalizing his father's terrible will. Because that's what harassing Lana had been about—teaching *Ike* a lesson.

How much longer was Ike going to let his father control a single thing about his life?

And did it even matter now that things with Jess were beyond repair?

When morning finally dawned, Ike managed to doze off for a while, but his sleep was so restless that he woke up more exhausted than if he'd just gotten up without sleeping at all. His guts felt like they'd been through a meat grinder, and a solid, blaring ache had settled into his head. He stayed in the shower until the water ran cold.

Ike exchanged some texts with Dare to learn that the meeting between the team and the leader of their mercenary enemies was that afternoon following a funeral for the brother of one of the SF teammate's girlfriends. That meant in a matter of hours they would know if this whole situation was coming to an end or about to get a whole lot fucking worse.

Finally, Ike had no other reason to hole up in his room. It

was going on ten o'clock, after all.

He was dreading seeing the disappointment and distance on Jess's face, but he was just pathetic enough to want to be in her presence anyway. Knocking on her door, he called, "Jess?" No answer. He knocked again.

Frowning, Ike set off to find her. It didn't take long. She was in the big industrial kitchen with Bunny, who was regaling her with a story about her and Doc when they were younger while she flipped pancakes on the big grill. Next to her, Jess was scooping scrambled eggs off the grill into a big tray, her discomfort in the kitchen even more noticeable next to Bunny. It might've made him smile if the expression on Jess's face hadn't fallen so hard when she noticed him in the doorway.

"Hey," Ike said.

"Hey, Ike. Good morning," Bunny said. "Coffee's on if you want some. And brunch will be ready soon."

Jess didn't say a thing, so Ike nodded and moved to the counter where the three-pot coffeemaker sat. He poured a cup and took a long sip, the hot liquid inside him making him feel incrementally better. Standing off to the side of the kitchen allowed Ike to watch Jess as she worked. She was wearing a loose white T-shirt pulled tight into a knot at the waist. Beneath it, a black bra was visible. On the bottom, skinny ripped-up blue jeans hugged her ass perfectly and ended inside her tall black boots. She pulled all of her hair into a thick side braid that laid over her left shoulder, the braid highlighting the red in her jet-black hair.

Jeans and a white T-shirt had never looked so damn good.

Jesus, he was a goner, wasn't he?

"You realize if you stand in my kitchen, I'm gonna put you to work, right?" Bunny asked after a minute.

"I'm at your service," he said.

She laughed. "My favorite words ever." No doubt, she heard a version of them often enough since Ike didn't know a single Raven who wouldn't drop everything to give Bunny a hand. As Doc's sister and Dare's great-aunt, she commanded a lot of respect within the club.

Put him to work, Bunny did. He set the table, earning some ribbing from Doc and Rodeo when they arrived soon after. He carted food out. He brewed fresh pots of coffee. And he didn't mind a bit of it—except that it gave him no time to pull Jess aside and apologize for…a damn long list of things.

The food was good for fuel, but Ike hardly tasted any of it. He kept trying to catch Jess's gaze, but she seemed to be looking right past him—or avoiding him altogether. When everyone was done and just sitting around the table shooting the shit, Ike's cell buzzed in his pocket. He checked it to find he had a missed call from Dare and had a text that simply said, *Call me.* But Dare hadn't left a message, which was strange.

"Excuse me," Ike said, pushing back from the table. Finally, Jess looked at him, questions clear in her gaze. She knew shit would be going down today, and no doubt she was nervous about it. Ike gave her a little nod. "Be right back."

Ike moved out into the lounge and called Dare.

"Ike," Dare answered.

"Hey, sorry I missed you. Bunny made up a big breakfast here and—"

"Ike," Dare said again, something in his tone making Ike's instincts blare. "I've got bad news here, man. And I'm really sorry to have to be the one to deliver it."

* * * *

Jess was in the kitchen helping Bunny wash the dishes. She almost regretted how much she liked the older lady because after all this was over, Jess couldn't see any reason why she'd get to spend time with Bunny again.

But Jess had been so happy to find Bunny up and around this morning because the lady's company would provide the perfect buffer between her and Ike. With Bunny around, the pair of them probably wouldn't fight and certainly couldn't fuck. And clearly Jess needed that kind of third-party intervention after she'd so easily given in to Ike's desire last night.

On the pool table.

Still mostly dressed and possibly more angry than she'd ever been in her life.

God, it had been so damn hot.

And another in a long line of mistakes where Ike was concerned. Maybe he was right after all—maybe Jess couldn't help but get in trouble, find trouble, and generally cause trouble.

One good thing had come from their rough-and-dirty quickie, though, and that was bone-deep resolve. Jess had known letting the sex happen—no matter how much she wanted it, too—had been a mistake. But she was done. She wouldn't make it again. Her resolve wasn't about revenge or playing hard to get, it was about protecting her heart before it got any more beat up.

The door to the kitchen swung open and Jess felt Ike's presence like a physical caress. Would she always be so aware of him? Footsteps told her he was coming her way, and then the hair rising on the back of her neck let her know he was right behind her.

"Jess?" he said. "I need to talk—"

"Not now," she said, rinsing a plate and bending to put it in the huge dishwasher.

"I'll give y'all some privacy," Bunny said, settling a dried pot on the stove.

"That's okay, Bunny," Jess said. "We don't need it."

"Yes, we do," Ike said quietly.

Something about his tone was…odd. He wasn't being his usual bossy self. She peered up at his face, and ice skittered down her spine. Ike's expression…was a breath away from being shattered. A soapy cup fell out of Jess's hands and clunked against the sink. "What's wrong?" she asked.

"Let's go outside—"

With wet hands, she clutched his arms. Her stomach squeezed. "No, tell me. Now."

Ike gently rested his fingers on her hips. "Everyone from Hard Ink went to the funeral for Emilie's brother this morning."

"Okay," Jess said, her thoughts scrambling. Emilie was dating Marz, one of the guy's on Nick's team, but otherwise, Jess didn't know her well.

"The mercenaries from Seneka showed up. There was a firefight. It was bad." As Ike spoke, Jess's heart was sinking to the floor. "Jess…"

"Oh, God," she said, time slowing, the room going a little wobbly around her. Not Jeremy, not Jeremy, not Jeremy. Without him, Jess wasn't sure she would've survived her father's death. And she couldn't imagine living in a world that didn't include her funny, generous, talented friend.

"Nick and his sister were both shot. And Jeremy…Jeremy sustained some kind of head injury." A moan spilled from her throat. Ike pulled her in closer, his hands gently cupping her face. "Jeremy and his sister were serious enough to be airlifted to the hospital for surgery. I don't know anything else yet."

Jeremy…with a head injury?

Jess shook and her eyes went blurry, and then the tears fell as a sob ripped up her throat. "Oh, my God," she said through thick tears. "Oh, my God. Not Jeremy."

"I know," Ike said, his voice strained. He pulled her against his chest and wrapped her in his strong arms.

"Ike," she cried.

He stroked her hair. "So damn sorry."

And then it occurred to her. "Oh, God." She pushed back far enough to meet his gaze. "What if Nick loses both of his siblings?" Since he'd come home from the Army, Jess had gotten to know Nick pretty good. He could be stubborn and opinionated and a pain in her ass, mostly playfully, but he was a good guy and a great brother, and she knew that his family meant the world to him.

Ike shook his head. "Don't think that way. They're getting treatment. There's no reason to think they won't pull through."

Did Ike really believe that? Jess let her forehead drop against his chest. He was probably right. They should stay positive. But the fear and looming grief were nearly suffocating. "I feel so far away," she said through more tears.

"I know. I wish we could go to the hospital, but some of the Seneka operatives got away, so the situation's still red hot." He settled back against the counter and pulled her to rest against him. He stroked her hair and caught the tears running down her cheek, and just held her as long as she needed him to.

For all the problems between them, there wasn't another

person she would've wanted to be with in this moment. Jeremy and Nick were both of their friends and coworkers. Ike knew exactly what she'd feel if either of the Rixey siblings didn't pull through.

Heaving a shaking breath, Jess pulled away, though she stayed within the comforting ring of Ike's arms. "Waiting for information is going to kill me."

He handed her a paper towel from the roll behind him. "That's the goddamned truth," he said.

"Thanks." Jess wiped at her face, but her stupid eyes wouldn't stop leaking.

"Come with me," Ike said. He took her hand, stopped at the fridge and grabbed two bottles of water, and then led her out the back door of the kitchen. A huge roofed porch ran the length of the building and overlooked a wide lawn, the rolling mountains, and the blue-green valley beyond.

Under any other circumstances, the view would've taken Jess's breath. But she just couldn't appreciate it, couldn't see it, not when her friends were fighting for their lives.

Ike pulled two cushioned lounge chairs close together and guided her to one. He took the other, and despite all her fucking resolve, she hated the distance between them. She leaned as far as she could into his chair and rested her head against his arm.

Ike sat up, gently grabbed her, and pulled her into the chair with him. "C'mere," he said, making room for her. "Is this okay?"

"Yes," Jess said, fitting her body in next to his so her drawn-up knee rested on his thighs and her head rested on his chest. "What do we do now?" she asked, suspecting the answer and hating it.

Ike sighed and pulled her in tighter against him. "Now we wait."

Chapter 13

The waiting was killing her. The minutes clicked by so slowly that it seemed like time wasn't moving at all. Jess lay in Ike's arms as morning turned into afternoon, and afternoon made the late-day stretch toward evening. Sometimes he dozed off, but she never did. She just stared at the view and silently fought back the yawning pain inside her. How had her world fallen apart so quickly? Again.

Hang on, Jeremy. Don't you fucking die on me! If miracles were possible, she willed him to hear her. To fight. To hold on to life and never let it go. Jeremy, with his dirty T-shirt collection and his flirtatiousness and his amazing art. She couldn't lose him. She just couldn't.

The thoughts beckoned more tears. Jess tried to stop them, but couldn't. What was taking so long? Why hadn't they heard anything else? It couldn't be a good sign, could it? Her eyes burned, her face ached, her throat was dry and scratchy. The more she tried to hold herself still so she didn't disturb Ike, the harder she shook.

"Aw, sweet Jess, don't cry," Ike said, his voice sounding like he was still half asleep. "I've got you. Everything will be okay." His hand gently rubbed her back.

"You don't know that," she said through thick tears. "You can't know."

Fingers cupped her chin and lifted her face to meet Ike's gaze. He stared at her a long moment, his thumb stroking her cheek and catching her tears. His eyes searched hers like he was looking for something. "I do."

"How?" she said. She hoped he did know because she needed some shred of hope to cling to.

Finally, in a very quiet voice he said, "Because we're together."

Confusion lanced through her grief, followed quickly by a tendril of hope she wasn't sure she should reach for. "Ike, what do you—"

His cell phone buzzed an incoming call. Jess gasped and her gaze clashed with Ike's.

This was it. Moment of truth time. Jess was so scared to hear the news that she could barely stand being inside her own skin.

Ike pressed the phone to his ear. "Dare, what do you have for me?" Pause. "Okay." Pause. "Okay." Pause.

Jess. Was. Dying. Literally dying. She searched Ike's face, hoping something in his expression would give her a clue as to whether the news was bad or good. But she just couldn't tell. "What's going on?" she whispered.

"Got it," Ike said into the phone, grasping her hand and pressing it to his heart. "Keep me posted on that and stay vertical, will ya?" Ike dropped the phone in his lap and exhaled like he'd been holding the weight of the world on his shoulders. "Jeremy and Kat are out of surgery and the doctors are optimistic about them both."

Jess blinked. It was like her brain couldn't process the information. And then finally, finally, it sank in. "They're going to be okay?" she rasped.

"That's what it sounds like," Ike said, rubbing a hand over his head. "Thank fuck."

"Oh, my God," Jess said, sagging against Ike's chest. "Oh, my God. Thank you." The tears started again and her shoulders shook. "I don't...know why...I'm crying now."

"It's the adrenaline letdown," Ike said. "The sheer relief of it."

"Yeah," she said. "I don't know what I would've done..."

Ike pressed a kiss to the top of her head. "And now you won't have to. None of us will."

The kiss resurrected her memory of what Ike had said before Dare called. That everything would be okay…because she and Ike were together. Jess forced a deep breath, and then another one, and finally managed to bottle up her tears. She pushed herself up so that she could see him. "What did you mean? Before…"

"Just what I said." Ike slipped his fingers between hers and clasped her hand. "When we're together, everything makes sense. And when we're not…" He shook his head. "It's like everything falls apart."

Uh, okaaaay. She liked the general sound of those words but had absofreakinglutely no idea what they meant, especially on top of everything else he'd said and done the past few days. "I like being with you, too, Ike. We've been friends for years and you're one of the most important people in my entire life. But—"

"That's just it," he said, frowning. "I don't want to be friends anymore, Jess. I want to be everything to you." He looked her square in the eyes. For the first time, she saw complete and total openness there. She saw fear. She saw pain. She saw sincerity. And it slayed her to get such a rare peek inside this man. Her heart tripped into a sprint. "I'm not sure that I deserve it. I'm not even sure that I'll be any good at it. But if you'll let me, I'd like to try."

* * * *

Ike's heart was about to beat the fuck out of his chest. From fear, from hope, from something else, something bigger, something completely overwhelming.

Love.

He loved this woman.

The clarity of his emotions had stolen over him in the quiet stillness of the night, and then they'd hit him like a tidal wave when he'd heard the news about Jeremy, Kat, and Nick. Once he recognized the emotion for what it was, Ike found it hard to understand how he hadn't realized what the hell had been going on inside him all along.

As he watched her, studying her every reaction, Jess pressed a hand to her forehead. "I...I..." She shook her head. "Are you serious?" she whispered.

Aw, fuck. What an asshole he'd been that she felt she had to ask. Voices echoed out from the kitchen. "Will you take a walk with me?" he asked.

"Uh, okay," she said, sounding confused.

He didn't blame her. But he didn't want an audience for this, either. He helped her stand up and took her hand, then he reached into the kitchen and grabbed a key ring off a hook. Ike guided Jess to a wide trail off the right side of the clubhouse. Within five minutes, they arrived at a row of six white cottages. Back in the heyday of the racetrack, they'd been additional accommodations people could rent out. Now, the club used them to house drivers during races, to help out a club member down on his luck, or to put up someone they were guarding or who otherwise needed their assistance.

Ike walked her to the third cottage and unlocked the door.

"What are these places?" Jess asked as she stepped inside. They were all the same—the main room had a bed and a tiny kitchenette with a small bathroom off to the side.

"The club uses them for different things, but I just wanted the privacy," he said.

She looked around the room. "It's surprisingly pretty."

"All Bunny," Ike said, following Jess's gaze. "She remodeled them a few years back. Wanted to make them nice for the people we guard who need to stay here. Apparently this is country chic."

Jess smiled. "It's very un-biker-like."

"Tell me about it." He stepped up close to her and cupped her face in his hands. "But I don't want to talk about that. I want to talk about us."

"Us," she said. "But what about everything you said? What about—"

Ike kissed her. "I was an asshole and a coward. And I'm really fucking sorry." He searched her pretty brown eyes. "I never realized how closed off I kept myself until you almost got abducted and we spent this week together. Both of which shoved my feelings right in front of my face and forced me to examine them. I didn't realize how much I'd been using the excuse of Lana's death to avoid opening myself up to getting hurt again. I didn't realize how much I was allowing those wounds to turn me into someone I don't want to be. And then nearly losing Jeremy on top of it all." He shook his head and swallowed the knot lodged in his throat. "Life can be lost in an instant. I've seen it, and I know you have, too. The idea that I could've lost you without you ever knowing…"

"Knowing what?" she whispered.

He took a leap of faith and hoped like hell that she leapt with him. "I love you, Jessica, and I want you in my life. I think I've wanted you since the day we met, and every day in between. I convinced myself that I didn't deserve you and wouldn't be good for you and that, once you knew about how I'd failed Lana, you wouldn't want me anyway. And, Jesus, the fact that I'm in this MC is a whole other issue that I—"

Jess grasped the back of his head and pulled him down for a kiss.

Was that a good sign? That had to be a good sign, right? Jesus, he was turning into a pathetic sap again. But it would be worth it if Jess wanted him the way he wanted her.

"Stop talking," she whispered against his lips.

"Why?" he said, dread snaking into his gut.

"Because if you keep talking then I can't tell you that I love you, too."

Warm, healing relief speared through him, her love gently stitching up wounds he'd carried for so long. "Fuck, yes. I'm so damn glad," he groaned, taking her in his arms and kissing her for everything he was worth. And while the heat was there, that wasn't all he felt between them. There was something deeper, something closer, something that filled the cold, lonely places inside him. Someone knew all the worst things about him and loved him anyway. Nothing meant more than that. Nothing felt more redemptive than that. "You need to know," he said, breaking the kiss. "I didn't mean any of that bullshit I said the other night. Being with you meant everything to me. Means everything to me."

"I know," she said, fingers stroking over his face. "I didn't mean what I said either. I'd dreamed of being with you so many times, but I never thought it would happen. I could've lived on those memories for the rest of my life if I had to."

"Well, you don't have to," he said, claiming her mouth in another hot kiss. "Not ever." He walked her back one step, then another, until her legs came up against the bed. "I want you, Jess. And I fucking need you so much. Right now."

* * * *

Jess couldn't believe this was happening. She couldn't believe that her world had gone from nearly imploding to giving her everything she'd ever wanted—all in the space of the same day. "I want you, too," she said. "And I love you so much."

"God, Jess," he rasped as he kissed her neck and slowly peeled off her clothing.

When she sat naked on the edge of the bed, Ike stood in front of her and tugged his shirt over his head. He kicked off his boots and stripped off his jeans. She drank him in with her eyes. His incredible height. The cut of his muscles. The huge black tribal on his arm, a red rose with petals that wilted and turned black on the side of his ribs, and so many other pieces she wanted to explore and ask him about, one by one.

The cock jutting out from his body.

Jess licked her lips. "Come here." When he stepped within reach, she grasped his hips and sank to her knees, her back against the bottom of the bed.

"Jess," he whispered, stroking his hand over her braided hair.

She bathed the length of his cock with her tongue and then sucked him in deep.

"Fuck," he rasped, dark eyes blazing down at her.

God, he was a thrilling mouthful. Heavy on her tongue. Thick in her mouth. Head meeting the back of her throat. Just the way she liked it.

She settled into a rhythm, swallowing as much of him as she could take, then pushing just a little further, and then sucking him hard on a fast withdraw. His groans and cursed words of praise were the sweetest fucking reward and turned her on so much that she reached a hand between her legs.

"Yeah, play with that pussy," Ike said. "Does sucking my cock make you wet?"

"Mmhmm," she moaned as her fingers circled her clit.

"Jesus, that's hot, Jess." A big hand curled around the back of her head. "So hot," he whispered. "I want to fuck your mouth so bad."

He took control of the movements, the strokes of his hips driving his cock deep into her mouth. His hand on her head giving him leverage, allowing him to move her how he wanted. She freaking loved it.

On a groan, Ike popped free of her lips. He lifted her from the floor like she weighed nothing and pushed her back on the bed. Like a predator stalking his prey, he crawled up the bed until he covered her, his hips settling between her spread thighs. "I wanna see you this time," he said. He took his cock in hand and smacked the head against her clit, and then he was sinking in, filling her, making her his.

Jess didn't really understand what he meant by the words until he started fucking her. But as he stared into her eyes and studied her face, and peered down between their bodies to watch himself moving inside her, she realized that between having sex in the dark that first night, and Ike taking her from behind the night before, she'd never actually seen his face during sex. And, holy crap, the way this man wore pleasure was so fucking sexy. He kissed her again and again, spilling words of encouragement and ecstasy into the space between their mouths. Though they'd kissed before, they hadn't done it while having sex, either time. And Ike had a particular skill at mimicking with his tongue what he was doing with his cock. God, he was a good freaking kisser.

He pulled back and met her gaze, and his eyes were absolutely on fire. "Love you so fucking much," he said, hips picking up speed, gaining urgency. He grabbed one of her knees and pushed it up, allowing him to sink deeper.

"I love you, too," she said.

He gripped her thigh hard. His hips ground and snapped against her pussy. His kisses became more aggressive, sucking, biting, tugging her lips. His other hand slid into her hair, pulling and guiding her head how he wanted it. But in addition to this roughness she craved, there was an intimacy about this act Jess had never before experienced. Staring into the eyes of her lover and whispering the depths of her emotions weren't things she'd ever done before. And it made the sex so much more than she ever knew it could be.

Healing. Bonding. Absolutely life-giving.

And it was all because of Ike.

"Oh, my God, Ike. So good," she rasped.

"Tell me what you need," he said, shifting to grind more delicious friction against her clit.

Jess moaned. "You. Just you."

"Fuck. That's right. Sounds so good." He gripped her harder and moved faster, his hips drilling his cock into her until she was gasping, moaning, coming so hard she could barely breathe. "Yes, yes," he grunted, and then he was coming too. Shooting inside her with the most fascinatingly erotic expression on his face—eyes closed, mouth open, forehead furrowed like he was almost in pain. Jesus, her man was hot.

When their bodies finally settled, Ike kissed her again. He was still deep inside her, and Jess wasn't in any hurry for him to leave. Not ever.

"I don't know what the future holds, Jess. But I know that right here is where I'm supposed to be. With you." He looked at her with such adoration on his face.

Jess hooked her ankles around his back, feeling the truth of his sentiment deep inside her. "That's all you gotta know, Ike. We'll work the rest out together." Ike nodded and kissed her, and despite all the uncertainty that still existed in their lives, Jess knew that she had a man and a love to hold onto for the rest of her life. And Ike was right. That was everything.

* * * *

Also from 1001 Dark Nights and Laura Kaye, discover Hard to Serve.

About Laura Kaye

Laura is the New York Times and USA Today bestselling author of over twenty books in contemporary and paranormal romance and romantic suspense. Laura's Hard Ink series has won many awards, including the RT Reviewers' Choice Award for Best Romance Suspense of 2014 for Hard As You Can. Her upcoming Raven Riders series debuts in April 2016. Growing up, Laura's large extended family believed in the supernatural, and family lore involving angels, ghosts, and evil-eye curses cemented in Laura a life-long fascination with storytelling and all things paranormal. She lives in Maryland with her husband, two daughters, and cute-but-bad dog, and appreciates her view of the Chesapeake Bay every day. Learn more at www.LauraKayeAuthor.com.

Also from Laura Kaye

The Hard Ink Series:
Hard As It Gets
Hard As You Can
Hard to Hold On To
Hard to Come By
Hard to Be Good
Hard to Let Go
Hard Ever After (1/19/16)

Hard to Let Go
A Hard Ink Novel
By Laura Kaye
Now Available!

Beckett Murda hates to dwell on the past. But his investigation into the ambush that killed half his Special Forces team and ended his Army career gives him little choice. Just when his team learns how powerful their enemies are, hard-ass Beckett encounters his biggest complication yet--a seductive, feisty Katherine Rixey.

A tough, stubborn prosecutor, Kat visits her brothers' Hard Ink Tattoo shop following a bad break-up--and finds herself staring down the barrel of a stranger's gun. Beckett is hard-bodied and sexy as hell, but he's also the most infuriating man ever. Worse, Kat's brothers are at war with the criminals her office is investigating. When Kat joins the fight, she lands straight in Beckett's sights . . . and in his arms. Not to mention their enemies' crosshairs.

Now Beckett and Kat must set aside their differences to work together, because the only thing sweeter than justice is finding love and never letting go.

* * * *

Time slowed and Kat's heart raced as Beckett slowly leaned in.

By the time her mind shoved through the haze of surprise and lust to react, his lips were brushing hers.

Just a brush of skin on skin, amazingly soft and tentative. So surprising given his size.

The world froze for a long moment, but then that little bit of contact set off a flash fire in Kat's blood. And apparently Beckett's, too.

Because the kiss turned instantly and blisteringly devouring. On a groan, his tongue invaded her mouth, and she sucked him in deep. Their hands pulled one another closer and their bodies collided. Their height differentiation was so great that Kat had to push onto her tiptoes and Beckett had to lean way down. Kat wasn't sure if she pulled herself up or Beckett lifted her, but the next thing she knew her legs were wrapped around his hips and his hands gripped her ass.

They stumbled into her room and Beckett kicked the door shut behind them. Kat moaned as her back came up against the wall and his erection ground against her core.

With his tongue in her mouth and his hands roaming her body and his hips pressing maddeningly against the center of her need, Kat was possibly more overwhelmed than she'd ever been in her life. Beckett Murda was all she felt, saw, smelled, tasted. Her mind was on a repeating track of Wait … wait … omigod … what's happening? But her body had totally left the station.

Whatever small part of her wanted to pull back or slow down gave way to the more urgent need to let go. Let go of worrying about Cole. Let go of the fear she felt for her brothers. Let go of the horrible images she carried in her mind of the Hard Ink roof collapsing and Jeremy going down with it, which was the scariest thing she'd ever seen.

Not to mention the conversation she needed to have, the one that would force her to break confidentialities and put her job at risk.

So she did. Kat let it all go in favor of letting Beckett pull her under the waves with him.

She plowed her fingers into his hair, which was just long enough to grip and tug, and squeezed her legs around his hips, bringing them closer. Creating more of that delicious friction. He groaned low in his throat, and the sound reverberated into her belly, causing her to grind her hips forward against him.

Wait …wait…wait…turned into want…want…want…

"Jesus, want you, too," he growled. He kissed and licked at her jaw, her ear, her neck.

"Beckett," she rasped as he trailed little bites down the side of her throat. She bowed off the wall, thrusting against him. And, God, he was deliciously hard and thick between her legs.

Suddenly, she wanted to know: Just. How. Thick.

Stroke of Midnight
A Midnight Breed Novella
By Lara Adrian

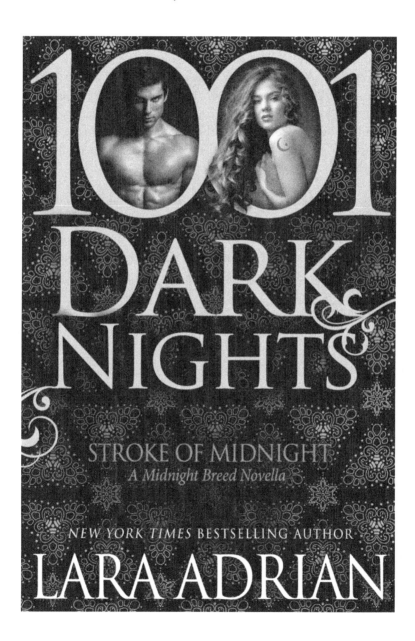

Acknowledgments

I am thrilled to be part of the 1001 Dark Nights collection for a second time with this novella in my Midnight Breed vampire romance series. My thanks to the awesome and endlessly creative Liz Berry, MJ Rose, Jillian Stein, and everyone else working behind the scenes at Evil Eye Concepts to make the project a success. Big hugs to my fellow 1001 Dark Nights authors as well. Every year, the lineup gets more impressive and the depth of talent more amazing. I'm grateful for your support and honored to call so many of you my friends.

And I have to send out lots of love and heartfelt thanks to my readers. I can't tell you what it means to me that you continue to embrace my characters and my work. I hope you have fun reading this new Midnight Breed adventure, and I hope you enjoy all the rest still to come!

With love,

Lara Adrian

CHAPTER 1

Screams shot up from one of the many narrow, cobbled alleyways in the heart of Rome's quaint old Trastevere ward. The shrieks of mortal terror pierced the night as effectively as a blade.

Or, rather, a pair of razor-sharp fangs.

Like the ones on the gang of lethal predators who'd shredded the throat of a human civilian in a dance club across the city only minutes ago.

Shit. Jehan swung an urgent look over his shoulder to the two other Breed warriors currently on foot behind him. "They're getting away."

He and his teammates from the Order's Rome command center had been in pursuit of the four blood-thirsty Rogues since their patrol had been alerted to the killing at the club. They had contained the situation before any of the other humans had realized what was going on, but their mission wouldn't be over until they ashed the feral members of their own race.

"Split up," he told his men. "Damn it, we can't lose them! Close in from all sides."

His comrade and good friend, Savage, grinned and gave a nod of his blond head before veering right to take one of the other winding alleys on Jehan's command. The other warrior, a hulking, shaved-head menace called Trygg, made no acknowledgment to his team leader before vanishing into the darkness like a wraith to carry out the order.

Jehan sped like an arrow through the tight artery of the ancient street ahead of him, dodging slow-moving compact cars and taxis who were getting nowhere fast in the district that was clogged with tourists and club-hoppers even as the hour crept close to midnight.

The public out and about tonight was a mix of human and Breed civilians, something that would have been unheard of just twenty years ago, before the Breed's existence had been revealed to mankind.

Now, in cities around the world, the two populations lived together openly. They worked together. Governed together. But their hard-won peace was fragile. All it might take was one horrific killing—like the one earlier tonight—to set off a global panic.

While every Breed warrior of the Order had pledged his blood and breath to prevent that from happening, others among mankind and the Breed were secretly—and not-so-secretly—instigating war.

Tonight's Rogue attack had the stamp of conspiracy all over it. And it wasn't the first. During the past few nights there had been a handful of others, in Rome and elsewhere in Europe. While it wasn't unusual for one of Jehan's kind to become irreversibly addicted to blood, the spate of recent slayings in all-too-public places by Rogues torqued up on some kind of Bloodlust-inducing narcotic had fingers pointing to the terror group called Opus Nostrum.

Just a few days ago, the Order had scored a staggering hit on Opus, taking out its newest leader, who'd been headquartered in Ireland. The cabal was hobbled for now, but its hidden members were many and their machinations seemed to know no bounds. They and all who served them had to be stopped, or the consequences were certain to be catastrophic.

Jehan was a blur of motion as he leapt over the hood of a standing taxi to vault himself up onto the tiled rooftops above the thick congestion on the streets.

His heavy black patrol boots made no sound as he traveled with preternatural stealth and speed over the uneven terrain of the buildings. He jumped from one rooftop to the next, following his instincts—and the trace, metallic scent of fresh blood that floated up on the night breeze as the Rogue attempted to escape his pursuers.

He lived for this kind of action. The adrenaline rush. The thrill of the chase. The conviction that came from doing something with real purpose, something that would have true and lasting impact on his world.

A far cry from the posh wealth and useless decadence he'd been born into with his family in Morocco.

That old life was still trying to call him back, even though he hadn't stepped foot on his homeland's soil for more than a decade.

It had been twelve months and a day since he'd received the message from his father. Jehan knew what that meant, and he couldn't pretend he hadn't heard every tick of the damned countdown clock in the time since.

With a growl, he pushed aside reminders of the obligation he'd been pointedly ignoring. Right now, his focus was better spent on the more urgent mission in front of him.

Down below in a twisting alleyway, Jehan spied one of the fleeing Rogues. Fingers gripping the handle of one of his titanium blades, he drew the weapon and let it fly. Direct hit. The dagger nailed the Rogue in the center of his spine, dropping him in his tracks.

Ordinarily, it took more than that to disable one of the Breed, but the titanium was toxic to vampires who'd gone Rogue, and as corrosive as acid to their diseased bodies. In minutes or less, the corpse would be nothing but ashes in the street.

Jehan didn't wait to see the disintegration happen. As he continued his dash across the rooftops, he spotted Trygg gaining ground on one of the remaining Rogues. The big warrior took the escaping vampire down in a flash of movement. The Rogue howled, then abruptly fell silent when Trygg severed its head with a slice of his blade.

Two down. Two to go.

Make that one left to go. Jehan's acute hearing picked up sounds of a brief struggle as Savage caught up to his quarry on a different stretch of cobblestones and delivered a killing strike of titanium.

Jehan leapt to another roof, racing deeper into the ancient district of the city. His battle instincts heightened as he homed in on the last of the fleeing Rogues. The vampire made a crucial mistake, turning into an alleyway with no exit. A literal dead end.

Jehan sailed off the edge of the rooftop and dropped to the

cobbled street behind the Rogue, cutting off any hope of his escape. An instant later, Savage emerged from out of the shadows, just as the feral vampire spun around and realized he had nowhere left to run.

The big male faced the two Order warriors. His fangs dripped with blood and sticky saliva. His transformed eyes glowed bright amber, the pupils fixed and narrowed to thin vertical slits in the center of all that fiery light. His jaw hung open as he roared, insane with Bloodlust and ready to attack.

Jehan didn't allow him the chance.

He threw his dagger without mercy or warning. The titanium blade glinted in the moonlight as the weapon sliced through the distance and struck its mark, burying to the hilt in the center of the Rogue's chest.

The vampire roared in agony, then collapsed in a heap on the cobbles as the poisonous metal began to devour him.

When the process had finished, Jehan strode over to retrieve his weapon from the ashes.

Savage blew out a low curse behind him. "Four Breed males gone Rogue in the same city on the same night? No one's seen those kind of numbers in the past twenty years."

Jehan nodded. He'd been a youth at that time, but more than old enough to remember firsthand. "Let's hope we never see bloodshed again like we did back then, Sav."

And all the more reason to take Opus Nostrum out at the root. For Jehan, a Breed male who'd spent a lot of his privileged life in pursuit of one pleasure or another, he couldn't think of any higher calling than his place among the Order.

He cleaned his dagger and sheathed it on the weapons belt of his black patrol fatigues. "Come on," he said to Savage. "I saw Trygg ash one of these four a few blocks back. Let's go find him and make sure we don't have any witnesses in need of a mind-scrub before we report back to Commander Archer at headquarters."

They pivoted to leave the alley together—only to find they were no longer alone there.

Another Breed male stood at the mouth of the narrow passage. Dark-eyed, with a trimmed black beard around the grim line of his mouth, the vampire was dressed in a black silk tunic over loose black pants tucked into gleaming black leather boots that rose nearly to his knees.

The only color he wore was a striped sash of vibrant, saffron-and-cerulean silk tied loosely around his waist. Family colors. Formal colors, reserved for the solemnest of old traditions.

Jehan couldn't bite back his low, uttered curse.

Beside him in the alleyway, Savage moved his fingers toward his array of weapons.

"It's all right." Jehan stayed his comrade's hand with a pointed shake of his head. "Naveen is my father's emissary."

In response, the dark-haired male inclined his head. "Greetings, Prince Jehan, noble eldest son of Rahim, the just and honorable king of the Mafakhir tribe."

The courtly bow that followed set Jehan's teeth and fangs on edge almost as much as his official address. From within the folds of his tunic, Naveen withdrew a sealed piece of parchment. The royal messenger held it out to Jehan in sober, expectant silence.

A stamped, red wax seal rode the back of the official missive...just like the one Jehan had received in this same manner a year ago.

A year and a day ago, he mentally amended.

For a moment, Jehan just stood there, unmoving.

But he knew Naveen had been sent with specific orders to deliver the sealed message, and it would dishonor the male deeply if he failed in that mission.

Jehan stepped forward and took the stiff, folded parchment from Naveen's outstretched hand. As soon as it was in Jehan's possession, the royal messenger pivoted and strode back into the darkness without another word.

In the silence that followed, Savage gaped. "What the fuck was that all about?"

"Family business. It's not important." Jehan slipped the document into the waistband of his pants without opening it.

"It sure as hell looked important to that guy." When Jehan started walking out of the alley, Sav matched his clipped pace. "What is it? Some kind of royal subpoena?"

Jehan grunted. "Something like that."

"Aren't you going to read it?"

Jehan shrugged. "There's no need. I know what it says."

Sav arched a blond brow. "Yeah, but I don't."

To satisfy his friend's curiosity, Jehan retrieved the sealed message and passed it over to him. "Go ahead."

Sav broke the seal and unfolded the parchment, reading as he and Jehan turned down another narrow street. "It says someone died. A mated couple, killed together in a plane crash a year ago."

Jehan nodded grimly, already well aware of the couple's tragic demise. News of their deaths had been the reason for the first official notice he'd received from his father.

Savage read on. "This says the couple—a Breed male from the Mafakhir tribe and a Breedmate from another tribe, the Sanhaja, had been blood-bonded as part of a peace pact between the families."

Jehan grunted in acknowledgment. The pact had been in place for centuries, the result of an unfortunate chain of events that had spawned a bloody conflict between his family and their closest neighbors, the Sanhajas. After enough blood had been spilled on both sides, a truce was finally declared. A truce that was cemented with blood spilled by another means.

An eternal bond, shared between a male from Jehan's line and a Breedmate from the rival tribe.

So long as the two families were bound together by blood, there had been peace. The pact had never been broken. The couple who perished in the plane crash had been the sole link between the families in the modern age. With their deaths, the pact was in limbo until a new couple came together to revive the bond.

Savage had apparently just gotten to the part of the message Jehan had been dreading for the past twelve months. "It says here that in accordance with the terms of that pact, if the blood bond is severed and no other couple elects to carry it forward within the term of a year and a day, then the eldest unmated son of the eldest Breed male of the Mafakhir tribe and the unmated Breedmate nearest the age of thirty from the Sanhaja tribe shall..."

Sav's long stride began to slow, then it stopped altogether. He swiveled his head in Jehan's direction. "Holy shit. Are you kidding me? You're being drafted to go home to Morocco and take a mate?"

A scowl furrowed deep into his brow at the very thought. "According to ritual, I am."

His comrade let out a bark of a laugh. "Well, shit.

Congratulations, Your Highness. This is one lottery I'm happy as hell I won't be winning."

Jehan grumbled a curse in reply. Although he didn't find much humor in the situation, his friend seemed annoyingly amused.

Sav was still chuckling as they resumed their march up the alleyway. "When is this joyous occasion supposed to take place?"

"Tomorrow," Jehan muttered.

There was a period of handfasting with the female in question, but the details of the whole process were murky. In truth, he'd never paid much attention to the fine print of the pact because he hadn't imagined there would be a need to know.

He didn't really expect he needed to understand it now either, as he had no intention of participating in the antiquated exercise. But like it or not, he respected his father too much to disgrace him or the family by refusing to respond to their summons.

So it seemed he had little choice but to return to the family Darkhaven in Morocco and deliver his regrets in person.

He could only hope his father might respect his prodigal eldest son enough to free him from this ridiculous obligation and the unwanted shackle that awaited him at the end of it.

CHAPTER 2

Eighteen hours later and fresh off his flight to Casablanca, Jehan sat in the passenger seat of his younger brother's glossy black Lamborghini as it sped toward the Mafakhir family Darkhaven about an hour outside the city.

"Father didn't think you'd come." Marcel glanced at Jehan briefly, his forearm slung casually over the steering wheel as the sleek Aventador ate up the moonlit stretch of highway, prowling past other vehicles as if they were standing still. "I have to admit, I wasn't sure you'd actually show up either. Only Mother seemed confident you wouldn't just tear up the message and send it back home with Naveen as confetti."

"I didn't realize that was an option."

"Very funny," Marcel replied with another sidelong look.

Jehan turned his attention to the darkened desert landscape outside the window. He'd been questioning his sanity in answering the family summons even before he'd left Rome.

His Order team commander, Lazaro Archer, hadn't been enthused to hear about the obligation either, especially when things were heating up against Opus Nostrum and a hundred other pressing concerns. Jehan had assured Lazaro that the unplanned leave was merely a formality and that he'd be back on patrol as quickly as possible—without the burden of an unwanted Breedmate in tow.

Marcel maneuvered around a small convoy of humanitarian supply trucks, no doubt on their way to one of the many remote villages or refugee camps that had existed in this part of the world for centuries. Once the road opened up, he buried the gas pedal again.

If only they were heading away from the family compound at breakneck speed, rather than toward it.

"Mother's had the entire Darkhaven buzzing with plans and arrangements ever since you called last night." Marcel spoke over the deep snarl of the engine. "I can't remember the last time I've seen her so excited."

Jehan groaned. "I'm here, but that doesn't mean I intend to go through with any of this."

"What?" Jehan looked over and found his only sibling's face slack with incredulity. His light blue eyes, so like Jehan's own—a color inherited from their French beauty of a mother—were wide under Marcel's tousled crown of brown waves. "You have to go through with it. There's no blood bond between the Mafakhirs and the Sanhajas anymore. Not since our cousin and his Breedmate died a year ago."

When Jehan didn't immediately acknowledge the severity of the problem, his brother frowned. "If a year and a day should pass without a natural mating occurring between the families, the terms of the pact specifically state—"

"I know what they state. I also know those terms were written up during a very different time. We don't live in the Middle Ages anymore." *And thank fuck for that,* he mentally amended. "The pact is a relic that needs to be retired. Hopefully it won't take too much convincing to make our father understand that."

Marcel went quiet as they veered off the highway and set a course for the rambling stretch of desert acreage that comprised their family's Darkhaven property. In a few short minutes, they turned onto the private road.

The family lands were lush and expansive. Thick clusters of palm trees spiked black against the night sky, small oases amid the vast spread of dark, silken sand. Up ahead was the iron gate and tall brick perimeter wall that secured the massive compound where Jehan had grown up.

Even before they approached the luxurious Darkhaven, his feet twitched inside his boots with the urge to run.

While they paused outside the gate and waited to be admitted inside, Marcel pivoted in his seat toward Jehan. His youthful, twenty-four-year-old face was solemn. "The pact has never been broken. You know that, right? Not once in all of the six-and-a-half centuries it's been in place. It's not a relic. It's tradition. That kind of thing may not be sacred to you, but it is to our parents. It's sacred to the Sanhajas too."

His brother was so earnest, maybe there was another way to dodge this bullet. "If you feel that strongly about it, why don't you pick up the torch instead? Take my place and I can turn around right now and go back to my work with the Order."

"Ohh, no." He vigorously shook his head. "Even if I wanted to—which I don't—without another mated couple occurring naturally between our families, the pact calls for the eldest son of the eldest male of our line. That means you. Besides, there are worse fates. Seraphina Sanhaja is a gorgeous woman."

Seraphina. It was the first time he'd heard the name of his intended. A silken, exotic name. Just the sound of it made Jehan's blood course a bit hotter in his veins. He dismissed the sensation with a sharp sigh as he stared at his brother. He couldn't deny that a part of him was intrigued to know more. "You've seen her?"

Marcel nodded. "She and her sister, Leila, are both stunning."

Not surprising, considering they were Breedmates. Although they didn't have the vampiric traits of Jehan's kind, the half-human, half-Atlantean females called Breedmates were flawless beauties without exception. His Paris-born mother was testament to that. As was Lazaro Archer's flame-haired Breedmate back in Rome, Melena.

"So, what's wrong with her, then?" Jehan murmured. "Let me guess. She's a miserable, bickering shrew? Or is it worse, a meek little mouse who's afraid of her own shadow?"

"She's neither." Marcel grinned as he eased the Lamborghini through the opened gates. "She's lovely, Jehan. You'll see for yourself soon enough."

"Not if I have anything to say about that." Crossing his arms, he sat back in the buttery soft leather seat. "I have a return flight to Rome tomorrow. I figure that gives me plenty of time to convey my regrets to our parents and get the hell out of here."

"You can't do that. Everything is already in motion. I told you, arrangements were made right after you called."

Jehan cursed under his breath. "If I'd realized our parents would charge forward without asking me, I could've saved everyone the effort. I should've told them over the phone that I wasn't interested in any of this and stayed put in Rome. Unfortunately, it's too late for that now. Whatever arrangements have been made will need to be canceled."

"I don't think you understand, brother." Marcel slowed the car as they rolled onto the half-moon drive of the Darkhaven's impressive arched entrance. "The handfast begins tomorrow. Which means the families assemble for the official meet-and-greet tonight. There will be formal introductions, followed by the traditional garden walk at midnight, and the turning of the hourglass to mark the celebratory commencement and the start of the handfast period."

Jehan's unfamiliarity with the process must have been as apparent as his disinterest. Marcel frowned at him. "You don't have any idea what I'm talking about, do you? For fuck's sake, the pact's been in place for centuries, but you never took the time to study the terms?"

"I've been busy."

Marcel's lips quirked at the droll reply, but it was clear that he took the pact seriously. Apparently everyone did, aside from Jehan.

For an instant, he felt a pang of loss for his absence all these years. It had been his choice to leave, his choice to make his own way in the world instead of being satisfied with the privileged, if stifling, one he'd been handed at birth. He'd yearned more for adventure than tradition, and supposed he always would.

"So, this handfast entails what, exactly?"

"A period of eight nights, spent together in seclusion. No visitors, no communication with the outside world in any form. Just the two of you, alone at the oasis retreat on the border of our lands and the Sanhajas'."

"In other words, imprisonment for a week and a day with a female who may or may not be a willing party to this whole forced seduction ritual. Followed by what—a public blood bond encouraged at sword point?"

"Forced seduction? Public blood bond?" Marcel gaped at him as if he'd lost his mind. "The handfast is all about consent, Jehan. Touch Seraphina against her wishes and her family has the right to take your head. Drink her blood without her permission and no one would balk if the Sanhajas took out their revenge on the entire Mafakhir tribe. This is serious shit."

Not to mention, archaic. Even though he had no plans to touch Seraphina Sanhaja or any other female who wasn't of his own choosing, Jehan's curiosity was piqued. "I thought the whole point of the pact was to seal the peace between our two families with a blood bond."

"It is," Marcel said. "But only if the handfast is successful."

"Meaning?"

"There has to be a mutual agreement. There has to be love. If there's no desire to bond as a mated couple at the end of the handfast, the couple is free to go their separate ways and the pact then moves on to the next pair in line."

"So, there's an out clause?" Jehan's brows rose in surprise. "That's the best news I've heard all night."

His brother released a frustrated-sounding breath. "I don't know why I'm bothering to explain any of this to you. The terms will be spelled out in detail at the ceremony tomorrow night."

The ceremony Jehan had no intention of attending.

Marcel parked in front of the opulent estate and killed the engine. The Aventador's scissor doors lifted upward and the two Breed males climbed out.

As they began to ascend the wide, polished stone steps leading to the Darkhaven's entrance, Jehan asked, "Who's the next pair in line after Seraphina and me?"

"That would be the Breedmate next nearest the age of thirty in the Sanhaja family, and the unmated eldest son of the second-eldest Breed male in our line. You remember our cousin, Fariq."

Jehan mentally recoiled. "Fariq, who prided himself on his collection of dead insects and snakes as a boy?"

Marcel chuckled. "He's not nicknamed Renfield for nothing."

And Jehan couldn't help but feel guilty that his refusal of the pact would mean some unfortunate Breedmate would eventually have to spend eight nights alone with the repulsive male.

But he didn't feel guilty enough to let the farce continue. He had to halt the whole thing before it went any further.

"Father's waiting for you in his study," Marcel told him as they reached the top. "Everyone else is in the main salon, where the formal introductions will be made."

Alarm shot through him at that last announcement. Jehan grabbed his brother's muscled arm. "Everyone else?"

"Mother and the Sanhajas. And Seraphina, of course."

Ah, fuck. If he thought this was bad enough before he stepped off the plane tonight, the situation had just nose-dived into a disaster zone. "They're here right now? All of them?"

"That's what I've been telling you. Everything is already in motion and ready to begin. We were only waiting for you to arrive, brother."

CHAPTER 3

The sound of deep male voices carried from the foyer. Until that moment, the small gathering inside the Darkhaven's elegant salon had been engaged in pleasant chatter about the weather and a dozen other light subjects. But at the low rumble of muffled conversation somewhere outside the gilded walls, a palpable spike of anticipation pierced the atmosphere in the room.

"Ah, my sons have finally arrived." Beautiful and poised, Simone Mafakhir smiled from her seat on a silk divan, her sky blue eyes lit with excitement. "I know Jehan will be delighted to meet you, Seraphina."

Sera's mouth was suddenly too dry to speak, but she gave a polite nod and returned the brunette Breedmate's warm smile.

"Seraphina's talked of little else all day," her mother said, giving Sera's hand a pat from her seat beside her on a velvet sofa opposite Simone. "She's been full of curiosity about Jehan ever since she arrived back home this morning."

On the other side of Sera, her blonde, twenty-two-year-old sister, Leila, barely stifled a giggle.

It was true. Sera had been full of questions since she'd been called home by her parents. She still didn't know much about Jehan, other than the fact that he'd flown in tonight from Rome, where he'd been living for many years. And that he'd come because he had been summoned to fulfill his role in the ancient handfasting pact that had existed between their families for half a dozen centuries.

The same as she had.

That is, if she managed to make it through the evening without bolting for the nearest escape.

She pressed the back of her hand to her forehead, which had gone suddenly clammy. Her heart was racing, and her lungs felt as if they were suddenly caught in a vise.

She stood up, not quite steady on the high heels she wasn't accustomed to wearing. The flouncy, blush-pink dress she'd borrowed from Leila on her sister's insistence swayed around her knees as she wobbled, lightheaded and fighting the wave of nausea that rose up on her.

"Would it be possible to, um...freshen up for a moment?"

"Yes, of course," Simone replied. "There's a powder room just down the hall."

Her parents both looked at her in genuine concern. "Are you all right, darling?" her mother asked.

"Yes." Sera gave them a weak nod that only made her wooziness worse. "I'm fine, really."

She just needed to get the hell out of there before she passed out or threw up.

Leila stood and grabbed her elbow. "I'll go with you."

They hurried out of the room together, Sera practically leaving her sister in her wake. Once safely enclosed in the large powder room, Sera sagged against the back of the door.

"What on earth is wrong with you?" Leila whispered.

Sera swallowed back a building scream. "I can't do this. I thought maybe I could—for our parents, since it's obviously so important to them—but I can't. I mean, this whole situation...the pact, the handfasting? It's insane, right? I never should have agreed to any of this."

It was all happening too quickly. Yesterday morning, an e-mail from her parents had reached her at the remote outpost where she'd been working. The message had been short and cryptic, telling her that she was needed at home immediately.

Terrified with concern, she'd dropped everything and raced back—only to learn that the emergency requiring her presence was a musty old agreement that would send her away with a complete stranger. A Breed male who may not understand or care that her carotid wasn't up for grabs, regardless of what the pact between their families might imply.

Oh, God. Her stomach started to spin again. She pressed her hand to her abdomen and took a steadying breath.

She paced the cramped powder room, her voice beginning to rise. "I need to get out of here. I can't do this, Leila. I must've been out of my mind for even considering coming here tonight."

Her sister stared at her patiently, her soft green eyes sympathetic as she let Sera vent. "You're just nervous. I would be too. But I don't think you're crazy for being here. And I don't think the agreement between our families is insane, either." She swept a blonde tendril behind her ear and shrugged. "It's endured all these years for a reason. Actually, I think it's kind of romantic."

"Romantic?" Sera scoffed. "What's romantic about a truce struck after years of bloodshed resulting from the kidnap of a virgin Breedmate from our tribe by a barbarian Breed male from theirs six-hundred years ago?"

Leila let out a sigh. "Things were different back then. And it's romantic because they fell in love."

Sera arched her brows in challenge. "Tragic, because despite their blood bond, they both died in the end and set off a long, violent war."

Sera knew the whole, tragic story as well as her sister did. It was practically legend in the Sanhaja family. And if she was being honest, there was a part of her that ached for that long-dead couple and their doomed love.

But it didn't change the fact that centuries later, here she was, standing in a locked bathroom in a borrowed dress and high-heeled sandals, while just down the hall, a Breed male she'd never even met before was expecting her to go away with him for eight long nights—all in their parents' shared hopes that they might come back madly in love and bound by blood for eternity.

Ridiculous.

Sera shook her head. "It might've been true centuries ago that the best way to guarantee peace was to turn an enemy into family," she conceded. "But that was then and this is now. There hasn't been conflict between the Mafakhirs and our family for decades."

Leila tilted her head. "And how do you know that's not because the pact was in place all that time? Since it first began, there's never been a time when there wasn't at least one mated pair between our families. Until now. What if the pact really is the only thing keeping the peace? It's never been broken or tested, Sera. Do you really want to be the first one to try?"

For a moment, hearing her sister's emphatic reply, Seraphina almost bought into the whole myth. At twenty-seven, she was a practical, independent woman who knew her own mind as well as her own worth, but there was a small part of her—maybe a part of every woman—who still wanted to believe in fairy tales and romance stories.

She wanted to believe in eternal love and happy endings, but that's not what awaited her on the other side of the powder room door.

"The pact isn't magic. And the handfast isn't romantic. It's all a bunch of silly, outdated nonsense."

"Well, call it what you will," Leila murmured. "I think it's charming."

"I doubt you'd be so enthusiastic if you were the one being yanked out of your world and all the things that matter to you, only to be dropped into some strange male's lap as his captive plaything." Sera considered her dreamy-eyed younger sister. "Or maybe you would."

Leila laughed and shook her head. "The handfast is only for a week. And you won't be dropped into anyone's lap or held against your will. You're meant to get to know each other away from the distractions of the outside world. That's all. Handfasting at the oasis retreat is symbolic more than anything else. Besides, I can think of worse things than spending a week in beautiful surroundings, getting to know a handsome Breed male. One who also happens to be a prince."

Sera scoffed. "A prince in name only. The old tribes of this region aren't any more royal than you or me." Which they weren't. Adopted by Omar and Amina Sanhaja as infants from orphanages for the indigent, there was no chance of that. Sera cocked a curious look on her sister. "How do you know Jehan's handsome? I thought you've never met him."

"I haven't. But being Breed, he's sure to have his mother's chestnut brown hair and incredible blue eyes. The same as his brother, Marcel."

Sara rolled her eyes. "Well, I don't care what he looks like and I don't care about his pedigree either. I'm not looking for a mate, and if I was, I certainly wouldn't be going about it this way."

Yet despite all of that—despite her unwillingness to be part of some antiquated agreement that had long outlived its expiration date as far as she was concerned—she knew she couldn't walk away from her obligation to her family.

Honoring the pact was important to her parents, which made it important to her as well.

And there was another, more selfish reason she had finally conceded to come.

Several hundred thousand reasons. The amount of her trust fund, which her father had agreed to release to her early. She would have it all at the end of the week—after her handfast with Jehan Mafakhir was over.

Sera needed that money.

As much as her father loved her, he knew she wouldn't be able to turn away from what he had offered. Not when there was so much she could do with that kind of gift.

That didn't mean she had to like it.

Nor did it mean she had to like Jehan Mafakhir.

In fact, she was determined to avoid him as much as possible for the duration of their confinement together. If she was lucky, maybe they wouldn't even need to speak to each other.

Miserable with the whole idea, she exhaled a slow, defeated sigh. "It's only for eight nights, right?"

Leila nodded, then her eyes went wide at the sound of measured footsteps and deep voices in the hallway. Putting a finger to her lips, she cracked open the door and peered out. She reported to Sera in a hushed whisper. "Jehan just walked into the salon with his father and Marcel. You can't leave him waiting. We have to get out of here right now!"

The bubble of anxiety Sera had been fighting suddenly spiked into hot panic. "So soon? I thought I'd have a few more minutes before—"

"Now, Sera! Let's go!" Grabbing her by the arm, Leila opened the door and ushered her outside. As they moved toward the salon, Leila leaned in close to whisper next to Sera's ear. "And I was right, by the way. He's beyond handsome."

CHAPTER 4

Jehan wasn't sure what had presented the most convincing argument for his consenting to take part in the handfasting: his brother's earnest persuasion on the ride to the Darkhaven, or his father's stoic greeting and his resulting obvious, if unspoken, expectation that his eldest son would shirk his obligation to the family.

If he'd been met with furious demands that he must pick up the mantle of responsibility concerning the pact with the Sanhajas, it would have been the easiest thing for Jehan to pivot on his heels and hoof his way back to Casablanca to catch the earliest flight back to Rome.

But his father hadn't blown up or slammed his fists into his desk when Jehan arrived in his study a few minutes ago to explain that he wanted no part in the duty waiting for him in the salon. Rahim Mafakhir had listened in thoughtful silence. Then he'd simply stood up and walked toward the door of his study without a word.

Not that he'd needed to speak. His lack of reaction spoke volumes.

He'd been anticipating Jehan's refusal.

He'd been fully prepared for his prodigal son to let him and the rest of the family down.

And as much as Jehan had wanted to pretend he was okay with that, the fact was, it had stung.

It had been at that precise moment—his father's strong hand

wrapped around the doorknob, his stern face grim with disappointment—that Jehan had blurted out words he was certain he'd live to regret.

"I'll do it," he'd said. "Eight nights with the Sanhaja female, as the pact requires. Nothing more. Then, after the handfast is over and my duty is fulfilled, I'll go back to Rome and the pact can move on to the next of our kin in line to heed the call."

Now, as Jehan entered the salon with his father and Marcel, he felt a small spark of hope.

She wasn't there. Only his mother and an anxious-looking couple he assumed was Omar and Amina Sanhaja. No sign of the unmated Breedmate he was supposed to formally meet tonight.

Holy shit. Dare he hope the Sanhajas' daughter had called a stop to this farce?

"Here we are!" An exuberant voice sounded brightly from behind him, killing his hope before it had a chance to fully catch fire.

The voice belonged to a leggy blonde with a megawatt smile and pretty, pale green eyes. Attractive. Certainly cheerful and energetic. As far as temporary housemates went, Marcel was right—there were worse sentences he could endure.

The blonde paused to glance behind her, and that was when Jehan realized his error.

"Come on, Seraphina!" She grabbed the hand of a tall, curvy brunette who'd hesitated momentarily just outside the threshold. "Don't be shy. Everyone's waiting for you."

The blonde was lovely, as Marcel had assured him. But her reserved, darker-haired sister was something far more than that.

Blessed with the figure of a goddess and the face of an angel, when she appeared in the doorway, Jehan could barely keep from gaping. He glanced briefly to his brother and met Marcel's *I-told-you-so* grin.

Damn.

Seraphina Sanhaja was, in a word, extraordinary.

Framed by a mane of cascading brown curls, a pair of long-lashed eyes the color of rich sandalwood flecked with gold lifted to meet Jehan's arrested gaze. Her face was heart-shaped and delicate, an exotic artistry of fine bones and smooth, sun-kissed olive skin that glowed with rising pink color as she stared at him.

How this stunning woman had managed to get past the age of twenty without some other Breed male locking her into a blood bond, Jehan couldn't even imagine.

His pulse stirred at the sight of her, sending heat into his veins. Even though he wasn't in the market for a mate, as a hot-blooded Breed male, it was impossible to deny his body's intense reaction to the female. He drew in a slow breath, his acute senses taking in the cinnamon-sweet scent of her and the subtle uptick of her heartbeat as he held her in his unblinking gaze.

For a moment, he was sorry he didn't have any use for tribal laws or ancient pacts that would put Seraphina Sanhaja in his company—better yet, in his bed—for the next eight nights.

Her sister tugged her forward on a light giggle. "Isn't this exciting?"

Where Leila crackled with unbridled enthusiasm, Seraphina was nearly impossible to read. Her lush lips pursed a bit as she made a silent study of him, her expression carefully schooled, inscrutable.

Standing before him, she was reticent and aloof.

Assessing and...*unimpressed?*

Jehan's brows lifted. He didn't want to admit the jab his ego took at her apparent lack of interest in him. With his thick, shoulder-length dark hair, tawny skin and light blue eyes, he'd never been at a loss for female attention.

Oh, hell. What did he care if she didn't like what she saw? The week ahead was going to pass a hell of a lot faster if he didn't have to spend it with a blushing, eyelash-batting Breedmate who couldn't wait to surrender her carotid to him.

Jehan stared her down ruthlessly as the formal introductions were made.

He was still trying to figure her out after what seemed like endless polite, if awkward conversation in the salon. Their parents made pleasant small talk together. Marcel and Leila fell into easy chatter about books and music and current events, both of them clearly striving to bring Jehan and Seraphina into the discussion.

It wasn't working.

Jehan's thoughts were back with his team in Rome. When he'd spoken earlier tonight with Lazaro Archer, he'd learned that rumors were circulating about Opus Nostrum moving weapons across Europe and possibly into Africa.

Even though he was only going to be delayed from his missions with the Order for a week, he already itched to be suited up in his patrol gear and weapons, not stuffed into the white button-down, dark trousers, and gleaming black dress shoes he'd worn from the airport.

As for Seraphina, Jehan got the feeling she was only seconds away from making a break for the nearest exit.

The otherwise cool and collected female jumped when the clock struck twelve. Smiled wanly as her mother erupted into excited applause.

"It's time!" Amina Sanhaja crowed from across the room. "Go on now, you two. Go on!"

As their families began to urge them out of the salon together, Jehan slanted a questioning look on Seraphina.

"The midnight garden stroll," she murmured under her breath, the first thing she'd said to him directly all night. She stared at him as if annoyed that she needed to explain. "It's part of the tradition."

Ah, right. Marcel had mentioned something about that in the car when Jehan was only half-listening. He'd much rather watch Seraphina's mouth explaining it to him again.

She softly cleared her throat. "At midnight, we're supposed to walk together privately to mark the turning of the hourglass and the beginning of our—"

"Sentence?" he prompted wryly.

Surprise arched her fine brows.

Jehan smirked and gestured for her to walk ahead of him. "Please, after you."

With their parents and siblings crowding the salon doorway behind them, he and Seraphina left the room and headed down the hallway, toward a pair of arched glass doors leading out to the moonlit gardens behind the Darkhaven estate.

The night was cool and crisp in the desert, and infinitely dark. Above them stars glittered and a half-moon glowed milky white against an endless black velvet sky.

It might have been romantic, if the woman walking alongside him didn't take each delicate step as if she was being led to the gallows. She glanced behind them for about the sixth time in as many minutes.

"Are they still there?" Jehan asked.

"Yes," she said. "All of them are standing in front of the glass, watching us."

He could fix that. "Come with me."

Taking her elbow in a loose hold, he ducked off the main garden path with her to one of the many winding paths that crisscrossed the manicured topiary and flowering, fragrant hedges.

The sweet perfume of jasmine and roses laced the night air, but it was another scent—cinnamon and something far more exotic— that made him inhale a bit deeper as he brought Seraphina to a more private section of the gardens.

She hung back a few paces, following him almost hitchingly in her strappy high heels. When he glanced over his shoulder, he found her pretty face pinched in a frown. Then she stopped completely and shook her head. "This is far enough."

"Relax, Seraphina. I'm not going to push you into the hibiscus and ravish you."

Her eyes widened for a second, but then her frown narrowed into an affronted scowl. "That's not why I stopped. These shoes...they're killing my feet."

Jehan walked back to her. Eyeing the tall spikes, he exhaled a low curse. "I don't doubt they're killing you. In the right hands, those things could be deadly weapons."

She smiled—a genuine, heart-stopping smile that was there and gone in an instant.

"Hold on to my shoulder."

Her fingers came to rest on him, generating a swift, unexpected electricity in his veins. Jehan tried to ignore the feel of her touch as he reached down and lifted her left foot into his hands. He unfastened the pretty, but impractical, shoe and slipped it off.

Her satisfied sigh as he freed her bare foot went through him even more powerfully than her touch. Gritting his teeth to discourage his fangs from punching out of his gums in heated response, Jehan made quick work of her other shoe, then stepped away from her.

"Better?" His voice had thickened. Along with another part of his anatomy.

"Much better." She was looking at him cautiously as she took the pair of sandals from where they dangled off his fingertips. "Thank you."

"My pleasure." And it was. More than he might have wanted to admit. He cocked his head at her. "How old are you, Seraphina?"

"Excuse me?"

He immediately felt rude for asking, but there was a part of him that wanted to know. Needed to know. "We're supposed to be getting to know each other, aren't we?"

The reminder seemed to calm some of her indignation. "I'm twenty-seven. Why do you want to know?"

"I just wonder why you aren't already mated and blood-bonded. You were raised in a Darkhaven, so you must know many Breed males. If any of the ones I know ever saw you, there'd be at least a hundred of them beating a path to your door."

She stared at him for a moment in uncertain silence, then shrugged. "Maybe I prefer human men."

Shit. He hadn't even considered that. "Do you?"

"To be honest, I haven't given the idea of a blood bond a lot of thought. My life is full and I keep busy enough with other things."

She started walking away from him, her bare feet moving softly, fluidly, along the bricked path. And he couldn't help noticing she hadn't really answered his question.

He strode up next to her. "What kind of things have kept you so busy that you're still unmated and nearing the ripe old age of thirty?"

She scoffed, but there was humor in her tone. "Important things."

"Such as?"

"I volunteer at some of the border camps, taking care of people who've been displaced by wars and other disasters. I guess you could say it's been something of a calling for me."

Well, he hadn't been expecting that. Granted, she didn't seem the type to flutter around in fancy dresses and high-heeled sandals all day, but he also wouldn't have imagined a stunning woman like her spending her time covered in dust and sweat. Or putting herself in harm's way in those turbulent areas that had never known peace, even before the wars between the humans and the Breed.

"What about you, Jehan?"

"What about me?"

"For starters, how old are you?"

"Thirty-three."

She glanced at him. "Younger than I expected. But then it's impossible to guess a Breed male's age. It's always seemed unfair to me that your kind never looks older than thirty, even the Gen Ones who've been around for centuries."

Jehan lifted his shoulder. "A small consolation for the fact that we can never put our faces in the sunlight. Unlike your kind."

"Hm. I guess that's true." She tilted her head at him. "What exactly do you do in Rome?"

"I'm part of the Order. Captain of my unit," he added, not sure why he felt the need to impress her with his elevated rank.

She stopped dead in her tracks again, and something told him it didn't have anything to do with sore feet. A chill rolled off her as Jehan pivoted to look at her. She barked out a brittle laugh and shook her head. "No wonder they didn't tell me anything about you."

"Who?"

"My parents." Her arms crossed rigidly over her chest. "If they'd mentioned you were part of that brutal organization, there's no way in hell I would've agreed to any of this. No matter what leverage they used to try to convince me."

Jehan's suspicions rankled along with his pride. "You have a problem with the Order?"

"I have a problem with cold-blooded killers."

Was she serious? "My brethren and I are not—"

She didn't let him finish. "I've devoted myself—everything I am—to saving lives. You're in the business of taking them." When he exhaled a tight curse and shook his head, she gave him a sharp look. "How many people have you killed?"

"Me personally, or—"

"I think that answers my question." She moved past him and started walking away at a swift clip.

He caught up in a handful of strides. "There's nothing cold-blooded about what the Order does. Are we brutal sometimes? Only when there's no other choice. But we call it justice. We're protectors, not killers."

"Semantics."

"No, it's reality, Seraphina." When she didn't slow her pace, he reached out and caught her arm. She flinched at the contact. He wondered if it was purely out of indignation or the fact that even though a chill had expanded between them, the heat of attraction still sparked to life the instant they touched. Her pulse fluttered at the base of her elegant throat, her heart pounding so hard and fast he could feel it through his fingertips.

His entire body responded to that frantic drumming, his veins heating, his fangs prickling as they elongated behind his closed lips. His cock responded just as hungrily, pressing in demand against the zipper of his trousers.

She pulled out of his grasp. "I can't do this. You need to know that I have no interest in any kind of handfast, and I'm not looking for a blood bond. Especially with you."

Jehan drew back. "You don't want to be part of this because you just found out I belong to the Order?"

Her lush lips compressed into a flat line. "I never wanted to be part of it."

"That makes two of us."

"What?" She gaped at him.

He shook his head. "I only agreed out of obligation. Because I feel I owe it to my family to uphold their traditions, even if they don't mesh with mine."

Her breath rushed out of her. "Oh, thank God!"

She didn't hold back her relief. She sounded like a death row inmate suddenly granted a full pardon, and his pride took another ding to hear the depth of her alleviation. "So, what do we do now, Seraphina? Go back inside and tell them we're calling the whole thing off?"

"You mean, break the pact? We can't do that." She glanced down at the bricks at her feet. "I can't do that."

"Maybe it's time someone did."

He studied her under the thin light of the moon and stars overhead. Everything Breed in him was urging him to touch her— to lift her chin and sweep the loose tendrils of her curly brown hair away from her eyes, if only so he could see their unusual shade again. But he kept his hands to himself, fisting them at his sides when the desire to reach out nearly overrode his good sense.

"You strike me as a forward-thinking, intelligent woman. You don't actually believe the pact holds any kind of sway over the peace between our families anymore, do you?"

"No, I don't. But it's important to my parents, and that makes it important to me. But..." Finally, she lifted her head to meet his gaze. "There's another reason I agreed to the handfasting. I have a trust fund. A sizable one. It's not due to release to me until my thirtieth birthday, but my father's promised it to me early. At the end of the handfast."

"Ah." Jehan lifted his chin. He hadn't taken her for the type to be motivated by money, but he supposed there were worse things. "So, you're here on bribery, and I'm here out of some pointless obligation to prove to my father that I'm not his greatest disappointment."

"That's why you're here?"

Her voice was quiet, almost sympathetic. The soft look in her eyes threatened to unravel his thin control.

He gave a dismissive wave of his hand. "It doesn't matter why either of us are here. Apparently, we both just need to get through the next eight nights so we can get on with our real lives."

She nodded. "How are we going to do that?"

Looking at her standing so close to him in the cool night air, her beautiful face and tempting curves making his mouth water and his blood streak hot through his veins, Jehan wasn't sure how the hell he was going to survive a week of seclusion with her. Not without putting his hands or fangs—or any other part of his anatomy—within arm's reach of her.

One thing was certain. They would have to set some clear boundaries. Rigid boundaries that couldn't be crossed.

And rules.

Jehan let his gaze travel the length of her, desire hammering through every cell in his body.

Oh, yeah. To survive the next week alone with this female, he was going to need *a lot* of boundaries and rules.

CHAPTER 5

She should have said no.

She should have trusted her good sense and left Jehan standing in the middle of the midnight garden alone last night, not helped him set down terms of their own for the ritual neither of them wanted to be part of.

Instead, that next evening, she found herself seated beside him at the head of a long banquet room in her parents' Darkhaven in front of a combined hundred members of their two families who had assembled to celebrate their send-off and the start of the handfast's first night.

In less than an hour, she and Jehan would be delivered to the private oasis retreat and left to fend for themselves until officials from both tribes came to retrieve them at the end of the eight nights. Until then, she would be trapped with him in close quarters. Intimate quarters.

Oh, God. She must be out of her damn mind.

Sera reached for her wine glass and drained it in one gulp.

"Pace yourself," Jehan drawled from beside her. "If you get too tipsy, I'd hate to have to carry you out of here tonight."

"Like hell you will." She smiled and spoke under her breath, doing her best to pretend he wasn't the last male she'd ever choose to spend time with. "And we have a deal, remember? One that specifically states no touching. I expect you to honor that."

A chuckle emanated from him, so deep it was almost a growl. "Don't worry, I have no intention of touching you."

She placed her empty glass back on the table. "Good. Then don't even joke about it."

"Trust me, Seraphina, you'll know when I'm joking."

She made the mistake of looking at him and found him smirking as he leaned back in his chair. But there wasn't any humor in his light blue eyes. Only a dark promise that made her pulse skitter through her veins.

According to tradition, he was dressed in a white linen tunic and loose pants. A long, striped sash bearing his blue-and-gold family colors was tied around his trim waist. He looked decadent and confident, sprawled against the back of his seat. As arrogant as a prince accustomed to having the world bend to his whim, even if his title was as musty as the pact that bound her to him tonight.

As for Sera, she had been clothed according to tradition too. Wrapped and knotted into yards of diaphanous red silk that somehow formed a body-skimming gown, she was also dripping in beads and bangles. Painted henna patterns swirled in delicate flourishes and arcs over the backs of her hands and up her limbs.

The dress constricted her breathing and the decorations on her skin made her feel like an offering headed for the altar.

Jehan's searing gaze beside her wasn't helping.

Even though they'd agreed to avoid each other as much as possible for the next week, Sera couldn't forget the heat that had ignited between them in the garden. Or in the moment they'd first made eye contact in the Darkhaven's salon.

He was attractive; she couldn't begin to deny that. With his luxurious chestnut hair and impossibly blue eyes, he was heart-stoppingly gorgeous. The fact that his massive, muscular body and powerful presence seemed to suck all the air out of the room only made the handsome Breed male even more magnetic.

The V-neck of his linen tunic was cut several inches down his powerful chest, baring a lot of tawny skin and smooth muscle, and the edges of his Breed *dermaglyphs*. The color-infused skin markings indicated the vampire's mood, and right now, the neutral hues of Jehan's *glyphs* told her that he'd recently fed.

Not surprising. It was customary for a Breed male about to enter the handfast to slake his blood thirst on a willing human Host before the week began. This to ensure that he didn't drink from his Breedmate companion and bond to her out of physical need instead of love.

A vision of Jehan drinking from the throat of another woman sprang into Sera's mind uninvited. His dark head nestled into the curve of a tender neck. His sensual mouth fastened to smooth, pale skin as his sharp fangs penetrated a pounding vein and he began to drink his fill.

Would he gentle a woman with coaxing words and soothing caresses when he took her carotid between his teeth? Or would he spring on her like the predator he was, dominating her with speed and force and white-hot power?

Some troubling part of her she didn't recognize stirred with the need to know.

Sera groaned. She squirmed in her seat as her pulse thudded faster and erotic warmth bloomed between her thighs.

She wanted to cross her legs to relieve the unwelcome ache, but the skirts of her ceremonial dress were too restricting. Elsewhere in the banquet room, her father was reciting the traditional terms of the handfast. She only half-listened, too distracted by Jehan's presence beside her and the heat of his gaze on her as she fidgeted and shifted in her chair.

It suddenly occurred to her that the room had gone strangely quiet. Expectantly quiet.

All eyes in the room were fixed on her, and her father was no longer speaking.

Jehan stood up and pointedly cleared his throat. "It's time for us to go, Seraphina."

"Oh." She rose to her feet, eager to escape the weight of everyone's gazes. Plus, she couldn't wait to put some much-needed distance between herself and Jehan.

But he wasn't moving. Why wasn't he moving?

"Don't forget the kiss!" someone shouted cheerfully from among the gathering. "It's tradition to seal the pact with a kiss!"

Leila. *Damn that girl.*

Sera shot a narrowed glare at her exuberant sibling but her grin showed no remorse.

"Kiss her!" she shouted again.

And then across the room, Marcel called for the kiss too. Someone else picked up the chant, then another. Before long, the entire place was applauding and thundering with the command.

"Kiss her! Kiss her! Kiss her!"

Sera turned a miserable look on Jehan. "We don't really have t—"

Before she could finish, he moved closer and his mouth slanted over hers in a blast of heat. His lips caressed hers, impossibly soft, achingly sensual. His hands held her face, and yes, they were gentle. His kiss was too, but beneath its tenderness was a possessiveness—a raw power—that rocked her.

He mastered her mouth in an instant, and every brush of his lips had her aching to be claimed by him.

Her thoughts scattered. Her knees went a little boneless.

Even worse, the coil of warmth that had gathered between her thighs a few moments ago blazed molten and wild now.

Sera raised her hands to grip his shoulders, if only to keep from sagging against him in front of a hundred onlookers. All the reassurances of their private agreement to spend the next week in separate corners flew away like leaves on the wind as Jehan kissed her. She couldn't help it. She moaned against his mouth, her pulse quickening, hammering even louder than the cheers of the gathering around them.

Jehan released her abruptly. His blue eyes glittered with sparks of amber heat, their transformation making his desire all too clear. He ran his tongue over his wet lips and she saw the points of his fangs, now gleaming in his mouth like razor-sharp diamonds. His breath rasped out of him, rough and raw.

"Let's go," he growled for her ears only. "The sooner we get this damned farce over with, the better."

Then he took her by the hand and stalked away from the table with her in tow.

CHAPTER 6

Jehan's body was still rock hard and vibrating with lust more than an hour after he and Seraphina were delivered to the oasis retreat.

Holy hell. That kiss...

As short-lived and chaste as it had been, it had gripped him in a way that staggered him.

He hadn't been able to deny how attracted he was to Seraphina from the instant he laid eyes on her. Now he knew she wanted him too. Her response to their kiss had left no question about that. The color that had rushed up her throat and into her cheeks couldn't be blamed on anything else, nor could her soft little moans. He'd felt her desire for him. He'd breathed in the sweet scent of her arousal, felt it drumming in her blood.

His own blood had answered, and now that his mouth had sampled a taste of Seraphina's kiss, everything primal and male in him—everything Breed—pounded with a dark, dangerous need for more.

Somehow, he'd managed to rein it in back at the Darkhaven celebration.

Now, he just had to make sure to keep his desire in check for the duration of their confinement at the private villa.

Eight nights, that's all, he reassured himself.

One hundred and ninety-two hours, give or take the few that had already passed tonight.

Which meant somewhere around eleven thousand minutes. All of them to be spent in too-close quarters with a woman who lit up every nerve ending in his body like a flame set to dry tinder.

Yeah, the math wasn't helping.

Everything they might need had been provided for by their families. Clothing, toiletries, a fully stocked kitchen for Seraphina. They would want for nothing from the outside world, and no one would interrupt their time together until the handfasting had ended.

They'd divvied up the place as soon as they'd been dropped off, negotiating territory and establishing boundaries where neither of them would cross. It only seemed right to give her the privacy of the massive bedroom. As for Jehan, he would inhabit the general living quarters, and use the big nest of cushions in the main room as his bed for the next week.

With Seraphina settling into the sole bedroom suite on her own, Jehan prowled the open space of the villa like a caged cat, taking stock of the unfamiliar surroundings. He strode across richly dyed rugs spread over terra cotta tiled floors. Above his head, the high, domed ceiling glowed with soft golden lights that glinted off a mosaic of gem-colored glass embedded into the white stucco plaster.

Down the wing of the hallway opposite the bedroom where Seraphina had sequestered herself was a traditional bathing room with a steaming, spring-fed pool surrounded by silk-draped columns and fat pillar candles.

In the adjacent, open-concept chamber, more beds of cushions and pillows were arranged around the room, some steeped in shadows, others strategically placed in front of tall, ornately framed mirrors. Erotic statuary and tables holding bottles of perfumed oils and incense jars completed the pleasure den.

Jehan frowned, shaking his head. The handfast agreement may forbid a male from forcing himself on the Breedmate sent with him to this place, but every room in the villa was obviously designed with sex and seduction in mind.

And try as he might to resist imagining Seraphina reclined on those cushions or stepping naked out of the steam-clouded baths, his mind refused to obey.

Eight nights.

He would be lucky to make it through this first one without losing his mind or tearing down the bedroom door she was currently hiding behind on the other side of the villa.

He needed fresh air. What he really needed was a hundred-foot wall between him and his unwanted roommate. A length of sturdy chain wouldn't hurt either.

Jehan walked back out to the main living area and headed for the French doors leading out to an oasis patio in back. As he crossed the room, he heard Seraphina hiss a curse from inside the bedroom.

He paused, listened. Told himself to keep walking in the opposite direction.

She swore again and he detoured for the passage leading to the bedroom.

"Are you all right in there?"

"Yes. Everything's fine." Her reply was quick, dismissively so.

He stood outside the closed door and heard her grumble in frustration. "I'm coming in."

"No. Wait—"

She stood in the center of the big room, tangled in the complicated yards of red silk that comprised her dress from the celebration. When he chuckled, she glowered. "It's not funny, you arrogant ass."

"Really?" He didn't even try to curb his grin. "Looks pretty funny from where I'm standing."

She huffed, narrowing a glare on him. "If you're going to stand there laughing at me, you might as well help."

He held up his hands. "No touching, remember? How can I help without breaking that part of our deal?" Of course, they'd also said no kissing, but that rule was already shot all to hell, even before they'd arrived tonight. "Ask me nicely and maybe I'll consider bending the rules."

Her shoulders sagged in defeat, but the baring of her straight, white teeth hardly looked submissive. "Jehan, will you please help me?"

He didn't want to admit how enticing his name sounded on her pretty lips. Especially when it involved asking him to assist in undressing her. His blood agreed, licking through his veins in eager anticipation as he stalked across the bedroom to where she stood.

She raised her right hand and gathered her long cascade of bead-strewn, soft brown curls off her neck as she presented her back to him. "There must be a dozen tiny knots holding this dress together. And I can't figure out where the ends of the long wrappings begin either."

Jehan stood behind her for a long moment, just looking. Just drinking in the sight of her graceful nape and elegant spine. She was blessed with hourglass curves and long, lean legs. The ceremonial dress hugged every inch of her in all the right places. Including the rounded swells of her beautiful ass.

How was it that his mouth could water, yet feel desert dry at the same time?

His gums prickled as his fangs swelled against his tongue. Another part of him was swelling too, pressing in carnal demand against the loose white linen of his pants. Heat rose in his blood and in his vision, swamping his irises with amber fire.

He reached out and began to loosen the first of the intricate knots.

There were eight of them, not a dozen. Each one was a test of his dexterity as well as his self-control. One by one, the fastenings fell away, baring Seraphina's naked back to his fevered gaze, inch by torturous inch.

Somewhere along the way, his lungs had stopped working. Desire raked him, sharp talons stealing his breath as he freed the last of the tiny knots and the scarlet silk slackened in his fingers.

Seraphina didn't seem to be breathing either. She stood unmoving, her mane of long hair still held aloft in her hand. Warmth poured off her skin, and he knew she had to feel his heat reaching out to her too.

Her heartbeat ticked frantically in the side of her neck, drawing his blazing eyes. The urge to stroke that tender pulse point—to touch and taste every enticing inch of her—nearly overwhelmed him.

Clamping his molars together, he fought to keep a grip on those urges. When he finally found his voice, it came out in a gravelly rasp. "There you go. All finished."

Seraphina paused, letting her hair fall. She turned a glance over her shoulder at him. "The wrappings too?"

Shit. He scowled and began a quick search for one of the ends of the lengths of silk. He tugged it loose and began to unwind it from around her bodice and waist. The damn thing was too long to pull free.

He swore and shook his head. "You'll have to turn with it."

"Like this?" She obeyed, pivoting in front of him. He nodded, then pulled the silk taut, letting the tail of it collect on the floor as she slowly spun before him. Around and around and around, her springy brown curls dancing as she turned, the beads threaded through the strands twinkling under the soft lights of the bedroom.

He couldn't take his eyes off her.

In some primitive part of his brain, he was the conquering desert warlord and she was his mesmerizing captive. His irresistible, stolen prize. He watched her spin, watched the ribbon of scarlet silk unwind, revealing more and more of the beautiful woman wrapped inside.

He wanted to keep undressing her.

When he looked at Seraphina, when he breathed in her cinnamon-sweet scent and felt the warmth of her skin with each dizzying turn she took in front of him... Damn him, but being near her like this, there was *so much* he wanted.

The drumming beat of her pulse vibrated in the small space between their bodies, and it made his own blood throb in answer. It made him hunger in a way he'd never fully known.

It made him want to burn the pact between their families and take her right here and now, willing or not.

Claim her.

Possess her in every way.

Make her his.

Dangerous thinking.

And a temptation he wasn't at all certain he would be able to resist.

Not for this one night, let alone seven more.

CHAPTER 7

She didn't know the exact moment when the air between them changed from simply hot and playful to something darker. Something so fierce and powerful, it made all of her nerve endings stand at full attention.

Jehan wanted her.

She'd have to be an idiot not to realize that.

She wanted him too.

And she was too smart to think for one second that he hadn't picked up on her staggering awareness of him as a man. As a dangerously seductive Breed male who could have her carotid caught in his teeth just as swiftly as he could have her legs parted beneath the driving pound of his muscular body.

Sera swallowed hard, her breath and heart racing as she slowed to a stop before him.

She glanced down, to where she was tethered to his strong hands by the unraveled length of red silk.

Although she was covered where it counted, there wasn't much of her dress left. Most of it lay on the floor at her feet; yards of scarlet pooled in the scant space between her body and Jehan's.

She licked her lips as she struggled for words. She should tell him to go, but everything female in her yearned for him to stay. She was no trembling virgin, no stranger to sex. But never with a Breed male. And the electricity that crackled to life between Jehan and her was something she'd never felt before.

It was arresting.

Consuming.

Terrifying in its intensity.

Yet it wasn't fear of him she felt when she held his piercing light blue eyes. It was fear of herself and of the way he made her feel. Fear of the things he made her want.

"Jehan, I..." She shook her head, unsure what she meant to say to him.

Leave?

Stay?

Forget the fact that neither one of them had come to this place willingly, nor intended to walk away from the archaic tradition with a blood-bonded mate?

But that's not what this moment was about.

What she saw in Jehan's amber-swamped gaze right now didn't have anything to do with their romantic surroundings or the expectation and hopes of their families. The things she was feeling had nothing to do with any of that either.

It was desire, pure and simple.

Immediate and intense.

Her body throbbed with it, longing pounding furiously in her breast and stirring a molten heat in the center of her. She drew a shallow breath—then held it tight as Jehan reached out to caress her cheek. His warm fingers felt hard and strong against her face, but he stroked her with such tenderness, she couldn't hold back the soft moan that spilled past her lips.

She stood rooted in place while her thoughts and emotions spiraled with rising anticipation.

The cool air of the room made her exposed skin feel even tighter. Her nipples ached behind the gauzy ribbons of silk that barely covered them. Goose bumps rose on her naked shoulders and arms with each second she endured under Jehan's hot, unwavering stare.

His fingers drifted away from her face slowly, then skated in a scorching trail down the side of her neck and onto the line of her left shoulder. She felt him trace the small red birthmark that rode her bicep—her Breedmate mark. His fingertips caressed the teardrop-and-crescent-moon symbol that signified she was something other than simply human.

That mark also meant that if she drank his blood, she would be bound to him and only him, for as long as either of them lived.

As if in answer to his touch, her veins vibrated with a primal quickening, pulse points throbbing in response to each tender stroke.

"You are...so incredibly beautiful." His deep voice was a growl of sound, tangling through his teeth and fangs. "But we made a deal, Seraphina."

She knew they had a deal. No looking. No touching. No physical contact of any kind. They had set clear boundaries and established separate corners where they could cohabitate for the week without having to spend any awkward time together. When the handfast was over, they would simply say their good-byes and return to their normal lives.

So why was she wishing so desperately that Jehan would pull her into his arms?

Why was she longing to feel the press of his muscled, hard body against her?

Why was the coil of smoldering need within her winding tighter, all of her nerve endings on fire and eager for more of his touch?

Eager for his kiss and everything that was certain to follow...

But he didn't kiss her.

A snarl curled up from the back of his throat. An animal sound. An otherworldly sound.

One of denial.

He shook his head, sending the thick waves of his dark hair swaying where they brushed his broad shoulders. His hand dropped away, down to his side. On a slow exhale, he stepped back, creating a cold vacuum of space between them.

He stooped to pick up the pool of red silk from the floor. He was retreating, yet when his gaze lifted to hers, his eyes still blazed with fiery desire, so hot it seared her. His fangs still glittered razor-sharp and hungered behind his lips.

He wanted her. It was written in his fierce expression and in the arousal that made itself obvious when she glanced down at the sizable bulge tenting his loose linen pants.

And he knew that she wanted him just as badly.

She could see that knowledge gleaming in his arrogant, knowing stare.

Damn him. He knew very well, and he was enjoying her torment!

He placed the mound of silk into her hands, a grin tugging at the corner of his mouth. "Goodnight, Seraphina."

He pivoted back toward the door. Then he strode out of the room without so much as a backward glance, leaving her to stare after him, half-dressed, fuming, and determined to avoid the infuriating ass for the duration of her confinement with him.

CHAPTER 8

For the next two days, he hardly saw Seraphina.

She spent her evenings behind the closed door of the massive bedroom suite, pointedly ignoring his existence. During the daytime, she slipped outside to the villa's sunbaked patio for hours on end, safely out of his reach and about as far away from his company as she could get.

She was pissed off, punishing him with frosty silence and deliberate avoidance.

Exactly as he'd intended when he'd left her high and dry—and as sexually frustrated as he was—that first night.

Better to earn her contempt than test his control under the desire-drenched heat of her gaze again. Her absence was a reprieve he welcomed. Better that than trying to withstand the temptation of her enticing curves and infinitely soft skin, now that he knew the pleasure of both.

Fuck. He'd only touched her for a few moments and the feel of her was branded into his fingertips. Her warmth and cinnamon-sugar scent was seared into his senses.

Even though she was out of sight now—rummaging quietly in the kitchen, by the sound of it—all he had to do was close his eyes and there she was in his mind. Standing in front of him in nothing but a few scraps of scarlet silk, her parted lips and heavy-lidded eyes inviting him to touch her. To take her.

No, pleading for him to do so.

But he'd shown her, right?

Pretending he was the one in control, denying both of them the pleasure they both wanted because he'd been too swamped with need to trust he could control himself. Now she was going to great lengths to ignore him, no doubt cursing him as a cold bastard. Meanwhile, he was walking around the villa like a caged animal with a semipermanent case of blue balls.

Damn.

He wasn't only a bastard. He was an idiot.

On a curse, he raked a hand through his hair and got up from the large floor cushion where he'd been unsuccessfully attempting to doze. It was just about sundown and he was twitchy with the need to be moving, to be doing something useful. Hell, he'd settle for doing anything at all.

He'd never been good at inactivity and the boredom of his exile was driving him insane.

More than once, he'd thought about slipping out in the middle of the night to run off some of his tension. Or say fuck the handfast and hoof it all the way to Casablanca and take the earliest flight to Rome.

With his Breed genetics, he could make it to the city in about as many hours as it would take to drive it. Maybe sooner.

Tempting.

But he couldn't leave Seraphina by herself out here. And as much as he wanted to get back to work going after Opus with his teammates at the Order, he wasn't about to abandon his honor or his family's by violating the terms of the pact.

If she could endure the week together and adhere to the ridiculous restrictions imposed on them by the ancient agreement—in addition to their own set of rules—then so could he.

And he supposed he really owed her an apology for the way he acted the other night.

Padding silently on his bare feet, Jehan strode toward the kitchen where he'd heard her a minute ago. She had her back to him, seated on an overstuffed sofa in the adjacent dining nook.

With her knees drawn up and her head bent down to study whatever she held in her hands, she didn't even notice him stealing up behind her from the kitchen. At first, he thought she'd taken one of the many books from the villa's library. But then he realized the small object was something else.

A phone.

In direct violation of the "no communication with the outside world" terms of the handfast.

The sneaky little rebel.

He opened his mouth to call her out on the breach, but then his acute sight caught the last few lines of a text message thread filling the display. Some guy named Karsten was asking her where she was and why she'd left him without saying where she'd gone. He was worried, he said. He needed her. Said he wasn't any good without her.

For reasons he didn't want to examine, the idea that Seraphina had another man waiting for her somewhere—that she wouldn't even mention that fact to him at any point when they talked—sent a streak of anger through Jehan's veins.

That she would look at him so wantonly the other night when this other male—what the fuck kind of name was Karsten, anyway?—obviously cared about her, needed her, made Jehan wonder if he'd read her wrong from the start.

Of course, she'd already confessed to him that she only agreed to participate in the handfast to collect a handsome payout at the end. So, why should it surprise him to realize she was already spoken for?

"You're breaking the rules." His voice was low and even, betraying none of the heat that was running through his veins.

She startled so sharply, the phone practically leapt out of her fingers. She scrambled to keep it and whirled around on the sofa to gape at him in horror.

"Jehan! I didn't hear you come in the room."

"You don't say." He gestured to the phone now clutched tight to her breast. "How'd you get that in here?"

She had the decency to look at least a little contrite. "I made Leila smuggle it in with the clothing she packed for me. She didn't want to, but I insisted. How was I supposed to go an entire week completely cut off from everything?"

"And *everyone*?" Jehan prompted. "Who's Karsten?"

Her face blanched. No need for her to ask him if he saw her texts. Her guilty look said it all. "He's my partner."

"Partner?" He practically snarled the word.

"My coworker. Karsten volunteers with me at the border

camps."

Some of Jehan's irritation cooled at the explanation. "For a coworker, he sounds very eager to have you back. He's no good without you?"

Her expression relaxed into one of mild dismissal. "Karsten is...a bit dramatic. Right now, he's concerned about a food and medical supply shipment that's being held up at a checkpoint near Marrakesh. Normally I make sure things clear without delays, but unfortunately this shipment didn't come in until after my parents called me home."

"What happens if the shipment doesn't get cleared?"

She crossed her arms over her breasts. "The food will rot and the medicine will spoil. It happens all too often."

"And this Karsten is unable to retrieve the supplies without you?" Jehan couldn't mask his judgment of the other man. If necessary food and medicine were sitting somewhere waiting to be delivered, he'd make damn sure it got where it needed to go.

Seraphina slipped off the sofa and walked to the marble-topped island where Jehan stood. "A lot of times, when things are delayed like this, my father's name helps loosen them up. Sometimes, it's a matter of finding the right palm to grease."

Jehan nodded. Corruption in local governments was nothing new. That Seraphina seemed comfortable navigating those tangled webs was impressive. She kept impressing him, and he wasn't sure he should like it as much as he did. "What do you think will free up this shipment of supplies?"

She shrugged faintly. "Does it matter? Karsten hasn't been able to get them on his own so far, and by the time our week is out here, it'll be too late. Food and medicine doesn't last long in the desert."

No, he supposed it didn't.

But maybe there was some way to fix the situation.

"You say you know the checkpoint where the supplies are being held up?"

"It's on the outskirts of Marrakesh. A lot of our materials pass through that same one."

Jehan considered. "That's only a few hours away from here by car."

"What are you saying?" She frowned. "Jehan, what are you thinking?"

"Let me borrow your phone."

She handed it over, still staring at him in question. Jehan entered his brother's number and waited for him to pick up. It took several rings, then Marcel's confused voice came over the line in greeting. "Hello?"

Jehan got right to the point. "I have a favor to ask of you."

"Jehan? What the hell are you doing calling me? And where did you get the phone? You know there's supposed to be no technology or outside communication—"

"I know," he bit off impatiently. "Where are you right now?"

"Ah...I'm home, but I'm getting ready to head out for a while. What's going on? Is everything all right with Seraphina?"

"She's fine. We're fine," Jehan assured him. "I need a vehicle. As soon as possible."

Marcel gasped. "What?"

Seraphina's eyes went about as wide as he imagined his brother's had just now.

"It's important, Marcel. You know I wouldn't ask if it wasn't."

"But you can't leave the villa. If you leave Seraphina alone out there, you'll be breaking the pact. Hell, you already are just by making this call to me."

"No one will know I called except you." Jehan glanced at Seraphina and shook his head. "As for breaking the pact by leaving her at the villa without me, not happening. She's coming with me, and we won't be gone long. No one will be the wiser."

"Except, once again, me." Marcel groaned. "I probably don't want to know what any of this is about, do I?"

"Probably not." Jehan smiled.

Marcel exhaled a curse. "Please tell me you don't want my Lambo."

"Actually, I was hoping for one of the Rovers from the Darkhaven fleet. With a full tank of fuel, if you would."

Marcel's deep sigh gusted over the line. "Does Seraphina realize yet what a demanding pain in the ass you can be?"

Jehan met her gaze and grinned. "I imagine she's figuring that out."

Marcel chuckled. "I'll drop it off at sundown."

CHAPTER 9

"Careful with that crate, Aleph. Those glass vials of vaccines are fragile."

Walking across the moonlit sand with her arm around one of the children from the refugee camp and a box of bandages held in her other hand, Sera directed another of the volunteers to the open back of the supply-laden Range Rover. "Massoud, take the large sack of rice to Fatima in the mess tent and ask her where she'd like us to store the rest of the raw grains. Let her know we have some crates of canned meats and boxes of fruit here too."

Behind her at the vehicle, Jehan was busy unloading the crates and boxes and sacks they'd just arrived with from the checkpoint near Marrakesh. Sera couldn't help pausing to watch him work. Dressed in jeans and a loose linen shirt with the sleeves rolled up past his *glyph*-covered forearms, he pitched in like the best of her other workers. Even better, in fact, since he was Breed. His strength and stamina outpaced half a dozen humans put together.

She still couldn't believe what he'd done for her tonight. For a village of displaced people he'd never met and didn't have to care about. All of the indignation and anger she'd felt toward him since their first night at the villa evaporated under her admiration for what he was doing now.

And it wasn't only admiration she felt when she looked at him.

There was attraction, to be sure. White-hot and magnetic.

But something stronger had begun to kindle inside her today. As unsettling as her desire for him was, this new emotion was even more terrifying. She *liked* him.

Jehan had intrigued her from their first introduction, even after she'd learned he made his living as a warrior. Their kiss at the banquet had ignited a need in her that she still hadn't been able to dismiss. And then, when he'd helped her out of her dress that initial night at the villa, she'd wanted him with an intensity that nearly overwhelmed her.

After he'd left her humiliated and awash in frustration, she'd almost been able to convince herself that he was simply an arrogant bastard and an aggravation she would just have to avoid or endure for the rest of their week together.

Now he had to go and do something kind for her like this. Something surprising and selfless.

Frowning, she turned away from him on a groan. "Come on, Yasmin. Let's go see if Fatima has anything good waiting in her kitchen tonight."

As they walked into the center of the camp, a Jeep was arriving from the other end of the makeshift village of tents and meager outbuildings. Yellow headlights bounced in the darkness as the vehicle jostled over the ruts in the dirt road into camp. The Jeep came to a halt several yards up and Karsten Hemmings hopped out of the driver's seat.

"Sera?" He jogged to meet her, a welcoming grin on his ruggedly handsome face. "I was down at the southern camp when I got word the supplies had been released." He gave her a quick kiss on the cheek as he took the box out of her hands. Then he reached down to pat the child's head with a smile. "What's going on? I thought you said you were going to be delayed with your parents for a few more days?"

She shrugged at the reminder of the small lie she'd told him. "I found an opportunity to get away for a little while, so I thought I'd run to Marrakesh and see what I could do about the supplies."

Karsten made a wry sound in his throat as he tossed the box of bandages to a passing camp volunteer. "How much did it cost this time?"

"A few thousand."

After haggling the checkpoint supervisor down as far as she

could manage, she'd arranged to have the money wired to the corrupt official's personal account. It simply was the way business was done in her line of work sometimes, but all of the "few thousands" had added up over the years. Her account was nearly tapped dry now—at least until she completed the handfast and her father released her trust.

A group of children ran past and shouted for Yasmin to join them in a game of tag. The promise of treats in the mess tent quickly forgotten, the little girl ran off to join her friends.

"Stay close to camp, all of you!" Karsten called after them, watching them go. Then he cocked his head at Sera. "It's good to see you. When I heard you'd left to go to your family without telling anyone what it was about, I was afraid something was wrong." He glanced down, finally taking in her appearance. "What the hell happened to your clothes?"

Seeing how Leila had outfitted her for a week of lounging and potential romance, before Sera left the villa, she'd raided Jehan's wardrobe for something practical to wear out in the field.

She couldn't show up wearing any of the dresses or peasant skirts her sister had selected, so Sera had appropriated Jehan's white linen tunic from the night of the banquet and a loose-fitting pair of linen pants. With the pant legs rolled up several times, the waist held around her by a makeshift red silk belt, and a pair of her own kid leather flats, her clothing wasn't fashionable, but it was functional.

It also had the added benefit that it carried Jehan's deliciously spicy scent, which had been teasing her senses ever since she slipped the tunic over her head.

She wasn't sure how to explain what she was wearing, but then Karsten no longer seemed interested. His gaze flicked past Sera now, to where Jehan had just unloaded the last of the crates and supplies.

His brow rankled in confusion. "Who's that?"

"A friend," she said, unsure why she should feel awkward calling him that.

"He's Breed." Karsten's eyes came back to her now, wariness flattening his lips as he lowered his voice. "You brought one of them into the camp?"

Even though it had been twenty years and counting since the

Breed were outed to mankind, prejudices still lingered. Even in her affable coworker, apparently.

"It's okay. Jehan is, ah...an old friend of my family." She waved her hand in dismissal of his concerns. "Besides, we won't be staying long. We have to get back to the villa tonight."

"The villa?"

Shit. She really didn't want to explain the whole awkward family pact and handfasting scenario to him. For one thing, it was none of Karsten's business—even if she did consider him a friend after they had dated briefly once upon a time. And maybe it was none of his business precisely *because* of the fact they had once dated.

Whatever the reason, she felt strangely protective of the time she'd spent with Jehan. It belonged to them—no one else.

"Once we get everything settled here in the camp, Jehan and I need to return. We're expected to be back as soon as possible." Which was about as close to the truth as she was going to get on that subject.

Karsten shook his head. "Well, you won't be leaving tonight. There's a big dust storm rolling in off the Sahara. It's moving fast, due here in the next hour or less. No way you'll be able to outrun it."

"Oh, no." A knot of anxiety tightened in her chest. "That's awful news."

"What's awful news?"

Jehan's deep voice awakened her nerve endings as sensually as a caress. He'd closed up the Rover and strode up behind her before she even realized it. When she pivoted to face him, she found his arresting blue eyes locked on Karsten.

"You must be Jehan." Instead of extending his hand in greeting, Karsten's fists balled on his hips. "I'm Karsten Hemmings, Sera's partner."

"Coworker." Jehan subtly corrected him. And as far as introductions went, his didn't exactly project friendliness either. His palm came down soft and warm—possessively—on her shoulder. "What's awful news?"

She tried to act as though his lingering touch was no big deal, as if it wasn't waking up every cell in her body and flooding her with heat. "There's a dust storm coming. Karsten says we may have to wait it out here at the camp. I know we need to get back soon, though. Your brother's waiting for us to return the Rover tonight—"

"Sera, if your friend has somewhere he needs to be," Karsten piped in helpfully, "then why don't you wait out the storm here at camp and I can bring you back to your parents' place tomorrow, after it passes?"

"Not happening." Jehan's curt reply allowed no argument. "If Seraphina stays for any reason, so do I."

Although he didn't say it outright, the message was broadcasted loud and clear. He wasn't about to leave her alone with Karsten, storm or no storm.

And if the protective, alpha tone of his voice hadn't sent her heart into a free fall in her breast, she might have found the good sense to be offended by his unprovoked, aggressive reaction to the only other male in her current orbit.

Karsten smiled mildly and lifted a shoulder. "Suit yourself, then. I'm going to start boarding things up ahead of the storm. If you need me, Sera, you know where I am."

She nodded and watched him walk away. Then she wheeled around to face Jehan. "You were very rude to my friend."

"Friend?" He snorted under his breath. "That human thinks he's more than a friend to you." Jehan's sharp blue eyes narrowed. "He was more than that at one time, wasn't he?"

"No." She shook her head. "We went on a few dates, nothing more. I wasn't interested in him."

"But he was interested in you. Still is."

"You sound jealous."

He exhaled harshly through flared nostrils. "Call it observant."

"I called it jealous." She stepped closer to him in the moonlight, weathering the heat that rolled off his big body and flashed from the depths of his smoldering gaze. His jaw was clamped hard, and the dark-stubbled skin that covered it seemed stretched too tightly across his handsome, perturbed face. "Why the hell should it bother you if Karsten is a friend of mine or something more? It's not like you have any claim on me. I could go after him right now and there's really nothing you can say about it."

A low sound rumbled from deep inside of him. "I would hope you don't intend to try me."

"Why? Because of some stupid pact?" Her voice climbed with her frustration. "You don't even believe in it, but yet you want to pretend we have to live by its terms."

"I don't give a fuck about the damned pact, Seraphina."

"That didn't stop you from using it as an excuse to make me feel like an idiot."

Sparks ignited in the shadowed pools of his eyes. "If you really think my walking away from you that night had anything to do with the pact, then you *are* an idiot."

She sucked in a breath, ready to hurl a curse at him, but he didn't give her the chance.

In less than a pace, he closed the distance between them. One strong hand slid into her loose hair and around her nape. The other splayed against her lower spine as he drew her to him and took her mouth in a blazing hot, hungry kiss.

Seraphina moaned as pleasure and need swamped her. Her breasts crushed against the firm, muscled slabs of his chest. Against her belly, his cock was a thick, solid ridge of heat and power and carnal demand. Hunger tore through her, quicksilver and molten. It burned away her anger, obliterated her outrage and frustration. As he deepened their kiss and his tongue breached her parted lips, all she knew was need.

She speared her fingers into his thick, soft waves and clung to him, lost in desire and oblivious of their surroundings. Willing to ignore everything so long as Jehan was holding her like this, kissing her as if he'd been longing for it as much as she had.

He drew back on a snarled curse and looked at her. His eyes snapped with embers, his pupils nothing but vertical slits in the middle of all that fire. His wet lips peeled back off his teeth and fangs as he drew in a deep breath, scenting her like the predatory being he truly was.

For a moment, she thought he was about to pick her up and carry her off to some secluded corner of the camp as if he owned her. She wouldn't have fought him. God, not even close.

But as they stood there, Sera felt a subtle sting start to needle her cheeks and forehead. Her eyes started to burn, then the next breath she took carried the grit of fine sand to the back of her throat.

The storm.

It was arriving even sooner than Karsten had warned.

She didn't have to tell Jehan. Pulling her close, he tucked her head against his chest and rushed with her toward the nearest outbuilding as the night began to fill with a roiling swell of yellow dust.

CHAPTER 10

By the time they reached the aluminum-roofed storage building several yards ahead, the biting wind had picked up with a howl. Sand churned across the camp, blowing as thick as a blizzard.

His body still charged with arousal, Jehan held Seraphina against him as he threw open the rickety wooden door. "Inside, quickly."

She no sooner entered the shelter than a muffled cry somewhere amid the storm drew both of them to full alert. The voice was small, distant. Unmistakably terrified.

"Yasmin." Seraphina's face blanched with worry. "Oh, God. The little girl who came to greet us when we arrived. She and some other children ran off to play a few minutes ago."

The cry came again, more plaintive now. There was pain in the child's voice too.

Jehan cursed. "Stay here. I'll find her."

Without waiting for her to argue, he dashed back into the night using the speed of his Breed genetics. The little girl's wails were a beacon through the blinding sea of flying sand. Jehan followed her cries to a deep ditch on the far side of the camp. At the bottom of the rugged drop, her small body lay curled in a tight ball.

"Yasmin?"

At the sound of her name, she lifted her head. Agony and terror flooded her tear-filled eyes. The poor child was shaking and sobbing, choking on the airborne sand.

Jehan jumped down into the ditch. Crouching low beside her,

he sheltered her with his body as the sandstorm roiled all around them. "Are you hurt?"

Her dark head wobbled in a jerky nod. "My leg hurts. I was trying to hide from my friends, but I fell and they all ran away."

Jehan gingerly examined her. As soon as his palm skated over her left shin and ankle, he felt the hot pain of a compound fracture. The break streaked through his senses like a jagged bolt of lightning. "Come on, sweetheart. Let's get you out of here."

He collected Yasmin into his arms and carried her up from the ditch. At the crest of it, Seraphina was waiting. A heavy blanket covered her from head to toe as a makeshift shield from the storm. She opened her arms as Jehan strode toward her, enveloping him and the child as the three of them made their way across the camp.

"She needs a medic," he informed Seraphina as she murmured quiet reassurances to the scared child. "I felt two fractures in the lower part of the left fibula, and a fairly bad sprain in the ankle."

Seraphina's brows knitted for a second, then she acknowledged with a nod. "The medical building is in the center of camp. This way."

She set their course for one of the glowing yellow lights emanating through the sand and darkness up ahead.

Jehan didn't miss the uncertain glances he drew as he and Seraphina brought the injured child into the small field hospital. Their wariness didn't bother him. Being Breed, he was accustomed to the wide berth most humans tended to give him. And it didn't escape his notice that one of the nurses carrying a cooler with a large red cross on it made an immediate about-face retreat the instant her eyes landed on him—as if her stash of refrigerated red cells might provoke him to attack.

The humans needn't have worried about that. His kind only consumed fresh blood, taken from an open vein.

And right now, the only veins that interested him at all belonged to the beautiful woman standing next to him. Even dressed in his worn shirt and oversized pants, Seraphina stirred everything male in him the same way she stirred the vampire side of his nature.

Just because their kiss had been interrupted by the storm and a distressed child, that didn't mean he'd forgotten any of that fire Seraphina had ignited in him. Now that the little girl was safe and in the care of a doctor, Jehan's attention—all of his focus—was centered on how quickly he could get back to where he and Seraphina had left off.

But he stood by patiently as she made introductions and explained to her fellow volunteers that Jehan was her friend, that he was the one who went out into the storm to locate Yasmin. Seraphina's vouching for him seemed enough to put the humans at ease, since it was clear that everyone at the camp trusted and adored her.

He was beginning to feel likewise.

More than beginning to feel that way, in fact.

After the medic and nurses went back to their work, Seraphina turned to look up at him.

"When you brought Yasmin out of the storm, you said her leg was broken." He nodded, but that didn't seem to satisfy Seraphina's curiosity. "Actually, you said her fibula had two fractures and that her ankle was badly sprained. You were right, Jehan. According to the field medic just a few minutes ago, you were one hundred percent accurate. You told me you *felt* her injuries. You can feel physical injuries?"

He shrugged, barely acknowledging the ability he so seldom used.

"Can you heal them too?"

"No. And now you know my curse," he murmured wryly. "I can inventory someone's wounds, but I can't help them."

She tilted her head at him, warmth sparkling in her eyes. "You helped Yasmin tonight."

Jehan stared at her, unsure how to respond. Seraphina couldn't know how his so-called gift had hobbled him in his life. He'd grown up feeling useless, aimless. It wasn't until he'd found the Order that he realized there were other ways to do something meaningful with his life. That his life had purpose.

She was still studying him, looking gorgeous and far too interested in him as she held his gaze. "The storm's really blowing out there. Do you want to wait it out in here or would you rather go to my place?"

He arched a brow. "Your place?"

"My tent." She smiled, and the warmth of it went straight to his groin. "It's where I stay when I'm here at the camp for any length of time. It's not all that comfortable, but it is private."

Jehan's grin broke slowly across his face. "Miss Sanhaja, are you trying to seduce me?"

She licked her lips, tilting her head as she held his hungry gaze. "I think I might be."

Holy hell. The promise in her voice had his blood racing so hard and fast to his cock, he wasn't sure he'd make it to her tent.

"Lead the way," he drawled thickly, his fangs already punching out of his gums.

He held the blanket aloft over them as they dashed out of the medical building and raced through the blizzard of sand. Seraphina's tent stood toward the far end of the camp. By the time they reached it and found their way past the zipper and ties that secured the shelter's entrance, they were coated in a thin layer of grit. They stumbled inside together hand-in-hand, Seraphina laughing and breathless in the dark.

She left him for a moment, bending to turn on a lantern.

The soft light put a glow on her pinkened cheeks and on the flush of color rising up the smooth column of her throat, making the fine sand that dusted her skin glitter like diamonds. Under the windblown tangle of her long brown curls, her sandalwood-colored eyes were fathomless and filled with desire. Her breath was still racing and shallow, the outline of her breasts teasing him from under the crisp white linen of his shirt.

He'd never seen anything so lovely.

With the storm howling all around them, sand buffeting the tent like rain, Jehan stood speechless, the sight of her like this branding itself into his memory forever.

He couldn't resist reaching out to stroke the velvet of her cheek. And then that wasn't enough either, so he cupped her face in his hands and dragged her into a fierce kiss.

The instant their mouths met, it was as if no time had passed between their fevered kiss before the sandstorm and this electric moment now. Hell, it was as if they were merely picking up where they left off that first night at the villa. All of the hunger he felt for this female, all of the desire...it was right there below the surface, waiting for the chance to reignite.

And he knew that Seraphina felt it too.

On a moan, she melted against him, her lips parting to give his tongue the access it demanded. Heat licked through his veins at the taste of her passion, scorching everything in its path. In an instant, his fangs punched through his gums to fill his mouth. Need hammered in his temples, in his chest. In the aching length of his cock.

He groaned with the intensity of it.

He had to pace himself. Wanted to take this slowly with her, despite his own impatience to have her spread out beneath him as he buried himself inside her.

But Seraphina was merciless. Her wet mouth and gusting breath tore at his resolve. Her soft curves and strong, questing fingers on his shoulders and chest, in his hair, stripped away his already threadbare control.

Sliding his hands under the loose hem of the tunic, he greedily caressed the firm swell of her satin-covered breasts. Seraphina gasped, arching into him as he flicked open the front clasp of her bra and cupped her bare flesh in his palms. Her nipples were tight little buds that pebbled even harder as he rolled and tweaked them between his fingers, hungry to taste them.

He released her, but only so he could take the shirt off and feast on her with his eyes.

He drew the linen over her head and let it fall to the floor of the tent. The red sash holding up her pants came off next. He untied it and watched as the slackened waistband of the linen trousers slid off her hips to pool at her feet.

"So beautiful," he murmured, reaching out to run the backs of his knuckles down her arm, then across the flat plane of her belly. He ventured further, toying with the lacy edge of her delicate panties. "This is what I wanted to do that first night with you, Seraphina. Undress you inch by inch. Pretend I had the right to look at you like this and think I could ever be worthy of having you."

She slowly shook her head. "I don't want you to pretend, Jehan. Tonight, I don't want you to stop. I didn't want you to stop that first night either."

A sound escaped him, something raw and otherworldly. He slid his fingers into the scrap of fabric between her legs, and...holy fuck.

She was almost bare beneath the lace. And wet. So damn wet.

Hot, liquid silk bathed his fingertips as he delved into her slick cleft.

She bit her lip, dropping her head back on a sigh. Holding on to him as he stroked her silky folds, she squirmed and shuddered against his touch. "Jehan, don't make me wait. Please, don't make me want like this again."

"No chance of that," he uttered, his voice like gravel in his throat, raw with desire. "Not tonight."

Not ever again, some possessive part of him growled in agreement.

He didn't know where it came from—the bone-deep sense that he belonged with this woman.

That she was *his*.

And that as ridiculous as the ancient pact between their families was, it had somehow delivered him to the one woman he craved more than any other before.

Jehan drew her mouth to his and kissed her again, as reverent as it was claiming. He broke contact only so he could strip out of his shirt and jeans, leaving both at his feet. He wore nothing underneath, and as soon as his cock sprang free, Seraphina's hands found him.

She stroked and caressed him, her fingers so sure and fevered, he nearly came on the spot.

Need twisted tight and hot with every slide of her hands over his stiff shaft, pressure coiling at the base of his spine.

Somehow, he managed to collect himself enough to douse the lantern with his mind. The tent plunged into darkness. Although the sandstorm raged outside, driving everyone in the camp indoors, he wasn't going to share Seraphina or this moment with anyone else.

Pulling her down onto the pallet of blankets and pillows with him, Jehan removed her panties, then smoothed his hand along every beautiful swell and delicately muscled plane on her nude body. The temptation of her sex was too much. The sweet scent of her arousal drenched his senses as he moved over her, parting her thighs until she was opened to him like an exotic flower.

One he couldn't wait to taste.

He lowered his head between her legs, groaning in a mix of agony and ecstasy as his tongue met her nectar-sweet, hot, wet flesh. His fangs were already fully extended, but at the first swallow of Seraphina's juices, the sharp points grew even larger.

The urge to bite—to draw blood and make her his in the most powerful way he knew how—rose up on him without warning.

No.

He tamped the impulse down hard, blindsided by the force of it.

Losing himself to carnal pleasure was one thing. Binding Seraphina to him for eternity was another. And it was a line he wouldn't cross.

He had no room in his life for a mate, and if she woke up in the morning with regrets, he sure as hell didn't want one of them to be irrevocable.

Tonight, he wanted to give her pleasure.

Selfishly, he wanted to give her the kind of pleasure that would ensure that every other male who'd ever touched her was obliterated from her memory.

Tonight, Seraphina was his—not because some ridiculous agreement said she should be, but because she wanted to be.

Because she felt the same undeniable desire that he did.

"Come for me," he rasped against her tender flesh. "I want to hear you, Seraphina."

"Oh God," she gasped in reply, arching up to meet his mouth as he kissed and sucked and teased with his lips and tongue. When she writhed and mewled in rising pleasure, he gave her more, sliding a finger through her juices and into the tight entrance of her body. She cried out as he added another, thrusting in tempo with his tongue's deep strokes.

He glanced up the length of her twisting body. "Open your eyes, beauty. I want to see you come for me."

She obeyed, lifting heavy lids, her gaze drunk with pleasure. "Jehan, please..."

Her hands tangled and fisted in his hair as he coaxed her higher, desperate for her pleasure—for her release—before he would let himself inside.

Ah, fuck. He'd never seen anything as erotic as Seraphina caught at the crest of orgasm. The sexy sounds she made. The unbridled response of her body. The tight, hot vise of her sheath, clamping down around his fingers as he flicked his tongue over her clit and drove her relentlessly toward a shattering release.

She held his gaze in the dark, and when she crashed apart a

moment later, it was with his name on her lips.

Jehan couldn't curb his satisfied grin.

He rose over her, pressing her knees to her chest as he guided his cock between the slick folds of her sex. Her eyes were locked on his, her body still flushed and shuddering with the aftershocks of her release. He tested her tight entrance with a small thrust of his hips, groaning as her little muscular walls enveloped the head of his shaft.

He grasped for control and found he had none.

Not where this woman was concerned.

And why that didn't scare the hell out of him, he didn't know.

Right now, with Seraphina wet and ready for him, the question damn well didn't matter.

With a harsh curse, he flexed his pelvis and seated himself to the root.

CHAPTER 11

She gasped Jehan's name as he took her in one deep, breath-stealing thrust.

His wicked mouth and fingers had left her nerve endings vibrating and numb with sensation, her body slick and hot from release. But each rolling push of Jehan's hips stoked her arousal to life once more. His cock stretched her, filled her so completely she could barely accommodate all of his length and girth. She closed her eyes against the staggering ecstasy that built as he moved inside her, his powerful strokes and relentless tempo driving her to the edge of her sanity.

She'd never felt anything as intoxicating as the naked strength of Jehan's magnificent body. That all of his passion—all of his immense control—was concentrated on her pleasure was a drug she could easily become addicted to. Maybe she already was because her hunger for him was only growing more consuming with every hard crash of his body against hers.

Reaching up between them, he drew one of her legs down from where it lay bent against her chest and wrapped it around his waist as he shifted into an even more intense angle. The new position gave her access to his *glyph*-covered pecs and muscled abdomen, which she explored with questing fingers and scoring nails. She lifted her head and watched him pound into her, mesmerized by the violent, erotic beauty of their need.

Jehan made an approving noise in the back of his throat. "Do you like the way we look, Sera? Your legs spread open so wide for me, my cock buried in your heat?"

"Yes." *Oh, God.* Had she thought she was already at the brink of combusting? His dark voice inflamed her even more. She tore her gaze away from their joining only to meet the crackling fire that blazed down at her from his transformed eyes. "Jehan...I didn't know it could be like this. Watching you push inside me like you can't get deep enough. I love seeing us together like this. I love the way we feel."

"Mm," he responded, more growl than reply. "Then let me give you even more."

He set a new pace that destroyed her already slipping control. Another orgasm mounted and twisted inside her, sweeping her into a dizzying spiral of pleasure. She caught her lip between her teeth on a strangled moan as the climax swelled, nearing its breaking point.

Jehan's rhythm showed no mercy. He rode her harder, deeper, his hips pistoning furiously.

She arched beneath him, unable to hold on any longer. Turning her head into her pillow, she let go of a scream as her release broke over her in wave after wave of bliss.

Jehan pumped furiously as she came, then a rough curse ripped out of him. He tensed, his muscles hardening like granite beneath her fingertips as she clung to him. His amber-lit eyes blazed hot, locked on her.

He hissed her name, torment and pleasure etched in his handsome, savage face. Then a roar boiled past his teeth and fangs. His hips thrust viciously, then he plunged deep on a curse as the sudden, scorching flow of his seed erupted inside her.

She'd never felt so sated. So deliciously fucked.

She caressed Jehan as his body relaxed and his orgasm ebbed. But his cock had lost little of its stiffness inside her. And as he murmured rumbling praises for the way she felt, his strong fingers petting her hair and cheeks and breasts, that lingering stiffness had returned to steel again.

She couldn't control her body's response to him, nor could she curb her shaky sigh of pleasure as his shaft swelled to capacity and the walls of her sex clenched to hold him. She moved beneath him, creating a slick friction.

"Holy fuck, Sera." He closed his eyes for a moment, head

tipped back on his shoulders as she invited him to take her again. When his gaze came back to hers, the fire that had been there before flared even hotter. "I should've walked away. Now, it's too late. It's too fucking late for both of us."

She nodded, knowing he was right. They should have resisted this heat that lived between them.

They should have refused the handfast and all that came with it.

They both should have realized that giving in to this desire would only spark a greater need.

For Sera, what she felt for Jehan went beyond physical need or even a passing affection. Tonight, she'd seen a new side of him. Not the arrogant Breed male who strode through life as if he owned the world. Not the Order warrior who dealt in ruthless justice and death.

Tonight, at the camp, she'd witnessed a different side of him. Jehan was a kind man, a compassionate man. She'd glimpsed the honor inside him, and now that she had seen those things, she would never be able to regard him in any lesser light.

So, yes. It was much too late for her to walk away from anything that happened between them tonight.

And if she should regret that fact, she never would.

Not when Jehan was looking at her the way he was now, with fever in his eyes and desire riding the furious arcs and swirls of his multicolored *dermaglyphs*. And not when his amazing cock was making her yearn to be taken all over again.

"On your knees this time," he commanded her, his deep voice husky and raw.

Her eyes widened in surprise, but she eagerly scrambled out from under him to obey. He loomed behind her, the heat of his presence scalding her backside. His fingers waded through their combined juices, wringing a desperate mewl from her throat as the wet sounds of his caresses joined the dry howl of the sandstorm still raging outside the tent.

She felt the thick length of his cock between her swollen folds. Then he grasped her hips in his hands and slowly impaled her on him, inch by glorious inch.

They set a less frantic pace now, somehow finding the will to savor the pleasure, making it last as long as they could hold out.

After they had both climaxed again, they dropped into a lazy sprawl on her blanket-strewn pallet.

For a long while, there were no words between them. They lay together in the dark, listening to the hiss of swirling sand as the storm continued to sweep through the camp.

Sera was stretched alongside him, one arm resting on his chest. She traced the pattern of *glyphs* that spread over his smooth skin, memorizing the Breed skin markings that were unique to him alone. They were beautiful. And so was he.

"I need to thank you for tonight, Jehan."

He grunted. "No need, trust me." His strong arm tightened around her, bringing her closer against him. "I should be the one thanking you."

She rose up to look at his face. "No, I mean for what you did tonight. For helping me bring the supplies here. For going out into the storm to find Yasmin and make sure she got the care she needed for her injured leg."

He shrugged mildly. "Again, there's no need for thanks. I did what anyone would do."

"Not anyone," she said. "And I never would've expected it from you. I misjudged you when we met, and for that, I also owe you an apology."

He cupped her nape and brought her down to him for a tender kiss. "Maybe we both were too quick to judge. When you told me you only agreed to the handfast to collect the trust from your father, I assumed you were willing to take his bribe because you wanted the money for yourself. And not that it should matter why you wanted it, but it did. Tonight at the checkpoint, I know what you did. I realized what you've been doing all along—using your personal funds to buy clearance for camp supplies."

She frowned. "It's only money. How can I keep it when those supplies mean life or death to the people who depend on me?"

"Your work obviously means a lot to you." There was a soberness in his eyes as he studied her in the darkened tent. "You told me that night we walked in the garden that your work is a calling."

"I did say that, yes." It surprised her that he remembered the offhand remark.

"What did you mean, Seraphina?"

She glanced down at her hand where it rested on his chest. "When I was eighteen, I volunteered one winter at an orphanage about an hour away from our Darkhaven. My parents encouraged it, since I was orphaned as an infant too."

Jehan made an acknowledging sound. "A lot of Breedmates find their way into Breed households as abandoned and orphaned babies or young girls."

She nodded. She and her sister were both adopted by the Sanhajas in such a way. "I was lucky. Someone saw my birthmark and recognized that I was different. There was a place for me because of that. But there were no Breedmates in the orphanage I went to that year. Only human children. Many of them were refugees whose parents had been killed in wars or died of famine and disease." She curled her fingers into a tight ball. "There was so much pain in that place. I felt it every time I held a crying baby or embraced one of those sweet, terrified kids."

"You felt it," Jehan murmured, understanding fully now. He reached up to take her hand, bringing her knuckles to his lips. "You felt their emotional pain, because, like me, you're an empath."

Every Breedmate, like every Breed male, was born with a unique extrasensory ability. Some were blessings, others were less of a gift. Where Jehan could register physical injuries, hers was the ability to feel emotional pain with a touch.

"I thought I could handle it," she said. "But everything I felt stayed with me. Until my time working at the orphanage that winter, I didn't know how to help. Now I do what I can."

He'd gone quiet as she spoke, and Sera knew he understood. Given his own ability, Jehan probably understood her better than anyone else could.

"You're an incredible woman, Seraphina." He shook his head, his thumb stroking idly over her jawline. "I think I recognized that the minute we met, but I was too busy looking for reasons to dislike you. I wanted to find hidden flaws, since it was obvious I wasn't going to find any on the outside."

His praise warmed her. "I haven't been able to find much fault in you either. And believe me, I tried. I called you a killer when I found out you were a warrior with the Order. That wasn't fair. I know that now. I also thought your biggest personal flaw might be an overblown opinion of your own charms. I think you've proven the point tonight, though. I suppose I have to give credit where it's due."

He chuckled. "If what I just did with you was charming, then just wait until you see my wicked side."

She grinned down at him. "When can I look forward to that?"

"If you're not careful, sooner than you think."

He grabbed her ass and gave it a playful smack. Then he tumbled her onto her back and covered her with his hard, fully aroused body. The crackling embers in his eyes promised he was about to make good on his threat right then and there.

CHAPTER 12

The storm had passed some time ago.

Jehan lay on his back in the dark tent, holding Seraphina as she slept naked and draped over him in a boneless sprawl. He'd been awake for a while, listening to the calm outside and trying to convince himself that he needed to get out of bed.

As much as he hated to disturb her sleep or forfeit the pleasant feel of her resting sated in his arms, he knew he should go out and check their vehicle, make sure it wasn't buried under a mound of sand. With the weather cleared, he was eager to get on the road.

He guessed it to be early morning, probably only two or three hours after midnight. If they didn't delay too long, it was possible they could make it back to the villa before sunrise. Otherwise, it meant spending the day at the camp, waiting until sunset when it was safe for him to make the drive again.

And while he could think of a lot of interesting ways to pass the hours with Seraphina alone in her tent, he wasn't ashamed to admit that he'd rather explore those options in the comfort of the villa.

Which meant getting his ass out of her bed ASAP, so he could expedite that process.

With care not to wake her, he eased himself out from under her and rolled away from the thin mattress on the floor.

Dressing quietly, he then slipped out of the tent to begin the trek toward the place he'd parked the Rover. He was the only one outside so soon after the storm. He hoofed it through the quiet camp, his boots putting fresh tracks on the sand-drifted road that cut through the center of the tents and outbuildings.

The Rover could have been worse. Sand coated the black vehicle and had blown into every crack and crevice. He dug it out and brushed it down as best he could and was just about to start it up when his preternatural hearing picked up the sound of men's voices elsewhere in the dark. Somewhere near the main supply building.

Jehan recognized Karsten Hemmings's dramatic tenor instantly. The other man sounded like one of the helpers who'd assisted in unloading the delivery earlier tonight.

Jehan listened, suspicion prickling his senses. On instinct, he reached into the Rover and retrieved the pair of daggers he'd stored under the driver's seat. Although he had busted Seraphina's pretty ass over the fact she'd brought her phone to the handfast, his breach of the terms by bringing his Order patrol blades was probably the worst of the two offenses.

Right about now, he was damn glad he had the weapons.

Tucking one into his boot and the other into the back waistband of his jeans, he stole around the rear of the tents and outbuildings, his senses trained on the pair of men. Sand sifted with their quick footsteps. Karsten issued orders to his accomplice in a low, urgent whisper.

"Pick up the pace, Massoud! My contact has been waiting on this shit for days. We've got less than an hour to make the drop and collect our money."

What the hell?

Karsten's Jeep was parked at the rear of the outbuilding. The back hatch had been swung open, while Karsten and the other camp worker were apparently loading the vehicle with crates taken out of the main supply.

Jehan crept through the shadows, peering at the contents of the Jeep while both men had gone back inside the building for more. Three crates labeled as canned meat sat in the back of the vehicle. Supplies that he and Seraphina had delivered earlier tonight.

One of the crates had been pried apart, several of the cans inside opened. An odd blue glow emanated from inside the containers.

At first, Jehan wasn't sure what he was seeing.

Not canned meats, that much was certain.

Each container held a palm-sized electronic object comprised of a metal casing and a glass center chamber. Inside the glass was a milky blue substance that glowed like a vial of pure energy.

Like a source of harnessed, weapons-grade ultraviolet light.

Holy shit.

The instant realization dawned on him, Karsten's cohort came around the back of the building. He was empty-handed, but the second his eyes lit on Jehan, he reached for his gun and fired a panicked round. Reacting almost instantly, Jehan let his blade fly, dropping Massoud dead in the sand.

The discharged bullet flew wild into the air. The cracking report of the gunshot echoed, shattering the sleepy calm of the camp. Screams and commotion stirred at once in some of the nearby tents.

Karsten raced out of the supply building. "Massoud, for crissake—"

He drew up short when he came face to face with Jehan holding his comrade's gun.

Jehan bared his fangs. "Doing a little dealing on the side, I see. What's the going rate on UV grenades these days?"

Karsten narrowed his eyes. "More than you could imagine, vampire."

The impulse to blow the human's head off was nearly overwhelming. But caution warned him that this was also Seraphina's longtime coworker. She considered Karsten Hemmings her friend.

As much as Jehan wanted to waste the bastard for profiting off Breed-killing UV arms and using Seraphina's goodwill to front it, that call wasn't his to make. Not like this.

"We both know you're not going to use that gun on me," Karsten taunted. "She'll hate you for it. Of course, if you pull that trigger, you'd better be prepared to die with me."

It was then that Jehan noticed the human held something tight in his fist. The blue glow poured out between his fingers.

"The detonator is already tripped," he confirmed. "The UV blast won't give me more than a sunburn. You, however..."

Jehan ignored the threat. He would deal with the fallout if and when it occurred. Right now, he wanted answers. If he had any chance of getting information to the Order, he needed answers.

"Who's waiting for this shipment, Karsten? Who's paying you for this shit?"

"Oh, come now. I think you know. Every warrior in the Order should know the answer to that question." He chuckled. "Yes, I know you're one of them. I did some checking tonight. Made a few calls. You're part of the Rome unit."

Jehan glowered. "And you're part of Opus Nostrum."

Karsten pursed his lips and gave a faint shake of his head. "Merely a businessman. And a like-minded individual. I despise your entire race of blood-sucking monsters. If Opus wants your kind eradicated and a war to make it happen, I'm only too happy to help send you all to your graves. Or into the light, as the case may be."

"Karsten?" Seraphina emerged out of the darkness, disheveled and confused. "Oh, my God. Jehan, what on earth is going—"

"Seraphina, stay back!"

Jehan's warning came too late. She had already strayed right into the middle of the standoff.

And Karsten seized his chance to let his weapon loose.

The UV grenade went airborne.

Jehan had precious little time to react. He dived under the Jeep as the light exploded all around him. The power of it was immense. Even from beneath the undercarriage of the vehicle, he could feel the searing energy of the solar detonation. It extinguished a moment later, plunging the desert back into darkness.

He was shielded.

He was alive.

But the act of self-preservation had just cost him dearly.

He heard Seraphina cry out, and he knew Karsten Hemmings had her.

The realization tore his heart from his chest. He couldn't let her be harmed. He couldn't lose her.

He never wanted to lose her.

On a roar, Jehan rolled out to his feet to face the bastard. Karsten had a pistol on her, held against the back of her head. And Jehan had dropped his gun somewhere in the sand.

"Let her go."

Karsten sneered. "Let her go so you can have her? She

deserves better than you, vampire. Better than anything you can ever give her."

Jehan wasn't going to argue when he was thinking the same thing now, miserable as he drank in the sight of her terrified face and her tender brown eyes pleading for him to help her.

"Let her go, Karsten. If you do, maybe I'll let you live. But only if Seraphina wants me to."

The human chuckled. "No, I don't think so. We're going to leave now. I'm going to make my drop and collect my money. Then Sera and I are going to get out of this godforsaken hellhole and enjoy our spoils." He nestled his open mouth against her cheek, the nose of the gun still pressed against her skull. "You'll see, my love. I can give you everything you need."

She winced and closed her eyes, a miserable sound curling up from her throat.

Jehan couldn't bear another second of her torment. He had to act. He had one chance to end this, but he couldn't do it without her total faith in him.

"Seraphina." He spoke her name softly, reverently. Hoping she could hear how much she meant to him. "Look at me, sweetheart."

Her eyes opened and found his gaze through the dark.

He couldn't say the words out loud without betraying his plan, but he needed her to understand. He needed her to trust him.

Do you trust me, Seraphina?

He said it with his eyes. With his heart.

Trust me, baby. Please...

She gave him a nearly imperceptible nod.

It was enough. It was all the permission he needed.

Moving with every ounce of Breed agility and speed he possessed, Jehan reached around to his back and pulled out the dagger he'd stashed there. He let it fly from his fingertips.

An instant later, Karsten Hemmings dropped to the ground, Jehan's blade protruding from the space between his wide-open eyes.

Jehan ran to Seraphina and pulled her into his arms.

In that moment, nothing else mattered.

Not Karsten Hemmings. Not the Jeep full of UV grenades, or Opus Nostrum.

Not even the Order mattered as he drew Seraphina close and

kissed her with all the relief and emotion—all the love—he felt for her.

He stroked her beautiful face and stared down into the soft brown eyes that now owned his heart and his soul. "Come on," he said, drawing her under the protection of his arm. "Let's get out of here."

CHAPTER 13

Sera was still numb with shock and disbelief several hours later, after Jehan had driven them back to the villa.

Karsten's betrayal cut deep. That he had used her to free up the supplies containing his hidden cargo was bad enough. But the idea that greed and hatred had poisoned his humanity so much that he was willing to kill—willing to traffic in weaponry designed for the wholesale slaughter of the Breed—was unthinkable. It was unforgivable.

Countless innocent lives were saved today, now that the UV grenades had been diverted from their buyer and stowed safely inside the villa.

As for Karsten and Massoud, when the other camp workers and residents came upon the scene and heard what the two men had been up to, there had been no shortage of volunteers offering to dispose of their bodies in the desert so that Sera and Jehan could get on the road as quickly as possible to beat the sunrise.

Sera had considered Karsten a friend for years, but there wasn't any part of her that mourned his death today even for a second. If not for Jehan's quick thinking and speed with his blade, she had no doubt that Karsten would have killed her.

He had almost killed Jehan too.

The terror she'd felt at that possibility had nearly gutted her as she'd stood helplessly in Karsten's grasp. Even now, the reality of how close she'd come to losing Jehan left her physically and emotionally shaken.

But he was alive.

Because of his warrior skills, they both were alive.

"Are you all right, Sera?" His deep, caring voice wrapped around her as they stood inside the villa together. "Is there anything I can do for you?"

She shook her head but couldn't keep from moving into the shelter of his arms. This was all she needed. His warmth enveloping her. His strong heartbeat pounding steadily against her ear as she rested her head on his muscled chest. She just needed...him.

"You should call your brother," she murmured. Marcel had left two messages on her phone in the past couple of hours, asking them to contact him as soon as possible. "We should let him know we've returned, at least so he can stop worrying that we're going to break the pact."

Jehan's chest rumbled with a sound of disregard. "I should call the Order too, and tell them what I'll be bringing back to Rome with me in a few nights. But my brother and everyone else can wait. The only thing I'm concerned about right now is you."

He pulled back and looked at her, a dark storm brewing in the pale blue of his eyes. When he lifted her chin and took her mouth in a slow, savoring kiss, it was easy to imagine that what she saw in his gaze—what she felt in his embrace and in his tender kiss—was something deeper than concern or simple affection.

It was easy to imagine it might be love.

"You're trembling, Seraphina." He reached out to caress her face and shoulder. "And you're cold too. Come on. Let me take care of you."

Maybe Leila had been right—that there was some brand of magic at work when it came to the pact between their families. Sera could almost believe it now because with Jehan leading her through the villa, his fingers laced with hers, it was far too easy to imagine that everything they shared since entering the handfast was somehow paving a path toward a future together. A future that might just last an eternity.

She hadn't missed his reference to the life waiting for him at the end of the handfast. She couldn't pretend that her own life wasn't waiting for her too.

But for the next few nights, she wasn't going to let reality intrude.

Jehan brought her into the cavernous bathing room with its towering marble columns and steaming, spring-fed bath the size of a swimming pool. He sat her down on the edge, then crouched down in front of her to remove her shoes. The soft leather flats were caked with sand and spattered with Karsten's dried blood. Jehan hissed a low curse as he set them aside.

When he lifted his head to meet her gaze, there was doubt in his eyes. "Can you forgive me, Sera?"

"For saving me from Karsten?" She shook her head. "There's nothing to forgive."

"No." His mouth flattened into a grim line. "I mean, for saving myself. For giving him the chance to get a hold of you in the first place."

Oh, God. Is that what he thought? Is that what weighed on his conscience now?

Sera leaned forward to take his tormented, handsome face in her palms. His anguish was palpable. She could feel the dull pain of it through her empathic gift. "Jehan, when I saw that flash of light as Karsten let the grenade go, I knew it would be lethal to you. I thought I was about to watch you die. If you hadn't protected yourself, we both would've been dead today. You saved me."

He studied her for a long moment, as if he wanted to say something more. Then he turned his face into her hand and placed a kiss in its center before drawing out of her loose grasp. "Let's get these clothes off and get you warm."

He stood up, taking her with him. With careful hands, he undressed her, peeling off the rumpled linen tunic and her bra. Then he drew down the loose-fitting pants and her lacy panties beneath. His gaze drank her in slowly, his eyes crackling with amber sparks.

When he finally spoke, his voice was dark and gravelly, rough with desire. "Earlier tonight, when I saw you naked like this for the first time, I said you were beautiful."

She licked her lips. "I remember."

She would never forget anything he said in her tent a few hours ago, nor anything he'd done. Arousal spiraled through her, as much at the reminder as under the intensity of his gaze now.

"I said you were beautiful, Seraphina...but I was wrong." He cupped her cheek in his palm, then slowly let his fingers drift down her shoulder, his thumb pausing to caress the Breedmate mark on her upper arm. "You are exquisite. The loveliest female I have ever, and will ever, lay my unworthy eyes on."

She started to shake her head in protest of his self-deprecation, but his kiss caught her lips before she could speak.

All of her desire for him—all of her tangled emotions—rose up to engulf her. She wanted him.

Loved him so powerfully it staggered her.

Only fear held her confession back.

Fear, and need.

She pulled back, breath heaving. Wordlessly, she unbuttoned his shirt and pushed it off his strong arms. Each swirl and flourish of the *dermaglyphs* that tracked over his powerful chest and muscled abdomen was a temptation to her fingers and her mouth.

She touched and kissed and licked her way down his immense body, finally lowering herself to her knees before him. His lungs rasped with the ragged tempo of his breathing as she unzipped his jeans and slid them down his hard thighs.

His cock bobbed heavily in front of her, the thick shaft and blunt, glistening plum at the crown making her mouth water for a taste. He groaned as she grasped his length in her hands, his muscles tensing, breath hitching, as she stroked him from root to head and back again.

When she leaned forward and wrapped her lips around him, his spine arched and he let out a tight hiss and guttural snarl. She'd never held so much force and power in her hands before, nor in her mouth. She couldn't get enough. And as his body's response quickened, it only made her hungry for more. For all of him.

She glanced up as she sucked him and found his fiery eyes locked on her. His pupils were thin and wild, utterly Breed. His broad mouth was pulled into a grimace, baring his teeth and the enormous length of his fangs.

She moaned, overwhelmed by the preternatural beauty of the male staring down at her. His large palm cupped the back of her head, his long fingers speared into her hair as she took the full depth of him into her mouth at a relentless tempo.

"Seraphina," he uttered hoarsely. "Ah, fuck..."

On a sharp groan, he withdrew from between her lips and scooped her up into his arms as if she weighed nothing at all. He carried her down into the steaming bath, fastening his mouth on hers in an urgent, fevered kiss as he sank to his shoulders in the warm water with her held aloft in his arms.

He tore his mouth away from hers, scowling fiercely. "I'm supposed to be the one taking care of you, if you recall."

She lifted a brow in challenge. "Is that your charming side talking or your wicked one?"

Sparks flared in his hot gaze. "Which do you prefer?"

"I haven't decided yet." Pivoting under the surface of the water, she faced him on his lap and wrapped her legs around his waist. The thick jut of his cock rose tall between them, the crisp hair at its root tickling her sex. She looped her arms over his shoulders and drifted close for a teasing kiss. "Fortunately, we've got all day to figure it out."

His hands gripped her ass and he smirked against her mouth. "All day, and another five nights after that."

"You think it's long enough?" she murmured, her lips still brushing his.

His answering chuckle was purely male and totally wicked. As was the meaningful shift of his hips that positioned his erection at the hot and ready entrance of her body. "Why don't you tell me if it's long enough?"

He lifted her onto him, and her laugh melted into a pleasured sigh as he sheathed every last inch.

CHAPTER 14

When he'd first arrived at the villa, Jehan had imagined what Seraphina might look like unclothed and wreathed in the steam of the bathing room as he made love to her. Now he knew. And none of his fantasies were any match for the true thing.

She met his rhythm stroke for stroke. Arousal arced through him with each rotation of her hips, making his vision bleed red as fire filled his gaze. This woman had ruined him for any other. She destroyed him with a smile, with every moan and gasp, and he hadn't even begun to show her what true pleasure was.

He rocked inside her, balanced on the edge of madness for how incredible they felt together.

Eight nights wasn't enough.

The part of him that was more beast than man snapped at that tether. Eight nights was nothing. And they had already lost three of them.

The part of him that was nearly immortal demanded much more than that. It wanted forever.

Something he couldn't give Seraphina.

Not when forever meant one of them would have to give up the life that waited for them on the other side of the handfast.

Real life—the one that she had devoted herself to, and the opposite one he was equally committed to. Real life, where her selflessness had nearly gotten her killed a few hours ago, and where he was the Order warrior whose work revolved around violence and death. Where cowardly men like Karsten Hemmings served diabolical groups like Opus Nostrum.

He couldn't turn his back on the things that mattered to him any more than he could ask Seraphina to turn her back on hers.

But it was damned tempting to think about forever when they were enveloped within the fantasy of the handfast.

With his arms around her and her legs circling his waist as they moved together, joined beneath the fragrant, steaming water, forever was the only thing on his mind.

Eternity with Seraphina at his side.

As his Breedmate.

Bonded by blood.

The thought sent his gaze to the smooth column of her throat. Her pulse fluttered, beating with a rhythm he could feel echoing in his own veins. His fangs, already elongated from passion, now throbbed with an equally primal need.

A dangerous, selfish need.

One bite and there would be no other woman for him as long as he lived. All it would take was a single taste. Everything Breed in him pounded with the urge to sink his fangs into her flesh and take that binding sip.

Equally strong was his need to bind Seraphina to him by blood as well. If she drank from him, she would belong to no other male. His forever.

He couldn't do that to her.

He wouldn't.

Instead he guided her toward a fevered climax, driving into her body with all the hunger that rode him in his blood. He gave her pleasure, moving relentlessly until she broke apart in his arms on a scream.

Then he pivoted her around and moved in behind her to follow her over the edge.

As he came inside her on a shout, he couldn't dismiss the cold knowledge that the clock on their time together was ticking—so fast he could feel it in his bones.

Eight nights with Seraphina wasn't enough.

But somehow, at the end of it, he was going to have to find the strength to let her go.

CHAPTER 15

Sera woke from a long sleep later that morning feeling drowsy and sated. Sore in all the right places. She couldn't curb the smile that crept over her face as she recalled the hours she'd spent in the bathing room making love with Jehan. Their sex had been exhausting and incredible—which, she was beginning to realize, was the norm where he was concerned.

He was a tireless, wickedly creative lover. When she'd lost count of her orgasms and was sure she couldn't take any more pleasure, he had lifted her from the steaming pool and carried her to one of several nests of plump cushions and silk pillows on the floor for another bone-melting round.

If she'd thought watching their bodies move together in the darkness of her camp tent had been erotic, it had been nothing compared to seeing every carnal nuance of their passion in the candlelit reflection in the bathing room mirrors.

Just the thought of their tangled limbs and questing mouths had her pulse thrumming all over again as she wandered into the villa's kitchen for a light breakfast. Jehan was awake too—if he'd slept at all. His deep voice carried in a low, indistinct murmur from the main living area in the heart of the retreat. He was on her phone apparently. She hoped he had gotten back to Marcel after his brother's repeated messages for them to report in.

Sera made some tea and grabbed a peach from a bowl of fruit on the counter. Her long curls poured loose around her shoulders and over her bare breasts as she padded quietly out of the kitchen in just her panties to join him.

Biting into the ripe peach as she walked, she considered how much sweeter the juice would be if she were licking it off Jehan's muscled body. Or sucking it off the hard length of his cock.

Oh God...she had it bad for this male.

He made her feel more alive than anything in her life ever had. Yes, she lived for her work. It had fulfilled her for a long time, given her purpose. But Jehan gave her pleasure. He gave her yearning and contentment, excitement and peace. He had opened a part of her she hadn't even realized had been closed before.

Most unsettling of all, he made her long for the one thing she'd never imagined she might need. A mate by blood. A bond that could never be broken, not even by time.

As he'd made love to her hours ago, there had been a moment when she almost believed Jehan might want that too.

She wouldn't have refused him.

They'd been drunk with passion, and in the heat of that limitless pleasure, he could have taken all of her—body, heart, soul, and blood. She would have surrendered everything she was. Without even knowing what a future together might look like once the handfast was over and they left the cocoon of the villa.

She would give it all to him now too, clear-headed and sober.

Not at the end of their eight nights, but now.

And as much as it scared her, she had to let him know what he meant to her. Even more terrifying, she had to know if what she'd read in his tormented eyes a few hours ago was anything close to the depth of emotion she felt for him.

If he loved her too, then nothing else mattered. They would find a way to blend their lives and form their future together.

But as she rounded the corner of the corridor and overheard some of his conversation, all of her hopes faltered, then fell away. He wasn't talking to Marcel. She hung back, out of Jehan's sight as he spoke with one of his fellow warriors.

"I appreciate your understanding, Commander. I'm eager to be back in Rome to assemble my team and put the new mission into action. I'll be there as soon as my obligation here is over." He paused to listen to the warrior on the other end, then exhaled a heavy sigh. "No, I haven't made Seraphina aware of my decision. To be honest with you, sir, my mind is made up where she's concerned. I don't intend to give her any room to disagree."

He chuckled as if he and his comrade had just shared a joke. Meanwhile, Sera felt as though she'd been punched in the gut.

He was going back to Rome. Eager to get back to his team there.

As for her, he'd just disregarded her as if she didn't matter to him at all.

Sickness roiled in her stomach, in her heart. She shivered, suddenly self-conscious of her nudity in the center of the romantic villa. Silently, she retreated back to the kitchen and dropped the half-eaten peach in the trash.

What a fool she'd been to let herself think this was anything more than a joke to him. It had been from the start. An obligation he felt compelled to fulfill.

One he just admitted to his commander that he would walk away from as soon as it ended.

Thank God she hadn't let herself look even more idiotic by confessing her feelings for him.

Now she had several more nights of torture to look forward to, knowing that Jehan couldn't wait to be finished with the handfast and leave her behind.

CHAPTER 16

Complaints of a headache had driven Seraphina outside to the sunshine for most of the afternoon. Jehan had tried to persuade her that another vigorous round of orgasms might make her feel better instead, but his attempt at humor—and seduction—had failed miserably.

If he wasn't mistaken, her escape to the daylight on the patio seemed no less deliberate now than it had that first full day they'd spent together at the villa. When she'd gone there in an effort to avoid his company.

Had he done something wrong?

Or had she realized how close he'd been to burying his fangs in her carotid the last time they'd made love and was now determined to steer clear of him?

Whatever it was, it bothered him that she didn't seem interested in talking to him about it.

Roaming around the villa alone while she avoided him outside was maddening. He missed her, and she had only been away from him for a couple of hours.

How empty would his life feel if she was gone from it for good?

That was the question that had ridden him most of the past twelve hours—ever since their escape from the danger at the camp. Now that he'd had Seraphina in his life, in his arms, how would he ever be able to return to his existence without her?

He thought he'd known the answer, but maybe he was

mistaken.

As twilight fell outside and she still didn't come inside to face him, Jehan decided he had to know. If she didn't feel the way he did, then he was ready to call off the rest of the handfast and try to save some shred of his sanity, if not his dignity.

He was stalking toward the patio doors when a knock sounded on the villa's front entrance.

Diverted from his mission, Jehan swung around and went over to see who it was.

Marcel stood there in the moonlight, grinning like an idiot.

And beside him—clinging to his arm with an equally besotted smile on her face—was Leila.

"You didn't return my call, brother."

Jehan raked a hand through his mussed hair and blew out an impatient curse. "Yeah. I, ah, was just about to do that."

"Bullshit." Marcel gestured to the Range Rover. "What the hell happened to the Rover? It looks like you drove it through a sand dune."

"Long story," Jehan said. "Suffice it to say things have been somewhat...interesting around here."

"Things have been a bit interesting with me too. With us." Marcel glanced at Leila, and she bit her lower lip as if to stifle the giggle that burst out of her anyway.

Jehan glanced at both of them. "What the hell are you talking about?"

Leila tried to peer around him, into the villa. "Where's Seraphina?"

"She's out on the patio, getting some air. Why are the two of you grinning like you've lost your damn minds?"

"We're in love!" Leila exclaimed.

"And we're blood-bonded," Marcel added.

"What?" Before Jehan could choke out his astonished response, Seraphina did it first. She stood behind him now in a long skirt and curve-hugging tank, a look of utter shock on her face. She crossed her arms. "What do you mean you're in love? How did that happen? And blood-bonded so soon? For God's sake, you only just met each other."

Jehan glanced at her, tempted to point out that they'd only just met too and he was already ruined for anyone else. But her pained expression kept him silent.

Marcel and Leila's excitement left no time for him to reply either. The pair stepped inside, practically vibrating with their news.

"We've been spending a lot of time together the past several days," Leila gushed.

Marcel wagged his brows at her. "And a couple of nights."

"Marcel!" She rolled her eyes, but her cheeks were flooded with bright color. "At first, we thought we only had the handfast in common. We both wanted it to be a success, of course. And honestly, we thought the two of you would make an adorable couple."

Jehan noted a cooler shift in Seraphina's posture as her sister mentioned the handfast. "How can you be sure you're not making a terrible mistake, Leila? You don't know anything about him. No offense, Marcel. You do seem like a good, decent male."

Unlike his brother? Jehan wondered.

Leila stared up at Marcel, warmth beaming from her eyes. "He makes me feel alive, Sera. He makes me laugh. He makes me feel special and beautiful, like I'm the only woman he sees."

Marcel cupped her face in a tender caress. "Because you are."

They kissed, leaving Jehan in awkward silence next to Seraphina. He glanced at her, but she stared rigidly ahead, refusing to meet his gaze.

"Congratulations," she murmured as the jubilant couple finally stopped devouring each other's faces. "I'm happy for you both. I'm sure our families will be happy to hear this news too."

"That's why we're here," Marcel said. "The handfast—"

Leila nodded. "Now that Marcel and I are blood-bonded, there's no need to continue with the handfast. It's over as of right now."

Marcel must have read Jehan's grim expression. He cleared his throat. "That is, unless you *want* to continue...?"

"Don't be ridiculous," Seraphina replied quickly. "Neither one of us wants that. We're both very eager to be done with this obligation and get back to our real lives. Isn't that right, Jehan?"

He scowled, uncertain how to answer. It seemed obvious that continuing the handfast with him wasn't what she wanted. He was impatient to get on with his life outside the villa too, but only if she would be part of it.

She stared at him as he struggled with the urge to tell her how he felt and risk her rejection in front of both their oblivious, elated siblings.

"Sera," he murmured.

But she was already pivoting away from him. "Now that this farce is over, I'll go collect my things."

When she sailed off in a hurry, both Marcel and Leila gaped at him.

"What the hell did you do to her, brother?"

Jehan shook his head. "I don't know." And then, the truth settled over him. Something about what she said. Something about *how* she said it...

She'd heard him today.

His conversation with Lazaro Archer back in Rome.

He cursed under his breath. Then he started to chuckle.

Marcel frowned at him. "She's pissed as hell at you about something and you're laughing?"

"Yeah, I am." Because now he understood her cold-shoulder today. He understood her anger at him now. And he'd never felt more elated about anything in his life.

Rounding up his brother and Leila, Jehan pushed both of them out the door.

"What are you doing?"

"Sending you on your way," he replied. "Don't come back for four more nights. This handfast isn't over until I say it is."

He closed the door on their confused faces, then turned to go after his Breedmate.

CHAPTER 17

Sera folded the red silk gown and placed it on the bed, trying not to let her heart crumble into pieces.

Outside the massive bedroom suite, the villa had gone quiet. As much as she wanted to celebrate Leila and Marcel's newfound love and bond, part of her was aching for everything she thought she might have had with Jehan.

Now that the handfast was over, she didn't even have those few remaining nights left with him.

Which was probably for the best.

Being around him now was its own kind of torture.

He was already making plans without her. Plans he didn't intend to discuss with or allow her any say in.

So why should she mourn the fact that their week together had just been cut short?

"Where do you think you're going?"

She froze at the sound of his voice but forced herself not to turn around. If she did, she was afraid she'd be tempted to run to him. With her heart so heavy in her breast, she was afraid she'd be unable to keep herself from whirling on him with pounding fists and streaming tears. Demanding that he explain how he could look at her so tenderly and make love to her so possessively if he only meant to leave her behind in a few more nights.

Although she didn't hear him move, she felt the heat of his large body at her spine. "I asked where you think you're going, Seraphina."

"Home," she said. "As soon as possible, I hope."

She walked back into the wardrobe to retrieve another of the pretty, feminine dresses that Leila had packed for her. Jehan was waiting when she came out. He had placed her bag on the floor, and now he sat on the edge of the bed, his sky blue eyes holding her in an unwavering stare.

Why did he have to look so intense and imposing, so impossible to ignore?

The sight of him waiting there, his handsome face grim with purpose, made her limping heart start to gallop.

She forced herself to move, walking over to pick up her bag and place it on a nearby chair so she could continue filling it. "Shouldn't you be packing your things too? If we're lucky, we might be able to get out of here in the next hour or so."

"I'm not leaving, Seraphina."

She glanced up at that. She couldn't help herself.

He stood up and walked over to her. "I'm not going anywhere tonight. Neither are you."

"What are you talking about?"

Her breath caught as he closed the space between them. As always, his presence seemed to suck all of the air out of the room. Right now, it was leeching away some of the resolve she wanted to hold on to so desperately.

"You heard it yourself, Jehan. The handfast is over. We've both made good on our obligations to our families, so now we're free to go."

He shook his head, his expression sober. "Eight nights, Sera. That's what we agreed to. I'm holding you to it. I don't give a damn if the pact terms say you can leave me now. I have four nights left with you, and I mean to claim them." He reached out and stroked his fingers down the side of her face. "I mean to claim *you*, Seraphina. As my woman. As my Breedmate."

"What?" Shock and confusion washed over her. "But I heard you on the phone today. You said you were leaving. That you had decided to go back to Rome. You disregarded me to your commander as if I didn't matter at all. I heard you—"

His thumb swept over her lips, stilling them. "What you apparently didn't hear was that I also told Lazaro Archer I had fallen in love with you."

No, she hadn't heard that.

And hearing it now sent spirals of joy and relief twisting through every cell in her body.

"You didn't hear me tell him that I needed to make a place for you in my life. Or that I couldn't leave the handfast without knowing you were mine." He caressed her cheek, eyes smoldering with affection and desire. "My life is with the Order, Sera. I can't give that up."

"I would never ask that of you, Jehan. I understand that you're doing something important, something that you're devoted to. After what we found at the camp, I realize your mission with the Order has probably never been more crucial."

"No, it hasn't," he said. "I can't leave my duty, but I know you can't give up yours either. I'm not going to ask you to leave your life behind to be with me in Rome."

She frowned, grateful that he understood what her work meant to her, yet unsure how their two worlds could mesh as a mated couple.

"That's why I've decided to pull a new team together here in Morocco. After last night, it's obvious that Opus has a strong presence here, so I've been tasked with pursuing those leads here on African soil. I'll work out the details with Commander Archer when I return to Rome at the end of the week."

She couldn't believe what she was hearing. She couldn't believe what he was doing for her. For them both. For the new bond he meant for them to share.

"Jehan, I don't know what to say."

He lifted her chin on the edge of his fingers. "You can start by saying you love me."

"Yes," she whispered. Then she said it again with all the elation in her soaring heart. "I love you."

He drew her close and kissed her, his lips brushing hers with such tenderness she wanted to weep. The next thing she knew, he had her spread beneath him on the bed. As he undressed her, then hurriedly stripped off his own clothing, his *dermaglyphs* pulsed with all the deep colors of his desire. His cock stood erect and enticing, awakening a powerful hunger in her—for his body, and for his blood.

Jehan clearly knew what she was feeling. His own hungers

blazed in his transformed eyes and in every formidable inch of his naked flesh.

His fiery gaze scorched her face as he looked at her in utter devotion.

And need.

So much need, it rocked her.

He lowered himself between her legs and entered her slowly, as he bent to lick a searing path along her jawline, then her neck. "You're mine, Sera."

"Yes," she gasped, arching into his abrading kiss as his fangs tested the tender flesh of her throat. "For the next four nights, I'm yours however you want me, Jehan."

He glanced up at her, baring those beautiful, sharp tips with his hungry, definitely wicked smile. He gave a slow shake of his head. "Four more nights is only the beginning. Starting now, you're mine forever."

She nodded, too swept up in love and desire to form words.

Emotion overwhelmed her as she watched him bite into his wrist to open his veins for her. "Drink from me," he rasped thickly, bringing the punctures to her parted lips.

Sera fastened her mouth to the wounds and stroked her tongue across the strong tendons of his wrist. His blood called to her, more deeply than she could ever have imagined. She moaned as the first swallow roared through her senses, into her cells. She drank more, reveling in the power of the bond as Jehan's essence—his life— became part of hers.

And all the while she drank, he rocked within her, creating a pleasure so immense she could hardly bear it.

"You're mine, Seraphina." He stared down at her as she fed, as she came on a shattered scream. "Starting tonight, you're only mine."

"Yes."

On a rumble of satisfaction, he drew his wrist to his mouth and sealed the punctures closed with a swipe of his tongue. His blazing eyes were locked on her throat.

Sera brought her arms up around him as he lowered his head to her carotid and licked the fluttering pulse point that beat only for him.

And when her handsome Breed warrior—her eternal love—

sank his fangs into her vein and took his first sip, Seraphina smiled.

Because whether she believed in magic or not, tonight she was holding the prince, the fairy tale, and the happily ever after in her arms.

* * * *

Also from 1001 Dark Nights and Lara Adrian, discover Tempted by Midnight and Midnight Untamed.

About Lara Adrian

LARA ADRIAN is the New York Times and #1 internationally best-selling author of the Midnight Breed vampire romance series, with nearly 4 million books in print and digital worldwide and translations licensed to more than 20 countries. Her books regularly appear in the top spots of all the major bestseller lists including the New York Times, USA Today, Publishers Weekly, Indiebound, Amazon.com, Barnes & Noble, etc.

Lara Adrian's debut title, Kiss of Midnight, was named Borders Books best-selling debut romance of 2007. Later that year, her third title, Midnight Awakening, was named one of Amazon.com's Top Ten Romances of the Year. Reviewers have called Lara's books "addictively readable" (Chicago Tribune), "extraordinary" (Fresh Fiction), and "one of the best vampire series on the market" (Romantic Times).

With an ancestry stretching back to the Mayflower and the court of King Henry VIII, Lara Adrian lives with her husband in New England, surrounded by centuries-old graveyards, hip urban comforts, and the endless inspiration of the broody Atlantic Ocean.

Connect with Lara online:

Website: http://www.laraadrian.com/
Facebook: https://www.facebook.com/LaraAdrianBooks
Twitter: https://twitter.com/lara_adrian
Pinterest: http://www.pinterest.com/laraadrian/

Also from Lara Adrian

Midnight Breed Series

A Touch of Midnight (prequel novella FREE eBook)
Kiss of Midnight
Kiss of Crimson
Midnight Awakening
Midnight Rising
Veil of Midnight
Ashes of Midnight
Shades of Midnight
Taken by Midnight
Deeper Than Midnight
A Taste of Midnight (ebook novella)
Darker After Midnight
The Midnight Breed Series Companion
Edge of Dawn
Marked by Midnight (novella)
Crave the Night
Tempted by Midnight (novella)
Bound to Darkness
Stroke of Midnight
...and more to come!

Masters of Seduction Series

Merciless: House of Gravori
Priceless: House of Ebarron

Phoenix Code Series

Cut and Run (Books 1 & 2)
Hide and Seek (Books 3 & 4)

BOUND TO DARKNESS

Don't miss the newest novel in the New York Times best-selling
Midnight Breed series
by Lara Adrian!

On sale now in eBook, print and audiobook

Chapter 1

Titanium spikes slashed the fighter's face, spraying blood
across the floor of the steel cage and thrilling the crowd of
cheering spectators inside the underground fighting arena. Gritty
industrial music pounded from the dance club upstairs, bringing
the din to a deafening pitch as the long match between the pair
of Breed males built toward its finish.

Carys Chase stood near the front, among the throng of avid
spectators as Rune's fist connected with his opponent's face
again. More shouts and applause erupted for the undefeated
champion of Boston's most brutal arena.

The fights were technically illegal, but highly lucrative. And
since the outing of the Breed to their terrified human neighbors
twenty years ago, there were few sporting events more popular
than the outlawed gladiator-style matches pitting a pair of six-
and-a-half foot, three-hundred pound vampires against each
other in a closed, steel mesh cage.

Blood was essential to Carys and her race, but sometimes it
seemed mankind was even more thirsty for it. Especially when
the spillage was restricted to members of the Breed.

Although even Carys had to admit that watching a vampire
like Rune fight was a thing of beauty. He was dangerous grace
and lethal savagery.

And he was hers.

For the past seven weeks—since the night she'd stepped
into La Notte with a small group of friends and first saw Rune
battling inside the cage—they had been practically inseparable.

She had fallen fast and hard and deep, and hadn't looked back for a second.

Much to her parents' dismay. They and her twin brother, Aric, had all but forbade her to see Rune, basing their judgment on his profession and reputation alone. They didn't know him. They didn't want to know him either, and that hurt. It pissed her off.

Which is why, with a full head of steam and a stubborn streak inherited from both of her parents, Carys had recently moved out of the Chase family Darkhaven and in with her best friend, Jordana Gates.

Leaving home to get her own place hadn't gone over well, particularly with her father, Sterling Chase. As the commander of the Order's presence in Boston, he, along with the Order's founder, Lucan Thorne, and the other district commanders, were the de facto keepers of the peace between the Breed and mankind. No easy task in good times, let alone the precarious ones they lived in now.

Carys understood her father's concern for her safety and wellbeing. She only wished he could understand that she was a grown woman with her own life to lead.

Even if that life included a Breed male who chose to make his living in the arena.

All around her now, the spectators chanted their champion's name. "Rune! Rune! Rune!"

Carys joined in, awed by his domination of the fighting ring even as the woman in her cringed every time fists smashed on flesh and bone, regardless of who was on the receiving end. And she could admit, at least to herself, that being in love with him had made her hope for the day he might decide to climb out of the cage for good.

No one had ever beaten Rune—and more than a few had died trying.

He prowled the cage with fluid motion, naked except for the arena uniform of brown leather breeches and fingerless gloves bristling with titanium spikes. The sharp metal ensured every blow was a spectacle of shredding flesh and breaking bone for the pleasure of the crowd.

Also crafted primarily for the entertainment of the sport's

patrons was the U-shaped steel torc around the fighters' necks. Each combatant had the option of hitting a mercy button inside the cage, which would deliver a debilitating jolt of electricity to his opponent's collar, halting the match to afford the weaker fighter a chance to recover before resuming the bout.

Although Rune had been the recipient of countless juicings when he climbed into the ring, he had never stooped to using the mercy button.

Neither did his opponent tonight. Jagger was one of La Notte's crowd favorites too, a black Breed male whose own record of wins was almost as impressive as Rune's. The two fighters were friendly outside the arena, but no one would know it to see them now.

Being Breed, Jagger healed from his injuries in seconds. He wheeled on Rune with a deafening roar, plowing forward like a bull on the charge. The contact drove Rune back against the cage. Steel bars groaned, straining under the sudden impact of so much muscle and might. The spectators directly below shrieked and shrank away, but the fight had already moved on.

Now it was Rune on the offense, tossing Jagger's massive body across the cage.

Game or not, the clash of fists and fangs brought out the savage in just about any Breed male. Jagger got to his feet, his lips peeled back from his sharp teeth on a furious sneer. His *dermaglyphs* pulsed with violent colors on his dark skin. He rounded on Rune, amber fire blazing from his eyes as he crouched low and prepared to make another bruising charge.

Opposite him in the cage, Rune stood tall, his massive arms at his sides, his stance deceptively relaxed as he and Jagger circled each other.

Rune's Breed skin markings churned with raging colors too. His midnight-blue eyes crackled with hot sparks as he studied his opponent. Rune's fangs were enormous, razor-sharp tips gleaming in the dim lights of the arena. But beneath the sweat-dampened fall of his dark brown hair, his rugged, granite-hewn face was an utter, deadly calm.

This was Rune at his most dangerous.

Carys's breath stilled as Jagger leapt, catapulting and cartwheeling in a blur of furious motion across the ring. One foot came up at Rune's face like powerful hammer, so fast, Carys could hardly track its motion.

But Rune had. He grabbed Jagger's ankle and twisted, dropping the fighter to the floor. Jagger recovered in less than an instant, pivoting on his elbow and sweeping Rune's legs out from under him with another smooth kick.

The move was swift and elegant, but it opened Jagger up for sudden defeat.

Rune went down, but took Jagger with him, tackling him into an impossible hold on the floor of the cage. Jagger struggled to break loose, but Rune's spiked knuckles kept the fighter subdued.

Howls and applause thundered through the arena as the clock counted down on the end of the match, with Rune about to claim yet another win.

As Carys cheered his certain victory, she felt a prickle of awareness on the back of her neck. She glanced behind her toward the back of the club. Two of her father's Breed warriors had just come inside.

Shit.

Dressed in the Order's black fatigues, Jax and Eli scanned the massive crowd, ignoring the spectacle inside the cage as they sought to locate her. She was getting used to seeing the Order's babysitting patrol every night, but that didn't make it any less annoying.

Maybe her father's patience had finally reached its end. She knew him well enough not to put it past him to send his warriors out to collect her and eventually bring her home. By force if needed.

Ha. Let them try.

As one of the rare few females of the Breed *and* a daywalker, Carys was every bit as strong as any male of her kind. Stronger than most, given that her mother, Tavia Chase, was a laboratory-created miracle comprised of half-Ancient and half-Breedmate genetics.

But she didn't need to resort to physical strength to avoid Jax and Eli. Carys had another ability at her disposal—this one inherited from her father.

As she stood among the crowd near the front of the arena,

Carys quieted her mind and focused on her surroundings. Gathering and bending the shadows around her, she concealed herself in plain sight. No one would see her so long as she held the shadows close.

She waited, watching the pair of Order warriors stroll deeper into the club to scan the hundreds of humans and Breed packed inside. Carys drifted deeper into the throng, unseen by anyone. Jax and Eli gave up after a few minutes of searching. Carys smiled from within her magic as she watched them finally leave.

Meanwhile, the match in the cage was over. Rune and Jagger had taken off their metal torcs and gloves. They clapped each other on the shoulder, both mopping the blood and sweat from their faces as the announcer declared the winner.

Carys let her shadows fall away then. The hatch on the cage opened to let out the combatants. She raced to meet Rune, shouting his name and applauding with the rest of the throng as her man collected yet another victory.

Rune's rugged face lit up with private promise when he saw her. The brutal, fearsome fighter stepped out of the cage and caught her around the waist, hauling her to him.

His dark eyes glittered with need he didn't even try to conceal. Ignoring the cheers and applause that swelled around him, he took her mouth in a possessive kiss.

Then he scooped her up and carried her out of the arena.

All Hallows Eve

A Krewe of Hunters Novella
By Heather Graham

Prologue

Come to me. Please, come to me.

The words seemed real to Elyssa Adair, like a whisper in her mind, as she looked up at the old mansion.

The Mayberry Mortuary was decked out in a fantastic Halloween décor, customary each year starting October 1. It sat high on a jagged bluff near the waterfront in Salem, Massachusetts. Just driving toward it, at night, was like being in a horror movie. Dense trees lined the paved drive and it was surrounded by a graveyard. The old Colonial building, when captured beneath the moonlight, seemed to rise from the earth in true Gothic splendor.

She shivered and looked around at her friends, wondering if the words had been spoken by one of them. Vickie Thornton and Barry Tyler sat in the backseat, laughing with one another and making scary faces. Nate Fox was driving, his dark eyes intent on the road.

No one in the car had spoken to her.

She gave herself a silent mental shake. She could have sworn she'd actually heard a whisper. Clear as day. Come to me. Strangely, she wasn't afraid. She loved the artistry of Halloween—the fun of it—and few places in the world embraced the day like Salem.

This was home and she loved Salem, despite the sad history of witch trials and executions. A lot of that was steeped in lure and myth, but the local Peabody Essex museum and other historic venues seemed to go out of their way to remind visitors of the horror that came from petty jealousy and irrational fear.

"Boo," Nate said, leaning toward her.

She jumped with a start.

She'd been deeply involved in her thoughts and the view of the old mansion. Nate, Vickie, and Barry all giggled at her surprise.

"Do you have to do that," she murmured.

He frowned, his eyes back on the road. "Elyssa, we've done this every year since we were kids. So are you really scared now?"

"Of course not," she said, and tried to smile.

She loved Nate. They were both just eighteen, but they'd been seeing one another since their freshman year. She was young, as everyone kept reminding her, but she knew that she would love him all of her life. Despite them being opposites. She was a bookworm, born and raised in the East, red hair and green eyes. He was from South Dakota, a Western boy, whose mom had been from nearby Marblehead but whose dad had been a half Lakota Sioux. He was tall and dark with fabulous cheekbones and a keen sense of ethics and justice. He was their high school's quarterback, and she was debate team captain.

"Don't be silly," she said. "Last year, I played a zombie, remember?"

And what a role. She'd arose from the embalming table and attacked one of her classmates who'd played the mortician, terrifying the audience.

Nate grinned. "That you did. And what a lovely zombie you were."

Please.

She heard the single word and realized no one in the car had spoken it. Instead, it had vocalized only in her mind. Incredibly, she managed not to react. Instead, she pointed out the windshield and said, "Looks like someone has decided to toilet-paper the gates."

White streamers decorated the old wrought iron, which seemed original. Time had taken its toll on both the gates and the stone wall that had once surrounded the property. She'd never minded that such an historic property was transformed each year into one of the best haunted houses in New England. And despite the decorations, the house remained open daily until

3:00 P.M. for tours. It had been built soon after Roger Conant—
the founder of Salem—moved to the area, around 1626, starting
out as a one-room building. Nearly four hundred years of
additions had blossomed it into a spacious mansion, the last
editions coming way back in the Victorian era. In the early 1800s
it had been consecrated as a Catholic church, deconsecrated by
the 1830s when a new church had been built closer to town.
Some said the site had then been used for satanic worship, taken
over by a coven of black magic witches, but she'd never found
any real support for those rumors. During the Civil War it served
as a mortuary—drastically needed as the torn bodies of Union
soldiers returned home. That continued until the 1950s when the
VA made it a hospital for a decade. Finally, the Salem Society for
Paranormal Studies bought the property. Along with historical
tours, it offered tarot card and palm readings and ESP testing of
anyone willing to pay the fee. The society had repaired and
restored the old place, eventually garnering an historic
designation, ensuring its continued preservation.

In the 1970s, Laurie Cabot came and created a place for
dozens of modern-day Wiccans, and the area soon become a
mecca for everyone and everything occult. Overall, though, the
society people were barely noticed, except by fundamentalists
who just didn't like anything period. Actually, the Wiccans had
brought a great deal of commerce to town, and that was
something to be appreciated.

Please, please, come. I need you.

Elyssa didn't move, not even a blink. Now she knew. Those
words were only in her head. Maybe she needed sleep.
Definitely, she shouldn't drink any more of the cheap wine
Nate's brother found at the convenience store.

Last night's overindulgence had been plenty enough.

They drove through the gates and past the graves. Like
every other New England cemetery, this one came with
elaborate funerary art and plenty of stone symbolism. One angel
in particular had always been her favorite. She occupied a
pedestal near the drive, commissioned for a Lieutenant Colonel
Robert Walker in 1863, there to guard his grave, on one knee,

head bowed, weeping, her great wings at rest behind her back.

They drove by and the angel seemed to look up—straight at Elyssa. Again, she heard the words in her head.

Please, help me. Find me.

"Look at the people," Vickie said.

The lines to get inside the haunted house stretched down the main walk to the porch, then around the corner of the house. The mansion was huge—seven thousand square feet over three stories, with a basement and an attic. Creepy windows filled the gables and projected inside dormers from the slate roof, like glowing eyes in the night.

"It's three days before Halloween. What were we expecting?" Nate asked. "This place is popular. But it looks like there are vendors walking by with hot chocolate. We'll have fun in line."

"Elyssa, can't you get us into the VIP line?" Barry asked. "Don't you still have friends here? Didn't they ask you back to work inside the haunted house this year?"

She nodded. "I just couldn't make it happen, not with getting the whole college thing going for next year. But, I'll see what I can do. John Bradbury still manages the place. He's a good guy to work for."

"Don't you know Micah Aldridge too?" Vickie asked. "Isn't he one of the main guys in the paranormal society?"

"He's never around at night. He and that weird, skinny lady from Savannah—Jeannette Mackey—have their noses up in the air at this kind of thing. They think they're a little above all this fun."

They parked far away, almost in the graveyard, and walked back to the line.

"Work your magic," Vickie told her.

Elyssa headed toward the makeshift desk and plywood shelter in the front where Naomi Hardy was working ticket sales. She was surprised to see that she'd been wrong. Micah Aldridge was there, helping with the sales.

Elyssa smiled at Naomi, then leaned down to talk to Micah. "I thought you hated this silliness."

He was a good-looking man who worked his dark hair and lean, bronzed features to add an aura of mystery to his appearance. His usual attire was some kind of a hat and long coat, reminiscent of a vampire, regardless of the season, and tonight was no exception.

"I don't hate what pays the bills," he told her, adding a smile. "Wish you would have worked this year. It's always great to see you."

"I just couldn't, not with college coming up." She drew in a breath. "Micah, I have some friends with me, and we're happy to buy tickets, but we can't afford VIP entrance and the line—"

Her words trailed off and she grimaced.

"Say no more, little one," he said.

To her surprise, he didn't let her pay. Instead, he set a BE BACK IN A MINUTE sign before his seat. He then whispered to Naomi Hardy, a pretty young woman of about twenty-five, who was selling the tickets to each person in line. Naomi was John Bradbury's assistant. She knew Naomi took a room in Salem for the month of October, but lived down in Boston.

Naomi smiled and nodded an understanding, then said, "Enjoy."

Micah led them up to the porch to wait for the next group to enter. She thanked him profusely, but he brought a finger up to his lips, signaling for quiet.

"Not even time for hot chocolate," Vickie noted, smiling.

"We'll get some after," Nate said.

In the mansion foyer they were greeted by a hunchback Igor-like actor who told them a tale about black masses in the house, mad scientists, and more. They then began the walk-through, starting with the dining room where skeletons had gathered together for a feast. One was a live actor who rose to scare each group as they entered. Next came the kitchen—where a cook was busy chopping up human bodies for a stew and offering the visitors a bloody heart.

Staged gore had never bothered Elyssa. She didn't mind the mad experiments in one of the bedrooms, or the Satanists sacrificing a young woman in the tarot card room. She didn't even mind the demented baby or the usual scare-factor pranks typical for haunted houses.

In an upstairs bedroom, they came to the mad scientist's lair where an actor was busy dissecting a woman on the bed, vials, wires, tubes, and beeping machines all around him. The woman—despite the fake gore—looked familiar.

Then she realized.

It was Jeannette Mackey.

Elyssa smiled and kept quiet, but when the rest of her group had filed out, she paused and hurried to the bed.

"What are you doing here?" she asked.

Jeannette grinned at her and replied with her sweet accent. "Darlin', when you can't beat'em, you've got to join'em."

Elyssa laughed, found Jeannette's hand, and squeezed it. "You and Micah working the show and Naomi Hardy on the ticket booth. Did they not get enough kid volunteers this year?"

"Gotta get back to work," Jeannette said. "New group is coming in. But, no, we're doing this just because we love the place."

Elyssa grinned and hurried out.

The other bedrooms on the second floor offered a Satanist mass, a headless tarot card reader, and two displays of movie monsters with ice picks, electric saws, and more scary weapons.

Then it was time to head down—way down.

Elyssa had always been oddly uneasy in the basement. That's where the embalming had once been done, and it hadn't changed much since the days when the house had served as an actual mortuary. The trestle tables were still there. The nooks and crannies where shelves with instruments had been kept remained too. Hoses above stone beds still hung, where real blood and guts had been washed away, the bodies readied for embalming. There was something sad and eerie about the place.

Vickie screamed and gasped delightedly. Barry kept an arm around her—except when he was jumping himself. There were motion-activated creatures in the arched nooks along the way. One, some kind of an alien creature, took Nate by surprise and he leapt back, causing them all to laugh.

But Elyssa's attention had been drawn to another of the basement nooks, a figure of a hanging man. She'd seen the group before them walk right by it—no blood, no gore, no actor to jump at them. To locals the image was nothing new. It could be seen throughout Salem, representative of men like George Burroughs or John Proctor, who'd also been convicted of witchcraft and hanged, like the women, during the craze.

Her head began to pound.

And she was drawn toward the image.

Yes, thank you. Come. Please, help me stop this.

She stared through the darkness and her first thought was how life-like the image was. But, of course, the man had been hanged. He was dead. No life existed. She could see every little hair on his head. He was dressed in Puritan garb, as if a victim of the witch trials. The nook had been painted to look as if it were outside at the hanging tree. He might have been about thirty-five or so in life, with dark hair and weathered features. And the smell. Rank. Like urine and rot. The area had really been done up to haunt all of the senses.

She moved closer.

Yes, yes. Help. Please, oh, yes, please.

The voice whispering in her mind grew louder.

One more step.

And then she knew.

The figure was real. Not an actor there to scare those who came so giddily through the house. And she knew him. He ran this place. He'd even given her a job here at the house last year.

John Bradbury.

Hanging, dead.

She screamed, which only evoked laughter at first. But she kept screaming and pointing. Her friends tried to calm her. Nate tried to show her that it was just part of the scare fest. A prop.

But he suddenly realized that it was much more.

White-faced and grim, he shouted, "That's a real body. He's dead."

The night seemed to drag on forever with the police, bright lights and horrified actors wanting to go home, Mayberry Mortuary haunted house closed down. Eventually, there was hot chocolate as they sat in the mortuary café, answering questions for cop after cop.

But, that wasn't the worse part.

That came when Elyssa finally made it home in the wee hours, lying in her bed, drifting in and out of sleep.

She felt her mattress depress and when she opened her eyes, John Bradbury was there.

Thank you. But you have to know. They're going to kill again, unless you stop them.

Chapter 1

"There?" Sam Hall asked.

"Oh, yes. Yes. Touch me there. Right there," Jenna Duffy moaned in return.

"Right here? I can touch and touch and——"

"Ohhhh yes. That's it."

Jenna rolled over and looked up at him, eyes soft, smile beautiful. He'd been straddled over her spine carefully balancing his weight as he worked his magic. Now he towered over her front.

"I think," she said, reaching up to stroke his cheek, her eyes filled with wonder, "that you missed your calling. The hell with the law. The hell with the FBI. You could have been an amazing masseuse. My shoulders feel so much better."

"You shouldn't spend so many hours reading without taking a break and walking around."

Jenna nodded. "I don't know how Angela does it. She has such an eye for the cases and requests, when we're really needed. I've read them over and over."

She was referring to Special Agent Angela Hawkins, case facilitator for the Krewe of Hunters at their main offices—and wife of Jackson Crow, their acting field director. Both he and Jenna loved their work. When they weren't in the field, he maintained his bar licensing in several states by working Krewe legal matters. Jenna assisted Angela in reading between the lines, determining where the team was most needed. The requests for Krewe help were growing in number; and while new agents came on all the time, it was still a race to keep up.

"We have tomorrow," he said. "Then vacation."

"Sun, sea, and tanning oils for exotic massages," Jenna said, laughing.

He stared down into her eyes—greener than the richest forest—and marveled at the way he loved her. Her hair, a deep and blazing red, spread out across the pillows in waves. It seemed incredible that this remarkable, beautiful, sensual woman could feel the same for him. That they could lie together so naturally, that laughter could combine with passion, and that they could live and work together.

And still be closer each year.

He smiled and kissed her.

Her fingers ran down his spine with a teasing caress, finding his midriff, then venturing lower.

"What are you thinking about?" she asked.

He groaned softly.

"Pardon?"

"Sex. Here, now," he said. "The perfect place. In bed— both of us on it."

She frowned.

"And you weren't?"

She smiled and caressed him in one of her most erotic and sensual ways. "There?" she whispered teasingly.

"Oh, yes. Right there."

"I can touch and touch and touch."

He kissed her lips, then her collarbone and her breast, moving lower. He loved her so much, truly loved her, and every time they made love, it seemed sweeter and sweeter. Her skin was satin, her hair the fall of silk, and her movements—

Those were the best.

They slept after, entangled in one another's arms, and he thought about heading to Atlantis and how he'd planned to ask her then if they shouldn't begin to think about a wedding in the near future.

What a beautiful night.

But in the morning everything changed.

With the phone call.

* * * *

A wickedly big and warty witch atop a broomstick rode above a sign that advertised "Best Halloween Ball Bash in the Nor'East."

New England. Halloween.

Nothing went better together.

And the holiday decorations would just increase as they neared Salem, Massachusetts, the days ticking off closer and closer to the hallowed day. Costume shops abounded, as if they'd sprouted from seeds of alien pods tossed down by a space ship. But people everywhere liked to party.

Unfortunately, this was not going to be a vacation in the Bahamas. Sadly, Sam thought about the tickets he and Jenna had changed and the rooms in the fantasy casino they'd canceled. He didn't mind. If Jenna needed to do something else, that was fine. As long as he was with her.

And he was.

"So," he said, frowning slightly as he glanced over at Jenna before looking back at the road. "Talk to me. We're here to see a relative but, somehow, I never met her when you and I first got together, back with the murders at Lexington House. And, a relative I also haven't met since."

Then again, they hadn't been back to Salem that many times over the past few years. Jenna's parents lived in Boston—when they weren't visiting friends and family in Ireland—so they'd only made it that far when they popped up for a weekend. Her uncle, Jamie O'Neill, her next-favorite relative, often came down to Boston when they were there.

Jenna didn't look at him. She was gnawing her lower lip, staring out the window. She'd grown more and more withdrawn since they'd left Boston's Logan Airport and started driving up US 1 toward Salem. He wasn't sure if she had even heard him.

Salem.

His home.

And while Jenna had come from Ireland as a child and grown up in Boston, her ties with Salem were deep. Her Uncle Jamie lived here, and she'd spent a tremendous amount of time, while growing up, with him. Salem was where he'd fallen in love with Jenna. And when they'd left, he'd assumed he'd open a law practice in northern Virginia. Instead, he'd found himself in the FBI academy.

And then part of the Krewe.

Thing was, though, until the call came, he'd never expected to be heading here. And he'd never expected that she'd close down. Jenna was an experienced agent. She dealt with a lot of bad things. She had a tremendous compassion for others and a stern work ethic. She'd been almost silent as they'd ridden to work, explaining only that they were going to have to change things up. No vacation right now. She'd gotten a call from an Elyssa Adair, someone he'd never heard her mention before. She was sorry, so sorry, about the trip, and she wanted to wait until they saw Jackson before explaining why this was so important. As soon as they'd arrived at work, he'd arranged for them both to speak with Jackson Crow at the Krewe of Hunters special unit headquarters.

He wasn't surprised that Jenna had so quickly been given permission for the two of them to travel to Salem. Krewe cases were often accepted on instinct, or because there was a particular reason a Krewe member should be involved. He was surprised, though, by Jenna, who was usually open and frank and outgoing, especially with him. They'd been together nearly five years. He'd changed his entire life to work with her and, of course, to deal with the fact that the dead seemed to like to speak with him.

And he loved her.

With all of his heart, with everything in him.

He knew that she felt the same way about him, which made it so strange that she'd seemed to shut him out, even while asking that he accompany her and assist on the case. At the moment, however, there wasn't a case. Not one that they'd been invited to join in on at least. A man was dead. He'd been associated with the old Mayberry Mortuary Halloween Horrors. Police were suggesting that he might have killed himself over financial matters. There was an ongoing local investigation. But, so far, the death was being considered a possible-suicide.

That much, he knew.

The minute Jenna had begun to talk about a cousin he'd never met, Elyssa Adair, and the fact that Elyssa had discovered the dead man in the haunted horror attraction, he'd probed for background.

John Bradbury, born in Salem, schooled in Boston, had returned to Salem to operate the mortuary under the business umbrella Hauntings and Hallucinations, Inc. The company was doing fine. However, the year before, Bradbury had gone through a tough divorce, and, apparently, due to past substance abuse problems, had lost all but supervised visitation rights with his three children. His ex-wife—while crying on a newscast—had told the world that it had been John's mental instability that had led to his self-medicating with drugs and alcohol and their subsequent divorce.

This was still New England, and while Sam held his own devotion to his home sector, he was aware that some of the old Puritanical values still hid in the hearts and minds of many. Mental weakness was kept to one's self. Everyone was shocked that the man killed himself, considering how calm he'd appeared to his employees and how happy he'd been when managing the mortuary in its guise as a haunted house. It would be easy to accept the death as an apparent suicide. Bad things happened around Halloween. Holidays seemed an impetus for those dealing with severe depression.

They were passing through Peabody—an old stomping ground for anyone who'd grown up in the area. Beautiful old Colonial and Victorian homes, big and small, grand and not so grand, were decked out in ghostly fashion, all the more eerie as night began to fall. Scarecrows, skeletons, ghosts, ghouls, black cats, and more abounded.

But the best was yet to come.

Salem prided itself on being Halloween central.

Jenna finally turned his way and said, "She's a little scholar. Elyssa was in Europe when we were here last. She earned six months study abroad before she was even a freshman. She's a great kid, a second cousin once removed or however you come about that. My dad's cousin's daughter's daughter. She's all grown up now, a senior and just turned eighteen. She's never seen a dead body—much less a hanged dead body."

Except in museums, probably. Many of Salem's attractions had scenes of life's finales, men and women convicted and executed after their so-called witch trials.

"I can imagine how bad it was," he said.

"She was nearly hysterical on the phone, and, of course, her folks are upset that she called me. They seem to think she's having a bad reaction to what happened. But I told her mom not to worry, that I was happy to come and see Uncle Jamie and that we had some vacation time coming anyway." She paused and looked at him apologetically. "I said I was happy to help her in any way that I can. The thing is—"

Her voice trailed.

He waited.

He knew her dilemma, listening intently when she'd explained the situation to Jackson Crow. Elyssa believed that a dead man had called her for help. Then that same dead man had appeared to her later to thank her for finding him, fading away with a warning that a killer had to be caught before more people died. Elyssa's parents would want Jenna to assure the young girl that what was happening in her mind was because of the horror she'd seen, not because a dead man could really speak to her.

"It's going to be hard," Jenna said. "I can't tell her that she's imagining things if, in fact, she's not. And if this man was really murdered, someone has to discover the truth about his death."

He reached across the car and squeezed her hand. "You'll do what's right. You always do."

She nodded and squeezed back.

They really hadn't talked about this much at all. Instead, they'd left the office, packed, and hopped onto the first plane. Angela had seen to it that a rental car was waiting for them. Normally, she would have seen to it that they had a hotel room too.

But, not in Salem.

Sam still owned a house here. His parents' home, where he'd grown up. Once, he'd wanted to sell the house and say good-bye to Salem. But Jenna and her Uncle Jamie had changed that. He'd learned something about his childhood home because of them, because of all of the bad that had happened.

Three things.

People made bad things happen.

Places weren't evil.

And when the dead remained, it was for a reason, usually to

make sure that the living finally got it right.

He entered Salem and drove down Walnut Street, heading into the historic district. People, off to early holiday parties, filled the sidewalks in costume. Around this time of the year it was difficult to tell the practicing Wiccans from all the amateurs.

"How cute," Jenna murmured, noting a group of children, all in costumes themed to *The Wizard of Oz.*

They stood at a stop sign, and Sam took a minute to look at the group and smile. He was about to move through the intersection when he suddenly slammed on the brakes. A costumed pedestrian had rushed into the street and thrown himself on the hood of the car, grinning eerily at them. He stayed for a beat while Sam felt his temper flaring. The person in the costume stared at him through the windshield, donning a red latex mask. It seemed the entire body was red beneath a black cape, the eyes blood-streaked yellow. The person suddenly pushed off the car, cackling with laughter.

"Ass," Sam yelled.

"Total dick," Jenna said.

"Vampire, demon?"

"Boo-hag," Jenna said.

He didn't know about a boo-hag. "What's that?"

"I guess it's a regional thing, from the Gullah people. They're from regions of Africa, mainly brought to this country as slaves. They got together and formed a group hundreds of years ago. They have a language, kind of like a Haitian *patois* joined with English, and all kinds of cultural stuff. And of course now, with time passing, the mix is African, Creole, and so on. They're known to have lived in the low country of South Carolina, down to north Florida at one time."

"And what do these boo-hags do?"

"To the Gullah, there is a soul and a spirit. The soul goes to Heaven, assuming the person was good, the spirit watches over the family. Unless it's a bad spirit. Then, it becomes a boo-hag. Like a spiritual vampire."

"A spiritual vampire?" Sam asked.

She turned to him, grave and knowing, a slight smile in her eyes. "When you slept eight hours and woke exhausted, that might have been a boo-hag. They suck energy out of the living.

Usually, they leave their victims alive so they can feast off of them again. If a victim struggles, that's when you find that person dead in the morning."

"And how do you fight a boo-hag?" Sam asked.

"You need to leave a broom by your bed. Boo-hags are easily distracted. They'll start counting the bristles and forget they came to suck your energy. To rid yourself of a boo-hag, though, you have to find their skin while they're out of it, and fill it with salt. That will make them insane with agony when they put it back on."

"Guess we need to sleep with salt and brooms," he said. "Easy enough to find at Halloween. How the hell do you know about all this? This is Salem, Mass, not the Deep South."

"You had to have known my mum's mother. She taught me all about the banshees and leprechauns. She loved legends. And she also had a dear friend from the low country who lived in Charleston."

"Wish I could have known her," Sam said. He was suddenly glad of the obnoxious drunk who'd thrown himself on the car. Jenna had finally become Jenna.

"Those eyes," she said, with a shiver. "Spooky."

"Contacts, most likely."

"Good ones, too. But there are a lot of great costumes at Halloween. You know that."

He did. "And no costume parties, huh?"

She grinned. "No costume parties. But you'd make a great John Proctor. He was supposed to have been a big, tall, strong dude."

"Before he was hanged," he said.

She grimaced at that.

They were nearly in the historic section.

He turned to her sheepishly. "I forgot to ask. My house? Or is Uncle Jamie expecting us?" Sam asked.

She turned to him, more relaxed than she'd been. "Uncle Jamie is expecting us."

"Okay, just so I know where I'm going."

She nodded, and he noticed a darkness settle over her again. There was something so pained about her eyes, and yet there was so much appreciation in them he felt a tug at his heart. He remembered meeting her when Malachi Smith had been accused of the brutal murders at Lexington House, and how strong and determined she'd been. Between her and Jamie, he'd found himself representing the young man pro bono. Even in the height of danger and true horror there, she'd never looked like this.

But this time her family was involved.

"I'm here," he said. "Jamie is here. And you're the best damned agent I know. Things will work out fine."

"Thanks," she said.

He drove to Jamie O'Neill's eighteenth century house, not much different from his parents'. Jamie kept the place in excellent shape. He was an exceptionally good man who'd almost gone into the priesthood. Instead, he'd studied psychiatry and donated an awful lot of pro bono work, always helping the underdog. Sam had known Jamie before he'd returned on the day of the Lexington House murders. He'd even met Jenna, though all he remembered of that day was being called upon by his parents to supervise a group of rowdy teenage girls.

Today, Jamie's house seemed strange as he eased onto the old stone drive in front. Like a dark cloud had settled over it. But the afternoon was waning. Massachusetts's autumns brought night quickly. Still, it seemed to Sam that clouds sat over the house and nowhere else. Jenna's family was certain that the property was haunted, but by nice ghosts they claimed. Ghosts that went about their business and left the living to their own. He was curious about Elyssa Adair and her family. Apparently, they didn't possess Jenna's mom's and dad's ability to shrug off anything that might be paranormal.

The door opened and he saw Jamie O'Neill step out on the porch. He wore a sweater and jeans, but cast a grave look about him that Sam could not remember seeing often. He lifted a hand in greeting, as Jenna ran up the walk to hug him. Sam opened the trunk of the rental car and grabbed their bags.

A young woman burst from the house behind Jamie. She had red hair, similar to Jenna's. Tall, lean, pretty, upset, yet relieved.

"Jenna. Thank you for coming."

Sam knew that the young lady had to be Elyssa Adair.

"That was never in doubt," Jenna said, engulfed in a tight and enthusiastic hug.

Sam moved forward, setting the bags down as Jenna disentangled herself and turned to make the introductions. "Elyssa, this is Special Agent Sam Hall. We work together and we're together, too."

"Uncle Jamie told me all about that," Elyssa said.

The younger woman stared at him with beautiful eyes that weren't quite as rich a green as Jenna's. Then she threw her arms around him and hugged him.

Withdrawing at last, she said, "I knew you would come, too."

He was puzzled. "Can I ask how?"

"The ghost told me. John Bradbury specifically said you were coming, and that was before Uncle Jamie ever mentioned you. He said he knew you when he was alive."

Chapter 2

"Come in," Uncle Jamie said after greeting Jenna and Sam.

Jenna looked at her uncle anxiously, wondering why she had such a bad feeling about what was going on. Elyssa had calmed and smiled at Jenna.

"Are you all right?" Jenna asked, hands on her young cousin's shoulders. She hadn't seen Elyssa for years, although they kept up on Facebook. Their lack of a visit hadn't been on purpose, just the way life had fallen into place.

"I'm fine," Elyssa said. "Now that you're here."

There was that unshakeable faith Elyssa seemed to have in her. Which was a lot to live up to.

"Let's talk," she said to both Elyssa and her uncle.

For a man who accepted just about anything on earth and maintained his faith with the loyalty of an angel, Uncle Jamie could be very matter-of-fact. "We need to, before Susan gets back."

"Susan?" Sam asked, following Jenna across the porch to the front door.

"Elyssa's mother," Jamie said.

A minute later Uncle Jamie had served them all coffee and they sat around the dining room table. Jenna felt Sam's hand on hers and met the strong gravity in his eyes.

"I'm here," he said softly.

She nodded, a thank you in the squeeze she returned on his hand.

"From the beginning," she told Elyssa. "Tell me

everything."

Elyssa glanced nervously at Uncle Jamie, took a breath and began. "Mom says I'm crazy. Dad is looking into 'trauma doctors.' I'm pretty sure he means shrinks." She paused. "Uncle Jamie came to the house. Mom thinks he's almost a priest—and he was almost—so she let me come here and she even said it was okay to talk to you because you're with the FBI. She thinks you'll make me understand the difference between a suicide and a murder. And Uncle Jamie has been the best person in the world for me because he doesn't think that I'm crazy. He seems to believe in...whatever it is."

Jenna thought about how much she really loved her uncle. He told her once that he believed deeply in his faith, so he had to accept that there was life after death. And who was he to declare that departed souls might not linger, trying to help others.

"What makes the police think it was suicide?" Sam asked.

Elyssa flushed uncomfortably. "There was a kicked over stool found near where he was hanging, right in the niche."

Sam shrugged. "Could have been planted."

"Why don't you tell us what happened exactly, from beginning to end?" Jenna said.

"We're open to hearing everything you have to say," Sam added.

Elyssa looked at Sam and nodded. She seemed to have taken an instant liking to him. Unlike Jenna, who'd admired Sam's stature and reputation from the beginning, but had not been all that enamored. It had been Uncle Jamie who'd known that Sam would come around to their way of thinking, and their determination to find the truth about the Lexington House murders. And then she'd been lucky. Sam had fallen in love with her, while she was falling hard for him. And now she couldn't imagine her life without him. It didn't hurt that he really was a gorgeous man, rugged, tall, smooth and dignified, with a rock hard jaw and a steely determination when he made up his mind to get something done.

Elyssa launched into her story. She'd just been out for a night of fun and heard a strange voice in her head, which she ignored. She'd tried to connect with John Bradbury when they'd reached the mortuary, but he'd not been around.

Then she found him.

Hanging dead.

The haunted attraction had been closed down and she'd answered questions over and over again. Back home, her mom had actually made her tea with whiskey in it so that she could sleep. But then she'd opened her eyes and John Bradbury had been sitting at the foot of her bed, telling her that he was grateful, but that she had to stop what was happening or other people would die.

"He didn't by any chance tell you what was happening, did he?" Sam asked.

"He doesn't really know. He was working downstairs in the embalming room when someone slipped a noose around his neck. He heard people talking, two people, he thinks. Then someone said something about the witch trials and wacky cults. Another voice said something about that person needing to shut up. And then the person who'd spoken first said what the hell did it matter? Bradbury would be dead. Who cares."

"The witch *trials*?" Jenna asked, adding, "Not Wiccans today?"

Elyssa nodded. "The witch trials, that's what he said. Someone was talking about the witch trials and cults. But, what they said exactly, I don't know." She looked hopeful. "Maybe now that you're here, John will come and talk to you instead of me. I can't remember all that he said. I'm not sure he knows exactly what he heard."

"We'll look into whatever new groups are in town," Sam said. "And, of course check out the older covens and groups too. Most of the Wiccans in town are good and peaceful people. They practice their faith like any religion."

"Good people come in all faiths," Uncle Jamie said. "Elyssa knows that."

"I mean, that's the thing. I couldn't figure out why he appeared to me. I'm in my last year of high school," Elyssa said. "I have midterms coming up. I'm not the police or even an investigator. Early this morning he came back. He wasn't a creepy ghost or anything. He didn't pop into the shower on me or anything like that. He appeared right when I'd finished dressing. Mom said I shouldn't go to school today. When I first woke up—that's when I called you, Jenna—I was still feeling freaked out. Then you said that you'd come and I was so relieved. I was finally hungry and was going to go out to get some breakfast when he appeared at my bedroom door. He thanked me again and said that you and Sam could help."

Sam smiled at her. "He came back and talked to you in your room and you didn't scream or pass out? Pretty brave kid."

Elyssa smiled. "Maybe I'm like you."

"Maybe you are—and it's really not so bad," Jenna told her.

"Should we have known this man?" Sam asked.

"He was from Salem," Jenna told him. "Five to ten years older than you. Do you remember his name from anything?"

Sam reflected for a moment and then shook his head. "I'm not really sure."

"He knew you, or about you," Elyssa said, staring at them both expectantly.

"We should start with the covens and cultists," Jenna noted. "Though that could be a long list. Seems like new things sprout up here every Halloween."

"I'll get Angela working on it back at headquarters," Sam said. "I'd like to get into the autopsy. I'll call Jackson, see if Adam Harrison has any sway up here."

"Adam has sway everywhere," Jenna assured him.

Adam Harrison, the dignified philanthropist who'd finally organized his little army of psychic researchers into an FBI unit, did seem to have sway everywhere. He was a good man, one who'd made a great deal of money and managed to keep his principles. His son, dead in a car accident in high school, had been one of those special people with an unusual ability. Eventually, Adam had learned that his son was not the only one.

"Excuse me," Sam told them. "I'm going to make some calls. You know Devin Lyle and Craig Rockwell are from this area, too. We might need some help covering the ground."

"Good idea," Jenna said. In all the rush she'd forgotten that her co-agents were also from Salem. Then again, Elyssa's hysterical call that morning had made her forget everything. "Hopefully, they're not already on assignment."

"We'll see," Sam said, and headed out to the living room

where he could call privately.

Uncle Jamie glanced at his watch. "Susan is due back soon. What are we going to say to her? I can't encourage a child to lie to her parents, but Susan and Matt will see her locked away in an institution."

"I'm not a child," Elyssa reminded them. "Come June, I'll be both a high school grad and over eighteen."

"And that means you'll stop loving and caring for your parents?" Jamie asked.

"Of course not. But Uncle Jamie, they think I'm crazy."

"It's going to be fine," Jenna said. "Your mom knows that you called me, right?"

Elyssa nodded. "I seem to have the gift. My mom doesn't, so she'll never understand."

"Some people never do," Jenna said. "But that doesn't mean she doesn't love you. So what we're going to do is this. You'll say you can't help but be concerned and worried. And I'll say that Sam and I have come because we've realized just how long it's been since we've been back here, so why not check out this situation for you. How's that?"

She looked at Jamie and Elyssa.

"Omission in itself can be a lie," her uncle said. "But, okay, it's not a lie."

The admission came just in time, as the doorbell rang. They could hear the door open and Sam's deep voice as he introduced himself to Susan and Matt Adair, Elyssa's parents.

"Jenna," Susan Adair said, hurrying across the room with a huge hug. "Have you had a chance to speak with Elyssa? You've explained that, while it's sad and tragic, poor Mr. Bradbury took his own life. All I think about are his children. This will be so hard for them."

"Not to worry," Jenna said. "We've assured Elyssa that we'll look into it all and that she needs to worry about school and midterms."

Sam laid his hands on Jenna's shoulders. "It never hurts to be thorough. That's what the bureau is all about. But Jenna is right. Elyssa doesn't have to worry or be concerned about a thing."

"See," Susan said, turning to her daughter triumphantly.

"That's all good."

Matt Adair had been hovering by the door, watching the reunion. He was fit—an athletic man, coaching football at the local high school. They were quite the odd couple. Susan, Irish-looking with carrot red hair and amber eyes, a ball of fire and energy. Matt, except for when he was on the football field, a model of quiet and calm.

He greeted Jenna with a hug, then said, "I never like to say there's nothing to worry about."

Elyssa let out a sigh. "He's worried because I was babbling, and he's afraid my peers are going to make fun of me. That's the least of my worries. Honestly, Dad. My feet are on the ground, and I've never been swayed by peer pressure."

And, to the best of Jenna's knowledge, she hadn't been. Elyssa was bright and happy. She made friends because she was honestly interested in others and enjoyed meeting people. Between them, Susan and Matt had raised her right. A daughter open to new experiences, but comfortable in her own.

"It's always smart to be cautious," Uncle Jamie murmured. "Now, how about some food. I've taken the liberty of ordering out. Italian. And I think the delivery person just drove up."

"I'll head out and get it," Sam offered.

"And I'll give you a hand," Matt said.

"Wait," Susan said. "Why does anyone need to be cautious? This was a suicide. Right? Our daughter found the poor man and that's that."

But no one answered her.

Jenna hurried to help Uncle Jamie with plates and Elyssa found silverware and glasses. The delivery order included lasagna, salad, and breadsticks and the next few minutes were spent passing food around.

"What's new in town?" Sam asked, when everyone was satisfied with a plate filled to their liking.

"They keep building ugly new structures," Matt said.

"It used to be so quaint here. But commercialism is ruining the place," Susan added, shaking her head.

"But a lot of the old shops are still around, right?"

"Oh, yes, and more." Susan said. "New England seems to be moving into an age of diversity. We now have a large Asian population."

"And Hispanic," Matt said.

"Russian, too. Mostly Eastern Europeans," Uncle Jamie said. "We have a new family from Estonia at my church these days, and a number of Polish."

Susan shrugged and smiled. "And islanders. South Americans and Southerners."

Jenna had to laugh. The way Susan spoke, it seemed that Southerners were the most foreign of anyone who'd moved to Salem. "The world moves all over these days. People go different places for work, to study, and some just to live."

"I actually love all of the different languages, the people and accents," Susan said. "But I have to say, if this weren't my home, I don't know if I would have moved here."

Jenna was curious. "Why?"

"Snow," Elyssa said. "Mom hates the snow."

"I don't hate the snow. I hate shoveling snow. And chipping the windows covered with ice."

"Oh, mom, you love Salem. We couldn't pry you out of here with a fire poker."

Elyssa seemed exceptionally happy. As if what had been so horrible was not half so bad anymore.

"Tell me about the new shops in town," Jenna said, glancing at Sam. No better way to learn the lay of the land than ask the locals.

"There's a great place called Down River on Essex Street," Matt said. "I love it. All kinds of books, new and used, and wonderful art and artifacts."

"It's owned by one of the silly Southerners who moved north to shovel snow," Susan said. "Pass the garlic bread, will you please?"

"And there's a restaurant and shop that opened near there," Matt told them. "Indian, from across the ocean. Great food. Beautiful saris and shirts."

"Too much curry, that's the way I see the food," Susan said.

"What about the old places?"

"Most of them are still around. And, of course, there are a number of covens. I think we also have people practicing Santeria or voodoo or something like that." Susan shook her head. "Evil spells." And her hand with the fork shivered halfway to her mouth.

"Most people," Uncle Jamie said, "whether they're practicing Santeria or voodoo or if they're Baptists or Catholics or Episcopalians, are good people. Today's Wiccans tend to be lovely, not wanting to hurt anyone."

"You really do see the good in everyone," Susan said.

"Most religions are good. What men and women do with that sometimes is the problem. I just don't go assuming they're out to do evil."

"I hope not," Matt said. "Halloween seems to bring out all of the kooks. Especially in Salem. And we did have that terrible incident with those murders just a year or two back."

"We know about that," Sam said. "We had colleagues involved with the investigation."

"We're going to hope that everyone behaves for Halloween," Susan said sternly. "And plan on all good things, right, Elyssa?"

The young girl nodded. "I'm going to the school dance, then a party at Nate's house. I'm going to be an angel. Not costume-wise. I'm going as Poison Ivy. But I'll be an angel."

When it was time for the Adair family to leave, Elyssa caught Jenna by the door and gave her a tight hug once again. "Thank you so much for coming. You've made me feel sane again."

Jenna smiled and watched the family go.

As the car drove down the street, Sam turned to Uncle Jamie. "Okay, so what's really going on around here?"

Jamie stared at him. "What do you mean?"

"I know you're in on everything happening. Santeria, voodoo. What else is there that we need to know about?"

The older man sighed and shrugged. "We do have two voodoo priestesses in town. They read tarot cards and do palm reading. But that's not new for Salem, as you know. A few neighbors have complained about chickens. I assume they're being used in their services."

"And the Wiccans? Have you heard of anything troubling there?"

"They're like any group, squabbling now and then."

"Were any of the groups upset about the things going on at the mortuary?" Sam asked.

"Now that I think of it, there was a town meeting. Quite honestly, it was all the usual. A woman complaining that having the mortuary be a theme park attraction for Halloween made fun of witchcraft. She objected to the image of everyone who practiced the Wiccan religion being portrayed as a broom-riding, warty old woman. Someone else was complaining that the haunted house took away from the historic value of the town. Another guy gave a great oratory about the freedom of being in America. Be Wiccan, a Buddhist, whatever, and accept all else. Some clapped for him, some said freedom came with responsibility and respect. But cooler heads prevailed. It's Halloween and every self-respecting town has to have a great haunted attraction. Besides, Salem makes a lot of money at Halloween."

"Think you can make us a list of names of people who seemed to be heading toward the fanatical stage on their speeches?" Sam asked.

"Absolutely."

"You talked to Jackson?" Jenna asked Sam.

He nodded. "Devin Lyle and Craig Rockwell are going to come straight here from a situation in San Diego. They'll be here by tomorrow night, or the next morning at the latest."

"That's Halloween," Jenna said.

"I'm off," Sam said, smiling at the other two. "Care to join me?"

"And where are you going, and what do you think you can discover at this time of night?" Uncle Jamie asked.

"Angela and the home office are online, seeing what they can find out. Thankfully, everyone has a blog or is on Facebook these days. They like to bitch, so we may find something out through their posts. So where else does one get the skinny on what's happening? The best local bar in the center of the action. Except, what would that be now? Hard to say. So I'll just hop from one bar to another and see what's there."

Chapter 3

"There," Jenna said, motioning with her head.

"Where, what?" Sam asked.

They'd entered a relatively new place on Essex Street called The Sorcerer's Brew. Nicely adorned with lots of carved wood and old kegs and trunks for tables and seats. The menu was full of old standards like clam chowder, scrod, fish, meat and chicken, many done up blackened, with cilantro or sriracha sauce. The signature cocktail was also called The Sorcerer's Brew, and they had taps for twenty different beers on draft.

Definitely a tourist stop.

The Peabody Essex museum was just down the street along with a number of the historic houses open to the public. Ghost tours left from the front of nearby shops and a number of store windows offered haunted mazes, 3-D haunted experiences, and slightly twisted versions of the ghosts of Salem, all which utilized various scenes of the condemned coming back to life to curse those who'd accused them. Like most new places that sprang up, the locals checked in now and then. Especially at Halloween, when they were working late and craved a quick bite, a drink, or a cup of tea after work.

Sam followed Jenna's pointed finger and saw a pair of young women seated in a carved wooden booth toward the windows at the front of the restaurant. He followed her as she moved through the crowd.

"Who are they?" he asked.

"Old friends," she told him, and then she grinned.

"Actually, you know them. You chaperoned all of us one day years ago."

And he remembered. Part of the teenage wild gang.

"Stephanie," Jenna said. "Audra."

The two women turned, then both sprang to their feet. There was a lot of gushing and hugs. Sam stood by and waited, then he was introduced. Stephanie had long dark hair and was dressed in black jeans and a black sweater. Audra too had long hair, dressed in a black-tailored shirt and long skirt. Stephanie still looked like a girl with big brown eyes and a gamine-like face. Audra cast a more sophisticated appearance.

"My God," Stephanie said, giving him a hug. "I'd heard you two were together now. I didn't get to see either of you when you were here on that awful Lexington House case. But, oh, a big-time lawyer, eh? Do you remember us? Audra and I were the other kids you had to watch that day. We tormented you, didn't we? But we all had these massive crushes on you. It's great to see you. Are you moving back?"

"Of course, I remember both of you," Sam said, lying. Actually, he didn't remember either of them, only Jenna. "It's great to see you. And no, we're not moving back. We're just here to visit."

"Sit down, join us, can you?" Audra asked.

Sam took a seat on the wooden bench next to Stephanie. Jenna slid beside Audra.

"We know why you're here," Audra said.

"We do?" Stephanie said. "I actually don't. What's going on?"

Audra drew an elegantly polished purple nail along the sweat on her beer mug. "The death at the mortuary. Elyssa Adair found the body."

"That's true," Sam said.

Jenna looked at him, shrugged, and went with his direction. "She was upset and called me. So that's why we're here."

"The whole thing is a little strange, isn't it?" Sam said.

Audra agreed with a shrug. "If that's what I did for a living, manage haunted houses, and I decided to do it all in, I would think that doing something like that would be a great final statement to the world."

Stephanie gasped. "You don't think he committed suicide, do you?"

"We don't really know anything at all," Sam said. "We're just here with the family."

"Did you two get married?" Stephanie asked.

"Not yet," Sam said. "But it's coming. What do you two know about the mortuary and the haunted house? Anything odd going on there?"

"You mean besides a man found hanged to death?" Audra asked.

"Yeah. Besides that."

Stephanie shrugged and said, "The paranormal people aren't happy about renting to the haunted house people. They're above all that, you know. And the haunted house people just think that the paranormal people are crazy. Micah is kind of a self-important jerk and Jeannette Mackey thinks that she's a serious psychic and that all the Wiccan palm and tarot readers in town are idiots. But when it comes to keeping the mortuary going, they force themselves to get along. Oh, my God. You don't think Micah murdered him, do you?"

"We don't know what to think," Sam said.

"But you've come home to solve this murder, haven't you?" Stephanie asked. "This is your home, Sam, right?"

He nodded. "Absolutely."

Jenna looked at Audra. "Are you in a coven?"

"I practice Wicca, but no, I'm not in a coven. I like practicing the tenets on my own. A lot of people don't really practice, they just join covens and then charge for tarot and palm readings and whatever else. Then they charge to be mentors. I don't like the charging part of it, so I practice on my own."

"Oh, come on, there are good covens in the area," Stephanie said.

"Some," Audra agreed. "But only a few."

"So do Wiccans argue with each other?" Sam asked.

"The only argument I know about is between Gloria Day and Tandy Whitehall," Audra said. "Old school versus new school, and all about money. Gloria runs the Silver Moon Festival throughout October. Tandy is much younger and has started doing some really wickedly wild parties. They're always vying for the most publicity. Everyone else is divided. Some support the new, others the old. But mainly they just bitch about each other privately."

"Then there's that idiot who went to court to support the drunk who killed a guy in the crosswalk. Said he was a warlock and that he was going to hex everyone," Stephanie said.

"Male witches aren't warlocks. They're witches, right?" Sam said, frowning.

"They are," Audra agreed, flicking a hand in the air. "At least, in my circles they are. But there are zillions of diverse ways to be a Wiccan or practice the Old Religion. There's Shamanic, Celtic, Gardnerian, and more, not to mention paganism, Pantheists, and Druids. What we all have in common is a love and respect for nature. Most of the holidays are about the same, speaking of which, Halloween is Samhain to us."

"Anything else going on?" Sam asked.

"I need another beer if we're going to play twenty questions," Stephanie said. "And you two haven't had anything to drink yet. What's happened to the service around here?"

"I'll take care of it," Sam said. "I guess they're swamped. What are you all drinking?"

"Local brew. Black Witches Ale. Give it a try," Stephanie said.

"Okay, four mugs of Black Witches Ale coming up."

Sam walked over to the bar and waited his turn, observing those who were there, some in street clothes, others in partial costume. Those were the ones who worked at the historical or Halloween venues, glad to be out of Puritan or creature garb for the night.

"Every place in Salem," an older man next to him said, and sighed. He shook his head, then glanced at Sam apologetically, as if realizing he'd spoken aloud. "Sorry—commercialism! Good for Salem, hard on those who live here!"

"It is almost Halloween," Sam said.

"Can't wait until it's over."

Sam offered his hand and introduced himself. "I'm from here; home for a visit with some family of a friend."

They shook hands.

"The place has changed. I remember when Laurie Cabot

started up with the first witch shop. You would have been young."

"I remember," Sam said.

"Nowadays, we got everything. This morning, damn if there wasn't a chicken head out on the embankment by my place."

Sam asked him where he lived, which was just a few blocks down from where they were, not far from the Elizabeth Montgomery *Bewitched* statue.

"We have Creole neighbors. Don't know what they're practicing, but come on, chicken heads?" The man sighed again. "My wife does say that Mrs. DuPont makes a heck of a chicken pot pie, though. Chicken heads and suicides. I'm telling you, the real stuff going on here now is worse than Halloween. Good for the economy, but crazy for regular folks."

"You're referring to John Bradbury's death?" Sam asked.

"I am. Sad thing. Nice guy. He'd come in here now and then. I'm a realtor and have some late nights. Anyway, Bradbury was always excited about bringing his artistic craft home to Salem. That's what he called it. He loved the old mortuary up there. He told me he wished he could buy it and, if ever he could, he'd turn it into a permanent attraction. Put more history in it, that kind of a thing. He loved the history of Halloween and how the Christian church managed to combine with the pagan ways."

The harried bartender came to them and Sam let the older man place his order first, then asked for the beers. The man thanked him and told Sam he'd be seeing him and moved on. As Sam collected the four steins of Black Witches Ale, he heard a couple at the bar arguing.

"Don't do it," the man warned.

"She's a bitch, and I'm going to take her down," the woman said defiantly.

"You're being ridiculous. There are enough people here to make everyone successful and happy. And, besides, that has nothing to do with practicing what we believe."

"It has to do with pride and with that nasty little bitch Gloria Day trying to take over from everyone else."

"Stop talking," the man said. "Someone will hear you."

"Maybe someone out there is practicing black magic. Not a

Wiccan religion, but pure Satanism. Bradbury talked against her, and look where he is."

"It was a suicide," the man said.

"Maybe. Maybe not."

Sam pretended to get thrown against the man's arm. When the fellow turned to look at him, he quickly apologized. "Sorry. It's so busy in here."

"It's okay," the man said.

"I don't remember it being this crazy. I'm from here, but…wow. Sam Hall, by the way. Nice to meet you, since I nearly sloshed beer on you."

The man frowned. "Sam Hall. You're that big-time attorney. Sorry, I'm David Cromwell and this is my wife, Lydia."

"Nice to meet you both," Sam said and decided not to tell them that he wasn't really practicing law anymore. "By the way, what should I do on Halloween? I hear there are all kinds of things going on and since I haven't been home in ages, I wouldn't mind some advice."

"Tandy Whitehall's Moonlight Madness," Lydia said. "Tandy has been here forever and she's the real deal. She gets fabulous bands and, if you get a reading at the party, it'll be a good one. It's just lovely."

David Cromwell had lowered his head and was gritting his teeth. Bingo. Sam knew that he had hit the core of their argument. Lydia was a huge Tandy Whitehall fan. In the morning, he'd find out how vicious and divisive that fight might be. John Bradbury was dead, and he'd apparently been vocal against the usurper as well.

"Thanks so much," Sam said.

He headed back to the table with the beers. Stephanie and Audra were bringing Jenna up to date on what was going on with their families. They all paused to thank him as he returned.

"Slow waiter," Jenna teased, looking at him.

He sensed she was ready to go, as he'd caught her glance at him while he talked to the Cromwells at the bar. A few minutes later, Jenna yawned and said that they needed to get some sleep.

"And who knows? Uncle Jamie might still have a curfew going for me."

Audra said, "If you think we can help you in any way,

please, don't hesitate to let us know."

"Thanks," Sam said.

"Don't look now," Audra said, "but that's Jeannette Mackey. See the athletic looking woman who just went up to the bar? She's Micah Aldridge's VP or whatever for the paranormal part of the mortuary."

"Really?" Sam muttered.

"I know her," Audra said. "She's older than we are by several years, but I know I've met her a few times. She was on the news a lot, even in Boston. Interviewed on her views on the past and the present and parapsychology."

"I remember when she first started talking about creating a 'true home for the power of the mind,'" Sam said.

He saw the bartender greet her and hand her a large glass of whiskey. "We should pay our respects on the way out."

"Definitely," Jenna said.

They bid her friends goodnight. Sam slipped an arm around Jenna and together they headed for the attractive woman swilling down the drink that had been poured for her.

"Miss Mackey," Sam said.

The woman spun around and stared at Sam, a little wild-eyed, then said, "Samuel Hall, attorney, right?"

"Correct. And this is Jenna Duffy. I believe you two have met somewhere along the line, too."

"Jenna, yes, how are you? You and Elyssa are cousins, right?"

"You have a good memory. We came up to support the family. I understand you and John Bradbury worked together. We just stopped by to say how sorry we are."

"Thank you. I had tremendous respect for John. It was an incredibly important job he had. His company was growing bigger and bigger and his ideas and management were brilliant. I can't tell you how much money the haunted house aspect makes, and what wonderful funds we received because of it. Survival, really. Oh, not that I like a haunted house. But, hey, it was so important I'd play a part in all the schlock when necessary." She looked at the empty glass in her hand. "We're all in shock. Of course, Micah is taking it in stride. I guess he is the stronger one, between us."

"If there's anything we can do, please let us know," Jenna
said.

"Of course. And if you need me for anything." Her voice
trailed. "A suicide. John. I still can't believe it."

"Actually, we're not sure we do believe it," Sam said.

"What?" Jeannette asked, sounding stunned.

"We'll be looking into it," Jenna assured her.

"Of course, you will, of course. As sad as it is, oh, my God.
You think that someone would have harmed him?" Jeannette
asked.

"Do you know of any enemies he might have had?" Jenna
asked.

"John? None. He was polite and courteous to everyone. He
had a bit of a problem with Gloria Day, but that's a long story.
Even so, he was still decent to her. She just didn't like playing
off Tandy Whitehall's thunder." She lowered her voice. "And
the Wiccans, you never know what they're up to." She let out a
soft sigh. "Excuse me, will you? I'm going to go home and try to
get some sleep."

"Us, too," Sam said. "I just want you to know that we're
sorry."

She thanked them, turned, and hurried out.

"What do you think?" Sam asked Jenna.

"I think we have a lot to look into."

The streets were still crazed with activity. It was nearing
midnight and there were parties galore around town. Children
and adults alike seemed to enjoy dressing up for the season.
They turned the corner to cut down by Burying Point and the
memorial to those who'd been condemned to hang along with
Giles Corey, "pressed" to death. They passed a few late night
ghost tours, the guides dressed in Puritan garb.

Many people believed Salem to be one of the most haunted
cities in the world. Easy to understand why. There were those
who'd been condemned to death, along with those who died
imprisoned, or others who went mad from fear or from what
was done to them. A rich history permeated, one that needed to
be remembered. Fear could cause normally decent people to do
terrible things. Or, even worse, to practice the sin of silence, too
afraid to speak out against injustice.

Jenna stopped by the memorial with its stone benches, each dedicated to one of the victims.

"John Proctor spoke out, and he died for it," she said. "I always think about that. He threatened Mercy Warren, his servant girl, with a beating if she didn't stop with the fits, and it worked once."

"You believe all of this has something to do with the witchcraft trials and the modern Wiccans?" Sam asked.

She shrugged. "The case that Devin and Rocky worked up here had to do with someone who'd been murdered before she could be tried. And, according to Elyssa, John Bradbury's ghost mentioned something about witches."

"I actually heard a woman back in the bar mention to her husband that John Bradbury had supported Tandy Whitehall against Gloria Day."

"May mean nothing."

"But could be everything. Another guy told me about finding chicken heads by his house. His neighbors, the DuPont family, practice Santeria or a religion that considers chickens to make good sacrificial offerings."

"Maybe they just like fresh meat at dinner?"

"At least we've got the feel for Halloween in Salem," he told her, slipping an arm around her shoulders as they continued to walk. "I want in on the autopsy. It'll take place tomorrow. Adam Harrison is going to work with the governor, who will call the mayor. I also want to get to the Mayberry Mortuary. It was closed once the body was found. The police and forensic people probably haven't finished with it just yet."

"If they suspect just a suicide," Jenna murmured.

"I don't know what they suspect. The lead detective on the case is a guy named Gary Martin. I don't know the man. I hope it's someone Devin or Rocky might know."

Jenna shook her head. "I don't know the name either."

"I should be able to meet with Martin in the morning and get into the autopsy."

"I'll head to the Mayberry Mortuary," Jenna said.

They came to the cemetery and Sam stopped. He could see the old tombstones with their death's heads, cherubs, angels, and other decorations, opaque and haunting in the moonlight. The main gates were locked at this time of night and it was, of course, illegal for anyone to enter. He thought for a moment he saw movement by one of the gnarled old trees.

"What is it?" Jenna asked.

He shook his head. "Nothing. Let's get back and get some sleep. It's been a long day."

She agreed.

The crowds had thinned, a few groups here and there, less as they left the cemetery and some of the major attractions behind and headed down the street that led to Uncle Jamie's house.

As they turned a corner, Jenna said, "There's another one, or the same guy on a costume bender. Another boo-hag."

She was right. Across the street, a group in costume was walking toward the wharf, heading back to one of the new hotels near the water. And there was someone in the same costume that had jumped onto their car.

A boo-hag.

Sam had been born and raised in Salem and he'd never even heard of a boo-hag before. Now he'd seen two in as many days.

The group was walking with their backs toward Sam and Jenna. Suddenly, the man in the boo-hag costume turned, stared their way for a moment, then headed off.

"That was eerie," Jenna said. "Movie monsters and most creatures seem almost ho-hum around here, but that costume gets to you."

"A boo-hag," Sam said. "Definitely creepy."

He didn't mention that there was something more. The way the eyes seemed to focus on them, the way they seemed to burn, even at a distance, as if they were formed of fiery red-gold, burning like the flames of hell.

Chapter 4

Sam knew that they often dealt with terrible things. That was the occupation he and Jenna had both chosen. Partly because of their "gifts," and partly because they wanted to make a difference. But this situation seemed more personal. He'd intended to give Jenna all the space she needed. But alone, in the darkness of their room at Uncle Jamie's, she turned to him with a sweet and urgent passion. The warmth of her naked body next to his, flesh against flesh, and the fever that seemed to burn in her became electric. No words, just her moving against him, touching, a feather-light caress at first, then a passionate love, both tender and urgent. He held her afterward, naked and slaked against him, and he thought that they both would sleep well.

Home was wonderful.

But home was also a place where nightmares could be rekindled.

He didn't want her facing any demons in her mind. But that night Sam was the one to dream. He saw something coming toward them out of a strange and misty darkness. Red, with shimmering golden eyes that seemed to burn with evil.

Then he realized that the thing wasn't coming at him.

He wasn't next to Jenna anymore. She was some distance away, sleeping, laid out on the bed, eyes closed, a half smile on her face.

And the thing was going for her.

He tried to run, to block the horrible menace from reaching the woman he loved. No matter how hard he tried, he was slowed down by the thick red mist.

The thing was now on Jenna, leaning over her, stiffening, inhaling, as if prepared to suck the life from her. The red mist became thicker and thicker. He realized he was fighting, straining, trying so hard to reach her. But it was no longer red mist that held him back. Instead, the barrier had become a sea of blood.

He woke with a start.

Morning.

His phone ringing.

An aura of fear stayed with him and he fought it; reaching for the phone and checking on Jenna, who was just beginning to rouse.

Jackson was calling. The right people had talked to the right people, and the FBI had been officially asked into the investigation. While suicide in the death of John Bradbury was a valid theory, the media had gone wild over the whole situation. Whispers of foul play ran rampant. He thanked Jackson for the assist and hung up.

"That's perfect," Jenna said, when he explained the call.

"I have to get to the autopsy," he told her.

"And I'll head to the mortuary."

"Maybe you should come with me," he said, recalling some of the dream.

"Don't be silly. We need to move fast on this. There are so many people we're going to have to interview, so much we have to find out. We have to divide the load. I know the mortuary, but we need to know the layout, how someone might have gotten in. That can only come from a visit."

She was right and he knew it.

He still didn't want to be away from her.

"Devin and Rocky will be here—"

"We can't wait on them," she said, frowning then smiling. "Sam, I'm a good agent. I was an agent before you were an agent, remember? I'll be careful. I promise."

He hesitated. "I had a nightmare," he said.

"You did?"

"A boo-hag was after you."

She smiled. "Sam, boo-hags aren't real."

"The one in the street was real. So we have to watch out."

"I swear, I'll be careful."

"Maybe—"

"Sam, I'm good at what I do. And when you're back from the autopsy, we'll meet up and go together from there."

He rose.

She was already up, heading to the shower. He started to follow her. She laughed, paused, and told him, "No time for that. I'll be right out. We need to move this morning."

"So you think you're that irresistible?" he asked her.

She grinned. "In a shower, you're irresistible."

And she closed the door on him.

"Nice lip service," he told her through the door.

"Lip service is later," she said.

He grinned at that, stared at the closed door for a minute, and then gathered his clothing for the day. He couldn't be unreasonable. He'd had a nightmare. Part of coming home, perhaps. And yet, in their world, nightmares could be real or, at a minimum, whispers of threats to come.

* * * *

"Hauntings and Hallucinations rents the space from us for the event," Micah Aldridge told Jenna.

It was just nine in the morning but she'd arrived at the Mayberry Mortuary to meet with Micah. Sam had headed for the autopsy and his meeting with Gary Martin. Adam Harrison had performed his usual magic. The FBI wasn't taking *lead* on the investigation—the situation didn't warrant it yet—but they were to be given access to information and leave to investigate. She hadn't met Martin and hoped that he didn't intend to dismiss the death as a suicide with no possibility of foul play. Things were always easier when everyone cooperated with everyone else. Most of the time it worked that way. But every once in a while they hit a local law enforcement officer who was more proprietorial, not wanting federal interference.

"I have to admit," Micah said. "I kind of loathed the idea of having something so schlocky here when we are trying to do real research. But bills have to be paid and we make enough from the

Halloween rental to carry us through the year."

She nodded. "Makes sense."

She studied the beautiful old building. By daylight, the skeletons, spiders webs, and jack-o-lanterns all appeared to be just nicely arranged paper and props, nothing more. By night, with special lighting, the place appeared eerie, especially the cemetery surrounding it. When it wasn't Halloween season, the place still cast a certain melancholy about it, a poignancy that perhaps reflected the shadows of lives gone by.

"You've been here before, haven't you?" Micah asked.

"I took an historic tour when I was about fifteen," Jenna said. "It's been a while. But I would like to take a look inside."

They entered through the foyer. Double doors led into a massive living room and to the ornate stairway that led up to the second floor. The living room was filled with creatures, spider webs, a giant tarantula, and other oddities. On one wall a painting had flesh when first looked at, but turned skeletal from a different angle. A grand piano, complete with a skeleton player, sat by the windows to the porch. By night, the interior lights would show him in an eerie symphony.

"They do a good job," Jenna said. "Where are the stairs down to the basement?"

"John made it all possible," a female voice said.

She turned to see a young woman entering from the foyer. Attractive, with a wealth of long dark hair and a pretty face, but her eyes welled with tears as she approached.

"I'm Naomi Hardy."

"Jenna Duffy."

"Naomi and John Bradbury worked hand in hand," Micah said. "His death has been hard on her."

Concern filled Micah's voice.

"John was a true visionary," Naomi said. "He went to shows across the country, always looking for the newest innovations in creepy, chilling, *fun* scares. But he insisted we keep some real history too, to go along with all the whacko legend and scary movie stuff. He was so good. Head of the artistic branch, and every year at Halloween, he managed this place himself. I still can't believe he's gone."

"I am truly sorry for your loss," she said.

"Jenna is with the FBI."

"You're here over a suicide?"

"Elyssa Adair, who found the body, is my cousin," Jenna said. "I'm really here to help her through this."

The explanation seemed to satisfy Naomi.

"John had the best job in the world. But then he'd had such a horrible divorce. His wife should have been shot. He'd had some drug problems as a kid and she dragged every bit of that into court, destroying his reputation. He had a hard time getting over it. All his success, and he could barely see his own children."

Which made the ex a definite suspect.

"Is the wife still around?" Jenna asked.

"No. That was the first thing the police asked. But she was nowhere near here. Home with the kids and she hadn't seen John since their last court date, months ago. She went on TV. Blamed his past, his drug problems, everything on him."

Tears welled in Naomi's eyes, which she brushed aside before asking, "What are you doing here at the mortuary?"

"Tying up the loose ends."

Naomi shrugged, as if uninterested. "If you'll excuse me, we're reopening tonight and now it's all on me. Micah, I'll be down at the ticket booth if you need me. Jenna, a pleasure to meet you, even under these circumstances."

She and Micah walked upstairs. Without darkness and actors, all of the haunting paraphernalia seemed worn and sad. Micah pointed out what was usually the tarot card reading and séance room. Another bedroom was used for psychic testing. She was interested in the entire layout, but really wanted to get to the basement to see if she could sense or feel anything. Elyssa wasn't lying. John Bradbury had appeared to her. But it would be helpful if that ghost would speak with her or Sam.

"Is there only one entrance to the basement?" she asked.

Micah nodded. "From the house, yes. The stairs are in the back of the kitchen. There's also an entrance from the back driveway that slopes down to a door. I guess it made for easy deliveries when the place was used as a funeral home."

Micah seemed fine about going down to the basement, but then again, he'd been alone here when she arrived. If the place was haunted in any way, Micah certainly didn't care.

She followed him to the ground floor landing and around the grand staircase to a door and more stairs that led down.

"It's a mess," Micah told her. "The police moved just about everything. Naomi will be taking over as manager and she'll see to it that everything is in order before tonight."

"Reopening already?" Jenna asked.

He shrugged. "I'm truly sorry. I liked John. He was a great guy. But life goes on and we have to pay the bills."

"Yes, I guess so," she murmured.

"The stairs are fairly narrow," Micah said. "In the old days, the dead came in through the back entry, and the coffins went back out that same way. Hauntings and Hallucinations carries some major liability insurance and we have strict rules about how many people can come through at one time. We're not the responsible party here, just the lessor, but we don't want anything bad to happen to anyone. Well, dead is bad, but the poor guy did himself in. You know, I saw John every day for the last couple of months and I had no idea he was so depressed."

Jenna didn't reply or correct him. Better to stay silent.

They'd reached the basement. The long stone embalming tables remained, each piled high with Halloween decorations. The police had indeed made a mess.

Micah pointed. "In the nooks and cubicle areas we have motion-activated creatures and characters. You can see the giant alien there, the werewolf over here, the vampire and mummy. That crazed killer over there scares the bejesus out of most visitors. Over there is where it happened."

She studied the cubicle, empty except for a giant iron hook that had long been attached to the ceiling above. The rope by which John Bradbury had hung had been removed, but the black lighting set up by the haunted house company remained. She thought that the basement, with its stone foundation pillars, wooden beams, and strewn paraphernalia seemed not eerie, but sad. The soft lighting made if look almost as if surrounded by a red mist. She walked over to where Bradbury had died.

"What were these crevices for?" she asked.

"I really don't know." He paused. "Poor John."

She stood still and wished Micah wasn't with her. Some

alone time might be beneficial here.

"The exit from the basement is over this way," Micah said. "We have visitors leave the house via the basement and walk back up the path to the parking lot when they've finished the tour."

He walked toward the back door.

Jenna hovered a moment, waiting, standing still, trying to imagine what had gone on when Bradbury had died.

"Jenna?" Micah called to her.

"Coming," she said.

She waited another few beats, then turned to join him at the exit.

And it hit her.

A movement in the air, a change in the temperature, the sense that they were not alone. She felt a brush against her cheek, and heard a whispered voice in the red mist aura.

I did not die by my own hand.

* * * *

The autopsy happened down in Boston where the Office of the Chief Medical Examiner was located. Sam was pleased to discover that the medical officer on duty was Dr. Laura Foster, a woman he'd worked with several times when he practiced law in Boston. She was bright, determined, and good at her job. There was even a Salem connection. Laura was the descendant of a woman accused of witchcraft during the craze. Her ancestor wasn't hanged. Instead, she died of the horrible conditions in the jail where she was held.

Detective Gary Martin was there too. He was pushing fifty, with short-cropped steel-gray hair. When he'd shaken hands with Sam, Martin had expressed surprise that the FBI had interest in an apparent suicide, but seemed to accept Sam's explanation that they were involved only because of family.

"If there's one thing I've learned," Martin said. "It's that you can never be sure of anything. With John Bradbury, it certainly appears he killed himself."

"It could have been made to look like suicide," Sam said.

Martin appeared skeptical. "Like I say. Anything's possible.

Maybe the autopsy will tell us something we don't know."

They stood off to the side while Laura Foster went through the preliminaries, then made a Y incision in the chest and dictated her notes. Death appeared to have come from a broken neck. Otherwise, John Bradbury had been a healthy, forty-five-year-old man, with a strong heart and clear lungs. The last meal remained in the stomach. Clam chowder, white fish, greens. Everything was recorded.

When she stopped speaking, Martin asked, "Suicide?"

"Could be," Laura said. "But, I doubt it."

Sam was listening carefully.

"I'm not a forensics expert," she said, "or a detective. The rope was taken and bagged as evidence yesterday. I saw it. From the way it was tied and the way he hanged, I can't see how he could have slipped it around his own neck. Also, these abrasions here, on the side of the neck. They suggest he was dragged while the rope was in place, choking him." She pointed at the body. "Marks here suggest he was digging at the rope before he died. This man was fighting and kicking. That's what broke his neck. He died fast, much quicker than simple strangulation."

"If he killed himself," Martin said, "he might have been fighting to the end. Perhaps regrets?"

Laura shook her head. "I can't say definitively death was by his own hand."

"So you're calling it a murder?" Martin asked.

Sam remained stoic, practicing something he learned a long time ago as a trial lawyer. Never let them know what you're thinking.

"I can't call this a suicide," Laura said.

"Just great," Martin said.

So much for an open and shut investigation.

"I'm sorry," Laura said. "I'll be doing more testing, but I suggest you start investigating this as a murder."

"Can you give us a time of death?" Sam asked.

"No more than sixteen or seventeen hours. So I'm saying between the hours of two and four, yesterday afternoon."

Martin left the room.

"He didn't want a murder," Laura said to him.

"No one ever does. Thank you for being stubborn."

"I'm not being stubborn, Sam. You know me. I call it the way I see it." She hesitated, nodding to her assistant, who was waiting to sew up the corpse. "It's just science—and justice, right?"

"Absolutely."

He stepped closer to the body. Sometimes, though not often, the dead could be reached by simple touch. But John Bradbury's spirit was not with them in the room.

He thanked Laura again.

"I hate it when people use Salem," she said. "When they do something like this, stringing a man up as if he was one of the victims from the old witch craze. It's mocking at its worst. Ignore Mr. I-Want-A-Suicide out there and catch this killer."

"Martin's not a bad guy. He was just going with what appeared to be obvious. The word was out that John Bradbury had been having a bad time lately. An excellent candidate for suicide. But we owe it to him to find the truth."

She nodded. "Glad you're on this, Sam."

He left the room. Martin had already stripped off the paper mask he'd worn inside. Sam did the same.

"Who the hell murders a guy like that?" Martin asked. "And how did you know?"

"I didn't," Sam said. "We're involved only because of Jenna's cousin, Elyssa."

Martin shook his head. "I guess that's your story and you're sticking to it. You Feds gripe my tail. You just come and go as you please, sticking your noses into what should be a local matter."

Sam tried to be diplomatic. He'd dealt with this attitude before. "We help local authorities solve a crime. That is all our jobs, right?"

"Yeah, I guess it is. You do know that I didn't want this to be murder. It's Halloween season. Patrol cops are going to have their hands full with corralling a ton of costumed drunks. Now there's a murderer running loose among them."

Sam pictured the boo-hag again from last night.

But no boo-hag had sucked the life out of John Bradbury.

No.

That poor man had been murdered.

Chapter 5

"During the afternoon, the only people here would have been me, Jeannette Mackey, John Bradbury, or Naomi Hardy," Micah told Jenna. "There are deliveries during the day. And when we're not open, the doors are supposed to be locked. Of course, we're open during the day in the afternoons for tours, but only if we have tours. They're by appointment only during October. That's not to say that someone might not have left a door or window open."

"No security cameras or alarm system?" Jenna asked.

"Yes, there's an alarm."

Whoever killed John Bradbury had done so in the afternoon before six o'clock since, by then, the actors and guides had reported and there were people coming and going from the basement. She asked Micah about who might have been at the mortuary that afternoon.

"It should have been locked. The only people there were the usual day workers. That's myself and Jeannette Mackey. During the season, it included John Bradbury and Naomi Hardy. I'm not sure when I first saw Naomi that day, but Jeannette and I both came in around eleven. I didn't see or hear anything. John had talked about taking a day off, so we assumed that he had. To be honest, while we like to be the "real" psychic deal and distance ourselves from Halloween hokum, it's all a little bit fun. So we like being a part of it. Participating. Watching." His voice drifted off. "We went through all of this with the police that night. They were dumbfounded that so many people who worked here, and then so many attendees went through, before anyone realized that our swinging corpse was real. There was always a corpse there and things are supposed to look authentic."

"And the police have said that you can reopen tonight?" Jenna asked.

He shrugged. "It seems part of the attraction now. You can rent the room in Fall River where Lizzie Borden hacked her stepmother to death. You can rent the room at the Hardrock Hotel in Florida where Anna Nicole Smith died. And someone died, at some time, in a good percentage of the homes in New England."

"I think it was more than two nights after before you could rent either room," she said. "So the people who should have been here during the day were you, John, Jeannette, and Naomi. And there is a security system. So if someone broke in, you should have known it?"

He shrugged a little unhappily. "Probably. But Jeannette and I were getting ready for a meeting of the Salem Psychic Research Society. We did find a college kid walking around, just looking, not doing anything bad."

"But with this hugely popular attraction going on, you have no cameras, no eyes on the crowd anywhere?"

"We have plenty of eyes," he said. "Every room has what Hauntings and Hallucinations calls 'security guides.' Someone not in costume, but in a black uniform, carrying a flashlight, there to help out in an emergency."

"And the police have a listing of these people? Did they interview the 'security guide' working last night?"

"Of course. It was William Bishop, and he was a basket case. The guides are just simple hires, like the kids who go in costume. Most of them are college aged, a few are retirees. Some are just high school students. We comply fully with all labor laws."

"Micah, I'm not concerned with labor laws. A man is dead."

"It's not my fault he killed himself!"

"But the point is, no one saw him do it."

Micah flushed. "I had no idea John was here. I was upstairs. I have some files beneath the dueling skeletons in the tarot room. Our computers and communications are still up in that room too. Jeannette was with me. Like I said, I don't know what time Naomi got here because I just wasn't paying attention. But she was a little distracted because she hadn't heard from John, and assumed he was taking the night off. I told her not to worry, I'd work the ticket kiosk with her if he didn't come in. She told me they were short a few actors, too. Sally Mansfield, a local housewife who does this every year, was sick with the flu. So Jeannette said she'd be happy to be chopped up or whatever."

"I saw Jeannette last night."

Micah looked at her, surprised. "She said she was going home to bed. She was really upset by what happened. We all cared about John. Poor Naomi. She has to keep this going or the monetary loss will be incredible."

"I've seen businesses closed down for weeks after a tragedy like this. But, I guess you're right, the show must go on."

He hesitated and looked at her suspiciously. "Why are you trying to make a bad situation even more difficult?"

"I'm a special agent with the Federal Bureau of Investigation, Micah. This is my job."

She preferred not to be so pretentious, but sometimes she had to be. And with Micah, it worked.

"Of course, I understand," he said. "But it was a suicide, wasn't it?"

"I don't think so."

"Am I a suspect?"

"Actually, you are," she said pleasantly. "So any assistance you can give me will certainly help in eliminating you."

"Whatever you need. But you know that John's personal life wasn't going well. Oh, my. There was a murderer in here with us? But how? When? I don't see how this can be possible. Oh, my God."

He was panicked, of no help any further. So she decided to leave. "Thanks for your help. I'll call you if I need anything."

She turned to head up the stairs, back to ground level, and out through the front. Micah followed.

"Someone could have come in through the back, through the delivery entrance, I suppose, and we wouldn't have known," he said. "You can't hear. I mean it is a big place."

Outside on the front porch, Jenna noted the quiet location and sad feel to the day. The ticket kiosks seemed cheaply thrown up, the Halloween decorations worn and frayed. Everything was much more magical at night. Naomi Hardy sat at the kiosk, head bowed. Jenna glanced over at the cemetery. Midmorning light was rising, sending streaks of yellow and gold down on the graves. Both the cemetery and house occupied a hill that sloped down to thick forest, the leaves a brilliant collage of orange, crimson, and gold. Past a decaying mausoleum and a weeping angel, she thought she saw something.

A strange flash of darkness and light.

Near the weeping angel and a worn tombstone stood someone in a black cape. Someone with a red face and body. The boo-hag they'd seen the other night. What would someone in costume be doing at the edge of a forlorn graveyard at this time of day, just looking up at the mortuary? She excused herself and headed down the rocky drive toward the cemetery. She leapt over a few tombstones and wove around ancient sarcophagi. But, when she reached the far side and the forest edge, the boo-hag was gone.

She drew her weapon and called out, "FBI. Get the hell out here, whoever you are."

She hadn't really expected a reply, not unless it might come from some holdover partier unsure of where he was from a function the previous night. She moved cautiously into the woods, alert and wary, careful of the leaves and twigs beneath her feet.

And then stopped.

No boo-hag was in sight.

Instead, a woman dangled from a tree limb.

* * * *

"Hanged by the neck until they be dead,'" Detective Gary Martin said, quoting from the death warrants handed down to those executed back in 1692.

Sam watched as a forensic photographer snapped pictures. The victim had been dressed up for display. Their male victim, John Bradbury, had also been decked out in Puritanical garb.

Whether this woman often dressed in period clothing for one reason or another, they had no way of knowing. He and Gary Martin had arrived on the scene within minutes of Jenna's call, both on the outskirts of Salem. Once again, Sam was plagued with a feeling of urgency and fear.

The boo-hag.

But Jenna hadn't mentioned a boo-hag. She just said that she'd left the mortuary, come through the graveyard, then walked into the forest, finding a dead woman hanged from a tree. She was calm. No surprise. She was one hell of an agent. She'd touched nothing, securing the scene until forensics and a medical examiner could arrive. They'd asked if Laura Foster might be sent, explaining that they might be looking at a serial killer. He and Martin stood next to Jenna, watching while the crime scene techs did their thing.

"Think this one is a suicide too?" Jenna asked Martin sarcastically.

"Kind of hard to hang yourself from a tree," Martin said. "Unless she climbed up there, then out on the limb, tied the rope, then jumped. Not likely."

Jenna smiled at him. "I'm sorry. I didn't mean to be a pain."

Martin moved around the tree, trying to get a better look at the hanging victim. A large white bonnet hid most of her face and it was difficult—without disturbing the rope—to get a good look at her face.

"It's Gloria Day," Martin said. "She's a big Samhain fest organizer and throws a witches' ball on Halloween. Or it's Samhain, to her, I guess."

"You knew her?" Sam asked.

Martin shook his head. "Not really. I know of her. Her face is on a number of advertisements. This is really going to shake up the community."

Sam and Jenna moved carefully around to where Martin stood to study the corpse too. As they did, the medical examiner's van arrived through the trees. When Laura Foster stepped out, Sam was grateful. They were going to need her on this one. Jenna had not met her, so he introduced the two women and then Laura went to work. Enough photographs had been taken from every angle so the rope was cut and the corpse lowered, laid carefully on a tarp that could be formed into a body bag. A temperature check indicated that the time of death had been somewhere between five and six A.M.

Laura provided as many specifics as she could from a cursory inspection, pointing out the corpse's coloration, the neck had not broken, and she was probably strangled to death, slow and excruciating.

"This is Gloria Day," Laura said.

"Did you know her?" Martin asked.

"I've only seen her. She runs an ad on the local news about her ball every year. She also has a shop and helps promote classes run by some of her coven members. She's kind of a big cheese around here."

"Like John Bradbury?" Jenna asked.

"That's right. But look at the way the rope was tied. It's exactly the same as with Bradbury. When you look at the photographs, you'll see what I mean. I don't believe that either victim tied a rope that way around their own neck." Laura shook her head. "This is going to be one wicked Halloween."

"What about the costume?" Jenna asked.

"She could have worn that herself. She ran the ball, owned a shop, and did some tour guide stuff. I know all that from the ads you can't help but see if you live here. I know she was thirty-eight years old, born in Peoria, Illinois, and a fairly recent transplant to Salem. She arrived in the city in a big way, though her commercial devotion was twitching away."

"Maybe we're looking at a rival coven, or group of covens, or even one of the other sects. Like the voodoo guys, the Haitians, or the Asian-Indians. Maybe I should throw the Catholics and Baptists in there, too," Martin said.

"They're not going to stop," Jenna said.

"Why do you say that?" the detective asked.

She looked up at him. "Someone is trying to recreate the witch craze."

"John Bradbury wasn't a Wiccan," Sam said.

"And neither were any of those executed long ago for signing pacts with the devil," Jenna noted. "People like Bridget Bishop, Rebecca Nurse, Sarah Goode, Susannah Martin—"

"You know their names?" Martin asked.

She nodded. "Elizabeth Howe, Sarah Wilde, George Burroughs, John Willard, Martha Carrier, George Jacobs, Sr., John Proctor, Martha Corey, Mary Eastey, Ann Pudeater, Alice Parker, Mary Parker, Wilmott Redd, Martha Scott, and Samuel Wardell."

"That's impressive," Martin said. "I can add Giles Corey—pressed to death. Had the reputation of being somewhat of a mean son-of-a-bitch, stuck to his guns. He had that famous line, *'More weight!'*" He studied Jenna. "Were you from here? You've got it down."

"Boston. But I spent a lot of time here while growing up. What I'm afraid of is some kind of large-scale plot, or sick deranged thing going on. They're both dressed. No man was hanged first during the real deal. Women got that honor. But there were men condemned and hanged as witches. From what I understand, John Bradbury had a love of local history, but he wasn't a Wiccan. Gloria Day was a big-time Wiccan, apparently famed for her classes and her ball."

Martin looked at Sam. "Let's get a search grid going."

"Sounds good to me."

Martin let out a whistle. A number of uniformed cops hustled over from the road area, around the outskirts of the trees, keeping their distance from the actual murder site until they were given instructions.

"I'm going back to the graveyard," Jenna said. "That's where I came in from."

Sam frowned at her. What had she been doing running around among the tombstones?

"No problem, whatever you need to do," Martin told her.

"I'll join her," Sam said, following Jenna.

To his surprise, Martin came too, leaving his crew to grid search the crime scene.

"You know," Martin said, "it's a 'graveyard' when it's by a church. It's a cemetery when it's freestanding or planned. Most of the plots have names."

Sam was trying to catch up with Jenna, but she was moving ahead quickly.

"Jenna," he called out.

She heard him and stopped.

He reached her. "Did the ghost of John Bradbury find you? What were you doing here? I thought you were searching the house."

She glanced back. Martin stood close to the edge of the forest. "I think he might have whispered to me down in the basement."

"The winged-death's-head is the most popular art on tombstones around here," Martin called, pausing at one of the graves. "The Puritans didn't want anything to do with icons that might suggest Catholicism. 'Life is uncertain, Death is for Sure, Sin is the Wound, and Christ is the Cure,'" he read to them. "Pretty succinct."

"That's a common epitaph in this area," Sam called back.

He looked over at Jenna, waiting for more information.

"It was bizarre," she told him, her green eyes intense. "I followed a costumed figure in there."

"But?"

"I came into the woods and didn't see a soul, except the woman hanged from the tree."

"Cigarette butt," Martin yelled.

"Great. Bag it," Sam called back. "Jenna, what happened to the person you were chasing? You think that they might have done this, or do you think it was a spirit?"

"No, nothing like that. And I don't know if they were a possible suspect or not. The guy in costume might have headed straight for the road, while I cut into the woods deeper. And it's Halloween. Finding someone in costume is going to be ridiculously hard. Half the world around here is going to be dressed up."

"What costume, Jenna?" he asked, holding her shoulders and trying not to grip too hard.

"It was a boo-hag."

Chapter 6

They were sitting in a meeting room at the police station when Craig Rockwell called Sam to say that he and Devin Lyle had landed and were on their way. Sam had seldom been more grateful to have other Krewe members around.

Lt. Bickford P. Huntington, Supervisor for the Criminal Investigations Unit, had called a meeting to inform a task force from Salem and the surrounding areas about the two murders and bring them up to speed on what was known. He had Gary Martin speak and introduced Sam and Jenna as representatives from the federal government. Some there were old friends, some on the force new, not around four years ago when the murders had taken place at Lexington House, which Jenna and Sam had worked.

Sam thought Huntington seemed competent as he laid out all of the information they knew. He also provided a good assessment for what they might be looking for. Someone with a deranged historical sense of revenge, or someone with a contemporary sense of it, or someone who just wanted to kill people. Huntington looked over at Sam and suggested that he provide the group his thoughts. Before he could speak one of the officers spoke up.

"This woman you found today, she was a major commercial-style star Wiccan. Does that mean that we're really looking for someone in a coven?"

The answer was probably yes, but Sam was careful with his reply. He couldn't say that a ghost had told a young woman that his killer had been talking about the witch trials and cults.

"It's my understanding that a feud has been ongoing. So I think it's going to be important to discover if there's someone in some kind of an offshoot cult that might be doing this, not necessarily Wiccan. We all know that today's pagan religions, especially here in Salem, believe in treating everyone with love and respect. Murder would be a terrible sin to anyone truly practicing the Wiccan religion. There are many ways to look at this without stereotyping anyone."

"But, the two victims were killed in the same manner as those executed during the witchcraft trials," another officer said.

"You all know your history here. Anything was witchcraft. If you looked into the future, silly girls playing at love potions, even goodwives trying medicinal herbs, all of that was considered witchcraft. Of course, none of those executed was a witch. It was hysteria, fueled over petty squabbles and simple hatred among the people who lived here then. The pagans, or Wiccans, we have in Salem today have nothing to do with all that. Should we look at strange cults and fundamentalism of any kind, be it Wiccans or another group? Absolutely. Do we need to question people spouting against Gloria Day? Definitely. But the medical examiner's office hasn't even started on the second autopsy yet. Let's see what comes of that."

Jenna was introduced—she smiled and greeted old friends and thanked those she'd worked with before, asking that they be especially vigilant in the areas surrounding the mortuary, graveyard, and forest, and to listen to what they heard around town. "You know Salem. You'll know when something isn't right or when it feels strange. We need to keep a close eye on the mortuary. The first murder apparently happened at a time when those in charge were busy or unaware. And we need to watch out for local situations. Crack pots, cults, culture clashes of any kind."

The meeting ended and Sam and Jenna wound up discussing their next moves in one of the conference rooms while Lieutenant Huntington went on to speak to the press. The community, Sam knew, would be talking about nothing else. But, none of it would stop Halloween or Samhain celebrations. Salem had a life of its own at this time of year. A pulse. A beat. Like a living entity.

Gary Martin was working hard. He hadn't wanted a murder, but he'd wound up with two. His men had retrieved a fair amount of evidence from the forest where Gloria Day's body had been found. All of the cigarette butts, cans, bits and pieces of hair, and everything else would go to the DNA lab. And while TV shows might get their results back in an hour, it would be days, possibly weeks, before these would be ready. Sam harbored no illusions. They were not going to get anything off an old cola can. Their killer wasn't sitting there enjoying a soda before hanging a woman. Results would come from walking and talking and discovering what was going on in the community. Someone had to have seen a car. The hill upon which the mortuary sat alongside the cemetery wasn't in walking distance from town. And Gloria Day's killer had not forced her to walk up the hill then into the forest to be hanged. It made sense that John Bradbury had been in the basement of the mortuary. He worked there. But Gloria Day was another matter. Her shop and school sat in the middle of town, down the street from the Hawthorne Hotel. Had she been lured up there to see something unusual? To participate in some kind of ceremony? Sam was anxious to get to her shop, but he also wanted to know more about the various groups in the community now. And much of it, he thought, needed to be done by himself and Jenna, or Rocky and Devin. The local police were good. But the Krewe team was better.

Alone with Gary Martin and Jenna in the conference room, Sam looked over the files on locals, along with the notes they'd received from Angela Hawkins, Jackson Crow's wife and top assistant. She'd found pages and pages of Facebook, Instagram, Google, and other social media communications that spoke of an all-out verbal war between two factions in the city. Two main rivals were clear. The Coven of the Silver Moon, Gloria Day's group. And the Coven of the Silver Wolf, Tandy Whitehall's people. Each of the two had hives, where the overflow went when there were too many people in a coven. Thirteen was considered the ideal number, but that wasn't etched in stone. Hives, he knew, kept their membership low so as not to become unwieldy, the perfect place for a newly ordained high priest or priestess. Both Day and Whitehall had enjoyed a lot of popularity, their hives numerous and, on occasions like Samhain, they gathered together. In Salem, that usually happened at Gallows Hill, which, frankly, Sam didn't agree with, and for good reason.

Just seemed the wrong place.

"There's been a lot of talk on the web," Martin said, reading through some of the notes Angela had e-mailed. "The word 'bitch' seems overly popular. Gloria Day seems to be accused of being a greedy, manipulative usurper, determined to rule all of Salem. She gives good cause for the world to believe modern-day witches to be old hags with saggy brooms and warts flying across the moon on broomsticks.'" He paused and looked at them. "Now that's just mean. She's old, yes. But certainly not ugly and doesn't have any warts."

Officers had tried to pay a visit to Tandy Whitehall, but she'd not been at her shop, Magical Fantasies, nor at her house. Everyone was on the lookout for her. If she wasn't found soon, sterner measures would be used. Sam believed Whitehall had to know they were looking for her. The media had sniffed out the latest murder with the speed of light. So quickly, in fact, that Jenna had wondered if they shouldn't be looking for someone involved with the media. But Sam kept remembering Elyssa's words. That the ghost mentioned the witchcraft trials and cults. That didn't necessarily mean modern-day pagans. But the well-publicized feud between the two most prominent covens could not be ignored.

Among the information Angela had sent was details on a legend. Sam had specifically asked about the Gullah culture and the boo-hag.

"Listen to this," he said, reading the information.

And he told them about an old folk story and a boy named Billie Bob who just could not find a wife. So his father fixed him up with the daughter of a swamp woman. He was stunned when he met her. She was gorgeous, with dark eyes, dark hair, and a beautiful body. She didn't want to be married by a priest, but was willing to stand before a judge. So they were married and she was the perfect wife by day. But at night she never came to bed. Suspecting the worst, Billie Bob, armed with sugar and honey and all manner of gifts, went to see a local conjuring woman. The old woman told him to pretend that he was asleep, then watch what his wife did. The next night Billie Bob did just that, following his wife up to the attic where she sat at a wheel and spun off her skin. All bloody muscle and bone, she headed out into the night. Billie Bob was terrified, so he went back to the old conjuring woman who told him he had to paint every window and door in the house blue, except for one. She also told him to splash salt and pepper on her discarded skin. He did both, and when she returned home, she found herself trapped, as the blue doors were a weakness. When she slipped back into her skin, the salt and pepper burned her horribly. In a panic, she crashed through an attic window and turned as bright as a falling star, her body exploding into chunks of flesh that were enjoyed by the swamp gators. Billie Bob was sad. The conjuring woman told him that he should not be. He'd had no wife, only a boo-hag. Once she'd tired of him, she would have brought him to her boo-daddy, who would have eaten his flesh, drank his blood, and gnawed at his bones.

"But Billie Bob didn't become chow," Sam said. "It's a bit like a vampire story, or even a story about our old concept of witches, bringing their new recruits to Satan. Their version of a boo-daddy."

"And what does a boo-hag have to do with Salem?" Martin asked.

"What about the Gullah culture up here?" Sam asked.

"We have a few transplants, but—"

A uniformed officer entered the room, escorting Devin and Rocky. Jenna rose to quickly hug and welcome the newcomers. As it turned out, Rocky knew Detective Gary Martin. They explained what had just happened.

"A second murder?" Rocky asked. "People are being killed in period costume. Not to profile anyone here, but—"

"We're looking for the head of the opposing Wiccan coven now," Martin made clear.

Rocky looked at Sam. "Divide and conquer? We've been reading the briefs on the murders all the way here."

"What do you mean 'divide and conquer?'" Martin asked.

"We'll go off and interview members of the opposing

team," Devin explained. "The more of us talking to people in a more casual manner, the better."

"And you think—"

Rocky leaned forward, "Gary, these are our old haunting grounds. We've dealt with murder here before. Bad things, involving people we knew. Out on the streets, we can do a lot of good."

Martin nodded. "But I need to be in the loop on everything. I was planning on heading to the mortuary tonight. I want to keep an eye on the place now that it has reopened. Two people are dead either in or near that place. But John Bradbury was no Wiccan."

"No, but he supported Tandy Whitehall," Sam said.

"How did you know that?" Martin asked.

"From hanging out in a bar."

"We don't have any viable suspects," Sam said, "except for Tandy Whitehall. And that's just because she seems to have a motive. She might also have an alibi."

"And unless we get out on the street, we'll have no idea about anything," Rocky said. "Hey, this is Salem. And Salem at Samhain and Halloween? That means hope."

"I'm pretty sure a little nook or hole-in-the-wall bar is where we'll find Tandy Whitehall," Jenna said. "Surrounded by those who'll protect her."

Martin seemed both indignant and worried. "And that could be bad. They could be armed with more than curses. Man kills his wife. Son-in-law kills father-in-law. Junkie kills for drugs. That's the usual things. But these people around here are fanatics. You don't think they'll turn this into a stand-off, do you?"

"This killer doesn't want to get caught," Devin said. "He, or she, or they. And as for my real thoughts, I can't help but think that it's not this Tandy Whitehall at all. It's too obvious. We have to be casual. Walk in like customers. Hey, I still own my great aunt Myna's cottage. I'm almost a real live local girl. And Rocky is from Marblehead. Let us do this our way. We'll find what we're looking for."

"I don't have a lot of choice, now do I?" Gary said, an edge in his voice alluding to the influence of the Krewe of Hunters agents. "I'll be watching things over at the mortuary. We'll keep in close contact."

"I'll hang out at the mortuary with Gary," Jenna said. "You guys handle the streets. How's that?"

Sam looked back at her, surprised and annoyed. He didn't like being away from her in Salem. But she was already up, ready to leave with Gary Martin. Sam stood as well, gently laying an arm on her shoulder.

She smiled at him. "I'll be fine."

He accepted that, just as he accepted who she was, what she did, how they were different, and how they were alike. He loved her. And part of that involved letting her be who she was. But there was still the matter of the boo-hag.

"Where are we meeting up? And when?" he asked.

"Last tour at the mortuary is midnight," Martin said. "We can do it then. The next two days promise to be long. The day before Halloween, then Halloween itself. We need to catch this killer quickly, before this goes any further."

* * * *

Apparently nothing stopped Halloween.

The Mayberry Mortuary was packed, the parking lot full. Jenna and Martin arrived in a police car, uniformed officers everywhere. Two at the entry, two by the ticket booth, one man watching the parking lot.

"I can only imagine the overtime," Jenna said, looking around.

"We don't really have a choice. Salem's economy would be totally in the trash if we had to start closing down things like this. Winter is cold as a witch's tit! Whoops, sorry. I'm sure that's politically incorrect now. But you know what I mean. Christmas is great, New Years, Wiccan holidays, we get people then. Summer is a fantastic time with school kids and families. But we can't lose Halloween. A lot of the locals only survive the off months thanks to what they make at Halloween."

"So the overtime is worth it," Jenna said.

But she doubted this killer intended to strike in the same place twice.

Martin used his phone, checking in with headquarters. Jenna paused in the parking lot, staring out over the cemetery, toward the trees and the edge of the forest. She'd volunteered to come with Martin only because she wanted to get back to the cemetery. She wanted the ghost of John Bradbury to come to her. She also wanted to know why she'd seen a boo-hag heading into the trees moments before she found a woman hanged.

"Still no sign of Tandy Whitehall," Martin said, hanging up. "Your coworkers are out, and we have officers trying to reach her. But she's seen the news by now and has to know we're looking for her. Probably long gone. I'm going in to do a walk-through. You coming?"

"I'll hang out here for a bit. I want to watch some of the people coming and going. I'll be in soon."

He left and she headed over to the busy ticket booth. She saw Micah working, but no Naomi Hardy or Jeannette Mackey. A young woman she'd never seen before sat next to Micah.

"Everything going all right?" she asked, watching him hand out tickets that were available from a pre-sale online.

He looked over at her. "We're sold out. But people get in line for cancellations. We're always crazy, but tonight is extra rushed."

Jenna overheard whispers from the crowd, where some of the visitors were commenting on how they could go to the place where the man's corpse had been hanged.

"You're a creep, Joe," someone said.

"Come on, creepy is fun. Afterward, we can go in the woods and find where that other corpse was hanging. The witch. Yeah, man, they hanged a witch."

Jenna grimaced at the nonsense. "Best of luck," she told Micah, moving down the porch steps, smiling and excusing herself as she moved through the crowd. Her smile faded as she made her way to the cemetery. She hated not being truthful with Sam. She loved him so much. He'd gone through the FBI Academy just for her, becoming a crack shot and a proficient agent. True, he talked to ghosts, and it wasn't a bad thing to be a lawyer who could talk to the dead. He seemed to be really worried about the boo-hag.

She entered the cemetery.

Most ghosts didn't roam around, moaning. Ghosts stayed for a reason, mainly to tell the living what happened to them. She'd seen fathers stay for children, mothers for a family, and children in a sad attempt to ease the pain of their parents. She knew ghosts who'd remained for centuries, hoping to see that history was not repeated. And, yes, she'd met a few in cemeteries. But, usually, they preferred being elsewhere. Tonight, however, one was here, following her. She threaded a path through the tombstones, glancing back to see the glow from the mortuary through the trees. If any of the visitors decided to head into the woods tonight, they'd be in for a surprise. The crime scene from the murder earlier was roped off, two officers watching over it. Finally, she stopped, noting a death's-head on the stone at her feet.

She turned.

John Bradbury faced her, still attired in his Puritan dress.

"We're truly trying," she said to him. "Elyssa tried to repeat what you told her. But we're not sure we understand."

He seemed to waver for a moment, gathering strength. Then he managed a weak smile. "I knew you would come. I tried hard to get someone to see, someone to know. It's not easy. I knew about you from Lexington House."

Jenna nodded. "Tell me exactly what happened."

He was a tall, nice-looking man, big enough that it must not have been easy to get his neck into a noose.

"I was working. Checking the connections on some of our automated monsters, readjusting the props on the embalming tables. I don't know where they came from. I just had a sense that someone was behind me."

"When you say you don't know where *they* came from—did they enter from the house or from the delivery doors? Did you smell something? Was anyone wearing aftershave or cologne? Or as if they hadn't bathed? Did you see their hands or anything about them?"

"I felt like I was hit by a bulldozer. I was standing there, then suddenly someone was behind me. I was slammed against one of the props, then I felt the rope go around my neck. They pulled it tight fast. I was struggling with the noose, trying to get it off. Then I was off my feet, being dragged and jerked. I couldn't really see anything but black. I think they were in costumes. Maybe capes."

"Were they wearing masks?"

"I don't know. But I never saw their faces. I heard them. The one said something giving 'dimension to the witch trials' and the other said 'to shut up.' Then the one who'd spoken first said, 'he's going to tell someone what we were talking about. The Wiccans, the cultists, the weirdos.'"

"That was it?" Jenna asked.

John Bradbury nodded. "They jerked the rope, and my neck snapped. I died. Then I felt like I was drifting, looking on, and I saw people coming through the mortuary. I kept trying to speak, but I realized they didn't see or hear me." He paused, smiling wistfully. "I worked with Elyssa. She had a way about her that reminded me of my oldest daughter. But I also felt that she knew things that maybe even she didn't know she knew. I felt her coming near me. I reached out with my mind. And she must have listened. Everyone else was pretty much just walking by me. She seemed to hear me. So I spoke to her. I then managed to follow her home. But I couldn't connect with her until the following morning. That was strange. But it happened."

"I am so sorry," Jenna said. "We're looking for two killers. But, John, I need you to think. Were they men, women?"

"I don't know. They were whispering. But you mentioned smells. I remember that it seemed absurd, but it was like I smelled a forest. Flowery, like an autumn breeze."

"Anything else?" she asked quietly.

"I was strangling, dying. And the thing is . . . my kids. They have to know that I didn't do this to myself. That I would never have left them, no matter how bad things seemed to be."

Jenna reached out instinctively, but touched nothing but a chilly breath of air. "They'll know. I'll make sure. You do know there was another murder?"

He nodded. "Gloria Day. I didn't like her very much."

"Did she have a lot of enemies?"

"On Halloween night, for years, Tandy Whitehall has been throwing a big gala. Gloria arrives in town and lures away half of Tandy's business. Gloria and I knew one another. We were never friends. She was more a bitch than a witch."

He was quiet for a minute. Jenna allowed him the moment of thought. She wondered what she looked like, standing in the graveyard, talking to herself. A number of family tombs were strewn between her and the mortuary, which probably blocked the vision of anyone who might have casually looked this way. The entire scene was vintage Salem at Halloween, complete with the giant old Victorian house, covered with webs and scarecrows and monsters, caught in an eerie glow that barely reached the cemetery.

"Red," John Bradbury said.

She waited.

"You made me think about that night. What I was feeling and smelling and I suddenly thought about the color red."

Jenna heard Sam from earlier with his story of a boo-hag. A body stripped down to muscle, bone, and red blood.

"Does that mean something?" he asked.

"I followed someone in a red costume into the forest. A red costume beneath a black cape. Does that mean anything to you?"

"What you mean…" a new voice said, "is that you followed someone in red and black into the forest, then found Gloria Day, the wretched bitch witch dead?"

Jenna turned toward the new voice. Female.

"Really, John?" Gloria Day said. "Bitch witch? How rude. I'm dead, too, you know."

The new ghost joined the party, wearing the same Puritan garb in which she'd died, standing with them among the lichen-covered tombstones. She'd been an attractive woman with dark hair, light blue eyes, a heart-shaped face, and a charming smile.

Gloria looked at Jenna. "You will find out who did this to us. And so help me, dead or alive, Wiccan, Catholic, Buddhist, whatever, I'll curse them in a fiery realm of hell where they'll burn for all eternity."

Chapter 7

"Where would a popular Wiccan head to avoid detection and the press?" Devin pondered, linking arms with both Sam and Rocky.

"Did you know her?" Sam asked Devin.

Sam knew that Devin had not started out as an agent. She'd first been an author of children's books—all based on a witch. She'd grown up in Salem and returned when her Aunt Mina left her a cottage on the outskirts of town. She and Rocky had met when Rocky had come to Salem. The murders they'd solved had traced all the way back to the days when Rocky had been in high school.

When the dead had first spoken to him.

Sam was fond of them both and had been glad when they'd become part of the Krewe. All of them were New Englanders from approximately the same area, hard not to share a few local peculiarities. For one, they all had the tendency to overuse the word "wicked." To a Brit everything tended to be "brilliant." In New England, things were just "wicked."

"I'd say she's hiding in someone's house," Rocky suggested. "The cops have a list of all her followers, so they'll be going door to door."

"Which doesn't mean much. There are no warrants. She's not under arrest, only wanted for questioning," Sam said.

Rocky grinned. "Can't get the attorney out of the agent, huh?"

"Thing is, once we get a murderer, we'd like to see he or she locked up, not free on a technicality."

"I just wish we could find this woman," Rocky said.

"Angela just texted me," Devin said. "There's a little place near the end of the Salem Harbor Walk, owned by a Wiccan woman who is in a hive that's an offshoot of Tandy Whitehall's coven. It's called the Goddess, serves a lot of Paleo foods, vegetarian offerings, homemade wine and beer. It's two blocks from Tandy Whitehall's house. Sounds like a place to start."

"Sound good to me," Sam said.

So far they'd managed to keep themselves out of the news. He and Jenna had been involved in the Lexington House case four years ago. It had been just a little more than a year since Devin and Rocky had met here to solve an old murder, which had been hard on Devin, since it had involved one of her old circles of friends. They needed to maintain their anonymity.

They headed down along the dark streets, avoiding revelers, costumed or not. Sam had loved Salem growing up. True, a lot had gone commercial. But the Peabody Essex museum was wonderful, teaching the history of fear and suspicion and distrust of one's neighbors and what those emotions could do to a community. The people who lived and worked here gave the place a pulse. And yet the old could still be found, along with the new. Quaint stood side by side with fun and the silly. So many restaurants had brought in excellent chefs. The House of the Seven Gables still stood, a testament to the past and a reminder that the past came alive through great literary works. Ships continued to ride high in the harbor, beneath the moon, the water seeming to stretch out forever.

Devin suddenly squeezed Sam's hand. "One way or the other, if we find Tandy or not, you need to tell Rocky and me what's going on with you and Jenna."

He looked at her with surprise. "We're good. We're great."

"You were acting a bit strange. You kept looking at her as if you're afraid you're never going to see her again."

Rocky nodded. "She's right." Then he paused and pointed. "There's our place. Rambling, with lots of rooms. Plenty of hiding places. Angela may be hundreds of miles away from here, but she can track like a bloodhound."

"Let's see what we find before we canonize her," Sam said, grinning.

The bar/restaurant was situated in a house where a plaque on the door informed them that it had been built in 1787. Plain dark wood on both the outside and inside. Booths offered hardwood benches, those along the wall with backs. Doors opened to additional rooms on either side of an oblong bar. Like everything else in Salem, it was decorated. No monsters here, though. Only pumpkins, Indian corn, and all manner of natural fall decoration. The place was busy, but not overcrowded, and a young hostess asked them if they'd like a booth or a table.

They opted for a table. Soon, they were sipping locally brewed brown beer with steaming bowls of chowder before them, listening to the snatches of conversations from those around them.

"Will the gala go on? I mean a woman is dead," a tall blonde at the bar said to her companion.

"Probably. There are sponsors, bands and tickets were sold. They can't cancel it," her male companion said.

"I heard this is a real Wiccan hangout," another girl said.

"Tourists," Rocky murmured, then he looked at Sam. "What's up with you?"

Sam hesitated, but these were his coworkers. They'd worked well together because they were straight with one another, even when it seemed ludicrous.

"Boo-hag," he said.

"What?" Devin asked, a frown furrowing her brow. "That's not like a redneck banshee or something, is it?"

"More like a vampire, a really creepy, ugly one," Sam said. "And we keep seeing one in particular. A boo-hag nearly threw itself on the car when we were driving into town. And Jenna saw one right before she found Gloria Day's body."

"You mean—someone costumed as one?" Devon asked.

Sam smiled. "Sure, what else. And I dreamed about one coming after Jenna. I couldn't get to her in time, and it was going to suck the life out of her. A dream, I know. But boo-hag keeps coming up, and it's bugging me."

"Where would one find a boo-hag in Salem?" Devin asked. "If we find someone in a boo-hag costume on the street, we can't just stop and search him."

"There's a community of Gullah people here who I want to

check out tomorrow morning," Sam said.

"Gullah?" Rocky asked.

"It's a blend of different African and island cultures, along with a Creole mix. The culture originally stretched from the coastal areas of the Carolinas to Florida. Now, it seems, they're mostly in South Carolina. The boo-hag is one of the demons, I believe, in their storytelling. It's hideous, shedding its skin, answering only to a boo-daddy."

"Ah, yes," a female voice said.

Sam turned and saw a petite, attractive woman standing behind him dressed in black and wearing a beautiful gold pentagram. Her platinum blonde hair was short and curled around a thin, lovely face.

Tandy Whitehall.

"Young and lovely women meet unwary men," she said. "They seduce them and use them, and, when the time is right, take their husbands or young lovers to their boo-daddy. He consumes them, down to gnawing on their bones. Every society has its monsters. The boo-hag is a bad one." She glanced around the table and smiled, then shook Sam's hand. "Emily told me you three were here. Would you care to come into the back where we can talk in private?"

"Tandy?" Devin said.

"Devin Lyle. You know, I miss your Aunt Mina. She was an amazing friend."

She drifted away from the table. They followed. Which seemed expected. They'd wanted to find Tandy Whitehall.

And had done so.

* * * *

Jenna knew this was her best opportunity to find out the truth.

"The oddest thing is that I don't believe Tandy Whitehall had anything to do with this," Gloria Day's ghost said. "You have to realize that some of the argument between us was all for hype and promo. We go about things differently—*went* about things differently." She looked at John Bradbury. "This is really so unfair."

"Tell me about it. I had children."

"And I'd hoped to have them one day, too," she said. "You didn't like me a whole lot, John. So don't pretend that you do now."

"I didn't like your Wiccan kick against haunted houses," he said. "You, I hardly knew."

Gloria made a face at him. "I just tried haunting the place, but no one could see or hear me."

"Could you two focus on the problem at hand," Jenna said. "We're trying to figure out who killed you, and disprove that it was two suicides."

"Hard to hang yourself over a tree," Gloria said. "You need some help."

"It's like with your death they want us to know a murderer is at work," Jenna said. "That might be because the killers have realized John's death isn't going to be accepted as a suicide."

"Either that," John said, "or someone is going about recreating the deaths of those condemned to hang, and maybe even Giles Corey's death, too. This could get really bad."

"Do they want it to look like a Wiccan war? If so, they missed the debate somewhere along the line. John and Tandy Whitehall were close," Gloria said.

"Gloria, I need to know what happened to you," Jenna said. "You didn't drive yourself out here, somehow make your car disappear, then hang yourself.

She wasn't meaning to be cruel, but Gloria seemed the type who wanted things straight.

And she did.

Gloria arched a brow with a shade of humor and said, "I don't know what happened. I was in the shop, just straightening up, and some kind of a bag was suddenly over my head. I was suffocating and passed out. I came to feeling the roughness of a rope around my neck, then agony and darkness. And I was here. On the other side. I wandered out of the trees and was surrounded by gravestones. I saw the mortuary up on the hill and had no idea how I had gotten here. And then, of course, I realized. I was dead. And I've been trying ever since to find someone who could hear me."

"Any smells?" John asked her.

"What?" she asked, looking at him, a faint wrinkling

forming above her brows.

"A smell, a feel, a sensation? Anything?"

"The trees. I remember the smell of trees. Something like a forest."

"I smelled the same thing," he said.

"Did either of you recognize the scent? From a store, a shop, either one of the big department store colognes, or anything more local?" Jenna asked.

"I know where something close can be bought," Gloria said after a minute. "A woodsy scent. At Tandy Whitehall's shop."

"You really think Tandy did this?" John protested. "I'm a big man, and even with a noose around my neck it would take more than a tiny woman like Tandy to take me down."

"We know from what you heard, John, that there were two killers," Jenna said.

"I don't believe Tandy did this to me. I really don't," Gloria said, looking at John. "We had our differences, but I respected her. No, I may be dead, but right is right, and I won't attack the woman, even if I am dead." She seemed to shake off her sadness and looked at Jenna with purpose. "But I know that scent, and it can be bought at Tandy's shop."

"Tandy has disappeared," Jenna said. "She's wanted for questioning. Would she have fled Salem?"

"Never," John and Gloria both said.

Jenna's phone buzzed and she glanced at it quickly.

Sam.

She answered and learned that John and Gloria were right. Tandy was still here, with Sam, Devin, and Rocky, and Sam's assessment was clear. *She's not our killer.* So everyone seemed in agreement, Tandy was innocent.

Jenna looked over at Gloria.

"I appreciate you finding my body," Gloria said. "I could have hung there a long time."

But it had been the boo-hag who led her. Had it intended for her to find Gloria?

She texted Sam.

Check Tandy's inventory. Find out who bought a woodsy scent that she sells. Find out about the Gullah community.

She finished her text and looked up.

"Someone is trying to make this look as if the Wiccans are evil," Gloria said. "As if the community should be hanging us again."

"Or trying to make it look like a feud," John added. "I was killed, so someone from the other camp had to die, too."

"What do either of you know about the Gullah community?"

"I know a number of folks who moved up here who are basically Gullah, but they don't really follow any special practices. There's one church in town that has a Southern twist, but it's basically Baptist. Most of them attend there. They're actually all great people," Gloria said. "Where do they fit in here?"

"I don't think they come into it at all. I think that boo-hag is being used."

"Boo-hag?" John murmured.

"Creepy, soul-sucking yucky demon," Gloria explained. "Gullah. Red. Woodsy. Mortuary."

"Red mortuary?" Jenna asked quickly.

"Maybe it's because you said boo-hag," Gloria said. "But I have an impression of red in my memory. For some reason, I seem to remember a whisper of the word mortuary."

Gloria paused and gazed across the graves to the mortuary on the hill.

John joined her, then glanced at his wrist and shrugged with an unhappy sigh. "I always wore a watch. But it stopped when I died. Go figure. Loyal watch, I guess."

"It's way past midnight," Gloria said. "The lines are gone and people are leaving. They try to have it all closed up by 2:00 A.M."

Jenna looked over at the mortuary, too, which appeared both dead and eerily alive, as if on a plain between the living and the dead. Haunting, opaque, sheathed in garish Halloween décor, in the moonlight it appeared decayed and faded.

Jenna was certain the answers she sought lay there.

"I'm going up there," she said. "Care to join me?"

* * * *

The back room at the bar/restaurant reminded Sam of an old brothel, especially the brocade cushions in gold and burgundy on the sofas and loveseats. Tandy served them an excellent herbal tea and talked about Gloria Day.

"I have to admit some of the bad feelings were jealousy. Every time I looked at her, I thought I should start singing *Memory*. But I actually liked her. We both managed to get people to ball-hop on Halloween, after the Sabbat on the Gallows Hill, of course. There was plenty here for everyone. So I want you to know that I'm not leaving town. I have no intention of running."

"Tandy," Sam said. "We need a list of people who wear, or have recently purchased a scent you make at your store. It's something woodsy, smells like a forest, that kind of thing."

She found her phone and tapped a message. "I'm getting it for you."

He leaned forward. "And what do you know about the Gullah community?"

"How did you even know we had a Gullah community?" Tandy asked, bemused. "They're usually in coastal South Carolina or Georgia."

"We heard there was a group here," Devin said.

"We do have a group here now. Almost a hundred," she said. "All good people. Some are more conventional; some have converted more or less to the Wiccan religion. They have their own language, a Creole similar to a Krio language spoken in what's now Sierra Leone. Their religion is based on Christianity, but includes a great deal of believing in the spirits of their ancestors. I buy a lot of merchandise from them to sell at the store. Beautiful, hand-crafted masks and totems, and jewelry."

"What about the boo-hag?" Sam asked.

Tandy smiled at that. "What about it?"

"It seems to be a popular costume."

"Wait here," Tandy said.

She rose and disappeared from the room, returning a moment later with a young woman, clad in black, wearing a beautifully crafted pentagram.

"Sissy, this is Special Agent Sam Hall, and Special Agents Lyle and Rockwood," Tandy said. "Meet Sissy McCormick. She's from Gullah country in South Carolina."

"Nice to meet you," Sissy said, joining their grouping by taking the chair Tandy had vacated. "My people are Gullah."

Sissy was striking, her skin coffee-colored, her eyes a soft blue. She had dark hair, queued at the nape of her neck, wearing a black cape over a long black skirt and tailored shirt.

"You've chosen to be Wiccan?" Devin asked.

Sissy nodded. "Something speaks to all of us, and not always what's in our heritage. But, basically, I follow the tenets of almost any creed. Be good to others, care for the elderly, sick, and injured, cherish all children, never offer violence. Be a good human being."

"Nice," Devin said. "Gullah is based on Christianity?"

"Of course, but so is voodoo," Sissy reminded her. "And look, many fundamentalists have caused tremendous harm to others in the name of traditional religions. Every faith out there has those who choose to take it too far, or read into it what isn't there."

"Or use it," Sam said. "Sissy, we're seeing a lot of boo-hag costumes, or at least one boo-hag costume, over and over again. The boo-hag is a Gullah demon, right?"

Sissy nodded. "Some manufacturer came up with that awful costume. Red latex to look like a fleshless body, a horrible demon face. My mother was so upset. She said it's just going to make people anti-Gullah. But it's just part of Halloween. People dress up as crazed movie characters. They know Freddy and Jason and all those fictional killers are just from movies. They'll know that a boo-hag is simply from legend, like a vampire or a werewolf. No true Gullah in this community would ever buy or wear such a costume."

"Here we go," Tandy said, slipping a pair of reading glasses from her pocket to stare at an incoming message on her phone.

Sam's phone rang. He didn't recognize the number, but it was local, so he answered. For a moment, there was nothing. Then he heard something like a snuffled tear.

"Sam?"

For a split second, he was confused.

Then he knew.

"Elyssa?"

He heard a sudden cry.

Then a whispered voice. "You want this one to live? Then get your wise-ass partner under control. All of you back down. Leave this alone. Let these murders go into the great cauldron of unsolved crimes. That is if you ever want to see this kid again. You back off, and she's free on November 1. You keep it up, she dies before Halloween."

Sam forced himself to remain calm, glancing at Rocky, who knew what the look meant. Trouble. So he worked to keep the caller on the phone, as Rocky called headquarters to run a trace through Sam's phone.

"We want Elyssa alive," he said. "But I have to have some kind of assurance that you're not going to hurt her regardless of what we do."

A soft laugh seeped through the speaker. "Trying to keep me on the line? You're on your cell, not at police headquarters. So you'll need some time to run a trace. It was nice that Elyssa kept this number in her phone. You were an attorney, so I would hope you understand the fine art of negotiation."

"So negotiate," Sam said. "I have to know that Elyssa remains alive."

"A call every six hours. But there'll be a new number each time. If I even suspect you're playing me, this pretty little girl will be hanged. Maybe by the witch memorials or the cemetery, right there amidst all the tourist attractions. Or I could find another cool place. So you need to find Jenna Duffy. Actually, I wouldn't mind seeing her hanged either. Now there's a thought..."

"Touch her," he said, "and you'll face hell a thousand times here on earth before going to the real thing."

Laughter followed his remark.

Cocky? Why not? Two people were already dead.

"Sam," the voice said, "I'm disappointed in you. I thought you were a negotiator."

"Okay, let's negotiate and not threaten other people."

He looked at Rocky, who was listening to his own phone, watching Sam with anxious eyes. Rocky nodded. They had a location.

"Okay. I agree. Don't kill anyone else and we'll back off. I'll get Jenna right now, and she'll back off."

"Six hours, you'll get another call."

The line went dead.

Tandy Whitehall seemed oblivious to the tenor of the call. But Sam had risen and stepped back where only Rocky and Devin knew who'd been on the other end of the line. But he was now really interested in that scent from Tandy's shop.

"It's popular with a number of men in town," Tandy said. "And a few women. Here's the list one of my cashiers just sent me. John Bradbury bought that scent, and I guess he suggested it to a lot of his friends and coworkers."

Sam took the phone and looked at it.

"Mortuary? Now?" Rocky asked.

"You got it." And he handed the phone back to Tandy.

"I'll turn myself in to the police now," Tandy said.

"No. Sit tight, right here. You too, Sissy."

"The call came from the mortuary," Rocky said.

He hurried out the door, wondering just which one of the people on the list was now holding Elyssa Adair hostage there. He didn't want Tandy calling the police. Not until he found out exactly who he was dealing with, someone that might even now be stalking Jenna, who may be stumbling into a trap.

Chapter 8

The mortuary was definitely clearing out. People were leaving in groups and singles. The ticket booth was closed. By the time Jenna walked across the porch and reached the front door, no one was around, the last of the visitors having reached the parking lot. She entered through the front door and no costumed actor greeted her.

"Detective Martin," she shouted.

No answer.

"Micah? Jeannette? Naomi?"

No reply.

The silence gave her a sensation of unease, one that had nothing to do with the fact that she was accompanied by two bickering ghosts. She ignored them, allowing them to follow her as she searched the ground floor rooms, amazed that the actors and staff could clear out so quickly. Also, no one had locked up. She passed through the dining room with its array of skeletal guests. On through the kitchen, where it appeared that a massacre had taken place. Fake blood leaked from a cauldron on the stove top, body parts lay scattered on a table, but no actor-chef or cook standing around with a plastic butcher knife to put chills and thrills into the bloodstreams of attendees.

"Goodnight," she heard someone call from the front of the house. "Last one out, lock up."

Jenna hurried to the front door. But whichever performer had just left had done so quickly. She could just make out a dark form heading to the parking lot. She hustled back to the kitchen.

"There's no one down here," Gloria said, following close behind her.

"We should check upstairs," John suggested.

"We should go to the basement," Gloria said.

Jenna was irritated. "Stop. I'll go up first, then we'll go down."

The stairway up seemed misty in the eerie black lighting used for the haunted house attraction. She moved carefully, unnerved, not wanting to be taken by surprise. One by one, she searched through the second floor rooms. Spider webs, creepy creatures, all manner of frights remained. But no one person. Where the hell was Detective Gary Martin? She heard the sound of movement coming from the back of the house. She hurried across the hall to one of the rooms that looked down over the delivery entrance to the old embalming rooms.

"Basement," she said.

"Told you," Gloria whispered.

"Where is everyone?" John asked.

"Good question. Detective Martin should be here," Jenna said. "Let's see what's down in the basement."

She moved quickly, hurrying down the blackened stairs. Portraits adorned the walls that started off as depictions of the living and changed to rotting skeletons from different perspectives. She ignored them and hurried around to the stairs to the basement. Her phone rang. Sam. She hit the answer button.

John screamed.

She whirled to see why.

A fist came out of the darkness, smashing against the side of her face. Her body crashing down the rest of the stairs, her phone disappearing into the misty darkness of the embalming room below.

Before the world vanished, she heard Sam's voice through the phone.

Calling her name.

* * * *

Sam spotted the mortuary, high on the hill, glowing opaque in the strange mix of moonlight and artificial electric haze. No cars filled the parking lot. The building seemed to be alive, its upstairs windows like soulless eyes. The front door appeared to be a gaping mouth caught in a strange and twisted oblong O of horror.

"Not sure how exactly we should be doing this," Rocky said.

"Maybe call the local police?" Devin murmured.

"No," Sam said. "We handle this ourselves."

The killer had threatened to kill Elyssa and now he probably had Jenna too. No time to wait for the locals.

"No police," he said.

And neither of his colleagues argued since, among those who bought the woodsy scent from Tandy Whitehall's shop was Detective Gary Martin. A cop gone bad? Sam didn't know. Especially since another man associated with the mortuary had purchased the scent, too.

The head of the paranormal research department.

Micah Aldridge.

* * * *

Jenna tumbled down the stairs, feeling every bruise to her body, but managed to roll out on the floor and draw her weapon.

She heard an eerie laugh.

"You have no idea how much trouble you're in," a voice told her in a hoarse, eerie whisper.

Then she heard another voice. Gloria Day. "It's a boo-hag."

Down the steps one came. But no demon. Instead, a living, breathing person in a boo-hag costume, armed with a Smith and Weston pistol gripped by red latex-clad hands.

"Stop," she commanded.

But the costumed person ignored her. "Throw down your gun. Now."

A snap of sound and a system was turned on that offered first eerie music, then the deep, rugged, masculine voice of the attraction's narrator. "And so Proctor died as well, for, as he was supposed to have said, the girls did, in the end, make devils of far too many a man and woman. It was in June of 1692 that the first of the condemned were hanged. Before it was over, nineteen would die in such a manner, and one man, Giles Corey, would be pressed to death."

A sudden flow of light sprang from one of the niches.

She heard a sob of fear and terror.

"Auntie Jenna? Help me. Please!"

Elyssa stood in the niche, supported on a stool, a noose around her neck, a second costumed boo-hag at her side ready to rip away the stool.

* * * *

Sam came through the mortuary front door. Rocky and Devin had slipped around the house, intent on entering the basement via the delivery entrance. He moved with care. What he wanted was to barge in with guns blazing and wrap his fingers around the throat of the killer now threatening Elyssa and Jenna. But he told himself to slow down, use caution. His head pounded, ready to explode. All he could hear was Elyssa's sobbing through Jenna's phone, from four minutes ago.

A lot could happen in four minutes.

He climbed the porch steps and saw that the mortuary's front door hung half ajar. He entered the foyer and looked around, certain from the acoustics and sounds made when he'd called her that the phone had dropped in the basement. He hurried through the garish decorations and around to the stairway.

A body lay on the floor right by the door to the basement stairs.

Not a prop.

Micah Aldridge.

He hunkered down and felt for a pulse. Faint. But there. He found his phone and dialed 911 requesting an ambulance and the police. He'd identified himself and asked for no sirens. His phone blinked for an incoming call. Rocky. He answered and told him the situation and that help was coming.

He left the fallen man and headed for Jenna and Elyssa.
Knowing now who he was about to encounter.

* * * *

"We'd been debating how to handle this, and honestly," the
costumed boo-hag said, "you weren't on our original list. But
that's okay. We had you running all over looking at Wiccans and
talking about the Gullah people, and don't you love our
costumes?"

Elyssa was still sobbing, but Jenna realized that struggling
just caused the rope around the young girl's neck to chaff more.
Elyssa's wrists and ankles were tied. Once the stool was kicked
aside, there'd be no recourse for her.

"It's not that I care," the boo-hag said. "I really don't care if
the kid—or you—live or die. You couldn't let a damned suicide
be a suicide. You just had to turn it into a murder investigation."

"You're so sadly mistaken," Jenna said. "The medical
examiner knew immediately that John Bradbury had been
murdered."

The boo-hag by Elyssa spoke out angrily, "That's because
your good buddy Sam Hall talked the medical examiner into
believing that. It could have been left a mystery, accepted as a
suicide. But that's all right. Eventually they would have blamed
the Gullah people or the Wiccans. But you! Bursting in here,
pushing everyone around. Here to pat poor baby cousin on the
back. What made you start running around screaming murder
anyway?"

"John Bradbury told Elyssa it was a murder and that you
would murder more people. Then John found and told me about
the way you two attacked him. And yes, you did have us
investigating what might be going on in Salem. But this has
nothing to do with the Gullah community or the Wiccans or
history, except in whatever way you thought you could use it.
This is all about greed."

John Bradbury's ghost floated over the niche where he'd
been hanged, and where Elyssa was now dangerously close to
meeting the same fate, swiping angrily at the air.

To Jenna's surprise, the boo-hag moved back, as if the

movement had been felt.

"Don't you understand?" the boo-hag behind Jenna said. "We're in complete control. So I'll only say it one more time. Drop your gun or my pal over there will kick the stool out from under your cousin."

"I don't think so," a new voice suddenly announced.

Sam.

The boo-hag whirled around. "Sam Hall. The great attorney, P.I. No—great FBI special agent now. Have you forgotten all about our negotiation?" stairway boo-hag said.

"Not at all."

The boo-hag beside Elyssa said, "We've still got all the cards, Special Agent Hall. Come down here. Now. Or this girl dies."

Jenna recognized the woman's voice. Naomi Hardy. And she knew that their suspicions had been right. This had nothing to do with the past, nothing to do with feuds or beliefs. "Naomi Hardy. You did this for a promotion? You killed people—you probably planned on killing more people to create a real Wiccan war and send a Wiccan to prison—all for a promotion."

The boo-hag's head whipped around. "She knows who I am."

"Shut up," the boo-hag on the stairwell said.

"You know, I thought at first that it was either Micah—or even poor Detective Martin," Sam said. "But, Jeannette, you and Naomi have to be the two dumbest murderers I've ever met!"

Of course, Jenna thought. Jeannette Mackey.

"Kill the stupid girl, Naomi. Do it," Jeannette yelled.

"They'll shoot me," Naomi said.

Jenna thrust herself up and burst toward the niche, trying to get to Elyssa. She could make that move because Sam had her back. Luckily, Naomi Hardy stayed hesitant. The boo-hag on the stairwell raised her red latex arm to fire, but Sam slammed his arm down on hers and the weapon went cascading down the stairs.

Jeannette screamed in fury.

Sam and the boo-hag went down.

"Kill the damned girl," Jeannette roared.

Naomi recovered her wits and kicked the stool.

Jenna lunged forward to save her cousin. Arms around the girl, she supported her weight so the rope could not tighten around her neck. Naomi's body began to jerk from side to side, as if being pushed hard. Gloria Day and John Bradbury were trying to have an affect on her, but it was another ghost who managed to stop her. He was in Puritan garb as well, a big man, heavy-muscled, broad-shouldered. He appeared before Naomi, who gasped and backed away.

Rocky burst through the basement door and helped Jenna get the noose down and off from Elyssa's neck. Sam wrenched Naomi Hardy aside. Devin Lyle appeared and cuffed Naomi, telling her that she was under arrest.

Sirens screamed from outside.

Help was coming.

The reign of terror was over.

* * * *

"Naomi Hardy thought that she had a brilliant way to become the head of the company? Get rid of John Bradbury? In the midst of the highest paying time of the year? Really? She did this for a job?" Devin Lyle asked.

"It was a pretty damned good job, from what I understand," Sam told her. "And trust me, I didn't get it until the end. I knew that both Detective Martin and Micah Aldridge had ordered that cologne—Scent of the Pine—Tandy Whitehall sold. And since both of our victims had smelled it, the scent seemed involved. But, as we would have learned had we had time to ask Micah about it, he bought it for Jeannette Mackey, who loved the scent."

They were all at Devin's place, a charming cottage on the outskirts of town. Devin had inherited the house from her Aunt Mina, who remained after death, still watching over Devin when she was in Salem. Mina was with them now, shaking her head over the terrible things an emotion like greed could cause a person to do. She'd done her best to make the ghosts of John Bradbury and Gloria Day comfortable in her house.

"How did she get Jeannette involved?" Rocky asked.

"Jeannette saw herself as a seer, a medium, the rightful

agent at the gate. Their agreement was that once Naomi became boss, she'd find another place for the haunted house company to operate. They were so obsessed with what they wanted to do that they were willing to kill," Jenna said.

"And," Sam explained, "Jeannette knew all of the legends about the new local cultures and communities beyond the Wiccans. She also hated both Tandy Whitehall and Gloria Day. What better way to get back at the two women than kill the one and get the other arrested for her murder."

"They planned on killing more people," Elyssa said.

Her parents, overcome with gratitude for Jenna and Sam and the Krewe members, had allowed her to come along with the adults.

"Who was next?" Rocky asked.

"Somebody named Sissy," Elyssa told them. "In case they didn't blame the Wiccans, they'd start looking at the Gullah people. They never intended for any of us to survive the night."

"I'm pretty sure they thought they'd killed both Gary Martin and Micah Aldridge," Sam said.

Martin had been discovered in the basement, a bad gash to his head. But both men were going to be all right.

"Here's what I understand," Sam said. "They had to kill John and make it look like a suicide. They figured that it might not work, so they planned an elaborate scheme to kill more people and make it look like an inter-Salem cultural war of some kind."

The ghostly presence of Gloria Day said, "So I died because of you, John?"

"It seems so. I'm sorry."

"You didn't die because of John," Auntie Mina pointed out. "You died because of two greedy, sick, demented women."

"Who really thought they could kill me, Sam, and Elyssa, and get away with it," Jenna said. She looked at Sam and smiled. "Thank goodness they underestimated you."

"They underestimated the Krewe," Sam said.

"I don't think Jeannette cared if she died," Elyssa said. "As long as she took us with her. But, you're right. Thank goodness for the Krewe. I think I'd like to be part of this one day." Elyssa leapt to her feet. "Gotta go."

"Where?" Jenna asked her.

"Party. It's Halloween. And I'm rather an important person right now. My guy is here for me. Don't worry, my parents love Nate."

She kissed and hugged them all, thanking everyone profusely, and then she was gone.

"What about us, John?" Gloria asked him. "Shouldn't we be going somewhere by now? Into the light or whatever."

John looked at her. "I'm thinking about sticking around for a bit."

"How lovely," Aunt Mina said.

Gloria reached for John's hand. "If we're going to stick around together, we're going to play give and take. Come on. It's Samhain."

"Where are we going?"

"Gallows Hill, of course."

John Bradbury groaned, then shrugged and took Gloria's hand. "Why not."

They said their good-byes and disappeared.

"I'm curious about one thing still," Jenna said. "There was a third ghost there last night. A powerful ghost. He was in Puritan apparel, big guy, like a hearty farmer type. Then he was gone. Who was he? There's not another victim somewhere, is there?"

Rocky shook his head. "The two women spilled everything at the station. No more victims."

"Big dude, powerful, looked like a farmer?" Mina said. "Might have been John Proctor, sick to death of watching more horror over petty jealousy and greed. Those bitter human emotions might have caused the hysteria once, but he wouldn't want to see it happening again. Could have also been George Burroughs. He was a big dude, too."

"I wish we could thank him," Jenna said.

"I'm sure he feels thanked," Mina said.

"Are we going out for Halloween?" Sam asked.

Jenna jumped up laughing and grabbed his hand. "No. We're staying in. Rocky, Devin, Mina, thank you for your hospitality. We're going back to Sam's house. Uncle Jamie is busy dishing out Halloween treats. We're going to be alone for a while."

Sam jumped up, ready to comply, but noted, "We'll all head back to Krewe headquarters in the morning."

And he told them all goodnight. Outside, the moon had risen over a beautiful, brisk, October night.

Jenna rose on her toes and kissed his lips.

"Trick or treat?" he asked.

"I intend to see that on this Halloween, every move we make is going to be one hell of a treat." She drew a finger down his chest. "Here, there, and everywhere."

He kissed her.

"I shall strive to make this a happy, happy Halloween too."

They drove to his house, and then they were alone.

There were all manner of treats...

And it was a very happy Halloween indeed.

Also from 1001 Dark Nights and Heather Graham, discover Crimson Twilight, When Irish Eyes Are Haunting, and Blood on the Bayou.

About Heather Graham

Heather Graham has been writing for many years and actually has published nearly 200 titles. So, for this page, we'll concentrate on the Krewe of Hunters.

They include:
Phantom Evil
Heart of Evil
Sacred Evil
The Evil Inside
The Unseen
The Unholy
The Unspoken
The Uninvited
The Night is Watching
The Night is Alive
The Night is Forever
The Cursed
The Hexed
The Betrayed
The Silenced
The Forgotten
The Hidden

Actually, though, Adam Harrison—responsible for putting the Krewe together, first appeared in a book called Haunted. He also appeared in Nightwalker and has walk-ons in a few other books. For more ghostly novels, readers might enjoy the Flynn Brothers Trilogy—Deadly Night, Deadly Harvest, and Deadly Gift, or the Key West Trilogy—Ghost Moon, Ghost Shadow, and Ghost Night.

The Vampire Series (now under Heather Graham/ previously Shannon Drake) Beneath a Blood Red Moon, When Darkness Falls, Deep Midnight, Realm of Shadows, The Awakening, Dead by Dusk, Blood Red, Kiss of Darkness, and From Dust to Dust.

For more info, please visit her web page,

http://www.theoriginalheathergraham.com or stop by on Facebook.

When Irish Eyes Are Haunting

A Krewe of Hunters Novella
By Heather Graham
Now Available!

Devin Lyle and Craig Rockwell are back, this time to a haunted castle in Ireland where a banshee may have gone wild—or maybe there's a much more rational explanation—one that involves a disgruntled heir, murder, and mayhem, all with that sexy light touch Heather Graham has turned into her trademark style.

* * * *

Chapter One

"Ah, you can hear it in the wind, you can, the mournful cry of the banshee!" Gary Duffy—known as Gary the Ghost—exclaimed with wide eyes, his tone low, husky and haunting along with the sound of the crackling fire. "It's a cry so mournful and so deep, you can feel it down into your bones. Indeed. Some say she's the spirit of a woman long gone who's lost everyone dear in her life; some say she is one of the fairy folk. Some believe she is a death ghost, and come not to do ill, but to ease the way of the dying, those leaving this world to enter the next. However she is known, her cry is a warning that 'tis time for a man to put his affairs in order, and kiss his loved ones good-bye, before taking that final journey that is the fate of all men. And women," he added, looking around at his audience. "Ah, and believe me! At Castle Karney, she's moaned and cried many a time, many a time!"

Yes! Just recently, Devin Lyle thought.

Very recently.

Gary spoke well; he was an excellent storyteller, more of a performer than a guide. He had a light and beautiful brogue that seemed to enhance his words as well and an ability to speak with a deep tone that carried, yet still seemed to be something of a whisper.

All in the tour group were enthralled as they watched him— even the youngest children in the group were silent.

But then, beyond Gary's talents, the night—offering a nearly full moon and a strange, shimmering silver fog—lent itself to storytelling and ghostly yarns. As did the lovely and haunting location where Gary spun his tales.

The group sat around a campfire that burned in an ancient pit outside the great walls of Castle Karney, halfway between those walls and St. Patrick's of the Village—the equally ancient church of Karney, said to have been built soon after the death of Ireland's patron saint. A massive graveyard surrounded the church; the Celtic crosses, angels, cherubs, and more, seemed to glow softly in a surreal shade of pearl beneath the moon. That great orb itself was stunning, granting light and yet shrouded in the mist that shimmered over the graveyard, the castle walls, and down to embrace the fire itself—and Gary the Ghost—in surreal and hypnotic beauty.

Gary's tour was thorough.

They'd already visited the castle courtyard, the cliffs, the church, and the graveyard, learning history and legends along the way.

The fire pit they now gathered around had been used often in the centuries that came before—many an attacking lord or general had based his army here, just outside the walls. They had cooked here, burned tar here for assaults, and stood in the light and warmth of the blaze to stare at the castle walls and dream of breeching them.

The walls were over ten feet thick. An intrepid Karney—alive at the time of William the Conqueror—had seen to it that the family holding was shored up with brick and stone.

"The night is still now," Gary said, his voice low and rich. "But listen if you will when the wind races across the Irish Sea. And you'll hear the echo of her wail, on special nights, aye, the heart-wrenching cry of the banshee!"

Gary—Devin knew from her cousin, Kelly—was now the full-time historian, curator, and tour director at Castle Karney. She'd learned a lot from him, but, naturally, she'd known a lot already from family lore. Kelly Karney was her cousin and Devin had been to Castle Karney once before.

The Karney family had held title to the property since the time of St. Patrick. Despite bloodshed and wars, and multiple invasions first by Vikings and then British monarchs, they'd held tenaciously to the property. So tenaciously that fifteen years ago—to afford the massive property along with repairs and taxes—they had turned it into a fashionable bed and breakfast, touted far and wide on tourist sites as a true experience as well as a vacation.

Gary, with his wonderful ability to weave a tale, was part of the allure—as if staying in a castle with foundations and a great hall begun in the early part of the fifth century was not enough!

But Gary had gained fame in international guidebooks. While the Karney family had employed him first for the guests of the B&B, they'd always opened the tours to visitors who came to the village and stayed anywhere there—or just stopped by for the tour.

"Indeed! Here, where the great cliffs protected the lords of Karney from any assault by the Irish Sea, where the great walls stood tall against the slings, rams, arrows, and even canon of the enemy, the banshees wail is known to be heard. Throughout the years, 'twas heard each night before the death of the master of the house. Sometimes, they say, she cried to help an elderly lord make his way to the great castle in the sky. Yet she may cry for all, and has cast her mournful wail into the air for many a Karney, master or no. Saddest still, was the wailing of the banshee the night before the English knight, Sir Barry Martin, burst in to kidnap the Lady Brianna. He made his way through their primitive sewer lines of the day, thinking the castle would fall if he but held her, for she was a rare beauty and beloved of Declan, master of Karney Castle. Sir Martin made his way to the master's chambers, where he took the lady of the house, but Declan came upon him. Holding the Lady Brianna before Declan, Sir Martin slew her with his knife. In turn, Lord Declan rushed Sir Martin, and died himself upon the same knife—but not until he'd skewered Sir Martin through with his sword! It was a sad travesty of love and desire, for it was said Sir Martin coveted the Lady Brianna for himself, even as he swore to his men it was a way to breech the castle walls. While that left just a wee babe as heir, the castle stood, for Declan's mighty steward saw to it that the men fought on, rallying in their master's name. Aye, and when you hear the wind blow in now—like the high, crying wail of the banshee—they say you can see Brianna and her beloved. Karney's most famous ghosts are said to haunt the main tower. Through the years, they've been seen, Brianna and her Declan—separately, so they say, ever trying to reach one another and still stopped by the evil spirit of Sir Barry Martin!"

There was a gasp in the crowd. A pretty young woman turned to the young man at her side. "Oh! We're staying at Karney Castle!" she said. "And the main hall is just so hauntingly—haunted!"

"Ahha!" Gary said, smiling. "Hauntingly haunted! Aye, that it is!"

"We're staying there, too!" said an older woman.

"Ah, well, then, a number of you are lucky enough to be staying at the castle," Gary said. "Ten rooms and suites she lets out a night! Be sure to listen—and keep good watch. Maybe you'll see or hear a ghost—there are many more, of course. It's been a hard and vicious history, you know. Of course, you need not worry if ya be afraid of ghosts—while the main tower is most known to be haunted, Brianna tends to roam the halls of the second floor, and that's where only the family stays."

Devin felt a hand on her shoulder and heard a gentle whisper at her ear. "You, my love. Have you seen Brianna?"

It was Rocky—Craig Rockwell, the love of her life, seated by her side, their knees touching. And it was the kind of whisper that made her feel a sweet warmth sear through her, teasing her senses.

Rocky was her husband of three days.

But though she smiled, she didn't let the sensual tease streak as far as it might. Oddly enough, his question was serious; partially because they were staying in the old master's suite, since they were family, through marriage—Rocky, through her. Devin, because her mother's sister April had long ago married Seamus Karney, youngest brother of the Karney family.

His question was also partially serious because they were who they were themselves—and what they did for a living, rather strange work, really, because it was the kind that could never be left behind.

She and Rocky had been together since a bizarre series of murders in Salem. Devin owned a cottage there, inherited from a beloved great aunt. Rocky had grown up in nearby Marblehead and had—technically—been part of the case since he'd been in high school. As an adult, he'd also been part of the FBI—and then part of an elite unit within the FBI, the Krewe of Hunters.

Devin had been—and still was—a creator of children's books. But, she'd found herself part of the case as well, nearly a victim.

Somehow, in the midst of it all, they'd grown closer and

closer—despite a somewhat hostile beginning. As they'd found their own lives in danger, they'd discovered that their natural physical attraction began to grow—and then they found they desperately loved one another and were, in many ways, a perfect match. Not perfect—nothing was perfect. But she loved Rocky and knew that he loved her with an equal passion and devotion.

That was, she thought, *as perfect as life could ever get.*

And, she'd discovered, she was a "just about as perfect as you were going to get" candidate for being a part of the Krewe as well. That had meant nearly half a year—pretty grueling for her, really—in the FBI Academy, but she'd come through and now she was very grateful.

Rocky had never told her what she should or shouldn't do. The choice had been hers, but she believed he was pleased with her position—it allowed them to work together, which was important since they traveled so much on cases. While the agency allowed marriages and relationships among employees, they usually had to be in different units. Not so with the Krewe. In the Krewe, relationships between agents aided in their pursuits.

While Devin had never known she'd wanted to be in law enforcement before the events in Salem, she felt now that she could never go back. She belonged in the Krewe because she did have a special talent—one shared by all those in the unit.

When they *chose* to be seen, she—like the others—had the ability to see the dead.

And speak with them.

It wasn't a talent she'd had since she'd been a child. It was one she had discovered when bodies had started piling up after she returned to live in Salem. The victim of a long ago persecution had found her, seeking help for those being murdered in the present in an age-old act of vengeance.

She still wrote her books, gaining ideas from her work. And being with the Krewe made her feel that she was using herself in the best way possible—helping those in need. She'd never wanted the world to be evil. And the world wasn't evil—just some people in it.

She did have to admit that her life had never seemed so complete. But, of course, that was mainly because she woke up each morning with Rocky at her side. And she knew that no matter how many years went by, she would love waking to his dark green eyes on her, even when his auburn hair grayed—or disappeared entirely. She loved Rocky—everything about him. He was one of the least self-conscious people she had ever met. He towered over her five-nine by a good six inches and was naturally lean but powerfully built, and yet totally oblivious to his appearance. Of course, he took his work very seriously and that meant time in a gym several days every week. Now, of course, she had to take to the gym every week herself.

Rocky was just much better at the discipline.

Better at every discipline, she thought dryly.

And also so compassionate, despite all that he'd seen in the world. When her cousin had called her nervously, begging her to come to Ireland, Rocky had been quick to tell Devin that yes, naturally, Adam Harrison and Jackson Crow—the founder and Director Special Agent of their unit, respectively—would give them leave to do so. And it had all worked out well, really, because they'd toyed with the idea of a wedding—neither wanted anything traditional, large, or extravagant—and they'd made some tentative plans, thinking they'd take time after and head for a destination like Bermuda.

They chose not to put off the wedding; in fact, they pushed it up a bit. And instead of Bermuda or the Caribbean, they headed to Ireland.

A working honeymoon might not be ideal. Still, they'd been living together for six months before they married, so it wasn't really what some saw as a traditional honeymoon anyway. And, St. Patrick's Day was March 17th, just three days away from their landing on the Emerald Isle that noon. Her cousin, Kelly Karney, had promised amazing festivities, despite the recent death of Kelly's uncle, Collum Karney—the real reason they had come.

A heart attack, plain and simple.

Then why was Collum discovered after the screeching, terrible howl of the banshee with the look of horror upon his face described by Brendan?

"They say," Gary the Ghost intoned, his voice rich and carrying across the fire, and yet low and husky as well, "that Castle Karney carries within her very stone the heart and blood of a people, the cries of their battles, the lament of those lost, indeed, the cry of dead and dying...and the banshee come to greet them.

Ah, yes, she's proven herself secure. 'Castle Karney in Karney hands shall lie, 'til the moon goes dark by night and the banshee wails her last lament!' So said the brave Declan Karney, just as the steel of his enemy's blade struck his flesh!"

Devin turned to look up at the castle walls.

Castle Karney.

Covered in time, rugged as the cliffs she hugged, and... Even as Devin looked at the great walls, it seemed that a shadow fell over them to embrace them, embrace Karney. A chill settled over her as she looked into the night, blinking. The shadow as dark and forbidding as the...

As the grave.

As Gary said, as old as time, and the caress of the banshee herself.

Rendezvous
Renegades 6
By Skye Jordan

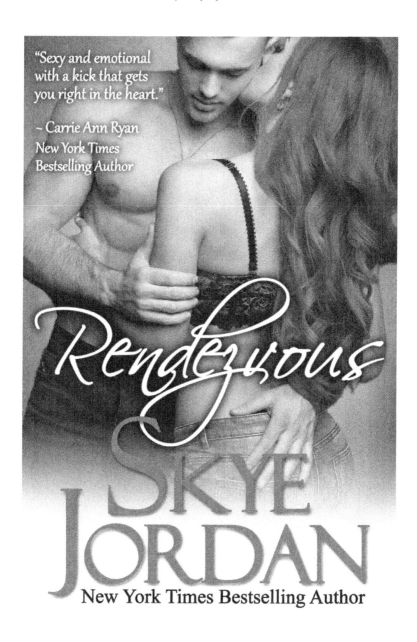

"Sexy and emotional with a kick that gets you right in the heart."

~ Carrie Ann Ryan
New York Times
Bestselling Author

Rendezvous

SKYE JORDAN
New York Times Bestselling Author

One

Keaton Holt avoided the blonde's palpable stare by riveting his gaze to the ball game playing on the television above the bar.

"They're looking at bringing a big league to Austin," he told the newest Renegade, Cameron Riggs, sitting beside him.

"Your chatter ain't gonna work," Cameron said, humor bubbling in his voice.

Cam had been Keaton's fight protégé for the last six weeks. With sixteen-hour days on the same set, doing the same job, and staying at the same hotel, they'd been, more or less, in each other's face constantly. On the upside, they got along. On the downside, the guy had the opportunity to see the dark side of Keaton's love life, something he'd been trying to forget for the better part of several months without success.

"Manfred's talking about expanding the league by two teams," Keaton continued without taking his eyes off the game, slowly spinning his glass on the bar. "They're saying Montreal will get the first."

"You can babble all you want, but it ain't gonna keep her on the other side of the bar."

Cam thought it was funny. So did all of Keaton's other friends. And for years, Keaton had found it amusing too. He could walk into a bar, a party, onto a set, and for reasons he'd never quite figured out, the woman with the biggest tits, the wildest tats, the most piercings, or the most crazy filling the space between her ears would zero in on him. So crazy, the Renegades had collectively nicknamed the women who hit on Keaton "them crazy bitches," a la Buckcherry's song "Crazy Bitch."

But the novelty had definitely worn off. Even the entertainment value had plummeted. And recently, Keaton's interest had flipped a one-eighty and now bordered on derision.

While he knew acting absorbed in baseball and conversation might be a delusional attempt at discouraging the triple-E— tattooed from shoulder to wrist—from hitting on him, he hoped it would allow him to at least finish his beer before he bailed.

This might have been one of Austin's many trendy downtown hotspots, but Keaton liked the bar anyway. Corner was upscale but not pretentious. It had great food without the snobbish foodie flair, and a wide variety of clientele sans the lowlifes and the nerds. The drinks were strong, the bartenders were honest and the barstools had cushy leather pads.

The location was also awesome for people-watching. With two of the walls making up the building's corner location missing, the bar became a foot-traffic funnel. And he was more than a little annoyed he couldn't just come here after a long day on the set and enjoy Austin's beautiful early fall weather, a beer and a ball game without dealing with the inevitable bullshit some Crazy Bitch would come up with.

"Some think Austin's a sure thing for the second team," Keaton said. "Others don't think this town can support a major league ball team. They think it should go to San Antonio, where they have a proven track record with the Spurs."

Cam took a swig of his beer, then started laughing with the liquid still in his mouth—which was how Keaton knew Crazy Bitch was on her way over.

Dammit.

Cam swallowed and bent his head toward Keaton with a raspy "How do you *do* that?"

Keaton had wondered the same thing so long, he'd finally asked the most outspoken and streetwise of all the Renegades women—Rubi. When Crazy stopped to talk to the bartender, Keaton told Cam, "Rubi said I managed to pull off some sort of confidence that she says sends a fuck-you attitude. Says I intimidate people who don't know me."

"That's very true."

Keaton frowned at Cam. "What the fuck? Next to Wes, I'm

the easiest-going Renegade in the bunch."

Cam lifted his brows. "To people who know you. Looking at you from the outside—especially when you're working, trying to get a stunt down right—you're intense, dude. Don't you remember it took me a month to talk to you?"

"I thought that was because Jax always had you working with one of the other guys."

"Some. But the other part was because you are fucking intimidating."

He sat back and held his arms out. "How? I don't have tats and piercings all over. I only have extreme haircuts when I need them to double someone for a long shoot. I shave my beard at least twice a week. I tip well. I say please and thank you. I open the door for others. I answer any question asked of me." He absolutely *did not* get this. And if his mother knew, she'd be mortified. "How in the fuck do I intimidate people?"

"But you've got your share of scars, which are even scarier." Cam grinned. "And look around you right now."

Keaton darted a look around the bar and found several people shooting nervous covert looks his way. But Crazy had her gaze homed in on him like a target, a hot little smile on her lips.

He dropped his hands to the bar and leaned on his elbows. "That's just ridiculous."

"You're built like a tank, but you move like a fucking panther. You've got a stare that could cut steel, and you use it whenever you're thinking about something. And I can't even tell you how many women who've told me how hot they think a guy's scars are."

Keaton cut a look at Cam. "Are you telling me I have perpetual asshole face?"

"Like that right there." Cam chuckled and pointed at him. "I wish I had a mirror. And you carry yourself with a don't-*even-think*-about-fucking-with-me air. A real one, not one you trumped up for the occasion. One that makes people take a step back. You're just an intense dude, man. Nothin' wrong with that. And it sure has been working like magic on the chicks."

No, it worked like magic on the *crazy* chicks. The chicks who dug trouble and drama and extreme shit.

"What can I say?" he muttered. "It's a fucking gift."

One he wished he could regift to someone else.

Anyone else.

"I don't get why you're not jumping on that shit," Cameron said. "Hey, I'm not complaining. I score every night you turn them away. But, dude, they're smokin' hot."

Keaton looked at Cameron. He was in his midtwenties, built, talented, smart, and good-looking. Coming on board with Renegades as a stuntman was going to net the kid a shitload of women. Keaton had been there. Done that. And had a few dozen T-shirts to show for it. It had been fun for a while. Those women had introduced Keaton to a whole different side of sex. A whole different side of himself. But it wasn't what he wanted anymore. If he were honest, it hadn't been what he'd wanted for a long time.

But that didn't keep the crazies from coming. And the really shitty part about that was the way those crazies killed interest from the normal women. Nice women. Women like his buddies had found. Like Jax's Lexi, Wes's Rubi, Ryker's Rachel, Troy's Ellie. Even the fucking OCD, pain-in-the-ass Marx, the Renegade's risk assessment manager, had landed a sweetheart in Grace.

His mind drifted to Brooke and that brief moment when he'd thought he might have found that kind of woman too. He'd been on the verge of starting something with her when a crisis with Brooke's sister had taken her back to Florida on short notice.

And Keaton went back to attracting these lunatics, like the tube-top, short-shorts, four-inch-platform-wearing woman now sauntering his direction.

Irritation twisted in the pit of his stomach. And something else. Something tight and vague and hollow. He'd never identified with the phrase "the one that got away," but he'd wondered over the last year if Brooke might have been that woman for him.

Keaton sucked down the last of his beer just as the lunatic's hip bumped the bar next to him.

She leaned close, giving Keaton a good whiff of cigarettes and powdery perfume. "Hi."

He didn't want to engage, but he didn't want to be an asshole either. "Hi." He didn't look at her as he pulled cash from his wallet and tossed it on the lacquered surface beside his beer to cover his bill. "I'm just on my way out."

Her hand curved under his forearm and hooked on. Irritation jolted through his body.

This was another thing—the way women touched him, like they had the right.

"That works for what I had in mind," she said, her voice sliding into a familiar, sultry tone. "Because since I set eyes on you, all I've been able to think about is strapping your hands to a headboard with your belt and giving you the best deep throat of your ever-loving life."

All consideration for her feelings flew out of his mind. Keaton huffed what should have been a laugh but that came out sounding like disgust. They just got bolder and bolder. And when the hell did that start turning him off instead of making him hard? He couldn't identify the turning point.

He met her eyes briefly as he pushed off the stool, and found them alight with the kind of raw sexual hunger that didn't thrill him anymore.

"How much is that gonna cost me?" he asked her, partly just to see how she'd respond, partly to make her realize how her approach made her look—because, honestly, these were the same kinds of offers every guy got from hookers in Vegas. The fact that no money would change hands now didn't make this offer feel any less sleazy.

His challenge took the edge off her cockiness. But instead of getting angry, she gave him a sassy "I'd ask that you return the favor."

Keaton looked at Cameron and slapped his shoulder. "Have fun, kid. Just don't miss the plane in the morning."

He grabbed his leather jacket from the stool and wandered through the milling customers, ignoring her taunt at his back. "What's the matter, stud? Don't like the taste of pussy?"

"Jesus Christ," he muttered, disgusted she'd said such a thing in public. If the situation was reversed and he'd done the same, he'd be in the back of a cop cruiser right now. But women could do any damn thing they wanted and men just had to be men and walk away.

So Keaton acted like a man, stepped onto the sidewalk, and started down the street.

The night was cool—a nice break from the heat they'd had here all summer—and he relaxed as he put distance between himself and the bar. Between himself and that ugly feeling he couldn't quite understand or escape lately.

The thought of heading home to LA and his friends helped smooth his rough edges. He let the soft air whisper over him as he rolled his shoulders, shook out his arms, then paused for a quick stretch of his calves against the curb, groaning at the relief sliding through his muscles.

It was a good hurt. The kind that confirmed he was learning and growing. That his skills were getting better. But it still hurt—even after he'd already taken a hot shower, stretched completely, and rested ice packs on a few key joints before coming out for dinner with Cameron.

"It's an ibuprofen kind of night."

It was also good he had some time off to look forward to. They wouldn't start filming the next season of this series for another three months, which would give Keaton time to switch up his workout to build different muscle groups.

He continued toward the river and his hotel, wondering how a guy got the wrong women to leave him alone and the right women interested. But based on Rubi's and Cam's assessment, it was beginning to sound like Keaton would have to change some very elemental parts of himself to accomplish that. Because how did you get other people to perceive you differently? It wasn't like he had control over others.

He paused as he passed a little restaurant called Vic's Diner, where the trunk of a live oak created the perfect place for Keaton to stretch his shoulders. With his hand planted firmly on the rough bark, his body set, he twisted away from the tree. The muscles across the front of his shoulder stretched from his pecs all the way to his biceps. It felt so good, his eyes fell closed on another moan. When the muscle released, Keaton worked the other arm.

The new position turned him toward Vic's, and as he stretched, his gaze focused on the warm glow inside, where a waitress stood at a table, chatting. She was middle-aged and African-American, with a round, youthful face and big, dark eyes. But what struck Keaton was her laughter—it lit her up and highlighted her animated, relaxed posture, making Keaton smile.

Another waitress joined the first. A younger, girl-next-door blonde, delivering apple pie smothered in vanilla ice cream to the table. She was as happy as her coworker and stayed to chat.

When the two girls broke out into laughter so loud Keaton

could hear it through the glass, he couldn't help but grin. He pushed his hands into the pockets of his jeans and wandered a little farther along the sidewalk, curious about the person they were talking to.

Their customer was another woman. Her hair was long and dark and waved loosely past her shoulders. She had her head bent in laughter, her hair hiding her face, but Keaton guessed she was closer to the younger waitress's age. She held a spoon in one hand while she held her head up with the other, her shoulders shaking with humor. And whatever the three women were talking about had to be universally funny, because even customers in booths around them started laughing and joining in the conversation.

Keaton found himself smiling and leaned his shoulder against the tree. The light, fun, easy atmosphere playing out inside the café churned a yearning inside him. What they were laughing about didn't matter—he knew with a certainty that this was what he wanted more of in his life. More normal. More sweet. More real. More hometown and apple pie.

He was done with superficial and temporary. Over being judged based on an expression or the way he carried himself. He wanted someone who really knew him. Someone who really got him. Someone who wanted more than a good or kinky or rough fuck. As much as he loved all that, *just* that wasn't enough anymore. And he certainly needed it with a whole different type of woman.

More laughter erupted inside the café among both workers and customers. The woman at the table was laughing so hard, she dropped her spoon in the dessert. A woman in the next booth reached out and clasped the hand of the older waitress, who was grinning when she said something in response.

The joy inside the restaurant was palpable and made Keaton smile even though his heart felt heavy. "Shit. Maybe I just need to start eating in cafés instead of bars."

The waitresses moved off to help other customers, and the woman at the table lifted her head, pulling her hand through her hair at the crown, exposing her face in a slow sweep.

As Keaton took in her face, Brooke filled his mind again. This woman was pretty, like Brooke. Her face open, happy, and glowing like Brooke's. Her skin smooth, her cheeks rosy, her lips full like Brooke's...

Keaton's smile faded. A lot of emotions conflicted at once—confusion, hope, denial. He tipped his head and narrowed his eyes, scrutinizing her face harder. He wasn't sure if his brain was distorting the woman to fit his memory of Brooke or if the woman was truly Brooke's doppelgänger, but it didn't matter. The sight sent Keaton's mind back to that night on the beach in Malibu, the night before Brooke had gotten that job offer in Florida. Strolling with her on the shore, under the stars. He remembered the full moon. The sound of the ocean.

Damn, he could almost feel the warmth of her mouth beneath his...

The ache tugging in his gut pulled him from the memory, and Keaton rubbed a hand down his face. He took a deep breath and reset his thoughts. Then laughed at himself. He couldn't remember much of anything about the women he'd slept with between the time he'd last seen Brooke and now. But he remembered every fucking detail of that one kiss on the beach with her?

Yeah, he was definitely ready for a life change. Unfortunately, that wouldn't help him where Brooke was concerned. His one revelation didn't change the distance between Florida and Los Angeles. But then he thought about Austin and how often he came here. About Austin and its development into nothing short of a mini Nashville, steeped in the music industry. Maybe that job she'd taken brought her to Austin occasionally. It wasn't a huge leap.

The city was also quickly becoming a mini Hollywood, with more television series and more movies being filmed there every year. Hell, maybe he and Brooke had already been in the city at the same time and didn't even know it.

He should just reconnect with her. See how she was. Check into her schedule. He had a good startup conversation. *"Hey, just saw your doppelgänger in Austin and thought about you. Was wondering if you ever get out this way."* Casual. Noncommittal. Good way to get back in touch.

He pulled out his phone, and scrolled through his contacts.

He found her name in the D's, and just the sight made him smile. "Brooke Dempsey."

So many fun memories flooded in from their few short weeks of knowing each other—dancing all night with friends, talking until sunrise, laughing, playing practical jokes, hanging out, barbeques, so many stories.

He might have gotten nothing more than one starlit kiss on the beach before she'd taken that job and disappeared to Florida, but looking back, Keaton was pretty damn sure they were some of the best weeks of his life.

He wasn't smiling anymore. "Fucking Florida."

Florida was the reason he hadn't stayed in contact with her. It was the reason he shouldn't call her again now. But after seeing this woman who brought Brooke's memory back so vividly at a time he needed it so badly, the urge to hear her voice overshadowed reason. And he hit Dial.

He exhaled and cleared his throat as he lifted the phone to his ear and looked up. The woman in the café was looking up now too, listening to the older waitress as the woman spoke. Keaton lost track of his phone call. A zing of excitement burned down his sternum. Even from where he stood, he could see the sparkle of the woman's bright blue eyes. Then she smiled, and dimples carved into her cheeks.

"Holy shit…" An ache pulled deep in his gut. "That couldn't be…"

She looked down and searched through her purse. The waitress wandered off. And Brooke's doppelgänger pulled out her phone, lifted it to her ear…

"Hello?"

Brooke's sweet voice vibrated against Keaton's ear at the same time the woman inside the café spoke.

Shock ricocheted through Keaton's system. His mouth dropped open, but no words came out.

She pulled her phone from her ear and frowned at the screen, then brought it back with a worried "Keaton? Keaton, is that you? Are you okay? Is everything okay? Can you hear me? *Keaton?*"

"Yes," he finally spat out. "It's me." Excitement, joy, relief, emotions he couldn't begin to identify, rushed through him with an intensity he didn't understand. "What the hell…? You're in Austin? How often do you come to Austin? How long have you been here? How long are you staying?"

Then he realized it was his last night, and all his excitement bottomed out. *Fuck.*

Brooke glanced around the restaurant, which was when

Keaton's brain kicked in and he realized he was still standing outside.

"How do you know I'm in Austin?" she asked.

He started around the building toward the entrance. "Because I'm here too. I'm coming in."

Pocketing his phone, Keaton paused a millisecond before pulling open one of the double glass doors.

Keep it together. Don't embarrass yourself. She hasn't called you since she left either.

That helped him cool the flash fire in his veins.

He pulled the door open and turned toward her booth. She was frowning at her phone, then glanced over her shoulder at the door. Keaton's feet halted, stopping him in the middle of the restaurant, and it took a long moment for his brain to catch up with his body to understand why. His conversation with Cam floated into Keaton's head. Then all the things Rubi had said. And he worried that seeing him again so unexpectedly, so suddenly, might frighten Brooke.

The thought was both stupid and real, making his usual rock-solid confidence waver. *Goddamn*, she looked amazing. And it felt freaking *euphoric* to have her eyes on him again.

"Oh my *God.*" She turned and pushed from the booth, and for a sickening second, Keaton was convinced she was going to freak out—and not in a good way. His heart dropped, and he started to lift his hands with words of reassurance forming on his tongue. But her shock flipped to excitement. The kind that bubbled into her laughter and sparkled in her eyes. *"Oh my God. Keaton!"*

Instead of putting up a wall or acting skittish, she ran toward him. Just freaking sprinted at him and jumped right into his arms, wrapping her arms around his neck, like this was some fucking romance movie set.

Catching and holding her took almost no effort. And it was all he could do with his brain shocked into shutdown by her reaction. Cascading warmth suffused his chest and loosened all the muscles strung tight with tension over the confrontation at Corner and Keaton's stress. He closed his eyes and held her tight, soaking in the beautiful feeling of her against him. He'd never even held her that night on the beach, and she'd left town so fast, he'd barely gotten a chance to say good-bye.

God almighty, she felt like wicked heaven beneath the smooth, silky fabric of the thin dress he'd barely had time to see. Only knew it was light with dark polka dots and ended midthigh. Her curves were supple and warm and couldn't have felt any more perfect if she'd been a supermodel instead of an assistant to celebrities of that caliber.

"I can't believe it," she kept murmuring at his ear. "I think about you all the time. I can't believe you're here. It's so good to see you."

"I was just thinking the same thing." God, he'd needed this. Hadn't known how badly until that very minute. "I was calling to tell you about your doppelgänger in Austin, then you answered the phone."

She laughed. A light, happy little giggle. She knew him. She got him. And when she pulled back to look at him, there wasn't a trace of fear or a nasty thought brewing in her eyes. Christ, her eyes were so blue. And so bright. And so much happiness lived there, just looking at her made him happy too.

And then she hugged him again.

Brooke was pure honey—fresh, real, raw goodness and sunshine. She instantly lightened the weight in his heart. And if she could do this for him after not seeing her for almost a damn year, he couldn't even imagine what his life would be like to have someone as awesome as Brooke around him every day.

This was exactly what he'd been missing for so long. Brooke was everything he wanted and needed all wrapped up into one sweet little package.

It had just taken him a year and three thousand miles to figure it out.

Two

Brooke had to let go. She knew it. But the last time she let Keaton go, she'd lost track of him for almost a year. Partially because all the Renegades were impossible to track, partially because she'd meant to. She'd had to.

"Am I choking you yet?" she asked, hoping to hide her painfully intense joy with a huff of laughter.

"Never."

His deep voice rumbled in her ear, and he kept his thickly muscled arms doubled around her, twisting just enough to rock her a little, as if hugging her wasn't quite enough. As if he could hold her forever. As if the overt show of affection in the middle of a café didn't embarrass the hell out of him. He made her feel safe and accepted and treasured, things she needed so desperately right now, it brought tears to her eyes.

She pressed her mouth to the soft cotton tee covering his shoulder and breathed in his scent. The smell of leather and wood and citrus and Keaton brought back a rush of wonderful memories and a sudden spill of emotion. "Damn, I've missed you."

They hadn't been lovers. They hadn't even dated. If Brooke had to put a label on their prior relationship, it would have to be friends, though she'd known from their very first meeting there was something special between them. Looking back, it had worked out for the best given how quickly she'd had to leave and move across the country.

And even though they hadn't acted on their mutual attraction—short of that one starlit kiss on the beach—she'd fallen a little bit in love with Keaton during those weeks. So holding him now brought both pleasure and pain.

He dropped his head back and smiled up at her. A relaxed, dreamy smile that turned Brooke's stomach into an Olympic gymnast and made her want to kiss him so badly, she ached.

"You're even more beautiful than the last time I saw you," he told her.

She laughed. "And you're even more charming." She glanced toward the restaurant's main door, and when she didn't see anyone standing there, she asked, "Are you in town for work?"

"Yeah. You too? That gig you took in Florida?"

He remembered. A little thrill bubbled in her belly. "Yeah. Can you stay? I'd love to catch up."

His smile was wide and warm. "I'm all yours."

Hers. Keaton Holt, all hers.

In her dreams.

Literally.

He lowered her feet to the floor, and Brooke soaked in every delicious inch of his body rubbing against hers. Especially the generous swell in the range of his zipper.

She slid her hands down his solid arms, curved her fingers around his, and stepped back, taking her first quick but full glance over him. Hunger stirred instantly. All the chemistry they'd built up in LA rushed back as if no time separated them.

She released him and turned toward the table, but Keaton grabbed one of her hands back and pulled her close again. "I'm not letting you go too far." He wrapped her close by his side before he moved forward. "You're like a leprechaun, disappearing just when I think I'm going to catch you."

That was an interesting choice of words, but she wasn't going to dig into them now. Not when she could slide her arms around his waist and press her head to his shoulder. "I'm certainly not going to argue."

He gave her a squeeze as they reached the table, then released her so she could slide into the booth. But when she expected him to take the seat across from her, he sat next to her instead. Angling to face her, he bent one knee, resting it on the cushioned bench, and laid his arm across the back of the seat.

Brooke was a little overwhelmed by his complete and focused attention. She hadn't had anyone this interested in her since…well, since him. She'd tried dating a couple of times in Florida, but between work, her sister, and her nephew, she just couldn't balance. And the men hadn't warranted enough interest to try.

Keaton inspired enough interest to get Brooke to leap tall buildings in a single bound.

She didn't even think about reaching out to touch him, she just did, laying her hand on his bent thigh. "So talk. Tell me everything I've missed. What movie are you working on? Who are you doubling? How long are you here? What's new? How is everyone?" She laughed at his growing smile. "I want it all. I have all night."

As soon as the words were out of her mouth, she heard their double meaning. But she didn't backtrack, because both translations were true.

Before Keaton could answer, movement at the edge of the table drew Brooke's gaze.

Lashonda, the sassy and utterly sweet waitress Brooke had been joking with earlier, paused at the table, and her dark gaze slid between her and Keaton. "Well, this is an interesting choice of company, Miss Brooke." To Keaton, she used a dry, deadpan tone to tell him, "I hope your sense of humor is as good as Brooke's, 'cause if it's not, you're gonna have to leave."

Instead of taking offense, Keaton started laughing, and the rich sound shivered through Brooke. He covered the hand she'd laid on his leg with his own and twisted toward Lashonda, turning on the charm he seemed to save for special occasions. "Now, why are you so nice to Brooke and so surly to me? I saw you through the window. I know how big that beautiful smile of yours can get."

A spark of surprise cut through Lashonda's dark eyes, and a reluctant grin tugged at her mouth. Keaton's intense exterior caused a lot of people to step back from him. He was a big guy and built like granite. And unless he was laughing or smiling, his expressions were serious, bordering on pissed off, when in reality, he was just thinking. On a lot of levels, Keaton Holt was one of the deepest men Brooke had ever met—and she'd met a lot of men in her time on the road with Ellie.

While Keaton tried to charm Lashonda out of her suspicion, Brooke's gaze drifted to the sight of her hand swallowed in Keaton's. His was big and scarred and tanned. He had a complex heritage of Japanese and Italian in his background with a smattering of European and Irish. She'd first set eyes on him at one of Ellie's mixers in Las Vegas. He'd been with his Renegade buddies at the time, and a little on the drunk side too. And with all his defenses down, the man was devilishly charismatic.

His olive complexion was already darker than Brooke's fair Irish skin, but his work outdoors made it that much richer and more golden. The contrast was striking.

"Brooke's been in for a couple of days, now," Lashonda told Keaton. "But I've never seen you."

"I'm sincerely sorry about that, and I'll make sure it doesn't happen in the future." He offered his free hand to shake the waitress's. "I'm Keaton. An old friend of Brooke's."

"Lashonda, and I like your manners." She shook his hand with the apples of her cheeks rounding as her smile grew. "Since Brooke seems to like you too, I'll give you the benefit of the doubt for now." She took her hand back. "Would you like a menu, Keaton?"

"No, thank you, but water would be great." His gaze settled on the mush that had once been a beautiful pie a la mode that Brooke had been looking forward to all day. Now, she didn't want anything but time with the man sitting beside her. "And how about a new...whatever that was before I interrupted Brooke?"

"Oh no." Brooke quickly dismissed it. "That's okay. I wasn't going to be able to eat it anyway."

It was a damn good thing she didn't have a wooden nose. She'd been so depressed before Keaton had walked in, she'd planned on eating the whole damn thing. In fact, she'd been threatening to buy out the restaurant so she could bring it back to her hotel room and bathe in their homemade apple pie and vanilla bean ice cream.

"I can," Keaton said. "It looks amazing. And I bet I can sweet-talk a few bites into you too."

Lashonda gave Keaton her full, approving grin and used her order pad to point at him. "It's official—I like you, boy."

He gave her that movie-star grin, complete with a knee-melting dose of charm. "Well, I like you too, Lashonda."

Their waitress broke into laughter and wandered toward the kitchen, muttering something about Keaton being a character.

He turned his attention on Brooke with a sigh. "Damn, I wish I'd found this place four months ago."

"You've been here that long?"

"Mostly." He kept one hand curled loosely around hers and used the other to scrape his fingers through his hair. His smooth, thick, jet-black hair. Hair she'd only felt between her fingers that one time on the beach. "I'm doing the fight and stunt scenes in *Rogue Justice*. Have you heard of—"

"*Really?*" She almost screeched, barely pulling her voice back a notch in time to save her dignity. She slapped a hand over her mouth and darted an embarrassed look around the restaurant. "I can't believe I just did that. You'd think I'd never met anyone famous before."

That made Keaton laugh, and Lord, when the boy smiled, really smiled, Brooke's heart could have been directly attached to a power plant. His looks put the man solidly in the tall, dark, and panty-melting category. Sometimes he looked Italian, sometimes Greek. His Asian characteristics were there—in his high cheekbones, in the slight taper to his eyes—but no one ethnicity ruled his looks. Not like Brooke with her dark hair, blue eyes, and white skin that burned before it tanned, instantly tagging her as one of the black Irish.

But what made Keaton unforgettable to Brooke was this quirky, funny, warm, intricate side of the man she'd gotten to know during her weeks in Los Angeles.

"I'll take your fangirling any day of the week," he told her.

"I love that show," she said. "Oh my God, I wish I'd known. I can't believe Ellie didn't tell me during one of our conversations. Now I'm *totally* going to marathon the whole season and fast-forward to the fight scenes just to watch you. That's so awesome. Wow, and intense," she added, thinking back through the episodes of the action-drama built around a political conspiracy plot. "Those fight scenes are...complicated and violent and *long*."

"Tell me about it." He rolled his right shoulder. "My body is screaming in agreement with you."

"Oh..." She winced, wishing she could massage out every last ache. "Ouch."

He waved it away. "Nothing a few meds can't fix." He wrapped both his big hands around hers, his fingers loose and warm—like his body. He had a way of being so alert, so intense, so focused, while also being so completely relaxed, so utterly comfortable in his own body. It was the sexiest thing Brooke had ever seen. "Let's talk about you. Tell me about this new job. How long are you in town?"

Oh yeah. That. That tedious part of her life that had driven her to the apple pie in the first place. The one that felt like an anvil locked around her ankle. She hadn't been proud of having to take the first and best-paying job she could find, and she was even less proud of who she'd had to take the job with, so she'd asked Ellie to play it down if anyone asked. Evidently, she had, and if Brooke didn't have to get into the ugly details of it with Keaton, she'd prefer not to.

"We're scheduled to be here eight weeks," she told him, pausing while she searched for ways *not* to talk about a subject so central to both their lives—work.

"Then back to Florida?" he prodded.

She smiled and nodded. "Yeah."

"So...?" he said, grinning in a *what's up?* sort of way. "You're awfully quiet. We always used to talk over each other. Tell me about this new gig."

She went for a vague approach. "It's the best-paying job I've ever had."

"Sweet." He paused, waited, lifted his brows. "But...?"

"Let's just say she's no Ellie."

His mouth compressed into a commiserating smirk, and he nodded. "Ellie does leave some pretty big shoes to fill."

"I guess a country music blockbuster with a heart of gold is a little hard to follow."

"And you hooked up with her from the very beginning. That creates a special bond. You can't expect to have that with every boss."

She nodded, dropped her gaze to their hands, and added her free hand to the pile, covering his. "You're right."

"You two were also more friends than employer-employee."

"True, but she was good to everyone."

"She still is. She's an amazing person. As are you," he said with a squeeze of her hand. "Which is why you two were so good together." He drew a hand from their knot and tucked her hair behind her ear with the softest look in those dark eyes of his. "Change is hard." He paused, searching her eyes, then asked, "Are you seeing anyone?"

She didn't understand at first. "As in dating?" When he nodded, she shook her head with a laugh. "Me, no. No time. Between the job, and my family..." She shrugged. Then forced herself to ask the same, even though she really didn't want to hear the answer. "You?"

"Nah."

When he blew off the idea, Brooke dug a little deeper. "Should I translate that into you're still just sleeping around."

He laughed. "If I had any kind of morals or values, I'd be hurt." But there was something subdued in his tone, and she wondered if she had actually hurt him. Before she could apologize, he added, "But, seriously, no, I'm not seeing anyone, even casually. I'm in..."

"A funk?" she asked with a grin, trying to lighten the discussion a little.

"More like a transition," he said.

Lashonda returned, interrupting the connection forming between Brooke and Keaton. He leaned back as the waitress set a glass of ice water in front of him, then a slice of golden-brown apple pie, partially hidden beneath a mountain of vanilla ice cream. She laid two spoons and extra napkins on the table.

"Good Lord," Brooke said. "It was supposed to be a *piece*, not a *pie*."

Lashonda propped her hand on her hip. "That's not what you were talking about earlier. Besides, that's a growin' boy right there. I got me three of 'em. I know one when I see 'em."

"Biiiiig tip comin' for you, girl." Keaton's greedy grin made Brooke laugh. He lifted a fist to Lashonda, who bumped it. "Biiiiiig tip."

Lashonda nodded, then winked at Brooke and added, "That one's a keeper," before she moved to another table, still grinning.

Keaton already had pie and ice cream on a spoon, lifting it toward Brooke, but he called to Lashonda. "Keep talking, beautiful. I'm just gonna leave my credit card on the table here for you."

Both Brooke and Keaton were laughing as he brought the spoon to her lips. She leaned back, shaking her head. "I can't."

"Oh, I think you can." He purposely bumped her bottom lip with the spoon, leaving ice cream there. She automatically licked at the cold spot, and the humor in Keaton's eyes converted to heat, his gaze clinging to her lips. "Open that pretty mouth, Brooke."

His low, suggestive tone, and the unmistakable sexual hum, licked Brooke's chest like flame. She opened and took the dessert from the spoon, and swore the world slowed to a fraction of normal speed.

Keaton's dark eyes watched every move of her lips and tongue—before, during, and after he'd delivered the bite. Brooke had never been so intensely aware of her mouth before. Never imagined she could be so wildly turned on by watching a man watch her mouth as she ate.

But she was so distracted by Keaton that the flavors of the pie and ice cream snuck up on her, coalescing all at once. Cinnamon and sugar. Butter and vanilla. Tart apple and sweet pastry. Pleasure overwhelmed her taste buds in one rich hit.

"Oh my God." Her eyes closed, head tilted back, and orgasmic, gooey bliss overtook her mouth. She moaned as she finished the bite. "Keaton, you have to—"

"—*taste this*" evaporated as soon as she focused on his face. He was still staring at her, but with a very different look. His that's-kinda-sexy interest had turned into something she could only label as animalistic white-hot lust. But it wasn't a look she'd ever had leveled on her before. In fact, she'd never seen such an intense display of desire on a man's face—in movies, on television, hell, not even in a porn video.

His mouth hung open a little, the tip of his tongue resting at the corner of his mouth, his eyes blazing with a savagely starved look of hunger. Brooke felt the heat of it all the way to the soles of her feet, and her body mirrored the craving.

When it came time to swallow her bite of pie, Brooke struggled against an extremely tight throat. Then cleared it before she tried to speak. "It's amazing. You should try it before it melts again."

"I really should," he agreed emphatically in a soft rumble.

Brooke got a very clear impression he wasn't talking about the pie. He was throwing off crystal clear, hard-core messages.

Messages Brooke didn't quite trust, because she'd never had them directed at her before. Especially not by a man like Keaton. And definitely not when, from what she understood, Keaton went for a very different kind of woman than Brooke had ever been or would ever be. She wasn't even sure how to address the messages, let alone what to do with them, and wondered how long she'd have to figure it out. Because she really didn't want to pass up this chance with him again.

She put her hand on his thigh and, with her stomach knotting, asked, "Keaton, how long are you in town?"

His eyes came into sharp focus. Thoughts churned. Then he looked down at their joined hands with a look on his face that conveyed the same feeling she'd had when he'd asked her about her job.

His voice was soft when he said, "We wrapped earlier today."

Which meant he'd be on the next plane out of town. Her heart deflated and dropped like a rock. Just her damn luck. But she forced a laugh. "Man, the universe does not want us spending time together, does it?"

He cut off another bite of pie and picked up some ice cream with the tines of the fork, then brought it to her lips again. But this time, he met her eyes. "Fuck the universe. We have all night, right?"

He popped the bite into her mouth and went back for another forkful for himself, asking, "Tell me all about life in Florida. How's your sister doing?"

Brooke kept the talk about Tammy's recovery from her husband's tragic death on an oil rig in the Persian Gulf short. Brooke didn't want to drag the conversation down, so she focused on the great strides her sister had made. And when she could, she steered the topics back to mainstream interests, which for her and Keaton was easy. They settled into a comfortable conversation that meandered like a stream, with no direction.

They talked about Keaton's many travels and his work. The people he met and the jobs he'd done. About the friends they had in common, the Renegades stunt company, its expansion and the jobs coming their way.

The pie was long gone by the time the topic came back around to how Brooke was adjusting to living in one place after traveling around the country with Ellie for so many years.

"I thought I'd go stir-crazy, you know?" she said. "But I love it. Not Florida as much as just finding roots. It probably seems weird, but just knowing the people you pass on the street, knowing the names of the waitresses who serve you breakfast, the clerks at the grocery store, the postman, the crossing guard, Justin's teachers, it's…comforting. Grounding. It's…hard to describe. But it feels good."

"Doesn't sound weird at all," he said. "I'm looking forward to going home for the same reason. I mean, not about the crossing guard or the teachers…"

She laughed, but the realization that he was leaving in the morning after she'd just reconnected with him sucked so hard, it created a physical pain beneath her ribs. One she tried to ignore, because there was nothing she could do about it, and she didn't want it to ruin this small window of time they did have.

"And your nephew?" Keaton asked. "How old is he now?"

Just the mention of Justin made Brooke grin. "Eight. He's so awesome."

Keaton looked concerned. "Hard time to lose his dad."

"It was. But he's adjusted well. Marc died his sixth year overseas, so he really spent most of Justin's life away. I don't mean to say that makes it easier to have your dad suddenly taken. Tammy said they Skyped almost every night, and Marc helped him with homework and read to him. But somehow that distance created a gap that allowed Justin to disconnect."

"And your sister? You sort of skated over all that in the beginning."

"Yeah, well, I feel a ticking clock on my time with you. I was trying to keep the conversation light."

"You're still always thinking of other people first. I'm sure that makes you an awesome assistant."

Brooke grinned and tipped her head both ways. "My current boss would probably disagree. But then she disagrees for the sake of disagreement, so…" She shrugged. "Honestly, Tammy's doing well, considering she's raising her son on her own with next to nothing. In fact, she just started her second year of nursing school. I'm really happy for her. She's got a rock-solid future ahead. I've just got to see them both through this last stretch."

"Damn impressive."

"Very." Brooke lifted her brows and shook her head. "The sheer number of hours she studies boggles my mind. She has classes on top of that, and her internship. It would overwhelm me."

His smile was soft. "I meant you."

Brooke laughed and was about to tell him that Tammy did all the work, but Lashonda stopped by the table.

"All right, lovebirds," she said, "I'd love to watch the stars twinkle in your eyes all night, but I'm sure you two have somewhere better to be locked up all night than here."

Brooke tapped the face of her phone and read the time: 12:05 a.m. "Oh my God. I'm so sorry. I didn't realize—"

"It's all right, sweetheart," she said, her voice smooth and sweet. "You two made my night. Haven't seen a couple as happy as you two in so long, I'm gonna be floating on air for a week. Now go on an' take all that lovin' home."

Embarrassment slid through Brooke's skin and heated her cheeks, but Lashonda's comment made Brooke realize that the instant heat between her and Keaton upon meeting again had cooled back down to a comfortable simmer while they'd been talking.

Keaton stood and took out his wallet. Brooke slid from the booth and put a hand over his as he placed three twenties on the table. "Keaton, no. Let me—"

"Sweetheart," Lashonda said, tapping her arm. "This is Texas. Let the boy pay."

She didn't have much of a choice unless she wanted to stand there and argue, which was the very opposite of how she wanted to spend any of her time with Keaton.

As they left the restaurant, Keaton swung his arm across her shoulders, and they started toward the sidewalk. Brooke thought ahead and realized if she wanted more than an awkward good-bye in front of her hotel, she was going to have to brush some of the cobwebs off those seduction skills she hadn't used since well before she'd moved to Florida.

Three

Keaton held back a moan of pleasure as Brooke leaned into him and wrapped her arms around his waist, but he closed his eyes, squeezed her shoulders, and pressed his face to the top of her head, inhaling the sweet scent of her shampoo.

Then asked, "Which way? Where are you staying?"

"Right. Four Seasons."

He let one of those "aren't you fancy?" sounds roll from his throat as he turned that direction down the sidewalk and strolled past the darkened commercial businesses toward the river. "Certainly coming up in the world, Miss Dempsey."

"If I could work for someone like Ellie again, I'd take a Motel 6 in a heartbeat."

He'd noticed that she'd shied away from any kind of negative conversation tonight. And he still couldn't believe they'd sat there and talked for three hours. *Three freaking hours*. He didn't talk to *anyone* for three hours. Not even his Renegade buddies. Not even about their jobs. Which were like a religion to them. Yet the time with Brooke had flown by. Just as if the year since they'd seen each other had never happened.

Keaton couldn't remember the last night he'd enjoyed as much as this one. If they only had more time. Or lived closer. Or…shit. He didn't know. So he stuck with safe subjects.

"Your boss is that bad, huh?" he asked.

She didn't answer right away, and when Keaton looked down at her, she had her face twisted up in a way that made him laugh.

"Shut up." She laughed. "I'm trying to think of something good to say."

"Stop trying and just say the first thing that comes to your mind."

Brooke groaned and said, "She's a crazy fucking bitch."

Humor exploded at the center of his chest, and Keaton burst out laughing. He laughed so hard, he stopped walking and pressed his free hand to his thigh to stay upright. He had the perfect image of the woman Brooke worked for in his mind. And he knew exactly why Brooke was so miserable. It wasn't funny. It was just so damned ironic.

"What did I say?" she wanted to know, half laughing at him as he caught his breath.

He shook his head and straightened. "Oh, this industry. I think it exposes us to more than our fair share of the crazies."

"Amen."

They'd reached the end of the street, where the pavement gave way to a trail leading along the river. One that also connected their hotels. He took her hand and started down the stairs.

"Hmmm, the river trail at night." Her hand tightened in his. "I wouldn't do this with anyone but you."

That made a few of his male feathers fluff. "Our hotels are only a quarter mile apart. With all the exterior lights between the two, the path is lit up pretty well."

"Where are you staying?"

"Radisson." He pointed down the trail on the right. "Can't really see it, but it's just right there. I've been running the trail in the morning."

They reached the bottom of the stairs, and even though the path was well lit, she released his hand and slid both arms around his waist, cuddling into his side. "I'd still feel better closer to you."

Damn, she felt so good. All soft and warm and curvy. She smelled like flowers and vanilla and honey. And then she tilted her chin up and the smile she gave him was so beautiful, it made Keaton think about things he'd never thought about—like more of these quiet walks along the river. Made him want things he'd never wanted—like the same woman to take those walks with every day.

"Baby," he said, "you *definitely* feel better closer to me."

She laughed and stroked one hand over his belly and up his chest. The move was innocuous in his world of casual sex with highly sexed women. But right now, with Brooke, the touch opened a floodgate of fire through his body. And even though he kept telling himself he wanted something different, even when his soul ached for more connection and more meaning, his body pushed lusty thoughts into his head.

After years of sex with uninhibited, wild, inventive, kinky, risqué women, Keaton's mind twisted toward adventurous sexcapades with Brooke, right here, right now—out in the open, up against a tree, at the risk of having anyone walk by. Sitting her on the dock railing, lifting that pretty skirt and burying his face in her pussy until her screams broke the night's silence. Letting her ride him on a bench along the path—

"Keaton?"

"Hmm?" He jerked himself out of the fantasies. "Sorry, what?"

She was standing in front of him, her body pressed against his in the sultry night. It was no wonder his mind had drifted that direction. She felt delicious against him. Like he-wanted-his-mouth-all-over-her delicious.

"Where were you?" she asked, her voice soft, laced with desire.

Or was that his imagination? He couldn't tell anymore. "Oh, you know. The end of filming, I'm a little brain dead at this point…"

"Are you? Because tonight sort of reminds me of our last night together in California." She grinned. "If, you know, you take away the humidity and the bugs…"

Keaton laughed.

Her hands trailed up his arms as she stretched up his body and wrapped her arms around his shoulders. Keaton's arms automatically circled her, pulling her close, and he groaned at the feel of her curves pressing against him.

"Mmm, baby." Fire spread between his legs, lit up his spine. He dropped his face to her shoulder. "You're going to blow my circuits."

Her fingers combed into his hair. The scrape of her nails on his scalp made his eyes roll back in his head.

"Do you remember?" she asked at his ear. "That night?"

"Can't forget."

"Is that where you were a minute ago?"

He shook his head.

"Then where were you?"

He shook his head.

"If you weren't there," she said, "where'd this come from?"

She rocked her hips against his erection, and the direct pressure pushed lust through his system. The kind of ecstasy that made him needy and hungry and a little crazy.

He growled and fisted his hands in her dress.

"Where?" she whispered at his ear. "Tell me."

"Right here, thinking dirty thoughts about you." He lifted his head, gripped her waist, and stepped back. "Which is why you need to go up to your room now."

Keaton looked at the winding stone staircase that led to a patio and an entrance into the Four Seasons. He knew because he sprinted these stairs in the morning.

"Those will take you to the lobby." He released her waist and fisted his hands to keep the hunger in the pit of his stomach from driving him to grab her back.

She stared at him as if he'd spoken a foreign language for a moment, then extended her hand. "Come with me."

The offer was so…sweet. It encompassed everything Brooke was—real and loving and warm and caring and honest. It encompassed everything Keaton thought he wanted.

"I…" He raked a hand through his hair, struggling against his habit to give in to desire whenever it suited him. "I can't. You're too…"

Her hand dropped, and a little frown creased her brow. "Too…?"

"Too sweet. Too good. Too important to me. Just *too.*"

She exhaled, closed the distance again, and pressed her body against his.

Keaton closed his eyes on a moan.

"Some men say," she told him, her voice a sultry hum, "that there's nothing like a good girl with a dirty mind. Where you're concerned, my mind is good and dirty."

Fire flared through his groin, and he forced his eyes open.

She was looking up at him with a gaze like the sparkling

Caribbean rimmed in thick black lashes. Eyes he wanted to see in every stage of pleasure. He wanted to watch her eyes light with fire as he teased her with the promise of wicked excitement. Soak in the need drenching her expression as he pushed her past her comfort zone until she begged for him. Lose himself in the wild passion unleashed inside her when he drove her to ecstasy. And finally, the shock and awe of bliss as she recovered.

But this was Brooke, not a casual hookup. If their situations were different...

But they weren't.

"Stop fighting yourself," she said. "I can see your thoughts battling behind your eyes. If you aren't interested, just say you aren't."

"I *am*," he said immediately, vehemently. "I've wanted you since I met you in Vegas. I wanted you in California. I want you now. But I'm backing off for the same reasons I did then. Because I'm me, and my life is this, and you're you, and your life is..."

He heaved a sigh, disgusted that he could talk endlessly and flawlessly about shit that didn't matter, but now, when he needed someone he cared about to understand, his words got all tangled.

"Okay, stop," she told him, her voice compassionate. Then she pressed her cheek to his chest, tightened her arms, and said, "Just stop talking and hold me."

He closed his arms around her and laid his head on hers, his gut aching with regret. "I'm sorry—"

"Shush." She cut him off. "Now count to twenty slowly."

"What?"

"Just do it."

She had to be the sweetest drill sergeant ever. So he did it. But somewhere around nine, her hands found their way under his tee, and her nails scored gentle patterns on his back, draining the stress from his body. And he lost count.

After another moment, she pulled back to look up at him. "Let me put something into perspective for you. We haven't seen or spoken to each other in a year. After tonight, I won't see you again for a long time. Neither of us knows how long. It could be another year. It could be longer. So the idea of not being together now to keep a vital friendship intact isn't very realistic."

He frowned, mulling that over.

"I think the reason you're twisted over coming upstairs with me is because you're a really good person and you don't want to hurt me. But I'm a big girl, Keaton, and I've been navigating my way through hookups for years. I may be sweet, but I'm very open to being whatever you want or need for the night."

Holy shit. Keaton's mind strayed deeper into those sexual thoughts again—undressing her, getting his hands on her bare flesh, pushing his hips between her thighs, having her completely and totally wrapped around him...

His resistance slipped a notch.

He lifted one hand and rubbed his face, hoping to pull himself from this haze. "I can't think."

"That's a good thing." Her hand slid down his chest, his belly, rested on the waistband of his jeans. "You've been thinking too hard."

And she flipped the button open.

Excitement stoked his blood, but Keaton's hand dropped to cover hers. "Brooke, slow down—"

"Is that really what you want?" She tugged her hand from his. "I think the best thing for both of us would be to push this, see where it takes us so neither of us spends another year wondering."

And she slipped her hand inside his jeans, beneath his boxers and covered his erection. Pressure, heat, contact—it all coalesced and flooded Keaton with lust. His eyes rolled back and closed.

And he and Brooke moaned at the same time.

The sound of her pleasure at the feel of him snapped Keaton's control.

He released her hand, cupped the back of her head, and held her steady as he kissed her.

She felt even better than he remembered. Her lips were full and plush and velvety soft. As soon as he eased the pressure, she didn't just open, she tilted her head back offering her mouth. And when he took her up on that offer, stroking his tongue into her warmth and circling it with hers, she instantly gave back with a purr so rich and so wanton, Keaton had to fight the need for instant gratification.

Just when he thought he had himself under control, she sucked on his tongue at the same time her hand made some sort of twist on his cock. The combination shot sparks off behind his lids and lit off warning signs in his brain.

He pulled out of the kiss and dragged her hand from his pants. But Brooke pushed up on her toes, leaned close, and rasped, "I'm hungry," against his neck, kissing him there and sending shivers over his skin. "I need a midnight snack. And I don't want to wait until we get inside."

She *did* have Keaton's dirty mind. How fucking dangerous was that?

"Jesus Christ." He was out of breath. The man with nine percent body fat, who ran five miles a day, worked out fighting twelve out of a sixteen-hour day, six days a week, was out of breath, all because Brooke had been kissing him, what, sixty seconds?

And what had happened to his brain? He couldn't find it in all the haze filling his head. The man who was always on, always focused, who could make split-second decisions on the fly couldn't even figure out what to do with her now.

"Brooke—"

"I have been dreaming about getting my mouth on you for *so...long...*" The way she moaned the last words made Keaton's cock surge. "Let's go out on the dock where no one can see us."

"No." Finally, some decision-making skills had returned. This was too much. He needed her too badly to walk away. She was right—he didn't want to go another year regretting not taking this chance with her. But he was going to do it right. "I need you in bed. Damn, I *seriously* need you somewhere private where I can focus on nothing but you."

Brooke stepped back and held out her hand. "I can arrange that." She smiled, a sultry, sexy smile he'd never seen on her gorgeous face before. One that showed him a whole different side of her. "And I will do my best to fulfill any other requests you have tonight, Mr. Holt. So, I hope you will make them, because it would absolutely thrill me to please you."

He took her hand and followed her up the stairs, watching her short skirt bounce around toned, creamy thighs.

When they reached the landing, he paused and pulled from her grip. "I probably shouldn't walk into the freaking Four Seasons with my pants tented and undone."

"You certainly wouldn't be the first."

His hands froze, and he looked up, brows lifted. A laugh

bubbled out of him. "Excuse me?"

"I've seen plenty."

He smirked and finished securing his pants, then grabbed her and swung her around in his arms, making her squeal and laugh. "Seen plenty, huh?"

"Uh-huh."

He kissed her. Kissed her again. Loved the way she framed his face, pressed her forehead to his, and smiled into his eyes. "Did you *cause* any of them?"

"Would it matter if I did?"

A distant pinch tugged somewhere deep in his body. A completely foreign sensation that he still somehow identified as jealousy.

And wasn't that a conundrum?

He cupped her cheek and gave her the only possible answer. "As long as what you're doing makes you happy, no, it wouldn't matter."

"Hmm." She kissed him. "I'm not the only sweet one around here." Then she turned and started toward the lobby with an extra sassy sway in her step. "But it wasn't me. Must have been another tramp stirring up the hopes of some celebrity loser staying—"

He caught up with her before she finished the thought and slung an arm around her waist. She was already laughing when he pulled her off her feet and hauled her back up against his chest. "Did you just call me a celebrity loser?" She giggled in answer. "Because I am *no celebrity*. And *don't you forget it.*"

She laughed so hard, he had to put her down so she could catch her breath. Only when he opened the lobby door for her did he think of the security cameras. "I'd better behave, or we might get a visit from Austin's finest over a misunderstanding."

She followed his eyes to the security cameras. A soft gasp pulled Keaton's gaze to the alarm in her eyes. "Oh, my boss would *not* be pleased if I were involved in anything that could reach the public."

He squeezed her waist. "Don't worry. I'll be good." He pressed a kiss to her neck below her ear and whispered, "In public."

She shot him a sidelong grin and crossed the lobby to the elevators. The hotel was quiet, with just one desk clerk on duty as they passed. Keaton moved behind her and pressed his body against hers. He loved the way she leaned into him.

"What floor?" he asked, barely above a whisper.

"Nine."

"Mmm. After you get on and the doors close," he said at her ear, "take off your panties."

She turned her head just enough to lift a brow at him.

"I'd do it," he told her, "but...cameras."

She grinned. "But it's okay if I do it."

"You'd be way more discreet. I'd get...distracted."

The elevator dinged, and the doors opened. When they entered, Keaton waited for Brooke to meet his eyes, then darted his gaze toward the camera's location. Grinning, she moved to the corner mostly hidden from view. And Keaton leaned back against the opposite wall, crossed his arms and watched this sweet thing inch her hands beneath her skirt, showing a little more of those luscious thighs. With her lip between her teeth and her beautiful eyes shining with the most adorable mix of both mischief and nerves, she tugged a pair of ocean-blue lace panties down her thighs and let them fall around her feet. Then exhaled and closed her eyes a second, as if that had been the biggest feat ever.

And Keaton softened to her just a little more. Which he couldn't afford—as she'd so accurately pointed out. He was leaving, and they didn't know when they'd see each other again.

But she was definitely his tonight. And he was definitely going to reward her for whatever that little escapade had cost her in dignity.

He pushed off the wall, dropped his arms, and crossed the elevator. He put both hands on the railing behind her and looked directly into her eyes. "Knowing you're standing here with nothing on under that dress is *unspeakably* sexy."

She smiled. A giddy, I'm-so-glad-I-pleased-you smile. The experience was so fresh, it shot a thrill up Keaton's spine.

He lowered the hand out of the camera's view to her side and slid it to her hip as he kissed her. "Are you wet, Brooke?" He kissed her again, not waiting for her answer, letting his hand drop until his fingers skimmed her thigh. "Can I feel you?"

That was something he did wait to get permission to do.

Her eyes darted over his head, then back. "Cameras?"

"I'm blocking the view."

She licked her lips. "Then, yes. Please." Her eyes closed briefly in a look of need, and one hand closed on his tee. "I ache."

Emotion surged through his chest. Desire, affection, things he couldn't name. She could make him feel so much with such little effort, it floored him. On some level, it scared him. But he'd think about that later. His physical need was too intense to worry about it now.

He held her gaze as he found the edge of her dress with his fingers. Delighted in the quickening of her breath as his fingers skimmed up the inside of her smooth thigh. Drank in the sight of her lips parting at his first touch between her legs. Savoring the heaviness in his gut as he eased two fingers between her closed thighs to stroke her.

Warm. Silky soft. And when his fingertips found her center, she soaked them.

"Fucking beautiful." He dropped his forehead to hers and lost himself in the slick feel of her, swollen and soft beneath his fingers. He didn't have room to do much more than stroke and rub and slide his fingertips between her warm folds, but she still clenched and gasped and moaned, making him high.

"Keaton…" She kept whispering his name, pulling at his shirt.

He followed every cue, tested out slow versus fast, steady pressure versus teasing, whispering touches.

"Jesus…Keaton… Oh God…"

"Are you a talker, Brooke? I hope so. I want to hear every little sound."

In the very short ride, her clit swelled beneath his thumb into a perfect plump pea. Her teeth worried her lips, turning them puffy and slick. Keaton's mind strayed toward pushing his cock between those lips, watching her suck and pleasure him. But when a surge of need shot up his spine and exploded at the base of his brain, blinding him with stars, he tore his thoughts away.

Plenty of time for that. All night, in fact. He needed to focus.

"You're so perfect," he murmured. "I can't wait to get you under my mouth."

"Oh my God."

"I can't even count how many times I've imagined tasting you."

"Keaton…I'm—"

She pressed her face against his shoulder, and a sound rolled from her throat. The arm around his neck—when had she put an arm around his neck?—tightened, and her body quaked while her pussy clenched.

The floor button dinged, and the elevator doors slid open. Keaton felt like he'd been thrust into the light from a dark cave. He'd been so lost in her sweet body, he'd not only lost track of where they were, but he'd missed the fact that Brooke had just climaxed in record time. And still hung on him, shaking and panting.

The elevator doors started to close, and Keaton stuck his foot out to block them. At least some of his brain was still functioning.

He drew his hand from between Brooke's legs and gripped her waist. "I'm gonna pick you up."

Her head wobbled as she tried to lift it from his shoulder. "What?"

"What room, baby?"

She wrapped her legs around his hips, laid her head on his shoulder, and sighed, "Nine-oh-nine."

Keaton might have been aching and tired when the night started out, but he couldn't have been wearing a bigger smile or sporting a heart filled any fuller right now. And Brooke had just given him the energy to run all fucking night.

Four

Brooke dug her hotel key from the outside pocket of her purse. Keaton swept it from her fingers and opened her door, all while carrying her. And he did it all with the same grace and ease and expertise he did everything—including bringing her to the quickest orgasm of her life the first time he touched her. In an elevator for God's sake.

She should have known he wouldn't have to ask any questions. Should have known he would be a master at everything involving women and sex and pleasure.

When she'd first moved to LA and stayed with Ellie and Troy, Brooke had listened to their stories about Keaton's exploits with lurid unable-to-look-away-from-a-train-wreck fascination. Back then, she'd been half-grateful she hadn't slept with him in Vegas and become just one more story, half-disappointed she hadn't gotten the chance to experience him.

But after a few days of hanging with Keaton along with the rest of the group, it was clear women were drawn to him. Not a surprise. Women were drawn to all the rugged, sexy Renegades. But according to the stories, the women who flocked to Keaton were all at the extreme end of the rough, risqué, and wild scales. The Renegades joked that the women Keaton had dripping off every limb were every man's fantasy—ridiculously hot, overtly willing, and eager to be wickedly naughty.

The real surprise had been learning Keaton had been wanting Brooke, little Miss Vanilla, the same way she'd been wanting him.

The door closed behind them, and Brooke rolled her head on his shoulder to press her lips to his neck. Tonight, vanilla was going to blend with rich, exotically spiced rum from some remote corner of the world where women like her rarely tread.

"I think this is bigger than my place in LA." His voice vibrated beneath her lips, and his view of the suite made her smile. She always left a light on somewhere in her hotel rooms, because she never knew what time she'd be back. This morning, she'd left on a small side table lamp, which was barely enough to throw a shadow.

"Probably costs as much for a night as you pay for a month," she said.

"Why?"

She laughed, knowing he was asking why anyone would need to stay somewhere so extravagant, not why it was so expensive. And she loved the way he didn't dwell on what just happened in the elevator. She hated men who were so insecure, they had to constantly check in for reassurance on their performance. Or worse, gloat over it.

She glanced over the living area, complete with a dining table and four chairs, a sectional sofa big enough to seat six, and a sixty-inch flat screen covering the wall over the fireplace. "Because this is where the high-maintenance stay. You have to pay people well to put up with annoying eccentricities."

"Well then, you…" He eased her to her feet, slid his hands up her back, under her hair, and cupped her head, "should stay everywhere free, because I've never met anyone easier to be around."

And he kissed her. "Can't believe how lucky I was to find you here."

And kissed her. "You're so beautiful."

And kissed her. "God, I love your mouth."

He made her feel like she was floating. Made her mind disconnect from everything but him. And with all the stress and turmoil in her life, that was the biggest gift anyone could give her right now.

When he pulled back again, she said, "Good. Because this mouth is going to be all over your body in about sixty—"

He growled and kissed her again, licking into her mouth with a strong, skilled, hot, playful tongue she couldn't help but want between her legs.

Inch by inch, he pulled her skirt into his hands, until his palms found her bare ass. He gripped her with both hands, and her skin tingled and heated beneath his fingers. A fresh wave of desire flooded her sex. His hard erection and rough jeans rubbed against her sensitive spots, covered in nothing but a thin layer of rayon.

She definitely needed to get him out of his clothes.

Pulling out of the kiss, she dragged at his shirt. "Naked, Holt. Now."

He laughed and let the shirt slide off his shoulders, over his head.

She leaned in to press her mouth to his chest, but paused and pulled back, looking at all the ridges over his abdomen. She'd seen him in swim trunks at least a dozen or more times in the weeks they'd been in California together. When he wasn't working, he seemed to live in them, but she'd given up hope of ever getting the chance to touch them or kiss them or lick them.

So she started by skimming her hands over his abdomen and experienced the unique sensation of warm skin over steely muscle...

Swoon.

God, she never swooned.

Over anything.

Or anyone.

After so many years in the music industry, it took a lot to impress Brooke. And Keaton knocked her for a loop in so many unexpected ways, she'd lost count.

His hands had found their way under her dress again, and stroked everywhere he could reach. His lips and tongue laid hot trails down her neck and across her chest as he stepped her backward until her thighs pressed the arm of the sofa.

With his hands at her waist, he leaned her backward over the arm.

"Keaton..." She laughed his name, clinging to his arms, but that didn't keep him from laying her back.

With her shoulders against the sofa cushions, Keaton stepped between her thighs, pressing them wide. He looked down at her with such blatant and overwhelming desire, her belly fluttered and her chest tightened. His dark gaze followed his hands down her body. He cupped her breasts, then caught the hem of her dress already at her hips thanks to gravity, and moved it up to her ribs in a deliberate shove. Brooke pulled in a breath of surprise and curved her hands around his forearms as Keaton's hot eyes raked her nakedness.

A long, low sound of hunger ebbed from his throat as he lowered his head and pressed his face to the soft space just beneath her ribs. The pressure and warmth, the intimacy, made her shiver. He pressed kisses to her skin in a direct line south. His earlier words echoed in her head—*"I can't wait to get you under my mouth"*—and the fire in Brooke's body flared into an inferno as she pushed her hands into his hair.

But he straightened, pulling out of reach to wrap his arms under and around her thighs. Without warning, he hauled her hips higher on the sofa arm and spread her thighs wider. His gaze remained rapt between her legs, and Brooke's breathing broke into another sprint.

He lowered his head again, pressing a kiss to her belly right below her belly button. Then lower. And lower. And lower.

Brooke curled the fingers of one hand into the sofa cushion at her side and reached forward with the other, combing her fingers through his dark hair. Loving the thick, soft feel of it while Keaton's kisses grew hungrier.

And he used his mouth like his hands, patiently, but with clear, deliberate purpose—to drive Brooke insane with pleasure. Each lick or swirl of his tongue made her tighten her grip on the sofa cushions. Every suckle made her arch and reach overhead, using the sofa to push toward him. Until he ate at her like he'd never get enough, driving her to a place where she bordered on insanity and writhed with need. Where the peak was so sharp, there was no way one orgasm would be enough to satisfy it.

When he drove her over the edge, Brooke fisted the cushions over her head. She arched and cried his name. The pleasure seemed to spike through her, ricochet, then hover, making it impossible for her to pull herself fully back to the present. To reality. To his fingers digging into the flesh of her thighs, his mouth eating at her with a ferocity that mirrored the hunger in her own body. But even when she was sure she couldn't climb another peak, he led her there a different way, drawing more pleasure from her body than she ever fathomed it could even possess let alone exude. Brooke continued to rise and break. Rise and break. And each climax brought something different, something new, something she'd never experienced before.

Then she felt the exquisite pleasure of his fingers joining his mouth. The tips stroking and rubbing, shooting a fresh thrill through her sex while his tongue lazily laved her, adding heat and pressure and friction. She was already choking out a moan and writhing toward his touch when the pressure of his fingers penetrated her body. Then moved inside her. And, bam, ecstasy slammed her like hurricane winds, knocking the breath from her lungs.

"So good…" She arched, dropped her head back, and moaned, "Oh fuck, don't stop."

He did the opposite. He created more pressure inside, teasing her outside. The multiple sensations were too much for her brain to absorb all at once, and it felt like it took forever to rise to climax. By the time she did, she was absolutely delirious with lust, swamped in a depth of pleasure she'd never experienced, and—she already knew—addicted to it.

"Keat—" He closed his mouth over her and growled. The sound vibrated through her. So erotic, so wild, she was out of her mind. "Need…it. Keaton, please…"

He added suction with his mouth, movement with his hand, and launched Brooke into the stratosphere.

The pleasure was so intense, Brooke's body exploded in a cluster of orgasms that wiped out her mind and ravaged her. She went limp. Her butt drifted off the arm of the sofa, and she sank into the cushions. Her breathing raced and her heart galloped. She had enough brain function to realize Keaton had moved away from her, but didn't have the strength to make her mind think about where he went.

The rip of paper pulled her mind into the present and brought her eyes open. "Keaton?"

"Right here." He bent over her, gripped her waist, and moved her up the sofa.

His jeans hung lower on his hips, and he pressed one knee

between her thighs, shoving all the loose pillows to the floor. Then he lowered his hips between her legs and propped himself up on his elbows. Brushing the hair from her face, he kissed her, slow and deep.

His hips moved against her, and the feel of skin against skin made her moan. He pushed one hand between them, stroked her with his fingers, then with the head of his cock.

"I put a condom on," he murmured.

Brooke tightened her arm around his shoulders. "I've waited so long for this."

"Me too." He dropped his forehead to hers. His eyes filled with lust, his kiss with affection and hunger. He brought his free hand to her breast, still covered in her rayon dress, stroked and squeezed. "I wish I could wait longer. I want to eat every inch of you, but you make me *insane*." His voice was raspy and more serious than she'd ever heard the lightest of the lighthearted Renegades. "I need you *now*."

His hips thrust, and his thick shaft penetrated her. A sound ebbed from Brooke's throat before it closed. Before her body arched in both pleasure and pain. Her head fell back, her mouth dropped open. And she could only describe the sensation as searing pleasure radiating along her walls. Burning through her sex.

Keaton's big body curved over her, every muscle taut beneath her hands where they dug into his shoulder.

"Ah, fuck, Brooke," he murmured against her exposed throat, his voice rough and strained. *"Fuck."*

She clutched at his shoulders with one hand, his hair with the other, caught up in the mind-bending thrill of all his sweat-slicked muscle sliding along her skin. Of his cock stretching her. Of his big body trembling with the effort to hold back.

He withdrew slowly, and the motion washed so much pleasure through Brooke's body, she moaned, delirious. Keaton's lips moved on her throat, and he kissed a path to her mouth, where his tongue dipped in to swirl and tease. Eyes open, tongues spiraling, he pushed back inside her. Stretching her until her breath caught. Then he held her gaze...and pushed even deeper.

The sound that rolled in her throat was almost animalistic. A sound she'd never heard come out of her mouth before. But she'd never been this...taken, this deep, this intimate with a man before.

Because this wasn't just about the sex. The way he looked at her, the way he held her, the way he *owned her* went much deeper than the physical.

He pressed one hot palm to her thigh, spreading her wider. Wound his arm behind her knee and leaned in, hitching her leg higher. Wedged his hips farther between her legs. And penetrated even deeper.

"Fuck," she breathed, the word hardly a whisper.

"Too deep?" he murmured, showing no sign of backing off as a trickle of sweat slid down his forehead, hit his brow, and veered along the top until it reached his temple.

"Just...so...much of you."

"You don't have it all yet."

"Jesus."

"Before I ask if you want me to back off, let me show you something I think you'll like."

He lifted one brow in a silent request for permission. When a smile quirked her mouth, Keaton used his body weight to push until she felt like he was so deep, he was at the back of her throat.

"Ah God..." she moaned.

And then he did...something...with his hips. Some dip or rock or...something that made shards of ecstasy rip through her sex. Her mouth dropped open, and sounds rolled out of her. Hungry, oh-my-God-don't-you-dare-stop sounds. She writhed toward him and dug her fingers into his skin, needing more of whatever he was doing.

"Keat..." She couldn't talk, couldn't think. Her mind and body were absorbed with seeking more and more of the intense pleasure. She tried to lift into him, but he had her pinned to the sofa.

"Brooke, baby..." His voice was a breathless rasp, and his micro-thrusts grew faster and stronger and longer until they weren't micro anymore, but burning ecstasy through her with each stroke. "*God*...you feel like fucking heaven."

Her orgasm grew inside her like a bomb. It was nothing like anything she'd experienced before. And her whimpers grew louder and louder...

"Don't...stop..." She didn't know what she was begging for, just knew she needed more. "Don't—"

He drew farther out, then hammered a couple of full thrusts

home, surprising a cry out of Brooke. But before she tumbled over the edge of ecstasy, Keaton changed the rhythm with one slow torturous deep drive into her.

"Oh my God… Keaton… Please…"

Reaching overhead, he threaded his fingers with hers and looked directly into Brooke's eyes. "I'm only going to last…for one…" He dropped his head and wiped his brow on her dress. "But I promise…more…after you let me…rest."

"Then give it to me." She flexed and tensed her fingers around his. "Because the sooner you get rest…the sooner I get more."

A split-second smile flashed across his mouth, before his lips crushed hers and his tongue worked her mouth the way his cock worked her body. He smothered her cry just before the climax hit, and Keaton pulled back, greedily drinking in the sight of her as the orgasm finally shook her to the core. Blinding light filled her head while wild pleasure zapped every nerve ending in her body. And for those extended seconds, Brooke lost herself in the absolute present—no future, no past, just that moment of utter bliss.

She was still clinging to Keaton when his orgasm swept through. The force of it, of the way it rocked his powerful body, humbled her. The way it drew guttural, savage sounds from a man she'd always seen as fun-loving and easy-going, surprised her. And the way it so completely took him over moved her.

Keaton released his grip on her hands and eased most of his weight onto one arm. He rested his face against her neck, and his hot breath came in quick, heavy pants. "Can't remember…last time I…couldn't fuckin' hold myself…together."

Her brain wasn't fully functioning yet. And she loved the feel of him against her. His heartbeat against her ribs, his belly against her belly, his soft hair against her neck.

She combed a hand through his hair. "I don't know what you're talking about, but I can't believe we're still dressed."

He lifted his head, laughing. "*That's* what I'm talking about. You had me so twisted around, I was too impatient to wait. You turned me into a fuckin' teenager again."

It took a second for his meaning to register. When it did, she turned her head, looked at him directly, and said, "Really?"

He propped his head on his elbow. "What do you mean 'really'? Is sex always this passionate for you?"

A laugh bubbled out of her, and one of his dark brows winged up.

"I'm sorry. You make it sound like I do it regularly." She stroked his face. "And I was asking because, honestly, I'm surprised I would be someone to instigate that reaction, considering who you usually hook up with."

He brought a hand to her face, cupped her cheek, and stroked it with his thumb. "That's exactly why. But..."—he winced a little—"can we not call this a hookup?"

"Um...sure." She drew out the word. "Why?"

"It's just... It doesn't fit us. Whether we ever do this again or not doesn't matter. You could never be just a hookup."

That spot inside her that warmed every time she thought of him opened and ached. And the affection in his expression seemed to take on more weight, causing Brooke a little bit of alarm. "You're right," she admitted, then pushed some of the hardest words she could imagine from her mouth. "But, just so we're on the same page, as much as the idea of something beyond a hookup intrigues the hell out of me, you know this can't be any more than tonight given our responsibilities. Right?"

His mischievous grin appeared and sparked her playful side. The one she'd put on hold last year. The one that had to stay on hold for a while. "That intrigues you, huh?"

She laughed but gave him the we're-adults-we-have-to-be-serious-sometimes look and repeated, *"Right?"*

He sighed, and his smile lost some sparkle. "I guess."

She stretched up and kissed him. "Now go clean up so I can officially undress you."

* * * *

Keaton was damn glad he didn't have to work today, because he'd be fuckin' useless.

He turned his head away from the sight of the sun rising over the Colorado River through the French doors of Brooke's suite and focused on the strands of her hair he was twirling round and round his finger. Rich, chocolate brown, with an occasional streak of deep red. As soft as silk.

He was propped against the headboard, and Brooke had fallen

asleep halfway on top of him, which gave him an incredible view. He could never get enough of the sight of her body from shoulders to ass. Of the white sheets tangled around her, framing her creamy skin. Of her chocolate hair spilling over her shoulder and down her back. Of her head resting on his belly, one rosy cheek, plump, pink lips, and long dark lashes accentuated in the morning light.

She was the most beautiful thing he'd ever seen in his entire fucking life.

He'd already taken so many pictures of her, his phone had run out of storage. He wanted some way to capture the night.

"Dammit," he whispered, dropping his head back against the headboard and squeezing his eyes shut.

He didn't want to go home.

No, that wasn't right. He *did* want to go home. He *didn't* want to leave Brooke. And who in the fuck expected *that* to happen?

He sighed and rubbed his eyes, shifting his hips to alleviate the nagging morning hard-on that obviously hadn't gotten the memo that he'd had more sex last night than he'd had in the last three months.

And every moment of last night had all been a-freaking-mazing. He couldn't say that about any of the sex over the last three months.

A phone rang, jerking Keaton from his thoughts. He sat forward, searching for the source, to silence it so Brooke wouldn't wake. But her head popped up before the second ring.

"What time is it?" she asked, her words slurred, voice groggy.

"Five thirty."

"You've *got* to be kidding me." She half crawled, half slid across Keaton to reach for the phone. *"Crazy. Fucking. Bitch."* Then answered, "Yes?"

She listened for a moment. "You can call— I understand that, but you're just telling me instead of—"

She hung her head, exhaled, rubbed her eyes. "Of course."

Keaton stroked her back, following the curve of her spine that he'd been admiring while she slept. So warm. So soft. So beautiful.

With other women, it was one-and-done. But Brooke kept refilling his tank, making him need her again and again.

"Mmm-hmm," she said into the phone.

She sighed and rolled her head, putting his erect cock directly in her line of sight. And even just having her eyes on him made his ache intensify. Brooke's hand swept that direction, her small, warm palm stroking his thick length like it was the most natural thing in the world.

Before he knew it, Keaton found himself focusing on her nicely shaped, nicely toned ass, then dipping his hand between her legs and brushing his fingers across the sensitive skin at the tops of her thighs, teasing her until she lifted and wiggled.

"Yes," she said, a little breathless now.

He rewarded her with a fingering treat that made her cover her mouth with her free hand.

His cock, standing at full attention now, drew her gaze, and she angled that direction so she could slide her free hand over his length. Sparks shot through his cock.

When he flinched, her bright eyes sparked, and she shifted position, sliding her belly down between his thighs. The little smile that turned her lips told him she knew he was hungry for her mouth. He'd become addicted to the way she gave head within two minutes of the moment she took his cock between her lips. Brooke was generous and erotic, and she loved it. And he craved her mouth the way she craved his fingers.

With her gaze on Keaton's, she took hold of his cock like a joystick and pulled gently, drawing his sac up until she could take one side into her mouth.

And erotic shock jolted Keaton to the soles of his feet. While her hand stroked the shaft, her mouth sucked and licked the sensitive skin of his sac, and his hands fisted in the sheets. *"Ah...God...Brooke..."*

He tried to stay quiet, but he really didn't have much control. Over anything.

She let him slip from her mouth, released his shaft, and Keaton experienced two seconds of relief from the intense pleasure.

Into the phone she said, "Okay."

Then moved the receiver away from her mouth to circle his head with her tongue and suck the tip in and out between her lips until Keaton's hands were tangled in her hair.

"Get off the phone," he whispered. "I have more important uses for your mouth."

She grinned, and into the phone she said, "Look, it's really early. Can we talk about this at breakfast? Great. See you then."

Brooke disconnected, tossed her phone on the nightstand, and took Keaton's cock in both hands with a sigh. She stroked him with loving intensity, "Now this is where I really want to concentrate my focus this morning."

She rocked to her knees, smiled into Keaton's eyes with so much affection, his heart swelled. Then she lowered her head, plunging Keaton's cock deep into her mouth.

Warm, wet heat. Pressure, friction, suction. They pushed pleasure through Keaton's package. His whole body quaked. Moans rolled out of him on waves, and he let them come, knowing the sound turned Brooke on. His vision doubled and blurred. "Ho-oly fu-u-uck."

She sucked. And sucked. And sucked. The amount of pressure Brooke could create with her mouth made his toes curl and his eyes cross. And she did it all while watching his reactions. All with affection and desire drenching her expression.

Keaton would drop to his knees and beg this woman to use her mouth on him. But she gave it willingly. Eagerly.

She closed her eyes and hummed, long and low, and the vibrations tore through Keaton's cock. "Brooke..." He curled toward her and slid his hands up her arms. "Come here."

She took her mouth off him long enough to say, "No more condoms, remember?"

"Ah, *fuck*." And dropped back, forearm over his eyes. He'd never used all his condoms in one night.

Ever.

Brooke laughed and pressed her flat tongue along him from his balls to his tip. Keaton shuddered and slid his arm to his forehead to watch. Her hungry eyes stayed pinned to his as she loved his cock with open lust and erotic intensity.

The connection he found in her bright blue gaze tugged in the center of his chest, and it was more than physical. Pleasuring him was her gift. One she went to great lengths to give well.

Among other things he'd learned over the last six hours, Keaton had discovered how to let down a few walls during sex. One of those walls was expressing his pleasure. There had been too many times when women had used pleasure as a carrot or a bribe or even a weapon, so he'd learned to keep that physical thrill hidden behind a wall of lust.

But Brooke gained so much joy and excitement from Keaton's pleasure that he did his best to show it. As a side benefit, the more excited he got, the more excited Brooke got. Which was why he hadn't been to sleep, why they didn't have any condoms left, why his cock hadn't been fully soft since he'd set eyes on her in the café, and why he rose to climax too damn fast now when he wanted to savor these last moments with her.

But as the affection in her eyes and in her touch joined his own feelings and drove him too high too fast and too soon, he said, "Brooke...baby...I'm gonna—"

She slipped her mouth off his cock, surged up the bed, and covered his mouth just as his orgasm broke. His brain whited-out. She drank in his growl of release and kissed away his groans of pleasure while continuing to pump him.

Then kissed lazy trails along his neck and over his chest as he sank against the bed and caught his breath.

"Baby..." he panted, letting his eyes fall closed as he stroked his hand over her hair and down her back. "I'm...never gonna...be the same."

He already wasn't the same. And he didn't fucking know what he was going to do about it. But he had about two hours before he had to head to the airport, which gave him very little time to convince Brooke to reconsider her "this can't be any more than tonight" so they could figure out how to see each other again.

They showered together, something Keaton hadn't done with a woman in eons. And the shower they'd shared was something Keaton had never done—a slow, drawn-out exploration of bodies with hands and mouths and finally soap, leaving them both starry-eyed and grinning.

While Brooke dressed, Keaton turned on the news and made coffee. He stood in the middle of the living area, looking out at the Colorado River, breathing in the scent of coffee. With the sounds of a woman getting ready in the other room, her voice touching his ears as she spoke with her boss, Keaton should be itching to get out of here. Should be feeling some sort of knot in the pit of his stomach over how he would end this cleanly.

But all Keaton felt deep inside was...

Stillness. Comfort.

Fuckin' joy.

Jesus Christ. He couldn't be more domestic or happier right this minute.

And who the hell had ever imagined that would happen?

"Are you a CNN guy?"

Brooke's voice pulled his gaze. The sight of her knocked all his thoughts out of alignment. She was wearing a sleeveless little black dress that fit her curves perfectly and ended at least four inches above the knee. And her black heels made her legs look like they went on forever.

"Whoa." He made a full turn and looked her up and down. "Hell-o, gorgeous."

Her makeup was soft, but it made her beautiful blue eyes pop and added color to her cheeks and lips. All that gorgeous brown hair had been straightened, parted on one side, and smoothed into a sleek knot at the base of her neck.

Smiling, she came to him, wrapped her arms around his waist. "Hell-o to you too, handsome." And she rose on tiptoe to kiss him. "Thanks for the coffee."

She turned, pulled two mugs from the cabinets, and poured, repeating her question. "Are you a CNN guy?"

He glanced at the television and shrugged. "I don't know, why?"

"Because I'm a FOX girl. I thought we might have finally found something to argue about."

Keaton laughed.

"How do you like your coffee?"

"Black is fine."

She handed him a mug, then slipped into a cropped taupe blazer with black piping. Damn, she looked stylish. She looked fuckin' New York City stylish.

Shit, he couldn't *get* used to this; Keaton was *already* used to this. "Those are some seriously hot work clothes."

She giggled and sipped her coffee. "Well, thank you."

"You have to dress up for this gig?" he asked, just holding his cup.

"Yes," she said, sounding less than pleased. "Especially when we're meeting a crew for the first time. Only after that will she let me dress down. Lately, she's been easing up. Even said I could do casual Friday."

She took another sip, then reverted to holding her cup as well. Their gazes held. And the gorilla that had been hanging on the chandelier all night, the one they'd successfully ignored until now, finally jumped down and faced them. It was time to say good-bye. And Keaton felt the physical drain of happiness as it slowly leaked from the room.

"You don't want to say it any more than I do," he finally said.

She pushed her mouth into a cardboard smile that lasted two seconds. Then glanced down at her coffee. "Sometimes we have to do things—"

Her phone rang. Again.

Brooke clenched her teeth and closed her eyes.

But Keaton's frustration spilled over. "You don't have to live like this, Brooke. Why don't you find another job?"

"It's not that easy. I—"

His phone rang. It was the first time the damn thing had made a sound since they'd been together, but it was still shitty timing.

"Sonofabitch." He set his coffee down on a side table, rubbed his eyes, and drew out his phone. "I'm sorry."

She shook her head. "No, go ahead."

He glanced at his phone with his hopes of seeing Brooke again plummeting and found Jax's name on the display. "Guess it's call-the-employee morning." And answered, "Hey, boss."

"Hey." Jax sounded upbeat as usual. "Great job on the series. Talked to Drogan last night. They want you back next season. But you probably already know all that."

"I do, but it's always nice to hear it from you," he told Jax while he watched Brooke wander to the kitchenette's counter and lean her hip there, scrolling through messages on her phone. "What's up?"

"Drogan's jumping over to the Avengers movie that started up a few weeks ago there. He's working with Copalli."

"Uh-huh." There were half a dozen series and movies being filmed in Austin at any one time. Keaton had run into crews and actors working on the newest Avengers film in town.

"You know Dupleaux, the stunt guy from France?"

"Uh-huh."

"He took a bad fall yesterday. Drogan and Copalli want to

know if you'll step in until Dupleaux's ready to jump back in."

Hell yes. The reaction was instantaneous, and excitement bolted through his body. He darted a look at Brooke, who'd abandoned her coffee and was staring off into space, looking restless. A sliver of insecurity opened in his chest. Was she ready for this to be over? He pushed the split-second thought aside. It didn't matter. He wouldn't say no to Jax either way.

But he answered with a far more subdued, "Of course."

After agreeing to check in on the set first thing to run through the day's stunts and meet with the actors and directors, Keaton disconnected.

Brooke looked over and smiled, but the sparkle in her eyes was gone. He hoped this news replaced it.

"Everything okay?" she asked.

"Better than okay." He strolled toward her, hoping his heart didn't get trampled in the next two minutes. At the counter, he pulled her into his arms. "Jax said another stuntman here hurt himself, and they want me to step in until he's back on his feet."

Brooke inhaled sharply. Her eyes brightened. Her hands curled into his shirt.

And just like that, Keaton's heart grew wings.

"Does that mean...?" she asked excitedly, then pulled back. "Wait. *What* does that mean?"

"If that spark in your eyes is any indication, it means I'm going to have to invest in a very large box of condoms at some point today."

Brooke broke into a smile and laughed. "So you're staying? How long?"

"Don't know." And right now, he didn't care. More time was more time. He cupped her face in his hands, kissing her. "I'll know more after I work with the crew today."

She pulled on his shirt to drag him into another kiss, her mouth open and warm. "Mmmm," she murmured between kisses, her lips curved with a sweet smile. "So happy."

Her phone rang. Her shoulders slumped. Her head dropped back. "Oh my God."

Keaton laughed and kissed her neck. Then murmured in her ear, "Rendezvous with me at the steps on the trail after work, and I'll make you forget all about her for the rest of the night."

Five

Brooke sat across the limo from Jillian, trying to hold on to her patience in the face of almost no sleep and Jillian's unreasonable demands.

"Ms. Dempsey?" The secretary for the *Entertainment Tonight* reporter they were supposed to be on their way to meet said on the other end of the line, "Are you still there?"

Brooke opened her eyes. "Yes."

"I'm sorry, but this morning is Hugo's only opening for the next six weeks. Are you sure Ms. Bailey can't make it?"

"Um…" Brooke's gaze skimmed across the limo to Jillian, and she tuned in to her boss's conversation with Charlotte, Jillian's agent.

"Look," Jillian was saying in her you-work-for-me, how-can-you-be-so-stupid tone, "this is very simple, Charlotte. It's not a negotiation. How many times do we have to go over this? You tell Blue Sky Airlines that if they want my face representing them, then free first-class airfare wherever they fly in perpetuity is part of the contract. Period."

"No," Brooke told the woman on the other end of the line, simply not up for attempting to rationalize her boss back to the interview today. "I apologize for the schedule change, but she's not going to make it."

"Oh, it's not a problem for me." The woman was perky and

friendly. "That means I can grab a latte from the barista next door, who also happens to be *really* hot."

Brooke thought of Keaton and smiled. "Lucky you."

She disconnected and double-checked the rest of Jillian's appointments.

Jillian didn't say good-bye to her agent. The only way Brooke knew she was done talking to her was the long-suffering sigh from across the car.

"Honestly," Jillian said. "The incompetence in this industry is unfathomable. I don't know how so many people make so much money."

Brooke had learned to stop commenting on Jillian's statements within the first week of working for her. She'd also learned which questions to answer directly, which questions to answer with questions, and which questions to ignore completely.

The ping on Brooke's phone hadn't even died out before Jillian barked, "What's that?"

"Confirmation of your cancelled interview with *ET*," Brooke replied smoothly as she read the text from her sister.

Another long night. These fall allergies are so hard on Justin.

That news made Brooke's heart sink. She instantly pictured her nephew curled up on the couch watching cartoons with an oxygen mask on, coughing and wheezing. And while Jillian bitched about something that didn't matter, Brooke asked her sister: *Are you seeing the doctor today?*

Yes. Follow-up appointment with the allergist. He's consulted with the pulmonologist who saw Justin in the hospital, so I'm anxious to hear what kind of treatment plan they put together. I'll get the final report they sent Provident too, but not for another week. I'll likely hear from the program before I get the report.

Tension crept into Brooke's shoulders. That report was the last element they needed to complete the file for Justin's entry into the bronchial thermoplasty research study for children. A procedure that offered Justin one last hope at a normal childhood.

Fingers crossed. Keep me posted, and hug Justin for me.

Will do. Don't kill you know who. At least not until after we find out about the program. If he doesn't get in, do what you need to. I'll always help you hide a body.

Brooke huffed a dry laugh. *Will do my best.*

"Are you texting privately during work hours?" Jillian wanted to know.

"No, ma'am," she lied.

"Then why are you laughing?"

Brooke lifted her gaze to Jillian's. Her boss's eyes were blue as well, light blue to Brooke's dark. And Jillian was a blonde. While the other woman was also twelve years older than Brooke, she looked the same age. Her skin was alabaster perfection, her makeup applied in a rigid routine every morning. Jillian was media perfection personified. The woman was absolutely gorgeous. And her body was as flawless as her face. Her looks had won her a lot of roles and earned her a lot of money. The glamorous facade had left the woman beneath bitter and bizarre and lonely.

"I was laughing because Hugo's secretary was all but licking my boots to get you back for the interview."

At first, the ease with which Brooke had learned to lie to Jillian had unnerved her. But she'd quickly realized that what she did and who she was with Jillian didn't affect who she was with the real people in her life.

And when a slow, haughty, satisfied smile came over Jillian's beautiful face, Brooke relaxed.

Someday, Brooke would get caught in a lie. And when she got caught, she'd get fired. Vanity wasn't Jillian's worst trait. Vengeance was. And for Jillian, vengeance stemmed from insecurity.

But if Brooke just kept all that in perspective, did her job, and watched her back, she'd make it through another year.

And that was all she needed. One more year.

Then she could take Keaton's advice and find another job.

"Rendezvous at the steps on the trail tonight."

Remembering his words murmured against her ear sent shivers through her again. She bit the inside of her lip to keep her smile at bay opened the cover of her iPad, and tapped into Jillian's calendar.

"I cleared your schedule this morning, but I haven't filled in this extra time on the set." Brooke glanced at Jillian, who was inspecting her manicure. "Did you have specific people you'd like me to contact for meetings? A schedule you want me to put in place, track, follow? What's the purpose of this change? And of going in early?"

Jillian's lashes, woven to extend them to a ridiculous length, lowered. Her lips, filled every three months with Botox, pursed, hiding a secretive smile. And Brooke knew with absolute certainty that whatever came out of Jillian's mouth next would be a lie. So she closed the cover on her iPad and waited.

"I heard someone special was going to be on the set. I thought we could scope things out." Jillian's foot swung a little, and her gaze traveled out the window with an evil little gleam. "There are a lot of big names and handsome men starring. I hope you won't get distracted."

Brooke had lost count of the number of movie sets, parties, and events she'd attended in Jillian's shadow, but never once had she acted inappropriately. And, oh, the opportunities… They appeared around every corner. This business was second only to a brothel in sexual activity.

Don't kill J. At least not until after the appointment.

Brooke ground her teeth and pictured her nephew.

Another year for Brooke was nothing. Justin still had a lifetime to face.

"You're always my first priority, Jillian." Brooke forced a smile and held Keaton in the back of her mind. Knowing she'd get to see him tonight would be what got her through another trying day. "I haven't heard you talk about anyone special in a while."

"Hmm. I *reconnected* with him last month at Steven's birthday party in Beverly Hills. The one you didn't attend because your nephew had a little…contest of some sort, remember?"

It had been a robotic competition that Justin had been working toward for six months, and he'd won first place in his age group for the entire county. So Brooke smiled at Jillian's attempt to make her feel jealous over missing Steven Spielberg's birthday party, which couldn't have meant any less to her. Nothing against Steven, but she'd never met the man. Justin, however, would have been crushed if she'd missed his competition.

"I do," Brooke said, remembering how excited Justin had been that day. And she also knew what Jillian meant by reconnecting, but she wasn't touching the topic of her boss's sex life, so she refocused on work. "I can check around when we reach the set to see if we can get some promo shots today, how does that sound? You look gorgeous today, and photos of you in blue always make your eyes pop in magazines."

"That's a nice idea," Jillian said, staring out the window. "Even nicer if we can find my friend. I'd love to get some…suggestive…candids with him."

Brooke frowned. Jillian was in a drawn-out divorce from a billionaire entrepreneur who had turned Jillian in for a much younger, perkier model two years before. It didn't help that the soon-to-be-ex himself was also younger than Jillian. Or that Jillian was struggling against a bulletproof glass Hollywood ceiling where the age limit was set so low, anyone too old to limbo might as well lie down and die.

But Jillian's narcissism had perpetrated a lot of her own problems. That coupled with vengeance for her husband taking up with a younger woman… Well, simply put, nothing good could come of Jillian's desire to see this mystery man—today or any day in the near future.

"At our last meeting with Charlotte, didn't she say it would be better if you didn't—"

"Charlotte doesn't understand publicity." Jillian waved Brooke's comment away.

In fact, Charlotte was one of the best publicists in the industry. And she'd told Jillian to lay off the younger men—for her career and her divorce. Pictures of herself in "suggestive candids" with this guy were Jillian's way of walking into the fire because she needed to feel the burn to know she was alive. She could be self-destructive in a lot of ways. This was only one.

"You two, I swear, you're both so young." Jillian sighed in exasperation, then looked down at her hands with an expression Brooke had never seen before. Confusion? Pain? "You'll both understand someday. It's not easy to get old. Especially in this business. It strips you down. Takes everything. Leaves you with nothing."

A pang of pity pulled in Brooke's chest. Pity was an emotion Brooke rarely experienced. Everyone had problems, and everyone chose how they dealt with them. She didn't have a lot of sympathy for people who simply chose poorly and wanted to sit around and complain about it.

But from Brooke's perspective, Jillian's life was hard in a lot of ways that weren't visible to the naked eye. She may have money, but money didn't provide the kind of security Jillian needed—job security, emotional security. Everything Jillian produced for her job came from inside her. Jillian created something out of nothing but raw Jillian. And when a person gave and gave and gave without some other source of support, without some other way to refuel and refresh their soul…shit happened. Addiction, depression, and suicide happened. Crazy happened.

Brooke had seen it in the music industry over and over.

"Sometimes you're put on a trajectory with the people you need most, right when you need them. Sometimes even before you need them," Jillian said, looking out the window, her gaze distant. "The perfect time, the perfect place, the perfect second chance. That's what this feels like."

This was stolen wisdom—it certainly wasn't Jillian's. Brooke knew if she pressed Jillian on what those words meant, she wouldn't be able to answer. Most of the time, Brooke felt like Jillian was living from the pages of a script, even when no one else was around.

But she didn't challenge Jillian or even speak to her for the rest of the short drive. Instead, she thought of Keaton. Of how their paths had collided. But this wasn't the perfect time or place for the two of them to connect. And they'd never had a real first chance, so this couldn't be the second.

Still…there was something magical about meeting up with him again. And about connecting so instantly and completely. Her travels with Ellie had introduced Brooke to a lot of people. More than she could ever count or than she'd ever remember. Yet she couldn't say she'd been so comfortable so instantly with many people in her life.

The limo turned into a lot and stopped. Their driver, Henry, spoke to the guard at the gate, and Brooke lowered a window so she could show the guard their passes. As soon as the glass was back in place and the car started moving again, Jillian had her mirror out to check her perfect makeup, searching for reassurance and accolades from Brooke.

And once the primping was done, the plotting began.

"Now, you just stay with me. Once I find him, you can make arrangements with a photographer."

As soon as Henry opened the door, Jillian hopped out and was gone. The older man offered his hand, and Brooke took it as she climbed out.

"Whoa," she said, tucking her arm through Henry's and pulling her sunglasses over her eyes. "I just stepped into the oven."

"Gonna be a hot one today."

She frowned at Henry. "Do you have a cool place to hang?"

"Yes, ma'am. A café about a block over. Free refills on iced tea, and they let me sit there as long as I like."

She smiled. "Okay, but only one glass of sweet tea. The others are unsweetened. Can't have your blood sugar spiking."

He chuckled. "Yes, ma'am."

They both squinted against the Texas sun toward Jillian posing for paparazzi with their lenses sticking through a side fence.

"I think she found the photographers," Brooke said.

"Some of 'em anyway."

Brooke felt tired today. Not sleep-deprived tired, though she was that too—pleasurably so. But worn-out tired. "How much longer are you going to drive for Jillian, Henry?"

"Just between you and me, Miss Brooke?"

"Always."

"Another year." He turned his head and smiled, his weathered face crinkling everywhere. "Till my youngest grandson graduates medical school. I'm helping out."

"That's fantastic."

"How about you?" he asked.

"Just between us, Sir Henry?"

He laughed at the nickname she'd given him on her first day. "Absolutely."

She returned her gaze to Jillian, who was now chatting with various people outside the studio in the warehouse district of downtown Austin.

"A year," she told Henry, then grinned at him. "Till my sister graduates nursing school. I'm helping out."

Henry laughed and nodded. "You're a good girl, Miss Brooke."

"Thanks, Henry. I needed to hear that today." She squeezed his arm. "Wish me luck."

"You won't need it, honey."

Brooke followed Jillian, knowing Henry was wrong, but she appreciated his faith in her. She scanned the staff clustered and milling outside the warehouse where parts of the latest Avengers movie were being filmed, but didn't recognize anyone right away. Brooke had looked over the names of the people involved in the film at the higher levels and knew about half by name, another quarter by reputation. But she usually worked hand in hand with the people who were never listed anywhere other than someone's payroll roster, which was always where most of the real work got done.

She paused a few feet behind Jillian as her boss sweet-talked an assistant director who had a tendency to hit on Brooke when he was drunk. That wouldn't have bothered her quite so much if he weren't married to a lovely woman with three adorable children at home.

With one ear on their discussion, Brooke scanned the area where crews moved equipment, a food cart worker stocked drinks and snacks, and staff conducted impromptu meetings in gaggles of threes and fours.

"We're doing some staged filming in warehouse B," Rob, the assistant director, told Jillian, "and there are several smaller mobile stages set up in warehouse A. The stunt crew is blocking out some scenes in there right now."

Brooke instantly pulled Keaton's handsome face to mind. She let the director's chatter about other resources fade, tapped the face of her phone, and wrote a quick message to Keaton.

Hope your new job is going well. I didn't get a chance to ask you what movie it was before I had to run. Can't wait to hear about it when I see you tonight. She paused, grinned, and added, *And I hope you won't need much sleep for your day tomorrow.*

"Judging by your grin, *that* text isn't about work."

Jillian's voice made Brooke want to roll her eyes. Instead, she hit Send and turned off her screen. "It's just *ET*, forlorn about missing out on your interview."

That got a placated smile from Jillian. "This way."

Jillian sashayed toward warehouse A like a queen bee. Brooke followed, curling her iPad toward her chest with one arm.

Rob's gaze latched on to her, and he stepped halfway into her path. "Brooke, I didn't see you." His gaze purposely roamed her, openly hungry. "You look...amazing."

"Hi, Rob." She intercepted his hand on its way to her hip and took it in a deliberate grip, shaking it firmly. "How are Amanda and the kids?"

The mention of his family seemed to knock him off balance. "O-oh. They're…good. Good."

"Great. Tell Amanda I said hello."

As she continued on, she heard his faint, "Uh…right…sure."

Walking into the warehouse momentarily blinded Brooke. It took several moments for her eyes to adjust from Austin's bright morning sunlight to the dark warehouse. Once she'd focused, it took her another couple of minutes to get her bearings. The space was cavernous, with several huge areas in the roof where the ceiling had been replaced with some kind of translucent material, so the sun filtered through, giving the warehouse an eerie, sci-fi sort of glow.

As the director mentioned, the warehouse had been broken up into different sets where various lighting and filming setups were arranged, but only the one taking up half the rear of the warehouse was being used.

Brooke took a deep breath and relaxed into the setting. Here, Jillian would be swept away by the activity, the energy, the excitement. The burden of coddling and soothing and entertaining wouldn't be on Brooke's shoulders. For a few hours, she could be free of those demands, and she anticipated the relief with a Pavlovian response.

She let her mind go and followed Jillian from person to person and group to group, where she was greeted with excitement and reverence. An action scene was obviously being blocked out at the back of the warehouse in a crazy maze of dark, multilevel metal madness. Brooke paused a good distance away from the action, her gaze wandering over the two smashed cars, the varied platforms of metal grates, the stairs…

"Hey, there."

Brooke turned to the female voice and found a production assistant she worked with often and who shared Brooke's affinity for chocolate, smiling at her.

"Hey." Brooke hugged her. "Great to see you."

"You too. Here for the duration or just a cameo?"

"Duration. You?" Schedules often fluctuated in this business with staff getting put on, pulled off, and moved around jobs as the norm rather than the exception. And actors' schedules were even worse.

"Same," Brooke said. "We'll definitely have to find a time to get together and scope out the best chocolate around here."

After Keaton leaves.

Brooke wasn't giving up a minute of the short time they had left. After that, she'd *really* need chocolate.

"Deal," she told Stacy. "So, get me up to speed on the film." Brooke's gaze strayed toward the back of the warehouse again, where several men planned out some kind of attack on the set with the filming crew. Jillian stood near the stunt crew, speaking with another director.

"The first thing you need to know," Stacy said, "is that we're behind schedule."

Brooke's attention was pulled from the shadowed corner. "Oh no."

"I know Jillian's going to be a bitch about it. I would have called you, but it just happened. Our stunt guy took a bad fall..."

The rest of Stacy's words faded in shock. The shock gave way to excitement. And giddiness was bubbling in Brooke's belly when she cut her gaze back to the darkened corner of the warehouse, where one of the men stood on top of a smashed military-type truck. But it wasn't Keaton. Her gaze dropped to the man pacing out in front of the truck. He was shirtless, well built, and had dark hair, but that's all she could see from where she stood.

Someone from the sidelines called, "Ready."

The dark-haired man dropped into a runner's stance and shook his body loose.

"Go."

He ran. Long, loose, easy strides that ate up the distance to the truck. One foot took a step to the bumper. The other foot leapt to the hood. One more effortless hop and he executed a jump-turn-kick move so fast, Brooke almost missed it, and the other guy on the roof of the truck flew backward.

Brooke knew in an instant the shirtless man was Keaton. She'd never seen him work. She'd never seen him fight. And during their weeks together in Los Angeles, she'd only seen a sliver of his abilities when he'd been goofing around with the other Renegades, but she knew without any doubt that was Keaton standing on that truck. Which meant not only did she get to have him in her bed at night, she also got to watch him work during the day.

She had to have excitement oozing from her pores, and she didn't have the first idea how she was going to lie about this to Jillian.

Up on the top of the truck, Keaton offered a hand to whomever he'd just knocked down, and the two busted up laughing about something. The rich, buoyant sound of Keaton's laughter inflated Brooke's chest with joy until it spilled over in her own laughter.

In that moment, the fluttering giddiness in Brooke's heart made her realize she wasn't just taking a swim with this guy the way she kept telling herself. She'd already jumped in the deep end.

"I want to be a stuntwoman when I grow up," Stacy said. "I've never seen anyone have so much damn fun at work."

"Right?" was all Brooke could think of to say.

"Brooke," Jillian said, tearing her gaze from where Keaton and another guy climbed from the top of the truck and dropped out of sight.

"The fire-breathing dragon beckons," Stacy said. "Good luck with that."

By the time Brooke reached Jillian, her excitement shifted to alarm over the deviously pleased glint in her boss's eye.

Jillian slipped her hand around Brooke's forearm and turned her toward the stunt set. "He's here, and he's even more delicious than he was a few months ago when I saw him last."

As they approached the set where cameramen and assistants and other staff gathered, Keaton and another man strolled out from around the side of the vehicles, talking to each other. Keaton used his T-shirt to wipe his face.

The sight of his chest and belly shining with sweat shot a streak of wild lust straight through her sex. Images from their night flashed in Brooke's brain—the way they flexed every time he thrust. The intensity in his expression every time he drove deep inside her. The darkness of his eyes as he watched every flash of pleasure slide over her face. The hunger in his mouth, in his hands, in his body...

Oh. *God*...

"If you don't want me to kick you on your ass," Keaton was saying, a grin splitting his handsome face, "then take three steps back like I told you."

The other man looked younger than Keaton. He was also very handsome, with more of an iconic American look with ash-blond hair and a square jaw. Definitely Jillian's type. And age-wise… Well, she'd been going for them younger and younger lately.

"Last time you told me to take three steps back," the younger man said, "I dropped ten fucking stories."

Everyone around them laughed.

Keaton shook his head and slowed as he came to the camera station with a playback screen. "I should have sent you home when—"

His gaze lifted and casually scanned the people around them, pausing on Brooke. Time stopped for a split second. A split second when she saw him in exquisite detail—his hair damp with sweat around his face, his dark skin glistening, his expression filled with joy. Pure joy—for his work and the people he worked with.

Then she saw a spark of excitement flair. And that lifted her happiness to new heights. It was the same spark she saw in Justin's eyes when she returned home from a trip, the same spark she saw in Ellie's eyes when they met again after being apart, and, she'd discovered over the last year, it was what life was really about.

"Hey," he said, drawing out the word with a little wait-you're-not-supposed-to-be-here confusion that transitioned into excitement as the realization she'd made a few minutes before hit him. "Are you—"

"Keaton Holt?" Jillian's overly excited voice cut through the myriad conversations, and she moved through the staff and crew as they parted like the Red Sea, allowing her a path toward Keaton.

Alarm skittered through Brooke's heart, and her gaze cut to Jillian.

"What are you doing here?" Jillian's face shone like a diamond. The picture of utter perfection. It was her all-in smile. Her nothing-can-compete-with-this smile. Her nothing-I've-done-wrong-in-the-past-matters smile. And she had 500 percent of her focus homed in on Keaton. Not the blond he'd been working with. The blond who was now wandering away like the rest of the crew, hoping to escape unnoticed while the she-devil was licking her chops over a different morsel.

"*I* reconnected *with him last month at Steven's birthday party in Beverly Hills.*"

Denial hit Brooke fast and hard.

Oh no. No, no, no.

Not Keaton. Not Jillian and Keaton. She could have anyone else. He was Brooke's only selfish desire. And they had so little time together.

Holding tight to the last flicker of hope, she darted a look at Keaton—and her stomach dropped to her feet. All the excitement there a moment ago—all the humor and life and happiness—gone. All locked behind a cool wall. One Brooke had seen others use when they were unpleasantly blindsided in public. One that often appeared in awkward and tense situations.

His reaction to Jillian confirmed the truth in Brooke's gut—Jillian and Keaton had been together. When, where, how—it didn't matter. Somewhere, at some time, they'd been together.

The images that flashed in Brooke's head made her stomach clench and burn. She purposely refocused somewhere else in the room to clear her head. Because this was a problem. A really big problem. A potentially *disastrous* problem. A cut that had the potential to bleed her dry if she didn't stem the bleeding.

She pulled her iPad into her chest and crossed her arms, as if that would help.

Jillian's reputation had preceded her, as usual, and the crew had skittered off in different directions. But Keaton was too much of a gentleman to bail, even though the look on his face told Brooke there was nothing he'd rather do right that moment.

"Jillian," was all he said.

And his voice was so deep and so cold, it made Brooke's stomach quiver. It made her hope she and Keaton never reached a point in their relationship or their friendship where he ever used that tone with her. Even the possibility stabbed at her heart.

But Jillian didn't seem to notice the antagonism. She swayed toward him like she moved toward everything she thought she owned, and Brooke's muscles tightened, preparing to witness them kiss.

But Keaton caught hold of her biceps when her lips were still inches from his. And Brooke stood several feet away in the most impossible, most awkward position of her life. If there were ever a moment she wished the earth would open up and swallow her, this would be that time.

"What...do you think...you're doing?" Keaton's voice was private, but filled with who-the-fuck-do-you-think-you-are menace.

Before Brooke could excuse herself, Jillian performed the perfect backpedaling, smooth-it-over routine. "I was just saying hello, of course. We *are* old friends after all." She pulled out of his grip but kept her voice light and adoring. "I'm sorry you're having a hard morning."

Keaton's jaw pulsed, but when Jillian didn't make another aggressive move, he shook out his T-shirt and tossed it over his head. Brooke's gaze slid down his torso on the way to the floor again, pausing on red marks. Red...scratches.

Her face bloomed with heat. Her sex followed. She hadn't seen those in the shower this morning. But she sure remembered making them last night. And *good God*, now she couldn't think of anything else.

Straddling his lap, his knees spread so wide, her hip joints ached, he thrust with all the strength in his butt and thighs. Unrelenting, consistent strokes that hit their mark and hammered whimpers of desire and cries of pleasure and screams of ecstasy from her.

With one arm wrapped around his neck, the other at his ribs, she'd been digging into him because, one—he'd been so sweaty, her grip kept slipping, and two—she'd needed the grip against the force of his thrust, and three—she'd needed the leverage to pull herself back into him so his next stroke would hit the same out-of-this-fucking-world spot inside her again.

"Come for me, Brooke," he'd demanded against her neck, even as she was just recovering from her last orgasm. *"Come again. So good. Love the feel of you coming around me. Come on, baby. Give it to me. Ah, yeah. That's it. Mmm, so good. Come on, baby. No limit. Give me another one."*

She shivered. Curled her fingers around the edges of her iPad until they numbed.

"Since we'll be working together..." Jillian's voice refocused her. "I certainly don't want to start out on the wrong foot. Brooke, this is Keaton Holt," she said, her tone light and charming and—dare she even think...sweet? "The only man who's ever truly stolen my heart. Keaton, this is my assistant, Brooke—"

"Yeah, I—" he started.

"Dempsey," Brooke cut in forcefully. She pried her hand from the computer and offered it to him. "Brooke Dempsey. It's nice to meet you, Mr. Holt." She pulled her hand from Keaton's overly hard grip and smiled at Jillian. "Mr. Holt and I met briefly in Los Angeles about a year ago. A friend of a friend."

He stared at her, lips parted as if he'd stopped before the words had come out. His dark eyes sharpened, flicked to Jillian, then returned to Brooke. And they were hard. He closed his mouth and rolled his shoulders back. Now he looked just as displeased with her as he had with Jillian. And yeah, she knew she deserved it, but shit... The way he closed off made it impossible to read his expression, and it hurt. Hurt like hell. She felt like she'd already lost part of him.

"Miss Dempsey," was all he said. Brooke could only thank God his voice didn't hold the same frigid ring as it had when he'd said Jillian's name.

She gave Keaton a nod and hoped he could read the gratitude in her eyes, but she'd never seen him look so miserable. Which seemed like the mood of the day.

Except for Jillian. The emotional undercurrents were lost on the narcissist. "Keaton, since I have time now, I thought we could block out the first stunt scene we're in together."

He planted his hands at his hips. "We're not in *any* scenes together."

"Oh, Copalli didn't tell you?" Jillian asked.

"What?" Brooke asked, frowning at Jillian, but her boss ignored her, and by the purse of Jillian's lips and the jut to her chin, Brooke knew Jillian was going to color outside those lines again.

"Told me what, Jillian?" Keaton asked with an I-know-what-you're-gonna-say-and-it's-going-to-start-a-fight tone. "Because if you think you're going to do your own stunts, I can tell you right now, that's not going to fly past risk assessment."

Jillian laughed softly, clearly happy with the fact that she'd ticked Keaton off. "We'll just see about that, won't we?"

Brooke was ready to climb out of her skin. She couldn't watch these two together anymore. She couldn't look at Keaton anymore, knowing the plans they'd had for tonight, for any night in the future, were history.

The day suddenly seemed to stretch out in front of her as ten, twelve, sixteen…long, hot, sticky hours of misery.

She cleared her tight throat and told Jillian, "If it's all right with you, I'll go check in with the production assistants now." Without waiting for her answer, she reminded Keaton of her need for their relationship to remain secret with, "It was good to meet you again, Mr. Holt."

Six

Keaton didn't know where the hell Brooke was or when she was going to come back to the hotel. And he felt like the biggest fucking loser on the planet waiting outside her room. The only reason the Four Seasons security hadn't called Austin Police on him was because Jax, the Renegade who was a Four Season's frequent-flier, had called and personally vouched for Keaton.

Which meant if he did anything to get into trouble, he'd get his ass royally kicked by Jax. And the only Renegade who was as good a fighter as Keaton was Jax.

He pushed to his feet and paced the hallway again, pausing at the end to stare out at the Colorado River reflecting the moonlight. Too bad he wasn't in a romantic mood. Once the shock of Brooke denying knowing him wore off, frustration set in. Frustration developed into anger as she went through the day without ever even looking his way. As his texts over the course of the day for explanations about her behavior went unanswered. As his question of whether or not they were going to meet tonight as planned was ignored.

And none of the images that kept floating into his head from the day were helping calm him down. The memory of her face floated into his head—of how happy she'd looked when she'd first seen him, contrasted against the shock and hurt in her eyes after she'd figured out he and Jillian had slept together.

"*Fuck,*" he bit out. That had been so goddamned long ago. He'd made some stupid decisions where women were concerned, no doubt. But Jillian was definitely one of his worst. It would have to be that one to come back and bite him in the ass.

And her stupid comment—*stolen her heart?* What a bunch of fuckin' *bullshit.*

The worst part was, he had no idea what was going on in Brooke's head. Could only guess why she'd played the "Hi, I'm Brooke Dempsey" card today, and absolutely hated the idea that she planned on pretending they didn't know each other while they were working together.

Talk about torture.

He wandered back toward her room, paused at another window, and pressed a fist to the ache in his gut, one created by a combination of acid from the stress and pure pain from the thought of losing Brooke so soon after thinking they'd get a chance to develop something.

Movement made him look left.

Brooke turned the corner, looking down at a keycard in her hand. She was wearing another dress. Black. But this one was more casual than the one she'd worn earlier. And sexier in a far more playful way. It had spaghetti straps and was fitted from her breasts to her hips, then flared into a short skirt. And it laced up the front through a double row of eyelets.

He wasn't feeling the least bit playful or lighthearted, and even though the comparison between the mood her dress evoked and his current mood was absolutely ludicrous, it still added heat to his anger. So did the fact that she looked ridiculously sexy in the damn thing. And the way his body surged at the sight of her.

It all blended to throw his emotions into a gear he didn't even know he had, let alone a gear he knew how to operate.

When he straightened from the window, she looked up and stopped. A gasp passed through her lips, and she darted a look over her shoulder.

His temper flared.

He didn't even *have* a fucking temper until today.

"Good to see you too," he said. "Been waiting all fucking night."

She turned back. "I was going to call you," she said, her voice hushed. "It's just, Jillian—"

"Isn't here. I made sure she left the building before I came. And I've been here over a fucking hour. Had my phone the whole time."

As if on cue, her cell rang. She exhaled, her shoulders rising and dropping. While she answered her own phone, she slid the keycard into the lock and opened the door to her room. "Hey, honey, I'm a little busy right now. Is everything okay?"

She had to be talking to her nephew.

"Okay, sure. I'll help you with that. Can I call you back in a little bit? Okay. Love you too. Bye."

She sighed and walked into the hotel room.

Still standing in the hall, Keaton was struck by an epiphany. He knew right that second exactly why he was so damned pissed. Because he didn't do this to women. Ever. He was up-front with them before they ever got close to a bed or an alley or bathroom or wherever they went to fuck. They knew when the fuck was over, *they* were over.

Brooke hadn't done that.

The realization made hurt ooze out beneath the anger, and things inside him got volatile. Keaton needed to downshift this shit and coast out of here.

He followed her in, saying, "Look, I wouldn't have liked hearing that we were done this morning, but I would have accepted it. What I don't like is having you act like you wanted things to continue and then pulling the shit you've been pulling today."

She put her purse and keys on the side table and turned to face him.

"I'm not pulling anything. I've been working my ass off all day. *Someone*, who shall remain nameless, put Jillian in a *mood* this morning, and she's been *bent* on taking it out on *me*. Suffice it to say, Jillian has been the crazy fucking bitch *from hell* today. And God forbid she settle for just any hairdresser. No, Jillian Bailey has to have the woman who did Mariah Carey's hair for the Oscars. Which means *I* have to fly her in, and *I* have to pick her up at the airport, and *I* have to settle her at the hotel. So forgive me if I'm not the picture of patience right now."

She crossed her arms and balled her fists, plumping her breasts over the edge of her dress and adding another edge of heat to

Keaton's frustration. "And I didn't answer your texts because Jillian is the queen of paranoia half the time and the queen of micromanaging the other half. I didn't want her reading over my shoulder."

"You seemed to be able to text me just fine before you got to the set this morning...while you were *in the car* with her."

"That's before *I knew*," she yelled.

"Knew what? That I slept with her? Is that where this is really going? Is that what we really need to talk about?"

She made a face and closed her eyes. "No. Don't." She shook her head. "I don't want to think about you with her. I don't care about that."

She didn't care? If she didn't care... He took two steps toward her, put his hands on his hips when he really wanted to run them over her body. "Then why did you pretend not to know me?"

"Because Jillian's a vindictive bitch, and, apparently, you are"—she rolled her eyes—"the only man who's ever stolen her heart. If she thought you were interested in me over her, *I'd* be the one to suffer."

"Why didn't you tell me you were working in the movie industry? I thought you'd signed on with another singer like Ellie."

"Because I didn't want to talk about work. Or about Jillian. I just wanted to forget about it all for one night."

That didn't ease his frustration. In fact, it made him angrier.

"So I was an escape." He moved closer until his body brushed hers. Until she had to tilt her chin back to look up at him. And Keaton could not fucking believe how badly he wanted her. His entire body surged with the raw need to feel Brooke again. "But now I'm a problem. So this is how it's going to be? You're just going to prance around the set in all these sexy little dresses and pretend I don't exist every fucking day?"

She pressed her lips together in determination, but her eyes closed in a look of pained desire. Then she stepped back and braced her hand on the dining room table. She took a slow deep breath and said, "If that's what I need to do to keep my job."

Anger spiked again. "Priorities. Is that it?"

She nodded.

That stubborn line of her jaw irked something deep inside him. He leaned in and pressed both hands to the table, flanking her. His body came into contact with hers—thighs, hips, chests. She let out a breath carrying the softest moan, it fizzed through Keaton's blood and made him high.

With his lips at her ear, he murmured, "So, what about me? What are you going to do about all the things I'm thinking during the day, watching you in these sexy little dresses?"

"Oh God..." The high-pitched words came out as barely a whisper, but they sang through Keaton's blood with the power of an opera.

"Sixteen hours a day. Every day." He pulled back to look into her eyes and found them drunk. He skimmed his gaze over the open neckline of her dress and all that creamy skin. "All that time just to watch you move, look at your body tucked into these"—he lifted a hand, pressed one finger to the side of her breast, and let it follow the curve of her body to her hip—"sweet little dresses."

"Keaton..." Her eyes opened, flooded with heat and lust and frustration. Her chest rose with quick breaths, and her breasts strained against the top of the dress.

"With skirts like these and all the hidden spaces around the warehouses," he said, "I could give you my hand and my mouth and bring you heaven in five minutes any time you wanted it, all day long."

"Oooooooh..." she groaned, her eyes sliding closed.

"You want it, don't you, Brooke?" he whispered.

"Yeeeees..."

The sweetest high flooded Keaton's chest. He lowered his lips to her temple and kissed her. Brooke leaned into his touch, hummed with desire, and fisted his T-shirt. Keaton was instantly high. "You want it now, don't you, baby?"

"Fuck..." Her hands tightened and twisted the cotton of his tee. "Yes..."

Keaton's eyes slid closed. He dropped his hand, found the hem of her skirt, and slid his hand up her thigh. "You're so warm."

The press of her lips against his brought his eyes open, and he found Brooke's rich blue eyes, heavy lidded and filled with passion and the same affection that had been there that morning, staring back at him. "I haven't been able to stop thinking about this all day." She kissed him softly, sliding the tip of her tongue along his lip and setting him on fucking fire. "I *ache*."

The breathy words, the insinuation that she needed him, wanted him, had waited for him, thrilled him beyond words. He kissed her back, teasing her lips while he held her gaze and slipped his fingers under her panties.

He passed a whispery touch over her, and she shivered. She was already on the edge. The fact that she was there because she'd been thinking about him all day turned a lot of his anger and hurt into pure, raw lust.

Starting with one finger, he moved over her. She was slick and hot and swollen, and suddenly all Keaton could think about was getting in there with his hands, his mouth, his cock.

"Oh my God… Yes. Yes, yes, yes… Mmmm."

"You like my hands, don't you, baby?"

"*Love* your hands… Mmmm… God… So good…" She whimpered and shivered.

Fuck, she was a goddamned drug. And Keaton was going to be addicted if he didn't back off the candy. Fast.

Brooke opened her eyes, tipped her head back, and looked up at him, lips parted, big bright blue gaze dripping with lust. "Make me come… Need it…"

That hit went straight to his fucking vein. Keaton pushed his fingers deeper, rubbed and stroked and pinched, purposely avoiding her clit to prolong this little treasure as long as possible.

"Ah God…" She rubbed all up on him, wrapped an arm around his waist, took his tee between her teeth. "Keaton… Pleeeeeeeease…"

She was fucking delirium personified.

Maybe he'd quit tomorrow.

* * * *

He was torturing her on purpose.

She probably deserved it.

God, this was an impossible situation. A situation she couldn't even think about because of what he was doing to her. And she didn't know how he did it. She'd touched herself; this sure as shit never happened.

He growled and pulled his hand from between her legs. Brooke's sex clenched at his absence, and a slice of irrational panic cut through her. "No, no, no..." she whispered, breathless, pulling at him. "Come back. Come back."

His gaze was so hot. So edgy. It probably shouldn't thrill her, but it did. This was a whole different side of the man. And, God, she should walk away. He was right. She should have just let him go this morning.

He had the right to be angry. Worse, he was hurt. She wanted to make it better, but she couldn't, not right now. The day had taken a physical and emotional toll on Brooke. One only Keaton could make her forget. He wanted it too. Wanted to know she wanted him. Wanted the distance and uncertainty that had built up between them over the day gone. Otherwise, he wouldn't be here. And he wouldn't be mad. And he wouldn't be pulling out his wallet.

The crinkle of foil made her need surge. Made her head go light, and she greedily jerked at the button of his jeans. She'd never wanted anyone like this. Never known she could. Knowing how badly it would hurt when things went south or they both went back to opposite sides of the country, or both, made her press her face to his chest and choke out a groan of distress.

By the time his hand moved under her skirt again, she had his jeans open, her hand around the cotton-covered heat of his erection. He pushed under her panties and between her legs with swift efficiency. A flash of cold shocked her. Made her gasp and brought her head up.

He had an unopened condom packet clenched between his teeth, making her realize he'd opened one of the little packets of lube he carried along with the condoms. Then his fingers glided over her sex, the lube instantly warmed by her body and his hand. Her eyes locked on his, and rough sound came from her throat.

"Fuck, fuck, fuck..." Her muscles clenched and quivered. Her eyes rolled back in her head.

His other hand gripped her jaw and gave her a shake. She gasped, opened her eyes, and curled the fingers of one hand around his wrist. But he pulled away, took the condom from his mouth, and tossed it on the table before closing his fingers on her cheeks again.

"You know why I love touching you?" His eyes were so close, she almost couldn't focus. His lashes were long, his brown eyes black in the dim light, all the angles of his face sharper with intensity. "Because of this. Because I can watch everything on your face. Watch all the pleasure you get from my touch slide through your eyes. Because I know *I'm* giving you that, and I can watch every…single…second of it."

The fact that he derived such a thrill out of delivering pleasure was a wicked turn-on. How many men cared that much about a woman's pleasure? She didn't know any. At least not intimately.

"And because your pussy is so…fucking…perfect."

Slow, deep slides. Shallow, stretching circles. A tug, a pinch. But nothing direct. Nothing repetitive. And nothing that would make her come. She was shaking and panting, leaning her butt against the table because her legs wouldn't hold her up.

She whined and rocked her hips into his hand.

He laughed. He fucking laughed. Low and rough. And reduced his touch to one finger. "Tell me what you like about it."

"You're…*so* good…at it."

A hot smile flashed over his face, and he rewarded her with a few direct, maddeningly gentle circles directly over her clit before sliding backward again and pushing inside her. God, it wasn't near enough. "What else?"

"Naughty."

"You like naughty?"

"With you."

His angry lust softened a little. "You want to be naughty tonight, Brooke? Want to be naughty with me?"

Her head dropped back, and a delicious stream of lust and desire and relief and excitement coursed through her. "God, yes."

A sound ebbed from his throat. His hand tightened on her face and jerked her gaze to his again. His hand stopped teasing and started driving. And where a feather-light touch might have lifted her to climax, this hard, demanding push and pressure worked her into a slow spiral toward implosion.

"Oh God… Oh God… Fuck, fuck, fuck…" She gripped the edge of the table. Fought to find the peak. Whimpered when it still didn't come. "Mmm… Please, please, please… Don't stop, don't stop… Ah…God…"

He dropped his forehead against hers and rasped, "We're gonna do this all fucking night."

She dropped her mouth open, panting. Her muscles burned.

She was already sweating. "Can't."

"Oh yes you can. Because I know you. You're going to need to come again right after you come now. Once isn't going to be enough."

She whimpered. He was right.

"And when I push you back on this table and put my cock in you, you're going to need to come again. And when I hover over you and kiss you, and kiss you and kiss you, you're going to beg me to hammer into you."

She dropped her head back. "Oh my God."

How had he figured that out in one night? Was she that predictable? Even she didn't know she was going to do that until he said it. Until it rang so true, she knew it was exactly what she would want.

"But I know," he said sliding his fingers deep into the folds on either side of her clit and stroking back and forth. Back and forth. Brooke's breath stuttered. "How easily and hard you come after the first. And since you're feeling naughty and frustrated tonight, I'll throw in a twist for you. Literally. We'll see how you like that. What do you think?"

His fingers tightened on the bud of her clit and gave a little twist one way, then the other.

"Ah…"

Tug, twist, twist, rub.

"Oh my God…"

Tug, twist, twist, rub.

"Ah…ha…ha…God…" She bowed backward as the orgasm took over, ravaging her like a hungry monster, and Keaton just kept feeding it and feeding it.

And just as he predicted, he'd spent so much time building her up, that even the release wasn't enough to satisfy her completely. Just the feel of his big hand still between her legs made her want more.

She groaned, rocked into him, and opened her eyes to his smug smile. "I hate you."

"Tell me that again in ten minutes, thirty minutes, ninety minutes, three-hundred minutes—"

She laughed. "Shut up."

The first smile she'd seen since he'd first set eyes on her in the warehouse that morning quirked his mouth. And it was hot. "Shut up and make you come, right? Shut up and fuck you?"

She was about to tell him that wasn't what she meant, but he pushed a full, leisurely stroke between her legs that made her eyes cross and slid the lube over her perineum and the pucker of her ass. "Ooooh…"

"Luckily," he murmured, easing one of her ass cheeks to the edge of the table and settling his fingers into a new and incredibly erotic exploration that tightened her throat. "Those are both extremely easy demands to fill."

Her breath came in sharp little pants as his touch pulsed surges of heavy pleasure deep into her pelvis. With his free hand, he took her face again and lifted it to his.

"Oh…God… Oh…"

He touched his lips to hers. Licked her upper lip. Sucked it. "Like it?"

She whined in response. Gripped the edge of the table with both hands to stay balanced while she writhed—because she couldn't hold still. He pulled her mouth to his with a hard hand on her jaw and kissed her. His tongue took hers hungrily with a matching, impatient groan, and he ate at her, while his touch revealed none of that. His fingers continued maddeningly slow and tantalizing circles and strokes, circles and strokes, circles and strokes.

Keaton pulled out of the kiss with a breathless, rough "Would you like me doing this while I sucked on you?"

"Oh my God." The thought was too incredible to fathom. She knew if she said yes, he'd drop to his knees right now. And, wow, part of her wanted that. *Bad.* But a bigger part was too anxious to get to that hammering part he'd mentioned. God, he made her so…fucking…what? She didn't know what to call it. But she felt a little rabid. "I need you inside me. So bad."

"I have the perfect solution." He withdrew his hand and stepped back.

"What—"

Both his hands disappeared under her skirt and dragged her panties down her legs. Then he gripped the back of her thighs behind her knees and lifted, taking her off her feet while spreading her at the same time.

"Keaton!"

He only lifted her to the edge of the table, but kept a grip on her thighs that turned the flesh white under his fingers. "We interrupt your regularly scheduled naughty program for a little extra naughty…"

He dipped his head beneath her skirt. Wet heat and pressure and movement assaulted her sex in the most decadently erotic way. Words and phrases and sounds spilled out of Brooke. She arched and gripped the table. Her head fell back, mouth dropped open, eyes closed. She cried out, shivered, shook, gritted her teeth.

The orgasm slammed into her and sent her spinning. Her hips lifted and spasmed, and Keaton continued to eat and eat and eat. And orgasm after orgasm after orgasm pummeled, rattled, and ripped through her body.

When Keaton rose from his knees, Brooke lay back on the table, shaking, one hand fisted in the hair she'd pulled over her face, the other white-knuckling the table edge.

"Oh my God…" was all she could manage. Her mind was completely white. She couldn't think at all. Her body was so completely aroused. Every nerve she owned felt like it was on the surface of her skin, just waiting for Keaton to stroke it. And he planned to do just that, judging by the condom he rolled onto his erection, so ready it arced toward his belly. And Brooke wanted it so much, she could taste it. She covered her mouth. "Oh my God." What had happened to her? She moved her hand to her tight throat. "Oh my God, want it. Want it now."

He stepped up to the edge of the table, reached for her, and dragged her to him by the waist. Lifting her, he pulled her upright until they were face-to-face, kissed her slowly, deeply, passionately.

When he pulled out of the kiss, he murmured, "Here's the naughty twist."

And he flipped her onto her stomach. For a shocked second, she stared at the wood. Then he tossed her skirt up, and a breeze of cool air licked her skin a millisecond before his hand cracked across her ass.

Brooke's gasp cut into the quiet and stalled her response. She pushed up on her elbows just as Keaton grabbed the flesh of her ass and hauled her to the table edge, impaling her with his cock.

And all Brooke's thoughts evaporated. All thoughts other

than—perfection, ecstasy, bliss, thick, hot, huge, mine, and orgasm, orgasm, orgasm…motherfucking *orgasm*.

The first of those orgasms hinted almost immediately. Keaton used the skirt underneath her to slide her across the table while he thrust and hooked one hand over her shoulder to both pull her into him and hold her while he hammered. His cock had to be the perfect size or shape or length or *something*, because she'd never been able to skyrocket like this. And unlike clitoral orgasms, multiple full-body orgasms weren't painful. They were…well…or-fucking-gasmic. And, she was discovering, addictive.

Highly addictive.

Like *majorly*.

In fact, she couldn't get enough. And when Keaton slowed his thrusts to drag at the straps of her dress and yank the bodice to free her breasts, Brooke rose to her hands and knees and rocked back, pushing his cock deep.

"Oh, yeeeeeees," she moaned. Gritting her teeth against the need eating her up inside, she used the edges of the table to push herself back and onto his cock. *Bang, bang, bang…* "Ah God."

Keaton bent over her, cupped and squeezed her breasts, bit her shoulder, then soothed it with his tongue. "You need it, baby?"

"Need it… God, need it, need it, need—"

He bit her neck, and pain made her complain. Then he released one breast and cracked her ass. *Hard.*

"Ah!" Her head fell forward, her mind spun with the shock, interrupting her rhythm. The sound split through the room, and the sting sang through her skin and sank deep into her ass cheek. Into her pussy. And melted into a pleasure so intense, she couldn't begin to describe it. She trembled, and whimpers hummed from her throat.

And when Keaton rasped, "Naughty girls, get spanked," at her ear, excitement spurted through her body and drenched her pussy.

He growled and dug his hands into her flesh, one at her hip, one at her breast. "That is *so…fucking…hot.*" He pulled out and slammed into her with a satisfied hum.

Pleasure spilled through her.

"Yes, yes, yes." She was insanely single-minded. She *had* to satisfy this craving. It was a necessity. And she put all her focus and energy on driving Keaton's cock right where it needed to be—hard and deep inside her.

Keaton gripped her hips and hauled her back against him. The rhythmic slap of flesh echoed the spankings he'd given her and shot sparks through her blood again. "Mmm, it's coming... Don't stop, don't stop..."

"You're fuckin' crazy sexy." His hand slid up her spine, collected her hair, and pulled her head back, arching her, forcing her ass higher. "Like that?"

"Yes... Oh God..."

He released one hip to smack the flesh of her ass, then dug his fingers in again and pulled her into him harder.

She cried out as the first wave of the orgasm hit, but kept pushing back into him, "Don't stop, don't stop, don't stop... *Fuck...*" And screamed as the next wave immobilized her.

But Keaton knew exactly what she needed. He wrapped one muscled arm at her hips and continued to thrust, igniting multiple orgasms like starbursts clustered together to explode in strings of ecstasy.

Keaton pressed his face to her neck. "Brooke, baby, so fucking good."

She closed her fingers in his hair and kissed his temple just as a violent climax slammed through him, drawing forth the brutally serious side of a man she was just realizing she'd only begun to know. The same way she was just coming to realize there was a whole side of herself she hadn't fully known about. One he'd only just introduced her to.

Seven

Keaton tried to massage conditioner into Brooke's hair, but she was so limp, she kept moving every time his hands moved. "The sooner you hold your head still, the sooner you can get out of here and lie down."

She groaned and let her forehead fall against his chest. He laughed. Then an unexpected rush of emotion swamped him, and he pressed his cheek to her head, wrapped his arms around her, and held her as tight as he could. Her hands circled his waist and hugged him back. And they just stood there like that in the elaborate Four Seasons shower, letting the hot water stream over them.

After a couple of minutes, she turned her head toward him and rested her cheek against his chest. "I'm sorry."

It was a big apology. An apology for everything that had happened, everything that had gone wrong that day, all that could still go wrong.

He lifted a hand and stroked her wet head. "Me too."

"It's just… It's so complicated."

The inflection in Brooke's words made it sound as if her inner landscape were all fire and brimstone. She'd never struck Keaton as the dramatic type, but it had been a year since he'd seen her, and she had been working for Jillian.

"I know Jillian can be self-involved," he said, "but I'm sure she'll understand once—"

Brooke pulled back and looked at him a little wild-eyed. "I hope your next words weren't going to include 'tell her.' Because we are absolutely not telling her there is anything between us."

Keaton let the rest of his breath release from his lungs and clenched his teeth in frustration as Brooke dropped her head back to rinse her hair. He felt like a rubber band continually being stretched to one extreme only to be snapped the other direction.

"This is ridiculous," he told her when she pulled her head from under the spray. "It was so long ago, I don't even remember anything about the night we were together. Like…" He fought to think back. "Hell, I don't even know how long ago it was. Before she was married to that billionaire asshole."

"In the limo this morning, she mentioned seeing you a few weeks ago."

He pounded the shower control with a fist, shutting it off. "If you knew about me in the limo—"

"I didn't know you were you. I mean…" She rubbed a hand over her face, pushing water from her eyes. "She didn't say a name."

He pulled a towel off the top of the door and wrapped it around her from behind, securing her in his arms. He pressed a kiss to her temple. "Unless you're going to tell me that what we've got here is over and we're never doing this again, which I'd never believe, she's going to find out eventually. Better to just deal with it up front."

"It's not just about her." She turned in his arms, and the deep apprehension darkening her pretty face worried him. "I need this job. I can't afford to risk that. And I know her. I've been with her day and night for a year. I know what makes her tick. And what makes her snap. And right now, with what's going on in her personal life, I guarantee even a *hint* of something between you and me would break her trust in me like a toothpick."

She pushed the shower door open, grabbed another towel from the rod, and handed it to Keaton. Tightening her own, she waited as he dried off.

"I thought having you in town longer would be a really great chance for us to spend more time together, but…" She ran both hands through her hair and shook her head, misery plain on her face. "How did everything go so bad, so fast? She can make the very best situation so damn miserable."

"Hey, hey…" He tightened the towel at his waist and stepped over to her, taking her in his arms again. "If she does this to you, why do you stay with her? Why haven't you found another job?"

She curled one arm around his lower back and the other up and over the back of his shoulder, as if she couldn't hold on tight enough. And Keaton's rubber band snapped the other direction again.

"Because it's not that easy," she told him, her voice tight with distress. Her phone rang in the bedroom, and she jumped like a plucked cord. "Oh, crap. What time is it?"

"Baby, relax," he murmured. "It's too late for Jillian to be calling you. Let it ring."

"It's not Jillian. That's my sister's ringtone." She turned out of his arms. "I didn't call Justin back. It's probably my sister, checking in." She tapped her phone and looked at it when she answered, but gave a surprised "Justin? What are you doing up so late? Where's your mom?"

"She's sleeping." The boy's voice that came over the line was definitely young, but he als sounded sick. Like he had a cold.

"Hold on a second, buddy, I just got out of the shower." Brooke put the phone on the bed and looked around, grabbing the first thing she found, which happened to be Keaton's T-shirt. Pulling it over her head, she picked up the phone and sat cross-legged. "So, what's going on? Why are you up while your mom's sleeping? Is she okay?"

"She's tired."

Now Keaton frowned. The kid sounded really sick. Brooke must have noticed it too, because her face creased with worry. She rested the phone on her bent knee, used both hands to rub her face, then propped her elbow on her thigh and her head in her hand. "Okay, I need really straight answers, Justin. Can you do that?"

"Yeah."

"Is your mom just tired? Or is she sick?"

Keaton finished drying himself off, knotted the towel around his waist, and leaned against the bathroom doorframe.

"Just tired I think," Justin said.

"Can you bring her the phone?"

Hesitation. When he spoke, he whispered. "But she'll get mad that I'm still awake and that I used the phone without telling her."

Brooke laughed a tired "Baby," and covered her eyes.

The amount of affection in her voice made Keaton smile, despite his lingering frustration. And fuck if everything inside him didn't go all warm and soft.

She uncovered her face. "Okay, just be really, really quiet," she said, lowering her voice to his level, "and point the phone at her so I can see she's okay. And then leave the room, and we'll talk more when you're in the living room."

"Okay."

Quiet fell. Brooke curled one hand into a fist and pressed it against her mouth, the other against her chest. After a moment, a smile curved her lips, and she exhaled heavily. She nodded to her nephew.

Then she smiled over at Keaton, and he saw tears glistening in her eyes. "She fell asleep with her anatomy book open and her glasses on," she told him, still whispering, and laughed softly as she dried her eyes on the shoulder of his tee.

Oh, man. This woman held a lot more inside than he'd realized. In fact, she probably had nerves of steel. At least until he walked into her life and upset the balance.

Keaton wandered into the bedroom and sat on the edge of the bed.

"Okay," she said to Justin, "now, where's your inhaler?"

"In my pocket."

"Then why do you sound like that?"

"Dunno."

Brooke sighed. "What happened to straight answers, Justin?"

"I really just need help figuring out what I'm going to do for the science fair." Now the kid sounded upset too, and when he got stressed, the wheeze in his lungs got worse.

"Okay, okay." She held up both hands. "Don't get worked up."

"But Derrick's doing skateboarding and physics, and he's calling it Popping an Ollie. It's all about doing these cool tricks. Trevor and his dad are building a freaking hover board. A hover board, Aunt Brooke. I have to turn in a paragraph on my project idea tomorrow, and I don't have one. I've been asking Mom to help me, but she never has time. She promised to do it with me tonight, but then she fell asleep."

"Oh my God," Brooke muttered, then closed her eyes, and framed her face with her hands. She pulled in a breath, blew it out, and said, "Okay, buddy, give me a minute. It's been a long day, and we all know I'm not that great on the fly. Let's think about this. Uuuuum…"

Keaton had heard countless friends and staff talk about this— their kids coming to them at the last minute with an assignment or project due the next day. In this case, it wasn't the child who'd procrastinated but the adult who didn't have the resources to provide the child the help he needed to do the work. And here this poor kid was, sick, up late, fighting to do his homework instead of blowing it off. That was a fighter. A kid with grit. One who could really make something of his life because he had the will. The determination. He also had a mom trying to get through nursing school to make a better life for all of them and an aunt who'd sacrificed part of her own happiness to provide security for him.

This was an amazing little family. And suddenly, Keaton felt selfish for wanting Brooke all to himself.

"I'm gonna fail…" Justin's pathetic wail pulled Keaton back and tugged at his heart. Especially when the kid started coughing. The raw sound made Keaton wince.

"Oh, come on. Stop," Brooke told him, but gave Keaton a helpless, pained look before telling Justin, "What about that one last year, where someone showed how a tooth disintegrated when it was left in a cup of Coke? You could do that…um, maybe. If you could get a hold of a tooth…"

Keaton made a face at the premise.

"Ew, Aunt Brooke…" Justin said.

"Okay, okay." She pressed her hands to her head. "It was just a suggestion. I'm still thinking. Take another hit on your inhaler, kid. Your Darth Vader impression is a little unnerving."

The combination of Justin's illness, the topic of a science fair, and her sister being asleep in the house was obviously unsettling for Brooke. Keaton didn't doubt she was also feeling the weight of another two months away from the boy on her shoulders right about now. If their situations were reversed, Keaton would be.

He reached out and clasped her foot, offering a reassuring squeeze.

She glanced at him and gave him a two-second smile, before telling Justin, "I'm not exactly a science genius. Maybe we should wake your mom."

That sounded like a cry for help to Keaton.

"You wouldn't say that if you saw the mood she was in before she fell asleep," Justin said.

Brooke laughed. "You can sound so old and wise one minute and like a whining two-year-old the next, you know that?"

"Whatever."

"And pissy teenager the next," she added.

"Mom doesn't like that word."

"I thought Mom was asleep."

While they sparred, Keaton found a notepad and pen, scribbled *What's he into?* and handed it to Brooke. Then he opened her iPad and googled science fair projects.

She handed back the answer. *Computers. Hates sports.*

Keaton nodded. With lungs like that, who could enjoy sports? Man, that made Keaton sad. He searched computer-related projects while Brooke and Justin continued to brainstorm a few minutes. But when the boy started coughing, the sound was so raw, it made Keaton pull his shoulders up around his ears and rub his chest.

"Baby, what's going on with your asthma?"

"You have to ask Mom."

"How long has it been this bad?"

"Just today."

"How long has it been getting a little worse every day?"

She'd obviously seen this pattern before, and Keaton was getting a deeper view of why she'd moved in with her sister. Brooke wasn't just a means of emotional support after the death of her brother-in-law. She obviously had a deep investment in her nephew, whose school and health took considerable time. Keaton's little fantasy of hooking Brooke enough to keep seeing him after his role in the movie was over, faded fast.

"Maybe a week?" Justin said.

"And your mom knows it's this bad?"

"Yeah. She talked to the doctors about it. They're trying something new. And before you ask what, I don't know. You really have to ask her."

Brooke sighed. "I want you to sleep in her room tonight."

"Oh, Aunt Br—"

"I know you hate it, but I hate the way you sound more. And if you don't sleep with your mom, I'm going to worry. If I worry, I'm not going to get any sleep. And I have to work tomorrow, buddy."

Keaton found a few video game–related projects and started scanning through them. He needed one the kid could do on his own, one that didn't cost much, one that didn't take much time…

Brooke got a long-suffering sigh from Justin, then a disgusted "Fine."

"Promise me."

"I promise. But I might not be sleeping anyway. I *need* a project."

Keaton spun the iPad toward her and pointed at the screen.

"Hold on. Might have found…" She scanned it, her brow furrowed, and she gave him a confused, are-you-crazy look. "What…?"

He smirked and lifted a shoulder.

"What?" Justin echoed, drawing her attention again. "Is someone with you?"

Which earned Keaton the most adorable look-what-you've-done look from Brooke before she told Justin, "I'm just chatting with a friend online. I'm going to put you on hold a second while I talk with them about this to see if it will work for you."

"Okay."

Brooke tapped a button and set the phone aside so she was out of the camera's view and groaned, covering her face with both hands. "I don't know how parents *do* it. He's so damn smart, it takes everything both Tammy and I have just to keep up with him." She scraped her fingers through her hair and scanned screen Keaton had pointing to. "I don't know anything about computer games. What's this?"

"It's an intermediate-level project studying animation and how its structure and implementation affects the viewer's perception of action in the game."

Brooke's eyes glazed over, and she gave him a pained look. "You lost me at intermediate."

Keaton grinned and shook his head. "He's a boy, he's into video games, and he's a brain. Trust me, he'll like this."

"Fine, whatever." She waved her hand over the screen as if to clear the whole idea from her mind. "You obviously speak his language. Why don't you just explain it—"

"Because you need to be the one to help him. He called you for help, and you need to be there for him and answer that call. It doesn't matter what source you get the answers from, what matters is that you bring the answer back to him."

Her eyes closed, and her breath leaked out. "I'm so tired."

"I know. This is going to be easy. I promise."

He gave her a quick rundown of the information available on the site and how Justin could use it to get his paragraph due tomorrow finished in ten minutes. Then Justin could dig deeper into the information to start building the project. And he told Brooke to give Justin his cell number and email to contact for support.

"And if he wants to whip the pants off that school, all I have to do is whisper the words 'secret project' to Rubi, and all hell will break loose."

Mention of their friend and computer guru Rubi Russo, girlfriend to Renegade Wes Lawson, made Brooke break out in laughter. "Oh my God. Rubi would probably make the animations come to life."

Smiling, Keaton cupped Brooke's face and stroked her cheek. "That's better." He kissed her forehead. "Now tell Justin what to do, and then tell him to get his sick ass to bed. Because you need to get your tired ass to bed."

Keaton stayed there while she explained the project to Justin, his hand covering one foot, his thumb massaging her instep. He had to hold back his laughter at Justin's excitement over the project idea, the amount of information on the website, and the fact that Brooke had a stuntman on call to help Justin out.

"Oh my God, Aunt Brooke, this is going to be the best project ever."

Both she and Keaton were smiling, but the sound of Justin's voice when it strained with excitement made them wince.

"Okay, okay. Ten minutes to write a few sentences, then bed. With Mom."

"Okay." He didn't sound as upset about it anymore. "Thanks, Aunt Brooke. You're the best. I love you."

Brooke's eyes sparkled with joy. "I love you too. Tell your

mom to call me tomorrow, okay?"

He promised he would, and they disconnected.

Brooke sighed. "Disaster averted." Her gaze swung to Keaton's and held. "Thank you. You saved the day and made me look like the hero at the same time."

"Oh, baby, you are definitely the hero." He shook his head. "I don't know how *you* do it."

"I'm not going to say it's easy, but's it's definitely worth every minute."

"I didn't fully appreciate how much Justin and your sister depend on you until just now. I'd just like to see you working for someone who makes you happy, or at least doesn't make you miserable. It's hard to imagine you couldn't find someone who would pay you—"

"Like I said, it's complicated."

"Explain it to me."

She heaved a breath. "I told you, Jillian pays me well. Still not enough to put up with her bullshit, but it doesn't matter, because I know how difficult it would be to find another job that pays me this well, or one that lets me live in Florida. And we *need* the money."

The way she said "need" told Keaton the financial situation wasn't just tight, it was dire. "Living is cheap in Florida. At least compared to California or New York where most big actors and actresses live. If Jillian pays you so well, the three of you should be able to live comfortably off what you make, even without Tammy working."

"It would be for normal, healthy people. But we're not normal, and Justin's not healthy."

It took Keaton a second to connect Justin's poor health with money problems. This was completely outside his healthy bachelor-oriented mind. "What do you mean? Justin doesn't have health insurance? Can't *everyone* get health insurance? Isn't that why we pay all those goddamned taxes?" Keaton stretched his mind to understand, but couldn't. "Don't all states have programs for kids whose families don't have the money for health insurance?"

"Like I said, it's complicated." She heaved a breath, the sound a combination of resignation and frustration. "When Tammy's husband died, she took the extension policy Brian's company offered to bridge the gap until she could find another solution. But the initial stress of Brian's death took a toll on Justin's system, and he got really sick. The gap policy had high deductibles and didn't cover some of Justin's medications."

Keaton's whole view shifted. His mouth dropped open. His breath left his lungs. "Oh, shit…"

"Between Justin's doctor visits, his treatments, his meds, and his hospital stays, the life insurance Brian had was gone in a matter of months. When she went for public aid, she was told she didn't qualify because the life insurance was considered income and put her above the need threshold. And because the system looks at your income for the previous calendar year to evaluate need, that meant Tammy and Justin would go uncovered for an entire year before she would qualify for coverage."

Keaton's stomach knotted and he rubbed his face with both hands. "You weren't fucking kidding. This is worse than complicated."

"Justin's been sick since the day he was born. Tammy never had a chance to go to school or start a career. She couldn't go out and get a job that would have paid enough to cover the specialty childcare he would have needed, let alone provided decent health insurance. She called me in California, bawling her eyes out because she got an eviction notice and was going to be out on the street in a matter of days. She'd stopped paying rent so she could hold on to the health insurance. She was terrified she'd be living on the streets with a sick kid. Terrified the courts would take him away from her. She never even had a chance to mourn Brian because she was always putting out fires and trying to take care of Justin."

"Jesus Christ." Keaton sank to the edge of the bed. The impossible situation crippled his mind. He couldn't even imagine a life so limited. "Is he covered now?"

"Yes. Ellie gave me the money to get them stabilized. When I got there, we found a little ramshackle house for the three of us. We found a better insurance policy that would cover Justin's meds and treatments, but it costs as much as the rent on the dump where we live every month."

"Which is why you took the highest paying job."

"And it's also why I can't lose this job. Because Justin was recently accepted into the final round of possible candidates for a research study. If he can get in, he'll get a procedure that, until now, has been reserved for adults with asthma. The doctors go into the bronchial tree with a laser and burn some of the lining out, making more room for air to flow. It's permanent and could promise Justin his only shot at a normal life."

Hope flared inside Keaton. "That's incredible."

"It is, but it's also expensive."

Keaton smacked a hand to his forehead and groaned. This family couldn't catch a break.

"Experimental procedures aren't covered by any insurance company," Brooke said. "Participation is an out-of-pocket expense."

"I'm afraid to ask, but..." He winced. "How much?"

She sighed. "The procedure alone, which is done in three different stages with a month in between each, costs twenty thousand."

"Ouch."

"Then there are additional medications and follow-up visits. We also have to agree to keep Justin in the study for the entire year so the researchers can gather their test data. In the end, it ends up costing sixty grand."

Keaton's mouth dropped open. "Holy shit."

"And to show we're committed, we have to pay half up front."

"Oh my God, Brooke..." Keaton had no words.

"I almost have it saved. I'm really close. A couple more paychecks and we'll have half. The rest can be paid over the course of the treatment, which will still make life tight for us. But after that year, Tammy will be out of school. She'll get a well-paying job with benefits, and she'll be able to stand on her own the rest of her life. She'll be able to provide for Justin until he can provide for himself. But I have to *get them there*. And if that means putting up with Jillian twelve more months, then I cross every day off on a calendar with a big black sharpie and suck it up."

"Jesus." He exhaled the word and sagged on the bed until he pressed his forehead to her foot. "I can't even imagine."

"So, now you know why I did what I did today," she said, her voice soft and sad. "And why we can't keep seeing each other."

He lifted his head. "What?"

"You're right. If we keep doing this behind her back, Jillian will eventually figure it out. We should have ended things this morning anyway. It's temporary, and our friendship—even if we only see each other occasionally—does mean a lot to me."

"Whoa. Slow down. Back up." His gut tightened. "When did we decide this was temporary?"

"What do you mean?" She stared at him with a confused look. "Temporary is all you do."

He pushed upright. "That's all I *did*."

She shook her head. "Did you hear any of what I just said?"

"Did *you* just hear me say I don't want to let you go?"

Anger and fear pushed his voice up a few octaves, and his words continued to ring in the silence. Their gazes held, and for the length of two extended heartbeats, Keaton wasn't sure who was more stunned by his admission—Brooke or himself.

Fear burned a circuit through his body, then vanished, mellowing instantly into warmth. Yeah. He was sure. He pushed himself up and slid his hand around her neck. Her eyes were still shocked and now watering.

"Brooke, I didn't mean to yell. I just… I've never, you know, done this before, so I'm probably not going to be very good at it for a while."

She closed her eyes, and tears spilled over her lashes. Fucking perfect, he'd made her cry. But she leaned into him, pressed her face to his shoulder, and wrapped her arms around his neck. And now Keaton's eyes stung. He pulled her onto his lap, rolling his eyes to the ceiling to banish the burn.

"Baby, you're different. You're special," he said into her hair. "I care about you, and I don't want to hurt either you or Justin. But, baby, I don't want to just let you go without trying either."

She sighed against his neck. Her body softened, and she melted against him. The feeling was so heavenly, Keaton moaned.

"How often do you get to Austin?" he asked her.

"This is our first trip."

"Does Jillian have the next year scheduled yet?"

"Mostly." She lifted her head and looked at him. Her dark lashes were clumped with wetness the way they had been in the shower and made her eyes look even bluer. "Where are you going to be?"

The fact that she asked shot a thrill through his heart. "Here until the other stunt guy comes back, then LA until they start filming here again, which will be about three months. In those three months, I'll probably be working close to home. Then between here and LA for the following three to four months of filming. Rinse. Repeat."

"I know Jillian's going to be in LA a few times, but I'd have to look at her calendar to know when." She sounded tired, but she was still talking. "I know we're in Vegas in a few months. I think we're filming somewhere in the Midwest in the winter…" She heaved a sigh, her shoulders sank, and she shook her head. "Keaton, this is so unrealistic…"

"Like you moving in with your sister and nephew, and paying all their bills to provide them with a place to live and the opportunity to live happy, successful lives? I bet that didn't sound very realistic when the idea came up either. But I know you're doing it, and I know it works. You don't plan to do it long-term, right? But it works for now."

When she didn't argue, he said, "Tell me this." He paused, mentally preparing himself for an answer he didn't want to hear. "Do you care about me enough to want something beyond temporary?"

Her eyes fell closed in a look of pain, and Keaton's protective wall started to crumble. But when she looked at him again, so much affection floated in her eyes, his heart flipped a somersault. "I have been crazy about you for a very, *very* long time There is nothing temporary about my feelings for you."

That made Keaton's lungs release a breath he hadn't known he'd been holding. Made a shaky smile ease the tension in his face. Filled his chest with joy and sent a calming warmth into his belly. He gathered her close, and rocked her, releasing a relieved breath.

Then fell back on the bed with her, stroked her hair off her forehead, and kissed her. "Then let's not worry about the rest right now." He ran his fingers over her cheek, twined his legs with hers, and just enjoyed looking at her beautiful face without a stitch of makeup. So fresh and real and honest. "We'll just have to manage as many rendezvous as necessary to keep us going until our situation changes."

Eight

The parking lot's disintegrating asphalt crunched beneath Brooke's sandals as she crossed the yard housing the actors' trailers.

She headed toward Jillian's trailer with her cell at her ear, her sister's groggy voice answering, "Hello."

"Oh my God, I'm sorry," Brooke said. "I didn't realize you'd be sleeping. I'll call back."

"No, it's fine." Tammy yawned. "I was up with Justin. How's the she-devil treating you?

"Same as always, but I have a little reprieve. She's got meetings all morning." Brooke glanced at her watch. She had at least three more hours before Jillian would be back. "I talked to Justin last night, and he sounded awful. That's why I was calling. I wanted to find out what the doctors figured out. He told me they were changing his medications? Trying something new? But he couldn't say what. Told me I had to ask you. And, God, Tammy, he sounded awful. It broke my heart to hear him like that again."

"I know. It's a hard transition."

"Transition to what?"

"That's the good news. I heard sooner than I expected. He was accepted into the first stage of the children's program for the bronchial thermoplasty. In anticipation of that, the doctors changed his medication, and that always throws him."

Brooke's feet stopped dead in the shadow of the trailer. She gasped, and a balloon of excitement instantly filled her chest. "Oh my God. He got in? Tammy, that's *fantastic.*" In the next breath, she said, "Why don't you sound more excited?"

"Probably because I'm exhausted. And because when I looked over the final documentation for the study, I discovered just how strict the guidelines are. He has to pass every segment of the study to continue on and get all three procedures."

When Tammy outlined all the hurdles, Brooke's excitement waned a little too. "You medical people," she teased. "You're all Debbie Downers, you know that?"

Tammy laughed again. "More like Realist Rosies. It's just part of the program—literally. And Justin's been through so much already. I don't want to get his hopes up with such high chances that he might not make it through—especially when he has no control over whether he makes it or doesn't."

"How frustrating," Brooke said. "This is supposed to be exciting."

"It *is* exciting. They're only taking fifty kids into this study, so the fact that he got in is all *very* exciting."

Brooke smiled and climbed the stairs to the trailer. "Yeah, I guess it is."

She pulled the door open, took the last two steps into the luxurious space—far nicer than the house Brooke rented with Tammy and Justin—and her gaze immediately drifted to a vase of vivid red roses on the granite counter in the kitchenette.

"Justin told me about the science fair project you helped him figure out," Tammy said. "Thank you for doing that. You have been such a lifesaver this year. You know when you leave, he's going to want to move with you, right? I think he's forgotten which one of us is his mom."

Brooke almost ignored the flowers but then saw a tall cardboard coffee cup and a pastry bag sitting in front of the crystal vase. Flowers for Jillian were common. Coffee and pastry were not. In fact, that was downright odd.

"Oh, stop. I'm the one who keeps leaving him for all these stupid trips. You're the one who's there with him every day. That's what really matters."

Brooke tucked the phone between her shoulder and cheek and peeked into the pastry bag. A note blocked the view of the pastry.

She pulled it out, and even before she read the note, she recognized the handwriting from the night before when Keaton had scribbled on the Four Seasons tablet.

For an extra sweet start to your day.

Her heart swelled and ached. Brooke laughed softly. Extra was right. He'd already started her day off as sweetly as possible by showing her just how many different kinds of sex he specialized in, and made sweet love to her before he'd disappeared from her room at daybreak.

"Brooke?"

"Hmm?" she said, tuning in to her sister's voice. "Listen, I'd better go. Lots of work to finish before the She Wolf returns to the den—"

"Not before you tell me about the stunt guy."

Brooke froze and thought back, wondering if she'd said something aloud to tip Tammy off about Keaton. "Uuuuh...?"

"Man, your head is really somewhere else." Tammy laughed. "The stunt guy you said Justin could call for help? He is so pumped over that. And I know you wouldn't give him just anyone's number, so what's the scoop?"

Brooke slid the note into the pocket of her jean shorts, then leaned in to smell the roses. Their rich scent instantly improved her mood. "Do you remember that guy I told you about from LA?"

"The one who's friends with Ellie's guy. The one you were hoping to hook up with before you moved?"

Brooke had told her sister about Keaton months after her move during one of those late nights, long after Justin had fallen asleep and the two of them had polished off a bottle of wine.

"Yeah, him. He's here. The project idea for Justin was actually his. So if Justin runs into problems, Keaton's happy to talk him through as much as he can. And if Justin gets stuck with any programming problems, we've got Rubi on call."

"Whoa, whoa, whoa," Tammy said. "We'll get to Rubi in a minute. Let's go back to Keaton. What's going on there?"

Brooke exhaled, nervous to talk about it, almost as if it would jinx their possibility at happiness. She also didn't like having to put everything into concrete words, because then it all became so unrealistic again. "I'm not sure. We're both interested, but there are a lot of roadblocks. The biggest of those right now being Jillian."

"Jillian? How is that bitch a roadblock?"

Brooke winced and closed her eyes. "She slept with Keaton once upon a time."

"Ew."

"It was a long time ago."

"Okay. I'll give him a pass on one ding. How is that creating a problem now?"

"She still wants him."

"God, that woman…" Tammy took an audible breath and let it out slowly. "Well, on the upside, that means he's über hot, or she would pretend he doesn't exist like she does with everyone she has no use for. But, yes, that could be a real problem."

Brooke heard the underlying guilt in her sister's voice and purposely forced herself to be positive. "But not your problem, because we're handling it. Keaton and I are on the same page. He doesn't want to do anything that could hurt Justin, so we're keeping things between us quiet. And to be honest, Tammy, I don't even really know what's between us. He's not a serious kind of guy, if you know what I mean. He's always been a typical breed in this industry."

"So were Jax and Wes and Troy—until they found the right woman. And not so typical if he's willing to hide in the shadows to protect a kid he's never met."

That was a good point. "One day at a time," Brooke told her sister. "Hug Justin for me, and keep me posted."

"If you'll give Keaton your all."

Brooke grinned. "I'll take that deal."

Before she'd said good-bye, the door to the trailer swung open, and Jillian stepped in, startling Brooke. She turned her back on the flowers, coffee, and pastry with a streak of fear shooting up her spine.

"Oh my God, Jillian." She pressed her phone to her heart, frowning at her boss's sudden appearance. "What are you doing here? You should be in a meeting with Phil Shriver."

"Phil canceled," Jillian said, her distracted gaze roaming the space. "Something about a sick brat at home. And Copalli wants to add in a shoot this afternoon."

Shit. Anxious to get her out of the trailer, Brooke turned her attention to her phone. "Let me call Jeannette and see when she and Percy can get you into hair and makeup—"

"The security guard said Keaton brought something in here earlier today

Fire filled Brooke's belly. Her mouth fell open to lie, but Jillian took the last step into the trailer and Brooke knew she'd never be able to hide the gifts from her boss.

While Brooke was still trying to figure out how she was going to spin this, Jillian pointed at the table behind Brooke. "What's that?"

Fuck.

Brooke pushed her mouth into a smile, stepped aside, and did her best Vanna White impression. "Your surprise."

Jillian 's eyes sparked to life. But as she approached the table her expression slowly soured. She propped a hand on her hip. "Is that it?"

"What do you mean?"

Jillian made an air circle around the gift. "That. Is that all he left?"

All? Brooke wasn't sure if she wanted to laugh or slap Jillian. She shrugged. "I just got here."

"Was there a card?"

"No. No card."

Jillian pursed her lips in one of those how-disappointing expressions. "Men." She shook her head. "Oh well. He'll make up for it in bed. He always does."

That grated along Brooke's already exposed nerves. "Oh, yeah? I've never had a guy like that."

At least not until Keaton. And she wondered for a distracted moment if she'd ever find another.

"Oh, honey." She gave Brooke a condescending, pitying look. "They're the only kind of guy worth spreading your legs for."

The image of Jillian spreading her legs for Keaton made Brooke's breakfast roll toward her throat. She shook it from her head and tapped into her phone. "If you say so. Let me give Jeannette a call—"

"I've already talked to her," Jillian said. The edge in her voice exposed her annoyance with Brooke's dismissal of a topic her boss obviously wasn't done talking about. "Keaton may not look like much in the grubby clothes he wears on the set. But, oh"—her voice turned dreamy and dripped with lust—"that man is a dark Adonis in a tux. Hair cut and styled, clean-shaven, smiling, those perfect teeth contrasting against his skin , those dark eyes of his twinkling with mischief…" Jillian put a hand over her abdomen and sighed a moan. "The man is irresistible." She tilted her head and smiled at Brooke. "I may not be the only woman who thinks so, but I'm determined to be the woman keeping his off-hours occupied during the next eight weeks. I'll have to talk to Copalli about holding him on the movie." Her gaze went distant as she pulled the top off the coffee meant for Brooke and lifted it toward her mouth. "The real trick will be keeping the other sluts' hands off him."

Brooke's stomach twisted tighter. "You don't think he can be a one-woman man?"

Jillian sipped from the coffee, made a disgusted face. "Godawful. That man is going to have to become my sexual slave to make up for this. She dumped the coffee in the sink, and Brooke fisted her hands in anger. "As for being a one-woman man, I couldn't care less. I only want him to distract me during this shoot. Besides, he's in his prime. And I mean *prime*. He's young, he has plenty of money, no responsibilities, and an exciting career. He travels everywhere, rubs elbows with all the most famous and wealthy, and the most beautiful women all over the world want to sleep with him—because he is truly a hell of a fuck. And unlike in the movies, that's a lot harder to find than you think. Oh, yes, he's the whole package." She met Brooke's gaze. "If you were him, would you want to settle for one woman? I wouldn't."

Brooke didn't know. She'd seen the uglier side of that beautiful fast life, and it didn't suit everyone. She and Ellie were perfect examples. Of course, they were also women. After so many years on the road with Ellie, behind the scenes in the music world, Brooke thought she'd seen a lot. Then she'd been introduced to Hollywood and realized she hadn't seen the half of it.

Now she wondered if she was being naïve by letting Keaton sweet-talk her into investing too much of her heart, when he really didn't know what it took to make a relationship work. When he himself admitted he'd never done anything but temporary before. Who was to say that in one of the millions of lonely moments they would spend apart, he wouldn't simply say yes to one of those hundreds of beautiful women who hit on him? And who was Brooke to ask him not to? These were the best years of his life. He should be out doing everything he ever wanted to do, not struggling to fit in a sketchy rendezvous with a part-time girlfriend on the fly.

"Is that what went wrong between you two?" Now Brooke's gut burned. She opened her iPad and clicked into Jillian's schedule to keep her hands busy and hide the emotions rising to the surface. "Why it didn't work out? Because he was always looking for the next woman?"

"Keaton?" Jillian asked, laughing softly. "No. Most men with his looks and confidence and swagger know they hold the keys to the kingdom." Jillian ran her fingertips over the edges of the rose petals. "They lie, they manipulate, and they use. They play games to keep themselves entertained at the expense of others. But Keaton has always been…just Keaton, which is probably why he's held my interest so long."

A strange discomfort settled in Brooke's chest. She opened her mouth to change the subject, but Jillian spoke again.

"Yesterday, for example. He didn't pull any punches when I tried to turn on the charm. He doesn't like me because I've spent my life acting much the way all those other people act. Any other man in that studio would have hugged me back, made a date for drinks, schmoozed me up and down." She lifted her brows at Brooke. "I am a movie star, you know."

"Then…you're in it for the chase?" Brooke frowned, confused by Jillian's perspective. "Why chase if you already know he doesn't like you?"

"Oh no." Jillian laughed, low and husky. "Hell no. This isn't about the chase. This is all about the catch. This is about the sex. And the sooner I get that boy into my bed, the better. He may think he's above all the bullshit that goes on in this business, but underneath that upstanding, solid, honorable facade, he's still a man. A man with a voracious sexual appetite. And I'm still the most gorgeous woman within a fifty-mile radius—maybe more. Even a forthright, tell-it-like-it-is, no-sugar-coating, up-front guy like Keaton wants to get laid. And the hotter the woman, the better."

Laughter bubbled up inside Brooke. Jillian might be beautiful on the outside, but inside, she was as ugly as a tar pit. And so damn superficial she couldn't even see there were people who valued inner beauty more than the outer beauty. "So, you think he'll overlook the fact that he doesn't like you or the way you operate, just to fuck you because you're beautiful?"

"Hell yes. He did it once, didn't he?"

"Once?" Brooke tried not to sound accusatory. "I thought you said you reconnected with him a month ago."

"I did. Just not the way I would have liked. I plan to change that this time around."

A knock on the door broke into Brooke's thoughts.

"That's Jeannette," Jillian said without making any move toward the door. "Percy's coming right after to do my hair."

Brooke moved to the door, greeted Jeannette, and stepped aside to let the slender woman in her fifties pass through the tight space so she could set up at the dining table.

"Where are you filming?" Brooke asked.

"Warehouse B."

Good. That meant Brooke could hang out in warehouse A and watch Keaton work. The thought made her smile. She could watch Keaton all day long and never get bored.

"Run along," Jillian said, dismissing Brooke like a child. "And double-check my massage, manicure, and pedicure appointments for tomorrow. I don't want anything to go wrong with my spa day after a hard work week."

The woman's condescension after she'd just confided in her like a quasi-friend fried Brooke's last nerve. She wanted to tell her boss a hard work week was spending two shifts on your feet at the hospital taking care of others, another twenty hours in the classroom cramming information into your brain, another thirty studying everything you'd learned over and over, and the remainder of the time raising your severely asthmatic, terribly brilliant eight-year-old when you had to calculate how much you could spend on dinner every night so you didn't run out of money before you could get a full-time job. With no fucking spa day in sight.

Instead, she offered a dutiful "Of course," exited the trailer, and headed straight toward the person who always made her feel better. About everything.

* * * *

Keaton wiped his hands on a towel and slipped his gloves back on. He glanced up and found Brooke still sitting off in a corner, talking on the phone, her face illuminated by the screen of her iPad.

He wished he had his phone so he could text her right now. Ask her to go out to dinner with him tonight. He wanted to take her somewhere nice. Somewhere she could wear a pretty dress and heels. Where they could get a bottle of wine and appetizers and sit for hours. Talk and eat and laugh and hold hands and kiss.

But it was just as well that he didn't have his phone. Because he couldn't ask her to do that. There were too many members of various film crews swarming this town to risk someone seeing them alone together. They couldn't chance starting a rumor. Their rendezvous would have to be private for the time being, which was fine with Keaton. There was nothing he wanted more. But he also wanted Brooke to know that this was about more than just sex for him. That he'd meant what he'd said last night.

Cameron came up to Keaton and offered him a bottle of water. Keaton took it and tipped it to his mouth, drinking deep.

The stagehand belaying the ropes for Keaton's fight sequence, Russ, approached to get Cam's news.

"Our stunt double's currently stuck in the Calgary airport," Cam said, taking a swig from his own water. "Her plane needs a part for the tail. And since it's a Swedish airline, and it seems there is only one of these parts currently in existence, take one guess where that part has to come from."

"You're fuckin' kidding me," Keaton said.

"Nope. And that one thing is backing up all the flights, so she can't get even get a decent standby spot until tomorrow."

"Where's FedEx when you need 'em?" Russ asked.

Cameron laughed. "She'll be here tomorrow." He looked at the set, then told Keaton, "I guess we could just skip over that part of the stunt and practice the ending fight."

"The last fight is easy. We barely need a run-through to be ready there. I want to get this film back on schedule."

Russ scratched his head and glanced around the warehouse. "What about pulling in a replacement? We've got a lot of fresh meat to choose from."

Keaton thought about that for a moment. He glanced at the

maze of metal, then scanned the catwalk to the jump point. From there his gaze darted to the landing point. "For you to get the pull on the ropes just right," he told Russ, "it would have to be someone very close to Jillian's weight. Otherwise, we'd be wasting our time. And Jillian's skin and bones."

"She's not that small," Russ said. "She's tall, so her weight is distributed, but I'd bet she weighs a solid one hundred and twenty. She was in here yesterday bragging about her weight-lifting routine."

Keaton huffed. Whatever. He wasn't even going there.

"Okay, who have we got?" Cam said, turning to scan the other staff and crew. "Alana? Grace? Hell, I don't think Mack weighs over a hundred and ten."

Keaton's gaze darted to Brooke. She was perfect. And just the thought of hooking her into safety lines and flying across the warehouse with her gave his belly a tingle. She would love it. But they were keeping their distance at work. So he said, "Sure, any one of those should—"

"I'd rather not use Mack," Russ told them. "Men are just denser than women, and it may sound weird, but I've worked these cables a long time, and there's a difference when I try to lift them. I think Alana's about twenty pounds too heavy, and Grace is a serious lightweight. She might be ninety-eight pounds soaking wet."

Keaton heaved a breath and rubbed a hand over his face, then pointed to a young intern. "There's Logan."

"Nah, too heavy." Russ said. "Hey, didn't I see Brooke over there in the corner? She's just about right."

There was no "about" to it. Brooke was perfect—in more ways than how her weight would work for this stunt. But Keaton wanted to keep her just right, so he said "She wouldn't be interested—"

"How do you know, man?" Cam said. "You haven't even asked. Yo, Brooke," he called before Keaton could stop him. She looked up. "Can you come over for a second?"

She hesitated, glanced around the warehouse, then stood and started toward them. She'd dressed down today—casual Friday, she'd told him last night—in jean shorts and a sleeveless blouse that gently followed the curves of her breasts and abdomen, stopping just beyond the low waistband of her jeans, teasing Keaton into believing he'd get a glimpse of skin if she moved just the right way.

The filtered sun from the skylights above created an ethereal halo around her. Her sandals made the softest clip, clip, clip across the cement and sparkled in the scattered light. She'd pulled her hair up into a ponytail, played down her makeup, and looked so fuckin' adorable, Keaton wanted to eat her alive. He wanted to take her somewhere tropical and secluded where she could dress in string bikinis—or nothing—twenty-four hours a day. Where they could lose themselves in each other for an entire month. In fact, he never wanted to let anything get between them again.

She slipped her hands into her pockets and came to a stop in front of them with a sweet smile on her beautiful face, her bright eyes alight with her characteristic eagerness to please. Keaton's heart rolled in his chest. He'd found his girl. His very own perfect match, the same way so many of his Renegades buddies had finally found theirs. He knew it with complete certainty, and the realization created an effervescent sizzle over his skin.

In that moment, as she shared a secret smile with him, everything inside Keaton calmed. And with all the chaos quieted, his emotions came forward, taking center stage, telling him that Brooke wasn't just his girl. Brooke was *The One*.

"What's up, guys?" she asked. "Can I grab you some water? Do you need a lunch run?"

"No, no," Cam said. "We actually need you right here."

"Um." She smiled, shrugged. "Okay."

"Not if you're in the middle of something," Keaton added. When she met his gaze, he said, "We know your work for Jillian comes first."

A smiled lifted her lips, and she gave him the slightest nod. "I'm okay there." Then to Russ, she asked, "What do you need?"

Keaton watched her expression as Russ explained the stunt. Her gaze met Keaton's, searching for security, then lifted to the catwalk, twenty feet in the air, and followed it to the end. "Out there? You want me to stand out there?"

"You really don't—" Keaton started, but she put up her hand.

"I'm just asking questions."

Cam shoulder-cocked Keaton a couple of steps sideways, then put a hand in the middle of his back and shoved. "Let's find a harness that will fit her."

Keaton twisted to knock Cam's hand away, and found his

fellow Renegade grinning. "What are you smiling about?"

"Never seen you caught up in a chick. It's fuckin' funny, man."

"Shut up. And don't even think about starting that rumor."

"Are you kidding?" Cam said, bending to pop the top on an equipment vault. "The way that cougar licks her chops when you're around? She'd eat Brooke as an appetizer on her way to you. I may be young, but I'm not stupid. I saw that triangle when Brooke and Jillian stepped in the door and both of them looked at you."

Cam pulled out a harness, tossed it aside, searched through, and grabbed another. Keaton knew this gear blindfolded. He pushed his hand into the dredges of the container, felt around, and pulled their smallest harness from the bottom.

Cam stood back, his face slack with awe. "How the fuck do you do that?"

"Practice. Years and years of practice." He looked up at Cam. "Can other people see it?"

"What? That the cougar has a hard-on for you? Or that Brooke is head over heels?"

Head over heels? Keaton darted a look over his shoulder. Russ was talking a blue streak, but Brooke didn't look like she was paying attention. She had a dreamy smile on her face, and her gaze was fixed on Keaton. The look ignited a burst of heat at the center of his body. One that filled his heart.

God, he hoped Cam was right. It would make getting Brooke to work with him on figuring out how to narrow their damn three-thousand-mile gap.

"Never mind," Keaton told Cam. He stood and closed the gap between them. "Just make sure you keep your mouth shut. Jillian will fire Brooke if she thinks there's something going on between us, and Brooke needs this job for reasons I can't explain right now."

"Sure, man. Okay. I get it."

"Not a word."

"Less than a word," Cam said, serious. "I understand confidentiality."

Keaton's vision cleared, and he saw the steadfast, confident, former marine standing in front of him instead of his happy-go-lucky fellow Renegade.

"I've got your back, dude," Cam said. "And I like Brooke."

"I know you do." Keaton exhaled. "I'm sorry. This situation

sucks."

Cam brought up his smile. "Brooke seems like the kind of chick who would dig this stunt."

Keaton laughed. "She is."

"Then let's have some fun."

When they returned with the harness, Russ was still explaining the stunt's short clip, walking her through the steps. By the time they returned to center stage, Russ moved off to talk with the cameramen, Cam grabbed cables, and Keaton fitted Brooke's harness.

"This is really a lot like zip-lining," he told her, fastening the straps along her ribs, lowering his voice to murmur, "Damn you smell good."

"I've never been zip-lining. And so do you."

"I do not," he laughed. "I'm sweaty and disgusting."

"I like you sweaty."

Her hungry whisper shivered down Keaton's spine.

He met her eyes, their blue hue bright and sparkling with mischief and desire. "I like you making me sweaty."

He finished with the last buckle and asked, "You've really never been zip-lining?"

"Nope."

"Okay, well, I kind of under-exaggerated anyway. It's really like zip-lining on drugs. If this feels overwhelming at any time, you just tell me and we'll stop."

He crouched to pull another strap between her legs and fasten it behind her. She turned her head and gave him that sexy smile. "I'm excited."

Grinning, he checked the harness over and over. Every clip, every buckle, every tie.

Cam came up behind her and hooked cables to the D-rings on the back of the harness. "I think someone's got that spark of adrenaline in her eyes."

She laughed. "I don't know about that." She ran her hands over the harness. "It's fun to watch, and I'm excited to try it, but...I'll leave the everyday life-defying acts to you guys."

"Have fun," Cam said before he moved to Russ's side off stage.

"Hey, where's your phone?" Keaton asked her.

"Oh, right." She pulled it from her back pocket. "Probably shouldn't have this on me."

"It would be cool to have one of the crew video it so you can show it to Justin."

"Oh my God." Her eyes lit up, followed by a gorgeous smile. "Great idea."

"God I want to kiss you so bad right now," he murmured.

Her gaze went soft, and her eyes lowered to his mouth. "I wish."

"Where's Jillian?" he asked, taking Brooke's phone.

"Next door, filming."

He nodded, then called to a stagehand. "Mack." He offered Brooke's phone. "Can you get a couple of good clips of this run-through for Brooke's nephew?"

"Sure."

Everyone moved back into position, and Keaton took Brooke's hand as she climbed the stairs to the catwalk. Since they weren't filming today, there was no director around to tell them what to do, so Keaton walked her to the end of the platform and up the steps at the end that led to nowhere and dropped off into nothing.

"Whoa," she said with a tight laugh as she reached the end. "Why does this look so much higher from up here?"

"Always does." He pointed at the blue mat covering the floor below. "If you fall, it's like a pillow."

"If you say so."

"I'm going to race down this ramp, jump these stairs, grab you, and launch myself across the opening and to the other side." He pointed to the other half of the ramp, which had been displaced six feet higher. The cables are going to help me make that leap. The finesse comes in on the landing. I need to land on the lip of that top step to start the next fight scene. Which is why practicing with the right weight is important for both the crew and me. Then we'll all know exactly what we need to do to make the landing right with the fewest takes. When the stuntwoman gets here tomorrow, we can film and move on."

"Okay, got it."

"I'm going to be coming at you hard and fast. I might knock the wind out of you."

She laughed softly, and her eyes heated. "I know the feeling, and I could never get enough of it."

A buzz kicked up in his belly. "Man, I like the sound of that. So, are you okay? Are you ready?"

"I'm always ready for you."

He laughed, joy sizzling through his veins. "Baby, you've got me juiced."

"Then let's do this."

He positioned her looking out at the warehouse and curled her fingers around the thin railing. "Don't hold tight, okay? You've got to let go when I grab you."

She nodded.

Keaton jogged back to his starting point He would never have believed having Brooke on the other end of a stunt with him could have brought such a thrill. But he was seriously stoked.

"We're ready," Russ called.

"Ready here," repeated the cameraman who'd be taking the test film.

"Here we go," Cam called.

Keaton shifted on his feet, scraped his running shoes against the metal until they gripped, and dropped into a ready crouch with his gaze on Brooke. And he definitely had a little extra fire burning at the center of his chest.

"Ready..." Cam said. "And... Go."

Keaton dug in and pushed into a sprint. He used his breath to take him the distance strong and fast. As he approached Brooke, he noticed everything in split seconds even though it was all happening at once—the whites of her eyes as they widened, the way her body tensed just before impact, the way her head ducked and her eyes scrunched closed as he grabbed her.

Her squeal vibrated in the air as he locked her body against his with one arm and launched from the top step with complete and utter faith in the men handling the ropes. And just as his foot left the rail, his harness pulled, his body lifted, and the cables carried him upward.

But Keaton immediately knew the guys handling the cables had used too much strength, and he and Brooke overshot the platform.

"Dammit," he muttered as they swung back toward the main stage. But as they dangled like a pendulum on their way to the ground, he added, "Oh, well, that just means we get to do it again. And again, and again, and again until we get it right." He tightened the arm at her waist, pulling her ass into his groin where heat and sensation tingled through his cock. "I'm all about getting it just right."

She sighed a little moan and slid her hand over his arm. Turning her head a little, she asked, "Are you going to get a break? I really want a secret little rendezvous with you right now."

Her eyes were wide and excited, her cheeks flushed, and her heartbeat pounded quick and hard against her ribs beneath his arm. The only thing that distinguished between fear and thrill was the sparkling smile cutting across her face.

"Uh-oh..." he teased, smiling at her. "Do I have a little adrenaline junkie on my hands?"

"I don't know about an adrenaline junkie, but you might have a nympho. Because, wow, that is a serious turn-on."

That struck a funny bone, and Keaton threw his head back and laughed. Which made Brooke laugh. They were just setting their feet on the ground and catching their breath when Keaton said, "Can you get away tonight? If we go out of town, we could find a place for dinner—"

"What in the hell is going on?"

Brooke's whole body went rigid at the sound of Jillian's harsh voice, and she whispered a tight, *"Fuck."*

The sound of her voice saturated in dread lifted the hair on the back of Keaton's neck. Cameron was already approaching Jillian with his all-American country-boy charm to explain the delay with the stuntwoman as Russ approached Keaton and Brooke.

"Let us take the heat," Keaton told Brooke, his voice low. Russ unhooked the cable at his back. "You didn't do anything wrong. Don't act like you did."

He started to step past her, but Brooke grabbed his arm. Tight. She didn't look up. "Please don't do anything to upset—"

"Nobody commandeers my assistant without asking." Jillian was slamming Cameron with condescension and attitude. Keaton started toward her. "Brooke," Jillian scolded, "what do you have to say—"

"Jillian." Keaton's tone cut her off and drew her gaze. Her anger turned sullen. "We didn't exactly give her a choice. And we did it to keep this film on schedule for you. Having this stunt ready to go when the stuntwoman comes will help get the film back on track."

Brooke came into his peripheral vision, and Keaton purposely kept his gaze riveted to Jillian.

"If you needed a stand-in, you should be using me. Brooke's hardly a substitute." Jillian rolled her shoulders back and added a little more attitude to her stance. Her gaze sent a clear you-stepped-out-of-bounds message to Brooke, and Keaton felt horrible for the stress he knew had to be boiling inside Brooke right now. "She can barely keep my schedule straight."

"You're not cleared for stunt work." He said it with a bite to draw her focus off Brooke. "The insurance would never allow it. And you should be filming right now."

"*Hmph.* At least the insurance company recognizes my value." She crossed her arms. "And one of the cameras is down next door. They're repairing it, so they gave us a break. I thought I'd come over and stay warm by watching you work. But you'll have to find another substitute for my double." She turned another one of those barely tolerable looks on Brooke that made Keaton fist his hands. "Brooke has more important things to do."

"I confirmed all your appointments," Brooke told her, voice level. "Answered all your mail, and completed the projects we talked about."

A slow smile curved Jillian's lips. A tight, you-little-bitch smile. "Great. Then why don't you go clean my trailer?"

The order took Keaton aback. Apparently it did the same to Brooke.

"Excuse me?" she said.

"Clean. My. Trailer," Jillian repeated, enunciating the words as if Brooke were an idiot. "Jeannette and Percy left it a mess. And since you dressed like trailer trash today"—Jillian's icy gaze roamed Brooke's outfit—"it fits."

Sonofabitch. Keaton's temper raged beneath his skin.

But Brooke just offered a subdued, "Yes ma'am," and walked back to the corner of the warehouse to collect her things. With her head down, she hurried to exit through a side door.

"Who the fuck have you become?" Keaton crossed his arms, set his feet, and stared Jillian down. "Is this what divorce does to you? Or is it the fame? Maybe the money? It has to be something that happened in the last few years, because you weren't like this when I met you."

"Like what? Strong, confident, straightforward? Oh, yes, I was. And you liked it."

"I also like common decency and compassion and kindness, which you don't have a trace of now. Now you're just *mean*. You're straight-up cruel. I hate this word, and I rarely use it, but, baby, you are a royal *bitch*."

She laughed, as if his slight meant nothing. "I'm a bitch because I discipline my staff for goofing off on my dime?"

"She *wasn't goofing off.* Didn't you hear me tell you why we put her in that harness? Didn't you hear her tell you she'd completed all the work you'd asked her to do? Then to send her on such a menial job to satisfy your own frustration—that's just sadistic, Jillian."

Her eyes narrowed. "So this is about Brooke."

"There's that hearing problem again. *No*, this is *not* about Brooke. This is about *everyone* here." He held his arms wide and realized everyone was listening and watching. Which was just fucking fine with him. "You talk down to *every* employee here. You complain about *everything*, no matter how well something is done or how hard anyone tries to please you. You ignore anyone and everyone else's needs and feelings. The truth is you don't give a fuck about anyone but yourself, and you do your damnedest to make everyone around you feel as small as possible. And I am fucking sick of it."

Rob, the assistant director, came up to them, alarm clear on his face. "What's going on?"

Jillian looked at Rob, then at Keaton. "Keaton was just telling me how thoughtless, rude, and bitchy I am."

Rob's gaze turned on Keaton with a please-tell-me-she's-kidding look.

"You've worked with me," he told Rob. He wasn't pulling punches now. "And you know I won't put up with this diva shit."

"You don't have to work with her," Rob said, then turned to Jillian. "You should be in the other warehouse, filming."

"They're fixing a broken camera." She turned her attitude on Rob. "As the director, you should know that."

Keaton pointed at her but spoke to Rob. "Attitudes like that kill morale. And you know as well as anyone that bad morale translates into the film." He held his hands up in surrender. "Not my problem. I'm out of here when Dupleaux recovers. Just keep her away from me."

He turned and stalked back toward the metal jungle, passing Cam with a grouchy "Let's get back to work."

Nine

Brooke stood at the French doors to her suite, watching the sun set over the Colorado River and wishing she could appreciate the beauty, but her nerves felt like they'd been double knotted all over her body.

"Tammy told me Justin was accepted into the program," she said to Lydia, the liaison within the research team handling the bronchial thermoplasty trial. "I can't tell you how grateful we are."

"When I saw his name on the final list I was thrilled." Lydia's warmth and enthusiasm touched Brooke. They'd built up a friendly rapport over the last six months since Tammy had discovered the project and Brooke had taken over management of the paperwork. Brooke and Lydia talked so often, Lydia felt like a friend now. "I was so excited when his name was chosen that I took a bathroom break just to go out in the hall and jump up and down."

Brooke laughed, and tears burned her eyes. Tears of joy. Tears of fear. "You've been so sweet to us, Lydia. I honestly don't know what we would have done without you through this process. You should be the poster girl for patience."

"Awww, thank you. I really haven't done anything but monitor the process, but I'm happy I could help. So where are you now? You're always in some exotic location, doing something exciting."

Not with Jillian. But she knew her life looked glamorous from the outside. "Not this time. Austin, Texas."

"Hey, almost out our back door." The research team was based in Oklahoma. "If you ever get up my way, you have to call. I'll take you out to lunch or dinner. I'd love to meet you in person."

Brooke smiled, and some of the chill Jillian had produced earlier in the day melted away. "I will absolutely do that. I'd love to meet you too. I feel like I already know you."

"Right?"

They laughed.

Brooke sighed, closed her eyes, and took the uncomfortable plunge. "Lydia, I have a hypothetical for you."

"Sure."

"Now that Justin's been admitted to the program, what would happen if, say, worst case scenario, I lost my job?"

A little gasp sounded over the phone, and Brooke's stomach fell.

"Are you afraid that might happen?" Lydia asked, her voice filled with concern.

"Oh, you know. These actors can be pretty temperamental. No matter how much you do for them, sometimes it's never enough."

"Oh, Brooke, I'm so sorry."

"Well, it hasn't happened yet. And I'm going to do everything in my power to keep it from happening, but I was hoping there would be a way to keep Justin in the program if my worst nightmare were realized."

"To be honest, it would be a real problem. The guidelines require payment in full or half the payment upon entrance to the program and a solid credit background and sufficient income to provide payments for the remaining half. That requires a solid work history and a current job that's secure."

Brooke winced. "What would be considered secure?"

"Employment with the same company for three years. If it's less, you'll need to have a letter from the employer stating that your employment is secure for the coming year."

Her stomach sank a little lower, and desperation released into her system. The thought of borrowing more money from Ellie made Brooke sick. She opened her eyes and found the sun gone, the night as dark as she felt inside. "I see."

"Let's take things one step at a time," Lydia said, her voice gentle. "Maybe things with your boss aren't as bad as you think."

Oh yes. They are.

"Sure. You're probably right." Brooke pressed fingers to her watering eyes. "I'm just tossing around what-ifs. I like to have all my bases covered, you know?"

"Of course."

"Okay, I'll talk to you soon then. And I will definitely call you the next time I get close to Oklahoma so we can meet."

They said good-bye, Brooke disconnected and pressed her free hand to the railing of her balcony. She took a deep breath, exhaled and accepted her reality. She just had to learn to live with Jillian treating her like dirt. And she'd have to keep a bigger distance between herself and Keaton.

Brooke had never been as mortified as she'd been earlier when Jillian had called her trailer trash in front of Keaton. The rest of the crew too, but Keaton...

She pressed her hand to her face, burning with shame. The memory still made humiliation swirl in her gut and rise in her throat. She wanted to get mad. She wanted to get spitting angry. She fantasized about telling Jillian exactly what she thought of her, about what Jillian could do with this miserable job—

Her phone vibrated in her hand.

Brooke pried her eyes open, took a steadying breath and looked at her screen, hoping it wasn't another apology from Keaton. Or another plea for a phone call. She couldn't even bring herself to talk to him. Not yet. Not until she faced Jillian again to get a feel for where she stood.

The text was from Jillian and simply said, *I'm back.*

Which was a summons. Jillian had been at dinner with a big producer who was passing through on his way to Los Angeles. Normally Brooke would have gone along to take notes, but since her fall from grace, she hadn't been invited.

She was definitely being punished. But instead of doing what she wanted to do, which was to walk in and quit, Brooke picked up her iPad and her notebook. At the door, she paused and checked her reflection in the mirror, smoothing her hand down the front of her straight navy skirt. She was back in full business dress, even though it was nine p.m.

Brooke kept her focus on getting from moment to moment. She strode to the end of the hall murmuring, "It's not a big deal.

I'm going to pretend it didn't happen. By now she's probably drunk on wine and high on attention."

Stopping in front of Jillian's door, she paused, took a steadying breath and knocked.

"Come." Jillian's buoyant voice floated through the door and had Brooke raising her brows.

"Okay..." So she wasn't in a foul mood.

Brooke stepped into the suite and caught the tail end of Jillian's side of a telephone conversation.

"That sounds *heavenly*. Lord knows I'm going to need a vacation when this is over."

Amen. Brooke would get a vacation just by having Jillian take one. She stood in the foyer for a moment while Jillian stared out at the night, pulling off her earrings and laughing at something the person on the other end of the phone was saying. She'd been back in the hotel room for at least a little while, because she'd changed out of her dinner attire and donned her black silk robe. Her colored and frosted hair was down, rolling in a smooth tumble past her shoulders.

A flash of Jillian, dressed like this, wrapped in Keaton's arms, one of his big hands tangled in her blond hair, the other locked around Jillian's small waist, assaulted Brooke out of nowhere. An ugly chill shivered through her body, but Brooke refocused on the Impressionist painting dominating the wall in front of her and shook off the insecurity. There was no mistaking how Keaton felt about Jillian now. And Brooke had made her share of less than perfect choices when it came to one-night-stands.

"I know, I know," Jillian said. "And I agree, Anguilla would be lovely, but I've always been partial to Barbados. There's always Bermuda... Oh, please," she laughed the words. "It is *not* the Hamptons of the Caribbean. Okay, okay. We'll talk soon. Bye-bye."

Jillian kissed into the phone and Brooke was so grateful her boss was in a good mood, her knees weakened with relief.

When Jillian didn't immediately launch into a tale about her night or the vacation she'd just planned or start issuing orders, Brooke clicked into work mode and moved to the sofa, perching on the edge of a cushion.

"I've printed out your schedule for tomorrow." Brooke opened her leather portfolio and pulled out a second copy, laying it on the coffee table. Normally, she would have asked about Jillian's dinner, let the woman preen about whatever she wanted to preen about. But after today, Brooke just wanted to find level professional ground again. "All your spa appointments have been confirmed and Henry has your schedule."

Jillian turned from the French doors and wandered toward the sofa.

"You have four hours between your last spa appointment, which is your massage, and your first interview. I've left a two-hour break between your massage for Jeannette and Percy to get you ready for your photo shoots."

Brooke paused and checked Jillian's expression. She stood beside the arm of the sofa with that cool holier-than-thou smirk, one hand absently twirling the tie to her robe. That gave Brooke another sliver of relief. It was Jillian's norm, and right now, Brooke would take the miserable known to the turbulent unknown in a heartbeat.

"I've laid out the periwinkle Vera Wang suit for your five o'clock interview with the Austin *American-Statesman*," she went on, returning her gaze to tomorrow's schedule even though she had it memorized. "The tailored red Donna Karan for your six thirty taping with *Access Hollywood* and the black sequined Anne Klein for the live cocktail party interview segment at nine."

She laid the paper on the table and lifted her gaze to Jillian's. "Jeannette and Percy have cleared their schedules and will be wherever you need them when you need them."

"Of course they will," was Jillian's response. "But your choice of outfits is all wrong."

Brooke mentally reached for some of the armor she'd let slide off. Jillian had never questioned Brooke's wardrobe choices before.

"I'll be wearing the periwinkle to the *Access Hollywood* taping, because, as you said earlier today, my eyes pop when I wear blue. And there's certainly no point in wearing something that makes my eyes stand out when I'm interviewing with a newspaper reporter from the *American-Statesman*. In fact, it really doesn't matter what I wear to that interview, so I'll be dressing down. Pull out my favorite jeans and one of my Marc Jacobs sweaters."

Jeans?

Brooke wasn't sure which fire to smother first—explaining that the journalist Jillian would be interviewed by was the stepson of a Los Angeles movie production mogul? Or reminding her that the ex-Miss America who'd be sitting in the chair opposite her on the *Access Hollywood* set always wore some shade of blue for the very same reason? And to knock the girl on her ass, Jillian would have to wear something stunning?

"Oh, well, um…" Brooke started.

But Jillian was done with the conversation and was already strolling toward one of the bedrooms.

"Get ahold of whoever you have to get ahold of at the hotel and tell them I still don't have the right flavor of Perrier in the refrigerator," she complained, her voice huffy, as if even having to address it was a ridiculous waste of time. "And if that maid comes in here before ten a.m. again, I'm going to have her fired."

"Wait, Jillian…" Brooke stood.

Jillian paused at the dining room table, turned and laid one hand on the back of a chair. "Oh, and speaking of fired, contact an employment agency and put in my request for a new assistant."

Shock hit Brooke like an ice storm and stole her breath. The freeze started at her shoulders and moved rapidly down her body. "Wh—what?"

"A new assistant," Jillian repeated. But the look on her face now was sheer ice. Lids low, jaw tight. "One who doesn't go behind my back and betray my trust. Put in the order, and I'll give you a decent letter of recommendation."

Brooke had a momentary battle between fury and terror. One thought of Justin and fear won out. "Jillian, what happened today was really just a misunderstanding." She rounded the sofa, clearing all barriers between them. Brooke knew Jillian responded to begging, but it went against everything Brooke was. Everything Brooke believed. "You know how badly I need this job. You know I would never do anything to jeopardize it."

Jillian crossed her arms and lifted her chin. "And I know Keaton. We've both been in the business a long time. I know his reputation, and I've worked with him often enough to know how he behaves. Which means I also know you're sleeping with him."

Brooke shook her head. She opened her mouth to tell Jillian it wasn't true, but the words wouldn't come out. It felt just as wrong to deny loving Keaton as it did to allow Jillian to treat her this way.

"You're a fool, you know," Jillian said in Brooke's silence. "He's the same as all the other men in this business. He'll fuck any decent looking woman who's available and suits him at the time. The bigger issue here is that I confided in you and you went after him."

"No I didn't—"

"That's deliberate betrayal."

"It wasn't, Jillian. You're wrong."

Her eyes flared with icy anger. She unfolded her arms and planted her fists at her hips. "Are you going to stand there and tell me you didn't fuck him?"

Brooke's words tangled in the barbed wired cutting her gut. "I…we…it wasn't like that—"

"I'm not an idiot, Brooke. I know exactly what it was like by the way he defended you after you left. Did you two lay in bed laughing at how gullible I am?"

"Oh my God, Jillian…" Brooke pushed a hand into her hair. This was ridiculous. Part of her wanted to slap the woman and tell her to pull her head out of high school. The other wanted to drop to her feet and beg her to understand. Then more of her words sank in and more confusion leaked through the dizzying combination of panic and frustration. "Defended me? He had nothing to defend me against. They asked me to help them out. I was done with the work you'd given me so I helped them out. That's all there was to it."

"If that was true, he wouldn't have berated me for belittling you in front of the rest of the staff."

Brooke pulled in a sharp breath. *That's* what this was about. Keaton standing up to her in public. Keaton taking Brooke's side over Jillian's. Keaton doing exactly what Brooke had asked him, told him, not to do.

Now her anger had a whole new target. And her pain dug deeper.

"You know me, Jillian. You know I would never do something so hurtful. And Keaton was having a bad day. The movie was behind when he stepped on the set. He'd just received word your stunt double wasn't going to make it. He was already tired from his previous job. He simply lost his patience."

"Neither of you looked the least bit unhappy when I walked

in."

She collected tolerance she didn't even know she had—for Tammy and Justin. "I understand that you're angry right now, but I wish you would just sleep on it. Just let your temper settle. Once you consider all the circumstances I'm sure you'll see things differently."

When Jillian remained unmoved, Brooke resorted to pleading. "You know how much I need this job. I just found out Justin got into the children's research program for the bronchial thermoplasty treatment. He's just a little boy with a long life of struggle ahead without this procedure. Please don't take that away from him. I've been a good assistant."

"I'm taking nothing from your nephew. You alone are responsible for that, Brooke. You and Keaton."

"I won't see Keaton again." She pushed the words out, confused with all the emotions swirling inside her—loss, pain, anger. But none of that mattered now. Justin had to come first. "Please give me another chance."

"If you want that letter," Jillian continued, dismissing Brooke's plea, "make a clean break with Keaton. Make sure he understands that what you had was a fling and that it's over. And you're not to contact him again while he's working on this set. I'll give you ninety minutes to get your things together and hunt Keaton down to say good-bye. He's probably out at the bars with the crew, hitting on the hottest woman within reach. Then Henry will take you to the airport."

Brooke panicked. Everything that mattered was crumbling around her. "Please, Jillian. Can't we discuss this?"

"We have." She turned and sashayed down the hall toward the bedroom. "And the discussion is over."

Fury consumed Brooke. Fury and fear.

"Fine," Brooke said. "But since you aren't willing to consider my wants or needs, I'm not willing to consider yours." Jillian stopped in the hallway. After a moment, she spun slowly to face Brooke. And the woman's hate-face was cemented in place. Brooke's stomach fluttered with anxiety.

"Excuse me?" Jillian said, her voice ice-cold and cutting.

Brooke's heart thundered in her ears and pounded in her chest. "Your letter of recommendation means nothing. We both know you'll be badmouthing me behind my back. We both know that when you feel betrayed, you're irrational and vengeful. And that if you had your way, I'd never work in this industry again."

Jillian crossed her arms. Her eyes narrowed and her lips pursed. "You've certainly earned that by talking back to me."

Brooke's emotions spiked past anger. Now she was livid. She took two steps toward Jillian before she forced her feet to stop. Before she forced self-restraint to kick in. "I've earned nothing but respect," she told Jillian in a low tone dripping with finality. "I've done everything you've asked and more. I've gone above and beyond to be the best assistant you could possibly want."

"You're the worst kind of assistant—the untrustworthy kind."

"And you're the worst kind of employer—the narcissist. And let me tell you exactly what's going to happen, Jillian. I'm going straight to Keaton, and I'm going to tell him everything. I'm going to tell him how you've treated me. I'm going to tell him what you've accused him of and exactly how you see him—as little more than a gigolo."

"Ha." Jillian huffed a disgusted laugh. "As if I care what he—"

"You should care, because everyone in the industry loves Keaton, and everyone in the industry hates you. Keaton is on every studio's list of the most desirable stunt fighters. There are a lot of beautiful actresses, Jillian, but there's only one Keaton Holt. So when a studio has to choose between you and Keaton because he refuses to work with you, who do you think they'll pick?"

Brooke was shaking with fury. But she was also bluffing—big-time. She had no control over Keaton. Nor would she ever tell Keaton those hurtful things. And she knew studios couldn't care less about the bullshit that went on between actors. Brooke was just hoping Jillian was insecure enough to believe it.

Her eyes narrowed; her jaw tightened. "You wouldn't."

"I would, and *I will*."

"I'll make sure you never work in this industry again."

"You're already going to do that," Brooke said, "so I've got nothing to lose."

Jillian fell quiet. Her jaw pulsed. "What do you want?"

I want you out of my life. I want the last year erased from my mind and heart. I want to forget I ever met you.

Brooke felt like she was going to shatter. She drew a slow

breath and reached deep for the courage to make her final demand. "I want a letter. And I want that letter to tell 'To whom it may concern' that my employment with you is solid. I want that letter to say you have absolutely no intention of letting me go within the next year."

Jillian laughed, the sound condescending and nasty. "Never."

Brooke turned on her heel and took two steps toward the door.

"Wait," Jillian said.

But Brooke didn't wait. She was done taking orders from Jillian.

She had her hand on the handle of the door when Jillian said, "Fine, you can have the letter."

Brooke paused, but she didn't turn around, waiting for the other shoe.

"But you'll talk to Keaton first," Jillian added.

Brooke shook her head and pulled the door open.

"Fine," Jillian said, her voice rising with urgency and anger. "But here's my final deal. I'll give you the letter. Then you'll sign another releasing me from responsibility for your salary for this fictitious year. And all this will stay between us. If you don't go to Keaton tonight before you leave, or if you tell him you leaving was my fault, you'll be hearing from my lawyer."

Brooke squeezed her eyes closed—in both relief and misery. Justin was safe, but Keaton would be hurt. She fought to shove her own loss aside, gather her frayed composure and turned.

And she told Jillian, "You'll write, print and sign the letter—*right now.*"

Ten

Keaton stared at the monitor above the bar in his hotel's lounge, but he wasn't watching the game. His mind kept twisting and spinning all the possible reasons Brooke hadn't texted or called him back yet. His fingers wound around his phone in a death grip so he'd feel it vibrate in case he couldn't hear it ring above the noise around him.

Still, he kept checking the screen.

Still, no contact from Brooke.

He hadn't decided if that was good or bad, but he was leaning toward the latter.

"Stop with the gloom and doom," Cam said before tossing another few kernels of gourmet popcorn in his mouth. "Cruella DeVille is probably punishing her by forcing her to polish all her shoes or making her clean out the chimney or something."

"That's only one of the options I'm afraid of."

"When she calls, she'll be a whimpering mess, and you can bring her to your room and make her feel all better. Think about that and stop pouting."

"I'm not pouting. I don't fucking pout."

Cam laughed, turned his head to the woman sitting next to him, and said, "Hey, gorgeous. Do you have a mirror I could borrow for a second?"

The woman grinned, her eyes bright. She'd been waiting for an hour for one of them to notice her. "Um, I think so…"

When she started looking through her purse, Cam said, "Good. I want to show this idiot what pouting looks like."

"God, you're an ass," Keaton told Cam. Then said to the woman, "He owes you a drink." He glared at Cam. "Buy her a drink, you idiot, and apologize."

"That's okay," she said, drawing Keaton's gaze. "I was really more interested in you. But I was hoping you weren't quite so…nice."

A hoot of laughter rolled out of Cam and fisted in Keaton's gut.

He turned on his stool and faced the woman. "What the hell is it about me that makes you think, at first glance, I wouldn't be nice?"

The sweet exterior melted away as the woman pulled out her attitude. She slid off her stool, crossed her arms, and tilted her head as she approached. When it was obvious she had no intention of stopping until she was between his legs, Keaton put out a hand and stopped her at arm's length.

"That rock-hard body. The grungy jeans and boots." Her hand took a fold of his light leather jacket between her fingers and rubbed. "The way you wear leather. The way you walk, the way you sit, the way you drink. Your scowl, those dark, intense eyes." She laughed softly, sensually, with a small shake of her head. "A better question would be what about you *doesn't* make me think rough, hard, screaming-great sex? Mmmm, and these scars. God, I love the scars…"

She lifted one hand toward his face.

Keaton grabbed her forearm, and her eyes widened a little. "Did I give you permission to touch me?"

A low laugh bubbled up from her throat. A hot, I-knew-it, you're-exactly-what-I'm-looking-for laugh that added fuel to Keaton's anger and hurt to his impending loss. Because if he couldn't work things out with Brooke, this was what waited for him.

Superficial, hedonistic fucking for physical release.

After experiencing the kind of connection he'd craved for years yet not even known he'd needed until he'd found Brooke, the thought of hooking up with strangers again left him absolutely hollow. The fact that his past and his actions today might have pushed him closer to that barren place tested his temper's limit.

"Yeah," she said, her voice low and hot. "Just like that. But let's do it upstairs—"

He shoved her hand away and opened his mouth to tell her to go to hell.

"Mr. Holt." A man approached, breaking Keaton's focus and defusing his frustration. He looked into the very familiar face of a desk clerk named Leroy. The man's dark eyes held Keaton's purposely, but the easy Southern air he always had was still in place. "A word?"

Cam took over with the woman, buying her a drink. Keaton turned his back to the others. "Hey, Leroy. What's up?"

"You okay, son? You looked like you were about to start a fight off the set."

By now, Keaton was on a first-name basis with everyone at the hotel from the managers to the maids. Leroy might have been a decade younger than Keaton's own father, but the man still called him son. "It's just been one hell of a long day. What's going on?"

"This was just dropped off for you." He held an envelope. "I saw you come in here, and I was on my way out, so I thought I'd swing it by on my way to the car."

Keaton exhaled and frowned, taking the envelope from him and looking at the smooth, swirly handwriting on the front. Even though the hotel was filled with movie people—production assistants, crew, minor cast members—only key people had his cell number. This could be anything from an interview request to a schedule change to a script modification someone wrote down at the last minute and asked their assistant to hand off to him.

Even though there was only one assistant he cared about right now, Keaton pulled open the unsealed flap and drew out the folded paper inside. "Know who it's from?"

"Pretty little thing. She came into the lobby, asked to leave it for you, and…"

Leroy's words faded as Keaton scanned the note and focused on the signature: Brooke. A lick of alarm burned in his gut, and he was on his feet, turning toward the hotel lobby, even while he read the note.

My time in Austin has been cut short. It was fun, but I'm on to my next adventure. Take care. Brooke

"What the...?" He looked up and scanned the hotel lobby. "Where? Where is she?"

"I don't know," Leroy said in that slow Southern drawl. "She was headed out when I started over here. Got waylaid at the door by one of those director types..."

Keaton rushed to the opening between the hotel lobby and the restaurant, but Brooke wasn't among those milling there.

He scanned the front doors and sprinted that direction. He hit the metal bar on an exit door, slamming the door open and scanning the drive. A black Lincoln town car sat off to the left, the engine running.

And Keaton caught the split-second sight of Brooke's dark head disappearing inside. Disbelief clashed with confusion and exploded in anger. He sprinted to the car as the driver turned to look over his shoulder, preparing to pull away from the curb.

"Stop!" he yelled at the same time he slapped his hand against the windshield on the passenger's side. But he didn't even pause to see if the driver looked his way before he lunged for the back door handle. "Brooke?"

And when he dragged it open and found a stunned, borderline-angry Brooke staring back at him, the wall Keaton had erected to hold his hurt back crumbled.

"*What in the fuck* is going on?" he demanded.

"Hey," the driver yelled back at him. "Get away from the car—"

"Henry," Brooke said to the driver. "It's okay. I know him."

That—like everything at the moment—hit Keaton wrong. "You *know* me? What, like you know the valet? Like you know the desk clerk? What does that mean?"

"Keaton, please don't—"

"What the hell is happening, Brooke? Why haven't you returned my calls? Why are you leaving? And were you seriously going to bail with nothing more than a *fucking note*?"

The truth showed on her face. She'd been about to do exactly that. But she didn't look guilty. She released her seat belt and stood from the car with an air of let's-get-this-over-with dread.

And when she met his gaze, those beautiful blue eyes that had always held such a spark or passion or affection were now flat and resigned. The sight stabbed at his heart. And he knew instantly what had happened.

"Jillian fired you, didn't she?"

Her gaze slid away, and she drew a deep breath to speak, but everything in her expression, everything in her posture, told him she was already gone. She'd already shut him out.

"It was inevitable," she said. "Bad timing, but there really wouldn't have been a good time."

She was working that positive streak hard, but she still sounded miserable. As miserable as Keaton suddenly felt.

"Why didn't you call and tell me?" he asked, guilt flooding into his gut. "I can talk to her. If I can't get her to change her mind, there are other avenues, Brooke, legal avenues—"

"No." Her rejection was sharp and resolute, and it sparked anger in the pit of his stomach. "You *cannot* talk to her. It's over. She's made up her mind." Brooke lowered her gaze, took a breath, and softened her tone. "Look, our time together was great, but we both knew it was ending soon. Like I said in the note, it's just time for me to move on."

"Move on?" The sparks inside him caught fire. He stepped around the door, took her by the arms, and turned her to face him. But even without the door between them, there were still barriers. Her barriers. "So you can find another *adventure*? Is that what I've been to you?"

"Keaton, this isn't a big deal." But now she sounded a little more like Keaton felt, distressed and upset. She tried to pull away. "Tomorrow you'll find someone new, and—"

"Don't." He held tighter, desperate to get her to listen. To admit she didn't want to walk away from him. "Don't minimize what's between us. I know it happened fast, but you know it's real. This isn't you. This is her. Don't let Jillian do this."

Brooke's gaze cut to his, and a flash of hurt there burned so deep, it stole his breath. "No, Keaton, *this* is *you*. *You* did this." Hurt gave way to anger, and she yanked her arms from his grasp. "You know what she's like. I warned you what would happen. I asked you not to confront her, but you did anyway. And just like I said in the beginning, if she caught even a hint of favoritism toward me, I would be the one to suffer."

"I *didn't* show favoritism. I purposely made a point to include her treatment of everyone on the cast and crew so I *didn't* look partial. You think I'd do that?" That cut him. Deep. "You think I'd deliberately hurt you?"

"Brooke, honey…" Their gazes both swung toward the driver, who was standing in the open driver's door. "We have to go, or you'll miss your plane."

She nodded and turned back around but didn't meet Keaton's gaze. "None of this matters…" Suddenly, she sounded broken, as if the bottom had dropped out of her fight, and another wave of guilt crashed through Keaton. "This is why I left you the note. Because I knew this would happen. Because I didn't want to end things like this."

"Miss the plane, Brooke," he pleaded softly, running a hand over her hair. He craved the feeling of her leaning into him. Yearned to hear the word *"Yes"* from her lips. "Let's talk about this."

A sound escaped her, part exhale, part sob. She shook her head, straightened her shoulders, and met his eyes in a soldier-like way that left Keaton bemused. "Sorry, I can't. I have to get home. I need to get back to my family."

Another stab cut Keaton, this one dead center through his heart. She turned away, but he grabbed her arm to stop her. "I'm only asking for enough time to talk this through, Brooke, because I already think of *you* as family."

A tremor passed through her small frame. Her free hand gripped the doorframe, and she turned back to him with the strangest expression, one he could only identify as a mix of agony and affection.

"It's over, Keaton…" Her voice shook, but the words cut Keaton straight down the middle. "Let me focus on what matters."

Eleven

Brooke wandered down the hospital hallway toward the new room assigned to Justin on the pediatric floor of Shriner's Hospital for Children, with two sodas from the vending machine in one hand, her phone in the other, and knots all through her stomach.

She stared at Keaton's name in her contact list and chewed on the corner of her lower lip, which was swollen and sore by the time she gave up on making the call—for what felt like the hundredth time over the last month.

Turning into Justin's room, she found Tammy in front of the IV pole, checking the monitor's settings. Her sister glanced over her shoulder, and her gaze sharpened. "That was way too fast." Her voice was lowered so she didn't disturb Justin's sleep. "You didn't call, did you?"

Brooke's mouth twisted in self-disgust. Instead of providing the obvious answer, she offered Tammy her favorite drink.

Her sister took the Dr. Pepper, then used it to point at Brooke. "You're just making yourself miserable by dragging it out. It's eating you up, Brooke."

"I know." She stuffed her phone into the back pocket of her jeans and paused at Justin's bedside to gaze down at him. "God, I still see him as a baby when he's sleeping. Did they say anything else before they brought him up?"

Tammy smiled down at her son and brushed his hair off his

forehead. "Just that he was talking about gummi bear angels right before he went under."

They both broke into laughter.

"One of the OR nurses saw me as we were coming up and told me it was another successful procedure. She said their other children have experienced an exponential improvement in their breathing capacity after the second treatment, something they haven't seen to the same degree in adults."

"Really?"

Tammy nodded, then shrugged. "No idea if that will continue to grow with the last treatment or not, but they're hopeful."

A giddy mix of excitement and relief jumped in Brooke's stomach, and her eyes stung with happy tears. "Oh my God, think what that could mean for millions of kids with asthma. That's so awesome."

Tammy turned to Brooke and pulled her into a tight hug. "*You're* so awesome." Her voice filled with tears. "He would never have had this chance if it weren't for you. And I wouldn't be halfway through nursing school either."

"Hey," she soothed, hugging Tammy back. "I love you guys. We're family. We stick together."

Tammy leaned away, smiling with tears sliding down her cheeks. She rubbed them away with the back of her hand. "We love you too. Which is why I want you to get on that phone and *call him* already."

"I will," she said, frustrated, then hedged with reservations, "...maybe..."

"Maybe? What's this maybe? We've talked this out. We agreed you'd—"

"I know, I know." She turned away, popped the top on her soda, and wandered to the window to look out over the lush green lawns surrounding the hospital. "I just...I wonder if it would just be better to leave it alone. I mean, it's been, what, over a month? Five weeks? He's probably forgotten all about it. Calling now and bringing it back up just to apologize seems..."

She released a frustrated breath and shook her head. Beyond smoothing over some hurt feelings, it seemed pointless. It wasn't like he'd want to see her again after she'd explained. And even on the one-in-a-million chance that he did, her new job involved just as much travel as her last. They'd never be able to make something long-term work. Brooke just wasn't sure if opening that door by calling without the possibility of something more was good for either of them. Then she realized how presumptive that was and got confused all over again.

"I don't know if it's a good idea," she said, agonizing over the decision the way she'd been agonizing over it for weeks—ever since she'd gotten the new job with an income to cover Justin's procedure and didn't need to abide by Jillian's brutal, self-serving rules. "And I still don't know what to say or how to say it or if it's even something I should say over the phone."

A beat of silence passed while Brooke worked over the conversation she wanted to have with him in her mind. But the thought of hearing that deep, rich voice over the line and not being able to see him or touch him... God, the pain ate at her. And it just kept getting worse as time passed instead of fading.

"You're right." The male voice sent a shiver down her spine. "It's not the kind of conversation to have over the phone."

Brooke's heart thumped hard. She pulled a sharp breath and turned.

Keaton stood just inside the door to Justin's room. He wore jeans and a black, hooded sweat jacket that zipped up the front, a white tee underneath. The sight of him made her feel like electricity arced through her body.

"Oh my God." Her gaze jumped from Keaton to Tammy, registered her well-you-don't-get-a-choice-now-do-you look, and back to Keaton. "What are you...? How did you...?"

She forced her mind to stop spinning, but that made her heart ache and yearn and hope. And God, that terrified her. What added to that fear was his expression, one she couldn't read. He didn't exactly look angry, but he definitely wasn't happy. Sober? Serious? Edgy? She wasn't quite sure, and that alone dragged Brooke's feet back to the ground—like a rock.

Regrouping, she dropped her gaze, and noticed something in his hand. A rectangular box about the size of a book, wrapped in bright paper.

A gift. For Justin.

Of course.

She'd almost forgotten about Justin's continued

communication with Keaton until the science fair project had been completed. One that had brought Justin stardom throughout the school and earned him an A plus.

Brooke swallowed the lump of disappointment, set her soda on the window ledge, and crossed her arms.

"I...um..." Tammy said, lifting her can of soda, "...think I need some ice for this. Text me if you leave or if Justin wakes up, but he should be out for another couple of hours."

On her way out, Tammy closed the door behind her. For a long moment, Brooke and Keaton just looked at each other. She swore she had a magnet the size of a football lodged beneath her ribs drawing her toward Keaton like a steel rod. And her chest ached with the effort it took to stay put.

She was just about to tell him how great he looked when Keaton's gaze slid toward Justin, and he asked, "How's he doing?"

The sound of his voice, lowered for Justin's benefit, moved something inside Brooke. It brought back memories of his voice beside her in bed from their short but intense time together and thickened her throat.

"He, um..." She took a steadying breath. "He was only awake briefly after the procedure, just about an hour ago, but they say it went great. Aftereffects of the surgery are minimal, and side effects of the new medications are manageable."

She realized the clinical approach wasn't going to work. Not when he was just two steps away. Not when she had to dig her fingers into her arms to keep herself from taking those two steps and throwing herself at him for the sheer relief of feeling his arms around her, feeling him supporting her again.

"So..." She took another breath, slow and deep, trying to keep her emotions from spilling over. "He's doing really, really well."

Keaton's gaze returned to her, still veiled. "Then it was all worth it."

His response hammered her composure. The answer was yes and no, but she didn't begin to know how to convey the depth of what seemed like such a simple answer on the surface into something sufficient to mend the rift she'd caused between them.

Only now did she realize why it had taken her so long to contact him again—because no matter why she'd done what she'd done, she'd still hurt Keaton in the process. And she knew in her heart there was nothing she could say to make that go away. It had happened. He'd felt it. The break between them had been made.

Words would not turn back time. Words would not change reality.

And the heaviness of that exhausted her.

"Is that for Justin?" she asked, weary and heartbroken over the potential of what they'd lost. "I'd be happy to give him the gift when he wakes up. You don't have to stay."

"If I just wanted to give him a present, I would have sent it in the mail. I'm here because Dupleaux returned to the set. I'm not working on the movie anymore."

She lowered her arms and pressed one hand to the foot rail of Justin's bed, trying to clear her mind enough to think straight. "I don't understand how that relates to—"

"Neither do I. At least not anymore." His jaw ticked. "I *thought* that was part of the agreement you made with Jillian—not talking to me while I was working on the set."

Oh shit. He knew?

He moved to the tray table against the wall where Tammy had piled her textbooks to study while Justin slept and set the gift on top of the stack. Then he met her eyes again.

"I'd planned on coming find you so I could tell you how sorry I am for fucking things up between you and Jillian. Because you were right. When I thought about it, I realized I did defend you a little too hard that day. And even though I tried to cover, Jillian saw through it. So that was my mistake, and staying away from you so you could abide by the agreement you made with Jillian and get the care Justin needed was my payment for that mistake. I almost ruined that for both of you once. I wasn't going to chance it again."

He wandered to the far wall, leaned his back against it, and crossed his arms, his gaze roaming the room. "But when I called Troy and Ellie to find out where you were, I heard about your new job. The one that's making this treatment possible and the one you had within a week of being fired. His eyes narrowed in consideration, or maybe discomfort; Brooke couldn't tell. "I didn't want to believe that you would stay away from me when you didn't have to. I didn't want to believe that you wouldn't contact me to tell me about the procedure and how Justin was doing when there was nothing stopping you."

He cut another look around the room, and there was no mistaking the raw hurt in his expression "But it looks like that's exactly what you did."

Her breathing hitched, picking up speed. Her mind started another spin cycle. "You...waited?"

He returned his gaze to hers and held it a long second before he said, "Yeah." A flash of pain shone in his eyes and cut straight through Brook's heart. "But it's pretty clear you didn't. So you probably had it right. This probably wasn't the best idea." He straightened away from the wall. "At least you know I didn't forget."

He turned and was halfway out the door before Brooke managed to grab a handful of his jacket. "Wait."

His free hand gripped the doorframe, and his body hummed with tension.

"Don't go." Brooke glanced at Justin to make sure he was still resting, then stepped close to Keaton and wrapped her free arm around his waist, squeezed her eyes closed, and pressed her head to his back. "I'm sorry. I'm so sorry. I didn't mean for things to—"

Keaton turned, breaking her hold. Then his arms closed around her and hauled her up against him so hard, all her air whooshed out. He pressed his face to her hair and exhaled heavily, the sound part agony, part bliss.

"Knock, knock." The soft, cheerful voice of the nurse on duty—Brooke was beginning to believe she knew them all—sounded as she passed into the room, as if she were knocking to interrupt their embrace, not to enter the room, because the door was still propped open by their bodies.

Keaton lifted his head and loosened his arms but didn't let Brooke go, and she wanted to weep with relief, with joy, with so much love, it swamped her. She kept her face pressed to his chest, where she breathed in the spicy, male scent of pure Keaton.

"Why don't you two take a break?" the nurse said. "Tammy's in the cafeteria. I have her number. I'll call y'all if Justin wakes, but I suspect he'll be out for most of the afternoon."

"Thank you." Keaton's fingers slid down Brooke's arm and clasped around her hand. "We'll be back."

He pulled Brooke from the room and looked both ways down the corridor.

"The elevators are—" Brooke started.

But Keaton turned the other direction. "I don't want the elevators. I want privacy."

Brooke wouldn't have been able to keep up with him if he hadn't been dragging her. She avoided the curious stares of hospital staff, her mind darting all over the place at dizzying speed. Within seconds, Keaton pushed through the door to a stairwell, and pulled Brooke out of the doorway and into his arms again. With his arms wrapped tight around her waist, he bent to pull her so close, their bodies connected from knees to shoulders, and he dropped his face to the hollow of her neck again.

"I've fuckin' missed you *so bad.*" His rasped words echoed the pain aching inside Brooke, and before she could respond, he pulled back and pressed his lips to hers.

Brooke hummed with relief so deep it was painful. Tears spilled from her eyes and added a salty poignancy to the moment. He tilted his head and kissed her deeper, and the hunger and longing Brooke had been stuffing away to get through every day overwhelmed her. She tightened her arms around his neck and opened to him the way she'd dreamt of kissing him every spare moment for the last month.

Keaton moaned into her mouth, lifted one hand to the back of her head, and caressed a hand over her hair. The sweet move choked Brooke with emotion, and she broke the kiss with an urgent need to explain everything, even though she knew it wouldn't erase the pain.

"I left Austin because she forced me to choose. It was horrible. I was torn apart. And there was no right answer. No matter what I did, someone I loved was going to get hurt. So I sided with Justin. I had to. It's who I am."

"I know," he said, wiping at her wet cheek. "It was the right thing."

"As soon as I got home," she said, "I called Ellie. I had to get a job so I could pay for the rest of this procedure. Ellie and Troy went to Jax. They put their heads together and got me a couple of interviews..."

She paused her ramble to draw air. "I've been crazy. I feel like I'm spinning. Trying to get used to someone new, still walking on eggshells, waiting for the next trapdoor to open under my feet, hoping I can get Justin through program before anything bad happens. I've wanted to call. I've had my finger hovering over the Send button a hundred times since I left—"

He kissed her again, this time gently, his lips lingering in a way that made the stress drift from Brooke's body and allowed her to lean into him. Finally finding a place to rest after doing so much on her own.

He lifted his lips from hers, pressed them to her forehead, and pulled her close again.

"I didn't want to hurt you, and I knew telling you I was sorry couldn't fix it. I didn't want to reopen a wound that I had no way of healing."

Footsteps on the stairs drew their attention, and Keaton moved them aside so the man in scrubs could pass. Then he sat on the steps near the wall and pulled her into his lap. "Ellie told me where you were, but she didn't tell me about the job. Who's it with?"

"Will and Leslie Crow."

"Oh, yeah. I've worked with Will," Keaton said. "Nice guy. Intense, yeah, but that's what makes him such a good actor."

Brooke nodded. "Definitely demanding, but also reasonable and appreciative and generous. They've given me the time I need to be with Justin during the procedures, and pay me well enough to make ends meet and still pay the monthly payment for the program. It's only been a few weeks, but they've been straightforward and honest."

"Refreshing."

"Right?" She laughed the word, relaxing into their conversation, into the feeling of having someone other than her sister to share her life with. "I'm cautiously optimistic. His wife Leslie is a fashion model, but she's pregnant with their first baby right now, so she's limited her jobs to maternity shoots until after the baby's born. They live here in Tampa, so I don't have to deal with the tiny airport in the Keys like I did for Jillian."

He frowned. "Did you move here?"

She nodded.

"That must be hard on Tammy and Justin."

"They moved too. The Keys are an expensive place to live. Tammy didn't want to leave the doctors she had established for

Justin right after Brian died, and then I came and had the job there with Jillian, but—"

"Now there's nothing keeping you there."

"Right. Prices here are so much cheaper which makes everything easier on all of us."

"What about Tammy's school?"

"They have a campus here—a bigger, nicer campus, actually. She just transferred."

He smiled and ran his knuckles over her cheek. "That's fantastic."

What was fantastic was the way she felt right this minute—so beautiful and wanted and loved. She covered his hand with hers and turned her head to kiss his palm.

A doctor in a white lab coat passed on his way up the stairs.

When he was gone, Brooke asked, "Did Ellie tell you about the arrangement with Jillian? Because she swore she wouldn't."

He wiped at her face a little more and tucked her hair behind her ears. "No. I heard about it on the set."

Shame burned in her gut, and Brooke's eyes slid closed. "Oh God." She shook her head and looked at him again. "I know it's your career and what you do is awesome, but that industry is not my favorite."

"I get it. Jillian never could keep her mouth shut, and it's going to come back to bite her big-time because her new assistant is the worst two-faced brownnoser I've come across in a long time. What happened with you was out within days of you leaving. How long do you think it will take for Jillian's deeper, more damaging secrets to come out?" He shook his head. "You were the best thing that ever happened to her."

She smiled and kissed him. "Thank you."

"You're the best thing that's ever happened to me too, baby. And I know I may not look real smart, but I'm not as thickheaded as Jillian"—he combed one hand into her hair, caressing her cheek with his thumb—"and I'm ready to do whatever it takes to keep you."

She sighed and covered his hand with hers. "Realistically, that's going to be a pretty tough gig."

"I'm aware. I'm also aware of these frequent-flier miles weighing down my airline account. And these lulls between jobs when Jax forces us to take R&R so we're sharp and fresh for the next job."

Brooke searched his eyes.

"Come on, baby, jump," he murmured, a smile sliding over his handsome face. "You know you wanna."

She laughed and cupped his cheek. "I really wanna."

He repeated the gesture she'd made just moments ago, covering her hand with his and turning his head to kiss her palm. "I know it's scary. And I know what a big jump this is for you." He curled his hand around hers and held her gaze. "But I know, together, we can make it work. And I can promise you, I'll never let you fall."

Her heart pulled, her stomach flipped. "Keaton, I can't move again. At least not right now. Between Tammy and Justin—"

"I'm not asking you to move. I would never expect you to move. You've made enough sacrifices. I think it's time someone went that extra mile for you for a change."

She tilted her head, frowning a little. "What do you mean?"

He grinned and ran his thumb over her bottom lip. "I got a hotel room nearby." His gaze lowered to her mouth, and his own lips tipped up in a hot smile. "I'd love to show you exactly what I mean first. We'll have plenty of time to talk over the details later."

A heat wave swept through her body. She lifted her brows. "You got a hotel room?"

"Yep. I was going to stay here as long as it took to convince you to give us another shot." He lowered his head and pressed his lips to hers. "But I'll keep it for as long as we need to negotiate the terms of the agreement."

Her heart filled. That giddy thrill fluttered in her stomach. "I do believe we have a perfect window of opportunity to start that negotiation right now."

Keaton's arm tightened around her waist, and he stood, carrying her with him. Brooke laughed in surprise as he set her on her feet. "You don't have to make that suggestion twice."

He took her hand and started down the stairs. Brooke had no idea where these side steps led and thought of her car in the main parking lot. "My car is—"

"My rental's right downstairs," he said, jogging the steps and pulling Brooke with him. "And my hotel is a block away. You can text your sister in the car."

She laughed with a fresh new joy filling her chest. They reached the ground floor in seconds. Keaton hit the landing three steps ahead of her and snatched her into his arms before her feet had a chance to touch the last two.

He kissed her long and deep, pulling away to set her on her feet.

Breathless and a little dizzy, Brooke leaned into him. "I've never looked more forward to a negotiation in my life."

Keaton grinned, the grin Brooke knew. The grin Brooke loved. The grin that set her world right and chased all the problems away, making room for hope and joy.

"Get used to it, baby," he told her "This is your new adventure."

Twelve

Seven months later

The cool ocean breeze blew gently across Brooke's face where she sat at a table on the patio of Jax Chamberlin's home on a Malibu beach in California. The setting should have eased her jitters, but tonight, she doubted there was anything short of a miracle that would make that happen. Watching Keaton and a couple of other Renegades work with Justin on fight moves wasn't helping.

"I'm not sure if I should be happy or terrified." She smirked at Ellie, who sat beside her, legs crossed, bare foot swinging, a hard lemonade in her hand. "Are they helping him or creating a monster?"

Ellie's smile widened. "Mmm, probably a little of both."

"That's what I'm afraid of."

She lifted her drink toward Brooke. "One of these would help you relax."

She smiled. "Not tonight, thanks."

"You okay?"

Brooke nodded. "Just tired."

"You've been tired a lot lately."

She shrugged. "Stress."

"You should get in to a doctor, Brooke. Make sure you're not anemic or vitamin deficient."

"Yep." There would be a lot of that in her future. "I will."

The summers in Southern California might be absolute perfection, but on the shore, when the sun dropped and the fog crept closer, Brooke found herself reaching for Keaton's sweat jacket. The one he'd brought especially for her even when she'd insisted she wouldn't need it. And tugging the jacket on reminded her it always took her a couple of weeks to acclimate from the East Coast's humid heat to the West Coast's dry warmth. Keaton seemed to know her better than she knew herself.

Keaton crouched and extended a hand toward Justin, palm out. "Aim and kick."

Justin tilted his body backward to balance on one leg and used the other to hammer a quick, hard strike. The slap of flesh against flesh sang on the breeze.

"Nice." Rich approval in Keaton's voice made a smile break through the concentration on Justin's face and warmed Brooke's heart.

All the guys were good with kids, probably because they were really just big kids themselves. But she'd been both impressed and moved when he'd stepped into a position of male role model for Justin so fluidly, so easily.

"Now pivot and jam Troy with a palm strike," he told Justin.

Her nephew's moves were strong and practiced. Moves Brooke had been watching him make for six months now. Ever since he'd recovered from his last procedure, his lung capacity had blossomed and Justin had taken up an intense interest in Keaton's love of martial arts.

Justin turned, set his bare feet in a solid scissor stance, and drove the heel of his hand up and into the hand Troy held just below his chin. Another slap of flesh sounded in the night, but Troy hammed it up. Performing the perfect stuntman's impression of a real hit, Troy snapped his head back with a grunt, reeled backward, and fell to the ground, rolling away.

The melodrama started Ellie giggling.

"Oh God," Lexi said with here-we-go lightheartedness. "Ellie's giggling."

"And after a couple of glasses of wine..." Rubi shook her head. "It's going to last the rest of the night."

"Come on, he's funny," she said in defense, and started

laughing again as she pointed at him rolling around on the grass, holding his face and moaning. "Look at him."

Jax chuckled and wrapped his arm around Lexi's shoulders. "He's an idiot."

"Yeah," Ellie admitted, "but he's an adorable idiot."

Troy went limp in the grass and looked at Ellie upside down. "Hey, you're supposed to be on my side."

"I am, babe. I said you were adorable and funny."

"This is no time to mess around." Keaton drew Justin's attention from laughing at Troy. "You've still got a guy at your back."

Before Justin could turn, Wes, who had to be ten times Justin's size, closed a forearm around his throat with a cartoonish growl.

"What the hell?" Rubi, Wes's girlfriend, made a face. "Was that supposed to be a pirate?"

Wes turned his head toward Rubi. "Baby, you don't watch near enough movies. Remember we had a talk about unearthly beings in sci-fi—"

Justin crossed one foot behind Wes's, ducked from under his arm, and used it to push him backward, tripping the Renegade. Wes landed on his ass. One second Wes was standing, the next he was on the ground. It happened so fast, Brooke's mouth dropped open in shock.

Keaton howled with laughter. He doubled his arms over his stomach and stumbled back a step, then bent at the waist, barely able to hold himself up.

"Oh my—" Brooke started, sitting forward in her chair.

"You little…" Wes laughed the words, jackknifed into a sitting position, and reached for Justin.

Justin screamed and jumped away, but Wes got ahold of his T-shirt and hauled him back. Justin was already laughing when Wes grabbed his waist, but then the tickling began. Justin squealed and giggled and cried for mercy.

Everyone was laughing—the guys even harder than the women. But Brooke heard a little rasp in Justin's cries that made alarms ring in her head, and she pushed from her chair. "I think that's—"

A hand closed on her shoulder. "He's fine."

Her sister's voice jerked her attention to the right. She was in a different pair of scrubs than she'd gone in to work wearing, and she looked tired. "Don't you hear—?"

"That's because he's screaming," Tammy said, her smile relaxed and happy. Which helped Brooke relax.

Until Justin's "No, no, no!" shivered over her spine. And she turned to find all three giant Renegades carrying a tiny Justin toward the pool.

All of Brooke's muscles tightened. She pulled in a breath to tell them to stop and took a step that direction, but again Tammy stopped her. "Brooke. He's fine. You've been so overprotective lately."

And just like that, her emotions went completely haywire and a push of irrational tears burned her eyes.

Shit.

The splash made her head swivel again, and Brooke piled her hands over her heart, caught between angst over the unknown happening in her body and more angst over Justin's ability to breathe. After so many years of watching Justin struggle for every breath, she still had a hard time embracing the fact that he could now act like a normal kid.

But all three men stood at the pool's edge, their humor now faded into intensity as their gazes homed in on the boy beneath the water, ready to pull him out on a second's notice. And a wave of deep, moving emotion rolled beneath her hands, rocking her foundation.

These men, really nothing more than acquaintances to Brooke, Tammy, and Justin, had taken the three of them in as if they had always been part of this ever-growing Renegades family. Brooke had experienced a sliver of this, just one way they showed their all-encompassing loyalty to each other, when she'd lived briefly with Ellie and Troy after Ellie had quit the road. But the way they'd taken Justin in like their own nephew and treated Brooke and Tammy like sisters for no other reason than because they were important to Keaton humbled Brooke.

And she was pretty damn sure this emotional roller coaster was going to kill her long before she ever found the courage to tell Keaton...

Justin's head broke the surface, his lungs filled with air, and the first thing he did was burst out laughing. The second thing he did was splash all three of the men standing there. Brooke released her own breath—air she hadn't realized she'd been holding—and her body sagged with relief.

Ellie walked to the pool edge with a towel and waited while the guys dragged Justin out of the water by the arms, then she wrapped the fluffy terry around him. Justin's face glowed with vibrancy and life and joy.

And tears swelled in Brooke's eyes out of nowhere.

"You're tired." Tammy rubbed her back and walked her a few steps toward the pool, frowning with concern.

"Me? You're the one who's been on your feet all day." She worked up a smile for her sister. "So? How was the first day at the big, fancy teaching hospital? What's with the different scrubs?"

Tammy's smile beamed, and she rolled her eyes. "It was amazing. All except the part where my last patient threw up all over me—hence the replacement scrubs."

The mention of vomit made Brooke's stomach roll toward her throat. She curved her lips over her teeth and focused on controlling the wash of nausea.

"But I'll tell you all about it later," Tammy said as they approached the guys and she thanked Ellie for the towel. She rubbed her son's wet head. "Time for this one to get to bed."

"Did you see me, Mom?" Justin chattered with excitement. "The guys taught me…"

Tammy walked back to the table with Justin, Troy, and Wes. Keaton stepped up to Brooke and reached for the zipper of the jacket, tugging it into place. "Cold?"

She snuggled close to him with the first real fear of driving a wedge between them since they'd gotten back together. "A little."

He turned her toward the house and wrapped an arm around her. "You don't feel good, do you?"

He didn't sound particularly alarmed, and Brooke felt guilty. This had suddenly become her new normal, which she neither liked nor could control. They stopped at the table where everyone except Tammy was comfortably seated again, opening another round of drinks.

"I'm fine," she told him, forcing a smile that seemed to drain her strength. "Just tired."

"I think we all need some good sleep." Tammy pulled a

Renegades logo sweatshirt over Justin's head and smiled at Brooke. "Ready?"

Brooke hesitated. She hoped she would find a moment to talk with Keaton alone tonight. Between the move, Justin's school, and Brooke's, Tammy's, and Keaton's schedules, they hadn't gotten much more than a few stolen moments together.

He'd just returned from a shoot in the Mojave Desert this afternoon and had a new shoot starting tomorrow on the other side of the LA basin. That meant he'd be working sixteen-hour days, six days a week.

Which left Brooke holding this secret time bomb until she saw him again.

That led her to fear and doubt and anxiety of how they would ever make this work. Spiraling into panic that she might have moved her sister and nephew to California only to have her relationship with Keaton fall apart when he found out—

Keaton gave her shoulder a squeeze. "I'll take her home."

It took a second for her to untwist her mind only to get confused again. "I live the opposite direction—"

"Yeah, well, I've been wanting to talk to you about that."

He used his foot to angle a chair and eased into it, pulling her onto his lap. Brooke couldn't look away from his face, from the intensity in his eyes. He was focused in a way that told Brooke this conversation had a very specific purpose. The fact that everyone else was also listening should have been weird. Brooke should have told him they'd talk about it privately, but instead of the others' presence feeling invasive, it felt supportive. Nurturing. And Brooke realized this was probably a lot like what it felt like to have a big, close family always butting into your business.

God, she understood why Ellie loved it so much. Brooke did too.

He pulled out his wallet, opened the fold, and drew out a key. "I think it's about time you gave your sister and your nephew some space." He grinned. "And come crowd me instead."

Her mouth dropped open, a fist of emotion grabbed her heart, and her eyes instantly blurred with tears.

"Awww," Ellie said. "That's so sweet."

A murmur of agreement passed among the other women while a mess of emotions jumbled with just as many conflicting thoughts.

"Oh my God." The words came out in a choked whisper, and she covered the tightness at the center of her chest with one hand. Tears spilled over, and embarrassment clouded the joy. She covered her face with both hands and huffed, "I'm sorry."

"Mom," Justin's bewildered voice cut into the moment. "Is Aunt Brooke moving out?"

"Shh," Tammy told him. "Let her answer."

"But she's crying," Justin said. "Can't we just have Keaton move in with us? I'd share my room."

Everyone busted up laughing, including Brooke. And when she cleared the tears from her eyes and looked at Keaton again, he was sharing one of those guy smiles with Justin. "Because I am just that cool, aren't I, Justin?"

"Totally," he said, utterly serious. "Aunt Brooke, I'd even clean the toys out of my closet to make room for his clothes."

"Dude." Keaton fisted the hand holding the key and held it out to Justin. "You are so freaking awesome." Justin beamed as he met Keaton's fist. Then Keaton gave Justin a secretive look and tilted his head toward Brooke, whispering, "But if Brooke comes to my house, then you have two places to live. How amazing would that be?"

His eyes went wide. "Oh, yeah."

Brooke turned into a broken faucet. More tears leaked from her eyes. She tented her hands over her mouth and murmured, "God, I love you so much."

He lifted the key again and gave her that look. The one that always floated in his eyes when he told her he loved her too. "Which is why you should take this. Because people who love each other should be together."

"Mom says that all the time," Justin agreed.

She reached out and stroked Keaton's face. "I need to talk to Tam—"

"No, you don't," her sister cut in. "You should do it."

"You should totally do it," Justin agreed.

Keaton's face broke into a beaming smile, and he laughed.

"Take it already," Ellie said. "What's wrong with you?"

"Thank you," Rubi said, her voice brimming with attitude. "I almost split a seam holding that in."

"Shush," Brooke told everyone. "Jeez. Keaton's spinning my

head fast enough."

"Welcome to Los Angeles," Rubi whispered with an evil little edge. "Jump into the fire, it's warm down here."

"Baby," Wes murmured, "save that good stuff for the bedroom."

"Hello," Tammy said, a reminder to Justin's presence.

"Gah." Wes rolled his eyes. "Kids."

And more tears burned Brooke's eyes. "Keaton," she said softly, "I think we need to talk before—"

"Okay, okay," he said with a dramatic you're-crushing-my-jam flair. "Girl, you're always demanding my A-game."

His fingers disappeared into his wallet again and emerged this time with...

A ring?

Brooke gasped, along with every other woman at the table. Her heart jumped, tripped, tumbled, then got up and did it all over again. "What... What..."

Wes, Troy, and Jax pushed to their feet simultaneously as if they were choreographed and leaned in.

"Is that a fucking ring?" This from Troy.

"Mom," Justin complained. "I can't hear."

"That's the point," Tammy told him. "Now be quiet so I can."

Brooke pried her gaze from the gorgeous sparkling band she couldn't even see because of the tears blurring her vision. Man, this wasn't falling into the right fairy-tale order of progression at all, yet that didn't make her want any of it less—no matter what order it came in.

"You bought her a ring," Wes accused, "and you didn't tell us?"

"What the hell?" Jax wanted to know.

"Girls, girls," Rubi told the three of them in her sweetest tone, "don't get jealous. You'll all get yours when the time is right."

Wes spun around and picked her up and threw her over his shoulder. Then smacked her ass. Rubi squealed and laughed, and as the other twittered with teasing and excitement, Brooke leaned in, pressed her cheek to Keaton's, and said, "We need to talk."

Rubi pushed against Wes's back, struggling to shoot a glare over her shoulder at Keaton. "You, mister, had better get that fine ass of yours out of that chair and drop to your knees. As in now."

Wes spanked her again. "Who's ass are you calling fine? Those words have my name stamped all over them, so don't be applying them to another guy. Understand?"

Brooke laughed at their antics, but everything inside her vibrated and jumped and snapped. She pressed her hands to her cheeks, utterly overwhelmed, whispering, "Oh my God, Keaton..."

"My knees are busy at the moment," he told Rubi without looking away from Brooke. "What's going on, beautiful? Talk to me."

"Do you feel those daggers piercing your skull?" Jax asked Keaton. "'Cause I'm pretty sure Rubi's eyes are registered as lethal weapons with every branch of special forces in the military."

"It's true," Lexi agreed. "You should really just do what she says. Besides, it's a photo op, and you know we always need promo material for the website."

"Hell no," Jax disagreed. "Don't you dare let our groupies know Keaton's off the market. We're droppin' like flies."

"And what, exactly," Lexi wanted to know, "is the problem with letting 'groupies' know you're off the market?"

"The more you're around them," Keaton said, referencing the other Renegades and their girls, "the easier they become to ignore. But the natives are getting restless, so you're going to have to tell me pretty quick, because the girls can only play smoke and mirrors for so long before those guys cut themselves loose again."

"Oh my God..." She curled his T-shirt into her fingers. "I don't think doing that here is a good idea. I'm not sure how you're going to react—"

"To you being pregnant?"

Brooke's breath caught. Her eyes locked on his. No one else seemed to hear what he said. They continued to chatter and tease, but it faded as a bubble seemed to close around Brooke and Keaton. Then her heartbeat grew really loud in her ears. And every breath she took sounded like a rasp across sandpaper.

"You...? How did you...?" Her stomach flipped so hard, she winced and covered it with her hand.

"That's one of the ways," he said. "Your exhaustion was another one. All these tears spilling out of you—when you're happy, when you're sad, when you're mad, when you're confused. The way you forget your keys and your phone. The way you keep knocking over your drinks at restaurants."

"That doesn't… How the hell do you…?"

"My sister is pregnant," he said. "I may not have mentioned it because I only found out about two months ago and I only remember it when I call home, which is usually when I'm on the road, because that's when I have time, hanging out in the hotel room. And every time I call home, all I hear about is the misery she's going through, which sparks tales of how hard my mother's pregnancies were with us. That, along with the way you've been feeling for going on two months, adding in that broken-condom episode about three months ago… Yeah, I've been suspicious for about three or four weeks. I've been pretty damn sure for about two."

"Jesus." She squeezed her eyes closed and rubbed her forehead. "I didn't even figure it out until yesterday."

"You're juggling a shitload of stress, Brooke. Your mind is in a dozen other places, and you always put everyone else first. It doesn't surprise me that your own needs weren't on your radar."

When she opened her eyes, the first sight that registered in her brain was his soft smile. "You're…not, I don't know, upset?"

"Hell no." God, his eyes sparkled with excitement. "I can't fuckin' wait."

Relief washed in. Only to be followed instantly by the realization that his proposal had been prompted by the pregnancy.

Fuck. This. Roller coaster.

"Well," she exhaled and pulled her whiny, pansy ass back into line. "That's good news."

"So…" He lifted his brows. "You're happy about it too?"

That wasn't exactly the right word. Shocked, terrified, already in love with the idea of having his child…but happy? She released a breath, and a smile fluttered over her lips. "Yeah." Then she added, "But, look, I don't want to rush into anything. Our schedules are crazy, we haven't been seeing each other when we live in the same town… Maybe we should just stay where we are for a while and see how things go."

A tarnish dulled his smile, but he ran a hand over her hair. "I bought the ring four months ago, Brooke. Long before any thoughts of kids came to mind." His fingers came around and slid over her jaw. "I knew those first few days after you'd left Austin, I wasn't going to be able to live without you. Like I told you in the beginning, I'm not good at this, and I'm going to make mistakes, but one mistake I will never make again is letting you go. Because I love you more than anything."

She dropped her forehead against his and started bawling.

And Keaton started laughing.

"Hold on," Ellie said. "I'm not tipsy enough to be hearing things. And I'm pretty darn sure I heard someone say pregnant."

"What?" A chorus of voices followed, both male and female.

Then hugs and high fives went around the group, while Brooke rested her head on Keaton's shoulder and let him support her and take care of her. And the feeling of having him there, wanting to be there for her, for them, for the family they would soon become...completed her in a way she'd never even known she needed.

And finally, Keaton pressed a kiss to her temple. "Are you ready to go home now, princess?"

"Princess?" She laughed the word. "No one's ever called me princess."

"Well, get used to it," he said, his cocky attitude swaggering through his voice. "Because you're going to get treated like effing royalty now, baby."

She was smiling when he set her on her feet, then dropped to one knee.

"Rubi has a point," he said. "We're only doing this once, so we should do it right." With his eyes on hers, he said, "Are you ready to do this with me? This crazy life? Together? Forever?"

She choked out a laugh. "As long as we're together forever—absolutely."

"Then let's get some princess-level bling on this pretty finger."

He slipped the sparkling band with a center diamond she'd have to appreciate in detail another time—maybe in another month or two when the hormones leveled out and she could stop crying at every little thing—onto her left ring finger so gently, she almost didn't feel it. But she felt a shift inside her. A grounding force. A deep and honest love.

And when he tilted his head back and looked up at her with the same love filling every inch of his expression, Brooke wished she could capture the moment in time.

He sighed, an utterly content sound that resonated inside Brooke. "I love you—"

She cupped his face and bent, pressing her mouth to his. When she pulled back, the cheers of their friends and family filtered in, and Brooke matched and finished Keaton's sentiment with, "—so very much."

About Skye Jordan

Skye's *New York Times* bestselling novels are all about enjoying that little wild streak we all have, but probably don't let out often enough. About those fantasies we usually don't get the opportunity to indulge. About stretching limits, checking out the dark side, playing naughty and maybe even acting a little wicked. They're about escape and fun and pleasure and romance. And, yes, even love, because Skye is ultimately a happily ever after kinda gal.

Skye is a California native recently transplanted to the East Coast and living in Alexandria, Virginia, just outside Washington DC with her husband of 25 years. She has two grown daughters in college in Colorado and Oregon. In her free time she's always taking classes and attending seminars. She currently loves rowing on the Potomac, exploring new places via writing retreats with friends, and classes in watercolor, baking and cooking.

Make sure you sign up for her newsletter to get the first news of her upcoming releases, giveaways, freebies and more! http://bit.ly/2bGqJhG

Also by Skye Jordan

REBEL, Renegades Book 2
RICOCHET, Renegades Book 3
RUMOR, Renegades Book 4
RELENTLESS, Renegades 5
RENDEZVOUS, Renegades 6

FORBIDDEN FLING, Wildwood Book 1
WILD KISSES, Wildwood Book 2

QUICK TRICK, Rough Riders Hockey Book 1
HOT PUCK, Rough Riders Hockey Book 2
DIRTY SCORE, Rough Riders Hockey Book 3
WILD ZONE, Rough Riders Hockey Book 4

INTIMATE ENEMIES, Covert Affairs Book 1
FIRST TEMPTATION, Covert Affairs Book 2
SINFUL DECEPTION, Covert Affairs Book 3

Get a FREE copy of THE RISK, Xtreme Heroes Book 1, by
signing up for Skye's newsletter here: http://bit.ly/2bGqJhG

Secret Sins

by

CD Reiss

Deliciously shocking. I couldn't breathe.
Laurelin Paige - *NY Times* Bestselling author of First Touch.

SECRET SINS
CD REISS

ACKNOWLEDGEMENTS

Lawyers are strange birds. The strangest of them is Jean Siska, who put Drew at the proper end of the table for his station, corrected my lingo, and made sure Margie was studying the right cases for the right exam, at the right time.

Erik, as always, found more typos than the most diligent proofreader and then formatted this book like a boss.

I was pretty terrified to have this beta'd, since the secret, while pretty shocking to most readers, would knock fans of *The Submission Series* right over. I didn't want it to get out. So thank you to the Camorra for their tight lips.

At one point, I doubted myself. The carefully constructed out-of-orderness of this story seemed like a conceit rather than a necessity. Laurelin Paige and Jenn Watson read a sequential version, assessed it as a bore, and set my doubts straight. Thank you.

Thank you Lauren, Laura, and Kristy for looking at the cover 100 times, and the girls in FYW for the same. Indie publishing really isn't all that indie, and that's a good thing.

My Goodreads group, CD Canaries, has a theory thread with spoilers and story possibilities for all things Drazen, especially Daddy/Declan Drazen. I hear it's razor sharp.

All the authors who blurbed, thank you.

The author community is shaken up regularly, and I'm thankful to the women and gentlemen who keep it about what's on the page.

Chapter 1

1982

"How old are you anyway?"

The guy asking had long strawberry-red hair and wore only shorts and a single sock. He'd tattooed a treble clef on his Adam's apple that started a symphony of notes all over his chest and abs. His name was Strat, and whenever his shirtless torso showed up in *Rock Beat*, Lynn went crazy trying to play the song he'd had drawn on his body. It sounded like crap.

"Eighteen, asshole," I snarled, letting loose a yard-long cone of cigarette smoke. I stamped out what was left of my cigarette. "You going to call or what?"

He and Indy snickered. I saw them look at each other over their cards. They thought they had my bra off next. They were wrong. Only two hands beat a full house, and if one of them had a straight flush or four of a kind, I was tits to the rail.

"I'll raise you." Strat tossed a ten in the center of the table.

We'd been going for four hours already. Indy had met me on the beach and, after a short chat, invited me to play poker. Yoni and Lynn were already in the hotel room for the possibility of a threesome, which was how I'd ended up on the beach alone. But poker? I could do poker.

My friends hadn't lasted long. Yoni and Lynn had passed out when they ran out of cash. Keeping up with a couple of cash-rich rockers who didn't know what to do with their first chunk of advance money was hard.

Indy/Indiana McCaffrey played guitar for Bullets and Blood. I'd met him on the beach first. I'd stayed cool even though he was completely gorgeous and charming, but when Strat came into the hotel suite, I almost had a coronary. I was a huge fan. I'd played their debut album, *Kentucky Killer*, for two weeks straight until Dad took my cassette. Took the Walkman too. I bought another of each but hid them.

"Call," I said, tossing in my ten.

Indy threw down his cards. "Y'all are too rich for me."

Indy had sun-kissed brown hair and a ginger beard. He was down to his skivs and a bandana around his neck, toned and tan from head to toe. I'd taken all of his money, and Strat and I had been pretty equally matched. Now I was going to break him.

"Too rich and too young," Strat said, popping a peanut.

Lynn coughed on the couch. Stretched.

God, please don't let her puke.

"I told you. I'm eighteen."

I don't know if I mentioned this. I wasn't eighteen. I won't say if I was younger or older. You can go figure it out.

Strat laughed. "Flygirl…"

Flygirl was a pretty common way to address a girl in the eighties, crossing race and geography, but I still felt as if it made me attractive to him. Strat chewed his peanut as if it had the mass of a pack of gum, chin up, looking at me in my bra. I felt naked.

I *was* naked, but I hadn't felt like it until his eyes swung around the curves of my body. I wanted to tell him to go fuck himself, but he finished before I could get a mental jacket on.

"You got a mouth like an old lady," Strat said.

His stare froze me in place. The backs of my thighs got sticky on the pleather.

"Never heard a girl talk like you."

Green was the rarest eye color, and his looked like precious Chinese jade.

He was so hot.

A hot rock star.

I put my cards down, snapping each one in the fan as I laid them out. "Aces full of sevens. You got anything in your hand besides your dick?"

Indy whooped. "She's got you, Stratty-boy. The pot and... what do you have left? Pants and a sock, bro. Go for the sock."

Indy was an amateur. He was beautiful and brilliant, but he didn't act twenty. He acted like the guys my own age.

Eighteen.

Or whatever.

Strat hadn't taken his eyes off me. Hadn't even glanced at my full house. Didn't even look down when he laid his cards on the table. I couldn't move for too many seconds. His look wasn't a look. It was a black hole. All gravity.

I tore myself from his gaze and looked at his cards.

Four deuces.

Fuck.

Losing to deuces was insulting.

Strat leaned back, the coils of his song all over his ripped body. The pot was his, but he didn't reach for it. He just worked me over with his eyes, arm over the back of his chair, knees apart, daring me to search for the bulge in his shorts. I breathed deeply but couldn't get enough air. My lungs had shrunk.

Indy looked at me under the table. "No socks, man. Shit. You're down to not too much."

I was in over my head. Way fucking over. Yet I liked it. More than liked it, I was comfortable when I was out of my depth. All the moving pieces, the inconsistency of the cards, the mess I was making excited and soothed me, a contradiction that translated into *belonging*.

I could fix it. I fixed it every time. My grades were amazing. I was the liaison for the Suffragette Society. I ran the school stage crew like a military operation. It was too easy. If you wanted an omelet, you had to break some eggs.

I'm not saying I chased musicians around after the sun went down because I sat on the edge of my bed and decided to make a mess of my life in order to fix it back up. Insight like that is no more than Monday morning quarterbacking.

I stood and put my hands behind my back, reaching between shoulder blades.

Strat licked his lips, taking his eyes from my crotch and leveling them on mine. I looked right at the motherfucker and pinched my bra hook. He was going to see my tits. The nipples were already hard from his attention. I had pretty good odds on a little damp spot where my panties had been on the pleather.

"Why don't you stop for a minute there?" he said.

I stopped. I didn't have to. Rules were rules. The bra came off. But he was effectively changing them.

Also, I didn't want to take my bra off.

Strat leaned forward a little. A blade of copper hair slid off his shoulder and swung in front of his cheek.

"What?" I asked. "Scared of a little tit?"

"Who are you?" he asked.

"Cinnamon." I flicked my head a little, and my own red hair got out of my eyes. "But you can call me Cin."

"Yeah. No. You got backstage last week from the admin office. I know you didn't fuck Herve Lundren to get there either. Then you and your friend show up places you shouldn't be. The loading dock behind the Wiltern. The thousand-dollar-a-plate dinner at Vilma. And Indiana here fucking stupids right into you."

"Stupid's not a verb, asshole," Indy said.

Strat didn't get distracted. Indy could have broken into the "Star-Spangled Banner" and it wouldn't have snapped the drum of energy between Strat and me.

"Cinnamon's not even a name," Strat added.

"Your mother name you Strat?"

"*Rolling Stone* revealed my name three months ago."

"Stratford Gilliam," I whispered.

He leaned back again, but he didn't spread out. He crossed an ankle over a knee. "Something's up. You have cash. Enough to play with us. No eighteen-year-old has a wad of twenties inside hundreds."

"I'm a fan. I like your music."

"What's your name?"

"You deaf? Cinnamon."

"I can call you Cin."

I touched my nose.

"Tell me your name," he said, "and you can keep the bra on."

He'd read me like a street sign. I didn't want to take that bra off. I wasn't ready for what that would lead to.

Yet I'd wanted to see if I could get out of it.

Dad asked me once why I loved trouble. Why I seemed to enjoy it so much. Why I made my own if I couldn't find it in the wild. I had no answer. Still didn't.

I didn't want it to get out that I was in a hotel suite with Bullets and Blood. If I told this guy my name, I could get into trouble, and not the enjoyable kind.

"Your name." The word *name* was silent on his lips.

My hesitation didn't seem to bother him. He played me at the right tempo, continuing when I thought I'd break and just snap my bra open.

"I've seen enough tits in my time," he said. "But you. Maybe you're a fan, but it's something else. You're different."

Show him your tits.

My fingers twitched on my sides. I was throbbing everywhere. My body wanted him, and my mind was running a four-minute mile in the other direction. I'd lost control of the situation, and as much as I dabbled in trouble, I never lost control of it.

Lock it down. Don't even think your name. Don't even think it. Don't even.

"What's your name?" he asked again.

I swallowed and decided to take off my bra. He'd try to fuck me, and we'd see where that went. I'd fought off men before. My hands crawled to my lower back.

He blinked, and in that split second his jade eyes were hidden from me, I changed course.

"Margaret Drazen," I said, putting my hands on my hips and leaning hard on one foot. "You can call me Margie."

"Nice to meet you, Margie." He lazily picked up the deck of cards. "Your deal."

Chapter 2

Five things about being me.

1. I come from a long line of money. I've got more money in my trust than most people see in a lifetime. I've never worried about having it or getting it. I don't have to work, but I like to. Really like to.

2. I'm connected. If I don't know who I need to know, my father does. I've never had much cause to call in favors or know the right people, except to get into concerts and parties when I was younger. But I can. And knowing that makes all the difference.

3. I grew up quickly. I was born mature. Strat had it right when he said I talked like an old lady. He said that before I was fed shit on sterling silver spoon, then the talk got real and I saw life for what it was. So the politics and backstabbing in law school were child's play. Intra-office bickering is white noise. I win. End.

4. Bullshit makes me really impatient, and drama is bullshit. Drama's never about right and wrong. It's about *feelings*.

5. Feelings are for children. See #3.

Chapter 3

1994

Law offices are snake dens. I learned that at Stanford when I butted up against the old boy network for an internship at Whalen + Mardigian. But I didn't bitch about the partners inviting the guys to a strip club and pulling interns from the group there, because I had the luxury of my own privilege. I felt bad for the women who didn't have my smorgasbord of options, but see... that was a feeling. See Chap. 2 - No.5

So I clerked at Thoze & Jensen, a multinational firm with twelve offices in the States and an impressive presence overseas. Tokyo. Frankfurt. Dublin. Johannesburg. Hong Kong. But the firm was still as backward as a third-world country. An impenetrable fortress for anyone outside the Harvard/Princeton/Yale Testosterone Mafia, meaning—women. All women, with or without Ivy League degree. We could clerk and we could be associates, but we'd never partner.

We'd see about that.

They hired me as an associate right out of law school but I had to clerk until I passed the bar. Until then, I got a six-figure salary even though I didn't need it.

How?

Easy. I brought them a client.

You thought it was going to be some scandal.

It could have been, but when choosing between sugar and vinegar, just remember vinegar works best as a preservative.

I was a clerk until I passed my bar, and despite what you may think, I couldn't buy that. Nor did I want to. I rented a house in Culver City and covered it in sticky notes. From the table where I kept my keys, (*Strickland v. Washington. Test for ineffective assistance of counsel. Performance objectively unreasonable. Reasonable performance would have gotten different result.*) to the bathroom mirror (*Ford v. Wainwright. No death penalty for mentally deficient*). Even my car had a note stuck to the windshield (*TORTS – Tarasoff v. Regents. Responsibility of psychiatrist to warn potential victims of harm. Responsibility can be litigated with commensurate award for damages.*)

I didn't have time for men or friends. No one understood me anyway. No one but my family, which was more than enough. I had six sisters and a brother. I was the oldest, and I'm still not telling you my age, or you'll start doing math in your head instead of paying attention.

* * * *

I was heading for a meeting with the senior partner on a copyright case I'd just been put on, rushing through the waiting room, which was a shortcut to the conference room, with an armload of depositions and pleadings, rattling hearsay exceptions in my head. There were ten categories, and I always forgot one. I walked across past the white leather couches with my folder, feet silent on the grey carpet.

Excited utterances.

Dying declarations.

Declarations against interest.

Present sense impression.

Present state of mind.

Doing good. Almost there...

Prior inconsistencies.

Public records.

Business records exception.

Ancient documents.

And....

And I beat my brain for the last one.

The man pushed himself off a couch as I was looking in my head for the tenth exception instead of out of my eyes for tall guys in suits.

I was midair, shouting, "Family records!" as if getting backed into reminded me that families couldn't be trusted to keep a story straight. The folder I was delivering to the conference room went flying. A shoe fell off. I landed on my butt bone with my legs spread as far as the pencil skirt allowed.

"Oh, shit, I'm so sorry!"

I put my knees together and got back up on my elbows to get a look at the clod who had knocked into me.

He was a god. The kind of guy who could model but didn't because it was too boring. Clean-shaven with brown hair pushed to one side. A bottom lip that had the same fullness as the top. Blue eyes. I had a metaphor for the color tooling around somewhere in the torts and procedures, but it all went blank when he put his hand down to help me up, and I saw a tattoo creep from under his cuff.

I looked at him again.

He looked at me.

"Cinnamon," he said.

"You can call me Cin." The words came automatically, as if coded in my myelin.

I took his hand, and he helped me up. My response might have sounded smooth and mature, as though I wasn't thrown off at all, but it was the opposite. I'd memorized that answer sober, drunk, and dancing. I even said it in my head when someone mentioned the spice. Back when I was a stupid, reckless, wicked girl, it was a calling card.

I got up, not making eye contact with the stares coming from the entire waiting room.

"I'm fine," I said, acting meek. When all the clients returned to staring at their magazines, I turned to the man who had knocked me down. "You going to stand there and let them trample my case file, Indiana McCaffrey?"

I smiled a little, and he smiled back. Wow. Had I been so unconscious when I met him that I'd thought he was only okay-looking? A close second to Stratford Gilliam? Seriously? How had he matured from twenty into this perfectly-chiseled version of a man?

I bent down to get my papers, and he put his hand on my shoulder.

"Let me be the first to get on my knees," he said, crouching before I could respond.

I couldn't believe he remembered me out of the thousands of girls who had thrown themselves at him. I knelt next to him and scooped up papers.

"I go by Drew now," he whispered. "My middle name."

"I go by Margie. My real name."

"I remember."

"I didn't expect you to," I said quietly.

He tilted his head just enough to see me, then he went back to picking up the files. I could see the tiny holes in his ears where he'd let his piercings close up.

"Who could forget you?" he said.

"Oh, please. Flattery only soils the intentions of the flatterer."

"Where's that from?" He tapped the stack on the carpet in an attempt to straighten them.

"My head."

He handed me his stack, and I jammed it into the folder.

"You haven't changed a bit."

I swallowed hard. I didn't have a problem with most of my misspent youth. I'd had fun and finished the job before I completely ruined my life. But I worked in an uptight law firm with a brand made of sedate blues and sharp angles. Former-rock-and-roll-groupie heiress wouldn't look good on them.

"Miss Drazen?"

It was Ernest Thoze standing by the reception desk, senior partner and my boss ten times over. I could have bought and sold him, but that wasn't the transaction I had in mind. I wanted to earn his respect.

I glanced at Drew then back at Thoze. Shit.

Thoze the Doze + Drew the Screw = I-Had-No-Rhyme-For-How-Much-I-Didn't-Want-That.

Thoze tapped his watch.

"Six minutes," I said. "I got it."

Thoze nodded and paced off. I was always ten minutes early, and fucktard over here had just given me seven minutes of reorganizing to do.

Fucktard smiled like a rock star. I remembered why I couldn't keep my eyes off of him or Strat.

"I knew you were meant for big things," he said.

I turned to face him, getting close enough to hiss. "It's been real fun reminiscing, but let's cut it short. I have a meeting. I'm sorry about Strat. That was fucked up. I wish I could have been there for you, but I didn't know until it was too late."

I didn't wait for a response, because seeing him made me *feel* things. Physical things. Emotions. Perceptions. He made me wonder if my hair looked all right or if my skirt showed enough/too much leg.

I paced off to my meeting, listing all the ways people could tell lies of perception.

Excited utterances.

Dying declarations.

Present sense impression.

He must be a client.

Present state of mind.

Prior inconsistencies.

Gotta be a hundred copyright claims after Strat split.

Declarations against interest.

Business record exception.

Just keep cool and don't give anything away.

Public records.

Ancient documents.

And motherfucking family records.

Boom. I pushed open the glass door to the conference room with finality.

I reorganized all the packets and laid one at each of the six seats with thirty seconds to spare. I opened the blinds that covered the windows looking out into the hall, letting everyone know the room was ready.

Life wasn't like books, not that I had time to read. But in books, there were fake coincidences and chances that changed fake lives. In real life, things happened because you made them that way. I'd never expected to see Indy again because I wasn't looking for him, and when I did see him, I assumed he was a client.

When he walked in ahead of Thoze and four other lawyers, plopped his briefcase down at the head of the table and smiled at me. My heart sank.

Not a client.

Chapter 4

1982 – BEFORE THE NIGHT OF THE QUAALUDE

It was the era of the deLorean with a car phone the size of a loaf of bread. The era of payphones and beepers. Reagan, *E.T.*, *Rocky III*, poisoned Tylenol, and Love Canal.

I lived all of it and none of it. I looked at the world through a peephole in the front door, outside to inside. Everything was tiny, far away, and in full focus.

My friend Lynn was the lens. She was a card-carrying groupie. She'd gone to Carlton Prep, same as me, and she was, unfortunately, dumb as a box of rocks. The product of two beautiful, stupid people who made a ton of money for being beautiful despite their stupidity.

She was entertaining as hell though. Connected. Older. Fully-sexed. I didn't want to be her, but I knew I had to go through her stage in life. And she needed me because she had a habit of getting her ass in trouble, and I had a habit of creating ways to get her out of it.

The Breakwater Club used to be stuffy and traditional but had changed to a venue for hip Hollywood parties on weekends. They let you smoke anywhere outdoors, but not inside. Which was annoying, especially on March nights when it could get down to fifty degrees by the beach.

Lynn struck a wooden match, hands shaking. She leaned on a concrete planter and cupped her hands over the flame. The corner of her cigarette lit. She sucked hard to pull the cherry. Behind her, the ocean crashed and the sand darkened close to the waterline.

"So fucking annoying," she said. "Like second-hand smoke ever killed anyone."

The guy smoking next to her checked her out with a smart smile. She wore a tube top and a skirt so short that her underwear showed when the wind blew.

I took the lit cigarette from her and pressed the tip to my own, filling my lungs with delicious nicotine. Yoni and Fred were inside.

"Are they both in there?" I asked.

"Yeah. The two of them. The hot ones."

That would be Strat and Indiana. Vocals and guitar, respectively.

And hot, for sure. Lynn and Yoni had been chasing them around for a week. Lynn had taught me so much about how to get through doors. How to ask person A for a favor because they knew person B.

I took it all back. She wasn't dumb as a box of rocks. She was dumb as a box of fox.

"I think tonight's the night," she said softly, leaning into me. She held up three fingers and twisted them around in a bastardization of "fingers crossed." Code for a threesome, which the two boys were famous for and what she had been trying to get herself involved in for a week.

"It's, like, fifty percent more romantic," I said.

She blinked. Didn't get it. I sighed.

"Yoni's in for girl-on-girl," she said. "I'd ask you but—"

"No thanks. Not tonight."

Not yet. I wasn't ready for that kind of thing. I'd done some low-level groping, but nothing close to the intensity of what Lynn chased after.

Yoni poked her head out. Her furry blond bob was held up with a big lace bow, and she wore fingerless, elbow-length gloves with dozens of silver bracelets at the wrist.

"Lynn," she said sotto.

Half the people on the smoking deck turned at the sound, then back to what they were doing.

"What?" Lynn asked.

We stepped to the door, and Yoni came out.

"They have a suite upstairs. Talking about a poker game. You got cash?"

"Yeah," Lynn answered.

"I'm in," I said.

Yoni's gaze sizzled over me, and I realized my error. I was going to be a buzzkilling interloper.

I stamped my cigarette out under my short boot. "Never mind. I'm going to take a walk. See you guys later."

I didn't wait for a response. If Lynn wanted to screw one or both of those guys, I could get a cab home. I didn't go to the street though. I went down the wooden steps to the beach. My feet felt the cold of the sand even through my boots. It had rained earlier in the day, and my steps made half moons of darker sand visible in the floodlights. I walked to the waterline out of reach of the light, not looking back, and sat with my knees to my chest, hugging myself against the cold.

The light disappeared and the night took over a few feet from the line where the sand got flat and wet, streaked with the movement of the tide and punctuated with intestinal piles of seaweed.

I didn't have any feelings one way or the other about the orgy. I wasn't interested. But I liked poker.

I dug my heels in the sand. Fuck this. I didn't know what to do with my body, with my place in the world, with my family. I was trapped in all of it. The water broke, foaming and hissing, a few feet from me. I didn't know if the tide was rising or receding. Didn't matter.

I didn't know what I believed in.

Desperation defined the lives of my friends. They were desperate to fit in, to make their families happy, or to decide who they were immediately. I didn't understand the hunger for approval or validation. The backstabbing and garment-rending over people with dicks made me uncomfortable. Men motivated tears and anguish that seemed unjustifiable. Weird. Out of character. I had friends who were normal one minute then started to have a freaking embolism when their bodies changed.

I felt it too. But we all took the same courses in school. We'd all known it was coming. Why act as if it was a shock?

I'd backed away slowly until I didn't have friends who couldn't cope. No one knew what to do with me. I didn't even know what to do with me. I knew I didn't fit in, and I didn't care. Maybe it was my version of rich girl ennui. Maybe I was just too smart, too good at too many things. Or too acerbic to make those warm girly relationships. I depended on no one. Didn't feel useful.

I felt as though I had more going on in my head than most people, then I thought I was out of my mind for believing that. So I reached out, trying to make more friends. Then I realized how empty relationships were. I realized I really did have more going on in my head than most people, and I started the cycle over.

Lynn had disappeared into the club, on her way to the suite to have a threesome or foursome, and I was left on the beach. I could have made it a fivesome, and why not? What would be the difference either way?

Screwing one or ten people didn't need to be an earth-shatteringly meaningful experience, but I should know why I wanted to besides boredom.

"It's not ennui then," I said to myself.

My face squeezed tight, reacting to having sand thrown in it before my brain fully registered that two shirtless men had run past me, kicking up sand. They dove into the freezing surf.

God damn. Los Angeles was pretty warm in March, all things being equal, but the water was fucking cold.

They swam to the place where the waves rose cleanly and treaded water, looking toward the horizon. When a big one rolled in, curling at the top at just the right moment, they flattened their bodies and rode it in. They got lost in the white froth, then they came up sitting. They high fived. The wave they had ridden continued past them, past the boundary of wet sand, to the dry line six inches from my boots.

Tide was coming in.

One of the men came toward me, pants heavy with water, hair dripping, short beard glistening in the lights of the boardwalk. "Got a towel?"

"No."

"Fucking cold."

"Shoulda thought of that before you went in."

Behind me, the other guy snapped a white hotel towel off the sand and gave it a shake before putting it around his shoulders. He had music tattooed all over his chest. That would be Stratford

Gilliam. Unbelievable in person. Even in the dark.

"She's got a point," he said and darted back to the club.

The guy with the ginger beard was Indiana McCaffrey, and he was supposed to be fucking Lynn and Yoni. Instead, he was standing over me, shivering.

"I have fire," I said, handing him my cigarettes and lighter.

He took them and sat next to me. "Thanks." He pulled out two cigarettes, handed me one, and lit both with trembling hands.

"You should probably get inside."

"I like being cold."

"Sure. That's why people move here."

He blew out a stream of smoke. It took a hairpin turn two inches from his lips when the sea breeze sent it behind him.

"You from here?" he asked.

"Los Angeles born and raised. Fermented in Pacific brine and air-dried in the California sun." I flipped my hair so the wind blew it out of my face. He was more beautiful in person than in any magazine. I didn't know how I got to be sitting on the beach with Indiana McCaffrey, but once the cigarette was done, he was probably going to split. Every second counted. "Your Southern accent's mostly gone. You could be a newscaster."

He nodded, or he could have been shivering. "My father didn't like me sounding like a hick, so he beat the accent out of me."

"What else did he beat out of you?"

He glanced at me. "Besides the shit?"

His pupils were dilated eight-balls with blue rings. He was on some sensory-enhancing drug. Quaaludes maybe. Supposedly the blue capsules made you horny and happy enough to melt the awkwardness out of the threesomes. That's what Lynn said. She got blued whenever she could. I kept away from blues. I didn't need to be any hornier or happier.

The top layer of his hair had dried, and it fluttered in the wind as he looked down, rolling the tip of his cigarette against the edge of the sand.

"Shit's the first thing to go," I said.

He smiled, looking up at me with a cutting appreciation. As if I'd touched him in a way I hadn't even tried. Asked him something real. I'd just been fucking around, but I'd hit a nerve, so I didn't shrug it off and ask something different or dismiss the question.

"Came a day," he said, putting the filter to his lips. "Came a day I stopped feeling anything good or bad. He'd beaten that out of me good. I like or don't like things. But everything else?" He flattened his hand and cut the air straight across our eyeline.

"I get it," I said. "I have the same thing. No beatings though."

"Everything's better with a beating."

I laughed, and he laughed with me. For a guy who had no feelings, I kind of liked him.

"I saw you play the KitKat Lounge the other night," I said. "And the party after."

He twisted his body to face me and looked me in the eye. "I knew I'd seen you somewhere."

"I didn't want you to think I was pretending to not know who you were."

"Fair enough."

"But you don't have to stay here to be polite. It's cold."

He shrugged. The shivering had slowed, and his skin had dried. "My friend's upstairs with a couple of girls, and I'm not in the mood tonight."

"I think those girls might be friends of mine."

He turned back to the ocean, mimicking my posture: knees bent, elbows wrapped around the peaks of his legs, shoulders hunched. "You want to go up there, it's room 432."

"I was on the beach to avoid that scene."

"Why's that?"

"Wanted to see if you two idiots would get hypothermia."

He turned to me again, chin at his bicep, hair bending over one dilated blue eye. "How old are you?"

"Eighteen. Why?"

"We're getting a poker game together at midnight. You in?"

I had nowhere to be until morning. And because I didn't give away my hand with my voice or body, I was very good at poker.

"I'm in."

Chapter 5

1994

The copyright case was pretty simple. Bangers, a UK-based pseudo-pop-rap band, had used a few bars of Haydn in their breakout song. Haydn wasn't protected under US copyright, obviously, but Martin Wright was, and he claimed Bangers had used his recording of Opus 33 repeatedly in the song.

Bangers countersued for libel, denying the claims and producing proof that they'd hired a string quartet to play the piece. Martin Wright couldn't prove it was his recording since he claimed they changed the speed so that they wouldn't sync up.

"By way of introduction, everyone, this is Drew McCaffrey," Thoze said.

Drew nodded at everyone, and I thought he lingered on me, but maybe I was mistaken. Maybe I lingered on him.

"Mister McCaffrey is here from the New York office, where he represents the interests of... god, how many musicians?"

"All of them, if I could."

Ellen giggled, sighed, caught herself. She was newly divorced, in her mid-thirties, and suddenly giggling. She was tall and attractive. Well put-together in her daily chignon and Halston suit. Closer to Drew's age and expertise. I had the sudden desire to lick him so I could call him mine.

Thoze continued. "Martin Wright, the cellist, was LA-based at the time of recording, and he's trying to bring this through a favorable court system. Thank you for bringing this to us, Mister

McCaffrey, but no one has a case." Thoze closed his folder. "I say we send Mister Wright on his way."

"They stole it," Drew interjected.

"You can't prove it," Peter Donahugh said, brushing his fingers over his tie to make sure his double-Windsor knot was still where it ought to be. "No one can. The cost to the client would outweigh the award."

Drew put his pen on the table, taking a second of silence to make his case. I'd known a musician puffy from drugs and alcohol. The guy across from me, taking three seconds to get his thoughts together, had the same blue eyes, but he also had a law degree. He still had guitar string calluses on his fingers and a tattoo that crept out from under his left cuff.

The *Rolling Stone* piece I'd read hadn't gone past Indy's devastation over Strat's death. I never heard about Indiana again. Didn't know his career choice post-mortem.

God damn. This suited him.

He pressed his beautiful lips together, leaned forward, and turned his head toward Thoze the Doze. I could see the tendons in his neck and the shadow the acute angle of his jaw cast against it.

I remembered how that neck smelled when I pressed my face against it.

"It was the most popular recording of Opus 33 when the song was mixed." Drew laid his fingertips on the table like a tent. "These guys, Bangers, didn't have a peanut butter jar to piss in. Moxie Zee charged an arm and a leg to produce, but he's a lazy snake. He billed the band for hiring a quartet that never existed, and I know him. He isn't searching out the least-used version of Haydn's Opus."

"A case is only as good as what you can prove," Peter said.

Drew kept his eyes on Thoze when he answered. "He's produced a bunch of paper. Not one actual cellist."

"We're not in the business of proving what isn't there." Thoze wove his hands together in front of him. "Absent something that proves malfeasance, we have nothing."

"What am I supposed to tell Martin? We don't care?"

"Tell him we're looking for something we can act on."

Thoze stood. His assistant stood. Peter and Ellen stood. I took the cue and gathered papers. I looked up at Drew to see if he was going to react at all, and he was reacting.

He was looking at me as if I had an answer. I couldn't move. Ellen tried to linger in the conference room, but in our shared stare and shared history there sat a thousand years, and Ellen didn't have that kind of time.

She cleared her throat. "Margie, can you grab me a coffee from the lounge on the third floor?"

"There's coffee right there," I answered from a few hundred miles away.

"It's better on three."

"I'm going for breakfast," Drew said, not moving. "I'll grab some coffee. Donuts too."

"Send the clerk. That's what they're for."

Was Ellen still talking?

"She can come."

Ellen paused then slinked out.

As soon as the glass door clicked, Drew spoke. "What are you thinking?"

"I'm thinking I had no idea you had a brain in your head."

It really was amazing how his lips were so even, top and bottom. How had I not seen that? Or the way his eyes were darker at the edges than the center?

"Things changed a lot since then."

I was feeling things, and now with his voice sounding like a cracked sidewalk, I knew he was too. That wouldn't do. It made me uncomfortable, as if my skin was the wrong size.

"I'm sorry. About Strat. I know you guys were close."

I'd broken the spell.

Drew pulled his gaze away and put his briefcase on the table, snapping it open when he answered. "Thank you."

"Was it bad?" I had no business asking that, but I had to because I should have been there. I should have done the impossible, leapt time and space, presumed a friendship I might have made up, and been there for them.

"It was bad."

He plopped his briefs in the case. I was supposed to get up and straighten the room out, but I couldn't stop watching him, remembering what he'd been to me for a short time and how those few weeks had changed me.

"What studio did Bangers record in?" I asked.

"Audio City." He slid his case off the table and went for the door.

Just as he touched the handle, I spoke. "Have you done a Request for Production?"

He didn't open the door but turned slightly in my direction, curious and cautious. "I don't see what that would prove."

I stood. "I'm only a clerk."

"I'm sure that's temporary."

I pushed the chairs in, straightening up as I was meant to. I didn't want him to feel pressured to take advice from someone who hadn't even passed her bar yet. Someone who had been no better than a smart-mouthed groupie all those years ago. But I wanted to be heard.

"You want to scare the hell out of them, you call in some favors at Audio City," I said. "Take Teddy out for some drinks. Be seen. And you file a Request for Production to aid discovery. Teddy hands over the masters."

"They'll be mixed down. They're useless."

"There's more to a tape than the music. There's pops and scratches. Match them to Wright's master. It's like a fingerprint."

"That's not true."

"It's true if you believe it is. You're not trying to prove anything. You're trying to get Moxie Zee to crack."

He took his hand off the door handle. I noticed then looked away.

"What you want," I continued, trying to sound casual, "is for your client to be paid for his work, right? I mean, cellists make a living but not that much."

"Not Drazen money."

I ignored the jab. One, he smiled through it. Two, though I tried to be as anonymous as possible in the office, it was nice to be known.

"No." I pushed the chair he'd sat in under the table. "Not Drazen money. If Moxie Zee is caught lying, most of his artists won't care. Some will think it's cool. But he works for Overland Studios as a music supervisor under his real name. Overland's risk averse. They're not keeping a guy who might have already exposed them to a lawsuit."

"And you think Moxie will pay off Martin under the table over a fingerprinting technique that doesn't exist?"

"People are pretty predictable."

He nodded, bit the left side of his lower lip, tapped the door handle three times, then looked me up and down as if he wanted to eat me with a dick-shaped spoon.

"You're still crazy," he said softly, as if those three words were meant to seduce me.

They did. He was half a room away, and every surface between my legs was on fire. I would have swallowed, but I didn't even have the spit to do it.

"How old are you?" he asked.

"Eighteen."

He walked out, letting the door slowly swing shut behind him, and I watched him stride down the hall in his perfect suit.

Men loved tits, legs, ass, pussy. Men loved long hair and necks. They loved clear skin and full lips. But some men, the right men—men like Drew and Strat—loved cutting themselves on sharp women, and I hadn't been loved for the right reasons in a long, long time.

Chapter 6

1982 – BEFORE THE NIGHT OF THE QUAALUDE

Bullets and Blood was on the verge. *Kentucky Killer* had caught fire and made the small label enough money to keep the lights on. But then the Big Boys went after Bullets and Blood, sending hip-looking A and R guys around with pockets full of promises. They introduced them to music legends like Hawk Bromberg, with his little flavor-saver and sideburns, who talked up his label and everything they'd done for him.

This was background noise in the weeks following, but the morning after I cleaned them both out at poker, I knew nothing. I'd kept my bra on, put my shirt back on, and stretched on the couch for a few hours. Woke up with a headache and a throat that felt like a bag of dry beans.

I had to get to school.

Lynn was gone. So was Yoni. The hotel room looked over the beach and, in the yellow of the rising sun, seemed expensive and luxurious in a different way than the night before.

"Morning," Strat said from the balcony. He leaned on the doorway in a shirt and stonewashed jeans.

Behind him, Hawk smoked a stubby brown cigarette as thick as a middle finger, looking at me as if he was eight and I was a piece of birthday cake. He was a legend, but I wasn't flattered. I was disgusted.

"Where's Indy?" I asked.

"Out for a swim."

Had Strat even slept? He still looked perfect, but maybe my standards were skewed. He looked as though he partied all the time, and that was what I found attractive about him.

"I gotta go."

"You should come around later."

Hawk nodded, picking the slick brown butt out of his teeth. He sang about heaven and earth with a voice like a fist, but I wasn't loving his real presence.

"Sure." I didn't have time to chitchat. My father was coming back from a business thing in Omaha, and I had to be home.

"Do you have my beeper number?"

"No."

I didn't have time to scrabble around for a pencil and a piece of cleanish paper so I could set off the little black box on Strat's belt. He wouldn't even answer it. He was a rock star.

"Eyebrow," he said. "Six-oh-six E-Y-E-B-R-O-W."

"Six-oh-six? Kentucky? I thought you guys were from Nashville."

"The beeper's from Kentucky."

I didn't move. Just waited for the long version.

"My dad moved to Kentucky. He's a doctor. He upgrades every six months."

Mister Big Rock Star was either too frugal or too busy to get his own damned beeper. Or too much of a kid. Or too attached to his parents.

No matter what angle I looked at that from, no matter how the light hit it, I found it charming.

* * * *

I had no intention of using that number for anything, though I'd never forget it. My driver was off. So I got a car at the hotel's front desk and sat back for the short ride from Santa Monica to Malibu. It was six thirty in the morning. I had ten minutes to get back.

Nadia, Theresa's nanny, would be up because she didn't sleep. Hector, the groundskeeper, was probably already working. Maria, Graciella, and Gloria. Definitely rousing Carrie, Sheila, and Fiona for school. Dressing them. Making sure homework was done. Deirdre, Leanne, and Theresa would be causing havoc. If I got right in the shower, there was a pretty good chance no one would notice I had even been out.

Except Mom. She was a wild card. She usually slept until eight, but if she drank the night before, she actually woke up earlier. And if she caught me out, she was unpredictable. She'd been pregnant six times since I was born, so she always seemed to be in a constant state of flux. Big. Little. Tired. Energized. Horizontal. Running. One person. Two. She was as likely to lock me out and act as if everything was normal as tell my father, which would be bad. Very bad. All bad. He did not like losing control. He seemed to have two emotions: cold calculation and satisfaction.

I loved him. I loved both of them. But I never knew what to make of them. In the end, I realized they didn't go on and on about how they felt but concerned themselves with actions. I respected that. It was what I thought it meant to be an adult.

I knew I'd pushed it. Playing strip poker with two guys in a semi-famous rock band in a semi-luxurious hotel room? And telling them my name?

My God. I didn't know what my parents would do to me, but everything about it was trouble. Dad cared about what people thought. He cared about appearances and chastity. Even if he wasn't in town, he had the nannies dress us all up and take us to church on Sunday. He made sure we had ashes on our forehead and palm crosses in our hands. He never mentioned God at all, but the Catholic Church always loomed as the ultimate authority.

I'd asked him why, and he said something odd.

He said, "Invisible gods are ineffective."

I had to hope that Strat and Drew had no reason to find out who the Drazens were. How old their money was. They wouldn't. I wasn't anyone to them. I made myself invisible in my mind when the cab got to my house. I gave the cabbie one of Drew's hundreds, ran into the side door, and made it into the bathroom without being seen.

I washed the night away with scalding water.

Six-oh-six eyebrow.

Go over pre-calc in the car.

History

Comp

Stupid's not a verb, asshole.

Forty minutes to memorize a hundred Latin conjugations
Tennis
Photography
Eat something
What's your name?
Catholic Women's Club
Chess Strategy Club
Then?
Then?
Then…

Chapter 7

1994

"I know everything comes pretty easily to me compared," I whispered to Drew/Indiana in the hall before swiveling into my cubicle. I had to pick up my things before doing Ellen's donut run. "But I put some work into being here. I'd appreciate it if you didn't mention we knew each other eleven plus years ago."

"Am I so embarrassing?" He smirked as if he had me over a barrel.

Typical man, thinking it was all about hard work now/today/this week. If word of our history got out, I'd be a slut and he'd be a hero. I'd be fending off advances in the copy room, getting censured for shit I did a decade ago, wondering why I never got the good cases, and he'd fly back to New York and get promoted.

"It's not shame and never was."

"That's my Cinnamon."

"It's Margie now." I spun to face him, my back to my desk and spoke quietly. Terry, the other clerk, was a foot away through the grey half-wall. "Full-time. This is my life. Like I said. I have plenty of privilege but no dick."

"It's 1994."

He said it as if we had entered the modern era and his dick didn't make a damned bit of difference in the workplace. Only a man could think something so utterly incorrect.

He must have seen me boil, because he put a hand up before I could explode. "I'm just giving you a hard time. I never intended to say a word about anything, but I'm in town for the week."

I opened the bottom drawer of my desk and got my purse out. "Fine." I slapped the drawer shut.

"Fine?"

"I have no feelings about it one way or the other."

"Good to see you haven't changed." He winked and slipped out.

Chapter 8

1982 – BEFORE THE NIGHT OF THE QUAALUDE
I didn't have to remember E-Y-E-B-R-O-W or six-oh-six, which I happened to know was a Kentucky number from a friend at Carlton Prep. I got a beep in the middle of chess strategy with a Nashville call back number. An hour later, I was in the passenger seat of a Monte Carlo driving into Pacific Palisades. Strat was behind the wheel, and Indiana was in the back with Lynn and Yoni.

I had no idea why I was there. I wasn't the prettiest girl who hung around them. I hadn't screwed either one of them, though apparently Yoni and Lynn had had a fine time with Strat before the poker game had gotten under way. I didn't understand why I was there because I didn't understand men.

Yet.

It came to me many years later, while reading *Rolling Stone*. During the interview, Indy was sitting in front of a mixing board they'd installed in the Palihood House (He was "producing" because that was always the story arc. Small-town beginnings>cohesion of the group>artistic satisfaction>commercial success>drug use>break up>The Bottom>redemption>rebuilding/branding). His hair was scraggly but intentionally so. His shirt was clean. He'd lost the puff around the eyes, and he was talking about Strat.

"He was like a brother to me, but more. A partner. And when he died, man, it was like someone ripped me open."

In the passenger seat of the Monte Carlo, with the two of them still poker-playing strangers, I didn't know they were like brothers. Years later, reading the *Rolling Stone* article, that Monte Carlo ride came back to me.

I'd been so clueless about how close they were and how lonely they were.

I always assumed I was brought into this world fully formed. Maybe I wasn't. Maybe I didn't understand people the way I thought I did. I chewed on that then forgot it, because it only turned up the heat on a cauldron of stew that had everything and nothing to do with the Bullets and Blood boys.

Indy leaned forward and pointed at a locked gate closing off a road into the foothills of the Palisades. "Up here. Code's fifty-one-fifty." He turned to me, and I could feel his breath on my cheek. "Wait until you see this place."

"It's nice up here," Lynn said before cracking her gum. She was in a black lace corset and tiered skirt. Red, red lips and black, black eyeliner.

"This is the ass-end though," Yoni chimed in. "It's the Palihood."

"Yeah, anything east of the park."

"South."

"East."

I rolled my eyes.

Strat ignored them. "He can't afford it."

"We just got a quarter-million dollar contract." Indy leaned back and kicked Strat's seat.

Strat shook his head. "Have you read it?"

"You don't read Greek either."

Driving up the hill under the clear spring sky, the fact that he'd read the contract and understood it made me look at Strat's arms, his music tattoos, the muscles of his legs, and respect him with a sexual heat.

We pulled up to a house made of glass and overhung with trees and surrounded by tall bushes. When we got out of the car, the shade was a welcome respite from the blasting sun, and the birds cut through the white noise of the freeway.

"It's nice," I said.

"And I can afford it." Indy pointed at Strat as he headed for the front door.

"Fuck you can," Strat muttered.

Yoni and Lynn had no interest. They'd started bantering about the coyotes in the hills, bouncing with excitement, as we went up the cracked steps onto the pocked flagstones.

"Ye of little faith." Indy opened the door. "I have the down payment next week. Made escrow already."

The black linoleum floors shined, and the sightline went through the house, over the west side, and to the ocean. Yoni and Lynn were already checking out the bean-shaped pool in the back.

You'd think a musician on the cusp of fame wouldn't want to be tied down to a house. He'd want to ride the tour bus and fuck a few hundred girls. That was the norm. But Indy stood in the empty space between the front door and the horizon and lit two cigarettes before handing me one.

"I can move in next week."

"Dude," Strat said.

"Dude," Indy snapped.

Strat turned to me, hands out, pleading. On the whole ride up, I'd wondered why they brought me, and I feared at that moment that they'd gone to the library or talked to their lawyers and found out who I was. Now they were going to ask me for money, and I couldn't give it to them. There was no other reason to put me in that car.

I liked them, but that house had to cost two hundred grand.

Would they threaten to tell Daddy things? The poker? The bra? The smoking? Would they tell him I drank and I kissed? Or that I was a cocktease?

When I brought the cigarette to my lips, my hand was shaking. I didn't know which scenario terrified me most. I inhaled the nicotine and blew out rings as if I had control of this. Whatever this was. It was my first cigarette of the day, and it made my palms tingle.

"Why the fuck am I here?" I asked.

Strat stepped forward, finger pointing at me then Indy. "Keep me from killing him."

"Fuck you," Indy retorted.

I didn't have anything much more intelligent to offer. "It's a nice house. Needs work. Get an accountant to tell him if he can afford it."

"Let me give you the short version." Strat's comment was directed at me but meant for Indy. "Two fifty minus fifteen percent to WDE. Two twelve and a half. Eighty-three grand. Minus three points to our producer. Two-oh-five. And by the way, we, you and me and Gary—the *band*—we have to recoup *their* points."

"We will. I'm telling you."

"Two-oh-five divided by three? Sixty-eight thousand dollars for a three-year contract. And you haven't even paid your taxes yet."

I rolled my eyes and looked at the ceiling. If Strat and/or Indy noticed me acting my age, they didn't say anything.

"There's income, fucktard." Indy patted his pockets and found a thick marker best suited to sniffing and writing graff. "I need a napkin. Fucking find me a napkin. An envelope. I gotta write on the back of it."

"Fifty grand for the studio we gotta pay back," said Strat the Sensible. "Recoupable. Producer. Recoupable. Equipment rental. Re—"

"Stop it!" I shouted.

I'd had it with the two of them. I didn't know much of anything. I didn't know how to run a business or how to make money, but I knew how to think like a rich person. Maybe that was why they'd brought me.

"You guys. You're so cute with your middle-class shitsense. You act as if it's money to spend. It's not. It's money to make more money. You." I pointed at Strat. "You move in here with Indy. You take your sixty grand, and you set up a studio in the garage or the living room. I don't care where. You." I pointed at Indy. "Get a commercial loan. You lay down the next record here and collect the fifty grand instead of paying it in recoupable expenses. You rent it out to your other musician friends and let them pay your mortgage, and you pay down that fucker because at eighteen percent interest, you're getting killed."

I took a pull on my cigarette. It was so close to the filter that my fingers got hot. Jesus, figuring that out felt good. Whether they did what I said or not, putting it together had been damn near orgasmic. "I need a fucking beer."

Chapter 9

1994

The San Fernando Valley, Van Nuys in particular, was a hell of parking lots and freeway-width avenues. Everything looked new yet coated over in beige dust. Drew and I had split right after the meeting, slipping down the back elevator. It was like the old days when I had a ten o'clock curfew I ignored.

We pulled into the back of Audio City, where the entrance was. Drew put the car into park and leaned back.

"You gonna open the door?" I asked.

"I haven't seen these guys in a long time. Give me a minute to think."

"Get back into your rocker head?"

He smiled, and something about that made me feel really good. "Yeah."

I switched my position so I was kneeling on the seat, facing him. I yanked on his lapel. "Take this off. You look like a fucking lawyer."

"Right. Okay." He wrestled out of his jacket and tossed it in the back. His shirt had light blue stripes and a white collar, and his tie was just skinny enough to be stylish without crossing the line into new wave.

I grabbed it and let it go so it flopped. "Come on, take this off."

He undid it. "I forgot how bossy you are."

"I still can't believe you even remember me."

"You're not forgettable."

"Please," I said. "There were hundreds of girls."

He yanked at the tie, slipping it through the knot. "I was obsessed with you the second you opened your mouth. You scared the fuck out of Strat. He thought he was going to lose me to you."

He leaned his head back on the seat, raising his hand languidly and touching my chin. My eyes fluttered closed, because I'd been too busy to let a man touch me in years, and this man knew how to touch. He ran his finger along the edge of my jaw, down my neck, and I grabbed it before it could move lower.

"We're working."

"What happened to you?" he asked in a whisper.

"I went to law school."

"Before that. You split. We couldn't find you. Strat hung out outside your house. We went to all the clubs. Your friends didn't know where you were."

He didn't know what he was asking. He thought he was going to get some reasonable, sane answer, but there wasn't one.

"It had nothing to do with you," I lied. It had everything to do with him. Every single thing.

"What did it have to do with, Cin?" His voice dripped sex and music, and I wondered if that was just his way of getting back into character.

I reached for his collar and ran my finger under it, revealing the stand of tiny white buttons. "The collar comes off."

"You need to tell me where you went."

"I took a trip."

"We waited, and you never showed up."

He moved his fingertip down my shirt. My breath got short, and I couldn't take my eyes off of his lips.

"Sorry. I flaked. You guys were too intense for me." I didn't know why I had to make it obvious that it was more than that. I could have kept my voice flat and subtext-free, but my inflection got away from me. If he couldn't tell I was hiding something, he was an idiot.

And he wasn't an idiot. That was shit-sure.

"You're not going to tell me, are you?" he said.

"No."

He took his hand away. Relief and disappointment fought for

dominance inside me as he flipped his stiff collar up and unbuttoned it.

"We had a good time," he said. "Good coupla months."

"Seven weeks."

"I wasn't even thinking about how long it was going to last. But I was so fucking stupid anyway. Strat was smart. He played at being a reckless musician, but man, he was sharp and fifty years older in his mind. He told me to chill out. He told me the thing we were doing was temporary, and I argued with him like a moron." He shook his head at his stupidity and got the last button undone, snapping the collar away from his neck.

"Looks better," I said, smoothing down the Mandarin.

He took my wrist and sucked me in with the tractor beam of his gaze. "I thought I'd be the one to lose my shit when it ended. But it was him."

I pulled my hand away. I couldn't pretend I didn't care for another second. "What happened?"

"I could ask you the same thing."

"You could."

But he didn't, and I opened the door to end the conversation.

Chapter 10

1982 – AFTER THE NIGHT OF THE QUAALUDE

Rich family. Pig rich. Six nannies, two cooks, and a cleaning staff rich. Multiple estates. We were our own economy. My dad wouldn't experiment with losing a chunk of it for another twenty-plus years.

My father had two brothers, and my mother had a sister she barely spoke to. She'd never said why. She never said much that was worth listening to. She hadn't seemed young to me until the autumn of Bullets and Blood.

This realization happened at a party. We had two hundred people in the house for my parents' anniversary. String quartet. Black tie staff. Open doors to our swimming pool with lotus blossoms and candles floating in it. Attendance was mandatory, so I had to tell Indy and Strat to get their laughs elsewhere.

All the family and business partners were there, all the wives clustered around the couches and most of the men hovering around the bar. Except Aunt Maureen. She never hung around the women. She was my "cool aunt" who ran a business and told the guy she'd been with for the past ten years that she saw no point in getting married. She was talking to my dad and a few guys in suits I knew by sight but not name. I was close by, hanging on every word, when I heard her say something about negotiations with a blue chip company. It was a bunch of numbers and percentages I understood because I remembered everything the adults in my family said about business. But at the end, she laughed.

The sound had a clear, tinkling quality her voice usually lacked.

She sounded so young.

Wait. She *was* young.

She was eighteen years older than me. A little less, give or take. And that made my mother fifteen and change when she'd had me.

Over the ice sculpture and through the floral arrangement in the center of the ballroom, I looked at my father and did more math.

I almost laughed at the symmetry of it.

But it wasn't funny. It took me too long to realize what had gone on, but I told myself I wasn't going to be like my mother. I didn't hate her, but I didn't respect her either. She was from a good family. She was beautiful and smart. But she was nothing. She did nothing. Her life was a vacuum that purpose had fallen into, never to be seen again.

I wasn't going to be that, but I was already on the way.

Me in my blue dress and little gold hoop earrings, dressed like a prim little miss. A chiffon-and-silk lie I let them believe. I felt sick.

I was thrown off balance by the impact of a small child. Fiona was five, and she had her arms wrapped around my legs. The others followed. Deirdre and Leanne hugged my legs too. Carrie and Sheila, at nine and eleven, stayed close, looking excited. I was only missing Theresa, who was a year old and had started walking two weeks ago. They looked up at me with eyes in varying shades of blue and green, hair from strawberry-blond to dark brown red. That was what happened when a redhead married a redhead, and my insides curdled like milk on the stove.

"Who's watching you guys?" I was talking about everyone but directed the question at Carrie, the oldest of them and most likely to put together a coherent sentence.

"Everyone's outside. Are you having cake or not?"

How long had I been staring into the middle distance?

Long enough for everyone to move to the garden, leaving a few clustered stragglers by the French doors. I let my little sisters lead me outside, where sibling hierarchy was determined by proximity to the cake. I'd lost any will of my own and hung behind all of them. I didn't really want cake. I'd been sick to my stomach for days, fighting a headache, feeling tender everywhere, but I had a compulsion to act as if dessert mattered.

My mother and father stood behind the cake, smiling for the

professional photographer. He wore an *LA Times* press pass. The camera was nowhere near me, but I felt exposed. They'd want a picture with me, and I couldn't. I just couldn't. I could stay relatively anonymous in the world, but people read the pages of news about the Reagan presidency, Beirut, Studio 54 closing, and Hollywood celebrities. After those, but before the stock ticker, came the society page. Weddings. Anniversaries. Deaths of monied men.

My father tapped his glass with a spoon. He was over six feet tall and looked every bit the oligarch he was, with a full head of dark-red hair. My mother was more strawberry, and she held her head high when he was nearby. On that night in particular, she beamed a little brighter.

The guests quieted, and even the photographer put his camera down when Daddy raised his whiskey.

"Ladies and gentlemen," he said, projecting to the back of the room, "thank you for coming. I hope you're all having a good time celebrating this, my anniversary with my beautiful bride."

A chorus of tinkling rose as more spoons met glasses.

A great sound, I thought. *They should try it in the studio.*

My sinuses filled up, and I almost started crying, but my father kissed my mother quickly and went back to his speech.

"We have an announcement!"

Let's hear it, Declan!

Hear! Hear!

"Eileen is about to make me a father for the eighth time!"

"Get off her, for Chrissakes!"

The shout from the back ended in uproarious laughter and cheers from everyone but the children, who didn't understand it.

Except me. But I wasn't a child. Never was, and never would be.

The photographer started snapping again. Dad and Mom indicated we should come behind the table so we could all smile in dot matrix patterns for tomorrow's paper, and I couldn't.

I'd hit my limit. I was going a hundred miles an hour, and the brick wall had appeared inches in front of me, without warning.

I'd taken a pregnancy test that morning. I'd put it away without looking at it and decided I wasn't going to think about it. Not until after the party. Pretending bad things weren't happening wasn't like me, but then again, nothing bad had ever happened to me.

I'd bought it as almost a joke because my period wasn't that regular. But it wasn't funny.

The compulsion to look at the results weighed like a rock in my chest, exploding in slow motion. I had to hide before the shrapnel shredded me from the inside.

My room was a good three-minute expedition across the house, and I took it at a run, slipping on the marble and righting myself. I was crying hard by the time I reached my hallway. Somewhere in the journey, I'd let it go. Everything.

Oh god oh god oh god

I was a sensible person. I knew I had options, and the first step to exploring them was to know what was happening. The nausea and headaches. The tender breasts and belly. The feeling at the root of my hips that something was *happening*. I had to scratch pregnancy off the list so I could move to the next possibility, but I knew I wasn't scratching shit off any list. I just knew.

And when they'd announced Mom was pregnant (again), I couldn't wait another second.

When I got to my room, breathless in my pale blue dress, I slapped open the medicine cabinet where I'd left the little plastic jar. If the liquid was one color, I could forget the whole thing. If there was a brown ring at the bottom—

"Are you all right?"

I spun at the voice in the doorway, leaving my back to the open cabinet. My father stood in the doorway, still thrust forward from his run up the stairs.

"I'm fine," I said.

"Your mother thought you'd take it hard. I told her you were made of steel." His smile was one hundred percent pride.

"I just ate something that didn't agree with me."

I spun and snapped the medicine cabinet door closed, but it bounced back, leaving an inch of the inside exposed. I turned back to my dad, hoping I wasn't disrupting the liquid. Taking the test with eyedroppers and test tubes, I'd felt as if I were in lab class. I didn't want to do it all again. And I didn't want Dad to see it. And I didn't want to be pregnant. And I wanted to rewind the whole thing, so I didn't stupid my way through life.

"You've been so busy with your extracurriculars, your mother is worried." His eyes left mine and went to the medicine cabinet. He wasn't looking in the mirror. They traced the edge, moving up and down.

"I'm a little tired. Can I skip the cake?"

"Be back down in half an hour for pictures."

His sharp expression meant that was an order. I could be green around the gills, and I'd be expected to smile for the camera.

"Okay." I wanted him to go away.

He looked from behind me to my face, scanning it. I felt made of thin blown glass, hollow and transparent. Too fine. Too delicate. Worth too much to be broken without everyone I cared about getting upset over the loss.

I tilted my head down and went around him, to the doorway, where the promised comfort of my bed waited. He'd have to follow me out and leave me alone for thirty minutes. I could do a lot of calming down in half an hour.

I'd just stepped onto the carpet in my room. It was mauve and grey. And by the second step, the colors became a woolen blur as I was pulled back and spun around.

Dad's face was beet red. He held a clear plastic vial in his left hand as he gripped my arm with his right. "What is this?"

"You're hurting me." I tried to squirm away, but he only gripped me tighter.

"What have you done?"

I was so scared I could barely think. My father had never raised a hand to me, but I'd always known there was an ocean of violent potential under his smooth veneer. A cold, deep sea that remained placid but was ever-threatening.

"It's negative!" I shouted, not knowing if that was true. I hadn't gotten a look into the vial before he stepped in.

"This?" He turned the vial toward me, open top to my face.

The yellow liquid had been slipped down. At the bottom, a brown ring of thicker membrane slid down, going elliptical before drooping into a line of accusation.

I didn't have an answer. Not an excuse or reason. Nothing but an explanation of what I'd been doing with my free time, which I was sure he didn't want to hear.

"Who is he?" Dad growled.

Wasn't that the question of the year.

"Let go!"

"Were you raped?"

"What?"

"I'll kill whoever did it."

"Dad! No!" I was crying now. I hadn't had enough time to process what I'd done to myself. I felt the spit and tears as if they were someone else's. Dad's face was lost in a wet, grey cloud, and my breath came in hard sobs. I choked out what I thought was a bit of reassurance. "It wasn't rape."

He twisted me around until I was facedown over my white footboard, the thin wood painful on my abdomen. While I was trying to navigate around that and the tears that flowed with the force of a storm, I felt a sharp pain on my bottom.

A strange clarity cut through my sobs, and my crying stopped as if I'd skidded to a stop at the edge of a cliff while the tears dropped to the bottom.

Dad spanked me again, and the impact turned breaths into grunts. I tried to turn, but he held me and whacked me again. I was confused, pinned. I looked around at him. His hand was raised with fingers flat, and elbow bent to strike me again, and he was looking at his hand as if it had done something he didn't understand.

Then in that split second, he looked down at me, and we made eye contact. He saw me but didn't. I didn't know what he saw. I didn't know what math he was doing in his head. The violent sea within him didn't calm. It didn't drain into a huge funnel and gurgle away, but the tide changed and moved like a lumbering beast, receding over the horizon to a place I couldn't see.

He let me go. I slumped over the footrail. I took two deep breaths, and only the first one was an incomplete hitch.

I had neither choices nor time. My family, for all their money, was very Catholic, very rigid, very traditional. I had tons of privilege but no rights. So if I was going to abort this baby, it was now or never. Let them disown me.

I had to run away.

Chapter 11

1994

Business had been rough for a few years, but Audio City was still the best music studio in Los Angeles. It had a certain something. Reputation-plus-talent-plus-acoustics-times-equipment-equals-hotter-than-hot. Before my parents' anniversary party, information like that had mattered to me. But sitting with the head engineer in a soundproof room that smelled of stale sweat and cigarettes, all that mattered was the plan—a ruse to get a settlement—and the client, a cellist who might have been ripped off by a wealthy producer.

"You were the only band in our history who canceled studio dates," Teddy said.

I vaguely remembered him. Back then, before Bullets and Blood, I'd slinked in with Rowdy Boys. Teddy'd had a full head of hair and a smile full of straight white teeth. When I sat in the booth with him and Drew (née Indy), Teddy was made of comb-over and nicotine stains.

"We got our own place," Drew answered.

"Still running from what I hear."

"Yup. Switching over to digital."

Teddy shook his head and snapped a pack of cigarettes off the mixing board. "Fucking digital." He pushed open the pack with his thumb and offered me one.

I took it. Then Drew surprised me by taking out his own pack and lighter.

"It's the future," Drew said, shaking out a smoke.

"Fuck the future." Teddy lit mine then his own.

I pulled on it, tasting the dry heat of tar and letting the nicotine run through my blood. I hadn't smoked in umpteen years, and I'd forgotten how much I liked it.

Teddy picked a little piece of tobacco off the tip of his tongue. "Digital wouldn't help you with your cello problem." He flicked the speck of a leaf away. "It's those pops and hums that make magnetic tape sound warm. It's what got you here. If we recorded on digital, it wouldn't mean shit."

"Yeah," Drew said.

"Digital's gonna kill music."

"Sure."

"But you don't care no more." He flicked his hand at Drew, from his fancy shoes to his conservative haircut. "Lawyer."

"Douche."

Teddy surprised me by laughing. "Yeah. Know thyself, right? I got it. Give me that production request or whatever you call it, and I'll show it to our lawyer. He'll get back to you." He held out his hand to shake Drew's.

Here was the problem. The request for production wasn't worth shit because the fingerprinting thing was made up. Even a shyster lawyer would figure that out.

"How about a deal?" I said.

Teddy's hand froze midway up, and he looked at me. Drew looked both surprised and curious.

I swallowed hard. "Let us down into the master archives for a Bullets and Blood record. The debut was recorded here, right?"

"Right."

"We'll just peek at the Opus 33 masters. See if it's worthwhile so you don't have to blow two hundred an hour on a lawyer. In return, Indy here will show you how they're going digital. Show you the right equipment. So you can decide for yourself if you can switch."

Teddy stubbed his cigarette into a half-full ashtray. I glanced at Drew. His head was tilted down and toward me, thumb to forehead to hide his expression. His cigarette burned hot to the filter as he smiled.

"Yeah," Drew said, looking up. "We'll do a consult. Above board. You can probably go digital without switching completely. I know you get people and lose people because you're analog. Let's see if you can't do both."

Teddy considered, looking away, then back at us. Shifting his box of smokes, shaking his foot, then nodding to himself.

"Yeah, why the fuck not?" He stuck his hand out again, and Drew grabbed it. "Why the fuck not?"

Chapter 12

1982 – BEFORE THE NIGHT OF THE QUAALUDES

They started getting that studio together almost immediately. They had recording and tour dates to keep. So during the day, the house was filled with workmen, artists, and sound engineers in leather Members Only jackets.

I was confused about Strat and Indy. For the next week or so, I was with them all the freaking time. Like a piece of furniture for the new house. Sometimes they beeped me, and sometimes I E-Y-E-B-R-O-Wed them. I met them wherever they were, and we proceeded to act as though we were all in some kind of relationship.

But they didn't make a move. Strat had eyes like fingers—they had a way of getting between my skin and my clothes. But he never did anything about it. Not in the week after I told them how to have their house and live in it too.

Once, when we were at a party in Malibu, Indy put his hand on my shoulder and said something in my ear. I don't even remember what it was, but the music was loud, so he had to talk in my ear if he wanted me to hear him.

Strat came up right after that, like a hawk, and put his finger in Indy's face, lips tense. Indy shrugged. It was the first time I saw them act like anything but best brothers.

Indy put up his right hand. "Pledge, asshole."

"Fuck you." But Strat put up his right hand. I could see the matching snake tattoos inside their forearms. "Pledge open."

"Nothing," Indy spat. "Nothing, okay?"

"Closed, dude. I'm sorry."

They put their hands down and hugged, back-slapping as if they'd had a whole conversation.

"What was that about?" I asked when Strat drifted off.

Indy shrugged, and someone came to talk to him. Male-musician-slash-producer-slash-A and R guy. Thirties. Black plastic sunglasses with red lenses hiding his blued-out dilated pupils. Cartoonishly hip. Guys like that were always talking to Strat and Indy, and they had a way of making sure I was treated like a life support system for a pussy. It would take three minutes for him to angle his body so that he was between Indy and me, then he'd turn his back to me.

Like clockwork, I was looking at the back of his jacket.

Fuck this. I didn't understand any of it. I went inside, picking my way through couplings and conversations on my way to the front door. I'd opened it, letting the cool West Side breeze in when Strat caught up.

"Where you going?" he asked, nipples hard from the night air.

I let my hand slip from the doorknob. "To buy you a shirt."

He gave me that look. The one that made me warm and tingly. The room was full of women wearing strings and little triangles, yet he was looking at me as if he wanted to devour me skin to bone.

Yes, it turned me on, but it also annoyed me.

"What was that about back there? With Indy?" I asked.

"What was what?"

"Fuck this."

I opened the door, but I didn't get far. He leaned over and pressed it closed.

"You don't know?" he asked. "You can't tell?"

"Since the first day you brought me to this house, you've treated me like a little sister—"

I had more to say. Much more. A speech worthy of Ronald Reagan, but he laughed. I just ate those words, chewed and swallowed them, because I'd seriously misread something. He opened the door, still smiling like a fuckhead.

"Beep us," was all he got to say before I left.

I had an orange button on my beeper. I pressed it, and my driver pulled up. Like magic. His job was to take me to and from whatever activity I had going on. His job wasn't to tell me where to go or tell my family where I was. I barely made it half a block back toward home before I knew I'd beep six-oh-six E-Y-E-B-R-O-W. Or Indy. It didn't matter. I was addicted to them the way Lynn was addicted to blues. The excitement of their company was the best drug in the world.

Chapter 13

Here's a comprehensive list of what it means to be mature for your age.

1. You see people through their lens, not yours. So there's less getting offended. Less reactive bullshit.

2. You have perspective but not experience. You know it all shakes out in the end. So small problems are small, and big problems are small.

3. You get cocky because you're mature and you know it. Stupid mistakes are other people's problems.

4. Your body is still a slave to your brain, and if your brain is thinking about grown-up shit, like sex, your body is going to be a hotbed. And if your body matures early... well, follow the yellow brick road. The Emerald City has its legs spread for you.

Chapter 14

1982 – BEFORE THE NIGHT OF THE QUAALUDE

The house in the Palihood had a thousand square feet of unpermitted add-ons. Some even made sense. Most didn't. One bedroom was five feet wide and had outdoor wood siding on one wall. One add-on was only accessible via five treacherous two-foot-high steps to an attic the shape of an inverted V, and another bedroom was only accessible from the outside patio and through a closet.

I arrived one afternoon after a respectable activity I could never recall in black pumps and a Chanel jacket. The house was dead except for the open door and obscure punk playing from the sound system the boys had installed over the lead-painted walls and chipped molding.

I didn't announce myself. I never did. I was a piece of furniture, more or less. I heard voices from one of the spare rooms. I passed through the third bathroom, into the closet, and almost opened the louvered door to reveal the sound when I stopped. A cry had come from the other side of the door.

The louvers gave me a choppy view, but I saw enough skin to make me take a step back. I heard panting. Groaning. A man's voice. Strat. I took a second step back. Stopped. The doors had a space between them, and I leaned forward and looked.

I recognized the girl from her silky brown hair. When she moved, it swayed over her shoulders. She was on her hands and knees. Strat was behind her, fucking her so hard my face flushed and my body's heat level went deep in the red. I could smell them. Their sweat and something funkier. The scent between my legs plus a man. I touched the wall. I needed it to hold me up.

Leave. Turn around.

"Take it, baby," Strat muttered, hands gripping her ass. His skin was satin with sweat.

I wanted him. I wished I was the girl with the brown hair, taking it. I shifted a little so I could see the place where their bodies met. His cock sliding in and out of her.

God god god I want it.

I was blocking the way, but I didn't want to go back and I couldn't go forward. All I could was hope that no one wanted to go into the spare bedroom right then. I shifted, nervous someone else was near me.

The second woman had curly blond hair and generous naked hips. I wished I was her, naked with them. Laughing about some whispered words.

You're nuts. This is so past what you're ready for.

"You want to eat her out, baby?"

"Yes," said Straight Brown Hair. She turned to Luscious Hips, still getting fucked, and her eyes lingered on the louvers for a moment.

She saw.

"Let me kiss your pussy."

No. She didn't.

Luscious Hips sat right in front of Brown Hair and spread her legs. I didn't think my clit could have been more engorged or my pussy wetter. I was glued to the scene as she laid her face between her friend's legs. I couldn't see what she was doing, but Strat, that voice...

"Eat her hard. Suck on it. *Mmf.* Yes. Make her come."

"I'm so wet. So wet," Luscious Hips shouted.

Strat put his hand between mouth and cunt. I didn't know what he was doing, but the intersection of those three things aroused me so much. I did the unthinkable. I stuck my hand under my skirt and tore my panty hose open to get under my cotton briefs.

I nearly collapsed at my own touch.

"Get it wet," Strat commanded as the girl on her hands and

knees sucked his finger. "It's going in your ass."

Did he say that?

I think I'm going to die.

The girl who was getting fucked had her face in Luscious's pussy as Strat stuck one finger in Fucked Girl's ass.

"Yes!" she looked up long enough to affirm.

Strat put in two fingers. She shouted, face planted in pussy. Luscious had Fucked by the back of the head, pushing her mouth into her cunt, pumping her hips across Fucked's face while Strat pumped away and got three fingers into her ass.

Oh god, I want that I want that.

But I didn't want to come. I pinched my clit to shut it up. I had more to see.

Luscious came, crying, "Eat my pussy eat me god yes baby yes eat me." She groaned and threw her head back in relief.

God, that was hot. I wanted someone to eat me out.

Strat held out his hand and said something to Luscious. She reached into the night table and pulled out a bottle of baby oil.

What are you doing, Stratford?

He poured it on Fucked. Down her back and in the crack of her ass. Then he massaged it inside.

"You ready?" he said, handing the bottle back to Luscious.

"Fuck me in the ass."

I swore the backs of my thighs tingled, and every nerve ending between my legs nearly exploded.

He pulled his dick out of her and moved it up between her ass cheeks.

He's going to do it.

Fucked's face tightened and she grimaced, eyes shut, teeth grinding, as Strat slowly but purposefully put his dick in her ass.

"How you doing, baby?" he asked.

"All the way," she said. "Take my ass."

I watched his dick disappear in her asshole, and I squeaked.

They didn't hear me.

I thought they didn't.

Luscious put her hand between Fucked's legs.

I didn't see the rest. I heard the squeaking bed, the shouts and moans, Strat barking when he came in her ass. My eyes were closed as I stroked myself to the most explosive climax of my young life.

As soon as it was done and the three of them were laughing and panting, I pulled my hand out of my panty hose. A line of pussy juice stretched between my second and third finger. I curled them into a fist and backed out of the closet.

Strat was right. I couldn't handle him.

Chapter 15

1994

"Aa-*choo*." I was on my fourth or fifth sneeze.

Audio City kept a rust-painted trailer-slash-shipping container in the north corner of the back parking lot. Teddy had given us the padlock key, and when we opened the back doors, we found a wall of banker boxes stacked to the ceiling. They were ordered by date, with the older shit deeper in the back, except when they weren't. We had to look at every box and hope that the label was correct. We found Martin Wright's Opus 33 sampler master box pretty quickly, about a third of the way through. It was labeled with his name and the year. Drew put it on a low pile and wiggled off the top. The box had become misshapen from dampness. The smell of mildew got sharper with every pile we unearthed.

Contracts. Invoices. Master tapes. A pencil case.

"That's weird," I said.

Drew handed it over. Shiny orange vinyl marked with pen. I pulled the zipper open. It was empty inside but dusted with fine white powder. I held it open for Drew.

When he looked, he laughed. "Of course. We could probably open up all these boxes and sell coke out of the back of this container."

I zipped it closed and tossed it back in the box. "He's a cellist. I can't even imagine what the rest of these have in them. We taking the whole thing?"

"More likely than not." He jiggled the top back on.

We'd found what we came for, but we were both hesitating. He looked toward the back, where another ten feet of solid banker box stood. A thick wall of musical history.

"You're thinking what I'm thinking," I said flatly. The container was hot and oppressive, yet I didn't want to leave it. "We did come for the *Kentucky Killer* masters."

"You have to get back to the office."

"More likely than not."

"You can't stay here with me. Already you've been with the visiting attorney too long."

"And a law clerk can't call in sick for the rest of the day or anything."

"You'd have to make it up over the weekend." He put his hands on a high box and slid it down, then he put it in my outstretched arms. It said "Neil Young – 1990."

"Yeah. I hate working weekends." I put the box with the rest of the early nineties. "Maybe five minutes. Then I'll grab a taxi back to the office."

"You should run into the office and call. I don't want you to get in trouble on my account."

He had dust on the shoulders of his shirt, and he'd rolled up his sleeves, exposing the tattoos on his inner arms. I'd done a good job stripping the lawyer costume.

"Five minutes." I held out my arms for another box. "Ten. Honestly, I already told Dozer traffic might keep me here. And I have a family dinner tonight. So they don't expect me until tomorrow."

"Saturday."

"Come on, you know the drill. Six days a week, et cetera."

He slid another box off the top. I'd never heard of the artist. He put it gently in my arms, still holding it. "I'm glad you got your shit together."

"You too." I whispered it because I wasn't just returning a nicety. I was speaking a deep truth.

Seeing him again wasn't just a happy coincidence. He scared the shit out of me. I didn't do feelings. They didn't rule me. I did what I wanted, when I wanted, how I wanted. But I was scared, and fear made me uncomfortable.

I decided discomfort was all right though. I wanted to be

around him.

His fingers grasped my elbows while he held the weight of the box. "I'm not together. I just have a law degree."

He wanted to tell me something, and I wanted to tell him something. We couldn't. We were different. We didn't know each other and we never had, but the pull was there. I wanted him to know me. I wanted to tell him my secrets. Not because of who we'd been, but because something about his puzzle pieces fit my puzzle pieces. I felt a clicking, like the snap of one piece into another.

I stepped back with the box, and his fingers brushed my arm as I pulled away.

That felt nice.

I turned away and put the box on the pile. Fear was uncomfortable, but the rainstorm between my legs wasn't much better.

Chapter 16

1982 – BEFORE THE NIGHT OF THE QUAALUDE

I happened to know that most stars, real stars, didn't get mortgages. They paid cash or had their corporations loan them the money, so they paid interest to themselves. But Drew and Strat, and Gary to a lesser degree, were normal guys on the brink of becoming real rock celebrities.

We lived on chips and pretzel rods because we were young and skinny. Indy lounged on the blue velvet couch, plucking on his guitar, and Strat scratched his head over the papers laid out over the coffee table. I had my legs slung over the arm of a matching blue velvet chair.

"Can you start booking the studio in August?" I asked.

Indy strummed his twelve-string. Even without an amp, the sound was thicker than a six-string, and he got his fingers into the narrow spaces between them as if he'd been playing since he was seven.

"Yup," Strat said.

He didn't have a shirt on, and I tried not to look at him. Strat was so beautiful it hurt. The promise of sex had diminished since poker night. Part of me said to hell with them, and the other part just wanted to know why.

Indy, Gary, and Strat were tight. Real tight. They'd grown up together in Nashville. Only sons in their families. Graduated from their local suburban high school. Like cupcakes dropping out of the same pan. Different, but all from the same batter.

An empty pack of Marlboro Reds landed in my lap.

"We're out," Strat said.

"There's a carton in the fridge," I said.

His knees bounced, and the swirls of musical staffs buckled where his body folded. A snake coiled around his firearm, biting inside his wrist. Gary and Indy had the same snake tattoo. Gary had married young and fathered up quick, so he wasn't around unless there was music to be made.

"Tell me what that snake's about," I said. I wanted to get him a box of smokes, but I didn't want to do it because he'd told me to. He was a bossy jerk. Sexy and powerful, but jerky.

"It's about you getting a fresh pack."

I didn't move. Indy ran his pick over his twelve strings. I didn't think he was paying attention.

"You all got matching tattoos so you could be a fucking asshole? Shit, I can get one too."

"Why? When you're a bitch already?" Strat's words and tone didn't match. The words were cruel and divisive. The tone was warm and friendly. His face invited me to kiss it, as if he was the only one who would tolerate Margie-the-bitch instead of Cinnamon-the-groupie.

It took me a split second to put together a snappy retort, but Indy cut it off by putting down his guitar and standing. He shot Strat a dirty look and paced out of the room. Strat watched him.

Something was going on, and Strat was too cool a customer to tell me.

I bounced off the chair and followed the guitarist. The house was barely furnished or painted. The guys didn't have the money or time to do the fancy stuff. They had parties, but everyone sat on the floor and in folding chairs. I crossed to the south side of the house where I could see the pool. They'd had that cleaned and finished because to have a party, you needed a pool.

The kitchen had nothing of use in it. Paper plates and plastic forks. The gas was hooked up but was used to light cigarettes and heat spoons of white powder. The fridge had beer, vodka, cigarettes, and a china tea saucer with blue pills arranged around the center circle.

Indy stood in front of the fridge, pulling out a carton. He flipped his wrist, and the box spun midair, dropping on the island counter with a *slap*. Red-and-white packs swirled out. I grabbed one before it fell off.

"It's not your job to do what he tells you," I said.

"Can I ask you a question?" He took a pack for himself and cracked the plastic, letting it flutter to the floor without a second look. Both of them were fucking slobs.

"Sure."

"What do you want?"

"Life, liberty, and the pursuit of happiness?"

He didn't respond, verbally or otherwise. He just wedged out two cigarettes and held the pack to me. I took one.

"Stop the bullshit. You're past that." He took a zippo from his pocket and clacked it open. "*We're* past that."

He lit me. I blew out a stream as he tilted his head to light his own, cupping it as if we were in a hurricane instead of a kitchen. He was unselfconscious in that second, and I admired his face and shoulders.

"Be more specific then," I said.

He clattered a glass ashtray between us. "You don't wonder what's going on here?" He pointed his finger down and made a circle.

Here. I knew exactly what he was talking about, yet he was so vague I could have kept the game going on long enough for Strat to stroll in for his smokes. But I couldn't. I was as tired of this shit as he was. Both. Neither. All. None. The space between them was getting uncomfortably tight.

"You mean that you guys are always beeping me, and you keep me around but no one's fucking me?" I ask.

"There you go."

"Yeah. I wonder that."

I wondered it at night, when I was home alone with my hands under the sheets. When I felt inside myself, the edge of the unbroken membrane tight on my finger. When I imagined some composite of the two of them was on top of me. Or one or the other. Or they fought over me, and both won. I didn't know what or who I wanted, but my body got wet for both Sexy Strat and Sincere Indy. Not that I knew what to do about it. I was old for my age, but there was nothing like actual experience.

"Little Stratford and I, we don't fight over women."

"Okay."

"That's the deal."

"You're implying you're fighting over me," I said.

"Yeah."

"You know what that does for a girl's ego, right?"

I didn't actually believe him. That was the problem. I was cute as hell, but come on.

"When I needed Strat, he was there for me. My father was a drunk fuck." Indy rolled the ashes off the tip onto the amber glass of the ashtray. "Still is. I needed this house for a reason. The guest house in the back? It's for my mother. To get her out of there. So when I finally talk her into leaving him, she has somewhere to go where she feels safe. If I'm hotel to hotel on a bus, that's great, but it's like leaving her to rot. And the guy in there"—Indy jerked his thumb toward the living room, where his best friend was probably still looking over paperwork—"he gets it. I can't do any of this business shit without him. My head's not in it. He's giving up a chunk of his advance to make this house and studio happen."

"I'm glad, Indiana. Really. He's a great friend." I stamped out my cigarette. "What do you want out of me?"

His frustration was bigger than anything we said. His fingers curled, and his teeth gritted. He stepped forward and put his hands just under my chin, an inch from touching them, as if it was as close as he could get. As if his palms and my jaw were the north sides of two magnets.

"I'm fucking nuts about you," he growled, then leaned down, so his face was level with mine. He smelled like tobacco and cologne, with a hint of music and risk. How many times had I watched his fingers on a guitar and wished they were on me? "You have to make a move," he said more softly but with urgency. "You have to choose."

"You're not supposed to have feelings." I said it as if "supposed to" mattered at all.

Strat's voice came from the patio. "Dude." He took the length of the kitchen in three steps, snapped up a pack of cigarettes, then pointed at Indy with the same hand. "Watch it."

"Is he telling the truth?" I asked. "You have a deal about me?"

"A deal?" Strat asked, ripping the plastic off his pack. "I wouldn't call it a deal."

"What do you call it?" Indy asked. "A pledge?"

"Call it a fucking truce."

"You guys are both…"

Insane.

Annoying.

Beautiful.

Looking from one to the other, knowing I could have either, I couldn't pick an adjective, much less a man.

I'd never liked feelings, even before I consciously pushed them away. They made me feel like seven people living in the same skin. Now I had these two guys looking at me as if I was supposed to say something.

What did they want out of me?

One or the other?

What was normal about this? I hadn't kissed either one of them.

Or anyone.

I threw my hands up. "Fuck you both."

I walked out. I didn't want the car to get me. I wanted to walk this off. This bullshit. This pressure. I couldn't admit I was in over my head. I'd never admit a situation existed that I couldn't handle, especially not something as basic as two guys wanting me to choose between them.

I was warmed by the setting sun, but the air chilled my skin. Good. I wanted sensory distraction. Anything to make this shit run in the straight line.

What did you expect?

Nothing. I hadn't expected anything.

No, I'd expected them to choose. I'd suspected that one of them liked me, and the other one kept me around as a courtesy to the other, and I expected that the one who liked me was Indy. And that brought about the bigger question.

Which one did I want?

Both. Neither. Either. Some fourth choice.

"Hold up!"

I thought about not turning around. Just walking to the nearest cross street and calling the driver. I got three steps while deciding what to do. I heard the footsteps quicken behind me, and I turned to see Strat. He was wearing the jacket he kept by the door.

"You got dressed. Nice going."

"Hold up," he repeated, grabbing my elbow.

I yanked away. "You guys need to work it out and get back to me."

"No, baby. You need to wake up. That guy back there? You're not going to find anyone better in your life. You turn your back on him, and you're an idiot."

I was surprised. Here he was, the god of them all, lean and sharp with a voice like a fallen angel, advocating for his friend.

"Why do I feel like a pawn in some game you guys got going?" I asked.

"It's not a game."

"What if I want you?" I didn't mean to say I wanted him, even though I did. I didn't mean to imply I'd made a choice because I hadn't even known there was a choice to be made.

"Sorry," he said, narrowing one eye and shaking his head slightly. "I'm not that kinda guy." He started to walk away.

"I saw you," I called, and he stopped. "With two girls. Couple of days ago."

"Yeah?" He tilted his chin up as if I could swing at it if I wanted, he didn't care.

"It was hot."

"That shit's not for you, Cin. That's a couple of blues and boredom. Not your scene."

"How do you know?"

"You're too good for that shit. He's too good. This is fucked up, the whole thing. I don't know who you are or what planet you're from, but it's not mine. It's his." Without another word, he walked back up the hill, long hair flipping as he stepped into the wind.

I watched him turn into the gate, then I hit the little orange button on my beeper. If I went right home to change, I could make it to the Suffragette Society planning committee. I needed to get away from this weird fucking scene.

Chapter 17

1994

I'd stopped sneezing. Either we had gotten so deep into the trailer we hit ancient allergens I didn't react to, or my body just gave up.

Drew's arms and shirt front were covered with dust, and he had a war-paint-shaped grey streak across his jaw. It was getting late and his cheeks were getting a dark shadow. I felt as if we were no closer to the box for Bullets and Blood, and I was close to giving up. But every time I thought to mention it, I stopped myself. I enjoyed Drew. His connection to my life before. The pain we shared. Even the shared pain he didn't know about.

"I kept the business going, even after the band broke up," he said. "Gary wanted to find another lead, but I was done. I just wanted that house." He picked up a box. Looked at the label. The handwriting had changed an hour earlier. Someone must have gotten another job.

"Did your mom ever move in?"

"Yeah. After my dad died of liver failure."

I took the box from him. *Rick Springfield.* "Fuck him then."

Drew laughed. "Yeah. Fuck him."

I laid Rick's box on top of the others. We'd developed a quick system so we could get all the boxes back in place, but it would still be a big job. We were deep into the woods.

I went back in to meet him. I was going to say something like, "Hey, I think we gotta ditch this," but he stood over an open box, looking at the contents with silent reverence, and I knew. I stood next to him. It was late, and the trailer's fluorescents flickered blue.

"Is this it?" I said, standing next to him, staring at the box's contents.

Master tape boxes. Ampex. Four of them. A folder. An envelope. He put his hand on a box marked *Kentucky Killer.* They'd recorded it for Untitled Records at Audio City before I came into the picture.

"Nothing happened," he said, more to himself than me. "When we did this, we could have been anyone. But nothing happened."

"You're not the first."

"Remember his voice? The way he grumbled then sounded clear in one breath? He developed that here. Before that, he sounded like a girl all the time. See, he could imitate any voice perfectly. Any accent. He could repeat Russian back to a Russian perfectly and not understand a word of it. But he didn't want to sound like anyone else. So he was trying to create this new sound during that first session, and he sucked. So bad. All over the place. And we were so fucking high. Really high. Everything sounded like shit. The studio smelled like pot and donuts."

He took a break to smile into nothing. He was beautiful. Radiant.

"What changed?" I asked.

His eyes moved toward me, and the answer was in his intensity. "After you left?"

"His voice. What changed his voice?"

"We were laughing at Gary. He was doing an imitation of his kid. She was two and said pickups instead of hiccups and fillops instead of flip flops. And…"

A smile spread across his face. He pinched the top of his nose between his thumb and first knuckle.

"Strat couldn't breathe. We thought he was still laughing but he was choking on a fucking donut." He took his hands away and looked at the ceiling. "Oh my God, what happened? I remember. I gave him the Heimlich. He spit up this wad of donut that looked like an oyster. We're laughing. I nearly broke his ribs and we were laughing. But his voice…his esophagus must have gotten shredded or something. Or his throat felt different and knew how to do it. He had a way of hearing that went right to his lungs. He did it once and never forgot it. Fucking gift."

He tilted his head back to the box and slid out a set of reels.

"You miss him. I'm sorry."

"I wish I could have stopped him."

I didn't expect him to put his arm around me, but he slid it over my back, up my spine, and over my shoulder, then he pulled me to him. I watched as he took the top off the smaller box. Inside was a clear plastic reel with brown magnetic tape. It didn't look magical, but to him it was, and we stood in silence for a minute as if praying to it. Then he put the top back on as if shutting out a thought.

His arm tightened around me until I had to loop my arm around his waist. From there, the rest was a dance. He turned. I turned with him. He bent down. I leaned up.

He smelled different. He was cologne and tweed. Sharp and clean.

I turned my head before our lips met, and though that movement came with the knowledge that I didn't know this man, I considered telling him what had happened to me.

Chapter 18

1982 – AFTER THE NIGHT OF THE QUAALUDE

I didn't know what to pack, but I knew I had to go. I yanked my smallest Louis Vuitton suitcase from the back of my closet and slapped it open. I didn't know what to put in it, so it was first-grabbed-first-served.

Outside, the anniversary party was breaking up. Long black cars headed down the drive, just moving dots of white and red lights. I didn't have much time.

I had to get out of there.

Out of that house and to an abortion clinic. I'd come to terms with being disowned. I wasn't having this baby. Not now. Not scared in my room with a party going on downstairs. Not with my mother getting a hundred congratulations for being just as pregnant as I was. Not with the spanking I'd just gotten still stinging my ass.

He'd never done that before. Would he do it again?

I picked up the phone to beep… who? Lynn or Indy or even Strat, who was the last guy I'd beep unless I was desperate.

Which I was.

Desperate.

Time was slipping away, and the consequences of my stupidity were going to land like an anvil in a cartoon. I'd be flat. I didn't know what my parents were going to do, didn't know if my father had even had a chance to tell Mom anything. But I couldn't get the last half hour back. I'd spent it staring out the window, trying to sort my head out. Identifying feelings for what they were. Useless.

This is fear.

Ignore it.

This is shame.

Pat it on the head and send it away.

This is regret.

Kick it.

I tapped the headset on my upper lip. Lynn's family knew my family. All my friends were from the same circle. I'd be sent right back home.

E-Y-E-B-R-O-W

I dialed so fast my fingers slipped on the buttons, and I had to start over. *Ring. Ring.* Three beeps.

I put in my number. They wouldn't know it. I'd always called from the car phone or a phone booth. Never from home. They didn't know where I lived. Smartest thing I ever did on one hand, because it protected them. On the other hand, when the beep came through, he wouldn't know who it was from.

So I waited.

When the phone rang, I picked it up in a rush. "Strat?"

He was outdoors. I heard traffic whoosh and the sound of music far away. A party? A show?

"Cin? What's up?"

His voice was rock candy, sweet and rough, making a beeline to the part of my brain that didn't do any of the good thinking. He must have caught the remnants of panic in my voice, because he didn't sound like his usual casual self. And what was up? What could I tell him over the phone from my own house?

"I need you to meet me at Santa Monica and Vine at midnight. At the gas station."

"What's wrong, baby?"

"Don't call me that." As I was finishing my sentence, the doorknob to my room turned.

"What—?"

I hung up before I heard the rest of the question.

Chapter 19

1982 – THE NIGHT OF THE QUAALUDE

Palihood wasn't even a word before my friends got snobby about the wrong side of Pacific Palisades. But it took Palihood House a week and a half to get a reputation, which Strat shrewdly made work in their favor.

Sound Brothers Studios. They trademarked it on a Tuesday and filed corporation papers by Friday. The sound boards weren't even set up yet, and they were already stealing business from Audio City.

Their parties were riddled with musicians. Some were at the height of their careers. They expected blowjobs. Hawk Bromberg could scream over classical guitar, which qualified him to get his dick wet within minutes of arrival. It was an entitlement, and that night, he got a look at me in my cutoff shorts and Marlboro miasma and decided he was entitled to me.

I clapped the heel of my denim wedge against the shag carpet and listened to him talk to me as if I wanted to fuck him. I didn't want to fuck him. I wanted Indy and Strat. I had the keen and unpleasant sense I'd lost them both by not choosing.

Hawk was telling me something about how record execs are all assholes and sellouts. Those cats weren't artists. They didn't understand the process (man) and those dudes are about money and not the music (man). Did I dig?

I did dig. His eyes were wet and his lips were dry, and I could dig it. I was as relaxed and happy as I ever got. Tiptoeing through fucking tulips.

"They got a bathroom in this place?" he asked.

"Yeah, sure. I'll show you."

I was like the lady of the house, even though I wasn't screwing either of the men who lived there. I was polite, I kept my pants on, and I kept my blood alcohol level low. I got to be in love with both of them without having to choose between them.

I wove through the crowd, Hawk behind me with his hand on my back, which I thought nothing of. He just didn't want to get separated. Indy saw me through the crowd, out of the corner of his eye while talking to Willie Sharp. Lynn winked at me when I passed her. We had to stop a few times to say hi to this one or that, but I was mindful of Hawk's needs and pulled away quickly to reach the quiet part of the house. Strat was in the kitchen, sitting on the counter with his feet on the island while two girls giggled at his side. One had her hand on his leg.

I told myself I wasn't jealous because jealous was a feeling—and I didn't have those. Also, Stratford Gilliam wasn't mine to get jealous over. That had been established.

The line for the bathroom was down the hall. I would have told him to just go pee in the bushes like all the other guys, but he'd said bathroom, not bushes. Maybe he had to do a sit-down session. Maybe he had a phobia.

"I'll take you to the bedroom suite," I said.

You're rolling your eyes.

I'm rolling my eyes too.

There are some mistakes you only make once because the stakes are so high, you don't know how to make them a second time. This was one of those mistakes.

I took him through the closet to the louvered doors. The bedroom had a futon and a night table from a thrift store. White blinds over the windows covered the view to the overgrown side driveway.

I pointed at the half-open door to the bathroom. It was done in pink marbelite and floral wallpaper. The house hadn't been redone since the 1960s, and the new owners were soon-to-be rock stars blowing their wad on converting half the building to a studio. No one had time for swanky bathrooms.

Hawk smiled at me and flipped his sunglasses to the top of his head. His eyes were red-rimmed and older than his years.

"It's over there." I pointed again and turned to walk back into the hall. I wanted to see what Strat was doing. It was a compulsion I didn't understand, but if he was going to fuck someone, I wanted to see it. See her. Or them. Just to make sure I'd completely lost him.

Hawk didn't go to the bathroom, and I was so lost in my own thoughts and intentions—again, you could see this coming a mile away—that when he grabbed my arm, I was annoyed, not scared.

"What?" I was still being polite, so I cut the sharpness out of my voice.

"You're really cute," he said, lightening his grip a tiny bit.

"Thanks."

"Sexy. Got a really smart mouth. I like that."

"You can let me go now."

He did. I was relieved about that for half a second because he closed the patio door.

I crossed my arms and leaned heavily on one foot. "Dude, I'm not watching you pee. Not my thing, all right?"

"What's your thing?" He stepped closer to me, tongue flicking his bottom lip the way it did when he played guitar. The girls loved that. They went nuts. But he wasn't my thing.

"My thing is getting a beer."

Oh, Jesus, that was what he was after? My thing. Indiana was my thing. Strat was my thing. Those two assholes made me feel so damn good and they barely even touched me.

"How do you like it?" His hand reached for me, and I curved away.

"I like it on Wednesdays. Today's Saturday. Sorry. My legs are closed for business."

I tried to get around him, but his hand shot out and gripped my jaw. He pressed his fingers together, and my mouth opened. I bent my knees trying to get away, but he held me up.

"Your mouth's open like a dick-shaped hole."

Did I mention he was a brilliant lyricist?

I grunted and pushed him away, and he slammed me between the wall and his body, his erection pressed against me. The first hard-on I'd ever felt. I squeaked.

He held two little blue capsules in front of my eyes. I tried to focus, but my entire face hurt from his grip.

"You're going to love this." He popped one capsule in his

mouth and jammed the other one to the back of my throat. "Swallow."

I shook my head, trying to scream and failing. He pressed my jaw closed. I tried to breathe, letting the weight go from my legs, but he wrestled himself down with me. I slapped his face, and he took it with a snarl.

"You like it rough. I knew it. I could tell."

I couldn't move. We were crouched in a corner, his knees and the hand on my mouth leveraged against the wall. His face was slick with sweat, and his tongue kept licking a dry spot on his lips.

I *hmphed* against his hand. If I spit enough, maybe it would slide off of my face. Maybe someone in the party would hear me scream over the music. But the extra spit dissolved the gelatin capsule, and my mouth was flooded in bitter juice.

"Good girl," he said.

If I'm so good, why are you still holding me down?

I couldn't say that with his hand over my mouth. If I could move before the Quaaludes took effect, I could get to Strat or Indy and they'd protect me. But once they were in my blood, I'd be high and horny. I wouldn't be myself. I'd probably open my legs like it was Wednesday.

He could fuck any girl he wanted. That party was full of pussy for guys like him. Why me? I wanted to ask, but he still had his hand over my mouth. The other hand pulled my knees apart.

"You're such a pretty little thing. Think you're so tough. Everybody wants you. Did you know? We talk about it. How we want you and you don't give it up. Well, now we can talk about how I got you to give it up."

I breathed hard through my nose, my hands curled into his jacket. I didn't know how to get away as he kept saying things meant to flatter and arouse me.

"I see those nipples under your shirt. So tight. Baby, you're so sexy. You're gonna want it so bad in a few minutes. You're gonna beg for it. Don't fight it." He pushed his hand up the inside of my thigh, fingers reaching into my shorts, touching my skin. My actual pussy.

I kicked, and one of my denim wedges came off.

"See?" he said. "Not dipped in gold."

I squealed and squirmed anew, and he got the crotch of my

shorts in his fist and pulled. I slid onto the carpet, and my shorts came down to mid-thigh. I opened my mouth to scream, but he shoved four fingers in it, blocking the sound.

There was a slap from somewhere, and I thought he'd hit me, but I was wrong. I could smell and hear the party, and suddenly Hawk was off me. I gulped for air. I pushed him away but only swung in the air. I was just completing an action I couldn't a second before.

"Hey, man!" Hawk shouted, but it was too late.

He bounced off the closet door, and Strat punched him in the face. The two girls from the kitchen were in the doorway. The one with a lipstick-smeared face ran away, and the other stood in shock and horror as Strat pulled his fist back again. The muscles of his back tensed and stretched, moving the musical staffs like undulating waves.

It landed with a crunch. The girl screamed and looked at me, which was when I realized my shorts and underwear were right above my knees.

"Tell him you wanted it!" the girl screeched from the doorway.

"What?"

"He's gonna kill him!" she shouted.

As if in answer, I heard a crack and the closet doors rattling. I tried to get up, and my hand landed on one of my denim wedges. I landed on my elbow.

I didn't feel anything. That was my normal state of being, but this particular numbness covered confusion and hurt. I got to my knees as Strat hit Hawk again.

The girl who had been in the doorway was pretty brave. She got between the two and tried to push Strat away. She definitely made it harder for him to get a clear shot, and the time she bought was enough to get Indy in the room.

It all happened so fast, with such complexity, that my shorts were still down. That's what stopped Indy in his tracks. Not the blood smeared across the Grammy-winner's face. Not his partner's pulled back fist. But me. My naked body.

Shit.

I pulled up the shorts.

Indy turned to Strat and put his hand on his shoulder and pushed, wedging himself between Strat and his punching bag.

"What's happening?" Indy said it so gently, it was a harmony of a hundred thousand heavenly tones.

"Fuck him." Strat spun to me, and Indy followed.

I was on my knees, butt-to-heels, arms crossed over my chest. "I'm fine."

"You are not fine." Strat's words were clipped.

With his eyes, Indy took me in, then his friend, then turned to Hawk, who was just getting his feet under him with the help of the girl with the smeared lipstick.

"Get out," Indy said, swinging his arm wide. "All of you. Out." Indy helped me up. He looked me in the eye. "What did he give you?"

"Lude."

He shook his head. "I wish Strat killed him."

Oh fuck. Was I going to cry?

For the love of fuck.

Stop it.

He put his hand on the back of my neck. The next thing he said was so gentle and strong, and his voice sounded like a layer of gravel floating on the deep blue sea.

"You're safe now."

The sea rose, moved forward, curved to bubbling white at the top, and dropped on me. I couldn't stop the stream of emotions any more than I could have used matchsticks to hold up a tidal wave.

* * * *

Feelings. Joy. Lust, fear, gratitude surprise arousalhatedisgustangerlovelovelove.

Lubricated with Quaalude and a narrowly avoided rape, they crushed me into sentence fragments. I couldn't get anything out that made sense. I was crying a flood of shit I'd held on to for months. Maybe years. Maybe forever.

The room was empty except for Indy and me. Strat had taken Hawk out by the collar. Indy had shouted *out* and closed the door behind all the gawkers.

Indy took me by the chin and looked in my eyes. It was getting dark, and I was covered in tears, but he saw enough to let my face go. "They're dilating already."

I'm fine. I thought it but couldn't speak.

He picked me up from the shoulders and under the knees. My other wedge fell off as he carried me

where are you taking me

to the futon, where he tried to set me down

I don't think so

but I held onto his neck and pulled him down until his face filled my vision

see? I'm not crying anymore

and he put me down but stayed close. He looked reluctant, but his pupils were like bowling balls. He was with me on whatever plane I was on. The pupils didn't lie. He'd popped whatever I'd been fed, or some other inhibition-reducing drug.

is it now? Make it now

He smelled like a man. My brain wasn't making sentences but

musk and sweat and chlorine from the pool

the scent alone drove a spike of desire between my legs so hard it was almost painful. I arched my back from it, and my eyes fluttered and my lips parted and

"It's the lude, Cin."

everything felt good while the potential for more good feeling seemed like a limitless void I could fill right now, right there. I put my hand between my legs and rubbed myself over my shorts because

oh God so good so good

all the void was inside me, and I had to fill it up. He had to fill it up. He had to. He was beautiful, and I loved him. The little voice inside my head that said that was the drugs talking. I knew that voice was on to something, but I didn't care.

I took Indy's hand and put it between my legs. I was so hot he sucked air between his teeth when his fingers landed there.

"I want you," I whispered, suddenly aware enough to put together three words.

"No, you don't. It's the—"

"The lude. I know. I can say what I feel."

I spread my legs and

are you really doing this?

moved his hand under the crotch, and his fingers pushed the

rest of the way through, until he felt how wet I was.

"Holy—"

"Oh my—"

"—shit."

"—God!"

He ran his fingers along my seam, and the second time over my clit, I exploded, mouth open, silent, muscles tightening, knees bent.

It was the most powerful, yet unsatisfying orgasm I'd ever had. I needed more. I was empty. Full of emotions. Full of joy and lust and a swirling ambition, and in the vortex of those was a centripetal void shaped like his body.

He thought for a second/million years and put his lips on mine, opening his mouth, giving me his tongue.

This is it.

I trusted him. The weight of his body, the thrust of his hips pushing the shape of his dick to me. I grinded against him as if it was my job. I was going to come all over again, clawing at his shirt, pulling it over his head. The arousal was so deep I couldn't see past it.

"How old are you, Margie?"

"Eighteen." I pulled off my tank top. "Give or take." I wasn't in the habit of wearing a bra, and I didn't even have the shirt all the way off before I felt his teeth on my nipples.

"I'm twenty," he said.

"Nice to meet you."

He pulled my shorts and underpants off in one move and kneeled between my open legs. His bare chest had a dusting of brown hair and a tattoo of a treble clef with a bird over his heart. I reached for his waistband, but my arms weren't long enough.

He grabbed my wrists and put them over my head, pressing them to the wall, and kissed me. "I've wanted you for a long time."

"I know."

"I shouldn't," he said. "You're not straight."

"Neither are you."

"True, true."

He rolled off me and lay on his back. He hooked his thumbs in his shorts, picked up his butt, and pushed them off.

His dick.

My heart dropped to below my waist. I wanted that beautiful thing. Maybe I did have a dick-shaped hole because it went on fire at the sight of it. I straddled him as soon as the shorts were off.

It was the lude. I couldn't even think. He pushed me down, the length of him on the length of my seam, rubbing where I was wet. I slid up and down, a tease of the act itself.

"Ludes make you come so many times," he said. "So do it. Come now."

The words. I didn't know what words could do. The permission cast a shadow with the light of inhibition. I ran myself against him, clit to cock, and came again, fingers digging into his shoulders. I took a breath to wonder if I was doing it right. I looked to him for cues and knew I must be all right because he was biting his lower lip, pushing against me.

Sex was so good, and I was still a virgin.

"Yes," I said. "Let's go."

"You're so hot. So hot." He took his dick by the base and shifted it to me.

I positioned myself over him then

this is it, Margaret

pushed down. His face knotted with concern when

now or later but now is better

we hit resistance but

"Wait," he said.

I pushed down hard, and something ripped. Something hurt. I froze for a second with him buried inside me, surprised at the stretching pain at my opening and the snug fit inside.

"You didn't tell me." He breathed it, gritting his teeth not in anger but a need to keep his head on straight against the knowledge that his head wasn't his own.

I needed him. I couldn't pretend I was experienced or even competent. I'd seen what I'd seen and knew what I knew, but it wasn't enough. The Quaalude made me eager and optimistic, flooded with the feeling that nothing could go wrong.

"Show me what to do now," I said.

He took me by the back of the neck and pulled me over him until I was an inch from his 33rpm eyes and I could taste the whiskey on his breath.

"I don't want to hurt you."

"I'll already remember you forever. You gonna make it count or what?"

He stroked my cheek with his thumb. His words were hard, but his tone was a caress. "Are you sure you don't have a set of balls somewhere?"

"You should be the last one to ask that."

"You're really special, Margie. You don't need me. You don't need anyone. That's what I was afraid of all this time, that I'd end up inside you and I'd never see you again."

How many minutes had passed since Hawk made me swallow? Fifteen minutes? Twenty? The room had gone from deeply angled sun to a wash of blue, yet time was nothing.

I didn't understand any of what I was feeling. The unmotivated elation caused by the drug I'd been force-fed was a bucking stallion behind a wood fence. With every kick, the lock bent. Soon the fence was going to crash down in a splintered heap and I was going to promise him an eternity together for another and another and another orgasm.

"Do I move like this?" I shifted my hips in a circle and drove down until I felt a pressured pain deep inside and my clit rubbed against him.

He groaned. That was good. He took my hips and shifted me up then down again.

"Like that," he said, hands running up my waist to my tits. He pinched them, and a new shot of pleasure ran down my spine.

I moved up then down until he was deep in me.

"Push against me here." He took a hand off my tit to press the front of me against him, so my nub rubbed against his body.

I gasped.

"When you come up, angle yourself so you get it the whole way. Go."

I did what he said, letting my clit feel the length of him. "Oh, God. That's. Fuck."

We moved slowly, up and down, pressing deep, the friction and pressure bringing me close to a third orgasm.

"If I make you come on your first time—"

"Gold star. Fuck. God. Gold star it's so good."

"You have to come soon. Please come soon I'm so-close-no-I'm-there." His eyes closed, and his jaw got tight.

I thought the drug had made me feel good already. I thought it had aroused me more than normal, but I wasn't even halfway there. The bucking stallion of emotion broke through the gate, and I was blindsided by a rush of joy. I cried out from the chest-bursting, brain-exploding emotional high. My world washed bright yellow, and as I dropped down on his dick, deep and hard, my orgasm flooded orange, deep red, explosive, centered on cunt and mind, mixing at the heart of something so vivid I couldn't see who I was past it.

I dropped on top of him, barely breathing. His chest heaved under me.

"Gold star," I gasped. "I'll remember you forever."

He laughed. "You haven't even started to remember me."

Chapter 20

1983

Strat died about six months after the last time I saw him, and I found out about it six months after that. I was in the library, catching up on schoolwork with a newfound ambition.

The library magazine rack was in front of my Debate Team materials, and I stopped when I saw Strat's music-strewn bare chest on it. I bit my lower lip. I'd been home a month and hadn't called him or Indy. I didn't want to explain about the baby or whose it was (or wasn't). I didn't want to revisit any of it. I was a new woman.

But he was majestic, and the photo was dark in a way that made it mysterious. I was curious.

Chapter 21

1982 – THE MORNING AFTER THE NIGHT OF THE QUAALUDE

The morning after I'd had a Quaalude shoved down my throat, I woke up on the couch with a headache. Indy was already in the kitchen, slogging down a glass of water.

"Where'd you go last night?" he asked.

"Good morning to you too." The light tasted too yellow. The air hurt. The floor and sky were too loud.

"Here." He shook three aspirin out of the bottle into my palm. The circles were too perfect and too white, the big B etched into them too capitalized.

He filled a glass of water for me. I washed the pills down and drank the entire glass.

"Thank you," I said, handing the cup back.

He took it then took my wrist and pulled me toward him. Bone creaked on bone, but it didn't hurt. I let myself lean on him.

"I have to tell you something." He spoke into my ear and stroked my back. That didn't hurt either.

"Mmm."

"I want to take another crack at last night, but without the ludes."

"Mm-hmm."

"Or Strat."

I swallowed.

Jesus.

Last night.

I hadn't forgotten as much as I'd woken up feeling like I had Dengue fever or something. But, yeah. Last night had happened.

I leaned back until I could see his eyes. "I think I just need to sleep today."

"Are you okay to stay?"

I shook my brain. Yes. I was supposedly on a camping trip. I hated camping, but I'd had to lie.

Right? I had to wrap my life in lies.

"Indy, I have to tell you something. After I tell it to you, you're never going to want to see me again."

He did something that took my breath away. He leaned over and swept my feet from under me, getting his arm under my knees. "Never tell me. Never say it."

His lips tightened a little, and without saying a word, I was sure he knew.

"Are you sure?"

"Yes."

I help up my hand. "Open pledge."

He laughed, and though it was loud, it didn't hurt my head. "My hands are occupied. Assume it's up."

"Swear you don't want to know. Swear you're already okay with whatever I was going to say."

"I do. Close pledge."

I slung my arm around his neck, rested my head on his shoulder, and let him carry me to his room.

I had a life in the weeks that followed, but not much outside Indy. I helped with the studio, hammering and painting, getting boxes and running cables. I could have done that forever, lost the world and gained my soul.

But there wasn't a soul to be had.

Chapter 22

1994

"Evidentiary privileges," Drew said, sliding a box up high.

I gave him the next one. It was after dark, but we were almost done. I'd spent the entire process watching the veins on his forearms, the way his biceps strained his shirt, the movement of his lips when he spoke.

"I just did that one," I complained.

"You don't get to stop until you can bill two-fifty an hour. Evidentiary privileges."

I picked up another box and brought it to him. They weren't heavy. "Attorney-client. Doctor-patient. Spousal. Priest-penitent."

He pushed the box to the topmost position in the pile, and I gave him the last one.

"Done." I slapped my hands together.

"Contracts, quick—"

"You can't go from evidence to contracts like—"

"Construction. Give me rescission remedies."

I put my hands on my hips. He was making it hard, and I loved it. "Builder in breach. No remedy. Owner in breach. Builder gets market value of work done."

He stepped toward me. "Land sale," he said in a velvety, non-demanding tone.

"Payments less land value."

He touched my elbows, pulling them toward him, so they weren't impatient angles on my hips. "Sale of goods."

I let my arms go around his waist. I wanted him right there, on a stack of boxes, breathing mildew and old air. I'd been with a few guys since Ireland, but I'd never felt so comfortable. Had he only been back in my life a day? Had it been just that morning when he knocked into me in the waiting room? I felt as though we'd picked up where we left off.

"Are we still in rescission?" I purred.

"You're really cute when you're buying time."

"The contract is canceled and either party can sue for breach."

I tilted my head up, breathing in his Drew/Indiana-ness. I could practically taste him.

"Not quite." He spoke in breaths, his lips grazing my face. "Non-conforming goods need to be established before cancellation and injunctive relief."

Our lips were going to touch on "injunctive." I was on my toes, leaning up, my hands feeling the tightness at his waist.

But when thunder ripped through the air and rain suddenly pattered on the windows, I jumped too far back for him to reach.

"Crap," I said.

Without a word, we scrambled to the two boxes we'd put outside. He put them into the trunk of his Audi rental, and we scrambled inside.

"Where are you staying?" I asked. "I mean… just…"

"They have me in a condo in Century City."

The firm had apartments for visiting clients. They must use them for visiting attorneys as well.

"That's across town from the office," I stated the obvious. For clients, Century City made sense. For an employee, it was stupid.

"I get the real Los Angeles experience, traffic and all." He started the car. "Where are you headed?"

"I live in Culver, but my car is downtown, and I have a family thing tonight in Malibu."

"That's a mess," he said.

"I can get a cab Downtown."

At rush hour, then I had to head west. I'd get to dinner with everyone after ten, and I wouldn't see my brother. He was having trouble at school, and though it wasn't my job to correct it, I was the only one he listened to.

Mostly, I didn't want to get a cab downtown. I wasn't done

with Drew.

I spoke before I thought it out. "Are the partners taking you to dinner tonight?"

"That was last night."

"Come to dinner at my family's place then. You can ogle the size of it. We have a great cook, and I have seven siblings to play with. If you like kids, that is."

"I love kids."

Of course he did.

Chapter 23

1982 – FIVE WEEKS AFTER THE NIGHT OF THE QUAALUDE

The pregnancy test was in my bag, a big square lump on a heavier lug of books. I didn't usually carry all my things. We usually bought a separate set of textbooks for home, so all I had to carry were my notebooks. But I had to hide that stupid test. The nannies and housekeepers had started looking suspicious of my comings and goings, and I never knew when one of them was going to innocently (or not so innocently) slip or snoop.

The band had gone to Nashville to meet with a producer. Two weeks. Perfect. I was supposed to get my period in that time.

But I didn't.

On the day the boys were set to return from Nashville, I got a beep from the Palihood house number. I went up there with my backpack and without a plan. I didn't know what to tell them. I couldn't even take the test until the next morning, so what did I expect? What did I want? Should I even tell them I was all of nine days late for my period? I mean, so what? I'd been late before. My schedule was all screwed up. What was the point of worrying them into thinking I was going to ask them for anything besides the number of an abortion clinic?

The side door was unlocked, and I walked in unannounced as always. I thought of putting my bag by the door, but the elephant in the room had been zipped into it, so I kept it slung over my shoulder.

I was about to walk into the kitchen because the beer and cigarettes were there, but I felt a vibration in the floor. Standing still, I listened. Birds. The freeway. The ticking of the clock. Men talking behind walls. And music.

I went to the side of the house I'd only seen down to the studs.

The studio was sheetrocked and painted. Floors down. Gold record and band photos hanging in the hall. The window to the isolation booth sealed and egg-carton-shaped soundproofing on the walls.

Strat stood in front of the mic, copper-gold hair tied at the base of his neck, unleashing a note I couldn't hear. The door to the adjacent engineering room was ajar. I peered inside. Indy sat at the control panel while a goateed guy I'd seen around untangled some wires.

"Dude," Indy said into the mic, looking at Strat through the window.

"Dude," Strat said into his own mic. "Really?"

"Warm as the girl in the middle," Indy replied joyfully.

My heart twisted once, sharply. I reprimanded myself. It was a metaphor, for Chrissakes. I told myself I didn't care. I had no feelings on the matter one way or the other. I liked Indy and he was fun, but only until he wasn't.

I didn't need to be special to him.

How much longer are you going to tell yourself that?

I opened the door before I could answer myself.

Indy turned. Then the engineer. The man whose baby I could have been carrying jutted his chin toward me in greeting then turned back to the egg-carton-lined room.

"Give me the next verse, Stratty." He jotted something in a notebook, not even looking at me when he said, "Close the door, Cin."

I closed it quietly and gently placed my bag on the couch behind the board as if a sleeping monster were inside it.

Strat wore a white T-shirt and black jeans with a chain that made a U from his front belt loop to his back pocket. It swayed with him as he sang. His voice was magic. It had been too long since I'd heard him.

"I need to talk to you guys," I said.

"I think we need to kill the preamp," Goatee said.

Indy moved a lever so slightly it could have been nothing at all. A low-level version of Strat's voice filled the room as he hummed to himself near the mic.

"No," Indy said, not even looking at me. "Make it work. We're not cheaping out on vocals."

"Sure, but..." a pentameter of technical terms I didn't understand followed.

Indy parried with another jumble of engineering nonsense, and Goatee thrust with his own as he counted a bunch of bills he'd pulled from his front pocket. My request for an audience had been denied apparently.

In the booth, Strat jotted notes, tapped his foot, and hummed verses.

I'd never felt like an outsider with them before, but I'd never seen them working either. It was a bad time. I'd come back after I did the test. Or not. But either way, I was doing what I had to with or without their permission.

I picked up my bag. When the handles got taut from the weight, I had to exert a little more energy to pull the whole thing up, and I wished I could lean on someone. I wished I hadn't always been so far removed, so cold, so non-demonstrative. I wished I was used to emotions because I was having them and I couldn't define them. They were moving through me so quickly I couldn't define them, much less cope with them.

I slung the bag over my shoulder and saw myself in the glass's reflection. I was translucent. Overlaid onto Strat's indifference.

I hated this. Needy. Childish. Whining. Grasping. Desperate. I saw myself from the outside. Out of control. Floundering. Hungry for validation. A few synonyms for "it's going to be all right" wouldn't cure me of the problem. Not even a little. So why did I want them so badly?

When I opened the door, Indy spun in his chair. "Didn't you want something?"

"It can wait."

I left, saving myself from myself. I could handle emptiness. I could handle solitude and isolation. This rush of neediness was going to kill me. If either one of them had started patting my head and saying he was going to help me/be there for me/whatever you want, baby, I would have told him to fuck off.

So when I heard Indy's voice behind me, I was tempted to just keep walking down the hall. But the needy part won. I turned to at least tell him, "No worries. I'm good." His posture, half in and half out of the engineering room, told me that would have been a welcome dismissal.

But I couldn't. That hot bubbling mess inside me wouldn't be silenced.

"You all right?" he asked.

I think I'm pregnant.

I'm sick in the morning.

"I'm fine. Welcome back."

"Thanks." He leaned back into the engineering room, and I took the opportunity to walk a few more steps down the hall, rescued and abandoned at the same time. "You coming back tonight?"

"Why?" I didn't turn around, keeping him at my back.

"Why?"

I didn't know how to answer. Didn't know how to move or think. I only knew how to blurt out my problems.

Something inside me feels like turned soil.

And I'm late.

And I knew how to shut myself up. I barely knew how to breathe without feeling the tension between breath and words.

"Yeah," I said. "Why?"

"Because we're back, and people are coming over. What's the problem, Cin?"

He wanted an honest fucking answer. He knew my fucking name, but he wouldn't even fucking use it.

Cin.

Cin, my ass. My fucking left tit. Taking my stupid stunt of a fake name and throwing it at me like a bucket of ice.

"You're working. We'll talk later."

If I'd been able to just walk away, things might have been different, but we were young. I had to offer him one chance to give me what I needed. But no, that wasn't to be. Indiana Andrew McCaffrey had to stake out his territory.

"Maybe." He waved at me dismissively, and with that, the potential to have my needs met went down the shitter.

"What do you mean maybe?"

"People come over, and it gets hard to talk. So it's cool."

I threw myself down the hall toward him, the weight of my bag pushing me forward, finger extended. "It's cool?"

He shrugged and looked back into the engineering room as if he was dying to get back in there. I'd never felt so alone in my entire life.

"Yeah."

"Don't you dare tell me you won't make the time to talk to me. I've never asked you for a goddamn thing, you—"

"That's fucking right." His tone was a cinderblock wall, and I shriveled inside even as I kept my own wall high and hard. "Look, if you're gonna turn crazy, you won't be the fucking first."

"What?"

"I'd be surprised. You didn't seem like the type. But before we 'talk,' I'm going to pull out what we said the night we met. Feelings aren't real, so we don't bother. Right? You're not getting crazy. Right?"

Crazy. The world and everyone in it was crazy. Because I had feelings. I didn't know what they were or who they were even for. Maybe I had feelings for a way of life that was about to end.

"Look," he said, rubbing his lower lip with his thumb. A little swipe of discomfort. "We're really busy right now. There's no time for this."

Whatever my feelings were, Indy wasn't going to help me sort them out, and fuck him. I didn't need him or his help. He didn't even know what to do with his own damned feelings.

"Better get back to work," I sneered.

I took my crazy and went down the hall without looking back.

Fuck him seven ways to Sunday.

Fuck both of them.

Chapter 24

1994

The Audi cut through the rain like a machete, and Drew drove as if he lived in a place where it rained more than two months out of the year. I felt safe. Again.

"I saw you in *Rolling Stone*," I said as if I was just trying to make conversation. I flipped through a black wallet of CDs. Doubtless a small fraction of what he had at home.

"That was such a joke."

"Too redemptive?"

"I did half the drugs they said I did."

"That's still a lot."

He smiled. "Yeah. There was plenty. It was the eighties. What can I tell you? I was a wreck. *Sound Brothers* was making a ton of money, and I was wrecked over Strat."

I slid a disc from the sleeve. *Kentucky Killer*. The album that turned me into a groupie and got them the deal that financed the studio. The one with the masters in the trunk of the car.

"I'm sorry about that," I said.

He shrugged and looked in the rearview before changing lanes as if he needed something to do with his hands and mind. "Yeah, thanks. I just... I didn't know. After you were gone, we started fighting. Bad shit. Fistfights. I don't know what was wrong with him. Or me. Maybe it was me. I think about it a lot. Was it all really my fault? I mean, he blamed me for letting you go. He said he wouldn't have. So I shut down. I didn't even want to look at him. I got very involved with the studio. He had the business head, and I kept just wanting to do shit my way."

"You made the studio a real success."

"I never felt like that without him. Feels like I'm treading water most days. He said the studio should be passive. It should run itself while we made music, and I just kept getting more and more involved in the day-to-day. I could barely show up to our own sessions, and Gary had a kid, so he was checked out. Strat just lost it. Went back to Nashville."

"It wasn't your fault."

"It wasn't. He had a bad heart. Congenital aortic valve something. If he knew, he might have decided to take too much heroin instead of amphetamines."

"Was that supposed to be funny?"

"Yeah."

"It was."

I'd mourned Strat's death. He'd died from only a slight overdose of uppers. His heart couldn't take it. I'd thought about that too deeply, reading too much into a heart that couldn't stand the exertion. I sought out details about his demise to avoid the sadness. I told myself he was a jerk, that he didn't matter, that he was in my distant past. But it did matter. A haze followed me, because he was indeed my past. I'd owned that life, that past, those stories that built me, and it all went and died while I wasn't looking.

"He cared about you," Drew said, glancing at me before he put his eyes back on the freeway. "We went to meet you on Santa Monica and Vine. And that neighborhood..." He shook his head. "Of all the corners to pick. We didn't know if you'd been dragged into an alley and murdered."

I shot out a laugh at how close to the truth he was. "I'm sorry I flaked."

"You didn't flake. We went to your house—"

I sat ramrod straight, eyes wide, adrenaline flooding my veins. "You did not."

"Did. We got a lawyer to find out where you lived, and we got ten different kinds of runaround. Then a guy with a gun and a badge opened the door. He flashed an order of protection and made threats. We stopped coming around."

"They never told me."

Of course they hadn't told me. I was indisposed and powerless.

"I'm sorry," I said, looking at my open hands as if I was trying to set the past free. "I just couldn't take it anymore. I..."

Deep breath.

This is important.

"I just needed to start over."

"I was an asshole to you," he said.

"You were fine. It was me. I was in over my head."

"We figured you weren't dead, so we just... well, we didn't forget. I let it go, but I didn't forget. Figured it was the way I'd talked to you the last time I saw you. Strat was pissed off. He was the one you called, and he insisted you sounded upset. I told him Cin didn't get upset. Cin is together. She never lets her feelings get the better of her. But he swore up and down. He paid a detective to watch the house until the day he died."

"Eight months after I flaked."

"You didn't flake."

"How do you know?"

"I know you. If you needed to get away from us, I get it. That's not flaking."

I made a breath of a laugh. He knew me. Sure. I always did what I said. If I said "meet me at Santa Monica and Vine," then I was going to get off the bus at Santa Monica and Vine with my smallest Louis Vuitton suitcase.

The rain pounded the windows, marbleizing them to opacity. The windshield wipers did nothing to break the stream. I gripped the edge of the leather seat because the red lights ahead of us got too big too fast.

Drew snapped the right blinker on to get off the freeway. It was miles too soon, but it was the only safe option.

He would have been a good father.

I covered my face with my hands. Did I steal that from him?

Note to self: "Not feeling" stuff doesn't mean you're not feeling it. Being unemotional and cold doesn't mean you don't have a pot full of emotions waiting to boil over. It means the heat hasn't been turned up enough, and the pot just hasn't been there long enough. It means the pot hasn't reached capacity.

But it will.

And your heart will beat so fast and hard you'll want to die.

Your eyes will flush with tears, and your throat will close like a valve's been turned. Regret will fill you on a cellular level until the very tips of your fingers tingle with self-loathing.

"I'm sorry," I said.

He parked the car and shut it off. "You didn't make the rain. Just give it ten minutes."

"No. I'm sorry I didn't flake. I'm sorry I didn't tell you what happened. I'm sorry I left you there. I'm just sorry for everything."

"Margie? What's happening?"

He put his arms around me, but I pushed him away violently. Once I told him, he would be sorry he'd ever touched me.

"I was pregnant."

I could see the entire diameter of his blue eyes as he looked at me in surprise, jaw slack, expression otherwise empty. Was it surprise? Was I wrong in thinking he already knew? Or was that wishful thinking?

I swallowed putty, looked into the pouring rain, and ground my teeth until I could breathe enough to speak. "I was going to meet Strat and get an abortion because I didn't want you to talk me out of it, and I was so damn mad at you. After I called, I tried to get to you. I climbed out of my bedroom window, but my parents caught me in the driveway and sent me away."

He shook his head, eyes narrowed as if I'd just dropped a bomb in his brain and he had to make sense of the pieces.

"Do not pass Go," I continued. "Right to LAX. A fucking convent in Ireland. I'm sorry. I'm so sorry. I should have called when I got back. But I was fucked in the head, and I couldn't deal."

He got a white handkerchief out of his pocket, and I snapped it away to wipe my eyes. It didn't even begin to do the job.

"Where's the baby?" he asked, pointing at the elephant in the room.

"Adopted."

"Where?"

"Jesus, Indiana! How the fuck should I know?"

He looked out his side window, probably so he wouldn't have to look at me.

"My parents came to Ireland during my last trimester to set up the adoption, so the baby's probably there."

Funny how I still thought of it as a baby. He or she had to be

Jonathan's age already.

Drew looked back at me, all the surprise and distance gone.

"My mom was really pregnant too, which was just great because she hated me for getting knocked up at the same time. She had her baby in the hospital, then I had mine in the convent, and Dad just took it. I didn't even hear it cry. A week later, they took me home. Mom had post-partum. Dad acted like the whole thing had been a fun trip and the bad shit never happened. Which, you know, I'll admit that worked for me."

The shadows of the rain fell on the curves of his beautiful face in an overlay of wrinkles and age. Yet he looked twenty again, an overwhelmed artist on the verge of a life of riches and fame. A kid with nothing but mistakes to make. He'd seen a lot. He'd lost his best friend. Faced the death of his father and the surrender of his mother. He'd been strong for his family even when all the perks and goodies of a life in the spotlight tempted him away.

And I hadn't given him a thought.

I'd been so wrapped up in my own problems for eleven years that I hadn't thought about what he would have wanted. Wasn't he as much a part of this as I was? Didn't he have the right to know? To claim what was his?

Well, there was that.

"It should have tried to find you. I was thinking about what was easy for me. And even when I saw you in the office... I was still thinking about myself. I'm sorry."

I didn't want him to speak, but that was the problem, wasn't it? I'd never wanted him to speak. I'd wanted him to go away. In the front seat of his rented Audi, with the rain pounding the glass, that changed. I wanted to know what he thought. I'd suffer the slings and arrows he threw at me if he'd just say what was on his mind.

He opened his mouth to speak, and I'd admit I flinched a little.

I wanted him to like me, to want me, to love Cin again and learn to love Margie. I should have felt like a little whiney bitch for that, but I didn't. I didn't have the energy to berate myself for wanting to be wanted.

"And..." he started, and I braced myself, "who were you thinking about when you invited me to a family dinner?"

It was crazy to laugh, but I did. I wasn't used to having this fucked up soup in my guts. I was off balance from the pendulum of emotion. Walking on a lubed-up balance beam. Of course I fell, but at least I fell on the side of laughter. If I cried another tear, I was going to have to wring out his hankie.

"Me!" I said. "I wanted to spend time with you again, and I was totally thinking of myself. But you look different. And we can call you Drew and never even talk about what happened. They won't know."

"But I'll know."

I stopped in the middle of a lateral mood swing. Just froze.

He wasn't talking about the baby and whatever right he had or didn't think he had to it. No. His face wasn't hurt or victimized. It was rigid with rage.

"Don't pretend it's about me," I said.

"Why not?"

"Just don't." I was almost screaming. I sounded crazy. Drunk on *feelings*.

"It's about you."

"No, it's—"

"Did anyone stand up for you? All this time? Has anyone—"

I couldn't hear another word. I yanked the door handle. It slipped with a deep clack. I grunted and pulled it again, even as Drew reached over to close the door.

Neither the downpour nor the unknown neighborhood slowed me down. I didn't care about my work shoes or the cold rain that soaked my white shirt. I was sodden before I got three steps away from the car.

I didn't expect him to pull away and leave me there. I figured I'd grab a cab or find a payphone while he stayed in the car and followed me. Because who would run out into this shitstorm? What normal person would leave the car running, the headlights on, and jump into a fucking monsoon to grab my arm?

"Let me—"

"Shut up!" he shouted, already soaked, hair flat on his scalp, eyelashes webbed with water. His shirt stuck to him, translucent enough to reveal the treble clef over his heart. "For once, shut that mouth and listen. I never forgot you. Never. Not a day went by in that studio without me thinking about you. How you think. How you talk. How you felt when I was inside you."

"You shut up! You forgot me, and you should have."

"I didn't."

"I was nothing." I jabbed my finger at him. "I was a short-term habit."

He continued as if I hadn't even spoken, water dripping from the angles of his face, along his cheekbones and jaw, meeting at his chin and falling in a constant silver line. "When Strat died, I couldn't save him. I wanted you there. I needed you. As soon as you called him that night, I should have had the balls to go right to your house and get you. Now that I know what happened, I know it was the biggest mistake of my life. I'll always regret it."

"Then you're a fool."

"I am."

In the urban dark of the street, with only the headlights of the Audi illuminating the diagonal sketch marks of rain, I didn't see him move, but I tasted rain warmed by the heat of his mouth. He was too fast and was kissing me before I knew what was happening.

He kissed my breath away.

He kissed my defenses to dust.

His lips dared me to feel nothing.

He turned me from solid to liquid.

One hand cupped my chin, and the other pulled me close from the back of my neck, and fuck him fuck him fuck him because I put my hands on his chest again, to his shoulders, his neck, the back of his head. My fingers dug into his wet hair. I felt close to him again, as I had all the years before, when I held his heart in my hands and someone else threw it away.

"I'm not abandoning you again," he said between kisses, running his face over my cheek like the water that spilled over it.

"Don't be stupid."

"Please. Let me earn this."

I pushed him away. His right eye was crystalline in the headlamps, bathed in light and rain.

"You've lost it, Indiana."

"I have. Slowly. Since I saw you this morning."

My teeth chattered as I looked him up and down. I didn't know what to make of him. I didn't know what to feel.

"I used you," I said, speaking the truth to myself as well as him. "I was looking for bad things to do, and you were there. I used you to fuck myself up."

"I know." His treble clef heaved under the wet fabric, a scar from a dream he'd once had. The footprint of a thing he'd loved and lost.

"I can see right through your shirt," I said. "It's indecent."

He pulled me to him, and we ran back to the car. He opened the door for me, and I leaned over inside and popped open the driver's door. It had barely closed behind him when he stretched across the seat and kissed me again. I put my hand on his wet chest, and he put his up my skirt. I let him, wrangling my body around his, opening my legs for his touch.

"That's not the rain," he said, sliding a finger inside me.

"God, no," I groaned. "It's you."

He drew his knuckles over my clit. "Look at me. Open your eyes and look at me."

His beard was soaked to dark brown, and droplets of water clung to his lashes. His hair stuck to his forehead.

"You're beautiful," I whispered. Then as he rubbed me again, I groaned, driving my hips forward. "Take me."

I reached between his legs and felt him. He sucked a breath through his teeth.

"We're not done." He yanked his belt open. "I'm going to fuck you right here, right now. But it's not the last time. Do you hear me?"

"Yes."

I would have promised him beachfront property in Nevada, especially after he took his dick out.

I wiggled out of my underwear while he reached into his wallet for a condom. Good man. No need to make the same mistake twice. I swung my leg over him, positioning him under me.

He pressed the head of his cock at my entrance with one hand, and with the other, he took my jaw. "This is not the last time. Say you understand."

"I do. I get it. I swear."

Was I lying? Maybe. But he was pressed against me, and every nerve ending between my legs vibrated for it.

"Say it."

"This is not the last time."

He pushed me down, entering me slowly.

"Look at me," he whispered again.

"You feel so good. It's hard to keep my eyes open."

"Feel it, Margie. Feel it."

He pushed me onto him, driving down to the root, every inch a reminder of what we'd had and what we were—a reimagined beginning with a past that ended us.

Chapter 25

1983 AFTER IRELAND

Eighteen, give or take. Mostly take. I could get away with a lot because I looked and sounded like an adult, and in a lot of ways, I was. I didn't take shit, and I knew my own worth. That went a long way, but I was still as greedy as a child. I craved experiences. New things. Broken. Unraveled. Unwound. I could test the world. See what I could make anew.

I would have been a sociopath if I hadn't learned to give a shit when I got back from the cold stone convent in the old country. I'd eaten the shit sandwich I'd been fed, shed my rock groupie skin, and I acted like the oldest of eight.

The first time my mother put Jonathan into my arms, she looked nervous. She hadn't wanted me to touch him for the first week. Anyone else could, but not Margie. Maybe because he was the precious only boy of her eight children, but she handed him over as if I'd drop him or something. Or my irresponsible behavior would rub off on him. I didn't take it personally.

Post-partum wasn't properly diagnosed back then, so she was treated like a hysterical female, and I wasn't treated at all. I felt as if my guts had been ripped out and replaced with sawdust. I didn't eat. I didn't talk much. We were both in deep pain and acting as if nothing had ever gone awry.

Eventually I took Jonathan from the nurse while Mom napped. He was everything. He had a little tuft of red hair and crystal-blue eyes that would eventually turn green. I'd held just about all of my siblings, but there was something about Jonathan. And the smell. Baby smell wasn't new, but his was different. It was the scent of heaven and earth. He held my finger with his tiny hand, and it didn't feel as though he did it out of newborn reflex. His grip felt like a plea. A connection. A deal rubbed with the salt of the earth.

I was going to make it my business to be there for him. To make myself useful if not to my own child, then to the brother born at the same time. I pledged it to him.

I straightened out so quickly, my family got whiplash. I never spoke to Lynn or Yoni again. I didn't make friends, but I made a few appropriate acquaintances.

It wasn't even hard.

"Did you breastfeed any of us?" I asked as Mom popped the bottle from Jonathan's mouth.

He was three months old, and I was still acclimating to my new life. Or my old life, depending on how you looked at it. It was the life a normal person my age should be living, not the life of someone who'd been whisked away to a foreign country to be tutored by stiff Irish nuns so she could secretly give birth to a baby she would never hold.

"Heavens, no. Why would I do that?" Mom handed the baby to the nanny to burp.

Her name was Phyllis, and she held her arms out but looked at me. She and I had set a pattern. Mom left before the baby kicked up his milk, and as soon as she was gone, Phyllis handed him to me. I slung him over my shoulder and patted his back, pressing my cheek to him so I could get a whiff of his baby smell. Best in the world.

I knew I was making Jonathan a replacement for the baby they gave away, but I couldn't help it. He smelled so good.

"I'll protect you, little brother," I whispered then put his little hand up against my own as if swearing on a stack of Bibles. "I pledge it."

I studied and behaved. I was a model of good and right behavior. I won my parents' trust back by staying in, helping my sisters with their homework, and finding a deep well of ambition.

You might think I was somehow browbeaten into good behavior. That I resented it. That I lost a wild part of myself to meet the expectations of others.

But it didn't feel like that. I felt wonderful. I helped Carrie and Sheila with their homework while Dad was off doing business and Mom was in her room. I wiped chocolate off Fiona's hands when she found the baker's cocoa in the back of the cabinet and ate the whole box.

I did everything but feed Jonathan. Mom insisted on feeding Jonathan until he started walking, then she abdicated, like with everything else. She was a figurehead, and oddly, I was okay with that. I loved her arm's-length parenting because she gave me room to fill my days with something meaningful to me.

Daddy was not an affectionate person, but after he spanked me for getting knocked up, he was never closer than half a room away. Even when I struggled in the back of the limo on the way to my flight to Ireland, he left the manhandling to an Italian bodyguard. He watched from the seats across with his jacket in his lap.

"One day," he'd said as Franco held me down, "one day you'll see this is for your own good."

I stuck my middle finger out at him.

"Who's the father?" he asked. "Who did this to you?"

I got my hand from under Franco's arm and stuck up my other middle finger.

"I'm going to find out."

All he'd have to do was dig around the groupie scene and he'd know, but he was so far removed from it, and I'd kept it so far away from my regular life, that I had hope he'd leave Strat and Indiana alone.

He sat next to me during the whole flight over. Just him, and he scared me. He checked me into the convent and left. They sent letters Sister Maureen made me answer. I said nice things, but I was shut down until he and Mom showed up three months before the baby was due.

"You look good," Mom had said. She was farther along than I was.

I felt gross being next to her like that. "So do you. How do you feel?"

"Better than ever." She smiled and rested her hand on her belly. She loved being pregnant. I didn't know how she felt about raising children, but she loved carrying them. "We found a family for your baby. They live here. It's a good home."

"Thank you."

I hadn't fought that part of it. I didn't want to be a mother at that point, and I had no choice anyway. I was sure they'd done all the diligence in the world.

"Your friends miss you. They come by to let us know."

"Who came?"

She rattled off a few girls I knew from the Suffragette Society and Jenn from the Chess Strategy Club, then she looked at Dad.

He sat in the corner with an ankle crossed over his knee, staring at me. The movement of his head was barely perceptible, but he gave her a definite no to whatever she was asking. Mom was a lion when it came to everything except Dad. So she acted as though no one else had come, smiling as if our family dynamic was as normal as peas and carrots.

I went into labor three days early.

Dad was there when I gave birth, not Mom. I hadn't expected him to be in the room. I tried to ignore him, and once the pain got really bad, I could pretend he wasn't there. The midwife handed him the baby still slimy with goop.

"Is it a boy or a girl?" I'd asked, trying to catch my breath.

He didn't answer. No one answered. Sister Maura just shushed me, and Dad took it away. By the time I delivered the placenta, I knew they'd never tell me a thing.

I'd flown home alone. My sisters had greeted me like a long-lost child. Even my mother had been overcome with happiness when I walked in the door.

Dad seemed cautious. He treated me as if I were a museum artifact behind a velvet rope.

When I got into Wellesley, he congratulated me with a handshake and a genuine smile, but he never touched me again.

I had to hang up a lot of my family duties when I went to Stanford Law, but I was always there. I called teachers when Fiona didn't understand her homework, chewed out Father Alfonso when he fire-and-brimstoned Deirdre, and tried to keep Jonathan inside the lines as he proved, time after time, that he could push every boundary with a cocky smile.

By the time I was studying for my bar, I felt as if the eighties were behind me. My parents had done their best, and I had a good life ahead. Sometimes I even felt gratitude.

Chapter 26

1982 – THE NIGHT OF THE QUAALUDE

I became enamored with the taste and feel of his nipples. The odd red hairs on his chest next to the brown ones. Quaaludes made you horny and happy, and we laughed a lot. I was getting ready to let him fuck me again. It hurt in a different way when he touched me. I was sore. But the internal pain had left.

I laid back and bent my knees, swinging them, smoking a cigarette. The cheap quilt under me felt good. Soft. Warm. Made for my skin.

And him. He was good. Very good. Kissing between my tits and down my belly. He was going to do to me the thing the girls had done with Strat. He was going to taste me. I tucked the cigarette between my teeth and put my fingers in his hair, spreading my legs for him.

When the door opened, I looked to see who came in but didn't move otherwise. I didn't jump or act ashamed, and neither did Indy.

"Dude," Strat said.

"Dude." Indy propped himself up on his elbows. "You get rid of Hawk?"

"Yeah. Party's over." Strat leaned down, plucked the cigarette from my lips, and put it between his own. He had no shirt, and the musical notations across his body curved around his nipples in a way I wanted to taste. "Said he gave you a blue lude. Looks about right."

"Yeah. Blue."

He blew out smoke.

I looked down at Indy, and he looked back up at me with a wicked smile.

"Naughty," I purred, reading his mind. I turned back to Strat and stretched, elongating my body, luxuriating in my nudity. I knew it was the drugs, and I didn't care. "You gonna give that back?"

He put the cigarette back in my mouth, peering down at me, through me, making some kind of calculation. I inhaled the delicious nicotine without touching the cigarette. Just sucking. Then I jutted my jaw at Strat. He took the butt from me and stamped it out in the ashtray on the floor.

"You're both luded," Strat said.

"Yup," Indy said then turned back to my belly.

I patted the mattress, staring at Strat. His long copper-red hair fell on each side of his face, and his jaw was rough with a day and a half of growth.

"Don't be a stranger," I said.

Strat glanced at Indy, who looked back at him intently and said, "You heard the woman."

The singer hesitated, looking from Indy to me. I'd never seen him hesitate before.

"I know you want to," Indy said. "One less thing to fight over."

In the seconds that passed, those two men who had grown up together and sacrificed for one another had a conversation without words. There had been a pledge, I knew that. But what was happening now?

I waited for what felt like hours but was probably breaths, and put one hand in Indy's hair while holding out the other to Strat. "Come on. It'll be fun."

I didn't think about the role reversal until years later, when I read about his death in *Rolling Stone*. Even then I smiled. I could practically taste him.

"Do what you want," Indy said. "But I'm eating this pussy right now."

And he did.

He opened my folds, exposing my clit. Even that felt good, but when he laid his tongue on it, my neck arched.

"Oh, *God!*"

As if called by my prayer, Strat leaned next to the bed and kissed me. Not just kissed. He put his tongue in my mouth and claimed me. Indy brought me to orgasm with his mouth while I cried out into Strat's, a conduit from man to man. I lay there gasping, wanting more.

"Yes," Indy said, kneeling.

Strat was over me, pants down, cock out. So fucking hard and straight, I had to reach for it.

"You sure, Cinny?"

"Yes." I stroked him. I didn't know what I was doing, but it couldn't have been that bad.

"I want your ass. I'll try to make it good for you."

"I know."

Indy pulled me up to my knees, and I kissed him.

"Say you're sure to me," he whispered. "It's a lot for your first time."

"I want it now."

Behind me, Strat kneeled on the mattress and stroked my body. I felt his erection on my lower back.

"What about you?" I asked Indy.

"Yeah. But, Cin. Margie. I'm crazy about you. This doesn't change that. I want to know you."

I didn't tell him I wasn't knowable because the ludes made me feel elated and open, with years ahead of me that were going to start with these two men, on this mattress—now.

"Okay."

He smiled then got me under the arms and threw me on my back. "This is gonna be fun."

I laughed, and the next minutes were spent in some kind of heaven. The two of them covered me with their mouths and hands. Strat put his fingers in my mouth and I sucked them, groaning for him while Indy sucked my nipples to exquisite pain.

"Wet, Cin. Make them wet."

I did, licking between his second and third finger.

Strat pulled them out. "Good. You ready?"

"Yes."

I didn't actually know what I was supposed to be ready for until he bent my knees so deeply, Indy had to get off my tits and my hips lifted off the mattress. I was completely exposed, and they looked at me. Both of them. Indy played with my cunt, and Strat rubbed my ass with his wet finger. They watched my face.

The finger pressed forward, and my asshole yielded. I felt it everywhere. My entire body reacted with a shudder, tightening around him at the same time as my clit engorged. Indy slid two fingers into my pussy and leaned down to kiss me. I took the kiss, ate it, moaned into it, even when Strat got two fingers in me, burying them inside.

"Going for three," Strat said a million miles away. "Relax."

I'd never been so relaxed in my life, but that third finger broke through the high with a shot of pain. I tightened.

Indy took his mouth off me and turned to Strat. "Lube, asshole."

Strat flicked his hand at the night table. The same one the girl with the luscious hips had opened. Indy opened the drawer and found the same bottle of baby oil. He handed it over.

Strat popped it open. "Open up."

I lifted my knees, and Indy leaned over me and spread me wide. Cold, dripping oil fell on me, and the two of them spread it around, inside, outside. Making sure I was slick and ready, talking like two lawyers making sure every t was crossed and i was dotted.

I felt like the center of the known universe, swirling a galaxy of pleasure between my legs.

"Guys," I groaned. "That's so nice. Please."

"She's ready," Strat said to his childhood friend. He scooted back until he was sitting against the wall, cock out like a flagpole.

Indy helped me up. "Okay, face me on your knees."

He maneuvered me until Strat was behind me and could get his hands on my waist.

"Open," Strat said. "Pull it open."

My ass cheeks were slick with oil, but I dug in and opened them as Strat put pressure on my hips to lower me.

"Slow," Indy said.

"Slow, baby," Strat said.

Indy kneeled in front of me, eyes still dilated black, biting his lower lip as I went down until I felt Strat's dick against my ass. It seemed no different than the last barrier I'd broken that night, so I pushed down.

"Slow." Indy demanded when he saw my face. "We have all

night."

It was different.

"Relax." Strat reached around and gently rubbed my clit.

Between the baby oil and my body's arousal, I was so wet that I didn't feel the least bit sore, and the pleasure relaxed me. My ass opened a little, and I bore down until the head was in. I stopped. Gasped.

"Can you take it?" Indy asked.

"Yes."

I got myself to a crouching position and lowered myself completely. Strat's cock went in all the way, and I continued down, down, stretching, taking every inch inside me. A sharp breath shot out of me with a crack of pain, but I didn't stop until he was rooted in my ass. Then I smiled, because I was stretched and full.

"So hot," Indy muttered, stroking his own cock.

I raised myself, feeling the sensation against the walls of muscle, then I went down again.

"That's it, baby," Strat said from behind me. "Take it. Take it hard."

"Indy?"

He took a deep breath and leaned forward. We shifted, realigned, and got my pussy right to take him. One hand on the wall behind us, one on my shoulder, he got his dick in.

It was a feeling I would never forget and one I never could repeat. All I had to do was stay still as they fucked me like two musicians with the same beat. One in, one out. Then both in at the same time.

Complete fullness. Stretched to my limit. Desired. Loved. Fucked endlessly everywhere. Both goddess and vessel.

"Touch yourself," Strat said. Neither of them had a free hand in the balancing act.

I jammed my fingers between Indy and me. I let out a long groan when I was close, but it was taking longer than I thought. It was too much. The pleasure wouldn't center where it needed to.

Indy put his nose astride mine and grunted into my cheek, exploding inside me.

I didn't think it was physically possible to feel any more pleasure or another slice of sensation, but I did, gathering vibrations between my fingers.

"Come, baby," Strat growled. "I want to feel it."

Indy pulled out and leaned back. His dick was slick with me and still stiff. "I got it."

He leaned down and flicked my clit with his tongue, then he sucked it hard as Strat pinched my nipples.

That was it.

As I screamed in pleasure, Strat pulled me down until he was deep inside me, and I came, ass pulsing around his cock.

"Ah, that's it," he groaned. "Fuck yes."

My orgasm was barely over when he pulled me up then slammed me down. Three, four, five times, then he came into me.

I leaned forward into Indy's arms, and we fell together, resting for fifteen minutes before we fell asleep in a heat of slick, euphoric flesh.

Chapter 27

1994

"I thought you were going to be the easy one," I said. The rain had lightened to dime-sized splats and rushing veins on the windshield. The inside of the car smelled of salt water and sticky tar.

"What's that supposed to mean?" Drew asked, brushing his fingers through his hair as he drove. It had loosened from its stiff lawyer-do and fell in his face the way it used to.

I'd settled into a mellow trust with him. The same zone as I'd fallen into eleven years earlier. "Strat was like an animal in a jungle. You were comfortable. Accessible."

"Accessible? That sounds a little demeaning."

"Just a little? Shit. When that flew out of my mouth, my subconscious was going in for the kill."

He smirked, elbow on the edge of the door, rubbing his thumb on his bottom lip. Had he done that before? At the Palihood house? I didn't remember. He seemed pensive and maybe a little hurt. I felt protective of him, even if I was the one I was protecting him from.

"If it's any comfort, you were the one who hurt me most." I put my hand on his knee. He put his hand over mine and squeezed my fingers together. "After that night, when it was just us, I really started to like you."

"That's no comfort whatsoever."

"Didn't think so."

The rain stopped as if God had flipped a switch. If it were

daytime, the sun would have come out.

"I wasn't out to hurt you," he said. "I was out to not get hurt."

"Get off here." I pointed at the exit, holding my next thought until I knew he wasn't going to drift on the slick road. "You know you don't have a case. Your cellist."

"Yeah. I know."

"Make a left here. And you knew I was working in the LA office."

"Read it in the company newsletter. Fine print on the last page. New hires."

"Martin Wright? Does he really think he was ripped off?"

"Every couple of weeks. Especially when he doesn't take his meds."

I closed my eyes and took a deep breath. If I was being honest with myself, I'd known it all along. The case was built out of ice cubes and set on a frying pan. He didn't have to come to Los Angeles for it either. He could have managed the whole thing with faxes. So why? I'd gotten easier to find. There were a few hundred TV channels and libraries had computers now.

Fuck it. He was a goddamn lawyer. He could have found me anytime.

"What do you want?" I asked.

His Adam's apple bobbed down and back up with a deep swallow. He squeezed my fingers again. "Something came across my desk. I don't do international cases, but I was helping an associate, and I saw your name."

"House at the end of the block with the hedge and the gate. Where did you see my name?"

"It wasn't yours. Your family's." He pulled up to the gate and stopped. The gate was closed, and outside his window sat a wet keypad waiting for my code. He put the car in park and shifted to face me. "I didn't think it had anything to do with you. I came to LA to see if you'd thought of me at all. Strat had all the girls. I did all right, but..."

"But? What came across your desk?"

"You were different. Cin—sorry. Margie. I never stopped thinking about you. When I saw your name twice in a month, I had to do something. I should have sent an interoffice or something, but I didn't want to freak you out."

"This has been so much more successful."

"Did you think about me? All that time? The baby—"

"No."

He looked stricken. Or maybe confused. Then he tilted his head a little as if he didn't believe me. Fuck him. But gently and sweetly. Again.

"Between having the baby and crashing into you in the hall, I didn't think about you once."

"Not once?"

"When I read about Strat dying, of course. Sometimes 'Blue Valley' comes on the radio. But otherwise, no. Not really. You haven't even existed to me."

Behind him, a tiny light in the corner of the keypad went from orange to green. The camera was on. There was a disembodied *bleep* a second later.

"Enter my code, or security's going to be out here with an agenda."

He rolled down the window.

"Sorry," I said. "I'm just telling it like it is."

"It's fine." He stuck his hand out the window. If his posture and tone were any indication, it wasn't fine. Not at all. "What's the code?"

"*My* code. We each have our own."

"Okay. What is it?" He looked at me expectantly, fingers poised an inch from the keypad.

I choked back a sob that nearly broke the speed barrier rushing up my throat. "Fifty-one-fifty."

I pressed my lips together to hold it all back and squeezed my eyes shut until little bursts of light exploded in the darkness.

"Just press it," I said, running my words together. "Just do it. I didn't forget you. I thought you didn't want me, and I was okay with that. I just took my lumps, but I think about you every day. Every time there's music anywhere. Jingles in commercials. Muzak in the elevator. You're there, and sometimes you're mocking me and sometimes you're holding me, but you're there. I didn't want you to know that. Ever."

He squeezed my hand, flipped it on his knee, and put our palms together. I didn't open my eyes, just felt him there. Heard the clicks and beeps of the buttons. When I opened my eyes, the windshield was clear, but my vision was fogged.

Drew leaned over and ran his thumb under my eyes. I pushed him away and flipped out his hankie. He smiled. I sniffed as I wiped my face.

"It's okay," he said. "It was a crazy time. We were both kids. And you had a lot on your plate. I should have been there for you."

The gate creaked open. God, the last thing I wanted to deal with was my family.

"I don't know how I feel."

"But you feel something." He rolled up his window.

"Yeah." I sniffed as he pulled forward.

"That was all I wanted to hear. Because I'd hate to think fucking in the front seat of a rental was our last time together."

* * * *

Drew pulled around the circular drive and planted the Audi close to the front door. The stones were wet and glistening in the front lights. The fountain tinkled, and the spring flowers leaned against the direction of the wind. Cars lined up on each side of the drive, and the valet staff hung out under the eaves.

Harvey, our butler, ran out with a black umbrella and opened my door. "Good evening, Ms. Drazen. I'm afraid they started dinner without you."

"Thanks. It's fine."

"Watch your step."

"It's not raining anymore." I indicated the umbrella.

"There's mist."

I'd grown up with this type of attention and found it was always best to let people do their jobs the best way they knew how.

Drew stood by the trunk of the car, trying to not look off-put by the butler and the huge span of the umbrella. But I knew better. Whenever a regular person saw the Malibu house and the staff, they had to hide their reaction.

I was about to tell Harvey that the fountain sounded louder than usual when Drew looked down. Water was pouring from the trunk.

"Crap," I said, keeping it clean for Harvey. "Aren't these things waterproof?"

Drew didn't know how sensitive the butler was, so he cursed up a storm as he opened the trunk. Three inches of water sat at the bottom, soaking the bottoms of the banker's boxes.

"We'd better bring them in," I said then turned to Harvey. "Can you find us some dry boxes?"

"Indeed."

I took his umbrella, and he dashed inside.

"Well, now your case against Moxie Zee is really dead," I said.

"And to think I was betting my career on this fingerprinting technique."

He picked up a box from the bottom. I held my arms out, and he placed it on them.

"Let's go in the side door. Avoid everyone. This way."

Drew took the second box and closed the trunk. "I was looking forward to meeting your family."

"No, you weren't. Trust me."

I took him to the side of the house, through the five-car garage I rarely saw because we had a valet to move cars around, to the part of the house the eight of us hid out in. The real kitchen. Not the ones the caterers heated up stuff in, the one everyone could see. But the kitchen the cook and his staff used. We curled up in the pantries and cooled off in the walk-in fridge. Sheila had made herself an apprentice and actually learned to cook there.

"Margie!" Orry shouted with a thick French accent, a clump of his grey comb-over flying up as he jogged to me. It looked like a parking barrier going up and down. He'd been our family chef for as long as I could remember.

The kitchen was alive with shouts, flames, *chopchopchop* for the night's dinner.

"Hey." I turned my cheek to him so he could kiss it. "This is Drew. He..." I caught myself. I didn't want to send the staff buzzing. "He works with me."

"Nice to meet you. You're not putting those on my butcher's block."

"I thought your bed would—"

"I'll laugh in advance. You can go in the wine cellar. Shoo. Before Grady forgets the blue in black and blue. *Grady!*" Orry was off, shouting to his grill chef about the temperature of the sea bass. Dad was picky about his blacks and blues.

"You running a restaurant?" Drew asked, juggling the box to keep stuff from falling out the bottom.

"It's Good Friday. Day of fasting and woe followed by gorging on fish. Come on." I jerked my head toward a narrow, half-open door and headed for it. He followed.

The lights were already on, which was good because I didn't have a free hand. We walked carefully down the creaky wood stairs to the cold, dry cellar, into the tasting room. It had only a few racks of seasonal wines that the sommelier decided should be consumed sooner rather than later, clean glasses, a refrigerator for cheese, and a metal table with stools. I put my box on the table, and Drew put his next to mine.

"Feel like a drink?" I said.

"Actually, yes."

I picked up two glasses and a bottle at random while he unloaded a box, laying the masters out in a line. The labels had fallen off.

"Are they ruined?" I asked, popping the cork.

"Yes, but no one cares about Opus 33." He found a file and opened it. Half-wet contracts. Runny-inked documentation. A package of bowstrings. "They must put away anything left in the studio. I had no idea they even cleaned the place. Ever."

He slid the top off the second box. Deep breath. His history was soaked inside.

"Here." I handed him his wine and held mine up for a toast. "To... I don't know what."

"To Stratford Gilliam. May he rest in fucking peace."

We clinked glasses. I looked at him over the rim as I sipped the red nectar. It went right to my head.

Stratford Gilliam.

May he rest in peace.

Chapter 28

1982 – THE NIGHT OF THE QUAALUDE
Six hours before I crawled out from under Indy, I'd been a drug-free virgin. But in the early morning hours after Hawk got kicked out of the house and I fulfilled a fantasy I didn't know I had, I had a sore asshole and a sour feeling in my bones. I'd seen Lynn's grouchy ass after she was luded, and I empathized for the first time.

The Palihood house was dead quiet and lit only by the moon through the windows. I padded to the kitchen naked, bold in my crankiness. I wasn't doing that blue shit again. Feeling scrambled and rancid afterward wasn't worth the happy hornies. I could get horny on my own, thank you. And happy was pure bullshit anyway.

At least that was done. I didn't have a single virgin part of my body anymore.

I filled a glass with water and slogged it. Refilled. Drank. Refilled. Drank more slowly.

The pool lights were on under the perfectly flat bean shape. Maybe a swim would cheer me up. It wasn't until I got to the screen door that I saw the orange pin of a lit cigarette making an arc from Strat's mouth to the side of the couch.

"I hear you, Cin."

"How did you know it wasn't Indy?" I asked from behind the screen.

He arched his back and neck until he could see me. "He walks like a fucking elephant." He lay flat again. "You're naked."

I opened the door. "Yeah. My ass hurts."

"Bad?" He looked over the pool and dragged on his cigarette.

I took his pack off the table. "No. Just irritated." I sat and lit one.

"That can't happen again."

"Did I blow your mind?" I dropped his lighter on the table with a *clickclack*.

"That guy's like my brother. He cares about you. Really cares about you."

He had a towel over his waist, but the rest of him was bare. The musical staffs on his chest rippled. I hadn't tasted them. I hadn't done much of anything but received him. I felt cheated.

"And what about you?" I said.

"He and I have a deal."

"Oh yeah?"

"You're his."

"You flip a coin or something?" I said it without breathing, half joking, half too far on the wrong side of a lude to be anything but negative. I emptied my lungs, letting the nicotine rush make my hands tingle.

"Played a few hands."

"You serious?"

"He pulled a straight."

I leaned back on the couch. "You could have asked me."

He stretched his arm out to the ashtray. The muscles were given definition by the tattoo. What a gorgeous thing he was.

"Nah." He stamped his butt out with a flutter of orange embers. "We didn't want to fight."

"How do you explain your dick in my ass then?"

He shrugged. "One night."

I leaned on the arm of the outdoor couch and stuck my cigarette in my teeth. Fuck them. I wasn't a baseball card to be traded around. "Fuck you guys."

"You did." He got up and stood over me. The towel was gone, and his cock stood straight and hard between us.

"One night," I said. "Did you agree ahead of time?"

"If the situation came up, yeah. That was part of the agreement."

"Fuck you twice." My voice dripped with honey. I hadn't intended it, but the sore feeling in my ass had abated, and the poor judgment of my cunt went live.

We regarded each other, above and below, half-drugged and young, looking for stupid excuses to do stupid things.

"You might get your chance. It's still night."

"For a few hours. Then, yeah, I'm his."

He touched the inside of my knee. No pressure, just a touch. "Open your legs, Cin."

I pulled my knees apart slowly. He kneeled on the couch and spread them, tilting forward to kiss me. He kissed like a man. As if he was marking territory with his tongue. I wrapped my arms around him.

Just once, I told myself. Just the once, I could trade them the way they'd traded me.

I let Strat take me. There was no other way to describe the way he held me down, pushed on my clit until I was close, then slowed down to keep me on the edge, kissing me tenderly right before I came and he exploded inside me.

Only then was I satisfied.

Chapter 29

1994

The wine was going to my head. It seemed as if Drew pulled the Bullets and Blood masters out with special reverence. I'd laid a towel out to soak up the water, and he placed the boxes on them gently.

I was going to have to tell him that the baby that had split us apart might not have been his. We'd been careless with our bodies then.

But when I saw him pull an envelope out of the box and I felt the bond that he'd had with his friend, I felt a real pull to tell him and a stronger pull to just bury it forever. Why bring it up? To what end would I risk hurting him with his friend's betrayal? I didn't fool myself into thinking I meant so much to him that my betrayal was equal to Strat's. The only thing I risked by telling the truth was damaging his memory of his best friend. I didn't want to turn that bond into a lie.

I was a coward. I owed him the truth.

"Drew. Indy… I—"

A young man's voice came from the top of the stairs, yelling in French. Orry shouted back. The door slammed. Feet scuffled along the wood, and a boy barreled into the room, shirt half untucked, ginger hair askew.

"What the—?"

"Jonathan," I said, noticing his frozen, terrified features.

"Margie. When did you get here?"

"This is Drew. He works with me."

They nodded at each other, practically grunting like apes. Little Jon was a man already, too tough for his own good.

"What's wrong?" I said. "You look like you just saw a ghost."

He swallowed. The kids came to the wine cellar when they needed to get away from the bullshit of the huge house. Sometimes to hide. Sometimes to sulk. I knew where to find Fiona during report cards' week, Leanne every twenty-eight days, Carrie whenever Dad was home.

"I'm all right." He started back upstairs.

Drew thumbed through an envelope.

"Wait," I said to Jonathan. "Try this."

I handed him my glass of wine. He was in fifth grade, but he was allowed to sip, and I wasn't ready to let him go back up to whatever was bothering him. He took the glass. Treating him like a grown-up worked, and he seemed calmer when he handed it back.

"It tastes fine," he said.

"Come in the storage room with me for a sec. I want to talk to you. Drew, do you mind?"

"It's fine." He looked up from a wet, runny note for a second and locked eyes on Jonathan.

I thought nothing of it. Not Indy's slack jaw or the way his eyes went a millimeter wider. I just pulled my brother into the inner chamber and sat him on a case of ancient vintage.

"What's wrong?" I whispered.

"Nothing."

"Jon."

"What?"

"Let's be efficient with our time. You're going to tell me. Might as well get it over with."

He pursed his lips, crossed his arms, jutted his jaw. I leaned on a low shelf and waited.

"You can't tell," he said.

"You know I won't."

"You need to really swear."

Jesus. To be in grade school again. To make the big little and the little big. To think you had control when you didn't and adulthood was just childhood layered over with manners and privilege. When lies seemed like easy answers to uncomfortable truths.

"All right," I said. "Let's do this. Let's take a pledge. We hold our hands up and swear anything we say is secret. When we put our hands down, we lock it closed and go back to normal."

He thought about it for a second, then with a short nod he said, "Okay."

"But there's another thing. We cannot lie. Not when the pledge is open."

"Fine."

I held my hand up, and he mirrored me.

"Pledge open," I said. "What happened?"

He took a deep breath and looked at the corner of the room. "Kerry and I were outside when it started raining, and we got stuck in the pool house."

Kerry was the daughter of one of Dad's associates. She was a year older than Jonathan and pretty smart.

"Go on."

"We started doing stuff."

Jesus Christ, use a condom.

He's not ready.

He glanced at me, tearing his attention from the corner for half a second, then planting it back. I didn't answer the glance or egg him on. I knew what was coming, more or less. Mom and Dad weren't very forthcoming about sex with the kids, thinking my early knowledge led to my early downfall.

He spit out the next line. "I think she broke it."

"Broke what?" I knew the answer, but my mouth ran before my brain caught up.

He wouldn't say but pointed at his crotch with both hands.

Do. Not. Laugh. Do. Not. Laugh.

"What makes you think it's broken?"

"She touched it. It got... it got weird then..." He looked at the ceiling.

I had to finish for him. Putting him on the spot wasn't working. He was in fifth grade, and though he'd started getting big, he was still a child.

"It got hard then felt tickly then white stuff came out?"

His eyes went wide. "Yes."

"It's not broken."

"How do you know?"

"Aren't you and your friends talking about this amongst yourselves? Girls? Sex?"

"I didn't have sex with her!"

I waved it away. "I know. Okay. I'm just going to assure you, it's not broken. You're fine. But tomorrow, let me take you to lunch and I can tell you why. All right?"

He took a deep breath of reprieve. "Yes."

"Until then, keep away from Kerry O'Neill."

"All right."

"Tuck your shirt in."

He did it, jamming the shirttails into his waistband as if Daddy was in the other room. He took a step toward the doorway.

"Jon. Stop."

"What?"

I put my hand up then down. "Close pledge."

"Close pledge."

We went back into the tasting room. Drew leaned on one of the benches, hair flopped over his face like a rock star, shirt dry like a lawyer, with a manila envelope in one hand and a white rectangle in the other. He looked at it then Jonathan.

"What?" I said.

Drew just shook his head as Jonathan bolted up the stairs with barely a wave.

"Strat mailed stuff to Audio City. I don't know why." He put down the manila envelope. Old stamps. Crap handwriting. He laid out the contents. "A note for me, and pictures of when we were kids. He was... he was so hurt. He couldn't show it because you were mine. But..." His voice drifted to silence.

"Drew?"

"When you left, he acted like it was nothing." He pushed the runny letter toward me.

I couldn't see much but my name, my real one, and phrases... *she was yours but... never wanted this... like a brother to me...*

"I knew about you and Strat. He told me in pledge," Drew said.

"In Nashville."

"Yes, but I—"

"That's why you were such a dick when you got back."

"I regret that."

"I deserved it."

He looked at the picture, shook it, pressed his lips together, and gave it to me as if it was the hardest thing he'd had to do in his life. I took it but kept my eyes on his. I had no idea what he could look so distressed about.

"What is it?" I asked.

"Just tell me what you see."

I looked at the picture.

Two boys about twelve years old, arms over shoulders, a suburban sidewalk stretching behind them. I recognized young Drew McCaffrey by the flop of his hair and the shape of his eyes.

And the other boy? I recognized him. I knew who he was. He was Stratford Gilliam, a kid with only a few more years to live, but that wasn't the kid I recognized. He looked like the three-dimensional kid had been transported from my house onto a two-dimensional surface.

I swallowed. None of this computed.

"It's a coincidence," I whispered.

Not unless Stratford Gilliam fucked your mother.

I couldn't do the math in my head.

Twelve-year-old Strat was a clone of my brother, Jonathan.

No. The other way around. Jonathan looked exactly like Strat.

I looked up from the picture. Drew stood above me, confident and together as if he knew something I didn't.

"Your family name came up in the Dublin office. Your baby's adoptive family is suing your father for breach of contract."

"I don't understand."

Don't you?

"They never had your real name. I presume it was to protect you. It took that long to find him."

"There would be two babies."

"We checked the public records. Your mother's eighth child was stillborn."

I took a step back, covering my mouth so I wouldn't scream. The calculus suddenly made sense. A sick fucking sense.

"I didn't know what I'd find here," Drew said. "But I didn't think this. I thought it was simpler. Not until I saw—"

I didn't hear anything else. Just my little brother's—

son's

—voice in my head as he spoke French with a perfect ear for tone. As I saw the lines of his body superimposed on Strat's—

his father's

—and the face which was unmistakably from the same gene pool.

I did the math with my senses. Heard the voice and saw the face. Smelled the new baby smell that seemed of my own body and knew, just knew, he was mine.

"I can't." My breathing got choppy. I was shaking.

Drew grabbed my wrists. "Margie."

"I can't tell him."

"You don't—"

"Oh, God."

"*Shh.* It's going to be all right."

He tried to gather me in his arms, but I pushed him away and I ran. I flung myself up the narrow stairs into the chaos of the kitchen. How many people were in the ballroom? Fifty? A hundred?

"Margie?" Orry asked, a piece of raw fish in his thick hands.

Everyone in the kitchen was looking at me, sauté pans frozen mid-agitation, break knives up, colanders dripping starch-thickened water into drains.

I heard Drew clop a couple of elephantine steps up from the cellar.

Cornered.

Your brother is your son.

I didn't even know what I was running from. I was a spider in a tub. I couldn't get up the sides. Couldn't get away, even on eight legs, from the glass bowl coming down.

"Margie?" Drew called.

A second had passed, and in that second, every feeling I was supposed to have in the past few decades dropped on me. I felt my shell break under the pressure as my insides got bigger than my outside, slowly giving way to hairline fractures. I couldn't do this here. I couldn't break with the kitchen staff staring and Drew climbing the stairs.

I ran out of the kitchen, following the map of my childhood.

Through the morning room, the library, the kids' playroom, and the breakfast room to the back deck. I threw myself down the wooden stairs to the beach where I almost collapsed on the cold sand. I got my feet under me and ran toward the wall of sound and water. The horizon. The darkness on the outskirts of the lights of civilization, where the water flattened the land.

I fell with my knees in the water and the rush of the tide in my ears. I stayed there and wept. I wept for what I'd done to sweet Drew. For acting as though Strat had no feelings. For my son who I was never, ever going to hurt by telling. For my misguided parents who had lost a baby and taken mine into their hearts.

The lip of the next wave reached me, soaking my calves and the top of my head. I wasn't mature enough for any of this. No one was. But I didn't cry for myself. I cried for everyone I'd hurt.

The water got louder than I thought possible, blowing at my ears so much that my lungs felt the pain, and the earth went out from under me. I spun in space, clawed the wet sand, tasted rough salt and foam. The sea wrapped around me like a vise, yanking me against it, pulling me to the air, where Drew had me in his arms.

He put me on the sand, and his voice became the sense inside the ocean's chaos. "Margie?"

He was cloudy and grey. My eyes couldn't focus. My chest couldn't hold my lungs, and I coughed. Sucked in a breath. Was I drowning or crying so hard I couldn't breathe?

His hands on my cheeks.

"Talk to me," he said.

"I don't know what to do."

"I know."

"I want to claw my heart out of my chest."

I realized I was gripping the front of my shirt as if I meant to literally claw through skin and bone.

He took my hands, leaning over. "It's all right. Margie. Can you hear me?"

"Yes. I'm sorry. I was young. I put you in a terrible position."

"No. Don't you dare. Don't you ever blame yourself. Ever. I was the one to blame. I should have known better."

"I never admitted I loved you."

"Neither did I."

"I was scared."

"I don't want you to be scared. Not ever again."

I reached for him, and he held me on the beach. I was cold,

but I wasn't. I was hurt, but I was healed. I was alone, but no, I wasn't. Not at all. I pressed my face to his neck and let him encircle me so tightly I thought he'd break me.

"I'm so sorry," he said.

I couldn't see his face in the embrace, but mine was scrunched with the push of sobs.

"I didn't tell you what I knew the minute I came to LA. I didn't know what I was walking into. I was afraid you'd shut down. I was afraid I'd still have feelings for you. And I do, Margie. I do."

I nodded.

"I know you just got blindsided tonight."

I choked out a laugh. We loosened our hold on each other until we were face to face. I brushed the sand from his cheek.

"Blindsided," I said. "Good word."

"I had no idea. I want you to know. I had pieces but didn't know the puzzle."

I nodded. "No one would believe the truth."

"What should we do?"

I knew he'd asked a broad question. He was talking about us, the world, the firm, my family, our past, our future. But I couldn't think past the tide of feelings. They may have gone back out to sea for the moment, but they'd be back. If I knew anything about emotions (and I didn't know a damn thing but this), they'd be back.

"Let's slip around the side and go to my place," I said.

"You've got a crappy track record of sneaking out of here."

"This time I have you with me."

He smiled and shifted a strand of hair from my face. "You do. You have me."

He kissed me with the passion of a promise. We stood and walked off the beach together.

Chapter 30

1994

Kentucky. More than halfway to New York.

I didn't dig graveyard scenes or talking to guys who weren't really there. I didn't understand putting flowers down for a dead guy who hadn't seemed to like them when he was alive. The young groupie hated downer shit, and the jaded law clerk—no, lawyer—didn't have the time.

And there was still the whole issue of feelings.

I told Drew when he opened the car door for me, "Doing something for the express purpose of making yourself feel sad is fake. The thing is fake, and the feeling is fake."

"The lawyer doth protest too much."

He held his hand out for me, and I took it, letting him pull me out of the car. I didn't need help, but he liked helping. Didn't take me long to figure that out, and who was I to refuse him his pleasure?

He'd given me too much in the past six months. He'd stood by my decision to let Jonathan stay my brother, to let my parents think I knew nothing about their loss. Though my father had masterminded the entire fairytale, his scheme to keep his grandson in the family was meant to protect my mother.

I couldn't refuse my father that, but mostly, I remained silent to protect my son, Jonathan. I'd die with that secret. I'd sew my own mouth shut before letting it pass my lips.

The only other person who knew was the man holding the flowers in the parking lot of a Kentucky cemetery.

* * * *

The little notes all over my house were long gone.

"I'll end you," I whispered to Drew one night, wrapped in sheets and darkness, my voice shredded from crying his name too many times.

He kissed me. I could taste my pussy on his face.

"You always threaten me before you fall asleep."

That was when the worry swept in. The worry that my family would be upended. That my brother would lose his mind. That my mother would go off the deep end. And my father, ever unpredictable, would hurt the messenger if the messenger wasn't me.

"You're the only one who knows." I touched his face in the dark. "I trust you. But I will end you."

He pinned my hands over my head. "I'll end you too."

We'd had this discussion a hundred times. In bed, over dinner, in earnestness and in jest. "I'll end you" wasn't a threat. Not really. It was a way of telling him how deeply I trusted him.

"Not if I end you first," I said, pushing my hips against him.

"How are you going to do that, Cinny-sin-sin?"

"Test me."

He let my hands go and wrapped himself around me. "Never."

"Smart guy."

He didn't move and barely paused. "Come back to New York with me. I can't live without you. The city feels like a tomb."

I sighed. We'd been long distance for too many months. "Speaking of testing... I'm sitting for the bar in February."

He got up on his elbows, eyes wide and blue, shocked and delighted. I'd waited to tell him so I could drink in that expression.

"The New York State Bar?" he asked.

"No, asshole, the old man's bar on Seventh and B. Of course the New York State Bar."

He was off me like a shot, sitting straight, suddenly awake. "You have to study. Have you been studying? We have to get on it."

"Relax. It's easy."

He scooped up my entire body and covered it in happy kisses.

I hadn't forgotten what had brought us together, but it was all drowned out by a feeling of safety and joy. I had to admit, as feelings went, those were pretty good.

* * * *

The parking lot of the Kentucky cemetery was empty but for a few beat-up trucks. Our shiny black Audi was the brightest object for miles. Drew had parked it in the middle of the lot, away from the wooden poles poking out from the earth at odd angles. The rusted chains between them were shaped like kudzu-wrapped smiles, one after the other on the edge of the rectangle—smile, smile, smile. The sky was the color of the asphalt, and the freight train clacking at the river's edge lumbered slowly, as if showing off its eternal length like a peacock showing off his blues.

I'd passed the New York bar six months after passing the California bar. I threatened to rack up forty-eight more states for fun, and Drew threatened to tie me to the bed.

That had worked out well.

Everything had worked out well. I was leaving. Maybe for a few years, maybe for good, but I was going. I never imagined I'd leave Los Angeles, but the thought of such freedom made me feel silly and lighthearted.

Me. Margaret Drazen.

I got goofy in the weeks before we finally left. Daddy hadn't been happy when we told him, and he eyed Drew as if maybe he remembered him from twelve years before, when a young man had shown up at the door asking for his oldest daughter.

But, you know, tough shit.

When Drew insisted we take 70 (apparently, I wasn't supposed to say *the* 70. Just 70 without the article), I didn't think anything of it. But he swung off the interstate and went south into Kentucky.

"Six-oh-six E-Y-E-B-R-O-W," I said from the passenger seat.

He glanced over. "I need to."

"I know."

We stopped at a light and he put his hand over mine. "I went to the funeral, but I didn't visit the... you know. The thing." He looked away.

"There's a florist up ahead. You don't want to show up empty-handed."

He'd bought a bunch of yellow flowers because they looked fresher than any of the others. Stillness shrouded us on the way to the cemetery. I pressed my hand on his, rubbing the rough patch on his fingertip where guitar strings had, calloused the skin.

I took his hand again in the parking lot, and we walked down the gravel path, counting lanes and ways against our printed map.

We found the grave exactly where it was supposed to be. Just another stitch in the houndstooth pattern of grey stones on the grassy hill. It said what it was supposed to say. His name. The relevant dates. Where the others had their defining roles—Father, Wife, Mother, Son, Baby—Stratford Gilliam had a clef like the one on his neck, short five-line staff and a quarter note tucked between the two lowest lines.

"I feel stupid," he said. "It's just a rock and dirt."

"Yeah. It's stupid."

That was why we were together. We shared a cold, calculating cynicism. We were immune to sentiment.

"I like the musical note," I said. "It's cute."

"I picked it. I drew it for his dad and faxed it over."

"Really?"

"Yeah. It's…" He swallowed hard. "It's F. The note." He blinked. Smiled with his lips tight in a thin line. "It's so dumb." His voice cracked.

"I bet."

He looked away from the grave and shut his eyes. "I picked F for…" He shook his head, shot a little laugh that was sticky with sadness. "Friend. I needed it to be F for friend. Like I was in kindergarten."

I put my hand on his cheek, thumb under his eye, ready to catch the tears that I knew were coming. "I'm embarrassed for you."

He opened his eyes. So blue. Bluer than the cloud-masked sky that day. He wasn't the man I'd met so long ago. The musician on the edge of fame. So close to the dream. So close he could save the world with it.

But he was. That man was still in him. Sometimes I forgot

about that twenty-year-old with the potential he had a lifetime to fulfill.

He laid the flowers down. I rubbed his guitar callouses as we walked back to the car.

"You should play music again," I said.

"No."

"You're not doing him any favors."

"It's not about Strat."

That was a lie, but I couldn't prove it.

"You're right. The world is better off without you making music."

He laughed a little and wrapped his arm around my neck, pulling me close and kissing the top of my head.

"I mean it," I said. "You're sexy with a guitar. Chicks dig it."

"You sure you could stand the competition?"

"Have you met me? I don't have competition." I walked backward in front of him, each of my hands in his. "You don't have to be a rock star. Just write some songs. See how it sounds. You might like it." I bit my lower lip. "I might like it. I could be your groupie all over again. I'll let you fuck me if you play."

He pulled me to him. "You're going to let me fuck you whether I play or not."

"I hear South Dakota has the easiest bar exam in the country."

"I'm not moving to South Dakota."

"Then you better get that guitar out, Indiana McCaffrey."

"You're threatening me," he growled with a smile. "You know what that does to me."

"What?" I reached between his legs, and we laughed.

I ran back to the car, and he chased me, pinning me to the driver's side door with his kiss. I pushed my fingers through his hair, pulling him closer. I wanted to crawl inside him and live there forever.

He ripped his face away from mine long enough to speak. "I love you, Cinnamon. You're too precocious. Too smart. Too much of a pain in the ass, and I love you."

"Even in South Dakota?"

"I'll play again!" He laughed. "I'll play if you love me."

"You bet your ass I love you."

"Case closed." He kissed me again, pushing me hard against

the car with the force of his erection pressed against me.

I groaned into his mouth.

"There was a hotel behind that florist." He spoke in gasps. "Wanna go make the bed squeak?"

"Yes."

We kissed again with an urgency that defied logic, as it should.

The freight train finally lumbered away, the bell on the last car dinging in victory. On the other side of the tracks, the rolling hills dissolved into infinity, and we drove right into it.

THE END

About CD Reiss

CD Reiss is a USA Today and Amazon bestseller. She still has to chop wood and carry water, which was buried in the fine print. Her lawyer is working it out with God but in the meantime, if you call and she doesn't pick up, she's at the well, hauling buckets.

Born in New York City, she moved to Hollywood, California to get her master's degree in screenwriting from USC. In case you want to know, that went nowhere, but it did give her a big enough ego to try her hand at books.

She's been nicknamed the "Shakespeare of Smut," which is flattering enough for her to put it in a bio, but embarrassing enough for her not to tell her husband, or he might think she's some sort of braggart who's too good to chop a cord of wood.

If you meet her in person, you should call her Christine.

Also from CD Reiss

Curious about Margie and the Drazen family? There's much more!

Jonathan's story is told in the epic *Submission Series.*

Beg
Tease
Submit
Control
Burn
Resist
Sing
Dominance
Coda

If sexy suspense is your thing, Theresa Drazen's all-consuming, life-threatening relationship with a hot mafia man is told in *The Corruption Series.*

Spin
Ruin
Rule

Celebutante Fiona Drazen lives a life of boundary-free debauchery. She's utterly forbidden to the one man who can save her.

Forbidden

Contemporary Romance standalones:

Shuttergirl: An A-list actor falls for a girl from the wrong side of the tracks. Second chances do exist, even in Hollywood.
Hardball: A pro baseball player falls for a buttoned up librarian. What could go wrong?

Sign up for the 1001 Dark Nights Newsletter
and be entered to win a Tiffany Key necklace.

There's a contest every month!

Go to www.1001DarkNights.com to subscribe.

As a bonus, all subscribers will receive a free
1001 Dark Nights story
The First Night
by Lexi Blake & M.J. Rose

Turn the page for a full list of the
1001 Dark Nights fabulous novellas...

Discover 1001 Dark Nights Collection One

FOREVER WICKED by Shayla Black
CRIMSON TWILIGHT by Heather Graham
CAPTURED IN SURRENDER by Liliana Hart
SILENT BITE: A SCANGUARDS WEDDING by Tina Folsom
DUNGEON GAMES by Lexi Blake
AZAGOTH by Larissa Ione
NEED YOU NOW by Lisa Renee Jones
SHOW ME, BABY by Cherise Sinclair
ROPED IN by Lorelei James
TEMPTED BY MIDNIGHT by Lara Adrian
THE FLAME by Christopher Rice
CARESS OF DARKNESS by Julie Kenner

Also from 1001 Dark Nights

TAME ME by J. Kenner

For more information, visit www.1001DarkNights.com.

Discover 1001 Dark Nights Collection Two

WICKED WOLF by Carrie Ann Ryan
WHEN IRISH EYES ARE HAUNTING by Heather Graham
EASY WITH YOU by Kristen Proby
MASTER OF FREEDOM by Cherise Sinclair
CARESS OF PLEASURE by Julie Kenner
ADORED by Lexi Blake
HADES by Larissa Ione
RAVAGED by Elisabeth Naughton
DREAM OF YOU by Jennifer L. Armentrout
STRIPPED DOWN by Lorelei James
RAGE/KILLIAN by Alexandra Ivy/Laura Wright
DRAGON KING by Donna Grant
PURE WICKED by Shayla Black
HARD AS STEEL by Laura Kaye
STROKE OF MIDNIGHT by Lara Adrian
ALL HALLOWS EVE by Heather Graham
KISS THE FLAME by Christopher Rice
DARING HER LOVE by Melissa Foster
TEASED by Rebecca Zanetti
THE PROMISE OF SURRENDER by Liliana Hart

Also from 1001 Dark Nights

THE SURRENDER GATE By Christopher Rice
SERVICING THE TARGET By Cherise Sinclair

For more information, visit www.1001DarkNights.com.

Discover 1001 Dark Nights Collection Three

HIDDEN INK by Carrie Ann Ryan
A Montgomery Ink Novella

BLOOD ON THE BAYOU by Heather Graham
A Cafferty & Quinn Novella

SEARCHING FOR MINE by Jennifer Probst
A Searching For Novella

DANCE OF DESIRE by Christopher Rice

ROUGH RHYTHM by Tessa Bailey
A Made In Jersey Novella

DEVOTED by Lexi Blake
A Masters and Mercenaries Novella

Z by Larissa Ione
A Demonica Underworld Novella

FALLING UNDER YOU by Laurelin Paige
A Fixed Trilogy Novella

EASY FOR KEEPS by Kristen Proby
A Boudreaux Novella

UNCHAINED by Elisabeth Naughton
An Eternal Guardians Novella

HARD TO SERVE by Laura Kaye
A Hard Ink Novella

DRAGON FEVER by Donna Grant
A Dark Kings Novella

KAYDEN/SIMON by Alexandra Ivy/Laura Wright
A Bayou Heat Novella

STRUNG UP by Lorelei James
A Blacktop Cowboys® Novella

MIDNIGHT UNTAMED by Lara Adrian
A Midnight Breed Novella

TRICKED by Rebecca Zanetti
A Dark Protectors Novella

DIRTY WICKED by Shayla Black
A Wicked Lovers Novella

A SEDUCTIVE INVITATION by Lauren Blakely
A Seductive Nights New York Novella

SWEET SURRENDER by Liliana Hart
A MacKenzie Family Novella

For more information, visit www.1001DarkNights.com.

On behalf of 1001 Dark Nights,
Liz Berry and M.J. Rose would like to thank ~

Steve Berry
Doug Scofield
Kim Guidroz
Jillian Stein
InkSlinger PR
Dan Slater
Asha Hossain
Chris Graham
Pamela Jamison
Jessica Johns
Dylan Stockton
Richard Blake
BookTrib After Dark
The Dinner Party Show
and Simon Lipskar

CPSIA information can be obtained
at www.ICGtesting.com
Printed in the USA
BVOW03s2132031116

466903BV00001B/1/P

9 781682 305690